LEGEND OF THE SILVER HUNTER

OMNIBUS EDITION

KETHRIC WILCOX

ISBN-13: 978-0-9965265-7-9

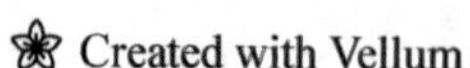 Created with Vellum

CONTENTS

VOLUME 1

VOLUME 2

VOLUME 3

PART I

VOLUME ONE

Kethric Wilcox

Tracker

Legend of the Silver Hunter

Book One

Kethric Wilcox
Copyright 2015 Kethric Wilcox

Cover design: Keith Martin
Cover Photography: Dan Skinner Photography
Edited by: Shannon A. Thompson

ISBN: 0-9965265-7-9
ISBN-13: 978-0-9965265-7-9

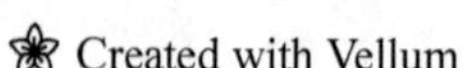 Created with Vellum

PUBLISHER'S NOTE

Welcome to the revised second edition. This volume fixes the typos and inconsistencies plaguing the first version. Here's hoping you find this version as enjoyable as the original. This is a work of fiction. Names, characters, places, and incidents are a product of the author's imagination. Locations and public names are sometimes used for atmospheric purposes. Any resemblance to actual people, living, or dead, or to businesses, companies, events, institutions, or locales is coincidental.

Tropical Smoothie Café, Cranberry walnut chicken salad sandwich, and mango magic are trademarks of Tropical Smoothie Café Franchise Distribution Company.

ACKNOWLEDGMENTS

I want to give a big thank you to my partner for giving me the time to focus on being creative over the last year. Thanks, tiger.

PROLOGUE

There once was a rich merchant, who had six children, three sons, and three daughters; being a man of sense, he spared no cost for their education, but gave them all kinds of masters. His daughters were extremely handsome especially the youngest. When she was little everybody admired her, and called her "The little Beauty;" so that, as she grew up, she still went by the name of Beauty, which made her sisters very jealous.

Beauty and the Beast by Jeanne-Marie LePrince de Beaumont, 1757 English translation

Not the exact way you remember the story of *Beauty and the Beast*. Beauty's heirs altered the lore through the ages. Even Madame de Beaumont's version doesn't come near to what happened at the end of the account. Under the influence of the family of Beauty, storytellers crafted a fable to teach how Beauty transformed the Beast back into the handsome prince with true love because it's the way magic in fairy tales works. In truth, Beauty's story is much darker, a history of conflict with a creature from the darkest of myths, a shape-shifter given to serving a corruption so foul it pulled spirits from the heavens.

The magic of the world was divided into three tiers of power. At the top was the mysterious Gold magic of the gods, which occasionally manifested as miracles performed by mortal prophets. On the middle tier were Silver magic for offense and Ebony magic for defense, designed to operate together in combating the corruption. On the lowest tier were the four elemental forms of magic—Amethyst (air), Ruby (fire), Sapphire (water), and Emerald (earth)—designed to make mortal life easier. But even the most powerful of mages is mortal and open to corruption. Ebony magic—originally meant to be one of creation's protectors—was warped into the darkest of the arts. Powerful practitioners twisted the souls of men and Beasts together into the first shifters. Ebony magic's opposite and equal, Silver magic, became creation's sole salvation. During the last major magical war, the most powerful silver practitioners led by their leader known as the Silver Witch banded together to weave a spell to lock shifter's powers to the phases of the moon. All magic carries a price, and the binding spell tied itself to the bloodlines of the casting mages. As long as at least one of these Silver mage families survives unbroken, the spell will keep the shifters bound to one animal shape, strongest when the moon is full.

The never-mentioned mother of Beauty and her siblings was a descendant of one of these Silver magic families. She passed the potential for Silver magic on to her children, but only in her youngest son was the ability to use the power active. Her line was a hunted family because they were the key bloodline in the ancient binding spell. She chose her youngest son to carry on the line because those who sought to break the binding were looking for a female witch. When Beauty went to take her father's place at the castle of the Beast, her little brother gave her a gift of the Silver magic. He triggered a change in her, which would allow her to cast one powerful silver spell in her hour of need. Searching the castle for the Beast, she found the prince locked away in his own dungeon, and together, they slew the Beast with the gift from her brother. The truth of what happened that day is hidden away behind the façade of happily ever after.

Down through the ages, the female descendants of Beauty and her prince became huntresses going up against the darkness. The gift of a one-shot use of Silver magic was passed down the line from mother to daughter until the origin of the magic was lost to time. Hidden even from Beauty's descendants is the family of her brother, whose male children carried the ability to use Silver magic at will and as often as needed. Every few generations, one of the brother's descendants marries one of Beauty's descendants. These marriages always arranged when the Silver magic began to fade from the line of huntresses. They also allow the descendants of Beauty's brother to remain in hiding from those hunting for silver mages. Once before this pairing produced a male hunter with the full gift of Silver magic. Since the hunter's time, ten generations of the lineage of Beauty have lived and died. Now, a new generation is born: five daughters and one son, all born of the huntress of her generation and a son of the hidden family line. This is their son's tale...

1

The ancient forest seemed gloomier than ever. The full moon flickered through the waving branches of the trees. Dark shadows stretched from tree to tree, blocking all but the faintest hint of light. A young man stepped on the path leading to the heart of the woodland. He wouldn't be going so far. The target of his test would meet him somewhere along the path and lead him off into the forbidding undergrowth. Wearing his dark leathers, the young man blended easily into the shadows of the forest. His long black hair was pulled back from his face, braided with a fine silver chain as light as his gray eyes. From his hips hung a matching pair of Hungarian sabers, and a long dagger was tucked into the top of each boot. Here he was on his eighteenth birthday, undergoing the test to become a full tracker of the House of Beauty, instead of being out celebrating with his few friends. The captain of the hockey team claiming to be his boyfriend wanted to take him out for a special birthday date—even hinted sex was part of the package—but had been told family obligations prevented their going out. Kieran didn't think the guy would ask him out again any time soon. Channeling his frustration into his tracking skills, he waited for the shifter's signal of the formal test's beginning.

A ragged human stepped out of the forest and barked, "Who are you and why are you here?" Kieran could tell, just from his voice, that he was no human at all. He was a shifter.

"I am Kieran Samuel Belle, tracker-candidate of the House of Beauty, come for the test."

"Of course, child of Beauty. By the ancient pact between your house and my pack, you get until sunrise to track me down and slay me. After I shift, I am allowed a ten-minute head start."

"What are you called shifter? I want the name of my target."

"I am called Grimfang."

"Shift when you're ready, Grimfang. I am ready."

"So you've never witnessed the shift before, young tracker?"

"No, you're my first live shift, Grimfang."

"Remember my name well, young tracker, for I will either be your first kill, or I will be your death."

Grimfang blurred and in his place, a dark-furred wolf stood for a moment before taking off into the woods. The shifter was definitely part of the pure dark shifter pack only the Ebony magic, which gave them the ability to change, could be sensed. Kieran, like the rest of his family, had heard rumors of packs whom were considered light shifters because they'd bred with elemental mages and pure humans trying to thin their blood and prevent the change. The young tracker drew a quick breath and swallowed hard after he witnessed the change.

Kieran waited the ten minutes dictated by the ancient rules before setting off in pursuit, moving with silent ease through the woods. He only paused to check for tracks and other signs of the shifter's passage. Deep into the forest, well off the regular paths, Kieran stopped short, sensing he was being spied on. While bending down to check for signs of spore and tracks, he slipped one of his long daggers into his hand and let loose a small trace of Silver magic. A faint silver mist formed over the track he was following, and the print blurred for a moment before a faint second outline was revealed by just a slight offset from the first print. Kieran whispered to the mist, and a vision of two wolves flickered before him. He snuffed out the Silver magic while putting away his long dagger so anyone who studied him would think he was using an enchanted blade instead of working magic himself.

Standing, Kieran drew one of his sabers and continued to follow the tracks. He ran his hand over the blade, letting another whisper of magic flow along the edge. This time, the magic was set to seek his quarry. Images flickered along the saber until the magic showed him an overhang along the trail. Two wolves hid themselves there, waiting for him to pass below. It was a clear violation of the ancient rules of the tracker's test, one tracker versus one shifter.

Kieran widened the view shown by the spell and found a trail, which came up behind the two wolves. It would allow him to use their ambush against them. After slipping from the main path, Kieran moved in silence behind the two wolves and drew his second saber. He moved up behind the two shifters but lost his footing on a patch of wet leaves. The shifters leapt at Kieran who just managed to get one of his sabers between the shifters and his throat. The shifters tore and clawed at Kieran, trying to get past his defenses. Silver sabers flashed as he held the shifters off. He dodged, trying to gain an opening. Kieran needed to put one of them out of the fight.

Ebony fire raked across Kieran's chest as the shifter's claws tore through his leather shirt. The skin beneath split. Kieran thrust the Beast off. He rammed a saber into its side. Falling, the shifter ripped the saber from Kieran's blood-soaked grip. The second shifter leapt on Kieran's back, driving him to the ground. Claws raked his back, inflicting searing pain as they tore leather and flesh apart. When the shifter tried to get its jaws around his neck, its teeth connected with the silver chain in Kieran's hair. Howling in pain, the Beast reared back. Kieran rolled out from under the monster as he slashed with his remaining saber. The silver blade opened a gash along the shifter's side as he tried to get away. Kieran regained his footing. He thrust his saber into the Beast's heart. Silver fire flared upon meeting Ebony-tainted blood, and the shifter fell dead. Kieran found the other shifter dead, his saber jutting from between its ribs. Pain burned across his chest and back. The wounds bled. Kieran pulled his sabers free. He removed the shifters' heads, grim trophies marking his passage into manhood. When he collected his trophies, Kieran cleaned his blades before sheathing them and heading home.

* * *

KIERAN WAS RESTING and recovering from the injuries received during his testing when he received a summons to appear before the Matriarchs. The Matriarchs, lead by his grandmother, ruled the House of Beauty, and they would decide whether he would become a full tracker of the house or not. Stiff and sore, he walked to the antechamber slowly, not wanting to pull open the stitches, and waited for permission to enter the council chamber. No magical healing for a mere son of the house, bandages wrapped him from shoulders to waist beneath his loose-fitting shirt. Kieran dressed in as much of the approved style without interfering with the bandages covering the claw marks across his chest and back. He hoped he passed, but didn't hold any high hopes considering his grandmother found fault with everything about him from his sex to his bad fortune of being the firstborn of his mother's six children. Standing in the antechamber, Kieran wondered if there was ever a time his grandmother had been happy with him, but all his thoughts only reminded him of the tasks she'd forced him to perform. A young boy of about ten stood outside the massive wooden doors, which separated the Matriarchs from the rest of the family. Kieran nodded to his young cousin, who was trying to act serious instead of looking bored.

Kieran remembered doing the same job when he was their age, *Goddess, oh how mind numbing.*

When Cousin Joey rang the little bell, it alerted another cousin on the other side of the door to Kieran's arrival. The door swung open on silent hinges despite its massive size and weight. Kieran stepped through and waited while the door was closed behind him before moving forward to the edge of the carpet, which marked the boundary between Matriarchs and all other members of the house. An elderly woman limped from somewhere in the back of the room to a throne-like chair at the center of the huge conference table. Other older women entered and took seats at the table, all facing Kieran as he stood before them. When all the women were seated, Kieran noted how only two of them still had any trace of Silver magic on them: the woman at the center, his grandmother, and a great-aunt who'd never married and hid a missing arm beneath a shawl.

Kieran's grandmother glared at him and fixed him with her stern gaze with her usual disapproval. "Kieran Samuel Belle, son of Miranda Belle, Huntress of the House of Beauty, you underwent the testing to become a tracker of the house."

"Yes, Huntress-emeritus. I tested and returned with the heads of two shifters. One belongs to the shifter Grimfang, who was sent to conduct the test under the pact. The other belongs to an unknown shifter who joined Grimfang in an attempt to violate the pact and kill this tracker-candidate."

"Your trophies are registered with the mistress-of-arms. We confer on you the rank of full tracker of the house. You will serve at the side of the next huntress of the house. Until there is a new huntress for you to track for, it will be your duty to begin training your younger male cousins to become trackers."

"I beg permission to speak my peace before the Matriarchs."

"You may speak within limits, Tracker Kieran."

"I wish the Matriarchs' leave to attend college until my cousins are of the proper age to begin the training. The eldest of my cousins is but a lad of eleven years. Tradition requires the training begin at fourteen."

"You began your training earlier than tradition requires, Tracker Kieran."

"Begging your pardon, Matriarch Desdemona, my circumstances were different from those pertaining to my cousins. I am the son of the last huntress and brother to the next huntress. My mother's brothers died before I reached the age of nine and the living trackers were too old to take their place at Mother's side. My services as a tracker were needed sooner so you authorized my training to begin early. The eldest of my sisters is three years shy of her majority and therefore ineligible to take the test of the huntress."

"So you wish to use the three years to attend college rather than attend to your duties to this house?"

"Huntress-emeritus, I desire to create rather than destroy. I wish experience in the world beyond this estate and Bangor. It is my desire to study graphic design and photography. I beg only a year's leave before I take up my duties to the house."

"Were you granted this year, would you take up your duties to this house, including marrying and producing children?" His Aunt Fiona's question was leading. Was she prodding him, knowing how his grandmother would react when he answered?

"Matriarch Fiona, I will take up all the physical and spiritual duties I am capable of fulfilling. Would you make me wed a woman and leave the marriage unconsummated? I'm gay, and short of my donating my seed for use in artificial insemination, my branch of the House of Beauty ends with me."

Kieran spotted the displeasure his honest answer brought out on his grandmother's face, but pressed his request. "One year's leave is all I ask for, honored Matriarchs, after which time I will dedicate my life to training my cousins and assisting the next huntress. Please, Grandmother, I shall never ask for anything again."

The moment he let the word grandmother pass his lips, Kieran realized he'd lost every hope of winning her permission. He caught her expression hardening more than ever.

"You will begin training your male cousins tomorrow. Should you leave this estate without escort by a member of this council, you will be banished from these lands until a new huntress decides otherwise. You are dismissed, Tracker Kieran."

Kieran retreated backward through the doorway from the council chamber, making plans and plotting his escape.

2

A somber mood filled the massive entrance hall of the Belle mansion. In the center of the hall, the young tracker paced. He was trying to memorize every log and carving, fearing this would be the last time he'd stand here for a while. Kieran was dressed to travel in jeans, a T-shirt under a denim jacket, and heavy work boots. After three years, the time had come for Kieran to cast aside his predetermined role as a male of the lineage of Beauty. Having recently passed his twenty-first birthday, he was determined to escape and go to college, until one of his sisters claimed the position of huntress. When his uncles and mother died during a mission, Kieran began training as a tracker well before the regular age, under the tutelage of his great-uncles, who were too old to go into the field. Three years ago, after passing the final test, he became a registered tracker of the House of Beauty. Shortly after his certification, he was assigned to train a new generation of tracker-candidates among his younger male cousins. If they represented the future after him, one of his sisters was going to be in trouble. After three years, not one of the boys deemed old enough by the Council of Matriarchs measured up. None of them possessed the talent to master the skills of tracking; in truth, they would be better off serving in the household and marrying to spread the bloodline.

Watching his father's approach, he envied the man's grace as he crossed the vast central hall. His father wasn't a weakling or anyone to underestimate despite his life of wealth and leisure. There was power behind his father's violet eyes.

"Kieran, are you sure this is what you want? You understand I'll do everything to help you. Your grandmother is furious with you. Once you leave, you're not welcome back so long as she lives."

"I want this, Dad. I won't live my life trapped here. If life would be any different with your family, I'd go there, but we both realize the life of constant training and fighting only continues in a different form. I need something of my own. I want to create, not destroy." He'd been repeating this phrase daily for the past three years.

"I understand, Son. Let's get you out of here before your grandmother locks down the estate."

"Thanks, Dad. I love you." They crossed the rest of the central hall together. Kieran reached out and grasped the handle of the ancient carved oak door. With a shrug of his shoulders to settle the weight of his backpack, he stepped out into the wide world beyond the bounds of the House of Beauty.

An hour later, Kieran and his father stood in line at Dysart's Travel Stop in Bangor, Maine to purchase Kieran's bus ticket to Little Rock, Arkansas.

"I made contact with some of your mother's former associates along your route to Little Rock. They are in possession of your number and will contact you if they are in need of your assistance. They can afford to pay you the going rate for a tracker of the House of Beauty."

"Thanks, Dad. I realize accessing the trust fund would let Grandmother find me and stop me from living my life."

"Just be careful; only some of these hunters are above board. You should be able to do your own thing in Little Rock. No hunter claims the area, and what intelligence there is says the packs are small and most were college students from creation-aligned clans."

"I'll keep my wits about me, Dad. I did manage to get into college without Grandmother learning I was applying. I can manage a couple of hunters."

"I worry about you since your mother is no longer here."

"Okay, Dad. Best thing you can do for me is to be there for my sisters in my place. I'm more worried about them than I am about myself. They're the ones who are going to face the dogs—"

"Where to, sir?"

"Little Rock, Arkansas, one way, one passenger with flex travel."

"That'll be three hundred."

Kieran's father slid cash across and scooped up the ticket.

"Your bus leaves in an hour. I'd better get back to the estate before your grandmother realizes I'm missing. Here's the leftover cash. With luck, one of the hunters will contact you before you run out."

3

———————

Seated near the rear of the bus, Kieran checked his phone as they pulled out of Boston. No hunter had contacted him yet, but he wasn't sure any would. The list of hunters who were cleared to hire a tracker of the House of Beauty was exclusive, which guaranteed those on the list were able to afford even the rare-gifted trackers of the family. Kieran knew it would be a hard sell to convince hunters to hire him. While he was a certified tracker of the House of Beauty, he lacked field experience; to hunters, he was untried, and they wouldn't know if he was truly worth the fee. His uncles once commanded fees ranging up toward fifty thousand dollars and they weren't gifted. While lacking his uncles' experience, Kieran kept an ace up his sleeve. Unlike most men of the House of Beauty, Kieran was actively gifted with Silver magic, a fact he'd had to hide from everyone but his father. Being gifted with any magic—save the dark magic of Ebony—made a tracker more valuable. The Matriarchs wouldn't care if he'd been gifted with any elemental magic like Emerald, Ruby, or Sapphire. Instead, he'd inherited Silver magic from his father's family, the Oisín Clan. Kieran sighed and thought if he could land one contract, the proceeds—even at the absolute base fee of ten thousand dollars—would get him through the school year.

The bus rolled out of Boston heading for Worcester, followed by Albany, New York, which would be its next stop. Kieran planned to refresh his storage of snacks and drinks in Albany. He read, slept, and ate during the ride. As the bus reached the outskirts of Albany, Kieran received a call from an unfamiliar number.

"Kieran Belle, can I help you?"

"Mr. Belle, my name is Richard St. Martin. I'm a hunter, and I understand your services as a tracker are for hire."

"I'm available for hire as a tracker. My fee is fifteen thousand, cash, half upfront, the rest payable at the end of the contracted period, whether you bag your quarry or not."

"You're expensive for an untried tracker. Why should I pay so much?"

"I'm certified as a full tracker of the House of Beauty."

"An impressive accomplishment, but you have no actual experience. Why should I pay so much for an untried boy?"

"Oh, I'm worth every penny of the fee. I'm a rarity among trackers of the House of Beauty. I'm gifted."

"Ah, I see," St. Martin paused, as if to contemplate the justification. "I'll give you a try. I agree to your fee, but I expect you to earn it. I'm in Amsterdam, New York."

"My bus will reach Amsterdam in about two hours."

"All right, I'll meet you at the station. I'll be wearing dark jeans and a black leather coat over a green T-shirt."

"I'm wearing jeans, a denim shirt, and you can't miss the long black hair."

"Since we know how the other is dressed, I'll see you in two hours. We'll eat, I'll give you the details, and we can work out a contract. The first seventy-five hundred will be on hand when you get here, and I'll get you the rest when the contract is done."

"Agreed, I will see you in two hours, Mr. St. Martin."

* * *

THE HUNTER, Richard St. Martin, met Kieran as promised, and they grabbed Kieran's bags from the bus. St. Martin took Kieran to dinner at Parillo's Armory Grill on Bridge Street. Kieran glanced at the menu and ordered Mom's Homestyle Lasagna and a Coke. He studied St. Martin while he ordered the Veal Français and a glass of wine. St. Martin was a slender man, about thirty-five, with long dark hair, glasses, and silver rings on each finger. A subtle power radiated around the hunter, a sign he'd survived encounters with shifters.

"I was sorry to hear about your mother; she was an amazing woman," St. Martin said once their order was placed.

"I didn't realize you knew my mother personally, Mr. St. Martin."

"She saved my ass when I was a kid. My dad was a hunter who got careless and led a powerful shifter to our home. He and Mom died because of his carelessness. If it hadn't been for your mother, I would have been dead alongside my parents."

"What happened?"

"As I learned later on, your mother had been tracking the same shifter as my father and that shifter led her back to our house. The damn thing was fast and took out Mom before Dad drew his gun. I was across the room trying to get out when Dad fired several shots at the shifter. Next thing I remember, a huge panther had me under its claws and was getting ready to tear out my throat when a sword arced through my line of sight and the monster's head went bouncing across the room."

"Sounds like Mom's style. She drummed it into our heads how guns are unreliable for making sure a shifter is dead. She was always harping on how important it was to make sure a shifter was dead by taking its head."

"She told me the same thing. Took me to my uncle's place after setting our house on fire to destroy the evidence. I asked her to train me, but she sent me to a local hunter instead."

"By policy and tradition, the House of Beauty doesn't train men to be hunters."

"Well, that policy never made much sense to me. Who trained me is another tale. I inherited my mentor's territory last year."

"So why do you need my services?"

"About six weeks ago, a new pack moved into the region. I can't locate their lair despite my own skills and talents. I suspect they're using Ebony magic to hide themselves from me."

"How strong is your gift for magic?"

"My talent in Ruby magic is weak. At best, I can light a campfire."

"If they are using Ebony magic, an elemental magic like Ruby won't help, but Silver can. I have access to some Silver enchanted items. Are you trying to locate them, or are you planning on eliminating them?"

"I want to locate them and figure out what their plans are before I move against them. Poor planning is what got my mentor killed."

"Good, because our standard contract only allows us to track for non-house hunters. A tracker of the House of Beauty only fights at the direction of the huntress of the line. I will fight to defend myself while on this contract but only if you're beyond defending me. Once you agree to these terms and pay the fee, I will track for you."

"We're agreed. You'll find the first half of your fee in here."

St. Martin slid a large envelope to Kieran. The envelope disappeared as food arrived. The pair chatted about what St. Martin knew about the pack's habits. When they finished, St. Martin paid the bill and they left. They drove out to Route 30, where St. Martin got Kieran a room at the Blue Moon Motel.

The following evening, Kieran stepped out of St. Martin's car in the driveway leading up toward the Georgian-style Guy Park House. The limestone house built in 1774 by Guy Johnson, the British superintendent for Indian affairs, was seized by the state of New York after Guy Johnson was declared a traitor and sold to a private owner. The state purchased the property in 1907 and created a historic site. The damage from flooding during Hurricane Irene left the property sitting vacant.

Kieran knelt and ran his hand over the drive. He sensed something and drew one of his silver daggers from his left boot. With a whispered command, silver mist formed around the dagger, and a foggy trail flowed along the drive with a sudden turn along the gate toward a missing section of the fencing.

Kieran rose and tracked the magical trail with Richard St. Martin on his heels. The wisp of Silver magic stopped at the break in the fencing. It swirled as though searching for the scent before pooling. Kieran stopped when he reached the pool of silver.

"Why did you stop?"

"The magic of my dagger pooled here. I believe this is where your shifters used their Ebony magic to break their trail. It will take me awhile to see if I can probe beyond it and find the trail again. Stay alert."

Kieran stood in place and called the Silver magic back into his dagger. He stepped to the break in the fencing, pushing the tip of the dagger into the gap. The Ebony barrier resisted the Silver magic of the dagger with explosive force, knocking Kieran backward into St. Martin. Shifters launched themselves through the breach, aiming for the hunter. Kieran rolled out of the combat as he'd been trained, leaving the hunter free to fight. The shifters were quick, but St. Martin was surprisingly faster. A panther shifter heading for Kieran was impaled on the hunter's silver long sword. Whirling, St. Martin launched the dead shifter into the rest of the pack. The hunter bought Kieran time to get out of range of the attacking pack. The young tracker raced back down the drive for the car. He skidded to a stop and dodged claws aimed for his face. Cursing only having the dagger, he dodged. The shifter he faced was another panther. Black fur and blazing yellow eyes followed Kieran's movements. It leapt at him. A silver arc caught the panther mid-leap. St. Martin stood over Kieran. The shifter's body landed in two pieces.

"She was the last one."

"Thank you."

"I'm just honoring my part of our contract."

"Now I'll finish holding up my end of the contract." Kieran set loose the magic of the dagger once again.

4

After finishing the job for Richard St. Martin, Kieran spent three more days traveling by bus, in part due to picking up a second tracking job. The other delay was to call a few places in Little Rock to find an apartment. On the third try, he talked with Mrs. Jones over the phone, a little old lady who seemed a little on the crazy side, but she offered him not one room but two in the large Victorian home she rented out to students. He didn't like not being able to see them beforehand, but she promised to give him a bedroom, a study, a bathroom shared with one other tenant, and access to the common areas of the house with the other tenants. It was the rent that sold Kieran on the place: three hundred dollars a month. At this rate, his money would stretch the whole semester. Kieran took the place, sight unseen.

After dealing with the leering truckers, drunks, and panhandlers in the public showers and rest stops, a tired and relieved Kieran arrived at the grand Victorian house he was sharing two days before freshman orientation with the little luggage he had. It was refreshing to reach a place he wanted to call home. He chose the University of Arkansas in Little Rock because it was far enough away from his family and the direction they wanted his life to go. The added advantage of no local hunter and only rumors of a loosely-organized pack of shape-shifters, whose families had served the forces of creation at school, made Little Rock perfect. He was the oldest child, and as a male, he was expected to become the tracker to whichever one of his sisters became the successor to their mother's legacy as huntress. Now twenty-one, he wanted a life of his own to become a graphic artist and photographer. To no one's surprise, his father sided with him against his grandmother and the rest of the Matriarchs. Besides serving as a tracker, Kieran, as a male of the line with what the Matriarchs assumed as a small gift for Silver magic, was expected to marry and produce children for the house. Coming out as gay while disputing with the Matriarchs hadn't proved an asset.

What little he had, his father had helped him pack in a hurry, getting him into town to catch a bus to Arkansas. His father promised to send more of his things later. Despite this, Kieran hated the sense that he was naked without a real weapon to wield for defense, just in case. After unpacking in his rooms, Kieran was settled down in the sitting room when a disturbance outside ripped him from his thoughts. Stepping outside, he spotted a group of jocks surrounding a slighter, older guy and his luggage. Slipping down the front walk unnoticed, Kieran positioned himself between the hedges at the end of the walk, which allowed him to see without being seen and to overhear what was going on. The older guy, Kieran noted, had golden blond hair, with eyes of amber. He was not as frail as Kieran first thought but had a lean and wiry build. The jocks were being idiots and harassing the guy. If there was one thing Kieran hated, it was a bully. Stepping forward got him spotted, so Kieran spoke up.

"Hey, guys, lay off. The guy has as much right to the sidewalk as you do."

"Who asked you for your opinion?" one of the jocks snarled at Kieran.

"Nobody offhand, but if you want to make something of it, I'll be happy to enlighten you about manners." Kieran's body language told the jocks he was serious.

"We'll deal with you later, punk. Move along, jerk, you're blocking our game."

Moving around the jocks and up the front walk of the house, the man now stood close to Kieran. The hint of a sexy musk caught Kieran's attention.

"Thanks, I'm Corwin Cooper. You can call me Cory," the man said, by way of introduction. "Are you renting from Mrs. Jones, too?"

This man was, apparently, one of Kieran's roommates. Kieran extended his hand.

"Pleasure to meet you, Cory. I'm Kieran Belle," he said as the men shook hands. "Can I help you with your stuff?"

He didn't wait for a reply before picking up one of Cory's bags, and Cory thanked him as he followed Kieran into the house. Setting the bags down in the entryway, Kieran showed him to the sitting room.

"Well, cross off meeting the neighborhood jerks, so let me introduce you to a couple of cool guys." Kieran slid open one side of the pocket doors leading to the house's large sitting room.

"Hey, guys, this is Cory Cooper, the tenant for the last set of rooms. Cory, this is George Harper and Theo Cronin. George is math and science, and Theo is music and business."

"Hey, an honor to meet you. So, Kieran, what's your major?"

"Graphic design and photography. Let's get you settled. We all share the downstairs. Second floor rooms divide two per tenant, a bedroom, and a study. Bathrooms are shared between sets of rooms. George and Theo are on the left of the landing, and we're on the right. There's another full apartment on the third floor, but I don't know if Mrs. Jones is planning on renting it or not. So what are you majoring in, Cory?"

"Painting and business."

"Cool, so these are your rooms. The bathroom is the door next to the landing, and my rooms are the doors on the balcony over the staircase."

"Did you say the bathrooms are shared?"

"Yes."

"So this one on the right is…?"

"Ours. Theo and George share the one across the hall. There's a door to the bathroom from each of our rooms as well as this one in the hallway."

"Okay, thanks for sharing."

5

——————

Early in the morning on the day before freshman orientation, Corwin Cooper or Cory as his friends called him, loaded up his 2000 Amazon Green Ford Focus with his clothes and personal items. He was ready to head off to college. Corwin Cooper pulled his car off I-30 at the 9th Street exit and drove with care as he looked for Spring Street. The drive to Little Rock from the family farm in Arkansas City was the usual long, boring drive. He found the address he was searching for, a huge Victorian house sitting on a large lot. He spotted several guys out tossing a football around as he got out of the car. Moving around to the trunk and bending over to get his bags, he wasn't paying attention to his surroundings. It was a surprise when one of the jocks crashed into him, knocking them both to the ground.

"Dude, what is your problem? Can't you see we're playing football here? What's so important you have to get in our way?"

"I'm renting rooms here, and was just getting my bags to move in."

"Hey, guys, we've got another faggot moving into the neighborhood. I think we should teach this one a lesson for interrupting our game."

Well, it seemed like he was going to get into a fight before he'd even attended his first class. Cory braced himself for the coming fight when he spotted a young man moving toward him and the jocks. Gracefully slender but muscular, the young man was beautiful as he intervened in the situation, saving Cory from a beating. The young man introduced himself as Kieran Belle before grabbing up one of Cory's bags and leading the way inside. Cory's eyes followed the flow of muscles beneath the tight fitting T-shirt Kieran wore, and wondered what the younger man would be like naked. He also wanted to see Kieran's long hair loose and flowing around his head as he lay in bed. Cory gave himself a mental shake as Kieran introduced him to their fellow roommates, showed him around the house, and deposited him at the door to what would be his rooms.

"Get settled in. George, Theo, and I were talking about where to go to get something to eat, since none of us had time to go grocery shopping."

"Okay. I'll be down in a few minutes."

"Cool, we'll celebrate your arrival, Cory."

"Same here, Kieran. By the way, thanks for the rescue out there."

"You're welcome. See you downstairs in a few."

Cory's gaze followed Kieran as the young man turned and walked away. Man, he hoped to convince Kieran to model for him sometime; he would make a wonderful figure study.

* * *

From the moment Kieran walked into his life, only moments ago, Cory had felt the itch to grab paper and pencil and draw him. It was almost a physical ache, this longing to draw him, long hair, slender waist, and muscular arms. *Who even looked like that?* He was perfection.

* * *

Kieran remained perfect, coming in and out of Cory's daily life, and to a lesser extent, Theo and George became part of the routine as well.

As a group, the young men had lunch together as often as their classes allow them. All four shared a few core classes, and Kieran and Cory were in drawing and ceramics together. The more time he spent with Kieran, the more Cory couldn't help his desires for the younger man. He wanted to spend even more time with him.

Cory noted Kieran rising early every morning for a run before breakfast and classes, but Cory preferred to study until it was time for breakfast. Sometimes, Kieran teased him that he'd gain more than the freshman fifteen if he didn't get some exercise, but Cory was a built young man from growing up on a farm. Completing daily chores, including tossing around hay bales, kept him fit. He rose well before the sun and was awake when Kieran got up to get ready to go for his runs. He sat in his window to watch and do figure studies of Kieran's body flexing and stretching, warming up for the morning's exercise. Kieran's body was lean and muscular without being overdeveloped. His long black hair reached to the middle of his back when it was pulled back into a braid to keep it out of his face. When loose, Cory figured it must cascade to just below Kieran's firm, round ass. What always caught Cory's attention were Kieran's eyes. They were a strange silvery gray color and seemed to gleam bright metallic silver whenever he laughed. It took coaxing, but Cory convinced Kieran to pose for him for his upcoming painting project. In trade, he would pose for Kieran's photography project, and Cory was the one to always bring it up.

"So, is there a theme for your photo project yet, Kieran?"

"I was thinking of doing something along the lines of the country boy lost in the big city."

"Sounds like me all right. Little Rock is a heck of a lot bigger than Arkansas City or Dumas. So where do you want to do the shoot?"

"I thought of starting downtown by the river market and working over toward some of the construction areas nearer to Main Street. All the construction makes the area interesting for gritty shots."

"Sounds good to me, so what do you want me to wear?"

"I was thinking work boots, beat up jeans, your faded denim shirt, your John Deere ball cap, and grab your long coat for a few shots."

"Okay. Sounds like your plan is all worked out."

"Yes, my plan is worked out. So what are you wanting me to pose in when you use me to model for your painting project, or dare I ask?"

"Well, I was hoping you'd do an action pose for me in just your running shorts with your hair undone. Sort of like you were fighting off some attacker."

"Am I fighting him off with my bare hands, or do I get a weapon of some sort?"

"I thought I'd add in the rest of the elements, like weapons and actual attire, once I had the figure down on the canvas."

"Well, it would be easier to give you the right kind of pose if you tell me what kind of weapon my fantasy self was going to be using. I'd hate to take up a shooting pose only to find out you're painting a swordsman or vice versa."

"I was thinking more of having you fighting off a werewolf with a long dagger."

Kieran stared at Cory for a moment before replying. "Okay, that wouldn't be my weapon of choice for such a fight, but I'll give you the pose you want. What made you choose the scene?"

"Professor Simms assigned a fantasy-action scene. Something made me think you would be perfect fighting off a werewolf."

Kieran's reply cut off when George and Theo entered the sitting room from the front hall with a huge crate between them.

"Hey, Belle, this just came for you. We signed for it and brought it in for you. Someone got a major care package from home. We call dibs on any cookies or sweets."

"If there's any in there, take them. They might kill you. I learned the hard way what happens if one of my sisters baked them. Well, let's find out what's in here."

Kieran pried the lid off the crate and found a note from his father inside on top of the packing material.

Dearest Son,

I hope this package finds you well. Your sister, Rosie, and I thought you might appreciate some more of your things, your special clothes in particular. Your Uncle Brom is working on the items you requested and will send them to you once they're finished. We'll talk more about how you came up with those combinations. Savannah and Amanda baked cookies for you and your roommates. I'd give them a pass if I were you, as I almost broke a tooth on the one they insisted I try. They send their love and they miss their older brother. Selene will test before Christmas. I realize this is earlier than we expected, but your grandmother and the rest of the council decided she's ready. Callie won't be ready until after the new year at best. With luck, Selene will pass the test and you can come home. For now, your grandmother's banishment on you still stands. We all love and miss you. Please stay safe and well, and call us.

Love,

Dad

DIGGING INTO THE CRATE, Kieran pulled out the tin of cookies and tossed it to George and Theo. "Be careful with those. Dad almost broke a tooth. If you try them, I hope there's a dentist on your speed dial."

"Thanks, bro." George and Theo high-fived and tackled the cookies. Kieran pocketed the letter and dug out the items in the crate. The scent of leather burst forth as he draw out a huge, heavy leather coat. More leather clothing followed, making a complete outfit. Beneath the leather lies a carved wooden box. Kieran pulled it out and set it to the side before he pulled out a bunch of regular clothes.

"Now I don't think I'm going to wear out everything I own, putting it through the laundry every week."

"What's with the leather? It's almost like armor."

"It's for special occasions. It's a work outfit of sorts."

"What kind of work do you do wearing combat leathers?"

"Track down werewolves." Kieran laughed to hide the fact he was telling the truth.

The leathers were his new tracker's armor, redesigned extra heavy for defense and layered with spells to protect and warn him. Having survived his own testing as a tracker with the scars to prove it, Kieran insisted on the new outfit. His chest and back would forever bear the scars left from his battle with the dark shifters of the forest. They'd broken the rules of the ancient pact by sending two shifters. The pack had failed in killing him. Kieran, aided by magic, had pierced through the deception. He'd found both shifters where they'd laid an ambush. Springing their trap on them, he brought home both heads as proof of his tracker skills. By the Matriarchs' reactions, Kieran knew something was off, but he didn't know what. He only knew they stared at him, some in fear and others as if they didn't know him at all.

"Will you model them for me?" Cory asked, ebbing all of Kieran's worries away.

"Sure. Help me get this to my rooms and I'll change clothes."

In his rooms, Kieran put everything away. He stripped to his T-shirt, boxer-briefs, and socks. Cory's eyes roamed his friend's body while he put on the leathers. Cory loved the smooth play of Kieran's muscles beneath his skin. Kieran straightened up from tying his boots, and pulled on the leather coat. Reaching up, he unbound his hair. He caught Cory's eyes roaming his body and grinned as his new friend gushed with enthusiasm.

"It's awesome and less campy than my original concept. I like the idea of a more modern hunter, perhaps you fighting with heavy handguns."

"You'll like these better." Kieran opened the carved box to reveal a pair of matching silver Hungarian sabers. "These are my weapons of choice."

"Wow, perfect. I want get some preliminary sketches down. Just let me grab my sketchbook. We'll find a place with good lighting, and you'll pick a pose."

"I'm starving. How about we grab lunch first?"

"Oh yeah, I'm kind of hungry myself. What are you wanting?"

"Tropical Smoothie Café. I discovered their awesome cranberry walnut chicken salad sandwich, and there's a location not too far a walk from here on Broadway in the old YMCA building."

"Okay sounds good to me. Do you want to change outfits first?"

"Well, I'll leave the coat and the swords here. I guess the shirt will be a bit much, so I'll leave it here, too."

Kieran fit actions to words and stripped off the coat and shirt. Cory loved Kieran in the T-shirt and leather pants, and found himself getting hard in his jeans. He had to pinch the bridge of his nose to break up his fantasy. When Kieran was ready, the young men left, heading uptown to get lunch. Once they'd placed their orders, they sat at one of the tables and waited, chatting about possible poses for the painting and more about what the photo shoot would entail. Both men were taking in the other, their thoughts moving beyond artwork and into the realm of fantasy, but neither said a word.

6

Returning from his morning run Kieran headed for the bathroom to grab a quick shower, realizing he was running late for class. As he pulled open the door leading from his side of the shared bathroom, he spotted Cory doing the same thing from his side. The second thing catching Kieran's attention was how lean and fit Cory seemed. Cory, like Kieran, was dressed only in a pair of boxer-briefs. They both stared in shock for a moment before they laughed at the situation. Kieran recovered first.

"I guess we're both running late this morning."

"Yeah, I was up late last night putting the finishing touches on my painting, and I overslept." Cory's voice lowered as his eyes took in the jagged scars on Kieran's chest.

"I'm not sure where my mind was this morning during my run. It was like I was a million miles away until my alarm sounded and I realized I was further out than normal." Kieran rambled as he took in the blond fur across Cory's chest. It flowed down his abs into the waistband of his briefs. Blond hair covered Cory's arms and legs. He had to bite his tongue to keep from laughing at his thought, *With all that fur, Cory looks like a wolf.* While Kieran admired how handsome his roommate was, Cory appreciated how smooth and tan Kieran was.

Pale scars slashed across Kieran's tanned chest. Sweat rolled down the valley between his pectorals and over-ridged abs. His boxer-briefs were darker along the lines of his crotch, and Cory was willing to bet there was a sweat soaked line between the cheeks of Kieran's ass as well. Kieran broke their mutual spell of lust.

"Why don't we share the shower?" Kieran's gray eyes sparkled with silver as he flashed his devastating grin.

Cory went beet red in embarrassment. Oh, how he longed to take Kieran up on the offer. He wanted nothing more than to take the younger man in his arms and kiss him while their bodies pressed together. Cory stammered out his reply, "Uh, you go ahead. You're all sweaty from your run. I'll grab one when you're done."

As Cory was closing his door, Kieran removed his briefs.

"You don't need to be shy, Cory. We're both guys. It's not like we have anything to be ashamed of, or the other hasn't seen before." Kieran straightened up his semi-hard cock, hanging thick over his haired balls.

His pubic region was well trimmed and revealed the same dark hair as his head. It was the only visible hair on Kieran's body besides his armpits. The door between the bathroom and Cory's bedroom closed, blocking his view of a blushing Cory. He heard Kieran chuckle through the door and called himself a complete idiot. Kieran was beautiful and somehow managed to leave Cory acting like a virgin crushing on his first man. He leaned on the door, listening to the water run in the shower, and imagined himself tracing the path of the water as it flowed over Kieran's body. Kieran was leaning on the other side of the door, waiting for the water to get to his preferred temperature and kicking himself for embarrassing Cory. His lust and desire for the somewhat older Cory had him acting like a fool. Kieran stepped into the shower, shaking his head as he thought monster fighting was easier. Hell, his grandmother at the height of one of her rages was less scary than asking Cory out on a date. He washed, dried off, and dressed before knocking on the bathroom door to Cory's room to let him know the shower was free.

* * *

LATER THAT DAY, clutching the preliminary drawings for his portrait of Kieran to his chest, Cory waited for his painting instructor to come around to him for the review. Uncertainty gripped him almost with a grip almost as tight as the one he had on his sketchbook. In all honesty, Cory didn't wish to show them to Professor Simms. The drawings seemed too private, as if he'd captured a secret about Kieran he shouldn't share with anyone. Kieran had yet to see the drawings.

"Mr. Cooper, what are you ready for me to review?"

"Here are the rough sketches for the fantasy scene, Professor." Cory, with reluctance, released the sketchbook into his professor's hands.

Professor Simms glanced through the sketches and sensed a connection to the subject, a desire to possess the model for himself. Cooper's emotions regarding this model were evident. Professor Simms almost experienced the mingled lust and love leaping off the pages. His eyes grew dark with desire.

"I'd like to meet your model, Mr. Cooper."

"My model should be here right after class. We're in history together next."

"Your model is handsome. These are good. Let's hope your painting turns out as well."

"Thank you, sir."

Even before walking away from Cooper, Professor Simms's thoughts were on how to acquire the mysterious Kieran, and they shifted between various plans while he reviewed the next student's work with only half his attention. Professor Simms recognized Cory as an attractive young man, one he wouldn't mind chaining naked to his bed. The boy's model, however, was a prize worthy of being added to the Master's collection, if Cooper's sketches bore any connection to Kieran's actual appearance. As much as he desired to please his master with the gift of a beautiful boy like Kieran, Simms also admitted to himself how much he wanted the pleasure of breaking the boy to his own sexual desires first.

Around the time class was ending, Kieran arrived at the door to the studio, and Cory waved him in as he packed away his painting materials. Professor Simms caught a glimpse of a flowing black ponytail and lithe muscles as Kieran crossed the room to Cory's station. Kieran had his back to the professor as he talked with Cory regarding their upcoming class, but Simms was enthralled with the view of the tapered back and beautiful ass surmounting strong legs. When Kieran turned to leave, this beauty struck Simms, yet something twigged the professor's senses, and he realized he would need more information on the young man. How amazing was the fact Cooper's sketches had captured the reality. It was time to make use of his minions. Once Coach Henderson and his pack of jocks proved their loyalty by capturing Kieran and Simms had sated his own lusts on the boy's flesh, he would turn the boy over to the Master. As a backup plan in case the jocks failed, he would offer a modeling job to Kieran. Professor Simms decided he would offer an assistantship, paying half tuition to Kieran. From his dress style, he wasn't one of the wealthy students. It should entice him.

Now feet away, Kieran and Cory were nearing the door of the studio when Cory stopped short. A puzzled expression crossed Kieran's face as Cory turned back toward the professor's office.

"What's up? We're going to be late for class, and you know how Dr. Arson is about students arriving late to his class."

"Professor Simms wanted to meet you."

"Why does he want to meet me? I'm not a painting major."

"I think he might want you to model for him. He just told me he wanted to meet you while he was reviewing my sketches for the painting."

"All right, let's make it quick. I don't want to be struck down by Zeus' lightning bolts by being late to Dr. Arson's class."

Cory knocked on the open door to Professor Simms's office. "Mr. Cooper, come in."

"Professor Simms, this is Kieran Belle, my roommate and model."

"A pleasure to meet you, Mr. Belle. Mr. Cooper did a remarkable job of capturing your likeness in his sketches."

"A pleasure to meet you Professor Simms. I wouldn't know. Cory hasn't shown me any of his sketches. Something about jinxing the final project."

"Ah, yes, most painters never reveal their work until it's finished. It's a superstition."

Kieran caught the way Professor Simms was sizing him up. Almost like a piece of meat or a prized item up for auction. Why did the man seem to be trying to figure out how Kieran would appear when naked?

"I wanted to meet you after seeing Mr. Cooper's sketches to see if you'd match up to a concept a client of mine commissioned me to paint. I'd like you to model for me, for payment of course."

"I appreciate the offer, Professor, but there are my own studies and projects to complete. There's a limited amount of time for modeling in my schedule, and it's reserved for Cory."

"Well, if you change your mind, I can pay you five hundred dollars a day to model for me. I should only need a weekend of your time to get my sketches and initial painting done."

"Again, thank you for the offer, Professor, but I'm not interested, and there aren't enough hours in my week to spare time for another modeling job. Now, if you will excuse us, Cory and I can just make it to class on time. Dr. Arson doesn't like tardy students."

Kieran grabbed Cory's arm and hustled them out of the professor's office. The encounter with Professor Simms left Kieran shivering like he'd been called before the Council of Matriarchs. The sense of being appraised like a painting at auction didn't go away until they reached the relative safety of the hall. Sweet Goddess, he wanted a shower; instead, he was rushing himself and Cory across campus to Stabler Hall. Beside him, Cory chatted about something Kieran didn't hear as they crossed campus, never noticing Kieran's discomfort. All his emotions were locked behind a mask of calm as he and Cory took their seats and settled in moments before Dr. Arson arrived to start lecturing on the Trojan War.

When history was over, Kieran and Cory parted to head to different classes. Cory was headed to his small business economics class, while

Kieran headed to English literature, two seemingly normal college guys who weren't in a normal situation at all.

7

Kieran sat in his English literature class, trying not to groan out loud as Professor Jaynes lectured on the themes and content of several classical fairy tales, including *Beauty and the Beast*. What a nightmare it was to listen to anyone talk about this particular story since, to Kieran, the fairy tale wasn't fiction but actual family history. Well, the real underlying story was family history; all the published accounts were so altered, they didn't resemble anyone in the family history books and for good reason. The real prince was an idiot needing to be rescued from his own dungeon by a mere slip of a girl, armed with a silver dagger and a one-shot spell, or so his dad's side of the family told the tale. Mom's side of the family pumped Beauty up to near Amazon status. Somewhere between the two accounts is hidden the truth. No matter which side told the story, the prince came out a wimp. Hell, the poor guy was lucky to survive the shifter taking over his castle. Imagine the embarrassment of having to be saved by some merchant's daughter from your own dungeon. According to the family histories and a few records from a court historian, Beauty never did let the poor guy forget it for the rest of his miserable life.

"Mr. Belle, you're being quiet today. Please give us your insight into the story of *Beauty and the Beast*."

"Which version, Professor? The original French, the later English, the Brothers Grimm version, or Disney's slaughter of the tale?" Kieran's tone was snarky and he knew it.

"Mr. Belle, I don't need attitude or lip in this class. Now, your insight on the tale."

"Sorry, Professor. It's a tale about accepting others despite all the faults you perceive in them. Beauty's family perceives her as an outsider because she's not greedy like they are. She asks for a simple flower instead of fine clothing and jewels. Her sisters hate her because she's beautiful in everyone's eyes. The prince is rude, crude, and socially unacceptable, but Beauty perceives a good and gentle nature lies hidden deep inside the gruff exterior. When the prince at last views himself through Beauty's eyes, the Beast is slain and the prince is handsome to everyone."

"Interesting perspective on the tale, Mr. Belle. Now, class, I want each of you to take one of the tales we've covered in class, and give it a modern twist. I'll expect at least fifteen hundred words from each of you. First drafts of your papers are due by the end of next week."

Kieran bit back a groan, while the rest of the class sighed. Realizing he wasn't going to get out of adapting Beauty's story into modern times, Kieran ground his teeth, waiting for the bell to ring. His fear was confirmed as he passed by his professor on the way out.

"I expect you'll give me an interesting take on *Beauty and the Beast*, Mr. Belle."

"Yes, sir, although I was thinking more of tackling *Snow White*."

"I think you'll do better with *Beauty and the Beast*. Yours is an interesting take on the subject. I anticipate a fascinating read, Mr. Belle."

Kieran nodded and headed off to his next class. He had to jog across campus to get to his photography class. They were doing reviews today, and he was anticipating the next assignment. To be honest with himself, he was also thinking about watching the hunky Professor Mason while he critiqued everyone else's work. Despite the baggy clothes the professor wore while teaching, Kieran guessed there was a fit body underneath. While crossing campus, his phone rang with a special tone he reserved for his father.

"Hey, Dad. What's up?"

"Hello, Kieran, I know you're likely on your way to class, but—"

"Yeah, just finished with English lit, and get to do a paper on you-know-who and her Beastly prince."

"Kieran, be careful with that topic."

"I know, Dad. I wanted to do *Snow White*, but Professor Jaynes likes my insight into the topic of the bitch and the critter after I spewed the family-approved crap about it being a story of acceptance. So why the sudden call, Dad? Did Grandmother come to her senses? Do I get come home for the holidays? I want to spend Christmas with you and my sisters."

"No, I'm afraid the news there is all bad. Your grandmother expressly forbids you to come home. She's even decided trackers were no longer allowed to assist huntress-candidates in the test. Selene will be facing the test without you."

"Dad, it's not fair to Selene, never mind how unfair it is to prevent me from being with family for the holidays. I'm sorry I'm not the prize-breeding stallion Grandmother wants, but she's never been happy I was born in the first place."

"I'm sorry too, Kieran. We'd go to my family's compound, but your grandparents and uncle are headed back to the old country during the season, and your grandfather is sealing the place off until they get back."

"It's okay, Dad. There are projects for school to work on, and I think the guys are going to do something before they scatter for the holidays. I'll be okay."

"I'll call you over the holidays, and we'll talk. I love you, Son."

"Love you too, Dad."

Kieran trudged to class in a deep funk. He tried his best to push it aside during class to give his classmates a fair shake during peer reviews. Professor Mason realized his prized student wasn't giving it his best go and asked Kieran to stay after class since he knew Kieran didn't have another class after.

"Are you all right, Mr. Belle? You didn't participate much during the review session, and when you did, you were a little harsh on poor Mr. Harkrider's work."

"I'm sorry, Professor Mason. I didn't mean to rip Harkrider apart like that," Kieran admitted, relieved to talk to someone he felt he could trust. Over the last two months, Professor Mason had become Kieran's favorite. They'd bonded over the use of film for photography while most of the other students felt film was a waste of time since digital photography was now the norm. "I got a phone call from my dad on the way to class. I'm stuck in Little Rock for the holidays." Professor Mason knew Kieran was apart from his family, although he didn't know all the reasons why, so Kieran said what he could. "My grandmother opposed my leaving home to go to college and has forbidden my coming home since I left against her wishes."

"I'm sorry to hear it, Mr. Belle. I guess your friends are all going home to their families as well."

"Yeah, so it's just me all alone in a large house for two weeks. Nothing at all exciting."

"Well, cheer up, Mr. Belle. I'm sure something good will come of the holiday."

"Thanks, Professor. I'm sure you're right."

"What are you doing for the Thanksgiving holiday, Mr. Belle?"

"No plans so far, sir."

"I'm hosting a small dinner party for some of my fellow professors and our top students. I'd like you to attend as my guest."

"Thank you, sir. I'd be happy to attend. Do I need to bring anything?"

"Just your portfolio of your best class projects to date. I don't often enter any of my own students at these parties, but you surpass all my more recent students."

"I'm not sure what to say, Professor."

"Here's my address. Come early. I'd like to set up your work before everyone else arrives."

"I get the idea this became a competition between you and the other professors somewhere along the way."

"Well, at least between the other professors. I always try to stay neutral. You're the first student in years whom I think is worthy to be included."

"Thank you, sir. Would you help me pick the pieces to display?"

"Of course, Mr. Belle. Bring your portfolio to my office tomorrow after your last class and we'll choose."

"Yes, sir. I'll see you tomorrow around 4:30."

* * *

THE STUDENT KIERAN RIPPED APART, William Harkrider packed away his photographs in silence when Professor Mason dismissed class. All the images were candid shots, because he'd been so careful not to catch Kieran's attention when photographing him to capture the image of a carefree and relaxed person. People's reactions still amazed William. He couldn't figure out what made Kieran so mad about the photo William had taken of him. In the photo, Kieran leaned against a tree with his shirt open to reveal his smooth, muscular chest. The black and white shot made the strange scars on Kieran's chest stand out in contrast to his dark tanned skin tones. Perhaps, he's self-conscious about the scars and didn't like other people seeing them. William thought, *I guess I embarrassed him.*

* * *

LATER IN THE WEEK, Cory stood at his easel in class, comparing his sketches to the work on the werewolf and the hunter in his fantasy painting. He knew why both were so realistic even in these rough forms. After all, they were both modeled on real people. The hunter modeled after Kieran and the werewolf on his older brother Jeff's beast form. But no one would know about that. No one could know. The Cooper family had kept their shifter heritage a secret for generations. It was too dangerous to let outsiders know what they were. There was a measure of relief in sketching it out in the open, hiding in plain sight, and in his painting, the dark gray wolf leapt at the rough sketch of Kieran in his leathers. The huge painting was a pain to lug back and forth to class, but Cory refused to leave it in the studio. The two jocks in class, Stevens and Riley, hassled him and a couple other students. Their advisor, Coach Henderson, seemed different around Professor Simms, opposed to the monster he was when on the field with the team. He seemed to defer to Professor Simms.

"Mr. Cooper, my office please."

"Yes, Professor."

"Stevens and Riley, I'd better see some progress on your assignment by the end of class, or you'll likely be warming the bench when Coach Henderson gets my report."

The two jocks started applying paint to their canvases. Cory crossed the room to the professor's office.

"What can I do for you, Professor?"

"Professor Mason is holding his annual Thanksgiving dinner party next week. It's become something of a competition between the members of the art faculty to bring their best student and an example of their work to be judged. I'd like you to be my student guest. Even unfinished, your painting surpasses the work of my best senior students."

"I'm honored, sir. I don't think I can finish it before Thanksgiving. Kieran's schedule is crazy busy, and he hasn't had a lot of time to model for me."

"It doesn't need to be finished, Mr. Cooper. We'll display it just as is with your color sketches next to it."

"If you think so, Professor. I'll put everything together. Where does it need to go?"

"Here's Professor Mason's address. If you leave the painting here the night before, we can use my van to pick it up and bring it with us to Professor Mason's home."

"I hate to leave it unattended, sir."

"It will be safe, Mr. Cooper. We'll lock it up here in my office at the end of class."

"Okay, sir. What time should we meet on Thanksgiving?"

"Meet me here at 4:00. We'll load up and arrive early enough to get a good spot in Mason's house. I know just the spot, and it's picked out."

"Okay, sir, I'll be ready."

* * *

THANKSGIVING Day dawned bright and sunny. Kieran rose early and went for one of his runs. Cory was pacing his room, worried about what Professor Mason's dinner party held in store for him. Only last night, he'd learned Kieran was attending as Professor Mason's guest. Nothing scared him more than Kieran figuring out how much Cory lusted after him, and he was sure the evidence was all over his painting. Cory wanted to back out of tonight's party, but after all Professor Simms had done, he wouldn't disappoint the man. He would go. The real worry was Kieran. *Was Kieran entering a piece? And if so, what photograph was chosen for tonight's display?* Cory dressed and left to meet Professor Simms at the art building to frame his painting and load it into the professor's van, ready to face the artwork and evidence.

* * *

KIERAN'S RUN took him through Little Rock's historic Quapaw Quarter to Professor Mason's stately Victorian home. He knocked on the front door and was greeted by the professor dressed in casual attire of jeans and a T-shirt, revealing the sculpted body Kieran had suspected lay hidden beneath Professor Mason's regular teaching attire.

"Hey, Professor, I hope I'm not too early to help with the set up."

"Good morning, Mr. Belle. I was just having a second cup of coffee and getting the turkey in the oven. Come in and I'll show you where I think we should put your photographs for display tonight."

"Yes, sir."

Crossing the threshold, Kieran glanced at the beautiful hardwood floors and slipped off his shoes.

Professor Mason caught this and smiled. Kieran blushed at the older man's approval and glad for his loose running shorts. The professor's regard was adding to his handsome features to make Kieran's cock stiffen. Kieran heard one of his grandmother's lectures in his head, and his looming erection subsided. Professor Mason led him into a living room with a huge fireplace. The space above the mantle was barren, and Kieran recognized a pattern of fading, indicating something had hung there for some time.

Professor Mason saw the question in Kieran's eyes as he stared at the blank space above the fireplace. "I took down the old landscape painting, which used to hang up there."

Kieran glanced over his shoulder at the professor. "Why would you do that, sir?" He asked, curious for the answer.

"It's a prime location for display. Several of my colleagues have asked for it in the past, and I've always said no."

"It sounds like the painting you had up there was special, sir. Why take it down for this party?"

"Because, Mr. Belle, I want to hang your photograph of the young man lacing up his boot against the backhoe in its place."

"Isn't this too large a space for such a print? We never do anything larger than what can be processed at school."

"I believe it displays your talent is the best of all your work thus far, so I had it enlarged to fit the space."

"Did you choose the one where his shirt is hanging from the back of his belt or with his shirt on, sir?"

"The one with his shirt off. Your talent for bringing out hidden emotions with the play of light and shadow on your subject stands out best in that version. In fact, I like it so much that I want to purchase the photograph from you when you graduate."

"I'm flattered, Professor. If you like so much, I'll give it to you as a gift."

"I'm honored, Mr. Belle, but I insist on paying you for it."

"Well, I hope you don't think I did a bad job when you meet the model. He'll be here tonight with Professor Simms." Kieran couldn't hide the dislike of the professor from his voice.

"I gather you don't care for Professor Simms."

"I met him once but couldn't help how it seemed like he was sizing me up like a piece of meat for market. Sorry, sir, I shouldn't talk about another professor in such awful terms."

"Why don't we drop the *sir* or *professor*? You can call me John and I'll call you Kieran."

"I'm never comfortable calling people in authority by their given names, sir. Being proper and polite was drummed into me at an early age. My grandmother is a strict woman when it comes to protocol."

"Well, I'm certain I don't want to make you uncomfortable, Kieran. Since you're majoring in photography, I expect you'll be my student for a while."

"Thank you, sir. So shall we hang the print?"

"Yes, and you can tell me all about the model. I can tell from the way you captured him, your feelings for him show."

"Cory is a wonderful guy, sir. He's my first real friend in ages. I think there's potential for more if I don't mess things up any further."

"What did you do?"

"I embarrassed both of us one day. I came back late from a run and went to go take a shower to get ready for class. We share the bathroom between our rooms, and we both walked into it in just our underwear. I think we were both checking each other out, and I asked if he wanted to share the shower since we were both running late. He fled to his room and closed the door, saying he'd wait until I was done."

"I imagine it was awkward."

"Yeah, it was. We've sort of made a joke out of it, and now we just leave the doors to the bathroom open unless one of us has company."

"So you check each other out often then?"

Kieran turned bright red, realizing he was discussing his crush on another boy to his professor and likely mentor.

"I guess we do, sir. So where is the print you want to hang?"

Professor Mason chuckled at Kieran's attempt to change the subject. He pointed to a large wrapped bundle leaning against the sofa.

Kieran crossed to it and removed the wrapping to reveal a large version of the portrait of Cory. A sigh escaped his lips as he glanced at the beauty of his friend in the photograph.

"He's beautiful, and I am eager to meet your friend, Kieran."

"Thank you, sir. You'll like Cory. He's a sweet guy."

Together, Kieran and Professor Mason got the portrait hung over the fireplace. They spent time arranging several smaller images around the room before a timer sounded from the rear of the house.

"Ah, time to go check on the turkey and get some of the other food going."

"Do you do all the cooking, sir?"

"Yes, Kieran. I love to cook, and I enjoy having company over for the holidays. If you're still stuck here in town for the Christmas break, I hope you will come and join my friends and I for Christmas Eve and Christmas Day."

"I think I'd like to join in, sir. Is there anything I can help you get ready for tonight?"

"If you don't mind, the formal dinning room isn't set up for tonight yet. You'll find everything on the sideboards. Are you any good with flower arranging?"

"My sister Rosie kids me about my magic touch with cut flowers."

"Is this your way of saying they all wilt when you touch them?"

"No, sir. She's always amazed at what I can create out of the assortment of flowers we get to work with."

"Well, you will find a couple of large vases in the butler's pantry and several dozen cut flowers in the walk-in refrigerator at the end of the pantry. Work your magic, Kieran."

"Yes, sir."

Kieran went into the butler's pantry and down to the walk-in refrigerator. There he found dozens of fresh cut flowers, many of them not even in season. Kieran wondered what florist had found the amazing array of flowers at this time of the year. When he picked up the first bundle, he sensed the magic in them. Emerald magic swirled around the stems and flowers, keeping them fresh and alive. The Emerald magic danced along his fingers, teasing his own Silver magic to play. He sensed the Emerald magic was connected to Professor Mason, and fearing detection, he silenced his own magic and brought the flowers out to the dinning room to arrange the huge vases Professor Mason had set out. When he didn't sense a reaction from the professor, Kieran set about arranging the flowers, letting them tell him where they wanted to go as he relaxed his hold on his own magic to hear the directions of the Emerald magic. Silver magic twined around the Emerald, reinforcing the life-giving magic and preserving it. Soon, two massive arrangements stood in the center of the table, and Kieran was setting the table for a formal dinner party.

"You do possess a rare talent with flowers, Kieran."

Kieran whirled, a butter knife held battle ready in his hand to face a shocked Professor Mason. The professor raised his hands up to show his hands empty of any weapons. Kieran did sense the professor's Emerald magic held in check.

"Sorry, sir. I guess I was miles away. You startled me."

"It's okay, Kieran. I didn't realize you'd lost yourself in your task. Those arrangements are beautiful. Your creativity is a real gift."

Kieran spotted the telltale sparkle of Emerald magic in the professor's sea-green eyes and wondered how he hadn't seen it before. His own sparkled silver as he laughed at the situation when he realized he was holding the professor at bay with a butter knife.

"Oh, sorry, sir. Reflex action."

"Your family must host some dangerous dinner parties."

"You would be surprised, Professor."

"It's not easy growing up in a mage family, is it, Kieran?" There was no point hiding it anymore.

"I wouldn't know, sir. My family aren't mages; they're hunters."

"Well, there's the reason for the lightning reflexes. I know I shouldn't ask, but I can sense Silver magic around you. Which hunter family do you belong to?"

"I can recognize your Emerald magic as well, Professor. As for my family, I can't tell you. If you don't know, you can't be forced to tell someone else, sir."

"I understand, Kieran. You're safe here, and I am an ally if you ever need one. The hunter's life is never easy."

"Thank you, Professor. I should go get ready for tonight."

"Kieran, a word of advice. Protect yourself. Some of my colleagues are not what they want you to think they are."

"Thanks, Professor. I'd better go. By the way, Professor, dinner is starting to develop a wonderful aroma." Kieran flashed one of his brilliant smiles as he headed for the front door.

Professor Mason was again struck by Kieran's beauty. His thoughts took a quick unprofessional turn. I'd love to have Kieran model for me, preferably a long session where he goes from fully dressed to totally nude. I couldn't help but sense his attraction to me, but did Kieran even realize his running shorts weren't hiding his arousal in the slightest? Okay, John, time to get your mind off undressing your student and breaking all the rules, and back onto getting things ready for dinner. Professor Mason headed upstairs to take a cold shower and refocus his mind on his dinner party.

* * *

CORY PACED around the painting studio, waiting on Professor Simms. The fantasy scene left Cory wishing for more working time; the painting's unfinished status bothered him. The werewolf leapt from the canvas, attacking an unfinished figure. Kieran's vague form on the canvas drew the eye away from the rest of the painting. For Cory, the worst part was he couldn't take up his brushes and paints to do any more work on the piece because the canvas was already framed for the party at Professor Mason's tonight. Cory turned when the studio doors open.

"So, Mr. Cooper, are you ready to go?"

"I wish it was in a more finished state. I also wish Kieran wasn't going to be there tonight."

"It's still a master work, Mr. Cooper. Once it's hung over the fireplace in Mason's living room, it will be the most talked about piece there."

"Well, I guess we should go get it hung before someone else takes the spot you want, Professor."

"The only one who with the time to claim the space will be Professor Mason, and I doubt he'd take up space with student-sized photographic prints."

"Is there anything in the rules of this little competition against having a larger print made of a photograph?"

"No, but your friend's photography would be something special for Mason to get a print as large as your canvas made up."

I guess we'll get your chosen spot. So I guess we should go."

Cory and Professor Simms loaded the huge painting and the smaller framed sketches into the professor's van and drove to Professor Mason's house. Kieran, who'd been home, returned dressed in his leathers, and he met them at the door. Professor Simms leered at Kieran for a moment until the wards woven into the leathers forced his eyes away. Kieran's silver eyes darkened to storm gray with a hint of silver lightning flashing with in.

"Cory, Professor Simms, welcome. You're early. Professor Mason wasn't expecting anyone and ran to the store to get a couple of things he forgot. Please come in. Do you need help with your painting?"

"Thank you, Mr. Belle. We'd like to hang this in the living room over the fireplace."

"I'm sorry, sir. Professor Mason claimed the space over the fireplace for my piece. The space over the fireplace in the study is available if you'd like."

"I'm surprised Mason would waste so much space on small works."

"The professor had my selection blown up to fit the space, sir."

"Well, the study will do."

Kieran led the way to the study, and left Cory and Professor Simms to hang their work in the space. He retreated to the kitchen to check on several items being served for dinner as Professor Mason returned.

"Hello, sir. Professor Simms and Cory Cooper are here, and they're hanging their painting in the study."

"I bet Simms is miffed he couldn't get the living room. Next to no one ever wanders into the study."

"He didn't seem pleased, even less when he learned you claimed the space for my work."

"Oh well, he'll get over his disappointment in time. Now, let's check on the turkey; it should be time to baste it again."

8

---

cting as co-host for Professor Mason's dinner party, Kieran greeted guests and helped them find places to display their works. He even made sure to direct the entire list of guests to visit the study to see his friend's painting, since there was no reason Cory should be punished because Kieran didn't like Professor Simms. The heaviest praise was directed at Kieran's photo of Cory, and he heard his friend getting lots of compliments and a few requests to model. Another professor's comment regarding his photograph was voiced loud enough for Kieran to overhear it.

"Mason, this is amazing work. I've never seen a photograph capture not only the beauty of the model but also the love of the photographer for his subject. Are the boys a couple?"

"As far as I know, Rodgers, they're roommates and good friends. Mr. Belle is a talented photographer. His portfolio of work is over by the couch if you'd like to see additional samples."

"Thanks, I'll check it out."

Kieran was stunned. He didn't think his crush on Cory was so obvious it showed in his work. He would check out the giant photo again after the party. He was turning to answer the door for another guest when he overheard a student guest commenting on Cory's painting.

"I'm surprised Professor Simms brought an unfinished piece to display. Perhaps if the figure of the fighter was the finished part instead of the werewolf, it would be a better piece."

Kieran bit his tongue and let the newest guests in. The current arrivals were Professor Crane, the ceramics professor, and his student, Marissa Holden. Marissa was carrying a large raku vessel, and missed the last step up into the house. The vessel went flying as Marissa fell. Kieran moved without thinking, and caught the vessel and Marissa. He handed the vessel off to Professor Crane, and helped Marissa to a seat, checking to make sure she was okay.

"I'm okay. Thank you for saving my piece. It took me weeks to get one to survive the firing process with the coloring I wanted."

"It's beautiful. Pots don't turn on the wheel for me; all I get is a mess."

"If you need extra help, come ask me. I'm Professor Crane's teaching assistant." Marissa smiled.

"I'll keep it in mind. Thanks. There's a spot in the living room to the right of the fireplace begging for a piece like yours. The lighting will highlight your raku to perfection."

"Thanks, I'll check it out. I'm sorry I haven't introduced myself. Marissa Holden."

"Kieran Belle, I'm Professor Mason's entry this year."

"You must be quite the photographer. Professor Mason hasn't entered anyone into this little competition in about ten years, or so according to rumors."

"Well, I hope I don't let him down. Judge for yourself. My entry is hanging over the fireplace in the living room."

"Now I know you're better than good. He wouldn't take down the painting from above the fireplace in there for anything."

"He told me it was something which had hung there for ages when we were hanging my photograph."

"Oh my, from what's been said, the painting over the fireplace in the living room was a landscape painted by his partner. They'd been together since high school."

"I sense a tragedy. One which might be better if Professor Mason tells me the story himself rather being the topic of student gossip."

"You're right. Well, I'd better get this displayed if I want a shot at second place."

"Don't sell yourself short, Marissa. I'd say you're in the running for first place."

"Not a chance, Kieran. Not when Professor Mason gave your work pride of place in his home. I'll see you around."

Marissa laughed and smiled as she slid by Kieran to take her pottery into the living room. He sensed a hint of shifter about her, but it was wrapped with Emerald magic, so more than likely she was a creation-sided shifter. Perhaps the reports to his family on the number of shifters in the area were out of date, but Kieran's curiosity disappeared as Professor Mason caught his attention.

"Everything is ready. If you'll help me get the food laid out on the sideboards, the hungry masses can get food, and eat and bicker over who's student created the best piece."

"I'm beginning to think you invited me so you'd get an extra set of hands instead of having to do it all by yourself," Kieran teased his professor.

"Ugh, you caught me. I can't resist free labor. It's been exciting to make use of the help."

"Will you tell me about your partner sometime, Professor? I bet she is someone special."

"Yes, he was special," Professor Mason corrected lightly. "We'll talk after everyone leaves, if I can convince you to stay and help me clean up."

Professor Mason's smile lit up his face in a way his colleagues hadn't seen in the last couple of years. From across the room, Cory noted the silver sparkle in Kieran's eyes. *He's happy*, Cory thought, fighting down a twinge of jealousy in his own feelings. *Well, he deserves to be happy with someone. I still can't believe how amazing he made me appear in his photos. I'd bet good money any photos he took of his professor would be even more beautiful. I wish Professor Simms had chosen another student's work.*

Kieran and Professor Mason disappeared into the kitchen to get the food out. Cory overheard a couple of professors starting to speculate on Kieran and Professor Mason's relationship. If their gossip spread, it would cause trouble for both the professor and Kieran. Cory crossed to the professors and addressed them.

"Do you think you should be gossiping about a fellow professor? How pure are your relationships with your chosen student? Kieran's my roommate and friend. I can tell you he'd never do anything like what you're suggesting."

"I guess someone's jealous. Lusting after your roommate? Seems you enjoy getting naked for him. What's the matter? Did he not make any passes at you once you were naked?" sneered Doctor Smythe, the art history chair.

"Smythe?" Professor Mason reentered the room, and by his expression, everyone knew he'd overheard. "Somehow, I'm not surprised you're attempting to smear my name. What was the name of the co-ed you were accused of sleeping with two years ago? Unlike some people, I remained faithful to my partner, even after he died. Can you say the same about your relationship with your wife?"

Professor Mason was angry. Even from the kitchen, Kieran sensed the man's Emerald magic rising with his emotions. Hearing the professor's voice coming from beyond the kitchen, Kieran paused his task. He glanced around the room, wondering when the professor had slipped out of the kitchen and returned to his guests.

Kieran made short work as he finished carving the turkey, and he went to find out what was going on. He was surprised to see his professor in a heated argument with another professor, which seemed to be about Kieran and some unnamed co-ed. A flash of Ruby magic caught Kieran's attention. Some other mage was pushing the anger in the room. The argument was reaching a dangerous flashpoint. If someone didn't do something to calm the situation down, Professor Mason's magic would be revealed to all of his guests. Stepping back into the kitchen, Kieran let out a soft whisper of Silver magic to wash over the room, using its superior powers to snuff out all other magic and create a sense of peace. Out of Kieran's sight, Professor Simms stiffened as Silver magic washed over the scene, erasing his work. He knew Mason's magic was Emerald and his late partner's had been Sapphire. Simms held back a scream of frustration as his carefully-crafted plan fell apart, and he was left trying to figure out where a Silver mage of such skill had come from. Try as he might, he couldn't find a way to trace the magic back to a point of origin, which meant that any of the several people absent from the room might be the mysterious mage. For a moment, fear gripped Professor Simms at the thought of having to face a skilled Silver mage. He needed better planning if he was going to capture the boy. Belle was a prize which couldn't be allowed to slip away. Presenting him to the Master as a gift would assure Simms of advancement in the Master's organization.

"Dinner is ready. If you will all please gather round, Professor Mason asked me to bless this gathering and the food." Kieran drew everyone's attention to him and directed everyone to hold hands, his own voice rising over the gathering.

"Ancient spirit of creation, we as your humble disciples, thank you for the outpouring of your gifts. You bless us with a spark of your wondrous creation. Let each of us gathered here go forth to spread beauty and art for your glory. Bless the food we are about to partake for the nourishment of your spirit within us all. For the glory and joy of creation."

The guests started making their way past the sideboards, choosing from all the wonderful foods and finding seats around the table and elsewhere in the house. Professor Mason took Kieran aside to warn him about the gossip.

"Kieran, we need to be careful."

"What's going on, sir? I sensed all the anger in the room."

"Some people are attempting to start a rumor about us being a couple and breaking school rules."

"I'm sorry, sir. I thought most people would pick up on how big my crush on Cory Cooper is. Like you said, my photograph of him is kind of a giveaway to my true feelings."

"They're looking at where I placed it. They also know I'm the one who had it enlarged to be a perfect fit for the space. Those inclined to think so, figure you're my new partner and I'm showing you off by replacing his painting with your photography."

"This is awkward, sir. It's too late to drop out of your class without killing my grades this semester. I can switch to Professor Haynes next semester."

"Don't you dare, Kieran. We'll talk about this after everyone leaves."

"I'll see if Cory can stay afterward. It might be wise not to add any more fuel to the rumors."

Professor Mason and Kieran brought out a few more food items. Kieran tested the tension around the room and found it was lower than it had been before he'd smothered it with Silver magic. For those with the gift, the lingering traces of Ruby magic could still be detected trying to fan a spark. He took a seat near Cory, hoping his friend would provide some comfort.

"Hey, how are you doing, Cory? I didn't get to talk to you earlier."

"Well, you were busy. You and Professor Mason seem to get along. I don't recall the last time you were this happy."

"He's a fantastic guy and a fantastic cook. He's worried his colleagues think he's crossing a line, which shouldn't be crossed. The tension is building, and I don't like the stress."

"Kieran, I'm worried about you and the professor. The gossip is horrible."

"I know. The professor mentioned the rumors while we were getting refills on some of the food. I offered to switch photography professors next semester, but he told me not to dare."

"I think you would only make things appear worse. The gossips would take your changing classes as confirmation they were right about you two having an affair. Once you're no longer his student, he can't be censured or fired for being in an inappropriate relationship with a student."

"Yeah, I get that. I like the professor, and I think he's hot, but he's not the guy I'm interested in."

"Watching you two tonight, I find it hard to tell your feelings are for someone else."

Cory appeared and sounded depressed that Kieran said he was interested in someone. Kieran caught Cory's chin in his hand and tipped the man's face so Cory was looking at him. His fingers enjoyed the soft sensation of hair against his hand, and for the first time tonight, he was aware Cory hadn't shaved in a while and a blond beard was now softening his face. He leaned in and kissed Cory.

Gasps echoed around the room. From the corner of his eye, Kieran spotted Professor Mason's smile.

"You're the one I'm interested in, dummy."

"You want me?"

"Yes, Cory Cooper, I want you to be my boyfriend and more. If you don't believe I want you, go to the living room, and stare long and hard at the photographic portrait of you hanging above the fireplace. If you can't tell me you get how much I admire you from the photo, I promise I'll leave you alone."

"I've been staring at your photograph most of the night. Yes, I want to be your boyfriend and more."

Cory dragged Kieran in tight and kissed him for everyone to witness. Professor Simms eyes flashed an angry red as he spotted his prized student kissing the boy he wanted to gift to the Master. Professor Mason pondered the blooming young love, and the background aura of gossip burned away. When Cory and Kieran broke their kiss, the guests all applauded. Both young men blushed a deep shade of crimson. Professor Mason rose and drew everyone's attention.

"I think it is time to adjourn to the living room and for everyone to cast their ballots for the best art projects."

The guests all left the table and headed for the living room where they found ballot sheets laid out for them to vote with and a box to put their sheets into. Kieran and Cory hung back to help Professor Mason clear the table and set it for dessert.

"I'm happy for both of you. I think you will make a fantastic couple."

"Thanks, Professor Mason. I hope Kieran can always call on you as a friend and mentor."

"I'm happy both of you stumbled into my life. Now, you two should go cast your ballots, while I set out the dessert."

Kieran and Cory left the kitchen, heading for the dining room, but ran into Professor Simms in the hallway. Kieran pulled out his phone and pretended to scroll for an app, even thought his sudden stance in front of Cory was obviously defensive. Still, the professor didn't budge. Kieran kept his eyes on the screen. "Is there something you want, Professor Simms?"

"Yes, there is, Mr. Belle. I want you to model for me in the nude. I'd like to see what Professor Mason's so attracted to. If you're a good boy and do what I want, Mason will escape a board of inquiry into his illicit relationship with a student."

"You are pathetic, Professor. Where's your evidence to prove your allegation? How many times must I tell you? I'm not interested in modeling for you, so let it go."

"First, I don't need proof to raise the allegation. Second, you will model for me or your lover suffers being discredited as a teacher. Third, if you don't model for me, Mr. Cooper here will fail the semester and be forced to repeat my class."

Cory drew a breath to reply, but Kieran cut him off.

"You disgust me, Professor Simms. You think you can hurt innocent people so you can sate your own perverted lust. I will not model for you. If you attempt to threaten Cory or Professor Mason, I will give the administration the recording of your threats toward us."

"You're bluffing. You will do it because you want to save your friends. My private studio on campus in the art building tomorrow at noon."

"Professor, there's nothing for you to use as leverage over me. This conversation is over. If anything happens to my friends, I wont hesitate to send a copy of the recording I made of this conversation to the school administration and to the police. Are we clear?"

Simms growled, stalking off.

Kieran pulled his phone from his pocket and stopped the recording. He sent a copy of the file to Cory and Professor Mason's phones.

"If anything happens to me, or he threatens you again, send the file to the school's administration and to the police."

Kieran kissed Cory before they went into the living room. Professor Mason had a puzzled expression on his face as they entered. Kieran led Cory past the professor and whispered in the professor's ear, "I'll explain later."

The pair cast their ballots for the best artwork. The box was emptied of ballots, and they were counted. Kieran's photographs were voted first place, Marissa's raku piece came in second, and a sculpture student's piece came in third. After the ballots were read, everyone went back to the dining room for dessert. The party broke up soon afterward, leaving Kieran, Cory, and Professor Mason to clean up. Kieran explained the reason for the file he'd sent to Professor Mason.

"Thank you, Kieran. I don't think any other student would think of protecting his professor like this."

"Professor, I'm doing this to protect us. Professor Simms is disgusting and should be dismissed from teaching. Besides, protecting people is what's natural to me."

"Remember to let others protect you in return, Kieran."

"Okay, enough worrying. Cory lets help get this mess cleaned up so the professor doesn't have to deal with a pile of dishes in the morning."

"You two go on home. I have a cleaning crew coming in the morning to straighten up everything. You need some time together, and I'm ready for some quiet time on my own."

"If you're sure, sir."

"I'm sure, Kieran. You guys have a good night. You can come back tomorrow night and collect your portfolio and painting."

"Thanks, Professor. Come on, Cory let's enjoy the walk home. You can spend the night cuddled up with me in my bed."

"How do you know I want to spend the night in your bed? I might want you to spend the night in mine."

"Are we trying to figure out who the top dog in this relationship is?

We haven't even had a real first date and we're standing here debating whose bed we're spending the night in."

"Okay, I guess we're moving too fast on the bed front. I don't even know how much experience you've got, Kieran."

"I was afraid you'd ask me about my experience."

Cory read between the lines as if he'd known Kieran for years. "Aw, how sweet, the little virgin thinks he can be top dog. Relax, Kieran I won't ever hurt you or force you to do anything you're not comfortable with."

"I never thought you would, Cory. Let's try moving at a slow pace. This is all new to me, and I don't want to rush into anything and regret ruining an amazing friendship."

"No rush, Kieran. Let's hang out tonight and go to our separate beds. We can go out to dinner and a movie tomorrow night as a first date."

"Sounds like a plan to me. By the way, I like the beard. You should keep it."

The two young men arrived back at their house and settled on the couch in the TV room. They kissed and cuddled for a while before deciding to head upstairs to their separate rooms for the night, finally together at last.

INTERLUDE: PROFESSOR SIMMS PREPARES PLAN B

Enraged to be defeated like an apprentice by a mere child, Professor Simms left the party without bothering to check if Cory possessed a way to get home. Pulling his cell phone from his pocket, he hit a programmed number.

"You've reached Coach Henderson. I'm either coaching or scouting, and can't take your call now. Leave a message at the tone."

"Henderson, it's Simms. Return my call at once or face punishment." Simms snarled into the phone before mashing his finger on the end call button. Simms had hardly disconnected the call when his phone rang with Henderson's number displayed on the screen.

"You wanted to speak with me, sir?" came Coach Henderson's question.

"I have two things I need you to do, you mangy cur. First, I want you to arrange to break a student's will and get him to submit to the Master's will. It can't happen for a while, so you will have time to plan and make preparations. Second, get your ass to my place, let yourself into the dungeon, and chain yourself to the St. Andrew's cross, ass on display."

"Yes, sir. Do I need to know the name of this student?"

"Not at this time."

"Yes, sir, I'll be on my way to your dungeon to service your pleasure."

"You're a good slave." Simms hung up.

9

During the rest of the Thanksgiving weekend, Kieran and Cory spent a lot more time together getting to know each other and trying to build a relationship. Kieran asked Cory out for a dinner that Saturday for the experience of a normal date. The young men seemed to enjoy themselves and each other. When the weekend was over, classes resumed, and both Kieran and Cory plunged themselves into their schoolwork and projects as the end of the first half of the school year approached. They were both so busy with schoolwork their budding romantic relationship drifted off to the sidelines, and they became more like close friends instead of boyfriends. After spending hours processing prints in the photo lab for final review, Kieran left school and headed back to the house. When he got home, Cory, George, and Theo were hanging out in the TV room erecting a Christmas tree. To Kieran, it appeared as though there were more lights wrapped around Theo instead of the tree. Cory and George were having a good laugh, hanging off each other. A small flash of envy flickered through Kieran's mind at the sight of George with his hands on Cory, and a small part of his mind screamed *mine* before he shook the emotion off as just two friends goofing around. Oh, how he wanted to run his hands over Cory's body and have Cory do the same to him.

"Hey, Kieran, give me a hand before these two decide to plunk the angel on my head and plug me in."

"You'd make an ugly tree, Theo. Hold still, and let me find the end of the light string."

It took a few minutes to get Theo unwrapped and the lights on the tree where they belonged. Kieran was in a better mood when the tree was all decorated. Kieran thought, *It's nice to have a tree in the house, even if the guys won't be around to enjoy it.*

"Hey, guys, where did all the Christmas stuff come from?"

"Mrs. Jones brought it by. She thought we needed some Christmas cheer before finals," George answered

"This is a nice gift from Mrs. Jones. Christmas cheer makes my day better," Kieran replied.

"What's the matter Kieran?" Cory asked.

"Family issues. I'm stuck here for the holidays because my grandmother doesn't get my not wanting to be part of the family business. I'm forbidden from going home to visit my dad and my sisters."

"I'm sorry. Hey, crazy idea, why don't you come and spend the break with me and my big family? There's plenty of room for another body on the farm," Cory offered.

"And your folks will go for you bringing home a total stranger? Cory, I don't think it's such a wonderful idea. I'll work on projects and keep myself busy around here, and there's an invitation to Professor Mason's for dinner on Christmas Day if I'm in town."

"Nope, I'm not going to leave you here to mope for two weeks. You're coming home with me and hanging out for the holidays."

"Hey, guys, you'd better kiss or move; you're hogging the mistletoe," George called out.

For the first time in almost a month, Cory wrapped Kieran in a hug, kissing him on the lips before releasing him to jog upstairs to his rooms. Kieran stood stunned for a moment before blushing and racing to his own rooms as Theo and George laughed at him.

Shock ran through Kieran as he pondered what, if anything, Cory's kiss meant. After Professor Mason's dinner party at Thanksgiving, they'd given dating a shot, but it had sort of fizzled out as their schedules got busier with projects. This kiss had been different from the other's they'd shared; it felt like there was a spark of something else in this kiss. Confused, Kieran buried himself in his homework to try and stop thinking about the kiss. He heard Cory in the shared bathroom but refused acknowledging the open door. They made a silent agreement to leave the doors to the bathroom open, flirting with silent glances and scoping each other out. Okay, this line of thought wasn't helping. He needed to either work or get out of the house. Cory's humming as he painted decided it for Kieran. He grabbed his iPod and fled the house for a long run.

* * *

CORY STOOD in front of the painting he was working on, not seeing what he was painting. While he'd never shifted, Cory had just enough of the blood in him to heighten his senses. Deep within him was the Beast, but his blood was too weak to shift. He paced, both wanting to claim Kieran and at the same time afraid of something about the man. Wondering if the fear was anything to do with the metallic tang in Kieran's kiss, Cory paced his small studio space. Cory heard a frustrated snarl through the bathroom and heard Kieran's study chair scrape the floor before the door slammed and Kieran raced down the stairs. Cory's focus shifted with Kieran's sudden departure from the house. Well, Kieran's departure made Cory certain he wasn't the only one affected by the kiss. Despite the frustration, the kiss created only one real question, and it ran through Cory's mind. *Would Kieran let himself be kissed again?*

In frustration, Cory forced himself to step back and stare at the painting he was working on. Kieran's face stared back at him, determined to meet any challenge. The painting seemed almost alive for reasons other than its life-size proportion. The portrait of Kieran stared back at him with a challenge in his silver eyes Cory somehow managed to capture in life-like splendor. Those painted eyes challenged, *Will you capture my heart with the same ease you captured my image?*

* * *

KIERAN'S FLIGHT from the house took him into parts of Little Rock best not traveled alone at night. He wasn't paying attention to his surroundings, lost in his thoughts about Cory and the kiss. Was it real or just because there was mistletoe and an audience? When he was knocked from his feet by a flying tackle from the side, Kieran realized he'd wandered into a bad section of town. His senses opened wide to his surroundings and the person who'd attacked him. He rolled away from a kick, avoiding broken ribs, and bounced to his feet. Kieran came into the personal space of a huge man who reeked of corruption. The shifter came at him again, and Kieran managed to dodge, and with a swift leg sweep, he sent the guy sprawling. In response, the shifter rolled and pulled up short when confronted by the glowing silver dagger in Kieran's hand.

"I'm so not the person you want to deal with now, shifter. So you get one chance to get the hell away from me before I nail your worthless hide to the nearest building."

"How the fuck do you know what I am?"

"Idiot, shifter, didn't anyone in your pack ever teach you about hunters and trackers?"

"Pack? I've been a lone wolf since I was twelve."

"Well, I suggest you find a pack or at least a mentor, because the next tracker you face won't let you walk away. They'll nail you to the wall and let their hunter take you out. It's your lucky day my huntress is out of state, or you'd be toast."

Kieran gave himself a mental kick in the ass when the shifter's eyes went from caution to blood lust.

"So the little tracker doesn't have back up from a hunter. Hey, boys, lets play."

Three more shifters emerged from the alleyway, just behind

Kieran. He swore under his breath as they encircled him. Four to one. Hell, one more and he'd qualify as a hunter in his own right. Luck was with him, the moon was far from full, so they wouldn't be able to take Beast form. Acknowledging this fact, his only option was to beat them to a pulp and leave them alive. Shifters retained whatever form they were in when they died. Killing them while human would result in murder charges if the police arrived. They pounced for him, and Kieran dropped and rolled so they collided with each other. He gained distance from them and called up a stun spell of Silver magic. He threw the spell at them and then headed for home as fast as possible. Kieran decided when he got back to the house he was removing all the damn mistletoe from the house. Misfortune caught up to Kieran, who didn't get far as a fifth shifter tackled him only a block later.

"Going somewhere, tracker?"

"Home." He slammed both hands blazing with Silver magic into the shifter's chest.

The shifter flew into the vacant lot behind them. Fortune didn't give Kieran a chance to recover. The other four shook off the effects of the stun spell and were on him before he picked himself up off the ground. Booted feet thudded into his ribs as he tried to roll away from them.

"Pick him up, boys. This little tracker needs to learn not to cross into our territory."

The two largest shifters grabbed Kieran's arms and hoisted him to his feet, holding him so his body was wide open for the fists hammering into him. The possible sound of his ribs breaking and the rising metallic tang of blood filling his mouth brought back unpleasant reminders of training session. Blow after blow slammed into him as the lead shifter unleashed his rage. Kieran let his own fury at the assault flow through him and raised his head in defiance, eyes blazing pure silver, just an instant before he cut loose with a wave of Silver magic and sent the five shifters flying in all directions. He sank to one knee, trying to draw a proper breath. His Silver magic sputtered and then was gone. It wouldn't help; Silver magic wasn't for healing. He needed to get to a hospital or to a Sapphire mage to get his ribs tended to. Staggering to his feet, he set out for home.

Bright Mother, please let me get home before I pass out, ran the silent prayer in Kieran's head. Intense pain staggered Kieran as he drew closer to the house, but he shoved the pain down and focused on getting home to Cory. Some instinct told him Cory would fix everything. *Why am I expecting him? I don't think he's going to kiss me again and make all the pain go a way like magic. Not likely.* In his head, he knew Cory was as normal as they came, not a secret mage or anything. He's just the first guy whose kiss meant something.

* * *

A NAGGING SUSPICION sent Cory out to the front porch. He paced, trying to figure out what was wrong. When he cast his thoughts on Kieran, the sense of something wrong staggered him. *Please be all right*, Cory breathed a silent prayer for Kieran's safety as he pondered the strange reactions they'd both experienced after the kiss under the mistletoe. Never had a kiss thrown him so off balance or left him reeling like this one. What the fuck was so different about this kiss from all the ones they'd shared back when they were dating after Thanksgiving? Cory spotted the shadows stirring at the end of the walkway to the house, and instinct told him it was Kieran coming home injured.

"Oh my god, Kieran what happened?" Cory raced off the porch to catch a sagging Kieran.

"Went running and ended up in the wrong part of town. I wasn't paying attention and got jumped." Kieran wheezed while holding his ribs.

"Let's get you to the hospital. Did you call the police?"

"No, I don't remember if I even had my phone with me."

"They'll call them when we get you to the hospital emergency room. Just lean on me." Cory cradled Kieran and got him settled into a car.

Cory sped to the nearest emergency room, which happened to be at the University of Arkansas for Medical Sciences. He got the attention of one of the attendants who brought out a wheelchair to help bring Kieran inside. Cory had to pass through the security station while Kieran was whisked into the exam rooms. Cory had taken Kieran's ID and insurance card from his wallet before the nurses whisked him away. He filled out as much of the paperwork as possible. He didn't know much about Kieran's medical history, and he didn't have Kieran's phone to be able to call his family. Once he'd filled out the paperwork and paid the insurance co-pay, the desk nurse had one of the floor nurses lead him back to where Kieran was lying on a hospital bed waiting for a doctor to come and examine him.

"I filled out most of the forms for you, Kieran."

"Thanks, Cory. I'm sure they'll have a million and one questions to ask. Sit. It will likely be a long wait."

"Do you want to use my phone to call your family?"

"Thanks, but no. I'm awake and aware of what's going on, so no need to bother Dad."

Kieran and Cory's conversation stopped as a doctor came in, and after asking the million and one questions, the doctor examined Kieran's injuries. The doctor helped Kieran get out of his shirt. Cory gasped at the huge livid bruises forming all over Kieran's torso. Kieran ground his teeth against the pain as the doctor poked and pressed on him to check for damage and internal bleeding.

"Well, Mr. Belle, we'll need to take some X-rays, but I don't think your ribs are broken, but several are cracked and close to being broken. Let's get you into a gown, and an aide will be up to take you down to X-ray. Your brother will stay with you until they take you in for the X-rays," he said, clearly mistaking Cory for Kieran's brother.

"Thanks, doctor." The doctor left. "Well, at least he thinks they're only cracked. I was worried they'd been broken."

"You're taking the news cheerfully," Cory said.

"I've had worse injuries at home."

"Like the one that gave you the scars on your chest?"

"Hey, you can only see those because I'm not furry like a wolf." Kieran's voice carried a tone of indignation, and then, without thinking, he added, "If you think those are impressive, you should check out the set across my back."

"What set across your back?" Cory rose and pulled open the gown. The loose ties pulled apart, and the garment slipped from Kieran's shoulders. "I can't find any scars under all the bruising."

"Trust me, they're there. Cory, relax. I heal fast. The bruising will be gone in a few days, and if my ribs are only cracked, they'll be fine before we go to your family's farm. If you still want me to come with you?"

"Idiot, of course I still want you to come with me. After a stunt like this, I can't leave you alone in Little Rock. Someone needs to keep an eye on you."

"So I guess the kiss under the mistletoe had more meaning than just a kiss because George and Theo were egging you on."

Cory flushed bright red and stammered. "I—I—I, yeah, I guess it did. I want us to explore the possibility of something more between us, and I want to do it right this time."

"I'd like to explore as well, Cory. I never had anyone who wasn't family take an interest or care about me. Besides, your kiss was kind of special to me, even more so now I know it wasn't just because of stupid traditions and an audience. You're the first guy to ever kiss me in a romantic way who meant it."

"I find your lack of romance hard to believe. Who couldn't love a stud like you and never kiss him?"

"It's the sad truth. Virgin here."

"Well, I'll protect and love you, Kieran. You're safe with me."

"I do feel safe with you, Cory."

10

____

True to his word, Kieran did recover from his injuries in a short time. A couple of his professors tried to send him home from class to rest and recover. The one professor who didn't try was Professor Mason, who took Kieran at his word when he told him he would be fine and didn't want to miss class.

The young men started their official dating again by marking the start from the time they left the hospital. For a first official date, Cory took him to the twenty-four-hour Tropical Smoothie Café on Rodney Parham and bought him a Mango Magic smoothie. Kieran found the change in their relationship kind of funny; the first time round, Kieran lead and held the protector role. Now, their roles were reversed. Cory led their activities, which included a lot of kissing. Somewhere along the way, Cory had become Wolf, in part because his thick chest hair was so much like fur. They were caught making out so often that Theo and George were making mock vomiting motions whenever they spotted the two of them together.

Christmas break was drawing near. Kieran's mood bounced between dark melancholy and glowing excitement. In many ways, he was looking forward to spending two weeks with Cory with fewer interruptions. He was also worried about his sister Selene, who was scheduled ahead of her time to take the test to become the huntress. If she succeeded, his grandmother's decree of banishment would be lifted and he'd be able to go home for visits, but Kieran's swings were getting on Cory's nerves. They'd been half fighting and half laughing about the trip as of late, all due to Kieran's nerves over spending two weeks with people he didn't know.

"Cory, it's two weeks of having a stranger in your house. How's your family going to deal with it?"

"They'll deal just fine. We're a big family. Plus, Mom and Dad are anticipating meeting you. They think you're the best thing in the world for me. I didn't have a lot of friends as a kid."

"Well, it's your own fault for being lazy in the morning. If you'd get up and get things done early, you'd have time to play later in the day instead of being stuck inside while everyone else is out having fun," Kieran teased.

"Now there's the Kieran I know. You haven't laughed with me in a week. Not since your dad's last call told you it was still a bad idea to come home for the holidays. Come with me and experience what life is like in rural Arkansas, and you'll understand why I ran away to the big city." Cory laughed.

"You call Little Rock the big city. Farm boy, you have a lot to learn about big cities. So, tell me how we get down to the family farm? Your car is in the shop, and I don't have a car."

"Mom and Dad are coming to get us on Friday. We'll spend three hours trapped in a car with them for the drive home. They'll ask you so many questions about life in Maine and your plans for the future, they'll forget I exist."

"Cory, I doubt they'll forget you exist. You're their son bringing home a strange guy to meet the family."

"I'm also the youngest of five boys. With all the chaos my brothers create, I escape their attention most of the time."

"So what time do I need to be ready by on Friday? I have class until two o'clock."

"I know. I told the folks to get here about four to allow you time to finish packing."

"It won't take me two hours to pack. I don't own many clothes."

"I know, but that gives us time to grab a bite to eat before we get hauled off to the middle of nowhere."

"I come from the middle of nowhere. Somehow, I don't think a farm with a family of ten counts as being a place of total tranquility."

"Better get to the bus stop or you'll be late to class, Mr. Smart-ass."

Kieran laughed, stuck out his tongue, and headed to the bus stop and his sculpting class. Cory gathered his own materials together for review of his biology lecture and lab notes. The last few days of the semester passed in a blur for both young men as they finished off projects, handed in papers, and took their finals. Friday dawned, and Kieran was a nervous wreck, thinking about meeting Cory's parents and staying with his huge family. He almost didn't make it through class. Catching the bus home, Kieran was a wreck, a walking basket case of nerves, when he got back to the house, finding Cory waiting in the sitting room with both of their bags packed.

"My folks called. They're going to be early, so I packed for you. They'll get here in just a few minutes."

"What? They weren't supposed to get here until four." Kieran was surprised. "Why are they arriving early?"

The world crashed to a halt as panic settled into Kieran's brain. This whole idea of spending time alone with Cory and his family was a bad idea. Perhaps staying in Little Rock would be a better plan. *Think about staying and getting your projects finished in peace, a big old empty house all to yourself, and on the plus side, Professor Mason invited you to join him for Christmas dinner if you got stuck in town.*

"Kieran, chill." Cory hugged him close. "It's not the end of the world. My folks will love you, so relax. Besides, they're busy with their hands full from dealing with my nephew Billy. He's twelve and hyperactive. So you won't be the center of attention we thought you'd be."

Kieran relaxed into the hug without even thinking about it.

"I don't know why the thought of spending time with your family makes me so nervous. I guess it's because this is the first holiday season away from my family. It won't be long before my eldest sister tests her fitness to inherit Mom's position in the family business. Am I bad for running out on her? When do I get to live my own life?"

Cory stroked Kieran's hair, relaxing both of them.

"I'm sure she'll forgive you. We'll make sure we find her a cool hand-crafted gift for the holiday."

"So how soon are your folks going to—"

The doorbell ringing interrupted Kieran's question, making him jump away from Cory.

"About now." Cory chuckled at Kieran's reaction before entering the hall and opening the door to admit his parents and a pint-sized version of Cory.

"Uncle Cory!" the boy screamed as he launched himself into Cory's arms.

"Hey, little man. How are you?" Cory replied.

"You must be Kieran," the woman appraised Kieran.

"Yes, Mrs. Cooper. Kieran Belle, one of Cory's roommates."

"A joy to meet you, Kieran. I'm Tamara, and this is my husband Jonathan."

"A pleasure, sir. Thank you for letting me tag along with Cory."

"What a pleasure to meet you, Kieran. We're glad Corwin's made such a friend. He's told us a lot about you. Are you boys ready to go?"

"Yes, sir. Cory packed for both of us because of the change of plans."

"He stinks Uncle Cory."

"Billy! Kieran had to run from the bus stop to get back here to be ready for us to head back to the farm. Now apologize to Kieran for being so rude."

"Sorry I said you stink."

"Nothing to worry about, Billy. I just got back here before you arrived. I didn't have a chance to shower or change, so I'm sure I stink pretty bad." When Kieran gave a small chuckle, Kieran's eyes flashed bright silver.

"Wow," Billy exclaimed. "His eyes sparkle when he laughs."

Mrs. Cooper put a hand on Billy's shoulder, almost to silence the boy, but she smiled at Kieran. "We'll wait while you go grab a quick shower, Kieran."

"Thank you, Mrs. Cooper. I won't be but a few minutes." Kieran headed upstairs.

Kieran found there were only two outfits left in his closet, his battered jeans and denim shirt or his tracker's leathers. He decided to dress smart for the trip and wrap himself in strength. He tossed the leathers on the bed. Snagging his towel and shower kit, he slipped through the doorway connecting his bedroom to the bathroom he shared with Cory. The door to Cory's room was wide open as usual. They'd stopped worrying about closed doors somewhere around the middle of the semester after they'd both opened the door from their respective rooms wearing little more than their boxer-briefs. They'd laughed about the event while both of them were scoping each other out. The thought of Cory's almost naked body had the blood flowing to Kieran's cock, making his flesh rise and beg for attention. Kieran stripped down and jumped into the shower. Water streamed over his toned body. The scars across chest and back from the narrow escape during testing were highlighted. The soapsuds flowed down his washboard abs to flow around his hefty cock and balls. He washed with speed and then dried off before making his way back to his room and getting dressed. His hair streamed behind him, drying in the air. Kieran put up his damp towel and tucked his shower kit under his arm before heading back downstairs to put the kit in his bag.

* * *

While Kieran was showering, Cory talked with his parents about Billy downstairs.

"Billy's dad isn't who we all hoped he was," Cory said, making sure the boy stayed out of earshot.

"No, and we can't deny how close to the surface Billy's Beast is, evidenced by his powerful nose," Tamara replied.

"Did he shift yet? Any indication what his Beast is?"

"Thankfully, no. But his next birthday is close, and he's under a lot of stress at school, not to mention when his mother visits," Jonathan, Cory's father, replied.

"Can you appreciate how much we're afraid Billy's father was a purebred dark shifter?"

Kieran's footsteps on the stairs ended their conversation.

"Okay, Billy, do I pass the odor test?" Kieran grinned at the young boy.

"Yeah, you don't stink now."

"Then, I think I'm ready to get out of here."

The group headed out to the Cooper's car. When they settled in, Jonathan put the car in gear and headed out of town back to their farm. Along the drive back to Arkansas City, the Coopers pointed out various sights to Kieran while asking tons of questions about him and his college plans. Tamara, Cory's mother, developed a mental itch she couldn't scratch. She sensed Silver magic and couldn't figure out where the sensation was coming from. The only new element on this trip the family made several times a year was Kieran, but she couldn't say the magic wasn't coming from him. On top of that, neither of the boys mentioned anything about if they were friends or boyfriends, so Tamara wasn't clear on the relationship status between the two boys. So far, it was just a mystery.

* * *

CORY GAVE Kieran the grand tour of the family farm, picking a few places for painting and photography work during their stay. Billy followed them everywhere. Kieran teased him by calling him Puppy, giving Billy the task of carrying his camera bag. Kieran never spotted the face Cory made when he first teased Billy with the new nickname. Cory wondered, *Does, Kieran have magic? Can he sense Billy's Beast?* Kieran found one spot he liked, so Cory and Billy posed together for a series of shots before Cory sent Billy back up to the house for his lessons with Tamara. With the boy gone, Kieran got a gleam in his eye and coaxed Cory out of his jacket and shirt for several more photos, playing with the way the light flowed over Cory's lean muscles.

Kieran used his considerable charms, but Cory resisted taking off any more clothes.

"The weather is too cold, Kieran. I'm going to get dressed, and we're going back to the house to get warm.

"Spoil sport," Kieran teased, packing up his camera equipment.

11

———

Cory took Kieran around the historic town of Arkansas City, once a bustling river port before the Flood of 1927 shifted the river a mile east, leaving the formerly busy port landlocked. They spent time helping around the farm, and Kieran did lots of photo studies for possible projects. Cory and Billy were often his models. One day while Kieran was out in the Cooper's fallow fields, he sensed the presence of a shifter. Reaching for his camera on the chance he might spot the shifter with his telephoto lens, he was interrupted by his phone ringing. He glanced down, and the number wasn't familiar to him.

"Kieran Belle, can I help you?"

"Mr. Belle, I was given your number by an associate. I'm in need of a tracker."

"Who referred you?"

"Richard St. Martin."

"What is your name? I'd like to check with Mr. St. Martin before I discuss business with you."

"Of course. My name is Alex Kincaid."

"I'll call you back, Mr. Kincaid, once I check your references with Mr. St. Martin."

"I'll be waiting on your call."

Kieran hung up and called Richard St. Martin.

"St. Martin Antiques and Collectables, how may we assist you?"

"Richard St. Martin, please."

"Speaking, how can I help you?"

"Mr. St. Martin, Kieran Belle here. I was calling about a referral you made to an Alex Kincaid."

"Kieran my friend, how are you? Alex Kincaid, did you say? No, I didn't give anyone your information."

"When he called me just a moment ago, he said you'd given him my number. Do you ever work with him?"

"I worked with him once, or I should say I cleaned up after him. You don't want anything to do with him, Kieran. He's dangerous and sloppy."

"Thank you, Mr. St. Martin."

"I told you to call me Richard, Kieran. Are you all right? There's something different in your voice."

"I'm fine, Richard. I thought I sensed someone spying on me, and then, I received the call from this Kincaid. I promised I'd call him back once I'd spoke to you. Thank you for revealing he's lied to me."

"You're welcome, Kieran. Call me some time and tell me all about how school is going."

"I will. Thanks, Richard. Good-bye."

* * *

KIERAN and the Cooper family were settling down for Christmas Eve dinner when Kieran's cell phone rang with the tone assigned to his father. Kieran excused himself and went to the living room to take the call.

"Merry Christmas Eve, Dad."

"I wish it was, Son."

"What's wrong, Dad?" Kieran swallowed the rising bile as a sense of dread filled his stomach.

"Your eldest sisters both failed the test to take your mother's place as huntress."

Shock locked Kieran in place and turned his father's words into a buzzing sound in his ear. Then, his brain finally absorbed what his father had said. His sisters were dead.

"Wait," he interrupted his father's rant. "Both Selene and Callie took the test?" He couldn't be hearing this right. "I thought only Selene was supposed to test."

"Selene was the only one who was suppose to test. When she failed, your grandmother and the other Matriarchs decided Callie was ready, so they sent her out to take the test. She wasn't even close to being ready. The shifters of the forest tossed her lifeless body back out of the woods ten minutes after she entered it."

Kieran flinched as his father's hatred for the Matriarchs burned in his ear. The Council's callous disregard of highly-trained Selene's failure and for Callie's lack of that same training only reminded him of why he'd run. *I want to create, not destroy; now this brutal test has swallowed two of my sisters.* Oh, how he wanted to sink to his knees and cry. He grew sick to his stomach as he tried to recall the sound of Selene's beautiful voice singing Christmas carols and Callie's bright smile as she handed him a huge present on his last birthday. *Gone, they're both gone.* Grief threatened to break Kieran; the only thing that pulled him back was his father's voice.

"Rosie and—"

"When?" Kieran interrupted, knowing where the conversation was going: his sisters that were left alive. "When is Grandmother going to make Rosie, Savannah, or Amanda take the test?" Kieran asked around the growing lump in his throat.

"Not until after the new year. They aren't ready either. Callie panicked and used her one shot of the Silver magic long before she was in any real danger. We're not sure what happened to Selene. We think she got to the clearing at the center of the forest before dark set in and the test got underway. The shifters didn't return her remains."

"Should I come home, Dad?"

"No, Son, there's no way for you to do anything for your sisters.

The Matriarchs wont allow a tracker aiding the candidate during the test. I'll do what I'm able to and make sure Rosie is prepared as much possible. Savannah and Amanda are still more than a year away from the birthday, which will make her old enough to be a candidate and another year from being ready to take the test. Your grandmother is still on the warpath about your taking off to go to college. All anyone gets is her rant about how you had the poor judgment to be born male. If she had a glimmer of the truth about either of us, she'd be on the warpath."

"If she'd lost the bad attitude against men of the bloodline, perhaps Great-Uncle Jack and Great-Uncle Mark would be alive. Make sure Rosie takes the sword I made for her and not the relic tradition requires the candidate use."

"You and I know where the fault lies, Kieran. We also both know you inherited my gifts and a better chance to survive backing up whichever of your sisters survives the test. Rosie's only choice is to take the one you made since the old relic is still in the forest with Selene's remains. Callie used one of your mother's old training swords."

"I'm afraid for my sisters. I get the sense I'm going to face the test myself before the year is out. Dad, only one other male ever became the hunter of the generation, and we both know I'm not likely to ever father children to carry on the bloodline. It's just not in my nature to marry and produce children."

"I know, Son, and I hope you find the man who makes you happy."

"I think I found him, Dad, but it's still too soon to know for sure."

"Tell me more about him later, Son. I'd better go before your grandmother blows a gasket when she learns I'm talking to you."

"Tell Rosie, Savannah, and Amanda I love them."

"I will. I love you, Son."

"I love you too, Dad." Kieran hung up.

He returned to the table saddened by the news of his sisters' deaths. The Coopers witnessed the change in his demeanor at once and moved to console him as he lost control of his tears. Cory wrapped him in a hug, threatening to crush the breath from his lungs as he sobbed into Cory's shoulder.

"Kieran, what happened? Who was on the phone?" Cory asked.

"It was my dad. There was an accident back on the family estate, and my two eldest sisters were killed. My grandmother is still mad so she won't let me come home to join the rest of the family for the funerals."

"Oh my god," Mrs. Cooper gasped, standing to bring him water. "How horrible."

Kieran numbly continued as if he hadn't heard her outburst. "Something went wrong with the special logging equipment we use to harvest timber on our land. My sister Callie was thrown from the equipment and died from her injuries. My eldest sister, Selene, was killed in the explosion following the accident, and the intensity of the fire destroyed her body."

"Kieran, I'm so sorry. I know how much you care about your sisters. You know we'll do everything to help you." Cory wrapped Kieran in a tight embrace.

"Thanks, Wolf." Kieran nearly choked at the sudden vocal use of his mental nickname for Cory.

There must be more to their friendship than they realized? He'd kind of been calling Cory "Wolf" in his head ever since the time he'd teased Cory about his furry chest in the hospital after Kieran's run-in with the group of shifters. Because the older guy was getting territorial around him and in part because of all the gorgeous fur on his body. Kieran let go for a moment and just let himself experience how good being held by Cory when he needed comfort was. Getting himself under control, he pulled away from Cory. Kieran didn't catch the puzzled glances on the faces of the Cooper family at his chosen endearment for Cory.

"Thanks again, Wolf. I'll be all right. I'm safe here like I'm with family."

"You're family, Kieran, and you're always welcome here. Please consider our home your home." Jonathan invitation was full of warmth.

"You're all so wonderful. Thank you. If you'll excuse me, I'm not hungry at the moment, and I'm going to take a walk and clear my head for a bit."

"Make sure you take a jacket; the weather is getting colder."

"I will, Tamara." Kieran rose from the table and grabbed his coat before leaving the house.

Outside, Kieran wandered around the farm with no destination, trying to wrap his head around his sisters' deaths. The long-time cover story for how they died spilled from his lips with ease. He hated how bad things were, leaving him no choice but to lie to Cory and his family. They'd been so kind; they were more like his real family. Wanderings took him out into the hay fields, and he slumped down at the base of one of the huge round bales. He held out his hands and let Silver magic form images of his sisters. The tears flowed unhindered as he let himself cry for his sisters. As he cried, he let the images of his sisters fade away.

* * *

IN THE KITCHEN, with Kieran out of the house, Tamara asked Cory, "What is he aware of regarding us, Corwin?"

"All he's aware of is we're a family from the Arkansas Delta. This whole calling me Wolf is a whole new thing."

"And you calling him babe is new as well?"

"Jesus, Mom, his sisters just died," Cory said, but catching the look of worry on his mother's face, realized she was worried about her own family first. He took a deep breath to regain his composure. "It's the first time I've ever called him babe."

"So what's going on between you two?"

"We're kind of dating but taking things slow. I don't understand why I'm so drawn to him. I want him as my mate. I sure don't get why he's calling me Wolf and Billy Puppy."

"Do you think he senses anything? Is he a shape-shifter? Do you sense anything to explain why you're drawn to him?"

"Hard to put into words the sensations I get being around Kieran.

He seems to fit somehow. I don't think he senses anything, since I've never shifted, so I doubt if I even have a Beast for him to sense. Billy's Beast is so close to the surface I'm still surprised he hasn't shifted. Something about Kieran makes me sure he isn't of shifter stock."

Tamara stiffened as she sensed something far off.

"Mom, what is going on?"

"There for a moment it seemed like someone used Silver magic, but only for a moment, now the magic is gone. Go find Kieran before the weather gets any colder."

Cory grabbed his heaviest coat and went to find Kieran. About an hour after Kieran had wandered off, Cory found him huddled at the base of a hay bale somewhere in the center of the field. With care, he slid in behind and wrapped Kieran in his arms. They sat in silence for some time, lost in each other's presence. Cory stroked Kieran's long hair marveling at the silky texture. Kieran lifted his head, drew a deep breath, and locked eyes with Cory's. His hands rose, cupping Cory's head and drawing him in to a kiss, which deepened as Cory relaxed and joined in. Breaking the kiss to breathe, Kieran managed a brief inhale before Cory drew him back into the kiss. After what seemed to be forever, they parted and gazed at each other. The sound of someone coughing alerting them they weren't alone. Jonathan stepped around the bale.

"Sorry to disturb you boys, but it's getting late and the temperature is supposed to drop pretty low tonight, so you might want to bring yourselves inside."

Cory rose, drew Kieran to his feet, and wrapped him in his arms. They broke apart except to hold hands and make their way back to the farmhouse. Once inside and divested of jackets, they made their way upstairs to Cory's room where they returned to their lip lock and deep embrace. Cory broke the kiss and the embrace, creating enough space to be able to unbutton Kieran's heavy flannel shirt. Kieran reached to do the same to Cory, but Cory stopped his hands.

"Let me do this. I think I started dreaming about undressing you almost from the moment we met at school, and watching you dress almost every morning, all I think about is wanting to stop you and drag you into my bed and make love with you."

A finger to Kieran's lips silenced any comment he might make before Cory resumed removing Kieran's clothes. Soon, Kieran was naked to the waist, and Cory marveled at his defined chest and abs. His fingers traced across his pectorals. Kieran trembled as his friend's fingers traced across the scars on his chest. Continuing their journey, Cory's fingers traced down his abs and lowered. He wanted to stop Cory from going lower almost as much as he wanted Cory to hurry further down his body. Both were surprised by the escaping moan when Cory's fingers brushed over Kieran's hard-on, as he lowered the zipper of Kieran's jeans. Neither figured out who moaned first.

Kieran pulled Cory close into a deep kiss as his lover's hands slipped into his jeans to cup his ass, and he sent the jeans sliding down his legs to pool at his ankles. Only his boxer-briefs separated him from his lover's touch. Cory pushed him backward on to the bed. Bending down, Cory pulled off Kieran's sneakers, socks, and jeans. Rising, Cory stripped himself down to his own boxer-briefs and joined Kieran on the bed. Their hands explored each other's bodies. Cory's tongue soon followed his hands across Kieran's body and down to the waistband of his green boxer-briefs. Fingers led the way, nudging the fabric down with kisses and lapping tongue, following the route plotted by his hands. Cory's tongue traced the ridges of Kieran's abs into his belly button, snaking down across his bush to the base of his trapped and rigid cock.

Sliding down to Kieran's feet, Cory drew off his lover's underwear, leaving him naked beneath his gaze. Cory moved his hands and tongue up Kieran's legs until he arrived at the juncture of his lover's legs and the rigid cock oozing pre-cum by the bucket. His tongue wrapped around Kieran's balls, teasing them as they drew tighter in their sack. Licking up the shaft, Cory got his first hint of the flavor of Kieran's pre-cum. He drew back at the strange tang. Shaking his head, he plunged back down on his lover's cock to give him pleasure. Kieran whimpered under Cory's tongue and sudden heat of his mouth engulfing the head and shaft. He'd never experienced such sensations.

Kieran grabbed Cory before he was taken too far out of his head with desire and dragged him up, kissing him with intense passion, sliding Cory's underwear off to bring pleasure to his lover's cock.

Once Cory was naked, Kieran explored his body until he reached Cory's hard and dripping cock. Tentatively, he lapped at the rigid flesh taking his first sample of man. Covering his teeth with his lips, Kieran took the crown of Cory's dick into his mouth and ran his tongue over the head, tasting Cory's pre-cum before taking more of the shaft into his mouth. Cory pulled away for a moment and shifted on the bed so they were in the sixty-nine position. Cory drew Kieran's shaft into his mouth and teased his balls with his fingers. Kieran mimicked what Cory was doing and ran his finger through the fur covering Cory's chest. Soon, their mouths were wrapped around the other's hard length, sucking and tasting. Reaching the edge of climax too soon, they slowed down and faced each other, sinking into deep kisses as they cooled down. Their hands slipped down, stroking each other, keeping them close to edge. Kieran broke their kiss, panting.

"Wolf, this is amazing."

"Babe, you're so beautiful, and I'm glad you're letting me be your first."

"You just make everything safe and special. Something deep inside tells me you'll never hurt me."

"I promised you would always be safe with me. Now relax and enjoy."

Cory drew Kieran in for a deep kiss and took both their cocks in hand, stroking them together right to the edge. Amber eyes locked on silver ones, they shuddered into climax together. Cory recovered first and slid out bed. Finding some tissue, he cleaned both of them up before sliding back into bed and pulling Kieran into his body, wrapping his lover in his arms, letting his instinct lead him into protecting the other man. They drifted off to sleep.

* * *

Morning dawned extra early when a small body crashed on the lovers' bed.

"Merry Christmas, Uncle Cory," Billy bellowed before realizing he'd landed on Kieran.

"Merry Christmas, Puppy. I think you should give us a couple minutes."

"Are you Uncle Cory's mate now?"

Kieran was mystified. Cory laughed at Kieran's expression before answering.

"I don't think we've gotten there yet, Billy. I'm hoping he'll agree to be my boyfriend for a while first. Kieran is someone special to me though." Cory had a huge grin on his face.

Kieran was stunned for a moment before he drew Cory in for a huge kiss and whispered *yes* in his boyfriend's ear. Billy bounded from the room, crowing about Uncle Cory giving him a new uncle for Christmas. The grins around the Cooper's kitchen table when they got downstairs made Kieran and Cory blush before they kissed each other to cheers from Billy. Tamara and Jonathan smiled. Kieran broke the kiss and blushed a furious shade of red.

"What's the matter, babe?"

"I just realized, I didn't get any of you gifts and it's Christmas day."

"Corwin this happy is all the gift we need, Kieran. Merry Christmas," responded Tamara and Jonathan in unison.

INTERLUDE: INFORMATION ON SHIFTERS

Over the millennia after the ancient war, the shifters sought ways to break the magic binding them to their limited forms. Only the most powerful shifters ever managed more than one shape. Of these, the legendary Beast was one of the most powerful, being able to take human, bear, a mid-way form of half-human and half-bear, and a few other shapes at will. The ability to take the half-man, half-bear form allowed him to create the illusion of being the prince under a dark spell. The Beast sired many offspring with powerful female shifters.

Weaker shifters grew more human as they mated with normal humans until several clans learned to suppress their Beasts, channeling the energy into other areas. Only at puberty or under overwhelming stress did the Beast escape control. These families hid their nature and selected mates who were pure human, mages, or diluted shifters like themselves.

12

Kieran and Cory settled back into college life after winter break and raised their relationship to a new level, asking their landlady, Mrs. Jones, about the empty apartment on the third floor and if she would rent the apartment to them. The young couple's obvious love tugged at Mrs. Jones' heart, so she agreed to open up the third floor apartment and lease the place to them. The apartment came furnished with a California-king bed in the master bedroom. The couple set aside the second bedroom as a painting studio for Cory with the beautiful light coming in from the windows in the east and south. Their class schedules diverged in this half of the school year, leaving them only history together. Cory grumbled over the heavier courses of his business major. Kieran sank into his computer graphics courses or lost hours developing film and printing photos. The young lovers managed lunch three times a week and dinner every night. After dinner one night, Kieran refused to let Cory get anything done until they'd stripped each other naked and made love.

"Wolf, I think I'm ready for you to be inside me. I spent time thinking about it, and I know what's between you and me is more than some passing thing. Can we make us a forever thing, because I-I love you, Wolf."

"Oh, babe, I waited for the right moment to tell you. I love you so much. You make everything so special. I want you and only you at my side forever."

"Please be gentle with me; this will be my first time. I never thought I'd be with anyone all the way, Cory"

"Relax, and we'll go slow and gentle."

Cory reached into the drawer and pulled out lube and condoms. He popped the lid of the lube bottle and slicked a finger, which he worked at a slow pace into Kieran's ass, preparing him for what was to come. He kept kissing Kieran, moving down along his jaw to gnaw and lick along his throat as Kieran whimpered in submission. More lube and a second finger worked Kieran open as Cory used his fingers to stretch the opening as much as possible. When Kieran was begging for more, Cory moved between Kieran's legs and slicked his cock before sliding the condom on and slicking the condom as well. Trying to be gentle, he lined himself up with Kieran's opening and pushed in. The sensation of being inside Kieran was a shock of heat and tightness. Kieran grimaced in pain as Cory first breached his virgin ass. Cory held still, letting Kieran adjust to having a cock in his ass. When Kieran's breathing returned to near normal, Cory slipped more of his hard cock into Kieran until the head of his cock brushed over Kieran's prostate. The whine of pain became a moan of pleasure as cock slid over prostate, giving pleasure and erasing pain. Both groaned from the depths of their souls as Cory bottomed out in Kieran, claiming him as his own. Once all the way in, Cory stopped and let Kieran get used to having a cock in his ass while Cory kissed him. When Kieran's breath settled down, he grabbed Cory's ass and urged him to fuck him.

"Take me, Wolf. I'm yours. Fuck me."

"It will never be fucking, babe. With you, it will always be making love. You are mine and I am yours. Now and forever."

"Now and forever, I am yours and you are mine."

To prove it was lovemaking and not a meaningless fuck, Cory withdrew until only the head of his cock was still inside Kieran and re-entered inch by inch. Cory made it last, for what seemed like ages to Kieran. Cory bit into Kieran's shoulder and Kieran did the same, claiming each other as mates. Their bites triggered something deep within each of them, and they climaxed together. Cory cleaned them both before pulling Kieran against his body, snuggling close as they drifted off to sleep.

* * *

THE BOYS WERE SURPRISED by how fast the second half of the school year was passing by. As they worked on projects, spring break was fast approaching, and the Coopers were wondering if they were coming down to the farm for the break. To find out how to plan, Kieran called his father about coming back to Maine for the break to visit his sisters. As expected, the conversation with his father for permission to come home hinged on his whether his grandmother was willing to forgive him for running off to attend college without her consent. Like so many of their conversations, Kieran's father promised to ask and call him back right away. When he didn't get a quick call back, Kieran took it as a sign his grandmother's mind was unchanged, so the boys made plans to head down to the Cooper farm for the break. Cory called his parents, and his mother answered the phone.

"Hey, Mom, is all right if Kieran comes home with me for spring break?"

"You'd better be bringing Kieran with you if you're planning on coming home for the break. He's family, too. Put him on the phone and I'll tell him myself," Tamara said.

Cory passed his phone to Kieran. "Here, Mom wants to talk to you."

"Hello, Kieran. I wanted you to know that you are always welcome in our home. My son loves you, and he's being stupid if he thinks we'd be upset with him bringing you home with him every chance he gets. Get your things packed and ready. Jonathan and I will be up to get you. Besides, if you miss Cory's birthday party, we'll never forgive you."

"I didn't know it was coming up. He's never mentioned when it was." Kieran's tone carried some irritation with Cory in it.

"I'll let you two sort that part out." Tamara chuckled, knowing her son was in trouble with his boyfriend and picturing the expression on Kieran's face.

"Thanks, Tamara. I've got to get ready for class," Kieran said, still glaring at Cory.

"I'll call you tomorrow with the firm details. Be packed and ready to go on the Friday before spring break by four in the afternoon."

"You'll need the van. Cory's paintings are due when we get back from break. He needs room for all the canvases he's doing over the break."

"Thank you. I'll let Jonathan know. Love to you both, and we'll talk later."

Kieran hung up and handed the phone back to Cory with a frown.

"You and I need to have a little chat about you withholding important information from me," Kieran said.

Cory paled, wondering if Kieran had guessed the Cooper family secret. "What didn't I tell you that's so important, Kieran?"

"Well, it seems you forgot to tell me you had birthday coming up during the break. How am I supposed to get you a birthday gift?"

"Oops, yeah my birthday is the 21st of April. Sorry, it slipped my mind."

"We need to talk more about these little details between us. I'll have to see what I can find as a gift suitable for a wolf," Kieran teased. "You know your mom is the best, Wolf. She's extended a permanent invitation to the farm."

"Well, that's good. I'm glad you mentioned they should bring the van; all those canvases just wouldn't fit in the car. Did she say when they'd be here?"

"Your folks will be here Friday before break at four to pick us up. She said she'll call me tomorrow with the final details."

"Why would she call you with the details? Oh, I bet she's up to something sneaky with birthday plans." Cory growled low in his throat.

Cory's growl sent a chill up Kieran's spine but also sent a flash of heat to his cock, making him adjust himself in his jeans. Cory caught the movement and licked his lips in a wicked grin. Kieran wagged his finger at his lover.

"I guess it's how moms are sometimes with their favorite child. I didn't get too much from Mom; she was always busy with my sisters. Dad spoiled me rotten, much to my grandmother's distaste. She was disappointed I was born first and a boy. Dad's family was overjoyed he and Mom had a son."

"Why not visit your dad's family instead of trying to visit your sisters, Kieran?"

"Dad's family travels a lot. Before the summer break, I'll get Dad to convince Gramps to let us stay at his compound on the coast. I want you to meet my dad and my sisters."

"It would be fun. I'd like to meet your family. I hope they will like me."

"They'll love you, Cory. My dad's family spoils me rotten, rewards of being the only grandson in a family, which prizes male children as much as Mom's family relishes daughters. Let's go get something to eat. I'm starving."

"Okay. So where do you want to go to eat?"

"Tropical Smoothie Café." It had become the couple's spot. "I'm thinking a Mango Magic and a cranberry chicken salad sandwich."

"Good thing they put one in the YMCA building. It's a good walk from here."

"The exercise will do us both good. We've been locked away in studios for way too long this semester. So come on, I'm starving."

"So you mentioned. Will you model for me again over the break? I want to focus on the human form this half of the semester."

"And how naked do I need to be for these paintings?"

"What are you talking about, Kieran?"

"Professor Simms still pretty much undresses me with his eyes every time I walk into his classroom. I had to give the dean a reason why I didn't want a stipend, which would pay half my tuition in exchange for modeling for Professor Simms' class twice a week."

"Wow, I'm sorry, babe. I didn't realize he was still hounding you about modeling after the way you rejected his request at Thanksgiving." The growl was back in Cory's voice.

"Easy, Wolf. I told the dean I didn't have time in my schedule, but thanked him for the offer. So, don't worry about it. Hell, I hated passing on the money, since I don't have any beyond what I put into savings when I got to Little Rock. I'm not comfortable with your professor perving on me, even if it's only as a painting. What's under the clothes is for your eyes only."

Another growl escaped Cory's throat. "You're mine and I won't let anyone else even think about touching you."

"Settle down, Cory. I told you when we first made love you were mine and I was yours forever. No one else is going to take me away from you or even lay a finger on me in the ways only you are allowed to. So, calm down and take a deep breath. I will model for you in whatever state of dress—or undress—you want me in. Remember, however far you make me undress, you're going to need to do the same for me during my next big photography project."

"Okay, I know I shouldn't be so possessive, but I'm always afraid I might lose you, and I wouldn't want to live if I lost you."

"You aren't going to lose me, Wolf, so put the thought out of your mind."

"Why do you call me Wolf?"

Cory enfolded Kieran from behind and nuzzled as his neck.

"Because you're territorial like a wolf, you have all the fun fur, and your nose is cold like a dog's, so cut out the nuzzling. Please, let's go get something to eat."

"I know you're starving. Come on, you big lug, let's go get you fed."

INTERLUDE: SHIFTERS HIDE IN PLAIN SIGHT

The young female shifter prowled around the edge of campus. After her rival succeeded in getting her banished from the pack, she chose to start over in a new town. Not even in town for a week, a strange mage approached her with an offer she couldn't refuse: do a job for him or die. Getting the job in the campus bookstore didn't take much effort. No. The hard part of her job was avoiding the do-gooder shifters of the campus pack and the few elemental mages she scented. They all used their abilities and magic for good. If they caught wind of her own pure Ebony magic scent, she'd be driven from campus, or worse, end up dead. The effort to keep hidden was stressing her out. While at work one day, she crossed the path of her targets, Kieran and Cory, as they were buying supplies for a class. Cory's scent confused her. What shifter buried their Beast so deep? Did he ever let it out to run? Cory didn't pay her any attention, but his companion caught her attention, his gaze telling her, *I know what you are and I do not approve of your existence.*

What was he? She studied them with care. When they came to check out at her register, the hairs on the back of her neck raised up. She stared into a pair of knowing silver eyes. Those eyes were filled with hatred for her being. When she took his money, Silver magic hit her like a jolt of electricity as it clashed against her Ebony magic. A hunter? Keeping time with a shifter? Confused, she escaped to the break room once they were through her line to rethink her plan.

13

———

The new checkout girl at the bookstore was a dark shifter. He could only read Ebony magic from her. Despite constant reminders it wasn't his place to do anything about her, Kieran's senses wouldn't come off as high alert. Okay, so this territory wasn't his to defend as a hunter, even if he were one. Shaking himself, he resolved not to do anything as long as she didn't do anything to draw his wrath, like attack Cory, he would let her be. The chances of her remaining on campus were slim given the makeup of the pack here; Kieran gave her about another week before she ran a foul of the light side shifters.

Kieran was sitting in the student union considering his options for lunch when he spotted the dark shifter from the bookstore following Cory out of the building without his lover realizing he was being followed. It was settled; the bitch had to die. Kieran was rising from his seat when a powerful hand slammed him back into the chair.

"What the hell?"

Marissa Holden slid into the seat across the table from Kieran, eyeing the man holding Kieran down. "Bruce, ease up," she ordered. "I think Kieran will listen without being held in his seat."

"Marissa? What's going on?" Kieran's voice was tinged with malice as he endured the presence of two shifters.

"I'm representing a concerned party. Our attention is drawn to a shift in the balances of magic from elemental to creation/corruption on campus. Our Alpha is concerned something is brewing, which will upset the peace on campus."

"Okay, so I knew you were a shifter, Marissa. I let it slide because I like you and you are a big help in ceramics. I'm gathering you know about the dark shifter working in the campus bookstore. I assume your Alpha plans to deal with her."

"She's on her own and she isn't a threat to our pack. No, this is about you. Your Silver magic concerns our Alpha," Marissa replied.

"You aren't a shifter and you're not a simple mage either. The Alpha wants to know who you are," Bruce said, hands still on Kieran's shoulders.

"Then direct your questions to me, Bruce. Playing the part of the muscle seems beneath an Alpha."

Marissa rose, and the hulking Bruce took her place in the seat across from Kieran. A bearish grin crossed his face at having been caught out by this strange young man.

"So who are you, Kieran Belle?"

"I'm a full tracker of the House of Beauty," Kieran responded with an evil grin.

The hulking shifter's eyebrows shot up, a curse of their own.

"That," he said, "sure as hell, is not what I was expecting."

"Well, I wasn't expecting to get pinned in my seat by an Alpha."

Bruce didn't laugh. "So where is your huntress?"

"Back home in Maine. I came here to get away from the killing and destruction. I don't have any beef with you or your ragtag pack. From what I've learned, every one of your families all served on creation's side during the ancient war."

"Well, you've done better research on us than we did on you. So what's your beef with the little dark shifter, other than she's a dark shifter?"

"She seems to have set her sights on my boyfriend for some reason."

Kieran's eyes flashed storm cloud gray, causing Bruce to flinch back. The Alpha recovered his composure.

"You do know your boyfriend isn't a pure human."

"Cory is pure human. I've never sensed anything out of the ordinary about him. Trust me, I would know if he were anything besides human. If anyone isn't pure human in our relationship, it would be me."

"All right." Bruce shrugged. "If the little dark shifter gets out of line with your boyfriend, you have my leave to track her down and deal with her. Little Rock doesn't have an actual hunter so we do our best to keep the shifters in check around town."

"Thank you. I'll try not to step on anyone's paws in the process. Just no promises." Kieran had a wide grin and a sparkle of bright silver in his eyes.

"Marissa was right," Bruce said, ignoring the fact that she was standing right next to him. "You are trouble, but I like you just the same. Come to Stickyz Rock 'n' Roll Chicken Shack on Friday night, and bring your boyfriend. You'll meet the rest of my pack and they'll meet you."

"We'll do it. Excuse me, I need to go track down my boyfriend and his shadow."

"Hey, Belle," Marissa called out. "Before you go, do you know of any places for rent down in the Quapaw Quarter?"

"Catch me in ceramics later. I'll give you my landlady's number."

Kieran left the shifter leader and his main beta behind as he left the Donaghey Student Center and tracked down the dark shifter. Cory, he knew, had an afternoon studio course, so Kieran headed toward the fine arts building. Rounding the Ottenheimer Library, he almost crashed into the woman he was trying to locate.

"Who are you and why are you following me?" she asked.

"Oh please, wolf-bitch, you're the one stalking my partner. I'm going to give you one warning to back off and mind your manners, or the next time I track you down, there will be lots of silver involved.

The local Alpha gave me clearance to take you down, so if I were you, I'd hightail it out of town before he decides to take you out himself."

"I haven't threatened anyone," she said, delight edging her voice. "You don't know what blood runs in your boyfriend's veins, do you?"

"I know it's nothing associated with corruption's side of magic. You, on the other hand, have next to pure blood of the dark running through you. Take my offer to get out of town. I won't offer it again."

"You're not a hunter, but you work with one. I sense the silver."

"I'm a tracker. Be glad my huntress isn't around or you wouldn't get the slim chance to escape with your hide. Now run, bitch, and don't stop until you're far away from Little Rock."

And she did. Taking a step away from Kieran, she shot him a wicked smile before disappearing into the shadows of the campus. Her smile told Kieran a lot. She wouldn't go far. Kieran was also puzzled as he headed off to find Cory. *Why does every shifter I meet on campus say Cory isn't human?*

14

The rest of the week sped past as they got ready for spring break and another trip to the farm. Friday arrived, and the young lovers were preparing to leave their house to meet Cory's parents for the ride. Kieran's cell phone rang with the special tone reserved for his father.

"Hi, Dad, what's up?"

"I have family business to discuss."

"Dad, I'm not free to talk family business."

"Sorry, Son, this is important. Your grandmother just cleared Rosie to take the test."

"She's not ready yet, Dad," Kieran said what he wanted to say to his grandmother. "She's not even of age to take the test."

"Well, she's taking it the middle of the week, when the moon is full."

There was no avoiding it. "Grandmother must let me come home this time. I'll change my plans for the break. Let me catch a flight this afternoon. I'll be in Boston tonight, rent a car, and be home by tomorrow afternoon."

"No, the woman holds a grudge. She's forbidden anyone and you in particular from helping Rosie with the test."

"If I'm not there, she'll fail without the additional training. Is there no way for you to help her?"

"No, I can't help and still be here for your other sisters. The old woman told me if I do anything to aide Rosie, I'd be banished from the estate, never to return. I've made sure she has spent all her training time with the sword you made for her."

"It will help. Tell Rosie I love her and I know she'll do it."

"I will, Son," he said, drawing in a shaky breath. "So how's your boyfriend?"

"Cory's doing fine. He's right here if you want to talk to him. His folks should be here soon to take us to the farm."

"Put him on. I'd like to talk to him."

Kieran handed his phone to Cory. "My dad wants to talk to you, Wolf."

"Hello, Mr. Belle?"

"Relax, Cory, I don't bite. Please call me Kellen. I'm only a Belle by marriage."

"Okay, Kellen."

"I need you to please protect my son for me, Cory. Love him with everything in your heart. I fear I'll be calling with bad news later in the week, and he'll need someone to get him through it."

"I do, and I will, sir. I promise."

"Thank you, Cory. Now tell my son I love him and take him for a roll in the hay."

Cory laughed as he disconnected the call, thinking how much he wanted to meet Kieran's father in person. He caught Kieran's expression and laughed again before kissing him and slipping the phone back into Kieran's pocket and copping a quick grope.

"Okay, what's so funny, Wolf?" Kieran asked once the kiss had broken.

"Your dad wanted me to tell you he loves you and we should go for a roll in the hay." Cory snuggled into Kieran.

Kieran laughed as he held Cory close for a moment longer.

"Sounds like Dad. Now, you need to make sure you pack all your paints and canvases, Wolf, or you'll never get the assignment done for your painting class."

"They're all packed and ready to go. Now where's your camera and film?"

"All set and ready, as is my laptop, so I might get my graphics project finished."

"So, time for just us before Mom and Dad get here."

"I think we do. So come here and—"

Frantic ringing of the doorbell interrupted Kieran as he was pulling Cory toward their bed. Kieran charged downstairs to answer the door followed by Cory. When he opened it, he was almost run over by a small boy. Billy burst past him and slammed into Cory, scared out of his wits. A larger body came rushing toward them, chasing after Billy.

"Come back here, you little brat. I'm going to hammer you into the ground."

Kieran slammed the door into the oncoming bully, sending him crashing into the floor of the porch. Kieran then stepped out on to the porch, blocking the bully's path.

"Get out of my way, faggot. I'm going to pound the little bastard into the ground for getting in the way of a perfect pass."

"Shut up and listen, you stupid jock. You try and lay a hand on the kid ever and I'll make sure your sports career ends before you ever get on the field."

"You can't hurt me, faggot."

"I'm not the one sitting on my ass from a door hitting me in the face. Get out of here before I decide to hurt you, jock boy."

"You and what army, faggot?"

Before the jock got back on his feet, Kieran lashed out with a sweeping kick, which sent the jock crashing back to the floor, nursing his left knee.

"Johnson, aren't you suppose to be next door getting a tutoring session from Lewis? It's the only reason you're ever in this neighborhood these days," Cory said from behind Kieran.

"He's not home from class yet, so I was tossing the ball around with my buddies when the little brat got in my way and tripped me up."

"Let me guess. He was behind you as you went for some fancy pass, and you crashed into him and fell on your face in front of your jock buddies. Get out of here before I call the cops and make you into an even bigger idiot than you are." Cory went back into the house.

"He means now, Johnson. Lewis is just pulling into his driveway, so you'll still make your lesson."

Kieran went back into the house and found Cory rocking Billy, trying to calm the sobbing boy.

"Sshh, Billy, it's okay. Uncle Kieran has taken care of the mean old bully. He wont let anyone hurt you and neither will I."

"I didn't mean to make anyone angry. It was an accident."

"Billy, it's okay. It wasn't your fault. Some people just can't take responsibility for their own mistakes. So how did you slip away from your grandparents?" Kieran asked.

"They were trying to figure out which restaurant to go to on the way home, and I just slipped out once Grandpa had parked."

"You know you're going to be in a lot of trouble once your grandma and grandpa get up here?"

Cory's parents came through the door just then. Tamara's eyes were blazing.

"William Henry Cooper, you are so grounded when we get back home. No Xbox and extra chores," Tamara growled. Billy hung his head, knowing it would do no good to argue with his grandmother. Tamara then rounded on Cory.

"The same goes for you, Corwin Samuel Cooper."

"What did I do wrong?" Cory asked, stunned by his mother's anger.

"You encourage the boy to be reckless, and it stops now."

Tamara's mood shifted as her gazed fell on Kieran who'd braced in a defensive position between her and Cory. A laugh choked off as her gazed spotted the silver fire in his eyes.

"Kieran, relax, dear. They've had this coming for a while now. Billy needs to learn his actions have consequences, and Corwin needs to learn to be more responsible when caring for children."

The silver fire in Kieran's eyes grew brighter as her tone reminded him of his own grandmother's lectures. Only with fierce control did he keep his magic in check.

"Tamara, Billy learned his actions have consequences just a few moments ago. He got into a small incident with a bully and came running here for help. I made sure the bully wouldn't bother Billy again. The whole encounter scared Billy enough. I think he'll behave from now on. Cory has been here comforting Billy while you and Jonathan were arguing over restaurants instead of paying attention to him. You let him slip away from you getting into trouble. You're the one who should be grounded, Tamara."

Cory took Kieran in his arms, glaring at his mother over his lover's shoulder. Kieran waited a moment before he continued.

"Tamara, Jonathan, I'm sorry I'm on edge. My own grandmother is being a coldhearted witch, preventing me from going home. Dealing with a bully and then hearing you attack Cory doesn't help."

Tamara bristled at the challenge coming from Kieran despite the visible sign of Silver magic in his eyes; Jonathan stepped in to defuse the situation.

"Kieran, don't be upset for standing up for Cory or yourself. You're right. We didn't pay attention on the street like we should have. Thank you for watching out for Billy and Cory." Jonathan placed his hand on Tamara's shoulder to calm her down.

"Why don't we get going? We have a long drive home."

Tamara gritted her teeth.

INTERLUDE: ROSIE'S TEST

Trepidation filled the young huntress-candidate as she entered the clearing at the center of the dark woods. Here the testing took place and here Rosalind "Rosie" Belle now stood like many of the daughters of each generation of Beauty's descendants. Each came here or to a similar place wherever the family had settled. One by one, each daughter was tested against a pack of shifters bound to the forest for this reason. When a daughter of the house killed five shifters without using her Silver magic, she became the huntress of her generation and her sisters would marry to spread the bloodline. The huntress and her sisters also formed the Council of Matriarchs, which governed the family. The death of the fifth shifter was the signal to the pack to break off and let the huntress leave the forest. Rosie now stood in the center of the clearing, holding the sword Kieran had given her for her last birthday.

"Uncle Brom helped me forge this sword special for you, Rosie. I've given it a special touch of Silver magic. It will cut through any shifter you meet and burn them."

Rosie hoped the man's magic would work. She wanted to save her own woman's magic for later in life. The pack emerged from the edge of the woods, led by a huge Alpha male. The Alpha shifted to half-man, half-wolf shape to speak to her. This was a powerful shifter. Rosie didn't think any shifters still had the power to hold the in-between shape.

"So the next would-be huntress has come for the test. I hope you're prepared to die, little girl."

"I'm prepared to fight and leave here as the huntress. Send your chosen five."

"You'll fight until we kill you, just like your eldest sister, or you'll run and die in the forest like your other sister."

"You broke the pact of the test. The battle is one versus five. How many of you attacked my sisters?"

"Enough of us to make them use their hated Silver magic. It will be the same with you. Only sunrise or my death will save you."

"Babe, hold still. If you wiggle, I'll never get the pose down."

"Do you have any idea how much hay itches against bare skin, Wolf?"

"Ah, yeah, grew up on a farm."

"Then cut me some slack, farm boy. This stuff itches and I'm wearing what can only be called shorts if you're generous over here. Where the heck did you find these things?"

"They belong to my brother Jeff. He used them when he went swimming with his gang of friends and wanted to impress the girls."

"I bet he got more than his fair share of guys checking him out in these things."

"He did mention a few times that he scored a blow job or more from guys when the beer was flowing and the girls weren't putting out."

"Careful there, Wolf. I don't think these things are going to hold me in if you get me sporting a hard-on. Even soft, these things are losing the battle to keep me tucked away. I should have worn a jock under them."

"A jock would ruin the effect of the shorts, babe. Be quiet and hold still. I've almost got this pose finished. I promise afterward I'll make it all worth your while with the hot roll in the hay your dad wanted us to have." Cory smirked as Kieran moaned and resumed the pose.

A half hour later, the boys were spread across a thick blanket on top of a stack of hay up in the loft of the barn. Naked, they were wrapped in each other's arms and locked in a deep soul-binding kiss. Their rampant erections ground together as their hands explored the other's body. Kieran's hands stroked up Cory's back to his shoulders and locked there as Cory's hand stroked down and across both of Kieran's ass cheeks. Cory's hands were stroking and spreading Kieran's ass until the boy was panting and begging Cory to take him.

"As much as I'd love to take you, we didn't plan this and didn't bring any protection or supplies with us."

"Outside pocket of my camera bag on the left side. I slipped in a small stash of supplies before the last field trip we took together, thinking we might find a secluded spot to do some private pics."

"Sneaky of you. I'm surprised you didn't try harder to find a secluded spot for us. Then again, with the way your mentor, Professor Mason, wanders around during those field trips, we wouldn't have any privacy. So grab the bag and let's have a roll in the hay, babe."

"You're evil, reminding me how easily getting caught in a compromising position by Professor Mason would be. I'm so glad you're mine, because by now, I'd have gotten the professor in so much trouble."

"I caught how much lust was in both your eyes during the Thanksgiving party. I wasn't thrilled with watching the two of you together. But that's enough talking about your professor; he's not the one I want to make love to. Get the supplies." The last came out in a Cory growl.

Kieran rolled away from Cory and found the camera bag. Cory pounced on Kieran's hot muscular ass, spreading the cheeks and dragging his tongue from taint to the top of the ass. He slid back down to focus on Kieran's rosebud, working his lover open with his tongue until he was buried deep and Kieran was moaning and panting hard. He then reached up and pried the tube of lube from Kieran's fingers along with the condom. He popped open the lube and applied some to

Kieran's hole and worked in a finger, dilating the muscles open further. One finger became two, spreading Kieran open wider and wider until the begging coming from Kieran became frantic and almost desperate. Cory rose up, tore open the packet, and rolled the condom on after slicking himself. He then slicked the outside of the condom and positioned himself over Kieran's back with his cock lined up on Kieran's hole before sliding inside his lover with care. Both their moans became full of pleasure as they consummated their love. The young lovers lost themselves in their lovemaking, and when they both reached their climax, they exploded simultaneously. They cleaned up as best as possible before collapsing back on the blankets and cuddling together in the hay. Cory wrapped Kieran in his arms as he spooned up behind him.

"Well, your dad will be happy we got this roll in the hay," Cory said, chuckling in Kieran's ear. "When did I last tell you how much I love you?"

"I think you moaned something about loving my tight ass around your cock," Kieran teased.

"Silly, boy," chuckled Cory. "I do love you, babe. I'm glad we found each other."

"I love you too, Wolf. I'm not sure what I'd do without you in my life." Below them, the boys heard the sound of someone entering the barn. A voice called out to them.

"Corwin, Kieran, are you in here?" Jonathan called out.

"In the hayloft, Dad. What's the matter?"

Cory and Kieran scrambled to find their clothes.

"Billy's missing, and he isn't in any of his usual hiding places. We need some extra help finding him."

"When did he go missing, Jonathan?" Kieran pulled on his jeans and reached for his boots.

"While you two were out in the field doing your painting project. His mother came to visit, and it went worse than normal. Billy got upset and ran off before she left. We thought he might search for Corwin like he tends to do."

"Guess we were in here by the time he escaped from Jillian. Hang on just a moment, Dad, and we'll be right down to help you search for him."

Kieran and Cory rapidly threw on their clothes and slid down the ladder from the loft to the barn floor. They followed Jonathan outside to join in the search for Billy.

"Where did he most likely go? Does he have any friends he might of run off to?" Kieran asked.

"Billy is pretty much a loner; there aren't many kids his age around here, and the farm is too far from town for his school friends to come here unless it's planned in advance. I know a couple of places he may have gone to hide that the others don't know. Follow me."

Kieran followed Cory as he took off across the farm and out toward the pond used for watering what little livestock the Coopers kept and for swimming in the heat of summer. Beyond the pond, a small grove of trees provided some shade and acted as a windbreak. The sun was setting as they reached the edge of the grove and plunged into the trees. The boys call out Billy's name, hoping to draw him out of hiding. Kieran put his tracking skills to use and soon found Billy's trail through the grove, and he led Cory after the young boy. Overhead, the full moon rose silver and bright, lighting the grove. They found Billy shivering against the base of the largest tree in the center of the grove. He was crying hard as Kieran and Cory wrapped him in their warmth and love.

"Easy, Puppy, it's okay. Cory and I are here; you're safe now."

"Mom hates me. She doesn't want me and wishes I'd never been born. She called me a monster."

"Your mother is wrong, Billy. You're not a monster. You're loved by so many people. One person can't take all the love away," Kieran said.

"She called me horrible, just like my father. She wishes she'd gotten rid of me before I was ever born."

Kieran stroked the Billy's back, trying to calm him down. Over Billy's head, he caught Cory's worried expression. Picking Billy up, Kieran carried him back to the farmhouse where Tamara got him ready for bed. Kieran didn't know whether to be angry with Billy's mother or to pity her.

"Wolf, what's going on? Why is Billy's mother so horrible with him?"

"Come and sit, babe." Cory led Kieran to a seat beside him on the couch and wrapped him in his arms. "Mom, you tell him everything. He needs to know what's going on."

"Sorry, we never did introduce you to our daughter, Jillian. She moved off the farm after giving birth to Billy. Not long after he was born, she had a nervous breakdown brought on by a delayed reaction to the trauma, which left her pregnant with Billy."

"She was the victim of a rape?"

"Yes, but it wasn't just a rape. She was on a date with her boyfriend, and we think he asked her to marry him when they were attacked. Their attacker took them prisoner and made them focus on each other while he raped them. Jillian witnessed him rip her boyfriend apart. The monster continued raping her for two more days before she managed to escape and made her way back here to the farm. We cared for her and got her treated at the hospital. The doctors ran every test and a full rape kit on her. We had to take her in for multiple appointments as they tested her for sexually transmitted diseases. On one of her visits, they told her she was pregnant. Jillian went into shock, not knowing if the child was her boyfriend's or her rapist's. If it was her boyfriend's, she didn't want to destroy the life growing inside her, as it was all she had left of him. But if it was her rapist's child, she didn't want a constant reminder of what she'd suffered."

"What a horrible choice to be faced with. So, she decided it was better to hope and believe the child was her boyfriend's?"

"She did, and we all encouraged the belief to help her keep her spirits up. We don't support abortion, but in this case, we figured we would support her if she decided to end her pregnancy, considering what happened."

"I take it Billy isn't the child of her boyfriend."

"We're pretty sure he's the child of her rapist, but he's our grandchild and we love him."

"Jillian must be trying to love him if she comes to visit him."

"Jillian comes to visit him to hurt him by reminding him he's the child of rape. She doesn't want or love him. At least, her visits always end in a bad way. Billy ends up in tears hiding somewhere until we find him, reminding him he is loved."

"The poor kid. I sort of relate. My mother's family was disappointed when I was born. They were hoping her firstborn would be a daughter. I've been the unwanted child since Mother passed away. Unless something happens to all my sisters, I won't inherit anything from the family estate because I'm male. My father's family has loved me from the moment I was born, and though I don't get to visit them as much, they've supported me in everything I've done. They even supported me when I came out to the family as gay. My mother's family was shocked because their prized-breeding stud vanished. I should try and spend more time with Billy when I'm down here."

"Babe, how kind of you, but we give Billy so much attention, he's smothered. I don't think he'd like one more grown-up to deal with."

"Ah, but you're all family. He's overprotected, wrapped in wool, and smothered because you're trying so hard to be both his mother and father. None of you just tried being his friend. As an outsider, I'll be just his friend, or since he's calling me his uncle, I'll be the crazy uncle everyone warns the kids to stay away from." Kieran grinned.

Kieran's little joke lightened the mood, even though Cory shot his mother a glance. They needed to talk. The Coopers returned to their normal routine as Kieran and Cory cuddled on the couch. Cory pulled Kieran over so he was wrapped in his arms and leaning against his chest. He sighed when they settled back on the couch in what he thought of as their proper places. They were relaxing and enjoying each other's presence, tuning out the rest of the world around them, when Kieran's cell phone rang with his father's special ring tone. Cory shifted, allowing Kieran to get his phone.

"Hi, Dad. What's up?"

"Are you sitting down, Kieran?"

"Yes, sir. Cory and I are sharing the couch. What's going on, Dad? Is Rosie okay?"

"I'm afraid she failed the test, Kieran. Even with the sword you gave her last year. She never got a chance to use her magic. We think the pack has found a way to break the rules governing the test. The evidence we found suggests Rosie was overwhelmed by more than the allotted five shifters."

"Bright Mother, what is Grandmother going to do to fix this? Will she let me come home?"

"She won't do anything. She ordered your other sisters to take the test together. The survivor will take your mother's place. Moreover, no, she won't let you come home. Not while either of your other sisters still lives."

"They're even younger than Rosie. They don't have a prayer of surviving the test. Tell Grandmother and the Matriarchs for me, if they go forward with this madness, I'll be testing this summer, rules or no rules."

"She won't let you come home, Kieran. She's afraid of you. The House of Beauty despises male children of the line. Worse, your birth was surrounded by omens they didn't want to live to be part of."

Omens? Kieran didn't have time to worry about something he'd never heard about before. Right now, he had to help his sisters. "The Council of Matriarchs will get over their disappointment because I intend to fulfill Grandmother's every last nightmare."

"I know how angry you are, Kieran. Please don't do anything rash just yet. You're the hope of two lines. While one fears you, the other loves you for everything you are. My parents want you to come visit over the summer break and bring your boyfriend with you. We will spend the summer together at their place on the coast and figure out how to deal with your mother's family. Now put Cory on. I want to give him some father-in-law advice. Love you, Son."

"Love you too, Dad. Here, Wolf, Dad wants a father-in-law to son-in-law chat." Kieran passed his phone to Cory."

"Hello, Kellen. I gather the news you gave Kieran was the bad news you warned me about."

"Hello, Cory. Yes, I'm afraid it was. His sister Rosie was killed in a violent attack last night. I want you to comfort him. He and Rosie were close, and his grandmother's refusal to let him come home is going to gnaw deep into his soul. Make sure he doesn't withdraw into himself. My parents are inviting you both to their home on the Maine coast; please come with him. There are things we should discuss in person. Besides, I want to meet the young man who's won my son's heart."

"I'm sure we will. I want to meet you as well, Kellen. I think Kieran wants to talk to you again."

"Put him back on. Protect yourself and my son, Cory."

"Yes, sir. Here's Kieran."

"Hey, Dad, would it be all right if we brought a third with us? I'd like to bring Cory's nephew Billy with us if it's okay with the Coopers. I think a new venue would do the kid some good, and adults who aren't his family spoiling him might be a big help."

"There's something special about this boy if he's wormed his way into your heart along with Cory. I'm sure your grandfather and the rest of the clan will be happy to make him welcome as well."

"Thanks, Dad. Please tell my sisters I love them and grieve with them."

"I will. Be safe, and make sure you keep an eye out for threats to Cory and young Billy. I love you, Son, and I will catch up with you this summer."

"Love you too, Dad. Tell Gramps thanks for the invite home for the summer." Kieran hung up.

Kieran's face was a mask as he hung up and silence filled the air. Cory stared at his boyfriend like he wasn't sure if he should hug him close or give his space. With three his sisters dying so close together, even Cory had to suspect something was off about Kieran's life, but Kieran pushed those thoughts away, wanting to—no, needing to— change to subject before an explanation forced its way out.

"Well what a surprise. I didn't think Dad's family would invite both of us to their place for the summer. They don't like to invite strangers to their compound."

Cory took it as a sign that Kieran didn't want to discuss another loss, so he went with it. "You think they'll be okay with Billy tagging along with us if they're doing this to get an idea about the guy dating their grandson?"

"They'll love the kid. They haven't had anyone young to fuss over since I was his age. Besides, how much trouble can Puppy get into?"

"You'd be surprised. Why do you call him Puppy?"

"Pay attention to how he follows us around when he thinks we don't realize he's tagging along. He's like a little lost dog in need of a place to belong. There's the reason why I call him Puppy. He'll be okay. Surprising and uncanny how my gramps always figured out when I was about to do something to get into deep trouble. The big question is, will your parents let us take him with us?"

"Take who with you where, Kieran?" Tamara asked as she came out of the kitchen.

"My dad's family has invited Cory and I to spend the summer with them at the family place on the coast of Maine, and I wondered if you'd let us take Billy with us if Gramps and company don't object. I think the change of scenery and a different set of adults might be a good thing for him."

"I don't think much of the plan, Kieran. Billy is a handful on his good days. If something goes wrong, he'll be miles from people who know how to help him. I think it would be better if he stayed here this summer."

"If you think so, Tamara. Billy is your grandson and I trust your judgment. Well, the offer is open if Gramps agrees."

"I'll think about your suggestion and talk with Jonathan. Thank you for thinking about Billy."

"You're welcome. If you will excuse me for a while, I'd like to take a walk by myself for a bit. Dad's call wasn't all good news."

"What happened, Kieran? Are your sisters all right?"

"Mom, not a good time."

"No, it's all right, Wolf. Rosie, the oldest of my surviving sisters, was murdered last night, and my coldhearted bitch of a grandmother stated my banishment from home is still in effect."

"Oh, Kieran, I'm so sorry. This is a horrible year for you."

"Not totally, Tamara. With your family in my life, it isn't so bad.

You're a second family to me. Without you, I'm not sure what I would do with all the grief in my life. You make it all bearable." Kieran took her in his arms and gave her a big hug. "Thank you for taking me into your lives."

"Oh, Kieran, you're always welcome here. You're like another son to us and even more to Corwin. Lean on us as you need to."

"Thank you. Wolf, come find me in the grove where we found Billy in an hour."

"Okay, babe. I love you."

"And I love you too." Kieran grabbed a jacket and headed out the door.

"You're worried Billy will undergo the shift when Kieran is around, aren't you, Mom?

"Yes, I'm not sure how he'll take it. I'm surprised it didn't happen tonight with the moon full tonight. With all the stress, Billy should shift. Something about Kieran and the sudden deaths of his sisters still nags at me. I don't know how to explain the sensation, like he isn't quite human, but he's not a shifter. I keep getting a sense of Silver magic about him."

"Mom, we're pretty well mated in every way it matters with the exception of my breeding Kieran or him breeding me and getting the pack's blessing. Are you worried he might be the source of the Silver magic you keep sensing? Do you think he's a Silver mage or just carrying an item attuned to Silver magic?"

"We're happy for the joy he brings you. Don't rush trying to decide which of you is the Alpha in your relationship, although it seems Kieran lets you take the lead more often than not. Silver mages are so rare they're almost a myth. I'm more worried he might be a hunter or related to one somehow."

"I don't think he's connected to any major hunting family. We all know there hasn't been a hunter in Arkansas since the Flood of 1927. I don't think Maine has a big shifter population. Dad's magic appears to be keeping us hidden from anyone figuring out what we are."

"Yes, I know your father's spell is likely the only thing keeping him from sensing the Beast in the few of us with enough of the blood to shift, in particular Billy. I think I'll ask around about hunting families in Maine."

"We need to tell him, Mom. Time for a heart-to-heart talk. I want the pack to approve him as my mate. I just don't think this is the time with his sister having just died."

"You're right, Cory. We should talk this out more. I know a delay is called for to take into account his sister's death. We don't get the time to delay. Alpha is coming to meet Kieran and make his decision about you taking him as your mate tonight as we requested. Moreover, we still need to deal with the issue of Billy. He's close to shifting. What we are is going to come a shock to Kieran."

* * *

KIERAN WENT to the grove where they'd found Billy hidden from the horror of his mother's visit. Crickets chirped in the center of the moonlit grove. Kieran took up a stick in place of a sacred sword and drew a circle around him. Finishing the first circle, he drew a second circle inside it. He filled the space between circles with arcane symbols. Setting aside the stick, he raised his arms and faced to the full moon above him. Kieran lifted his baritone voice in a chant, releasing Silver magic. It set the circles and symbols afire with power.

> *"By earth and water, air and fire,*
> *I call to you to aid my desire,*
> *Let all, which is hidden now be found.*
> *Huntress of the silver moon,*
> *Hunter of the winter snows,*
> *I bid thee welcome.*
> *By my will, so mote it be."*

Power answered power. His chanting finished with a brilliant flash of Silver magic. Before him in place of the stick was his sister's sword, given as a gift to celebrate her last birthday. He retrieved the blade. The

Silver magic of the blade flared as it touched his magic. He brought the blade upright before his face, whispering a brief command.

"Show me what I need to know."

Silver mist formed around the blade, spreading out enough to become a screen on which a picture of his sister appeared. Before him, his sister's last battle played out. He studied the scene as she fought. Rosie used every skill of a huntress of Beauty's line, plus several tricks Kieran had taught her from his lessons with their Uncle Brom. Silver blade flashing, shifter blood splashed. She fought. Claws swept out, slashing his sister. The wave of bodies hit her, bringing her down. Under a heap of bodies, she fell. She tried to call her magic. Shifter claws slashed across her throat. They ripped her open. Her life bled away before her Silver magic answered. They left her to rot on the field. He counted twenty shifters getting up from the pile, which took his sister down. He also counted fifteen dead shifters around his sister's body. Rosie died a huntress of the House of Beauty.

The rules of the test were broken. The one-time use of Silver magic would never protect his remaining sisters. He was the only hope for the main line of Beauty's descendants. They had distant cousins, but the magic was weak and faded in those lines. It was one of the reasons the Matriarchs wanted him to marry one of his cousins. They wouldn't stand a chance if he fell. It was time to come clean with Cory and his family about who he was. Hearing Cory's approach, he sent the sword back to a clearing in the forest at home and dismissed the circle. Kieran stood and waited for his lover/boyfriend/consort to come into the clearing. Cory stopped short right at the edge of the outer circle as if he sensed the Silver magic. Shaking his head, Cory came forward into Kieran's arms and they kissed.

"I gave you a little more than an hour to allow time for you to walk out here, babe."

"Thanks, Wolf. I appreciate it. I needed the time to wrap myself around Rosie being gone. We were always the closest. We cared for each other after Mom died, even more so when Dad wasn't around. She advocated for me when Grandmother went on about what a disappointment I was for being born male."

"Your grandmother sounds like a hard woman."

"She's bitter. An injury took her out of the field and trapped her on the family's business board early in life. Mom had to take on the active part of the family business before she was ready. Mom had just started dating Dad and hadn't even brought him home to meet her family. She decided to surprise him and asked him to marry her on their fifth date and to come back to Maine with her."

"Must have been a shock to him. It's hard to imagine someone asking me to marry them on only the fifth date."

"It was a shock, but Dad told me he wanted to ask her to marry him after just meeting her. I think it was the fact she asked him, which shocked him. Dad has his traditional side, but they were happy up until I was born. Grandmother made their lives miserable for having a son. Dad's family always made me seem like I'm the greatest thing since man learned how to microwave food."

Cory laughed and pulled Kieran in for a deep kiss. An anguished howl pierced the night, breaking the lovers apart. The brush along the path to the grove cracked and shuddered as something large forced its way through. A huge black-furred wolf broke into the clearing and uttered its heartbroken cry. Kieran, sensing a shifter, acted on instinct, pushing Cory to a protected position behind him as his sister's sword appeared in his hand. He braced himself to hold off the wolf. More brush broke and parted. A pack of wolves emerged from the woods around the grove. Cory tried to placed his hand on Kieran's arm and hold him from attacking, but pain drove his hand back as it contacted Kieran's Silver magic.

"Please don't, Kieran. If my guess is correct, the black wolf is Billy. The rest are my mother, my siblings, and the pack my family belongs to. We were afraid Billy's shift would happen while you were here."

"What? How is this possible? You can't be. I never sensed shifter blood in any of you before. How am I now sensing shifter in everyone but your father?"

"Until tonight, we've never connected you to the Silver magic we've sensed," Jonathan spoke as he stepped into the clearing with a large gray wolf at his side.

Kieran's heart shattered as he realized he'd given his heart to someone with shifter blood. Granted, it was so weak as to be non-existent, but then he realized, with the exception of Jonathan, all the rest of his lover's family members were shifters. Silver magic swirled around him, forming armor. How had he not suspected? He bit back a sob, betrayed by the man he loved. Would he need to kill the Coopers?

"Kieran, we need to talk about some things," Jonathan said.

"You're not a shifter, Jonathan? What are you? How does your family go undetected?" Kieran's voice broke in anguish.

"I'm a Sapphire mage. They were hidden from you because of my magic. I cast a spell, keeping my family safe from detection as long as they never injure a human being. It also keeps me safe from detection as well. I'm guessing the stress of Jillian's visit caused Billy to shift, which triggered the breaking of my spell. We never wanted to deceive you, Kieran. We were hoping Billy wouldn't shift while you were here. Cory escaped Tamara's family curse; he's never shifted."

"It doesn't matter, whether he's ever shifted or not. Shifter blood taints everything between us. He can't even touch me right now because of that taint. Do either of you realize what's been done? Because of your magic, Jonathan, he's broken my heart. Cory, I only spare your family because my broken heart still belongs to you."

"Babe, please, your magic is painfully proving I'm not completely free from the taint the rest of my family bears. Mom's family has spent generations of breeding trying to end the curse, and they thought I was the first success. We're most worried about Billy. His shift proves his father was the rapist as we've all feared."

"So, Wolf, your family is one of the factions seeking to purge the Beast. My family has heard rumors of the existence of clans who wanted to free themselves of the Ebony magic."

"The rumors are true. Now I need to know what you are. Is your Silver magic your own or is it from powerful artifacts?"

"My magic is my own. I learned to hide it behind various items so no one would guess what I am, even when I'm tracking shifters."

"So you're related to a hunting family. Mom and the Alpha were afraid you were. We've never heard of a hunter family carrying so much Silver magic. Tell me who you really are, Kieran?"

"I'm surprised by your family's and pack's lack of information. I figured every shifter clan would have heard of the House of Beauty. I'm a full tracker of the house. My mother was the last huntress and my sisters have been dying during the test to take her place."

"Oh my god, if what you say is true, we should be enemies, not lovers," came Cory's shocked response.

"Kieran, please shut down your magic. I promise the pack won't hurt you. Billy came seeking you and Cory for comfort. Even in Beast form, he seeks you out," Jonathan said, trying to divert attention from Cory.

"Is that black wolf truly Billy? By the Goddess, so much Ebony magic. What was his father?"

"A pure-born Alpha of corruption's side. One so powerful, he possesses a midway shift form. An Alpha who claims to be a direct descendant of the legendary Beast and distant kin to Tamara's family."

His magic faded. Kieran sank to his knees sobbing. Cory wrapped his arms around his boyfriend, wanting to comfort him. Kieran shrugged him off. The black wolf sat close to Kieran, whining for attention. Kieran started to reach but withdrew his hand. Cory spread his arms out and welcomed the young wolf into his embrace.

"Cory, I'm sorry for hiding my heritage from you. If I'd had a hint you were of shifter blood, I'd have revealed who I was. I thought you were a regular human. I wanted to protect you from the dangers of my life. Hell, I ignored all the signs. Bruce and Marissa told me you weren't pure human, and I dismissed what they said out of hand. We can't be. We have to end this relationship here and now. Gods, we make *Romeo and Juliet* seem normal."

"I'm sorry I didn't tell you about us sooner. I don't want to end our relationship, Kieran. You and I are mated. I have just enough of the wolf in me. If you leave me, I'll die. You know wolves mate for life. By loving you, I've endangered my whole family."

"Billy poses a bigger danger. I think he's imprinted on you and

Cory as a pair. If you leave, he'll loose any and all control and have to be put down," Jonathan added.

The wolf beside Jonathan shimmered, and a naked Tamara stood next to her husband.

"Kieran you have every right to be angry with Jonathan and me. We bind our family to silence until they find their mate. Cory told me you were his chosen mate when we planned on you coming down for this break. I should have let him tell you then. I thought we'd have more time before Billy shifted. I was hoping binding him would prevent the shift, but Jonathan keeps reminding me Sapphire magic isn't powerful enough to bind a shifter of Billy's purity. It would take Silver magic to bind Billy to one form. He needs your help, and I have no right to ask you for it."

"You're right, Tamara. You don't have the right to ask me for anything. Not even to help Billy. Take your pack, and leave this grove now." Kieran rose from his knees.

"I'm not the Alpha of this pack, Kieran; they aren't mine to command. They came to help catch Billy and because Cory has something he wanted to ask you, which requires the pack's approval."

"What did you want to ask me? What needs to be approved by your pack, Cory?"

"I want you to be my bonded life mate. I wanted to ask their approval of you as my true bonded mate. I still do."

"Even knowing what I am? You want me as your bonded mate? You want to marry me? Let your Alpha face me. Let's get his disapproval over. Then you will find a mate the pack approves. Come and face me, pack Alpha. Are you brave enough to face a child of Beauty?"

A silvery gray wolf shimmered and was replaced by an old man who faced Kieran across the grove. He approached and stood before Tamara and Jonathan. The rest of the pack forced the shift back to human form. They gathered in the clearing, facing Kieran. Cory and wolf Billy placed themselves in front of Kieran as if to protect him from the pack.

"I am pack Alpha. Corwin and Billy Cooper, you will step away from the child of Beauty."

Billy refused to budge from where he stood. Kieran knelt next to him and urged him to go to Jonathan and Tamara. Cory stood to the side.

"I'll be all right, Puppy. He's your pack leader. You belong with the pack. I'll be fine."

With a backward glance, Billy moved toward the pack. The Alpha stepped forward and placed a hand on Cory's head, checking if a bond existed. Kieran forced himself to stay where he was. Part of him yearned to protect Cory with every fiber of his being, but he'd have to cut through the pack to get to him. The pack was facing him now, behind their Alpha. Billy remained the only wolf.

"How are you called, child of Beauty?" the Alpha asked Kieran.

"My full name Kieran Samuel Belle Oisín, a tracker of the House of Beauty on my mother's side. On my father's side, I am the heir to the ancient lineage of the Silver Witch."

There was a gasp from the pack.

"Speak only the truth here, tracker. The Silver Witch is a myth."

"I speak only truth, Alpha." Silver magic flared around Kieran like a visible aura. "Once I take the test, I will be the on the path to become heir to the most powerful line of Silver mages. I will be the Silver Witch of my generation. I am no myth."

"Well, tracker. Who has chosen you as their mate?"

"I, Corwin Samuel Cooper, have chosen him as my mate, Alpha."

"You have chosen dangerously, Corwin Cooper. The House of Beauty is our enemy, and it is said that because of the Silver Witch and Silver mages like him, our kind has but one shape and must fear the hunters. I will not approve your choice of mate. You bonded without the pack's consent. The bond must either be broken or you must leave the pack."

"Hear me, Corwin Cooper, before you answer your Alpha's choice. You bear the shifters taint for which both sides of my family would kill you, should they discover what you are. I do not have the authority to protect you, and by all rights, I should be fighting to kill you all," Kieran said.

"Kieran, we promised to love each other forever. We mated. We've bonded. I won't live without you. I'll take my chances with your family."

"I'm sorry, Cory. If you won't do the right thing, I will. I'm a child of the House of Beauty, not a shifter. I have a duty to protect the purity of my house. You should be with your own kind. It breaks my heart to let you go, but it has to end this way. I've made my choice. I refuse to be your mate. By the huntress of the silver moon and the hunter of the silver snow, I send this bond back from whence it came. By my will, so mote it be."

Kieran made a gesture and Silver magic surged from his heart to Cory's, seeming to burn away the mating bond between them.

"I return your love to you and take the price of an indifferent heart for myself."

Kieran gathered his power like a cloak, casting a spell to transport him away from the pack.

"Kieran, no! Please come back! We can work this out," Cory shouted before turning to face the pack. "He would never have hurt any of us. Why must I live with a broken heart? Why are you punishing me?"

"It's for the safety of the pack. The descendants of Beauty are the most powerful of all the hunter families. They would kill us all," the Alpha proclaimed.

"You're an old fool. Kieran ripped out his heart instead of cutting off our heads. I think we're more likely to be in danger from the House of Beauty now that he has nothing personally invested. You've destroyed two lives this night and possibly a third. Billy is as attached to Kieran as Cory was, in a different manner. If he shifts back, it will be hard to explain to him why Kieran doesn't love Cory anymore," Jonathan replied in anger.

"You overstep your place, mage. I'll not be challenged by a human."

From amidst the pack, Cory's eldest brother Jeff stepped forward.

"Time I challenged you for leadership of the pack, old wolf," Cory's brother Jeff growled.

"Why should I accept your challenge mate-less cur?"

"Mate-less no longer, old wolf. Your daughter gave herself to me as mate last night."

Howling, the old man shifted and lunged for Jeff. Two wolves collided, locking jaws and rolling, fighting for dominance. Cory stared in horror as his brother fought for control of the pack. Wolf Billy pressed against Cory's leg, whining in fear. Cory caressed his head between the ears, trying to calm the wolf boy as the two men fought to the death.

INTERLUDE: TRANSPORTED TO TROUBLE

Silver mist wrapped Kieran in fire as it whisked him away from Cory and the pack. The magic of the transportation spell should be beyond Kieran's level of spell casting. The old grimoire, which contained the spell, contained a record showing only a mage of his father's or grandfather's level should be able to cast the spell. Perhaps because his heart ached from the magic of breaking the mate-bond to Cory, he now possessed the strength to cast more powerful spells. Time seemed to stop for Kieran and visions appeared before him.

Once the silver mist wrapped about him, Kieran gazed at a scene out of the dimmest legends of his own family. Before him, he witnessed the moment the first male Silver Witch gave his youngest sister Beauty the gift of Silver magic. It wasn't a gift so much as an awakening of a dormant ability. He caught the twist in the magic the Silver Witch made, which limited women to one spell of Silver magic. In his own way, the first male Silver Witch was as jealous of his beautiful younger sister as were their older sisters. He chose not to wake the full potential of Silver magic in his sister. Kieran knew he would unlock the power if he got back to his remaining sisters before they took the test.

Pain ripped a scream from Kieran in the place between worlds, as he experienced the pain of knowing his grandmother had sent his sisters to their death. He was the last hope for the House of Beauty. Destiny was closing its hand around him, transforming him from tracker and witch into the Silver Hunter of legend. Just as he was about to materialize from the spell, a large hand of Ruby magic tinted with Ebony hijacked his spell and cast him into darkness.

Kieran woke slumped on a hard concrete floor with chains binding his hands to the wall. Pain both physical and emotional wracked his body from head to toe. He tried to pull himself upright but fell back on the floor. He sensed others drawing near. Lifting his head, he received a slap across the face.

"No slave lifts his eyes above his master's feet. Keep your eyes on the floor at all times."

"Go to hell. I'm no one's slave."

Blows fell. The pain left Kieran unconscious.

16

"Dad, help me get him inside. Cory, snap out of it." Jeff shook his brother.

"Your brother just lost the love of his life, Jeff. Cut him some slack. Take Billy inside and get a warm bath running," came Jonathan's directions.

Cory just let his father drag him along and into the bathroom. A hand touched his forehead and soothing coolness flowed through his body. They carried him inside and undressed him. He was lowered into a tub of warm water, like being wrapped in Kieran's arms. He heard a whine and scratching at the bathroom door as Billy tried to get to him. Jeff rose and let Billy pad into the room.

"It's getting crowded in here. Billy, you keep an eye on him. I'll go get some of his clothes. Just let him relax; he needs time to process what's been done to him and Kieran." Jonathan left the bathroom.

"We'll be downstairs when you're ready, little brother."

"Thank you, Jeff. It's hard to believe you're the new Alpha. I'm sorry you challenged for my sake."

"You aren't the reason I challenged the old man, little brother. I dated Danica on the sly for the last three months. The old man never approved of me. He sensed another Alpha and discouraged my mating.

I did it for Danica. You and your tracker, I will decide about you later," Jeff responded. "We'll talk more about it when you're ready." Jeff left Cory and Billy alone.

"Billy, what do I do? Kieran was everything, and now there's this huge ache in my heart. I'm so sorry we hid what we are from him. I never wanted him to rip his own heart to pieces to protect me. I want him back and whole."

Billy gave a low growl and nudged Cory. Cory rubbed between Billy's wolf ears and got out of the tub, grabbing a towel to dry off with. He dressed and went down the hall to the room Kieran used to house his clothes, computer, and photo equipment. Cory found Kieran's heavy leather duster, and pulling it over himself, he lay down on the bed in the guestroom. Billy settled himself on the floor, out of reach of the magic woven into the coat. Cory sobbed himself into a sleep where he dreamed of Kieran.

Kieran stood in what had been his room on the second floor of Mrs. Jones' house, surrounded by a circle of Silver magic. On the floor before him were three items, his leather duster, a small square box, and a long rectangular box. He seemed to be muttering something, but Cory couldn't make it out. The scene faded away and was replaced with an image of Kieran looking sad as he began to speak.

"Cory, I love you whole-heartedly. If you're hearing this, you're wrapped in my coat. I'm hoping that a question that's been nagging me for a while isn't what has separated us. A couple of different shifters have tried to tell me that you're not the human you claim to be, that you have shifter blood. By now you likely have questions about my own heritage, especially if my sisters have started dying in freak accidents. If it turns out you do have shifter heritage, I don't care. I love you and I will always love you regardless of what I may have done that has left you wrapped in my jacket trying to hold on to me. I'm likely the last of my direct family line, a line of shifter hunters. I'm currently a tracker for the House of Beauty, and I hope things haven't reached the point where I'm the hunter-candidate of the house. Bright Goddess, I hope we are not of opposing heritages. It's bad enough being descended from a fairy tale heroine without adding a Romeo and Juliet twist into our story.

I'm hoping as I enchant this coat that we're only temporally parted because of warring houses and not that I've been given a chance to take the test of the huntress, as silly as that title sounds, and failed, which will mean I'm dead. Know that if I made some grand gesture about setting you free and taking on an indifferent heart, I was casting a spell to hide all my love for you inside your heart so you could use it to find me, if the transport spell I'm sure to cast right after that goes wrong. I've never cast the transport spell before, and it's very powerful.

I've left you a couple of items, one I've been carrying for a few years now and the other I've had my Uncle Brom forge for me in case that nagging question had the answer I didn't want to hear. When you wake up, reach into the inner pocket on the right side of the coat; you will find two boxes. One is a box containing the ring I forged for my one true soul mate. I know it will fit you and never come off as long as we are both alive and true to each other. The other item is a chain with a wolf's head pendant. Uncle Brom has enchanted the chain with a binding spell I developed. If that nagging question about your family is answered—yes, you are shifters—then Billy might need the chain to aid him in making a difficult choice. The spell will bind a shifter to one shape as long as he never takes the chain off. The choice of shape is his alone, human or Beast. If I have joined my sisters in the next world, the ring will fall off and vanish. Please remember me and care for my heart; use my love to help you find a new love. Come find me if we've only parted ways because you learned I'm from a hunter family and I learned you're a shifter. Just use the ring to follow my heart's love back to the source.

The phantom Kieran kissed Cory on the lips and faded away. Cory awoke fumbling with the coat, which was wrapped around him like being in Kieran's embrace. It was heart wrenching to unwrap himself from the sensation, but he needed to know if Kieran did this. He found the pocket and reached inside to find two boxes one small and square in shape and the other a long flat box. Cory pulled out both boxes and sensed Billy studying him from where he was curled up on the floor. Opening the smaller box, Cory gazed on the gleaming silver ring Kieran had forged for the day when he found his soul mate. Cory slipped the ring out of the box and slid it on to his left ring finger, where it seemed too loose to remain. The ring pulsed with Silver magic, which tingled across Cory's hand before it tightened and transformed from a plain band to a wolf's head with two diamond eyes. Cory gave it a tug, but it refused to budge from his finger. He swallowed a pang of grief. Kieran hadn't been the one to place the ring on his finger. Some deep sense awoke in Cory, telling him through the working magic of the ring that Kieran was still alive. A renewed sense of confidence flowed through Cory, so he dressed and slipped into Kieran's leather coat. With Billy following him, he went downstairs to face his family and the pack, which were waiting for him.

* * *

KIERAN SHUDDERED as the cold water splashed against his bruised and battered face. His tormentors took to making sure he didn't get any rest even when the pain drove him into unconsciousness, the frequent bouts of which had left him with no sense of time, no reference for telling if it was day or night. Someplace nearby, an item enchanted with Ebony magic kept him from accessing his own Silver magic in nothing but tiny trickles. Kieran suspected it was either the collar or the cuffs around his wrists. He knew his captors were trying to break him, although he didn't know why. The whole affair left Kieran with suspicions of being in a bad TV show revolving around some sort of sexual slavery ring, although knowledge of the slavery scene was way out of Kieran's frame of understanding. He only knew they kept demanding he acknowledge them as his masters. By shifting his emotions from his heart to Cory's, he made his captors' task next to impossible. With no heart, he didn't care about anything. He spat blood and defiance at his current tormentor and sent a tiny trickle of magic to test the collar's lock.

INTERLUDE: A HIDDEN LINEAGE REVEALED

Kellen Oisín stood in the hall of the Belle Matriarchs, facing down his mother-in-law with murder in his heart. When he'd returned home and found his youngest daughters missing from their classrooms—and after checking their rooms in the family suite were also empty—he'd marched down to the council's chamber and demanded an audience with the council. Behind his blazing violet eyes, the vast Oisín reserve of Silver magic was held contained by an extreme act of will as he stormed into the council chamber when the doors opened just wide enough to slip through.

"What have you done, old woman? Where are my youngest daughters?"

"They're gone to the test. We must have a huntress. Do not interfere; it is not your place."

"You've sent them to their death. Congratulations, you've just brought about what you fear most, old woman. Kieran is your last hope. You've destroyed your own house in your haste to have a new huntress when you knew the pack broke all the bonds holding them to the rules of the test. You should have cleansed the pack before sending my daughters out there. It was your duty as the huntress of your generation. Crippled or not, you should have gone in their place. Now, only my son survives. I hope you're ready to deal with a legend being born. It serves you right."

"If you talk about the ancient fairy tale of the Silver Hunter, Kieran doesn't come close. He'd have to be the child of both the huntress of her generation and a son of the line of the mythical Silver Witch. My daughter assured me you were as normal as humans come."

"Because I swore her to secrecy and bound her oath with magic. I am the heir to the Silver Witch, and Kieran is the son of both lines."

"Why have you sought forth the Silver Hunter? Do you know the disaster you're bringing down on our heads?"

"Do you know what dwells within your own forest? There's a new Alpha in your forest, one not bound to the rules of the test, an Alpha whose monstrous power screams an ancient lineage. The Silver Hunter is the only hope of protecting the magic binding shifters to their single forms. It thinks it has eliminated the lines of the ancient mages who cast the binding during the last mage war. The House of Beauty and the line of the Silver Witch are the last of the Silver mage lines involved in the binding spell. Truth is the House of Beauty has always been a diversion. You've never mattered, save to help keep our line hidden and as breeding stock to bring forth the Silver Hunter when the time was right."

"Damn you, Kellen Oisín. Go and bring my grandson home. Let him be tested."

17

Cory clad in Kieran's leather coat entered the living room where the full pack waited, his brother Jeff seated at the center. Wearing part of Kieran's tracker armor gave him the confidence to face anything; beside him, Billy padded along.

"Corwin Samuel Cooper, you brought a tracker into a gathering of the pack. Is this how you show respect to your Alpha?" Jeff asked.

"No, Alpha, I brought my chosen mate before the pack for approval by your predecessor. His being a tracker is beside the point."

"What do you seek now?"

"Not a damn thing from this pack. I'm not a shifter but for a minor taint in my blood. In the morning, when Billy has returned to human form, I'm going to give him the choice Kieran planned to offer him. Kieran suspected for some time the secret we were all hiding from him. He left me a message spelled into his coat. Along with the message, he also left me the ring he forged for his soul mate and a collar, which will give Billy a chance at a normal life."

"He broke your mating bond before us. You're delusional, little brother, if you think he still loves."

"You're wrong. He didn't break the bond. He hid his heart within me to protect it and our bond. I'm wrapped in his love and I have this to prove I'm his soul's mate. Take if from me if you're able," Cory challenged as he extended his ringed hand up before the pack.

"Corwin, stop this nonsense. You're grieving over the tracker's betrayal and departure. Take the ring off and get rid of the coat. The tracker is gone, and he doesn't love you," Danica, his brother's mate, ordered him.

"Fuck off, Danica. Kieran is as much member of this family as you are, and he will always be welcome here. Mate to my brother or not, you don't get a say in my life. This family confirmed Kieran's fears in such an abrupt manner and didn't give him the normal time to adjust we give a mate-candidate to decide. This ring will not come off my finger until Kieran and I are no longer soul mates. This collar will give Billy peace by binding him to one form, and the choice is his, to be boy or wolf. Do you want to take the chance away from him, Danica? It's not your place to decide anything other than how many children you'll bear for Jeff, so just be quiet."

Danica appeared as if she would retort, but Jeff's raised hand stopped her. Cory continued his speech.

"Kieran is still watching out for us. His family has cast him out because he was born male and because he's gay. Are you going to reject him because he's tracker and not a shifter? It would be a laugh since the family mated for generations to breed the shifter out of you. For some of you, Kieran might be able to purge the last of the taint out of you. Are you ready to throw it away because of who his mother was, of who his father might be?"

"Cory, what do you need from us?" Jonathan asked.

"I need help getting back to Kieran. He needs me. Is there a fast way of finding him?"

"There are plenty of things belonging to him; we'll scry for him. I'll do everything to help you track him down."

"Thank you, Dad."

"What will you do when you find him, little brother?" Jeff asked.

"Love him with every fiber of my being and support him when he goes back to his family to claim his place."

INTERLUDE: MONSTERS IN THE DARK FOREST

In the deep dark woods of the Belle estate, the dark pack swirled around their Alpha as he attempted to shift his shape into something besides his monstrous bear form. Try as he would, no other animal shape would his body transform into. He settled into the half-man, half-bear form and growled his frustration at his failure.

"They're all dead. No huntress-candidate lives. The cursed line of Beauty is broken. Why am I denied my victory? All the major families of the cursed Silver magic are broken. Their ancient spell should be as dead as those pathetic children."

One of the pack omega males approached, head bowed in submission before the Alpha.

"Ancient one, there is one child left to the House of Beauty: the elder brother of the huntress-candidates. He is but a tracker of the house."

"The men of Beauty's cursed line don't carry the Silver magic. Somewhere we missed an heir to the magic of another line."

"What of the Silver Hunter of the prophecy?" the omega asked.

"The Silver Hunter is a myth, a fable told to frighten shifter children. The prophecy holds no meaning. No hunter would ever choose to mate with a shifter, and to fulfill the prophecy, this fictional hunter must take a male shifter as a mate."

"Our sources report the son of the last huntress left because he was driven out for being gay. He doesn't fulfill his role in the breeding plans of the House of Beauty. If he has found a mate, he might be the one to fulfill the prophecy."

"Either mated or not, if he is the be the hunter, he must come to the test. When he does, he shall die like his sisters."

18

—————

Kieran didn't recall his captors moving him from his cell; they must have moved him the last time he lapsed into unconsciousness. Ice-cold water hit his face and brought him back to an alert state. When he came to this time, he found himself strapped to a St. Andrew's cross under a bright spotlight. He gathered his captors were getting more upset with him, and their failure to break him must be pissing off their higher ups. Perhaps they were handing him over to a more skilled torturer, one who wouldn't be afraid to use rape or the threat of rape to get Kieran to break. Despite the pain, Kieran focused and sent the tiny trickle of magic he was able to summon into the lock on his collar again. One last twist and he heard the faint snick of the lock popping. The spell holding his magic in check split and vanished. A huge man entered the room, and Kieran waited, gathering his power. Shock almost caused Kieran to falter when the man stepped into the light shining on Kieran. Coach Henderson stood before him dressed in a pair of heavy leather combat boots, leather pants, and a chest harness, which screamed torturer in a bad horror movie. His previous captors might not have used rape, but the coach's attire said he wouldn't hesitate to use rape to further his agenda. However, what was scary about Coach Henderson was not the way he was dressed but the fact Kieran sensed the man was a dark shifter.

"You've been giving the boss' boys a run for their money, Belle. I never thought you'd prove to be so tough. Didn't think I'd have to come and break you in person. The Master who bought you is impressed by your strength. However, he's grown tired of the fact you aren't serving him as he desires."

"An Alpha like you is a servant? How it must gall a shifter of your status to be someone's bitch, Coach. This master must be powerful to have you licking his boots. Your pack must be so disappointed in you," Kieran's answer rasped from his parched throat.

"What can a mere boy comprehend about shifters?"

"I got a whiff of what you are, Coach. You can't break me. Your master is wasting his time if he thinks I'll serve him. He can't keep me here any longer."

"You're bound by his magic, and his Ruby magic will keep you in place."

"Stupid shifter, I see no one ever bothered to explain that Ruby magic can't bind. Even if it could, your boss hasn't got the juice to bind me. He should have hired a more powerful Ebony mage if he wanted to bind me. Because the one who made this little enchanted collar was useless. I broke his toy, and now, I'll give you the chance to tuck your tail and run shifter, or I'll nail your hide to the wall."

"You've been beaten and starved for over a week. Do you think you'll beat me in a fight? Even in my human form? You can't even stand, much less fight me," Coach said.

Silver fire burst from Kieran's hands and slammed Coach Henderson into the wall. Silver magic bands held the coach to the wall. More magic broke the final bonds holding Kieran. When the final bond popped, Kieran fell to the floor. He managed to push himself up to a sitting position and grimaced up at the struggling Coach.

"Still think I can't beat you, Coach? The spell holding you is the most minor of Silver magic's collection of bindings. So why don't you tell me who your master is, although I think I can make a guess and say Professor Simms. Confirm my guess and I'll kill you fast."

"And leave a human corpse behind? I don't think so, mage. You won't draw the attention to yourself," Coach sneered.

Coach Henderson continued to struggle against Kieran's magic, while Kieran attempted to stand. Their standoff was interrupted as a shadow stretched across the room from the open doorway.

"Then I'll kill you for him and even take the rap for your death, Coach. I'm betting I'll walk free when the jury rules my actions as self-defense." Cory's voice came from the doorway, followed by the click of round chambering in a pistol.

"Cory, get back. This is between me, the coach, and whoever is behind this operation," Kieran urged.

"I've been searching for you for over a week, Kieran. Do you think I'm leaving you now?"

"Damn it, Cory. I can't even stand and fight. If we're attacked now, we're both bound for the sex slave market."

"It's just us and the coach; the rest of the complex is empty, and Billy is guarding the hallway."

"You left a thirteen-year-old boy to guard the hall?" Surprise pulled the question from Kieran's mouth.

"Nope, I left a large wolf guarding the hall," came Cory's smug reply.

"Fuck, help me up. We need to get out of here. Don't think you're safe, Coach Henderson. If you haven't left campus and town before the next full moon, I will find you in your Beast form and kill you."

"You still don't scare me, kid. You won't be safe on campus. My boys will make sure of it," Coach Henderson growled, knowing the jocks of his football team would lash out at both Belle and Cooper without his having to say a thing.

Silver magic flared around Kieran's hands, and the bands holding Coach Henderson to the wall tightened and burned into his flesh. Kieran let the magic sink in beneath the skin and used it to form a pattern like a tattoo.

"Enjoy the pain the spell will cause you from now on, Coach. If you send any of your jocks near either of us, the magic will enter your bloodstream and burn you to death from the inside."

Cory helped Kieran from the room, and Billy's wolf form joined them as they made their way out of the old abandoned warehouse. When they got outside, Kieran blinked and flinched from the brightness of the sun. Cory got him into his car and then covered him with the leather coat. Kieran settled and was asleep by the time Cory had Billy settled in the backseat and got behind the wheel. He started up the car and headed for the nearest hospital.

"Just take me home, Wolf. They'll ask too many questions at a hospital. Food, water, and sleep are the things I need most. Well, a hot shower would be good too." Kieran chuckled.

"How did you end up here, babe?"

"My transport spell was hijacked. I'd targeted the farmhouse, but I got swept up in a vision, and then, there was this searing pain, and when I came to, I was chained to a wall and someone was telling me I was a slave and needed to call him master. It took me this long to get enough magic into the lock on the collar keeping me from using my full magic."

"Sounds like we found you just in time."

"It's a story I want to hear at some point. Why did Billy choose wolf form?"

"He wanted to stay with us, just not as a little boy. Mother wasn't happy and tried to order him to stay a boy. Dad stepped in and told her you'd left the decision up to Billy, not to anyone else. Then, he told Billy whatever he decided, the family would support him, and not only did he stare down Mom but also my brother Jeff. Who, by the way, is the new pack Alpha."

"I suppose I've got to go through the ritual you were going to make me face when you confirmed my suspicions you were shifters."

"Nope. I told the pack I didn't want and didn't need their approval of my choice of mate. I think none of them are in a hurry to meet you again. You being a tracker of the House of Beauty scares them no end. They think the Huntress of the House of Beauty will come sweeping down on them and kill them all."

"Won't happen. All my sisters are dead, and I'm the new hunter-candidate for the House of Beauty. I'm tired and want to sleep."

"Sleep, babe. We'll be at the apartment soon. I'll wake you when we get there."

"One thing before I sleep, Wolf."

"Anything, Kieran."

"Kiss me. I want my heart back."

19

———————

Kieran awoke, flailing at the sensation of bonds tightening around him. When Cory's calming voice penetrated his mind, he realized some of the bonds were Cory's arms. When Kieran settled down from his fright, Cory hugged him tight before stroking his hands down Kieran's body to soothe him further.

"Babe, you're safe. You were having a bad dream."

"I was having nightmares again. I dreamt I'd lost you. Your family wouldn't let us be together anymore. You howled as I broke our mate bond. I felt my heart breaking. Then everything was silver fire and pain. All my sisters are dead."

"Your mind is still trying to deal with what happened almost a month ago. You're safe now. It's just you, me, and Billy."

"Oh, Bright Mother, I keep hoping it was all a dream. I just want to be Kieran and Cory. I keep expecting my grandmother or my father to show up to drag me back to Maine."

"Take it easy, we'll be just us for as long as possible. We don't have to be anything else. We're back at school in our apartment and just a couple of college students. For us, neither the House of Beauty nor the Cooper pack exists. There's just the Belle-Cooper family."

"I love the sound of it, Wolf, I do. I want to make it official soon. I just wish it were simple, Wolf. If my sisters are all dead, then either my grandmother or my father will be coming to take me back to Maine for the test. The House of Beauty must have an active hunter. A life of serenity isn't in the cards for us, Wolf."

"As long as I'm with you, babe, I have everything I need. Oh, I almost forgot. This little package came for you this morning. Theo signed for it and brought it up."

Kieran sat up, took the package from Cory, and glanced at the address. He gave a little chuckle before opening the package.

"It has been awhile since I heard you so happy, babe."

"It's from my Uncle Brom. He taught me how to forge and enchant items. His Silver magic only works when he uses a metallic focus. It's why even though he's the older brother, my dad is the Silver Witch's heir. He sent me a ring to match yours. When you put it on my hand, the magic will activate."

"So, how come you weren't needed to put this one on my finger to activate the magic? Why do you need me to put this one on you? Don't get me wrong. I'm not saying I don't want to put a ring on your finger."

"The reason is because I had a hand in forging the one on your finger and my magic is woven into it, Wolf. Uncle Brom forged this one alone, without the assistance of the one who'd won my heart. It needs your touch to know you're my soul's match, otherwise the magic will lie dormant."

Cory took the box and opened it to reveal a ring matching the plain band, which had been his ring from Kieran before it transformed into the wolf head ring locked to his finger. He took the ring out of the box and experienced the tingle of Silver magic. Taking Kieran's left hand, he slipped the ring on to his lover's ring finger. The magic flared as it mixed with Kieran's own magic. The ring transformed to match Cory's wolf's head, but the eyes were amber instead of diamond. Kieran reached out and took Cory's left hand in his own left hand so their rings touched. Silver magic flared around their hands, and both rings changed once more; now both rings sported twin wolf heads, one with diamond eyes and one with amber eyes. Both men sensed a light touch on their heads as the magic finished.

Kieran grabbed Cory and drew him in for a deep kiss. Cory melted into his lover's embrace and returned the kiss with a passion. They were sliding into position to make love and consummate their new status when Billy poked his nose into Kieran's side, wanting attention. Kieran broke the kiss with a yelp as the cold nose touched him. He rolled over and scratched Billy between the ears as Cory spooned up behind him.

"I'd better take Billy for a walk before we get ready for classes."

"Today is Saturday, babe. I'm worried this is the third time this week you experienced nightmares and not remembered what the day is. I still think we need to get you checked over and make sure nothing is wrong with you."

"I'll be all right, Wolf. Besides, how do we explain how I got this way? I can't accuse Coach Henderson of kidnapping, not after the team just won the Sun Belt Tournament."

"The shifters on campus might find someone to examine you without raising all kinds of awkward questions."

"I'll text Bruce. Bet the pack keeps in touch with someone who won't ask too many awkward questions. I need time in the photography lab I have a lot of work to do to get ready for finals."

20

———

While taking Billy for a walk, Kieran still wondered about Billy's choice to remain a wolf instead of being human, Kieran realized Billy's life as a boy was hard. With a mother who didn't love him, grandparents who smothered him in protections, the stress of school, and friends who lived too far away to visit after school without making special arrangements, his choice made sense for him to choose the escape offered. If given a choice like the one he gave Billy, Kieran thought he would jump at the chance to be free and loved. Given the choice, Billy picked being with the two men who cared for him with just the right amount of love and concern; his wolf form gave him a freedom he would never get as a boy. Pride shone in Kieran's gaze as he took in the wolf walking at a calm pace beside him like a big puppy, and he smiled even though he still envied Billy for being so free of responsibilities.

"I agree with your choice, Puppy. I'd choose to be free like you, if I were allowed to make the same choice. I just hope the chain and spell aren't causing you to much pain."

Billy snorted and gave him a huge doggie grin, tongue falling out of his mouth as he panted his joy. Kieran laughed, and they continued their walk.

* * *

KIERAN LOCKED himself away in the school darkroom for hours at a time in his efforts to please his teacher. His professor was old fashioned. Professor Mason's concept of a strong photo required understanding how to frame an image, give it the correct exposure, and then process film. Until you mastered film photography, Professor Mason forbid the use of a digital camera. Kieran enjoyed the solitude of the processing room, which he managed to snag for himself by working late.

Down the hallway from the photography studio, Cory was locked away in the painting classroom. The life-size paintings of Kieran in the hayfield stood on easels as Cory worked to put the finishing touches on them.

Unknown to Kieran, Cory was being harassed by a couple of Coach Henderson's jocks, who were trying to get into his good graces and win his sponsorship into the frat he belonged to. The spell cast by Kieran, which should be burning Coach Henderson and alerting Kieran, never kicked in because the jocks acted on their own initiative. All magic comes with loopholes and blind spots.

* * *

CORY CONTEMPLATED how much time Professor Simms was spending on commenting on his paintings, focusing on the ones Kieran had modeled for in tight shorts. Professor Simms's praise of Cory's work made the harassing grow worse.

"Now, class, I want you to study Mr. Cooper's work. His paintings exhibit what I've been trying to explain to you all semester about letting your emotions flow in your art. Mr. Cooper brought his subject to life in these paintings, and you sense the deep emotions in every brush stroke."

"Yuck, who cares about how some faggot paints pictures of his faggot boyfriend? It's disgusting. It should be burned, and the faggot should get the crap beaten out of him," Cory's jock classmate Stevens complained.

"I made a note on what little you did over the break, Mr. Stevens, and it's not worth my time to grade. Since neither you nor Mr. Riley care enough to even attempt to do the assignments, you will both leave now. You'll both receive an F for this assignment and for the semester."

"You wouldn't dare fail us. Coach Henderson will kick us off the team if we fail any of our classes."

"You should rethink your attitude before you decided to slack off and not do the assignments."

"This was supposed to be an easy A. Everyone claims as long as you put paint on the canvas, it's easy to pass painting. Fuck, Coach is going to kick your ass when he finds out some faggot art teacher failed two of his personal recruits."

The two jocks left muttering about getting even with the faggots. Professor Simms dismissed the class. Cory lingered behind to speak with his professor.

"Professor, you do realize Coach Henderson is going to kill you for flunking them."

"Don't worry about me, Mr. Cooper. Coach Henderson and I have an understanding. They'll be in more trouble with him than they are with me. I think you're ready for a showing of your work, and I'd like for you and your model to come to my home for dinner tomorrow night to discuss possible works for a show."

"I'm not sure Kieran will enjoy the idea of dinner with you, Professor. You make him uncomfortable. I had a tough time getting him to keep modeling for me."

"He doesn't trust me because of the little incident with Professor Mason. It's understandable, but he does need to move past it. He is beautiful, and I'd still love to use him as a model for a project I have in mind. Please bring him. I'd like to apologize in person and ask him if he'd reconsider modeling for me if you keep us under your watchful eye. Besides, I have a surprise I think both of you will enjoy."

"I'll ask him and let you know, Professor."

"Thank you, Mr. Cooper. I'm sure your model wants you to succeed."

Cory gathered his materials and put them away before gathering his books for his afternoon classes. Professor Simms returned to his office just off the painting studio, firing up his computer to input the failing grades for the two jocks. Once done, he focused on his plans for Cory and Kieran.

* * *

KIERAN EMERGED from the film processing room; even the dim light of the outer room was enough to hurt his eyes after the total darkness of the inner room. He glimpsed a shadow moving toward him. Before Kieran reacted, a hand groped his crotch and a mouth pressed against his for a kiss before vanishing.

"Who the hell are you?" Kieran demanded of the shadowy figure.

"Just a fan of your beauty and photography. I've wanted you since the first day of class this semester," came a voice Kieran recognized as belonging to William Harkrider, the guy whose photos Kieran had savaged in the last critique session. "I think your flavor is better in real life, a definite improvement over my fantasies."

"What the fuck, Harkrider? Get off me. I have a boyfriend and you're not him."

"Cooper is so hot and sexy in your photos. I love how you find just the right combination of light and shadow. I wish I had someone who gazed at me the same way. I need the secret of how to take pictures like you do; then Professor Mason's attention will fall on me."

"Fuck, this sure wasn't the right way to ask, Harkrider." Kieran's anger was almost physical. "What would you have done if I'd been Johnson or one of his jock buddies? They'd have beaten you to a pulp. For the record, Professor Mason appreciates your work, Harkrider. If he didn't think you had potential, you wouldn't have a key to let you in after hours. He only gives those to his best students."

"I'm sorry. I get it. I am being stupid and taking a risk even with you. Hell, you're always with the monster dog, and he's scary. I wish I had someone special like you have Cooper."

"I'll forgive and forget this time, but you need to focus on somebody else for your crush. I've got some time before I have to get to a make-up lecture with Professor Jaynes, so grab your camera. I'll show you a couple of tricks to play with lighting."

"You're such a beautiful couple. I'm sorry I lost control and helped myself; I figured I would pretend you were mine for a moment. Will you show me your lighting tricks?"

"Don't be afraid of Billy. He's just a big puppy and won't hurt you. Yeah, I'll show you some of my tricks. Just no more kissing or groping. Come on, while there's still light outside to work with."

Leading the other boy outside, Kieran showed him to a place where the sunlight was filtering through the trees, creating areas of light and shadow playing across their skin. Kieran took out a digital camera, setting William up in a spot where light and shadow played, bringing out a dark and mysterious side instead of the geeky, and he snapped a few shots. He showed the other boy the shots and explained what he scanned for when framing an image. William swapped with Kieran who posed for him in the same area of light and shadow, and helped by releasing his hair to cascade around his face and down his back.

"My major trick is to use the digital camera to check if I like the shot first; then I use a film camera to capture the final images, Will," Kieran encouraged.

"Wow, this is amazing. I know I shouldn't ask, but would you let me take a couple of you with your shirt either open or off?"

"I think we'd better stick to what's in your camera, Will."

"Okay, I just thought I'd ask. Your body is fantastic. Professor Mason will be amazed by this set. Thank you so much, Kieran."

"Any time you need help, just ask for it, Will. I'm happy helping when I'm not buried under my own pieces. Let me check your digital shots." Kieran gathered his hair back into a ponytail to get it out of his face.

William put away his film camera and brought his digital over to where Kieran was sitting, getting his hair back under control. William handed Kieran the digital camera, watching as the older boy reviewed the images. Kieran blinded poor William with a fierce smile.

"These are wonderful. Professor Mason is going to embarrass you in class if your film prints come out as amazing. He'll remark on how your emotions for your subject are obvious."

"Oh lord, now I'm embarrassed."

"Don't be, Will. If you work at it, I'm sure you'll find the person meant for you. Let me talk to Cory. I'd like you to come by our place later and hang out with us. If you bring your camera, we'll see if I can convince him to pose for you. You have a good eye. Cory and I don't have any good pictures of us together as a couple; you would be doing us a big favor."

"I'm amazed you'd let me hang out with you. Cool. Let me give you my number. Text me and let me know if Cory's okay with me hanging out and taking pictures of you guys."

"Sure thing, Will. Here's mine back at you. If you won't make it, let me know. I need to get back; my film should be ready to make prints." An alarm sounded on Kieran's phone to remind him of an appointment. "Oh hell, I need to get to going. I have to get to a make-up English literature lecture with Professor Jaynes. Will you do me a huge favor?"

"Well, after the stupid stunt I pulled on you in the lab, I owe you a lot for not beating the crap out of me and then for showing me all these great techniques," Harkrider said. "What do you need?"

"Will you check my film and find out if it's dry? If it is, will you cut it and put it in sleeves. Here are the keys to my locker. Use my supplies and put everything away for me. Thanks so much. We'll catch you later." Kieran shook Will's hand.

William Harkrider stared at the keys in his hand and was surprised how easy it was to get Kieran to trust him with access to his art locker and personal items. The Master would be pleased.

21

Kieran and Cory both arrived back at the house, which held their apartment, exhausted but excited. Cory swept Kieran into a deep kiss right in the front hall. Their roommates catcalled and shouted "Get a room," so the lovers raced up the two flights of stairs where Cory fumbled, opening the door to their apartment, and the two stumbled inside. Book bags and supply bags hit the floor as the two kicked the door shut and resumed their journey toward the bedroom. Breathless, they fell on the bed still wrapped in each other's arms.

"I missed you," they breathed almost in unison.

Cory took his usual place against the headboard with Kieran wrapped in his arms.

They just soaked in the presence of the other for a while.

"So how was your day, Wolf?"

"Well, kind of strange and hectic. Stevens and Riley were giving me grief in the studio this morning before Professor Simms stepped in and threw them both out of class with Fs for not only the assignment but for the semester."

"Coach Henderson won't like it. I'm surprised we can't hear his howling in pain across campus. The spell I burned into him should have been rendering him near incoherent with pain. Oh hell, he recruited them personally. I'm betting they did it of their own accord, which means the spell won't affect him. Their failure just means they're cut from the team. Still, I hope Professor Simms has his insurance in order."

"The strange part, babe, is Professor Simms wasn't worried about Coach's opinion on the matter. He told me they had an understanding and not to worry about him or the two idiots."

"Wow, odd. Sounds like some of the campus rumors may be true. Well, what else happened to you today?"

"Professor Simms offered me my own showing. He wants us to come to his house tomorrow for dinner to discuss it, and he wants to personally apologize to you for his scoping you out. He wants you to model for him for a personal project he's planning. I'd told him I'd ask you."

"I think he's got hidden strings attached to the offer of a show for you. Like, if I don't give in and model for him, you won't get the show."

"I don't know. We can find out if we go hear him out. If posing is a condition, we'll pass. I've got a couple of leads at galleries around the Hillcrest area which might be interesting."

"Okay, we'll hear him out."

"Thanks, babe."

"Anything for you, Wolf."

"So how was your day?"

"About as weird as yours. William Harkrider kissed me when I came out of the darkroom this afternoon."

"He what?"

"Easy does it. He admitted he's had a crush on me since the first day of classes. I've given him the riot act and sorted everything out. What he wanted was help with photography. He thought he'd found a way to ask and fulfill one of his college fantasies."

"I'll tear him apart. How dare he touch you?"

"Down, Wolf. He's more embarrassed about it than anything. I put him in his place and I gave him the help he wanted for class. I invited him to come over, hang out with us, and do us a favor of taking a photo of us together. He is pretty good with a camera."

"You are unbelievable. A guy kisses you uninvited, knowing you have a boyfriend, and you end up inviting him over to hang out. How hot and sexy is this guy?"

"Oh, my word, you're jealous. How cute. He's a total geek. He's skinny as a rail, rocking the total nerd thick glasses with no sense of fashion. Not my type at all. Here, let me grab my digital out of my camera bag. There are a couple of photos of him. I used the digital to show him how to capture the play of light and shadow I love to use when you model for me."

Kieran grabbed his camera and turned on the review screen before handing it to Cory, who flipped through the images of William Harkrider and frowned at the images.

"You call this a total geek? He's all dark and mysterious. You're telling me you don't care anything for this guy when your demo shots of him are so good?"

"Wolf, you know the only person I care anything for is you. Part of my magic seems to bring out the most potent traits in the person I'm photographing. You've seen the photos I do of my other classmates and the ones I did of the homeless couple. Tell me, do any of them compare in any way at all with the images of you? Honestly, Will has a dark and mysterious side to him, so dark and mysterious is what came out in the photos. Delete them, babe. They were to show him how to capture light and shadow. I don't need them for anything, and they bother you. I'll text Will and tell him you aren't cool with hanging out."

"No, tell him to come. I'm being as irrational about him as you are about Professor Simms. Besides, I want a photo of us together."

"Okay, I'll text him about coming over now while we still have some natural light to work with."

"Let it wait until tomorrow, babe. It's the weekend and we have all day to hang out with him tomorrow. Tonight, I want to make love with you and forget about the crazy day we've had."

"Now there's something I agree with." Kieran relaxed into Cory's embrace, letting his lover hold him.

Cory was undoing the buttons of Kieran's shirt when there was a large crash and the sounds of Billy howling from the backyard. Kieran rocketed off the bed, Silver magic flaring to life around him. He grabbed his sabers from their spot by the door. Cory moved to follow him but found his way blocked for a moment by a shield of magic. A scream rose from downstairs from either Theo or George, and Kieran dropped the shield between Cory and the rest of the house. Kieran was out the door of their apartment and racing for the stairs. Cory followed his lover. Kieran was heading down the stairs for the first floor when Cory reached the landing to the second floor. Silver magic was flowing all around Kieran, forming armor, and he wasn't stopping. Cory spotted the shattered front door as he hit the landing for the stairs to the first floor. As he reached the first floor, he spied Theo huddled on the floor near the sitting room. He caught the panic in Theo's eyes as the hair on the back of his neck crawled. Cory rolled to his right just as a huge paw whistled past where his head had been. A silver booted foot shoved him further away from the combat, and Kieran stood over him in silver armor. A huge black wolf faced them from across the room. He heard Kieran swearing about checking the phase of the moon. Cory backed away toward Theo, giving Kieran room to maneuver. He kept his eyes on the large wolf and spotted the flaming silver brand on its shoulder. Holy fuck, it had to be Coach Henderson in his Beast form; he must be powerful to be fighting with Silver magic in him.

"Get out of here, Cory. He's got a mage helping him, who's trying to keep my magic contained. Get to Billy; get Theo and George out of here as well."

The huge wolf lunged at Kieran and had to retreat as the silver sabers drove him back. Kieran advanced, trying to buy Cory time to get Theo moving and get out of the house. Strike and counter strike, Kieran kept Coach Henderson's wolf form back, scoring wounds on the huge Beast. The shifter was powerful and was shaking off most of the wounds Kieran inflicted; he also left few openings for Kieran to exploit. It was as if he anticipated Kieran's attacks. Kieran sensed only the coach and he were left in the house. Ruby magic swirled around the coach. Coach lunged for Kieran, and the young tracker dropped below the leaping shifter. He slammed both sabers up and into the wolf's chest. The Beast's momentum ripped both blades from Kieran's grip. It sailed past him, crashing into the wall. Kieran rolled to his feet and studied his foe. Damn, he'd missed Coach's heart. The shifter writhed on the floor, trying to dislodge the blades piercing its sides. Kieran gazed on in horror as Ruby magic flowed around the blades, melting them. It left puddles of silver on the floor. Ebony magic swirled around the coach, and his wounds healed. Kieran let Silver magic flow and shield the entire house. He cut off the Ruby magic. He couldn't do anything about the Ebony magic since it was part of Coach's nature as a shifter, but he must be of a powerful bloodline to heal wounds inflicted by silver weapons. Kieran's magic also transformed the gauntlets of his silver armor into weapons. From a spot in front of the elbow to a similar length beyond his hands, silver blades extended from the armor.

"Now, Coach, let's find out how tough you are without the aid of your Ruby mage."

The beast howled in rage and leapt for Kieran. The young tracker dodged and swung his left arm out and down against the shifter. Silver fire burned along the wound he inflicted on the beast. Whirling, Kieran struck, slashing with his right arm but missed as the Beast dodged. The death dance continued for several minutes until Kieran managed to spear the shifter through the ribs and score a lucky shot to the heart. The Beast crumpled to the ground and lay still. Kieran struck one last time and severed the Beast's head. He dropped the Silver magic barrier and let his armor vanish. This was a mess and because the Beast had likely woken the neighbors, the police were sure to be called. Disposal of the beast wasn't possible. Surveying the damage to the house, he heard police sirens pulling up in front of the house. He summoned his sister's sword and slid it through the beast's blood, because he needed something to explain how he'd killed the beast. Police burst through the damaged front door, and he heard them headed his way.

"Clear."

"Clear."

"Freeze. Police. Drop the weapon."

Kieran let the sword down easily and slid it out of reach.

"Keep your hands up. Don't make any false moves."

The cop approached him and then spied the beheaded wolf on the floor.

"What the hell is it?"

"It's the wild animal, which broke in and was going for one of my roommates."

"You killed it with a sword?"

"Yes, officer, I did."

Right in front of the police and Kieran, the body of the Beast burst into Ruby flames tinted with Ebony. When the flames were gone so was the body of the Beast.

"Well, it's going to make filing a report difficult at best. What the hell is going on here?"

"You don't want to know, officer. The explanation would just seem crazy. What if we just report it as a wild animal, which escaped after trying to attack a couple of college students?"

"It's about all anyone would believe at this point since we don't have a body to deal with. Are you and your roommates okay?"

"I'm fine, and I think my roommates are just a little shaken up. We'll let our landlady know about the door and then lock up as tight as possible. I think I'll get Theo and George to stay at a hotel tonight."

"Sound advice. You and anyone else living here should do the same."

"Hotels won't take a dog, and I can't leave mine behind. Not sure if the monster might come back and try for him."

"Well, be careful. If you have any further problems, here's my card. Call me."

"Thanks, Officer Roberts. We'll call if there's any more trouble."

22

Kieran and Cory bundled up Theo and George and packed them off to a hotel. Once they left, Kieran and Cory checked the house and called Mrs. Jones to let her know about the damages. Mrs. Jones told them she'd send her handyman over in the morning to assess the damages and make the repairs. They brought Billy into the house and did their best to secure the front door.

"Take Billy into the sitting room and keep him there, Wolf."

"What are you planning to do?"

"I'm going to seal the front door with magic to make sure we don't have visitors we don't want."

"Will it keep out everything?"

"Well, not everything. I can't keep out another Silver mage of equal or greater power, and it won't last long against a powerful Ebony mage. It will keep out shifters and lesser mages. Mostly, it's there so we have a chance to get someplace else."

"You've gotten comfortable about using magic around me, babe."

"Not so much comfortable as resigned to the fact both you and magic are parts of my life, which can't be kept separate anymore. Just need to keep major magic away from Billy."

"Okay, babe, we'll go get the sitting room cozy."

Kieran faced the hastily repaired door. Chanting and weaving his hands over the frame, Kieran wove a web of Silver magic to trap and bind anyone who was a threat to his loved ones within the house. The spell shimmered for a moment and vanished from sight. Kieran shuddered as adrenaline rush wore off. Death had been much too close to the ones he cared about. He returned to the sitting room where Cory was lighting a fire. Several blankets and the cushions from the couches were arranged before the fireplace to make a comfortable nest. Billy was lying there watching the doorway for Kieran. He huffed once to alert Cory to Kieran's presence. Crossing the room, Cory caught Kieran as his knees gave out and he gave into the shakes.

"Babe, it's okay. You've made sure we're all safe. Relax, let me be the one giving you shelter and peace now."

"I'm worried something else is going to come crashing into our lives before I'm ready. I'm worried I won't be able to protect you and Billy. I don't want to lose you, Cory."

"You're not going to lose either of us. You're my hero, and the hero always wins in the end."

"I need to remember to cancel your subscription to the sappy book of the month club." Kieran laughed at the pained expression of Cory's face. "I don't know how you read such sappy love stories. The heroine always seems to have mush for brains any time the hero steps into the room, even when she's the CEO of a major company."

"I don't read the ones with heroines. The one's I read have hot cowboys trying to figure out how to get it on in the barn and still be all butch afterward."

"Okay, now those sound a little more sexy. I don't want us ending up like some cliché romance characters."

"Nope, it's not how we're going to end up. We're going to be remembered for our true love and our happily ever after, the way all fairy tales end."

"Ugh, a fate worse than death. I don't care how many fairy tales you read. When you grow up in a family whose history descends from one, there's no such thing as happily ever after."

"Was Beauty's life with her prince bad, Kieran?"

"Her life was a mess, and she made her prince miserable until the day he died. A man's place in our family is spent in servitude. If you don't have a talent for tracking, you get all the menial tasks around the estate. The men of the House of Beauty are mainly there to keep the line going, prized breeding studs."

"Wow, now I know why you loved your time on the farm. I just wish we'd told you about our family secret before you learned it the hard way."

"It's okay, Wolf. I have the best parts right here with you and Billy."

Kieran drew Cory into a deep kiss. They settled into each other's warmth and the glow of the fire, drifting on the foggy edges of sleep. Billy stretched his wolf body out across the lovers' feet. Contentment filled the room, leaving only the fire crackling and the relaxed breathing of the two young men and the large wolf.

Bang, bang, bang.

All three sleepers jumped into wakefulness. Billy growled and lunged for the front door. Kieran was half a step behind the wolf. Cory, stunned, followed behind. Kieran skidded to a halt in the hallway before an older version of himself. The gasp from behind him told him Cory had caught a glimpse of the man in the hallway, while Billy stood there growling.

"Kieran Samuel Belle Oisín, is this how you greet your father?"

"Billy, down. Now, boy, he won't hurt you."

The wolf settled and sat, but he still blocked the path between father and son.

"A loyal dog you have, Son."

"Not a dog, Dad."

"A wolf. No, not just a wolf, a boy as well. Bright Mother, you have a shifter as a guard dog."

"Dad, I'd like you to meet Billy Cooper, guard dog."

"This will be a tale worth hearing. I'm guessing the young man behind you must be Corwin Cooper."

"Yes, sir. You must be Kellen Belle."

"No, I'm Kellen Oisín. I married into the House of Beauty, and Kieran uses his mother's family name."

Kieran closed the distance and hugged his father. Billy relaxed but still seemed alert. Cory stood next to Billy, watching his boyfriend with one of the only family members he spoke of with such fondness.

"I'm glad to see you, Dad, but why are you here?"

"Your grandmother sent me to bring you home. She's decided you should take the test and take your mother's place."

"Right, she's called me home to let a pack of rabid shifters tear me apart."

Cory's arms wrapped around him and drew Kieran into his strength. Billy put his head below Kieran's right hand and leaned against his leg.

"You're not in this alone," Cory said.

"Thanks, Wolf. Knowing I have you makes facing what I have to do easier. Dad, you need to know. Cory and I are two halves of the same soul. We're mates."

Kieran held up both their left hands, revealing their rings. Kellen frowned at the twin wolf heads before glancing at Billy and then at Cory. The smile, which broke across his face, reached his violet eyes, and they lit in the same way Kieran's silver eyes did when he smiled with joy.

"Your grandparents on both sides are going to have heart attacks when you bring your mate home, Son. I'm not sure if your Uncle Brom will laugh or get angry."

"Well, one of them is welcome to hers. Uncle Brom has always understood me, better than most of the family; it's one of the reasons he's my favorite uncle. I think he'll be happy for us."

Cory was gazing at both of their rings, still trying to guess what was going on. Kellen took pity on Cory's lost expression.

"Cory, my son has told you what you're getting into, I hope."

"Well, I know he's a full tracker of the House of Beauty and he's a Silver mage. I also know he found out the hard way my family is a shifter clan trying to purge the dark taint from our bloodline."

"Oh, my poor little boy, you have know idea what you're getting into. Kieran is so much more than a mere tracker and a Silver mage. He's now the direct heir to the House of Beauty from his mother's side. This summer we'll test if he's strong enough to claim his heritage from me. If he does, he'll become the legend destiny is calling him to be."

"You still believe in the old prophecy, Dad? I never wanted to be a legend. I still don't want to be one."

"What legend, babe?"

"The Silver Hunter. The son of a Huntress of the House of Beauty and the Silver Witch."

Kieran stepped free and reversed his position with Cory so he now wrapped the older man in his embrace of support.

"Let me introduce you properly to my father, Wolf. This is Kellen Kieran Oisín, the Silver Witch's heir and a descendant of Beauty's youngest brother. Their mother was from the strongest of the lines of Silver mages who cast the ancient binding spell on shifters."

Cory gasped.

"Father, I present my soul's other half and my life mate, Corwin Samuel Cooper, first of the Cooper line who seems to be cleansed of the shifter taint."

Kellen extended his hand toward Cory, who took it, and they shook hands.

"Welcome to the Oisín Clan, Corwin."

"Thank you, sir."

"I think you boys should pack. You'll come stay with me at my hotel. We'll start back to Maine after you've had a good rest."

"Dad, we can't leave yet. Cory and I still have finals to take. I want to finish what I started this year."

"Your grandmother won't like it, but do what you need to do. Let me get my things from the hotel and move in here until you're free to come home."

"Dad, as much as I love you and want to spend time with you, I need to do this on my own. I will protect Cory, Billy, and this house. We'll replace Cory's clunker of a car and then drive up to Maine when classes are done."

"Well, you definitely are your mother's son. I haven't heard her tone in ages. I'll expect you to be home a week after finals are over."

"We'll be there three weeks after finals are over. Cory and I need to settle things with his family before we come to Maine."

"Well, it sounds like you have everything planned out, Son."

"I do, Dad. I love you, but I need to do this my way."

"Then I will see you three in Maine in a month." Kellen vanished before their eyes. Kieran drew Cory into a deep kiss as Billy rubbed against both young men.

"Let's put out the fire down here and go up to our rooms. I want to make love to you in our bed, Wolf."

"Will we be safe? Your father just waltzed in here past your magic."

"I told you, it wouldn't stop a more powerful silver mage. Dad's one of the most powerful there is. We'll be fine. I'll spell the stairs and the door to our rooms. We will have plenty of warning."

INTERLUDE: PROFESSOR SIMMS'S PLAN B FOILED

Across Little Rock, Professor Simms stood within his circle of power, cursing Coach Henderson's uncontrollable need for revenge against Kieran Belle. Even with the use of the ancient artifact crafted by a powerful Ebony mage, it was next to impossible keeping Henderson one move ahead of Belle's Silver weapons. The boy was fast and skilled, and then Silver magic cut off his link to Henderson. Where did the Silver magic come from? Was the boy the source of the magic? No, Belle couldn't be a mage; he never sensed any when the boy came near. Belle being the source of the Silver magic would explain why all his plans to get rid of Professor Mason kept failing. Damn, now Henderson was dead. Explaining his disappearance was going to be difficult with the body of the shifter destroyed. The Coach proved not to be as powerful a shifter as he claimed, despite Henderson being an Alpha with his own pack and possessing more power than the local riffraff of dark shifters in the city. Belle proved to be something more powerful, and because of that, Henderson failed.

The old warehouse shook with a blast of dark power. Before a shaken Professor Simms, the image of a dark figure wrapped in the shadows materialized.

"Your shifter and his pathetic pack have failed to procure the merchandise."

"The shifter is dead and his pack is scattered, Master. The merchandise is more than he seems."

"Yes, he is. His potential borders on legendary. Exploit his weakness and bring him to me before the semester ends. If he escapes back to Maine untainted, creation will have its savior. He must be broken and tainted before he returns to face corruption's champion."

"I will do everything in my power to bring him to you, Master. However, there is a Silver mage interfering with my plans. My Ruby magic isn't a match for Silver. I may have to recruit another magician to assist in creating a trap to hold the boy."

"Do what you must. Just make sure he remains undamaged physically. I won't have his beauty marred in any way."

"Yes, Master."

The dark figure faded away. When the Master was gone, Professor Simms began plotting. With a wave of his hand, the Ruby mage set the warehouse on fire, destroying any evidence of his presence. The trap would also require more shifters as bait to lure a tracker.

23

———

Kieran sat in his English class waiting for Professor Jaynes to return their modern retelling of a fairy tale. Reshaping *Beauty and the Beast* proved to be a major pain. Transforming the story without giving away family secrets was next to impossible. After talking with Cory, Kieran settled on changing Beauty and her prince into a gay couple and making society the Beast trying to tear them apart.

"Excellent and well done, Mr. Belle. This was an interesting twist on the old tale. Making society the Beast was excellent commentary on the modern world."

"Thank you, Professor." Kieran stared at the A+ on his final paper and an A+ for the semester. He wanted to race out and show his grades to Cory. It was like he was twelve he was so excited about the grades.

"Okay, class, your semester is almost over; this paper counts twice, once as your final paper, and if you scored a B+ or higher, it counts as your final exam. You're done for the semester with this class. Enjoy your summer break. For everyone else, I'll see you next week for the final exam."

* * *

CORY STOOD in front of his final paintings of the semester, including the one of the werewolf hunter. He and Kieran agreed to make some changes to the hunter in the painting starting with the model. The subject of the painting was a redhead, wearing jeans and a T-shirt, and wielding silver Glock pistols. His other paintings with Kieran as his model remained unchanged since they revealed nothing of his secret background. They revealed a whole lot of Kieran's body, and Cory witnessed the effect it was having on the students he knew were gay as well as the glares of envy from several of his female classmates. It wasn't like Cory had painted over the original painting he done of Kieran fighting the werewolf; it was safely hidden in their apartment. He'd spent the last week with a different model posing for the one in his final portfolio. His heart hadn't been into painting this one and it showed. The painting was cold and lifeless.

"Mr. Cooper, your fantasy combat scene isn't the piece I remember you working on earlier. Why the change?"

"The original was damaged beyond salvage when the house I'm living in was broken into a couple of weeks ago, sir. Kieran's been to busy to model for a reproduction, so I had to hire a different model."

"A shame. I would bet Mr. Belle made a stunning hunter."

"It was a better piece, Professor."

"Well, perhaps you'll get a chance to recreate it next semester."

"Perhaps."

EPILOGUE

Wrapping up their school year, the young lovers met with Mrs. Jones and paid rent to hold their apartment for them through the summer months and into the first months of school. The guys helped Marissa Holden move into Kieran's old rooms on the second floor. Earlier in the year, Marissa had mentioned needing a place for the summer and next semester to Kieran when she'd cornered him with her Alpha. Kieran and Cory finished packing their clothes and personal items and got them loaded into the van they'd purchased in part with a trade-in of Cory's dying car and with the rest of the money coming from Kieran's savings account. He'd put back money from his tracking jobs in case of emergency. Once they were all packed, they loaded Billy the wolf into the van and headed out for the Cooper farm to settle matter with Cory's family. When Kieran and Cory pulled into the Cooper farm, Jonathan and Tamara, who gathered them into a family hug, met them. When the hug broke, the questions began.

"Are you boys all right?" Tamara asked.

"Mom, we're fine. The bond between us is restored and strong. See? Here's the proof we're meant to be together." Cory raised his and Kieran's left hands to show off the double wolf-headed rings.

"We were worried your bond was broken beyond repair," Jonathan added.

"It was never broken, Jonathan. It was only hidden away from those who would have used it against us. Now it's complete and unbreakable as long as we're faithful to each other. Cory wants us to get Jeff's blessing for our mating. It's why we've detoured south before we head north to spend the summer in Maine."

"You're going to test to become a hunter, aren't you, Kieran?"

"Not just any hunter, Jonathan. The test I take will make me the head of the House of Beauty. Before I take the hunter test, I have another test to take. I need access to the full powers of my inheritance from my father's family to be able to do what needs to be done as the head of the House of Beauty. I have to become the Silver Witch first."

"Let's get you boys settled in before supper. Jeff will want to talk with both of you before the rest of the pack gets here to witness the ceremony."

"Thanks, Dad."

"Hey, Wolf, can you manage our bags? I think Billy needs to go for a run before we all settle in."

"I can manage, babe. Go have a good run. I'll see you inside."

* * *

KIERAN CAME downstairs from the room set aside for him and Cory, dressed in his full tracker leathers; silver chains were braided into his hair, and the mate to Cory's double wolf-headed ring was on his left hand. From his boot tops protruded the hilts of his silver daggers. He came to stand beside Cory in front of the fireplace in the family room where the pack the Cooper family belonged to awaited. Several of the pack members drew back as the presence of so much silver made itself felt. Jeff Cooper, pack Alpha and Cory's older brother, sat in his chair like it was a throne. He glared at Kieran, and a soft growl escaped his throat.

"Oh, knock it off. You all know who I am and what I am," Kieran sneered back at the growling pack members.

"Corwin, are you still insisting he's your perfect mate?" Jeff snarled.

"Yes, Jeff. Kieran is my soul's mate and I'm his."

"What benefit does the pack get from this mating between a shifter and a tracker?"

"I'm now a hunter-candidate, Jeff. The first benefit is you all get to live free and protected from other hunters. The House of Beauty places you under our protection."

"We're not pets. You won't put us on a leash like you do with my nephew Billy."

"Relax, I have no intention of turning you into house pets. The House of Beauty needs a new pack to test future hunter-candidates, and I choose your pack for the honor."

"What happened to the old pack?"

"It's about the be put down to the last pup in a few months when I take the test."

"What happens if we refuse this honor?"

"Cory, Billy, and I leave, and you'll never see us again. While we live, your pack will be safe from the House of Beauty, but the protection ends when I die."

"Not much of an option package, so I'll bless your mating on behalf of the pack."

"Good. Cory, Billy, and I will be leaving in the morning. It's a long drive to Maine."

VOLUME TWO

Kethric Wilcox

Witch

Legend of the Silver Hunter
Book Two

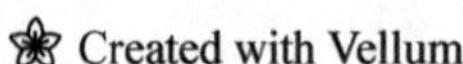 Created with Vellum

PROLOGUE

Kieran strode into the council chamber with such force the doors slammed into the walls. The Matriarchs rose at the interruption of their meeting. All except Kieran's grandmother who remained seated in her throne-like chair. When he reached the end of the conference table, Kieran smacked his hand down on top of it, and the room echoed with the sound.

"We did not summon you, boy. A tracker does not bring business before this council."

"Shut up, Aunt Fiona. I'm not here as a tracker of the House of Beauty. I'm here as the hunter-candidate. Time is up, Grandmother. You are all out of granddaughters to send to their deaths. The pact is broken, and the mongrels of the forest murdered my sisters."

"Sit down, now! My grandson makes a valid point. We lived to witness a cursed generation when we must allow a male to test as a hunter. We must also resign ourselves to this fate. Kieran is the last of the House of Beauty. With his death, our line ends."

"I'm not dying any time soon, old woman. I've got too much to live for. Oh, I'm so much more than my sisters."

"A disappointment is what you are, boy."

"Only to a closed-minded old woman, who couldn't do what was needed to be done before she let an entire generation of huntresses be slaughtered. Serena and Rosie both died as full huntresses. My other sisters were never given the chance to properly test. The Alpha who rules this pack now is a direct descendant of the Beast himself. I'm the only one who stands a chance to defeat him."

"Male arrogance. Your chances of defeating a monster of such an ancient a lineage are less than even your sisters."

BEAUTY'S TALE

All at once, the merchant lost his whole fortune, excepting a small country house at a great distance from town, and told his children with tears in his eyes, they must go to there and work for their living...Poor Beauty at first was sadly grieved at the loss of her fortune; "but," said to herself, "were I to cry ever so much, that would not make things better, I must try to make myself happy without a fortune." When they came to their country house, the merchant and his three sons applied themselves to husbandry and tillage; and Beauty rose at four in the morning, and made haste to have the house clean, and dinner ready for the family. In the beginning she found it very difficult, for she had not been used to work as a servant, but in less than two months, she grew stronger and healthier than ever. After she had done her work, she read, played on the harpsichord, or else sung whilst she spun. On the contrary, her two sisters did not know how to spend their time; they got up at ten, and did nothing but saunter about the whole day, lamenting the loss of their fine clothes and acquaintance. "Do but see our youngest sister," said they, one to the other, "what a poor, stupid, mean-spirited creature she is, to be contented with such an unhappy dismal situation."

"Beauty and the Beast" by Jeanne-Marie Le Prince de Beaumont, 1757 English translation."

Those of you who follow me as chronicler of the House of Beauty must continue the tradition of keeping the truth in these records secret from all but the huntress of the house. In some cases, keeping secrets will be best if even the huntress remains unaware of some events. Mother became a bitter woman when she founded our house. I am aware how the stories portray her as bright and cheerful. After all, I helped craft some of those stories. She resented her life and her sisters most of all. She never expected to marry into royalty. At best, she figured on marrying a farmer. Shortly after, mother convinced father marriage to her would be in his best interests and lost touch with her youngest brother. No trace of my youngest uncle can be found, although rumors are often carried to us of his marriage to the daughter of a count in a distant land.

The first entry from the first chronicles of the House of Beauty, translated in the nineteenth century from the original French.

1

———————

The brown minivan pulled into a gas station in Bangor, Maine after a week and a half on the road from Little Rock, Arkansas. The trip shouldn't take so long, but the young lovers driving the van stopped often to explore the sights and to work a couple of tracking jobs. After rolling the van to a stop at the pumps, the driver put the van in park and shut off the engine. After opening his door, Kieran, a tall man in his early twenties, dressed in blue jeans, a black t-shirt, and sneakers, emerged; his long black hair flowed down his back to below his firm ass. Out of the passenger side stepped Cory, a man in his mid-twenties, his blond hair and beard trimmed short, also dressed in jeans, a t-shirt, and sneakers. The blond opened the rear passenger door and a huge black wolf leapt from the car, a silver collar with a wolf's head clasp hung around its neck. The boyfriends glanced at each other across the roof of the station wagon, and with a knowing nod, Kieran turned to the pump, putting gas in the car. Cory signaled the wolf and crossed the parking lot to an open grassy area where the wolf relieved himself. Once the wolf finished, they returned to the car, and the blond put him back in the car before heading to the gas station's store for supplies and the restroom.

Cory returned and put the supplies into the car as Kieran finished pumping gas. His dark-haired companion crossed the lot to the store for his own turn in the restroom; when he returned, they continued on their way.

As they left the gas station, Kieran glanced at his boyfriend and could tell what he was thinking.

"We still need to drive for about another hour, Wolf," Kieran said, calling his boyfriend by the nickname he'd given him over Christmas break. "Granddad's family built the place on a secluded section of the coast so no one would bother them."

Cory reached into the backseat and stroked the wolf's head between the ears. Only a few months back the black wolf had been his barely thirteen-year-old nephew Billy Cooper. After Billy's very first shift, the boy had opted to stay in wolf form in order to remain with his Uncle Cory and with Kieran. The silver collar with its wolf head design contained a powerful binding spell, which kept Billy in animal form.

"I hope we'll get time to relax and check out the ocean while we're here. Billy and I would love to visit the ocean."

Cory's voice held a bit of a nervous tremor, causing Kieran doubt over the idea of introducing his boyfriend to his father's family. Perhaps introducing his shifter-related boyfriend to his magic-wielding grandparents and uncle didn't rank as a brilliant idea.

"I'm sure we'll find time to play in the ocean. Granddad's estate owns about two miles of private beach. We can camp out on the beach one night and make love under the stars."

Unless, of course, Kieran thought, *Dad's chasing me around the estate, and I'm dodging the spells he's hurling in my general direction. I can imagine all the fun of trying to make out with my boyfriend while ducking fireballs and other dangerous spells.*

"Camping on the beach sounds like fun. Did you ever go before?"

"Not since I was a kid. Dad and Uncle Brom took about a dozen guys from school and me out camping on the beach one weekend. The trip didn't go well. Turned out a couple of the guys were allergic to shellfish."

Kieran's thoughts refocused on his paternal heritage from his father and grandfather; he was a descendant of the Silver Witch, a figure so wrapped in secrecy not even fairy tales made any mention of the most powerful line of mages the world had ever known. Part of the reason for traveling to Maine was the coming magical challenges. *I wonder when Dad will start the test. With my luck, Dad started the test when we called to tell him we left Arkansas. I hope I can keep Cory and Billy safe until I can go on the offensive.*

2

———————

The minivan stopped before an impressive iron gate, the only passage through the looming stone wall, which divided the estate from the rest of the world. Cory winced and Billy the black wolf howled in pain as they crossed through the barrier of Silver magic. Kieran reached out and caught his lover's hand.

"I'm sorry, Cory, the pain will only last a moment longer."

The dark-haired young man quickly keyed in a sequence on the security system. The gates parted, and when they opened wide enough for the van to fit, he drove through. Cory rubbed as his head throbbed with a headache, and Billy the wolf continued to howl his pain as they passed through the barrier. Kieran pulled the van over and pulled his lover to him to help ease the pain. He also reached back to caress the wolf between his ears.

"I'm sorry. I didn't think to shield the van before we got here."

"I think we'll survive. But this is our first time being exposed to so much Silver magic."

"The barrier is designed to keep out shifters and warn of enemy mages. Every generation adds to the power. I didn't get to add to the magic of the barrier yet, which is why you both experienced so much pain."

"Well, we're through, and I'm sure your family will be ready with the pitchforks and flaming torches when we get to the house."

Kieran laughed and put the van back in gear, heading for his grandparents' house. After nearly twenty minutes of driving, Cory wondered if the family put the house on the ground or if Kieran's family lived in trees. Kieran brought the van around yet another bend, and a huge clearing opened up before them. A huge log and glass structure worthy of any high-end resort sprawled across the clearing and back into the woods.

"This is your grandparents' house?" The question escaped Cory's mouth before he stopped himself.

Kieran laughed at his lover's expression. "What? You expected a castle where Sleeping Beauty would be right at home?"

"To tell you the truth, I couldn't imagine what to expect. Don't ask why but the only picture in my mind is of your grandparents living in a dark forbidding castle with a moat and a dragon guarding the gates. So I guess you're more the woodsman than Prince Charming."

Cory couldn't help laugh at Kieran's expression as the Prince Charming line sank home.

"Your sense of humor is tragic, Wolf. As a shifter, you should be careful about any references to stories with a big bad wolf in them. Remember, what's a fairy tale for you is family history for me."

Cory cut off in mid-laugh as Kieran's comment registered. Try as he might, Cory still didn't think of *Beauty and the Beast* as based in historical fact. How do you deal with a fairy tale made flesh and blood?

Kieran pulled the van up to the front of the giant cabin. Kieran's father and another slightly older and bearded man of similar appearance met the young men. Kieran seemed to teleport from his side of the van to wrap the second man in a fierce hug. The man hugged back as Kieran's father shook hands with Cory and patted the wolf on the head.

"Welcome to my family's home, Cory."

"Thank you, Kellen. The place is impressive."

Kellen's laugh rang silver off the walls of the cabin. Kieran and the older man he hugged glanced over at Kellen and Cory, and Kieran's laugh joined his father's as he recognized the expression on Cory's face. Releasing the older man, Kieran crossed to his lover and drew him into a fierce kiss.

"Forgive, Cory, Dad. He thought Gramps and Grams lived in a dark and forbidding castle. He's got his fairy tales mixed up."

"Well, with a little warning beforehand, we could have whipped up a good glamour of ancient and dusty ruins for him. A moldy old castle appears kind of silly in the middle of the Maine woods, but anything to excite the tourists," said the older man Kieran hugged on arrival.

"So, introductions. Cory, you already met my father, Kellen. This rogue here is his older brother and my favorite uncle, Brom. Uncle Brom, this is my boyfriend, Corwin Cooper. Cory for short."

"A pleasure to finally meet you, sir."

"You can call me Brom, or even Uncle Brom, Cory."

The two shook hands, and Brom stopped and raised Cory's hand so he might study the ring on the young man's finger. He grabbed Kieran's hand and brought the matching rings up to examine closely. The rings on the boys' fingers flashed as the sunlight caught the amber and diamond eyes of the nearly twin double wolf heads on both rings. He was surprised to see what the spells he'd forged into the plain silver bands had transformed them into. Kieran had designed special spells for what he called his true love rings. While he'd crafted the rings and cast the spells into them, Brom didn't even begin to think he understood the magic his nephew had designed. Brom glanced at his younger brother before turning his focus back at the young men before him. Before he spoke, the huge black wolf, which arrived with the young lovers, nudged his head, searching for attention.

Uncle Brom started looking over the young man his nephew had brought home with a more discerning eye before voicing his concerns. "Okay. I'm confused. Since when does a tracker of the shifter hunting House of Beauty take a shifter for a boyfriend and another as a pet? Talk about being in the wrong fairy tale."

Kieran laughed at his uncle's confusion. He drew Cory into a hug before speaking again. "We moved out of fairy tales and into

Shakespeare, Uncle Brom. Some days, our relationship is more of a *Romeo and Juliet* than *Beauty and the Beast*."

"Nephew, your romance sounds more like *Romeo and Juliet* meets *Beauty and the Beast*. I hope this isn't going to end like either of those tales."

"No, sir. Kieran and I are going to get the happily ever after," Cory answered for the young men.

"Well," Brom said to Kieran's father. "Why don't you get your son and his boyfriend settled in? I need to get back to my work at the forge." Brom turned his attention back to his nephew. "I want your input when you get a chance, Kieran."

"Of course, Uncle Brom. You know I can't resist."

Brom hugged his nephew and shook hands with Cory before striding off toward the woods. Kieran turned from watching his uncle walk off and faced his father.

"I guess Cory and I are in the guest cabin."

"Yes, your grandmother thought you boys would like the privacy. Your grandfather would toss you into your old room here in the main house, despite the fact you last used the room when you were fifteen."

"Yeah, the intensity of my training to become a tracker put an end to visits here. I bet nothing in my room changed since the last time I was here, Dad."

"Your grandparents left both our rooms alone, Son. Why don't you two—" A head butt from the wolf reminded Kellen of the third member of the boys' party. "Sorry, why don't you three go get settled into the guest cabin? Dinner will be at seven. Don't be late."

"Yes, sir."

Kieran bundled Cory and Billy the wolf back into the van and set off for the guest cabin hidden behind the main house.

BEAUTY'S TALE

The good merchant was of quite a different opinion; he knew very well that Beauty outshone her sisters, in her person as well as her mind, and admired her humility and industry, but above all her humility and patience; for her sisters not only left her all the work of the house to do, but insulted her every moment. The family had lived about a year in this retirement, when the merchant received a letter with an account of that a vessel, on board which he had effects, was safely arrived. This news had liked to have turned the heads of the two eldest daughters, who immediately flattered themselves with the hopes of returning to town, for they were quite weary of a country life; and when they saw their father ready to set out, they begged of him to buy them new gowns, headdresses, ribbons, and all manner of trifles; but Beauty asked for nothing for she thought to herself, that all the money her father was going to receive, would scarce be sufficient to purchase everything her sisters wanted.

"What would you have, Beauty?" said her father.

"Since you have the goodness to think of me," answered she, "be so kind to bring me a rose, for as none grows hereabouts, they are a kind of rarity." Not that Beauty cared for a rose, but

she asked for something, lest she should seem by her example to condemn her sisters' conduct, who would have said she did it only to look particular.

*   Beauty and the Beast by Jeanne-Marie LePrince de Beaumont, 1757 English translation*

The founding Huntress left to her eldest daughter the position of Huntress. Across the ages, the line remained strong until the time of the tenth Huntress. Celestine de la Belle was a woman blessed with many daughters and cursed with a few sons. Her daughters competed to decide who would succeed their mother as Huntress and leader of the House of Beauty. To prevent her children from spilling each other's blood, Celestine created the pact and the test. Celestine found a wolf-shifter clan and bound its Alpha and his line to her service with her gift of Silver magic. The clan would be free to hunt on her lands so long as each generation provided warriors for a test she devised for her heirs. When a daughter of the house reached the age of eighteen, she would be sent out to a special clearing on the first full moon after her birthday to face five shifters in combat. If she killed all five without using her magic, she would become the Huntress of the next generation. Celestine also decided her sons would serve a purpose as well and trained them to track shifters. She also established the test of the tracker, where each male of the line would track down and kill a shifter of the pack to prove his worth.

An entry from the Fifth Chronicle of the House of Beauty, translated from the original German in the twentieth century.

3

———

Cory stood in awe in front of the guest cabin. The cabin appeared to be about the size of his parents' barn back home. He gazed at his reflection in the wall of glass, which made up the front of the cabin. He also watched his lover as Kieran unloaded their bags from the back of the minivan. Hopping from the back seat of the van, Billy the black wolf padded over to sit beside Cory and pressed his huge head against Cory's leg.

"This place is pretty big, don't you think, Billy?" Cory stroked between the wolf's ears.

Billy huffed his agreement. Kieran placed the bags at the foot of the stairs leading up to the front door of the cabin. Looking at his lover, he only chuckled in amusement at the awe on Cory's beautiful face.

"You realize you gave me the impression of a struggling student trying to make ends meet back in Arkansas, Kieran? Now you show me you come from a family with more wealth than most of the state."

"Oh, I don't think Gramps is richer than everyone in Arkansas; after all, the Walton family lives in Bentonville. None of the money from either family is mine to do anything with—at least, not at the moment. So I needed to earn my own money for school."

"This is still overwhelming, Kieran."

"I realize this is all a bit much, but at least Gramps and the rest of Dad's family don't flaunt their wealth. I think they're embarrassed by how wealthy they are. Each generation goes out and makes their own fortune before they get to enjoy what they will inherit."

"Why bother if they're so rich? Why go out and add more to the pile?"

"Both sides of my family are descended from a merchant family, Cory. The concept of proving you can make your own way in the world is drummed into the genetics of Dad's family for centuries."

"Well, rich or poor, I still love you, Kieran Belle."

"Good, because I love you too, Corwin Cooper," said Kieran in one of his rare usages of Cory's full name. "Come on and help me get our stuff inside. Grams will take our heads if we're late for dinner the first night we're here." Kieran decided not to mention to his lover about his concerns regarding his father and uncle. Something about their demeanor when he'd arrived with Cory seemed off. He wondered if Gramps was pushing the prophecy again.

INTERLUDE: FAMILY PLOTS

Brom arrived at the main house an hour before dinner was scheduled to start at the request of his father and brother. He entered to find the house filled with the aroma of his mother's cooking. From the smells, she'd gone all out for the return of her favorite grandchild. Brom found his father and brother in the living room discussing the ancient prophecy of the Silver Hunter. How he hated this topic. His hatred of the topic grew when he discovered the generations of magical breeding, which had already gone into the project. Now it looked as if prophecy was coming to pass in the person of his nephew, Kieran.

"Brom, there you are," his father said, looking up from a copy of the prophecy. "We were just discussing the development of Kieran's choice of boyfriends on the path of his journey toward becoming the Silver Hunter."

"Cory's inability to shift troubles us," Kellen said, directing his brother's attention to the page containing the prophecy. "He's supposed to have a shifter at his right and left side."

"Then maybe Kieran isn't the one destined to be the Silver Hunter, after all. Have you given him any time to grieve his sisters? The only reason Kieran's even in a position to become the Hunter of the House of Beauty is because they were all sacrificed to this prophecy. Hell,

Kellen, have you even taken time to mourn your daughters or have you shut off your emotions?"

"How I grieve my daughters is none of your business, Brom. Kieran has to be my focus. If he doesn't survive this, then everything for generations will have been for nothing. He's the last of the prime bloodline of the House of Beauty. None of the collateral branches will ever produce a candidate for the prophecy any time in the next twenty generations. A couple of Kieran's cousins are pregnant and might carry the Belle potential."

"You are so fucking cold, Kellen. You've lost five daughters and you haven't shed a tear for any of them because, like Dad, all you really care about is this cursed prophecy. This piece of insane ranting has driven this family for more generations than we can count. Take some time and become human again, little brother. Your son needs his father, not another slave driver. Dad has done enough of that over the years, never mind what the House of Beauty has done to him."

"Stay out of how I deal with my son."

"Why? So you can drive him insane with the damned prophecy? Let him live his life how he chooses and with the person he chooses."

"So I should stand back and let him take his beloved uncle's path and end up with his magic ruined because he didn't use a condom when getting fucked by a shifter with high traces of Ebony magic? No, Brother, I'm not letting Kieran fuck up his life like you did."

The argument was devolving into name-calling and cross accusations between the brothers when their father called it to an abrupt halt; he had spotted Kieran and a young blond man enter the room.

4

Kieran and Cory arrived at the main house for dinner to find Kieran's father and uncle arguing in the living room. The energy in the room screamed of a long-running argument between the men. He noted that from the sound of things, they'd moved beyond whatever topic had started the argument into more personal and long-simmering disagreements. In a chair on the far side of the room sat an older version of both men, puffing on a pipe. He listened to both men argue without intervening until he spotted Kieran and Cory in the doorway. Kieran glanced at his grandfather and thought it odd that the man seemed to be enjoying the division between his sons. It was almost like watching Grandmother Belle holding court back at the House of Beauty. Kieran's blood ran cold at the thought of adding Cory to this mixture.

"Enough out of the both of you. My grandson and his boyfriend are here at my invitation. Behave yourselves or I'll send you both to your rooms without dinner."

"DAD!" two shocked voices rang out.

"If you're going to behave like you're both children, I'll treat you like you're children."

"I would give up now, Dad. Gramps always wins in the end," Kieran interjected, trying to draw attention away from Uncle Brom.

"This is between your uncle and I, Kieran, so mind your manners and introduce your boyfriend to your grandfather."

Kieran grabbed Cory's hand and dragged him across the room to stand before his grandfather. Cory glanced back over his shoulder at Kellen before he returned his gaze back to Kieran and his grandfather. Cory beheld the progression of how his lover would age over the years. Cory seemed impressed at how well the men of Kieran's family aged.

"Grandfather, this is Corwin Cooper, my boyfriend and partner. He's a member of a clan of shifters trying to breed the curse out of their lines, like the rumors we keep hearing. Cory, this is my grandfather, Aodhfin Oisín."

"Meeting you is a pleasure, sir."

"So you're the little shifter who snagged my grandson's heart. Well, you're easy on the eyes. From the reading I get of your aura, you can't shift."

"Thank you, sir. No, I've never shifted in my life. My parents think I may be the first to break the family curse. Of course, they were a little disappointed when I came out as gay. I'm sure the pack and clan hoped I would help breed the next generation."

"Yes, I'm sure the news hit them hard. Kieran's coming out gave us a bit of a blow as well, but we love him beyond measure. As long as you're good to my grandson, you're welcome in my home."

"I promise to always be good to him, sir."

A rich female voice called from the next room. "If you boys are done yelling and inspecting the merchandise, dinner is served. Come eat before all my hard work gets cold."

Kieran led Cory into the family dinning room where a table groaned under the weight of the food placed upon the surface. They found each place setting marked with name cards, and the boys found themselves seated next to each other opposite Kellen and Brom with Kieran's grandparents seated at the head and foot of the table. Kieran caught the beautiful silver-haired lady by the apron strings and wrapped her in a bear hug before she escaped into the kitchen.

"Kieran Samuel Belle Oisín let me go this instant. I still need to put food on the table."

"Honestly, Grams, if you put any more food on the table, the thing will collapse under the weight. I want you to meet someone special to me first."

Kieran turned them around to face Cory, who couldn't hide the grin on his face at the interplay between Kieran and his grandmother. He introduced Cory to his grandmother, Líadáin. After the formalities of introductions wrapped up, the family sat down to dinner. The tension between his father and uncle resonated in the room, leaving Kieran to wonder what might be causing problems between them. He decided on cornering his uncle after dinner to discover the problem. Decision made, Kieran turned his attention to his grandmother, and the two traded stories about the things going on in their lives.

Across the table from the boys, Kellen and Brom focused on their plates and on ignoring each other. They both resolved not to argue over dinner and ruin their mother's reunion with her favorite grandson. Líadáin came to Kieran's side when he came out as gay and there'd been no coming between them since. The kitchen became the first place to search when Kieran went missing from magic lessons with his grandfather. The boy's cooking nearly matched his grandmother's. Around the table, various dishes of familiar foods passed back and forth. Brom added helpings of his favorites to his plate while his thoughts turned darker and darker.

He opposed the plan to direct Kieran along the path to fulfill the ancient prophecy. The boy didn't choose to take the first steps along the path of prophecy when he took the test of the Tracker. Being born male in the House of Beauty dictated he serve as a tracker or servant. His gift from the Oisín side of his heritage made being a tracker inevitable. Step one down the path to prophecy. After running away to college, he returned home with a shifter for a lover and another for a guard dog. Step two and possibly three down the path. These supposed signs convinced his father and brother the events foretold in the prophecy might be coming to pass. They needed to make Kieran ready to face the predicted darkness. By opposing his family's plan, Brom hoped to give the boys a chance at a normal life. He must talk to the boys later and try to steer them off the path of prophecy. He focused back on the conversation going on between his father and Cory.

"My family would never attack you. We're trying to break the curse on our bloodline. Breaking the curse is one of the reasons Billy accepted the collar to stay in wolf form," Cory said.

Gramps' face flashed pale in shock before the crimson flush of anger began to spread across his face and his gray eyes began to flash silver at Cory's admission of the wolf in their party being another shifter. Kellen reached out to calm his father, even as he offered an explanation.

"The collar is Brom's work and Kieran's spell, Father. From what they told me of the boy, he loves his Uncle Cory and Uncle Kieran so much, he defied his grandparents and pack leader's order to choose human form and instead chose to become a wolf so he might stay with the boys."

The expression on Aodhfin's face warned Kieran and Kellen that further discussion would come and soon. Kieran took Cory's hand and held on tight. His grandmother dismissed them from the table, and Kieran dragged Cory out of the house.

"I think you made a mistake bringing us here, Kieran. Billy and I aren't going to fit into your family. We don't belong here."

"Of course you belong here. My grandmother is smitten; she loves you. You realize Dad approves of you, and I think you'll find Uncle Brom is on our side."

"I don't think your grandfather was thrilled when he learned Billy is a shifter locked in wolf form."

"Wolf, listen to me, you and Billy are my chosen family. Gramps will come around. I won't let anybody drive you and Billy away from me. Let's go back to the cabin and we'll curl up in front of the fireplace and cuddle."

"I guess I'm more tired than I thought. Let's shower and go to bed. Today proved to be a long day."

Taking Cory's hand, Kieran led them back to the guest cabin. Drawing his partner inside, Kieran took them to the huge downstairs bathroom, which contained a giant Jacuzzi tub. With practiced fingers, the dark-haired tracker made quick work of stripping down his blond lover. Kieran's fingers danced through the forest of dark blond chest hair traveling downward along Cory's treasure trail to the dense bush above his thick manhood. Lips and tongue soon followed fingers until Kieran knelt before his lover, tongue-flicking teasing licks across the tip of his lover's cock, bringing the beast to life. Before pleasure overwhelmed him, Cory pulled Kieran back to his feet and stripped him down so his smooth, lean body became exposed. By mutual agreement, they came together in a fierce kiss, which threatened to spark a fire. Lips moved along jawlines, seeking the pulse points along exposed necks, where tongues licked in sync to the heartbeats below. Hands explored as if for the first time they had touched each other's naked flesh. Cory made his way down his lover's smooth body to the right nipple, which he bathed with his tongue until the nipple became a firm peak capping the powerful pectoral muscle, before swiping across to render the same treatment to the left.

Kieran pulled Cory back up into a fiery lip lock as his hands roamed over his lover's firm back, moving down to his tight furry ass. Cory's hands found their way to cup and knead Kieran's smooth ass cheeks and to trace a finger down the valley between the cheeks. With a moan of pleasure, Kieran tried to focus enough to use his magic to start the tub filling as Cory's lips again moved over his throat and across his left shoulder. He experienced Cory's teeth brush against his collarbone. Would Cory try and bite him like wolves did when they mated? His lover's mouth moved back up along his neck and reclaimed his lips as his hands lifted Kieran by the ass and wrapped his lover's legs around his waist as he stepped over the edge of the tub and settled them both into the warm water.

Kieran reached back until his fingers found the controls to the jets and started the water bubbling around them. The change of position brought Cory's erection into contact with the valley of Kieran's ass, and the head slipped in to rub against Kieran's hole. Pleasure surged through both lovers as they embraced in the swirling waters. Kieran's fingers slid along Cory's neck, digging deep as they buried themselves in the thick blond hair. Cory's fingers played along Kieran's ass, teasing his rosebud along with the tip of his own cock before sliding up Kieran's back to tangle in the thick clump of Kieran's braided hair. The braid came loose under Cory's manipulation, spreading a dark curtain around the pair as they lost themselves in another soul-deep kiss. The jets of the tub shut down, and Kieran broke the kiss, rising and drawing his lover with him out of the tub. He grabbed a thick fluffy towel and began to dry Cory off.

When both of them dried off, Kieran led Cory naked through the cabin and upstairs to the loft, which held a huge king-sized bed. On the nightstand beside the bed gleaming in the moonlight coming in from the skylight was a bottle of lube and several condom packages. While the boys practiced monogamy, they agreed to practice safe sex until they understood what each other's magic-tainted blood would do to the other. Kieran drew Cory down on top of him, and the two resumed their interrupted lovemaking. To the world outside their bedroom, their relationship would seem as if Kieran was the dominate in the relationship, but in the bedroom, Kieran let go of all his take-charge persona and let Cory be in control. They didn't define their roles in lovemaking; Kieran didn't always bottom and Cory didn't always top. Often, Cory led Kieran into topping him so they remained equals in their relationship. Tonight, Cory kept full control, and after prepping Kieran, he took him for the ride of his life. When they were spent, Cory cleaned them up, snuggled up behind Kieran, and wrapped him in his arms as they drifted off into sleep.

5

For the first couple of days during their visit to the Oisín compound, Kieran and Cory relaxed and explored the forests around their cabin, dined with the family in the evenings, and returned to their cabin to make love. During the family dinners, Uncle Brom would drop hints as to the project he was working on, hoping to entice Kieran to come out to the forge and work with him again. Gramps still brooded over Cory's welcome to the compound and remained distant from the boys.

On their second Saturday at his grandfather's estate, Kieran couldn't contain his curiosity any longer and dragged Cory along with him to Uncle Brom's cabin and forge located on the opposite side of the compound from the boys' cabin. Drawing closer to the clearing, they detected the sounds of tools hammering on metal and inhaled the scent of burning coals. Brom stood over an anvil, hammering out a length of iron into the rough shape of a highland dirk.

"UNCLE BROM!" Kieran screamed so his uncle would be aware of him over the din of his work.

Brom turned and smiled at his nephew and his boyfriend. Cory contemplated the scene before him as Brom grabbed a towel to wipe away the sweat from his naked torso and his face. As he moved, his muscles rippled under his skin. Where Kieran was smooth, Brom had a thick mat of dark hair across his pectorals, thinning to a trail down the center of his abs to the top of his jeans. The family resemblance between Kieran and his uncle seemed to be the face and the silver eyes. Cory shook himself when he realized he was staring at his boyfriend's uncle like a prospective date or trick. He blushed when he caught Kieran watching his reaction to Brom. Kieran merely smiled at him, which never failed to melt his heart.

Kieran leaned into Cory's side and whispered into his ear, "He affected me the same way once, Wolf. One of the reasons why I love all your fur."

Cory blushed harder and Kieran laughed.

"So what is this mystery project you wanted my ideas on, Uncle Brom?" Kieran asked to direct his uncle's attention away from Cory.

"Well, the principle is based on the collar we designed for Billy. I'm trying to figure a way to change the spells enough to allow such a design to be used against hostile shifters. Adaptive spell-shaping isn't my strong suit," Brom confessed.

"I don't suppose another collar like the one we made for Billy or my notes are laying around any place handy?" Kieran asked, looking around.

"Check the middle drawer of the drafting table. I think I put your notes in the drawer after I forged the collar and the spells."

Cory, standing closer to the drafting table, pulled open the drawer only to leap back, shaking his fingers from the sting of Silver magic. Kieran moved quickly to his side, drawing the Silver magic out of his lover's hand.

"Sorry, Cory. I forgot to warn you about the ward," Kieran said before kissing each fingertip.

"I should realize something important like designs would be warded with magic."

"Yeah, Wolf. This might not be a comfortable place for you between the heat and the magic."

"I can tolerate the heat and I need to build up a tolerance for your magic. We won't always have time for me to get to some distant place so I can avoid your magic."

"All right, but if the magic gets to be too much, head back to our cabin and I'll find you in the bedroom when I'm done here." Kieran drew Cory in for a deep kiss and unbuttoned his lover's shirt to expose his furry, sweat-slicked chest. "You're going to melt if you keep this shirt all buttoned up." Kieran's actions reminded his lover of the heat pouring off the forge.

Cory flushed from both the heat and desire for a moment before yanking Kieran's t-shirt over his head, leaving his lover bare to the waist. To add a bit of a tease, Cory used Kieran's shirt to wipe the sweat from his own chest before tucking the tee into his back pocket. Kieran's face took on an indignant expression for a moment before laughing and returning with the notes to work with his uncle. Cory regarded the two shirtless men as they put their heads together to study the notes regarding the collar and how to change the magic from voluntary to involuntary. The magical technical talk and the heat finally began to bore Cory, so he wandered off and found a quiet spot down by a creek, which flowed past Brom's clearing. He sat on the bank and took off his shoes and socks before dangling his feet in the cool water. He pulled Kieran's tee out of his pocket, took off his own shirt, and folded them together into a pillow as he lay back on the bank to study the clouds through the tree canopy. The mix scent of his and Kieran's sweat on the shirts invaded his senses as he let himself drift, and soon, his cock got hard in his jeans. Cory reached down, stroked himself through the dense fabric of the jeans, and grew harder. He repositioned himself in his jeans, undid his belt, and pulled down the zipper to expose his bulging boxer-briefs. The fabric grew damp from sweat and pre-cum. Cory found himself glad he wore a colored pair of underwear because a white pair would be transparent from the moisture. His left hand tucked up under his head exposed his hairy pit and the curve of farm labor toned muscle; his right hand stroked down his furry chest to the waistband of his boxer briefs and over the bulge of his thick full cock to cup his balls. Cory drifted in self-pleasure as his hips rose. His hand slipped his jeans and his briefs down below his balls before rising to stroke the turgid length of his cock with a lazy, teasing stroke. His fantasy thoughts started out with slowly undressing Kieran, kissing and licking his exposed skin, slowly running his fingers through Kieran's hair while he nibbled and sucked on one of his tender nipples. Running his tongue across the firm and furry pectorals to the other nipple before following the treasure trail down to where the folded leather apron lay still wrapped around the trim waist. Hearing Brom's deep voice as the man moaned his name in pleasure.

Cory sat bolt upright, all the pleasurable thoughts vanishing from his mind as he found Kieran transforming into Uncle Brom in his fantasy. Even worse, he realizes Brom's deep voice was actually calling out to him.

"Hey, Cory, come on back to the cabin. Kieran and I are going to take a break for lunch." Brom's voice echoed through the woods.

Dressing quickly, Cory headed back toward Brom's cabin and lunch with his boyfriend and the man in his sudden fantasy. He was worried Kieran would sense his thoughts had strayed to another man. Cory thought to himself, *In some ways, I'm as naive about sex as Kieran is. I never made love to anyone older than I am, so I guess I dreamed about what having a more experienced partner would be like.* He arrived back at the forge and Brom's cabin to find Kieran sitting alone on the front stairs with a couple of cold bottles of water at hand. Cory didn't like the expression of concern on Kieran's face as he glanced up at his lover. He hoped the expression was something to do with the spells for the collar and not anything that bled through the deep bond they shared. Kieran handed him one of the bottles of water and patted the section of stair beside him for Cory to sit.

"I think we need to talk, Cory, because I'm surprised you didn't come back when I called for you."

Cory bowed his head and nodded, while his hands destroyed the label on the water bottle.

"You realize I love you deeply and truly, Wolf. This bond between us is new to both of us, and because I deal with magic all the time in my life, I experience things more intensely than you do. I shared your pleasure and your intense feelings of guilt. I don't understand what caused the sudden shift in emotions."

"I was daydreaming about making slow love to you, but for some reason, your body became your uncle's. I don't understand why, other than he's as beautiful as you are but in a more mature way. I love you with everything in my heart. I don't get why thoughts of your uncle invaded my daydreams of you."

"Okay, I admit I didn't expect you to be replacing me so quickly in your sexy daydreams. I'm guessing Uncle Brom turns you on because he's older and more experienced than I am. I suppose being in love with someone who was a virgin when you met them is hot for a while, but you miss sex with someone with maturity and experience."

The sad expression on Kieran's face tore Cory apart. He set down his water bottle and took his lover's face in his hands, lifting his chin so they looked each other in the eye.

"Kieran, I don't care about experience. I care about love, not sudden bouts of lust. I'm sorry for being human in such a way. You said yourself your uncle is sexy. You're the one I love, and to me, you're the only person who matters. I can't promise my eyes won't wander, but you possess my heart and my heart will never stray."

"I hope not, Cory. I gave you my heart and soul. If I lost you now, life wouldn't be worth living. I guess I can't hold your fantasy against you if you want to jack off to thoughts of what Uncle Brom would do to you in bed, but I hope I can blow fantasy away with the reality of me later."

"My love, you're better than any fantasy will ever be." Cory drew Kieran in tight and kissed him. "I think I'll go back to our cabin to get cleaned up and wait for you to come back to me when you're done here."

"You could at least stay for lunch, Cory. Uncle Brom should be bringing it out in a moment."

"I think we both need a little space to deal with my wandering mind. I'll grab something from the fridge back at the cabin." Cory kissed Kieran one more time, got up, and walked back across the compound to the cabin where he and Kieran were staying. Kieran stayed seated on the steps of his uncle's cabin, waiting for the older man to come out with lunch.

* * *

BROM on his way out to the porch overheard Kieran's conversation with Cory and the part about his abrupt appearance as Cory's fantasy lover, and Brom's heart ached for Kieran and how mature he sounded as Cory tried to apologize and patch things up between them. He waited until Cory left before making noise as he juggled the plates of sandwiches through the screen door of his cabin.

"Hey, give me a hand here or the ants will get lunch instead of us," Brom called out.

Kieran grabbed the plates and set them down on a nearby table before grabbing his uncle around the waist in a fierce hug and letting go of his grip on his emotions. Sobs wracked the younger man as tears soaked his uncle's shirt. Wrapping his arms around his sobbing nephew, Brom's heart shattered anew at the pain, which struck so close to home. He stroked Kieran's back and let the boy sob himself out. He didn't cry like this. Not since his mother's funeral. When Kellen brought him here, as far as Brom recalled, Kieran lost control and cried.

Kieran settled against his uncle, seeking the comfort only the older man gave him. Kieran didn't let his emotions control him and he never let them get the better of him, not even in private. Brom ushered the boy over to the rustic couch with its overstuffed cushion on the porch and settled them both down. Kieran curled up against his uncle, as he'd done when he was a little boy needing comfort or whispering secrets he couldn't tell his father.

He never revealed the causes of his heartaches to anyone other than his beloved Uncle Brom.

"All right, *mo stór*, tell me what's tearing you up like this. I can tell when you're bottling things up again."

"I'm glad you still think of me as a treasure, Uncle Brom. I experience times when I think you're the only one who does despite all the protestations of how much I'm loved around here. There's tension in the air that's never been here when I've visited before. You and Dad are fighting over something I think has to do with me, because you stop when I enter the room. Even Gramps is acting odd. I get the feeling he and Dad are hiding some ulterior motive behind everything they do of late."

"Not true, *mo stór*, they love you as much as I do, and trust me on this, if your grams didn't love you more than she loves her own children, she would never teach you how to cook her most secret recipes. As for your father and I, let's just say I don't like the fact that he hasn't stopped to mourn your sisters or given you time to mourn them either. So what's bothering you?"

"I'm worried I don't possess Cory's heart, like he says I do. While he was off in the woods, the pleasurable experience he gave himself resonated through our bond, but when he broke off, I got this intense flash of guilt overriding everything. When he came back, it was after you called out instead of when I called him, as if he didn't hear my voice. He had this guilty expression on his face, and he confessed to having an erotic dream, which started off with him making love to me but ended up with him in bed with you instead." Kieran blurted out the last part of his admission before hiding his face against his uncle's chest.

"Well, his confession is a shocker, and I confess I overheard his apologies to you for having a wandering eye. I didn't realize I'm the source of his distraction. What he finds in a old guy like me is beyond me."

"He discovered how hot and sexy you are," Kieran mumbled against his uncle's chest.

"Something tells me, *mo stór*, someone else experienced a crush on me."

Kieran merely nodded against his uncle's chest. Fear sent shudders through Kieran's body before he sat up and put a little distance between himself and his uncle.

"I couldn't help crushing on you. I was ten. You are the first male to show any concern for me besides Dad. You were a strange man who opened his heart as well as his arms to a broken little boy, who lost his mother. I fell in love with you the moment you wrapped me in your arms and called me *mo stór* for the first time. Dad broke the spell by introducing you as his brother and my uncle. I was crushed to discover all the fantasies about growing up to marry you couldn't happen between blood relatives. Best and worst five minutes of my childhood."

Brom chuckled at the flush of color on Kieran's face at his admission of his juvenile crush on his own uncle. Brom realized male role models were seriously lacking in Kieran's life, as was male-male affection. He took Kieran's left hand and studied the ring intensely. He noted the wolf's head representing Kieran appeared a bit smaller than the one depicting Cory. The dynamic seemed odd with Kieran being the beta of the relationship; from everything Brom witnessed, Kieran was more an Alpha personality and seemed to lead Cory around. This might be part of the problem. Kieran didn't yet realize his position in the relationship and tried to stay Cory's equal. Brom made a mental note regarding the rings seeming a little loose, which meant one of their hearts strayed, and he figured the wandering heart belonged to Cory's, given the details of the boy's confession to Kieran.

"What should I do, Uncle Brom? I don't want to lose Cory, because deep down, we are made to be together, but what if all this is infatuation and not real love?"

"I can tell you this is real love, *mo stór*. You crafted the magic of those rings, so it wouldn't work for anything less. You need to talk with Cory and find your footing. I think your spells worked better than you realized. Take a close study of your ring. Do you realize the wolf representing Cory is slightly larger than the one that represents you?"

"I never realized the size difference before. I always thought they appeared equal in size. This means Cory and I aren't equals, and he should be the Alpha in our relationship."

"Yes, *mo stór*. Be careful. Until we can test his blood, raw sex with a shifter might damage your magic and put you in danger when you undergo the initiation to become your father's and grandfather's heir to the power of the Silver Witch."

"I want a normal life, free of magic and shifters. I don't want to be the legend some stupid destiny is trying to make me. Besides, I don't recall any tales with the hero or legend as the submissive half of a relationship."

"I think you might be surprised at how the dynamic works, Kieran. The hero goes out, does all heroic stuff, and comes home to someone who reminds them they're only human after all."

"I guess you make sense. I promised Cory I would always protect him. How do I be protective and let him be the dominate in our relationship? He doesn't possess magic, he can't shift, and the people who seem to want to hurt us can do both. How does an almost-normal guy protect a tracker and witch like me?"

"You need to talk to Cory about how to handle any situation which arises, *mo stór*. Now eat your sandwich before the ants discover free food."

Kieran ate the sandwiches Brom put on his plate. He put away more food than either of them expected him to consume. After they finished eating; uncle and nephew sat in companionable silence for a while. Kieran rose and excused himself.

"I think I better get back to our cabin and talk with Cory. We need to talk before either Gramps or Dad shows up to start the initiation process. Thanks for listening, Uncle Brom."

"I'm always here for you, *mo stór*."

Kieran dashed off for his own cabin to find Cory and talk. Shortly after he left Brom's cabin, Kellen arrived at his brother's place. The brothers settled in on chairs on the porch for what Brom realized was going to be a long discussion about his nephew and Kieran's boyfriend.

INTERLUDE: UNCLE BROM DRAWN INTO
THE FAMILY PLOT

Kellen settled in on his brother's porch and sighed because what he needed to ask of his brother would put them at odds over Kieran and Cory. The brothers sat in growing silence before Brom finally spoke.

"All right, Brother, what are you and Dad cooking up to do to my nephew and his boyfriend?"

"We need to keep them separated for about a week so I can initiate Kieran and test his limits."

"Kellen, you do realize they're bonded. Those rings on their left hands are ones I forged to Kieran's specifications. I don't think even Kieran realizes the adaptive power of his spells. Understand this, Brother, as long as their bond lasts, those rings won't come off."

"I understand better than you realize, Brom. What I need you to do is to help us block their bond so they can't experience what's happening to the other."

"No, Kellen. They're having a rough enough time of things already. I won't add to their problems. Cory isn't sensitive to the bond like Kieran is. The boy doesn't possess magic, and since he's not a full on shifter, he only experiences the connection on a primal level."

"What do you mean the boys are having a rough time already?" Kellen asked his brother.

"They were both here earlier today; in fact, you missed Kieran by a few minutes. Seems Cory's baser instincts got the better of him when he caught me all hot, sweaty, and shirtless working at the forge. He wandered off when Kieran and I got down to heavy magic talk and ended up out by the creek having erotic daydreams. Only problem is halfway through his hot dreams about Kieran, his mind took a sudden left turn and replaced Kieran with me. Passion turned to guilt, and Kieran sensed it all and confronted him about the daydream."

"I'm sure the conversation didn't go well."

"Actually, Kieran was mature about the whole situation, and Cory admitted the details without Kieran prodding him. He pledged undying love to Kieran but not faithful eyes, and I think he hurt Kieran more with his confession than with the fantasy. They need to work things out, and they do not need us mucking things up for them."

"I need to judge Kieran's limits without interference from Cory's shifter heritage. I need to determine if the shifter heritage he inherited from his mother's line is going to mess things up. If they're fucking without protection, Kieran's magic might be damaged or lost."

"I warned Kieran about the possibility of damage to his magic. He wants a normal life more than anything, Kellen."

"I get where he's coming from, but I'm afraid he can't. The Alpha in control of the pack on the Belle estate is a descendant of the damned Beast. Kieran is destined to be the Silver Hunter, or we're all lost."

"Sounds like you need to work on transforming Cory into an actual shifter instead of worrying about Kieran's magic. Doesn't your prophecy say something about a silver and ebony shifter on his left and right hand?"

"Yes, if you go by dad's translation of the prophecy, but silver shifters don't exist, so I'm guessing white is the proper translation of the passage, so unless Cory's animal form is a white wolf or something arctic, we're going to need to find a different shifter. Billy fulfills the ebony shifter."

"But the prophecy also said something about the white or silver shifter being the hunter's mate in one of the stanzas. I think you're stuck with Cory. I don't understand why you or father can't go and kill this Alpha. Either one of you is more power than any six silver mages."

"Because, like any other mage, we would never get through the forest of the Belle estate to confront this Alpha. The pack would tear us apart. Only Kieran possesses the skills to get to the heart of the forest and face down the Alpha. He's the only one with the proper bloodlines to do this, Brom."

"So are you asking me to block or break the connection between Kieran and Cory?"

"Break the bond if you can, but block the connection at the least."

"Go away now, Brother," Brom growled. "This power play makes me sick, but I will block the connection as best I can. Remember, Kieran is a more powerful silver mage than I am. He can break my spells with ease," Brom said as he stalked into his cabin and slammed the door behind him.

6

___

Kieran arrived back at the guest cabin to find Cory sitting on the front stairs in a pair of shorts and flip-flops. The sight of his boyfriend waiting for him made his heart skip a beat until he caught the expression on Cory's face. Cory was angry and his anger was directed at Kieran. Stopping short of the bottom stair, Kieran gazed up at Cory as the man stood.

"I was thinking while I waited for you to come back here. I shouldn't need to experience guilt over one stupid fantasy daydream. I'm not Mr. Perfect. I'm human. Therefore, my mind wandered while I was jacking off, big deal. I can't help your uncle is fucking hot, and yes, I do wonder what the experience would be like to be with someone older and more mature, Kieran. Every guy I ever dated was close to my own age or younger. So if my mind wanders from time to time, you're going to need to deal."

Kieran tried to keep the hurt from showing in his face and from flowing down the bond to Cory. He'd been all set to forget about the stupid fantasy and try to get their relationship back on track. Now, as he stood facing an angry Cory, he experienced the anger flowing down the link and feeding his own rising anger.

"Well, I guess all the crap about wolves mating for life is a lie after all. If you're so hot for Uncle Brom, go ahead and make a move. I'm sure he'll let you down as easy as he can. I guess I was the naïve little virgin, and now you get to add taking my virginity to your list of accomplishments, so I guess you're done with me. I should remember to never trust my heart to a shifter."

"Oh right, as if giving my heart to a fucking hunter wannabe was a brilliant idea. I moved my things to the downstairs bedroom for now. With luck, your father or uncle will be kind enough to take me to where I can catch the bus home to Arkansas."

"No need. You can take the van and drive your ass back to Arkansas, and take Billy with you. I'll leave my copy of the key on the island in the kitchen. Take the van. I won't need transportation."

"Oh, sure, and I won't be five minutes down the road before you call the cops and report the van stolen since the registration is in your name."

"The registration is in both our names, but I'll sign the title over to you as well. I'm done having my heart stomped on."

A flare of power surged through both boys' left hands as the rings on their fingers tightened with a painful squeeze before becoming loose and threatening to slip off.

"I would let this whole stupid incident go, Wolf. I do love you, but if you want to go, I won't hold you back," Kieran said, looking up with a mournful expression at his boyfriend.

Cory gazed down at Kieran, and for the first time, shared the true surge of emotions through their bond. Love, anguish, and loss slammed into him from Kieran, whom he realized was prepared to let him go if leaving was what Cory wanted.

"I love you too. I need time to cool down, and we can talk about this relationship with rational minds in the morning. I don't want us to be one of those couples, which argue and use sex to think they fixed everything. I'm going to sleep downstairs tonight so I can think."

"Fair enough. We can both think our relationship over and discuss where we go from here in the morning. If you want to leave, I won't stop you."

* * *

FOR THE FIRST time since their relationship reached the sleep together stage, Kieran and Cory went to separate bedrooms. They were both so depressed neither of them went up to the main house for dinner. A fact not missed by Grams, who asked pointed questions of her husband and sons at dinner.

"All right, you three, what's going on? Why aren't Kieran and Cory here for dinner?" Grams questions were sharp.

"The boys are having a bit of a relationship issue, and I'm sure they chose to stay at their cabin to work their problems out," Kellen replied before Brom said anything.

"What kind of relationship issue would keep either of those boys away from dinner?" Kellen noted his mother didn't let this topic go away.

"Kieran sensed a disturbance in their bond this afternoon while the boys were visiting me at the forge. When he asked Cory what was going on, Cory admitted to having a brief sexual fantasy, which started out with Kieran as the focus but somehow shifted to me being the focus. Cory's not as sensitive to the bond between them as Kieran is, so he couldn't tell how upset Kieran was about the whole thing," Brom confessed before Kellen interjected.

"I'm sure the boys will work this out and be fine by breakfast," Kellen said, trying to get his mother off the topic.

"But you would prefer they stayed apart until after Kieran's been tested and you discover if he can inherit the power of the Silver Witch, Brother. I don't like your plan to disrupt their bond. They need the bond to find the proper balance in their relationship," Brom growled at his brother.

"I'm not going to sit back and let Kieran repeat your mistake. We can't wait for me to find a new wife and produce another son. Besides, no child I produce now would possess the proper bloodlines to become the Silver Hunter," Kellen retorted.

"I keep telling you to do your own dirty work. You want the dark shifter dead so badly, get old lady Belle to protect your ass while you make with the major magic," Brom shouted back at Kellen.

"Both of you be quiet. Camille Belle is too old and broken to act as Huntress anymore. If one of Kieran's sisters had lived to become Huntress, we might take the risk of doing this ourselves," Gramps interjected.

"But all the girls are dead and only Kieran is left of the direct bloodline of the House of Beauty. I don't like any plan which puts my grandson in harms way, and I forbid you all from messing with the boys' relationship. Let them work things out and figure where their relationship goes." Grams tone invited no further argument from any of the men at the table.

The Oisín Clan finished their dinner in silence.

7

After a nearly sleepless night, Kieran finally heaved himself out of bed and padded naked into the bathroom. After relieving himself, he stepped into the shower and realized how much he hated fighting with Cory as the water soaked his hair, forcing him to remember to use magic to get his hair clean and dry. *Cory loves taking the time to wash my hair, and I love the sensation of his hands stroking my hair and massaging my scalp.* With a frustrated growl, Kieran ran his fingers through his hair, letting Silver magic bind the dirt to his hands before releasing the magic under the spray of the shower. When he stepped out of the shower, he bound the moisture in his hair to the towel. He returned to the bedroom and donned a pair of shorts before grabbing a plain leather band, which he used to bind his hair into a loose ponytail. Padding barefoot downstairs, Kieran headed for the kitchen. Soon, the aroma of coffee filled the air while Kieran began rummaging in the fridge for ingredients to turn into breakfast. With his ingredients assembled for stuffed omelets, Kieran set to work chopping ham, cheese, peppers, onions, and tomatoes into tiny cubes. After getting his *mise en place* assembled, Kieran set the kitchen table for two before turning his attention to cooking the bacon.

The rich aromas of coffee and frying bacon reached Cory's nose, and he gave up the pretense of trying to read the book he'd found on the nightstand in the spare bedroom. He padded barefoot down the hallway to the kitchen doorway where he stopped and studied Kieran move with the grace of a dancer as he tossed things in pans and made delicious scents fill the air. Kieran was so beautiful Cory couldn't understand why his eye had wandered to the man's uncle. Cory waited until Kieran set down the chef's knife and moved over to the sink to wash his hands before he approached. He slipped an arm around Kieran's waist and used his other hand to move Kieran's ponytail out of the way, so his hairy chest pressed against Kieran's smooth back as he pulled the man he loved against his body. Using his left hand, he found and captured Kieran's left hand and intertwined their fingers so their rings came together. A faint spark of power flashed as the rings touched, and he received an abrupt experience of Kieran's fear of losing his love and the deep sadness of the younger man.

Kieran broke the embrace and crossed to the stove to flip the bacon. He turned and faced Cory; for a moment, tears sparkled at the corner of his silver eyes. Open and vulnerable, his soul laid bare for a brief second before a stoic mask slammed down on his beautiful face. Cory's heart shattered at the pain he'd inflicted on Kieran. Worse was the knowledge he'd shattered Kieran's trust in him. Before Cory spoke anything further, Kieran raised his hand and placed his index finger on Cory's lips to stop him from speaking.

"No, I don't want any more apologies, no matter how sincere they are. I want you to take a good hard glance at the wolves on your ring and study the sizes carefully."

Cory raised his left hand and stared at the silver ring with the two wolves heads, one with amber eyes representing him and the other with diamond eyes representing Kieran. The inspection took him a few moments to discover Kieran's wolf was slightly smaller than his own wolf. He raised his head to peer at Kieran as he realized he was meant to be Kieran's protector and Alpha to Kieran's beta. When Kieran sensed the understanding dawn on Cory's face, he sank to his knees and tilted his head up and to the side, barring his neck in submission.

Cory sank to his knees opposite Kieran and reached out to raise Kieran's head back to a normal position.

"Babe, I'm honored by your submission, but I hurt you and broke your trust in me. I don't deserve your submission at this time. When I earn back your trust, I'll claim my Alpha rights."

"Wolf, by admitting you're not worthy to claim your rights as a pack Alpha instead of taking them as is an Alpha's due, you proved I can still trust you. I want you to claim me totally as your mate. I don't care if mating damages my magic."

"No, I won't ruin your magic. Surely we can find a way for us to complete the mating without hurting you or your magic."

"I remember hearing of two ways which might protect my magic, but I don't think either Dad or Gramps will go for them. Uncle Brom might help, but he's not strong enough anymore to do this alone."

"What are these ways, Kieran?"

"We bind my powers so I can no longer use them, sort of like we bound Billy to one form. The other is a ceremony, which strips my powers from me for a time. This ceremony is used to seal a committed relationship. The problem is they both require a Silver mage more powerful than I am, which means only Dad or Gramps are able to perform the ritual for us."

"So we need a way to get them to use their magic without knowing they're binding your powers. What if your uncle crafted some piece of jewelry and got them to cast the power-binding spell on the piece?"

"I'm sure he would, but the spell is specific to the magic being bound, and they'll wonder why he wants to bind a Silver mage more powerful than he is."

"I don't understand all the workings of magic, but sometimes Dad uses a talisman when he needs to cast a spell on himself, yet retain the ability to break the spell. What if you use me in the spell like a talisman so you're able to cast the magic yourself, remembering I can break the spell if we need your powers back?"

"I'll need to do some research on this one."

"Let's begin your research after breakfast. I think you're going to need a do-over on the bacon. From the aroma, you went beyond extra crispy."

"Ugh, I'm a better cook than this, honestly."

Kieran got up off the floor and quickly took the smoking pan of incinerated bacon off the stove and dumped the ruined pan in the sink. He found another pan, while Cory poured two cups of coffee and prepared them how he and Kieran both enjoyed it. He placed Kieran's on the counter beside the stove and took his own over to the table. After rearranging the settings, placing them next to each other, he sat down to study his lover as he cooked. Cory let his love for Kieran flow through him, hoping his lover would sense the emotion through the bond they now shared. Kieran smiled at him with one of his billion-watt smiles, and this one reached his lover's eyes, making them sparkle. Getting playful, Cory focused on an image of Kieran naked on his knees with Cory's cock buried to the pubes in his throat. Kieran moaned, his cock going rigid and tenting his shorts as he flushed red all over. Cory teased Kieran further with a thought of him on his back with his legs up on Cory's shoulders as his lover teased his hole with the tip of his hard cock. The moan from Kieran got deeper and more need-filled than before as his flush deepened, and a wet spot began to form on his shorts near the head of his cock. The click of the burner being shut off was the only warning Cory got before he found himself on the floor with his shorts vanishing with a tingle, which told him of Silver magic's involvement, before a warm wet heat wrapped around the head of his cock. Kieran swallowed his lover's cock to the root on the first go. Now came Cory's turn to moan in intense pleasure. Kieran worked Cory's cock with tongue, throat, and mouth until his lover struggled to draw a proper breath. The abrupt stop left Cory teetering on the brink of orgasm. Kieran rose and smirked at his prostrate lover. Cory's quick recovery and his reaction caught Kieran off guard as he turned back to try to make breakfast. Kieran found himself on his back with a naked Cory pinning him down and a raging hard-on staring him in the face. Cory snarled in his sexy lust-filled voice.

"You don't get to walk away with the job unfinished, lover. Now open wide and get your hot mouth back on my cock."

Kieran whimpered in submission and swallowed Cory's cock to the root, once again taking his lover to the edge, but this time, Cory kept him from stopping, taking control of the blow job and transformed the service into a skull fuck until he blew a huge load down Kieran's throat. Kieran swallowed and kept going until Cory pulled free as his cock reached a level of sensitivity even he couldn't take. Cory stretched himself full length on top of Kieran and nuzzled his lover's neck at the join to the shoulder where he bit down hard enough to bruise. Kieran moaned and turned to expose more of his neck in wolf-like submission, letting Cory lick and nibble leaving his scent all over Kieran.

"Mine," Cory growled in Kieran's ear.

"Yours," Kieran whimpered as he nuzzled back.

Cory got up and scooped Kieran from the floor, carrying him up to the main bedroom where their supplies were. Once in the bedroom, he made short work of stripping off Kieran's shorts before tossing his lover on the bed. Kieran bounced once before Cory pounced on him and pinned him to the mattress. Kieran moaned as Cory's tongue went to work on his body, erasing all traces of Kieran's own scent before Cory smothered him with his body, coating him in Cory's musky scent. Cory flipped Kieran over and repeated the process on his lover's backside. After making sure Kieran was covered in his scent, Cory slid down and began to rim and tease open his lover's ass, getting him loosened up for a deep mating fuck. Before long, Kieran was a moaning puddle of jelly from the rim job. Reaching over to the nightstand, Cory grabbed the lube and a condom package settled in to suit up. He ran a lubed finger over Kieran's twitching hole and lightly teased into his lover's body before shifting his position to let the head of his thick heavy cock rest on and tease his lover's entrance. Whimpers from beneath him drove his now actively dominant nature to sink into the tight warmth of his lover's body, claiming him as mate. Slow and gentle quickly transformed into hard and fast as Cory's love and lust collided with and was influenced by Kieran's through their bond. At the height of passion, as they were cresting toward mutual orgasm, Cory once again bit down on Kieran's shoulder with bruising force, triggering their mutual explosive orgasm. Cory collapsed on top of Kieran panting as his cock was milked dry by the spasms of Kieran's ass muscles. When they both came down from the world-rocking orgasm, Cory reached down and grabbed a hold of his condom to keep the thing from slipping off as he withdrew. Even for a second orgasm in a short period, his load bloated the end of the condom. He tied the condom off and dropped the used item in the trash. He rolled over on his back and pulled Kieran in tight so his lover was pressed into his side with his head on Cory's chest. Kieran, for his part, snuggled in and drifted in satisfied contentment, inhaling his lover's scent. They drifted off to sleep wrapped in each other's arms.

* * *

KIERAN AND CORY woke late in the afternoon but stayed cuddled in bed for a long time, enjoying being in each other's company. Finally, they decided to get up and shower together, even though Cory wanted to keep Kieran covered in his scent so others would recognize Kieran was his mate. Kieran rubbed against Cory letting him understand he would always be his. Once in the shower, Cory took to washing Kieran's hair properly, working the shampoo deep into Kieran's scalp and massaging down his neck before going to work on the rest of length. Kieran was purring like a cat as Cory worked on his hair. The task took awhile to get the length cleaned and the shampoo rinsed out, but Cory enjoyed every moment of his task almost as much as Kieran did. With Kieran's hair washed, Cory started in on washing his lover's body and realized the places where he'd bitten down on Kieran's shoulders didn't show the faintest trace of bruising.

"I'd expected to find my bite marks on your shoulders. You should be sporting a couple of huge hickeys on you considering how hard I bit down on you."

"Only by breaking the skin would you leave a mark, Wolf. Remember, I heal fast, and surface bruises fade fast. I love how you tried to mark me as yours, Wolf. I am yours, so you don't need to worry about marking me."

"I want others to recognize you're mine. I'm in a serious wolf-like state of late almost as if my beast were moving closer to the surface."

Kieran turned in concern and gazed deep into Cory's amber eyes, which brought a surge of the beast up in Cory until Kieran dropped his gaze in submission and offered his throat.

"Sorry, I don't understand where this is coming from," Cory said as he licked along Kieran's throat from shoulder to earlobe, making Kieran shudder.

"Your beast is closer to the surface, Wolf. I'm beginning to suspect your inability to shift isn't from sudden miraculous breeding by your parents. I think someone bound your ability with magic and the binding spell is breaking down."

"Do you think Dad did something after my birth?"

"He would be my first guess. Silver magic isn't binding you or you would have been in incredible pain all your life. I think we'll quietly ask Grams to scan you after dinner tonight, and if the binding is Sapphire magic, she can fix—or at least strengthen—the spell."

"I don't want to shift."

"I don't want you to shift either, Wolf. We're tied into the stupid prophecy enough. I want a long and normal life, not a short legendary one."

The lovers got out of the shower, dried off, and returned to the bedroom to get dressed for dinner with the rest of the family.

* * *

KIERAN LED Cory to the back of the main house and through a vast herb and vegetable garden to the door leading into the kitchen. He wanted Grams to check Cory over before they ran into any of the other Oisín family members. Both boys sniffed deeply of the heavenly scents coming from the kitchen door as they entered.

"Wipe your feet and wash your hands, boys. I have work for both of you," Grams said as she placed a bowl of potatoes fresh from the garden on the work island in the center of the kitchen.

"Yes, Grams," both young men replied as they complied with her directions.

When they finished washing their hands and taken a place at the workstation, Grams placed a bowl of water, a scrub brush, and an empty bowl in front of each of them. The bowl of potatoes between them, Kieran sighed knowing they're tasked to clean the potatoes. Grams' philosophy, *idle hands get young men in trouble*, which she applied to Kieran at age ten when he came and stayed with his father's family until things settled down on the Belle estate after his mother's death.

She did her part to keep young Kieran out of trouble. Líadáin taught him how to work a magic she guaranteed would win him the person of his dreams. Kieran learned to cook, use herbs, and set a proper table. He returned to the Belle estate less rebellious and with a purpose once again.

His goal firm in his mind, he managed to convince Grandmother Belle to let him spend every other summer with his paternal family. The stern old woman permitted him two weeks to visit his father's family the summer he turned eleven as a reward for his performance during training. When he returned home with a beautiful handcrafted silver broach as a gift for her, she agreed to allow him to spend one month each summer with his father's family until he turned fifteen, and his training as a tracker for the House of Beauty began full time.

"Something serious is on your mind, *mo stór*, for you to sneak in the back way. The last time you did such a thing since you were twelve," Grams said, pulling Kieran from his memories. "So what brings you and *mac tíre óg* to my kitchen? You can both work while we talk."

Cory seemed puzzled by the Irish words, which he guessed meant Grams was talking about him. Kieran glanced at him and smiled.

"*Mac tíre óg*, means young wolf in Irish," Kieran said as he picked up the first potato and dunked the spud in the bowl of water before attacking the skin with the scrub brush. "Grams, Cory's wolf is getting closer to the surface, and we think his lack of shifting isn't due to genetics but rather a binding spell, which is breaking down."

"Why come to me, *mo stór,* and not your father or grandfather?" Grams said as she started chopping some herbs while giving Cory a glance, which made him blush and start cleaning potatoes.

"Because this binding isn't a Silver magic binding spell. The sensations are more akin to Sapphire, which means Cory's father most likely, cast the binding. Since Sapphire magic is your talent, I figured we would be better off to coming to you. Besides, Gramps will get all upset about the barrier spell and go all end of the world on us."

"Well, the barrier spell needs to be taken into consideration, Kieran. The barrier keeps us protected from dark shifters and others who wish for Silver magic go the way of Gold and Amethyst."

"I understand, Grams. I keep waiting for Dad or Gramps to come and tell me my turn has come to add to the layers of the spell."

"Once you undergo the ritual to link you to the power of the Silver Witch, Kieran, you will take your turn adding to the layers of defensive magic in the barrier. Now, *mac tíre óg,* give me your hand, and let's discover what sort of interesting things I can learn about you." Grams reached across the worktable to take Cory's right hand.

Kieran tried to focus on cleaning potatoes as his grandmother's magic washed over Cory, searching out the spell, which bound his shifter abilities. The room grew colder as Grams' magic worked and Cory's shiver was visible. Grams muttered words in Irish under her breath as she ended her scan of Cory. Kieran set aside the potato he'd finished peeling and stared at his grandmother in expectation.

"Don't stare, dear. Yes, *mo stór*, you were right to be worried. A binding spell of Sapphire magic is at work holding Cory's abilities as a shifter at bay, and the spell is breaking down because he's been ingesting Silver magic. I'm guessing you boys aren't using a condom when you perform oral sex on each other."

Kieran and Cory both blushed at the comment from Grams. She clucked her tongue in disapproval before continuing.

"The Sapphire magic of the spell is being eroded but at the same time is also working with the Silver magic to eliminate the Ebony magic in Cory's blood as well. He's balanced between the three types of magic."

"Grams, how does this relate to his beast being so close to the surface?"

"Had Cory's shifter genes not been blocked at an early age, his wolf would be dark, and yes, Cory, your animal form is definitely a wolf. I suspect not as dark as young Billy's wolf, since they don't share the same strain of the lineage. Your beast is fighting to stay dark, but the dark is losing the battle. The dark will lose for sure as long as you don't shift before the balance tips further toward Silver magic."

"Will I shift if the balance becomes more Silver magic than Ebony magic?" Cory was desperate for the answer.

"I can't say for sure, Cory. The shifter gene is a creation of Ebony magic. While some shifters possess traces of the other types of magic, no shifter ever possessed Silver magic."

"So if we tip the balance to Silver magic, I might never need to worry about shifting?"

"I can't promise, but if you keep the transition gradual as you're doing—even though you didn't realize what you were doing—I'd say your chances are good. You'll come as close to human as you will ever get. Be careful, you two." Grams moved around the worktable and drew both boys into a fierce hug. Kieran and Cory linked arms and held the woman fast between them.

"You'll never get dinner ready if you squash my wife between you boys," Gramps declared as he entered the kitchen.

Kieran and Cory let Grams go from their hug and scurried back to washing and peeling potatoes.

"Kieran, I need a word with you in private," Gramps called from the far side of the kitchen.

"Be right with you, Gramps," Kieran replied as he jumped off his stool and kissed Cory.

Kieran followed his Grandfather out into the herb garden and to a spot, which was reserved for Gramps to smoke his pipe. Grams hated the stink of the thing and had long ago forbidden him to smoke the pipe in the house. Gramps settled in his chair and Kieran sat on the ground, facing him as he'd done when he was much younger. He called this little corner of the gardens the wisdom patch, because here was where Gramps brought him when profound things were to be discussed. When they were both settled and Gramps had his pipe lit and drawing to his satisfaction, he gazed down at Kieran.

"Your father and I have been discussing your purification and initiation rituals, and we've decided I should be the one leading you through both."

"I'm honored, Grandfather. I always thought when the time came Dad would be the one who would be my guide for these rituals."

"Normally, Kellen would be acting in the role of guide and priest for these rituals. Family tradition plans for a father to initiate his son as his rightful heir to the power. We think you would be better served by becoming one of my direct heirs in case something happens to me."

This turn of events caught Kieran off guard. Worry crossed his expression. Might something be physically wrong with his grandfather?

"Gramps, what's wrong? Are you okay?"

"Oh, don't worry. My health is good, Kieran. I'm concerned these are dark times and so much of the ancient prophecy seems to be centering on you. I want to give you access to the full powers of the Silver Witch, not what you can draw on now or the slight bit more power you might get as your father's heir."

"Okay, Gramps. When do you want to do these rituals?"

"We'll do them next week. You must leave Cory behind. This is only for the Silver Witch and his heir."

"You do understand he's going to sense what's happening to me through our bond, Gramps. I can't take off this ring as long as he and I are truly bonded."

"Yes, Kieran. Your father will make sure Cory doesn't come looking for you or interfere with the rituals."

"Well, I'd better get back to helping Cory and Grams get things ready for dinner." Kieran rose and hugged his grandfather before heading back into the house. The idea of his father looking after Cory while he went with Gramps didn't sit well with Kieran. He decided as a precaution to ask Uncle Brom to keep an eye on Dad for him.

* * *

DINNER WAS a quiet affair without either his father arguing with Uncle Brom or Gramps debating with either of his sons. Kieran wondered what was up with his family. He sensed something off but couldn't figure what was wrong. When dinner finished, he led Cory out into the deep woods and along a hidden path to Uncle Brom's cabin. Letting themselves into the cabin was easy since Brom never locked the place. Kieran settled them down on the couch in the front room in what he thought of as their proper places. Cory leaned up against the arm, and Kieran snuggled in between Cory's legs, resting against his chest with Cory stroking his hair. They kicked their shoes off and got comfy on the couch as Uncle Brom came in through the backdoor, yanked open the refrigerator, grabbed a beer (from the sounds of the clanking bottles), and stomped into the front room. He was startled for only a moment when he realized he wasn't alone in his own home and figured out who reclined on his couch.

"You boys surprise me. I figured I would be *persona non grata* around you two."

"We worked things out, Uncle Brom, and our bond is stronger than ever. Thank you for giving us the reason to make our bond stronger," Kieran replied.

"Well, this is a first. Actually, I expected your father to be here, *mo stór*. Instead, I find you two camped out like you own the place. Do either of you want a beer?"

"No, thank you, Uncle Brom. Kieran doesn't do well with beer and I don't drink." Cory's firm response came for the two of them. "What we want to understand is what's going on behind the scenes. Your father pulled Kieran aside earlier tonight to tell him something private, and everyone got so quiet at dinner tonight. The day has been kind of unnerving."

Brom scrutinized his nephew as the young man nodded along in agreement and snuggled in tighter to Cory, almost using the older boy as a shield. They accepted their bond and their roles within the bond. Kieran let Cory be the Alpha and take the lead.

"Did Kieran explain anything about the rituals he's going to be undergoing soon?"

Cory shook his head in the negative as his left hand caressed Kieran's hair; somehow never catching on the ring both boys wore. Kieran remained quiet; he wasn't allowed to speak about the rituals to an outsider. Brom glazed at him for a moment, silver eyes meeting silver eyes before he glanced up into the amber eyes of Kieran's lover. He witnessed the fierce source of protective strength in those amber eyes. He smiled at the boys, took a swig from his beer, and began a long explanation of purification and initiation rituals for Cory's benefit.

"So I can't be part of any of these rituals, but I'll experience everything done to Kieran through our bond, won't I?"

"Yes, Cory, you'll likely experience everything Kieran does. What worries me is the part of this where my father will invest Kieran with access to the power of the Silver Witch. If you absorb the magic through Kieran, the ritual may cause you harm because of the Ebony magic in your blood from your shifter heritage."

"Can I be shielded from any of this?" Cory asked.

"Tell me you recall a way, Uncle Brom." Kieran's eyes pleaded with his uncle as he spoke.

"You ever use the love displacement spell, Kieran?" Brom asked.

"Yes. Back when we first discovered how opposite our heritages are, I used the spell to hide my feelings away inside of Cory so I gained time to figure things out without my emotions getting in the way. Turns out the spell helped save me from some powerful dark force, which wants to enslave me."

"What you need to do is cast this spell again—only this time, draw your bond out of both of you and place the link someplace or into something safe until the rituals are complete. Removal of the bond is the only way to make sure neither of you will experience what's happening to the other until after you restore the bond," Brom said and hated himself for playing along with his father and brother and their plans.

"I'm not a fan of this idea. We can find some other way?" Cory asked Kieran.

"I might put a block on our bond, Wolf, but I'm not sure my block would hold against the power, which will flow along the channel and down the bond. Dad might be able to cast the spell, but I don't want to ask him to mess about with our bond. I can lock our bond into our rings, and you can hide the rings someplace safe until I come back from the rituals."

"Why don't you boys go home and discuss this further? Plans like this should be between the two of you," Brom said as he got out of his chair to encourage the boys to leave.

Kieran and Cory got up and put on their shoes before hugging Uncle Brom and heading back to their own cabin. Shortly after they left, Kellen came into the main room from the door leading to Brom's bedroom.

"I don't like how powerful their bond is, and I don't like seeing Kieran take second place to Cory."

"Kieran's role is partly the nature of their bond and partly due to his upbringing in the House of Beauty. All the strong men in his life—you, Dad, his uncles, and great-uncles on the Belle side—are like most of the women in his life, disciplinarians. Face the facts, Brother. To survive in the House of Beauty, even you needed to become a doormat. Kieran loves and respects you, but he doesn't relate to you as someone who will comfort him when the world beats the crap out of him. I figured you realized why he comes to me when he needed answers and solutions to his questions and problems. I'm the guy he's free to talk and do fun things with."

"I hate when you're right. Old Lady Belle was hard on Kieran as a boy, his training was so rough, and all I did was keep the worst punishments from falling on him when he failed some task. I guess I was wishing he would come to me for advice like a son should come to his father."

"Oh please, how many times did you go to Dad for advice when we were kids, Kellen? Every time I turned around, you were running to Uncle Padraig for advice. Asking uncles for advice runs in the family, Kellen."

"Yes, I suppose so. So what will they do, come and ask me to block their bond or will Kieran cast the emotional removal spell?"

"I chose to send them back to their cabin to discuss what they want to do, so we wouldn't be forewarned. I want the boys to be happy. After almost wrecking their relationship, I don't want to be part of anything that drives them apart."

"I don't want them hurt either, Brom. I love Kieran with all my heart, and he's the last bit left of his mother. We need him more than you can imagine."

"I still say we should handle this shifter problem some other way."

I wish we only needed to deal with the shifter problem, but an Ebony mage is involved in this somewhere. If Kieran doesn't possess all the pieces to the prophecy and all the power we can give him, we're doomed."

"Okay, but one last question before you get as bad as Dad with the doom and gloom, little brother. What did the boys talk to Mother about before dinner tonight?"

"I didn't even realize they'd spoken with her."

"Well, you might want to find out before you muck about with their relationship too much. I only caught Mother mentioning something about a slow transformation process before I ducked out when Dad came toward the kitchen."

"You do understand Mother won't say anything to betray their confidence. We'll hope Dad's plan works and Kieran pulls their bonds out into their rings."

"You're planning to try and destroy their bond. Answer me this, little brother. Are you so sure Cory isn't the mate your precious prophecy talks about? Did you or Dad stop to think of a reason he never shifted? Sapphire magic can be used to bind as easily as Silver magic can."

"Sapphire magic wouldn't hold off the change of a born shifter. No Sapphire mage is powerful enough."

"What if the binding spell was layered over years and years of close contact? Stop and think, Kellen. You don't possess any information about Cory's family other than some of them are shifters. Talk to Mother before you ruin your son's life."

"I don't possess the time, Brom. I can only hope he'll forgive me," Kellen called back as he fled from Brom's cabin back to the main house.

8

———

Things were quiet around the compound for the rest of the boys' third week. Near the middle of their fourth week, Kieran exited the cabin to find his grandfather standing in the clearing in front of him. He was dressed in what Kieran had come to think of as training clothes, sturdy leather boots, pants, and shirt. At Aodhfin's side were silver hiking staff, a travel pack, and large leather-bound book. Kieran took all this in with a quick glance before turning around and retracing his steps into the cabin to change into his own training gear. He also explained to Cory their plans for the day had been changed by Aodhfin's desire to start training with Kieran again. Kieran changed from his jeans and t-shirt into his leather tracking clothes, including the heavy leather duster. On his hips, he wore the matching pair of silver Hungarian sabers; twin silver daggers poked their hilts from the tops of his boots. Kieran kissed Cory with all the intensity of their love for each other and the promise to be back as soon as he possible before he left the cabin and joined his grandfather.

Aodhfin took up his hiking staff, the book, and his pack, leading Kieran off into the woods while Cory's eyes followed their departure from the porch with Billy sitting at his side. In silence, Kieran followed his grandfather into the forest for hours until they arrived in a clearing he didn't recall being to before. In the center of the clearing stood an altar-like table on top of which was a bookstand. Aodhfin placed the large book he'd been carrying on the stand before facing Kieran. Grandfather and grandson stared at each other for a long moment before Kieran knelt before his grandfather without a word being spoken.

"Tonight we will begin your initiation into the ranks of the Silver Witches of the House of Oisín. You will be consecrated to the ancestors, after which will begin your training to become the Silver Witch and assume command of the grimoire our family has spent centuries crafting. First, you must be cleansed in the scared springs; strip and leave your clothes and your modesty behind as you follow the path laid out by our ancestors."

Kieran rose and stripped, leaving a pile of clothes, weapons, and silver chains behind him as he padded barefoot across the clearing to the pathway leading to the sacred springs. His grandfather beheld how Kieran had developed in body and had a flash of pride pass through him as his grandson passed naked before him. He hoped his grandson would forgive them for what they planned to do to Cory while Kieran was undergoing the purification ritual. Aodhfin went and tidied up Kieran's pile of clothes, weapons, and silver chains before taking a different path down to the sacred springs. He espied the double-headed wolf ring lay on top of the pile. Aodhfin's path led to a special alcove, which housed the herbs and oils needed to begin the cleansing ceremony. Here, Aodhfin stripped away his clothes and weapons, donned a white loincloth and a silver pendant, which marked him as the Silver Witch before continuing to the springs.

When Kieran arrived at the sacred springs, he stood on a stone overlooking the three pools. The pool to the left was a hot spring, which appeared to lie directly above its heat source as the water steamed and nearly bubbled with the heat. The pool to the right seemed to be a cold pool; the stone edge appeared to be rimmed with ice despite the heat of the season. The central pool lay below both of the others, and here, their waters mixed to a perfect temperature. In front of this pool, Aodhfin stood wearing only a pendant and a loincloth;

behind him on a table about waist-high rested several towels and sacred oils. Kieran made his approach and knelt before his grandfather, a supplicant before the font of purification.

"These pools are sacred unto the goddess of the moon and her consort the god of the sun. What seek you here?"

"I come seeking purification before undertaking an important quest for knowledge and power to be used in the defense of mankind."

"What knowledge and power do you seek, O mortal youth?"

"I seek the knowledge of my ancestors and the power of the Silver Witch."

"You seek much, O mortal youth. By what right do you seek such knowledge?"

"By my descent from the last woman to hold the power of the Silver Witch, she who was mother to both my mother's line and my father's line. I claim the heritage of both the House of Beauty who slew the Beast and of the House of Oisín."

"Step into the pool until you are submerged to rinse away all earthly impurities."

Following the instructions, Kieran stepped into the pool and sank below the surface. His hair spread out as the small current in the pool swirled around him—first hot, then switching to cold—before enfolding him in a comfortable warmth like the fluid of the womb. Slowly he rose to the surface as the pool raised him up on a platform of Silver magic and allowed him to step off on to the ledge where his grandfather stood, face now hidden behind a silver mask with no features. The mask was a silver mirror to Kieran, but its magic allowed Aodhfin a clear view of everything from within. Aodhfin pointed to the table, and Kieran lay down on the surface face up, hair streaming down a trough behind his head. He closed his eyes as Aodhfin placed a white cloth over his face. Aodhfin, now in the full role of high priest to the goddess, took up the sacred oils and began a massage of consecration starting from his grandson's feet and working upwards to his neck, skipping over his grandson's hardening cock and tightening balls for the moment. He chanted the special prayers to open both his grandson and himself up to the powers of the goddess and to the Silver magic.

Power rose along his spine, flowing back and forth, as his grandfather's hands worked across his body until the power began to pool in the lowest of the ancient power points in his groin. Kieran experienced both the power and an orgasm building in his manhood. Would his own grandfather bring him to physical orgasm or was something else intended to release the power and his seed? From behind the veil of fabric covering his face, Kieran sensed a power rising outside of his body in the place where his grandfather stood and realized his grandfather was transformed by the presence of the goddess' consort the god. Now the divine spirit made use of the earthly flesh to keep the ritual pure and removed from the taint of incest. The god took hold of Kieran's cock, and with three sacred strokes, brought forth an orgasm of both magic and physical seed, which left Kieran drained and sore.

"Your sacrifice is accepted and banked against the needs of your sacred line, Kieran of the Oisín and the Belle."

The power vanished from the grove, and Kieran found himself on the edge of blacking out as he sensed his grandfather slump down next to him. After a time, Kieran stirred as he listened to his grandfather moving about the area. He opened his eyes to find himself lying on a sleeping bag in the first clearing. Sitting up slowly, Kieran examined the scene and found his grandfather had started a fire, and he sniffed food cooking. The sound of a stomach growling announced Kieran's recovery to Aodhfin who handed his grandson a plate of bread with honey smeared on the slices.

Even chewing slowly and washing the bread down with spring water, the plate was empty in mere moments. Kieran experienced some of his strength flowing back into balance with food in his system again.

"I don't recall ever being this off balance from a cleansing ritual before, Gramps."

"This was the most powerful one you will ever be involved in, Kieran. We only used this version when the Silver Witch dedicates his successor."

"I sort of tingle as if I'm a live wire, while also being as empty as a drained battery."

"The live wire sensation is your newly opened channel to our ancestors' magic, and the dead battery sensation is your personal power, which drained away when you reached orgasm during the ritual. The first will fade into the background in a day or two, and your personal power should return after a good night's sleep."

"When all this training is done and the rituals are completed, am I only going to be one of your successors, Gramps?"

"Yes, Kieran, but you possess access to many of the powers of the Silver Witch, but in truth, you will still only be my successor as your father is still only my successor."

"So the full powers of the Silver Witch still belong to you?"

"Yes, only the death of the Silver Witch or a deliberate severing of the power will transfer to his successor the full powers of our family line. Only one Silver Witch at a time is the way of our family since Beauty's brother became the first male Silver Witch following their mother's death. Get some rest now, boy. You'll get more family history as we continue your training."

Kieran settled back into the sleeping bag to get some sleep. He tossed and turned in the bag for a while before sleep final overcame him. He'd learned early last week he didn't sleep well alone anymore; he was used to Cory's solid form wrapped around him.

9

When Kieran went with is grandfather, Cory had been left to his own devices to entertain himself and Billy. His wolf-shaped nephew was content after going for a brief walk to settle down on the porch of the cabin and sleep. Cory made his way up to the main house in his wanderings where Kieran's father met him. Kellen wanted all the details of how he'd met Kieran and about his own family and clan. Cory spent the better part of the day reliving his relationship with Kieran for his lover's father. Grams brought them food and drink, while Kellen poured on the questions, probing for details about the Cooper family's quest to purge the shifter blood from their line, Billy's birth, and choice to become a wolf instead of a boy and dozens more.

Finally, Grams took pity on him, and after packing him a late night snack, he sent him back to the guest cottage. Cory put his snack away for later and made sure Billy had water and food in his bowls before climbing the stairs to the loft. If the cabin seemed empty without Kieran to share the place with, their bed seemed even more so. Cory cuddled Kieran's pillow to himself, seeking the scent of his lover to ease him into sleep. A fitful night's sleep finally overtook Cory until a dream dragged him under.

In his dream, Cory viewed from a distance Kieran stepping out of the trees onto a beach. Under the light of the full moon, the sand was silver. Cory beheld his lover in torn clothing, barefoot, breathing hard, and surveying his escape routes, looking to evade his pursuers.

His lover appeared worried as if something dangerous were pursuing him. Kieran's expression in the dream made Cory wonder what pursued his lover in his dreams.

Cory trembled in his sleep as in the dream he listened to brush crack behind Kieran, alerting him to the presence of his pursuers. Grabbing a stick, dream Kieran moved further out on the sand. He drew a circle around himself and waited. The direction of his eyes led Cory's dream vision to the edge of the forest, revealing at least six wolf shifters stalking him. The Alpha was a huge, dark gray beast, at least twice the size of the other wolves. Its eyes glowed bright yellow in the moonlight, and its vicious canines flashed silver. The beast prowled forward with the rest of its pack close on its flanks. Cory followed the events in fear as the beast scented Kieran and let loose a fierce howl of victory. Kieran braced himself, and silver began to flow along the length of the stick down to the circle around him. The Alpha coiled and leapt at his prey, hoping to drag Kieran down so the rest of the pack can close in and help finish him off.

As silver flashed in a circle around Kieran, Cory blasted from the dream into a waking state by an instinct telling him he's not alone in the bedroom. He rolled from the bed ahead of sword blade slicing down where he'd been a moment before. From the shadows on the far side of the room, Kieran's father emerged with a long and deadly silver sword. Cory sprung to his feet, racing for the stairs, ignoring his own nudity. He grabbed Billy by the silver collar to keep him from charging up the stairs to confront the mad man with the sword.

"Tonight is a full moon wolf-boy. Shift and fight me."

"I can't shift. Are you forgetting I don't possess enough shifter blood to make the change possible? What will Kieran do when he finds out you're attacking me, Kellen? You're his father. How can you betray him like this? If you hurt me, Kieran will never forgive you, and he'll never do what you want him to do."

"You must be tested to determine if you're truly worthy to be my son's partner."

"Tested? I would give my life to protect Kieran. You're mad if you think attacking me will cause me to abandon Kieran." Cory backed up a few steps looking for something to use as a weapon. Beside him, Billy growled defensively.

Kellen charged swinging his sword like the mad man Cory named him. Billy and Cory barely escaped its path. Cory grabbed the table lamp and swung the lamp like a club at Kellen. Turning to make another pass at the pair, Kellen found he was blocked as another figure ran in room wielding a heavy silver broadsword. Short dark hair and a heavier frame revealed the man to be Kieran's uncle.

"Stop, Kellen. The boy proved himself to my satisfaction. He stood his ground and refused to let the beast attack you."

"So now you want me to spare Kieran's pets? Get out of the way, big brother."

"I had a vision while I was working at the forge, Kellen. The boy will help Kieran along the path destiny chose for him to walk. Kieran and Cory possess the potential to be truly mated, because unlike our line, the House of Beauty carries the contamination of shifter blood."

"Impossible, they're bred to hate and to hunt shifters? When did they ever mate with one?"

"According to my vision, Beauty herself is the source of the contamination entering the bloodline. Her idiot prince and the Beast shared a mother who was half-shifter. Their mother's blood is what makes Beauty's descendants such good trackers and hunters. The prince's shifter blood gives them heightened senses and speed."

"So why can't Kieran shift?" Cory asked

"Beauty's daughter used her gift of the Silver magic to bind the shifter genes in such a way no child of the house would ever be able to shift. Cory, this is something you must never tell Kieran."

"Oh, goddess, what do I do now? Brom, Dad doesn't possess any of this information, does he?"

"Now we wait to find out how young Kieran fares in the tests to become the next Silver Witch. We should go so Cory can get some rest."

Brom led his brother from the guest cabin, bidding Cory good night. Cory led Billy upstairs, put on some sleep pants in case of any more surprise visitors, settled into the bed, and let the wolf spend the night in the bedroom. *I wish we didn't strip away our bond, I need to be sure Kieran is all right and to be sure he's aware I'm all right as well. I wish the removal spell didn't work. If the spell failed, Kieran would be here by my side instead of out in the woods somewhere.*

10
___

Kieran and Aodhfin spent several days out in the forest engaged in training both magical and physical. Aodhfin focused a lot of the lessons on breaking the habits Kieran had developed from his training with his mother and the senior trackers of the House of Beauty. Kieran had a disturbing tendency to rely on physical tricks instead of letting his magic flow in the open. Aodhfin blamed Kellen for some of Kieran's lack of freedom with magic. Kellen helped train the boy to hide his power from his mother's family, in part to keep the Oisín hidden. The natural inclination of the House of Oisín was to keep hidden from the rest of the world to protect the most powerful of all the binding spells ever cast.

Aodhfin was impressed by Kieran's creative streak at using his magic as an extension of some other act.

"Kieran cast the spell and forget about masking the magic. You won't be able to mask the more powerful spells in the family grimoire." At Kieran's puzzled expression, Aodhfin said, "Yes, I understand I'm contradicting everything your father taught you."

Kieran pulled himself up short from the maneuver he'd started and let the magic flow. He scrutinized the spell while the magic took form and fizzled. He took a stance and attempted to cast the spell again without trying to disguise what he was doing. Again, the spell took form and fell apart. After several more attempts to cast the spell without hiding its form, Kieran stood frustrated.

"Plain casting doesn't work, Gramps. I don't think straightforward casting is how my version of the Silver magic works. If I'm going to become the Hunter of the House of Beauty, I'm going to be casting in combat. I won't get the time to stop and cast a spell."

"You're going to learn the proper forms of spell casting, Kieran. Learning the proper forms will be on you. The burden is yours. You must prove to me you can cast the most powerful spells from the grimoire in the traditional manner."

"The way to go about this is to skip over the spells I cast on a regular basis and go to spells I'm not familiar with. I need to learn spells which aren't combat focused."

"Well, put away your weapons and come over here. We'll start with a simple locator spell and focus on a target you're acquainted with. I think young Cory will hold your focus."

"I think you're cheating, Gramps. With the rituals over, all I need to do is put my ring back on and I'll find where Cory is through our mating bond. Hey, do you recall where I put my ring, Gramps?"

"You mean this ring?" Aodhfin said, holding up Kieran's bond ring.

"Yes, my bond ring," Kieran, said as he crossed to take the ring from his grandfather.

"This bond must end. Someone like Cory isn't meant to be at your side, and he certainly shouldn't be in your bed. Prophecy says you must take a shifter as your mate. We will find you a female shifter, so you can produce children to continue Beauty's line."

Kieran's expression turned to horror at his grandfather's words and outright shock when his bond ring twisted and melted in his grandfather's hand before vanishing. His grandfather stood stock-still for a moment, as if listening to a far away voice.

"According to the message spell I received from your father, your Cory is still alive. Apparently, Brom had some sort of vision at the forge last night and stopped your father from completing his task. Your father is upset and confused now. Seems your shifter put up a good defense before Brom stepped in. I guess I can let you keep him as friend."

Kieran's horror and shock turned into anger at his grandfather's betrayal.

"What gives you the right to get between Cory and I? I'm supposed to be around to protect him. I gave him my word I'd always protect him. Now you tell me I not only failed to protect him, but I failed to do what I promised from someone in my own family. I would expect this crap from my mother's family, but I never for the life of me figured you would pull this on me, Gramps. Wipe away your sense of smug satisfaction about destroying my bond to Cory, Gramps. You are not the only one who can plot against family when the need arises. You cannot understand what life is like for a child of the House of Beauty. So, while I cast the emotion separation spell, I didn't lock the bond into our rings."

Kieran crossed the clearing to his weapons and gear, quickly packing them up so he could get back to Cory and Billy. As he grabbed up his coat, his grandfather's magic grabbed his arm. Kieran exploded in fury at the binding spell and shattered the spell without a thought. Anger turning his beautiful face into an ugly mask of rage, Kieran whirled on his grandfather, a magic blade blazing in his hand. Aodhfin took a step back from his grandson and raised both hands in a warding off gesture.

Slinging his pack over his shoulder, Kieran turned and left the clearing, heading back to the guest cabin. As soon as he was far enough away from the clearing, he took off at a run. He raced back to the cabin so he might find Cory and find out what had happened. He crashed into the front room to find Cory sitting in front of the fireplace talking with his grandmother. When Cory spotted Kieran, he launched himself across the room, his fist catching Kieran in the jaw. Kieran staggered backward. After the first fist, Cory's entire body crashed into him. His lover's anger at him rode down the mating bond from Cory's ring, shattering the spell along with Cory's ring. When the spell shattered, it returned to Kieran all the feelings of their connection. Cory's anger flowed through him and joined with his own fury. In his confused state of intense rage, Kieran's magic surged between them, sending Cory flying across the room with a scream of combined rage and agony.

Both young men regained their feet with near inhuman speed. Before they raced at each other to clash in close quarters again, a wall of sapphire ice formed between them.

"Stop this at once, both of you," Kieran's grams said as she thickened the ice between the enraged lovers. "You two are the last ones who should be at each other's throat."

"Where were you when your insane father tried to kill me? I poured my fear and love into the bond to call you back. You promised me I would break the spell if I pushed hard enough. You promised me I'd be safe here with your family despite my heritage. You promised me by our bond, Kieran."

"I did, and I failed you. Only now has the spell broken. I didn't figure they'd try to kill you while the bond was suspended. We discussed what we thought were the ways needed to protect you from the amount of Silver magic pouring through me. Neither of us considered a physical attack on you into our plans. I love you more than anything, and I would never let them harm you. I don't even have my ring to prove how unbreakable our bond is to you. Gramps destroyed the symbol of our bond. I love you, Wolf."

Before Kieran dropped to his knees in submission, Cory stopped him.

"Go away, Kieran. I can't deal with you now. I don't understand how the mating bond chose so wrong when instinct picked you for my mate."

Cory turned his back on Kieran, refusing to meet his lover's anguished face. He raged at Kieran for failing his promise, and his words cut Kieran to his emotional quick. Spell or no spell, Kieran failed to protect him from Kellen's madness. *No,* a voice in his head screamed, *you're the one who should be protecting him; you are the Alpha of this relationship. You're the one who is supposed to be guarding Kieran's heart.* He sensed Kieran's emotions as he turned and fled the cabin. Cory understood the pain he inflicted on his mate. A voice like ice cut him from across the room.

"Those last words were totally uncalled for, young man. My grandson loves you with every fiber of his being. Do not blame him for something, which is not his fault. The training to become the heir of the Silver Witch is intense. You would do well to find him and forgive him before he does something you'll both regret."

"He promised me he would always be around to protect me. When I needed him most, he wasn't here. How do you forgive so many broken promises?"

"Don't blame my grandson for the actions of his elders. You're the Alpha in your relationship; you should be protecting yourself and Kieran, not expecting him to come running to your rescue. These are dangerous times, Cory, and I'm sorry, but Kieran is the focal point. You are either his strongest support or his Achilles' heel. Only you can decide where you stand. I suggest you take back those hateful words."

Turning, Cory found the ice barrier gone, so he raced from the cabin with Billy on his heels as the wolf came as if sensing his need. Billy passed Cory and sniffed the air before setting off along a path deep into the forest. Cory followed, hoping to find his love before Kieran found time to inflict deep wounds of self-loathing on himself. What seemed like hours later, Cory and Billy found Kieran sitting on the bank of a clear pool at the base of a small waterfall. He sat, stripped down to his boxer briefs, and his hair was wet. Despite the breaking of branches beneath Cory's feet, Kieran didn't move until Cory touched him on the shoulder. Kieran turned and buried his face in Cory's chest, wrapping his arms around his lover, and sobbed. The sorrow Kieran experienced washed down the mating bond and into Cory like a flashflood. Wordlessly, he enfolded Kieran in his arms and in his heart, letting his love wash away the words said in anger and fear. As the agony of heartbreak and failure was replaced by the joy of love and acceptance, the lovers found themselves stretched out in the soft grass along the pool's bank. Kieran rested his head on Cory's chest and let his hands wander his lover's body.

"I'm sorry I said what I did back at the cabin. Mating bonds don't ever choose wrong, and I don't need a magic ring to prove how much you love me."

"I guess not needing a ring is a good thing since both of them are gone. Wolf, what I still can't understand is how your mating bond would have chosen me in the first place. I'm a descendant of two of the most pure mage lines in existence. My bloodline contains not a drop of shifter blood."

"Listen, bloodlines aren't important now. What's important is we're together and we need to find a way to keep anyone from breaking us apart again. If you want a consolation prize, Uncle Brom is pissed at your grandfather for getting your father to attack me."

"You're trying to make me forgive Dad for attacking you, aren't you, Wolf?"

"I guess I am a little. He is your father, after all. No point in ruining your relationship with him."

"Thanks. I'll talk to him. I promise. For now, I want to enjoy us and let our love wash over us both."

"We can do better. Make love to me and let your love wash through me, and let's purge the last of the Ebony magic from my blood."

"If we do this, Wolf, we will change the dynamics of our relationship. Are you sure you want me to be Alpha?"

"Yes, make love to me and forget the condom. I want you to be the true Alpha in our relationship. Since you swore to protect me, I want to be your true mate and submit to you in all ways."

"Wolf, this trust is special, and I'm afraid. I realize everyone seems to think I should be the Alpha in our relationship, but I actually relish giving you control. If anyone should be submitting, I think I should be the one. I'm still worried about what might happen when our opposing magic collides. I want our true mating to take place someplace special. Forgive me for asking for a little time to set things up to make for a night we'll never forget."

"Kieran, you realize I'll wait for you forever. I'm glad you trust me enough to give up control, but I think we can do this and still keep our balanced relationship. Understand this, Kieran Samuel Belle Oisín, I'm not letting you out of my sight until after we've truly mated and nothing will ever block us from knowing when the other needs us."

The lovers cuddled together for a while longer before Kieran rose, stripped off his still damp briefs, and pulled on his other clothes. He pulled Cory to his feet, and with a sharp whistle, called Billy in from his romp in the forest. He led the way back to their cabin where they cleaned up and got ready for dinner at the main house with Kieran's family.

INTERLUDE: THE APPRENTICE AND THE MONSTER MEET IN SHADOW

A dark cloaked figure stepped out of the ancient forest into a clearing the reeked of death. Before him lay a pile of bodies, both human and wolf, in various stages of decay. The figure in the dark cloak made a gesture, and Ebony magic swirled around the clearing, speeding up the decomposition and leaving only bones. The magic gathered the bones and bound them into the form of a throne with a canopy of wolf skulls. The finials of the throne's arms formed from human skulls. The cloaked mage settled into the throne to await the arrival of the dark Alpha shifter who claimed descent from the legendary Beast.

Across the clearing, dozens of amber and green eyes reflected the light of the full moon as the shifter pack moved out of the tree line. In the middle of the pack strode a huge beast, half-man and half-wolf or bear. From the distance, the mage couldn't tell which, though he leaned toward bear. *Well, seems the legendary claims of this Alpha shifter regarding his ancestry were true.* Only a shifter with a dark and powerful lineage would be able to hold the midway form of a shift. To be both beast and man during the full moon took incredible power no lesser line possessed. The pack stopped a distance from the enthroned figure while the Alpha continued forward to stop a few feet from the throne. Definitely a bear—a grizzly from the appearance and size of the Alpha—surprising given the pack was all wolf-shifters. The mage and the monster stared at each other for a moment longer before the shifter spoke.

"You are late, shifter."

"Do you bring me word of the boy who would be a hunter?"

"He and his boy toy along with the cur managed to lose my agents somewhere in Virginia. The boy took an assignment from a local hunter who turned out to be more talented in Emerald magic than she appeared. She masked the boy's trail from my agents."

"Why are you here?"

"I am here because my Master discovered the boy made his way here to Maine. Powerful spells now keep them hidden. Most likely he is hidden away by his bitch of a Huntress grandmother."

"The boy did not return to the House of Beauty. If he came here, we would not be meeting."

"So sure you can kill the boy like you did his sisters. He's not like any of his sisters. You won't spook him into wasting his magic."

"He's a male of the House of Beauty; he doesn't possess magic of his own. He will die faster than his sisters. The middle one made a formidable Huntress; pity she failed to survive our trap. Go now and find the boy. Beauty's accursed bloodline must end so the spell may be broken and shifters may be free."

11

—————

fter sending a note the previous evening to the main house advising the rest of the family they wanted to take time for themselves, Kieran, Cory, and Billy went for a hike the next morning. They stepped out into the glade on the near side of a creek. Kieran carried a picnic basket his grandmother packed and left on their porch, a blanket thrown over one shoulder and his camera bag over the other shoulder. The boys and their wolf settled down near the creek, spread the blanket, and set down the picnic basket. Unslinging the camera bag from his shoulder, Kieran surveyed the glade and found a couple of spots he wanted to use as background for photos of Cory and Billy.

The young men and the wolf settled down to eat their picnic and enjoy the peace and quiet of the deep forest. Kieran's grandmother packed all kinds of food in the basket for the boys and the young wolf. Kieran shook his head as Cory and he pulled out enough food to feed ten people. They tucked in until they were full and couldn't eat anymore; then, they repacked the basket. Cory resettled the blanket near the base of one of the old growth trees near the creek and sat with his legs in front of his and his back against the tree. Kieran settled on his back with his head in Cory's lap, while Billy flopped down in the grass between the boys and the creek.

The lovers rested in each other's presence, enjoying being normal. Cory ran his fingers through Kieran's silky dark hair and let them play lightly over his lover's face, almost as if he tried to memorize Kieran's features like a blind person learning their sighted friend's facial structures. His fingers eventually trailed down Kieran's neck and under his shirt collar to the scars on his lover's chest. Cory's fingers eventually wandered across Kieran's chest to find one of his nipples and tweak the nub playfully. Kieran reached up and pulled Cory down into a tongue-filled kiss. They shifted to lay side by side on the blanket to continue kissing and touching each other with ease. Their kisses deepened, and they became so lost in each other they didn't sense the arrival of Kieran's grandfather from the opposite direction. The first indication of Aodhfin's attack came from Billy's yip of pain as Aodhfin zapped him with a cantrip. Kieran reacted fast. Cory found himself flat on his back as Kieran surged to his feet; Silver magic flaring to turn the creek into a barrier. Aodhfin's found his counter spell deflected and himself swept off his feet as Kieran bounded over the creek and tackled him. A gleaming silver dagger appeared against Aodhfin's throat.

After making his point, Kieran got off his grandfather and helped the older man back to his feet. As he turned to cross back to Cory, his grandfather's power wrapped around his chest and pinned his arms to his side. Rage surged as his eyes followed Aodhfin across the creek headed toward Cory and Billy, a silver staff materializing in his hand. Fury powered Kieran's reaction, and his grandfather's binding spell shattered as silver armor formed, and Kieran vaulted the creek powered by Silver magic to land between Aodhfin and Cory. Scythe-like blades ran from both elbows to a similar distance beyond Kieran's wrists. Silver magic swirled around both grandfather and grandson as they faced off. As grandfather and grandson glared at each other over weapons, another voice rang across the clearing.

"So this is how you decided to continue with the testing, Father? We all realize the enemy won't give the boys a chance to rest and be happy if given the opening, but aren't you pushing things a bit hard?" Kellen said.

Before Aodhfin or Kellen might react, they found themselves flung across the clearing and each of them bound to a tree. Kellen actually experienced his own power draining away from him and flowing into Kieran.

"If you think for even a moment I'm letting either of you get anywhere near Cory or Billy again, you're dead wrong. If you ever come anywhere near them with a weapon or magic raised to harm, the fact you're my blood family won't matter. I will kill you. They are my family as much as you are, and for the remainder of our stay and the rest of these tests, they are off-limits."

Kieran released his father and his grandfather and dropped the barrier across creek. As he was turning to face Cory, he caught movement out of the corner of his eye as Kellen charged him with his long sword raised for a deadly strike. Kieran spun and set himself into a defensive position with one deadly scythe blade ready to block and the other held back for a counter attack. Kellen swung with all his strength behind the weight of the blade. Kieran blocked the attack and directed his father's sword along the edge of his own weapon, but didn't follow through with his own counter attack; instead, he lashed out with a powerful kick to the back of his father's legs. Kellen staggered from the blow, but recovered and was quick to strike back at Kieran. For his part, Kieran blocked with his weapons beating back the long sword between the two scythes. With magic powering his strength, he forced his father back toward the stream, their blades still locked together. While Kieran seemed distracted, Aodhfin leapt over the creek and went for Kieran's exposed flank. Surprise caught Aodhfin as a heavy branch swung by Cory intercepted the heavy staff. Billy launched himself at Aodhfin's legs, trying to bring the man down. The contest brought Kieran and Cory back to back against Kieran's father and grandfather with Billy snapping at both older men from outside the combat. Kieran shoved his father back, disengaging their weapons. Off-balance, Kellen fell backward into the creek with his long sword sinking deep in the earth. With Kellen out of the fight,

Kieran whirled to find Cory managing to hold off Aodhfin's attacks with his branch. When Cory slipped and fell, Kieran leapt over his lover and caught his grandfather's staff in the X formed by his crossed weapons. Knowing he was off-balance, Kieran dropped to one knee, still trapping his grandfather's staff between his own scythe blades. With an unknown strength, Kieran shoved his grandfather's heavy staff up and out, and lunged into the older man with a shoulder, driving the air from the man's lungs. Aodhfin landed on the ground, gasping for air as a single scythe blade stopped short of his throat.

"Give up, both of you, and stay down. You may have taught me magic, but Mother and her family taught me to fight in real combat. Neither of you are skilled fighters, nor are your hearts in the fight, while we're fighting to defend someone we care about. This battle is over, you two."

Kieran let his own Silver magic fade away, releasing his armor and his father at the same time. The power he'd taken from his father flowed back, leaving him weak. Cory was by his side as he started to sag from the energy drain. Billy placed himself between the boys and the older men as Kellen rose from the creek and came to help his father. Cory helped Kieran back to the blanket they'd laid out and got him seated with a bottle of water. He glared over his shoulder at Kieran's father and grandfather before deciding to ignore both of the older men and focus his attentions on his lover. He handed Kieran a second bottle of water when he found the one in Kieran's hand empty. He rummaged in the picnic basket and found some bread left over from their lunch. Kieran shook his head at the bread before leaning back against the tree and closing his eyes. Kieran stirred only when he made out his father lifting his grandfather to take the man from the clearing.

"No more tests, Gramps. I think we all understand what I did here today. Tomorrow, I'm taking Cory down to the beach, and we're camping for a week. When we get back, you both need to be ready to do whatever rituals are needed to make me the next heir to the Silver Witch."

"I'll make the arrangements, and we'll be ready when you boys get back," Kellen replied.

Aodhfin and Kellen put away their weapons and limped away from the glade. Cory snuggled in next to Kieran on the blanket and hugged his lover tight. Kieran lightly stroked his hand down Cory's side and held his lover.

"This next week is for us, Wolf. We're going to hide away from the world and make love to each other and complete the mating bond when the time is right."

INTERLUDE: THE PROFESSOR AND A HUNTER SPEAK ON THE PHONE

The renegade hunter, Alex Kincaid, sat in a booth at the back of a seedy dive bar in Boston's South End, trying to drink away his troubles. No matter how hard he tried to get close to the Belle kid, something kept blocking him. First, the hunter, Richard St. Martin, warned the kid off from working with him. The next interference came from the damned Emerald witch and her disruption spell throwing him off Belle and his cur of a boyfriend's track. So here he sat, drinking and trying to figure out how to find Belle so he might deliver the kid to the crazy Professor Simms. He took his time getting hammered, and his frustration grew at a rate where any little thing would set him off. Kincaid pounded back his whiskey and slammed back his beer. Before he signaled the waitress for another round, his phone rang.

"Kincaid."

"Did you find the boy yet?"

"You're aware I didn't fucking find the boy yet. If I did, he would be lying naked at your feet."

"I suggest you get out of the seedy bar you're in, sober up, and get back on his trail."

"His fucking trail is a month cold, thanks to the fucking Emerald bitch."

"She's been dealt with, so sober up, and start hunting him again. The compass in your possession will find him now. The witch who cast the disruption spell is dead."

"Hope you're right this time, cause if I need to find him without magic, I can't promise he'll be in pristine condition."

Kincaid's whiskey glass burst into flames and went out fast.

"A reminder, Mr. Kincaid, I can reach you anywhere."

"Fuck you, Professor Simms! You're easy to find as well. Don't threaten me with your parlor tricks. I'll deliver the Belle kid to you. Make sure my money is ready." Kincaid hung up and jammed his phone back in his coat pocket.

Now he was pissed. Taking orders from a mage rankled Kincaid. The wimpy professor giving him his marching orders would never be the kind to get his own hands dirty.

Like hell, I'll show the fucking pansy ass mage how a hunter finds his prey. Kincaid slapped enough bills down on the table to cover his bar bill and leave a tip for the waitress who kept his glasses full without him having to signal her. Calm, clear thinking is what he needed to be doing, if he planned to hunt a trained tracker such as Kieran Belle.

Rough, hardcore sex always served to calm him down. He could imagine the male prostitute as the professor as he fucked and beat him until he achieved orgasm.

12

To regain his strength, Kieran took a day longer than he thought he would need after his confrontation with his father and uncle. Cory did his best to spoil him by bringing food up to their bed and feeding Kieran in between rounds of kissing and snuggling, among other things. Once his strength came back, he rummaged around the cabin for the supplies they needed for their stay down at the beach. Kieran packed everything into two backpacks, and by the afternoon, the young men got on their way to the beach part of the Oisín compound. Before they left, Kieran took both his own and Cory's cellphones and put them on the night stand by their bed in the cabin. Billy trotted along and roamed off into the woods along the path to chase the local wildlife.

After walking for a couple of hours, the sound of the surf pounding reached their ears, and they soon reached a point on the path overlooking the coast. Kieran stopped to let Cory take in the view of the ocean waves crashing into the rocky coast. The sea spray reflected rainbows as the water splashed off the cliffs. The white caps danced on the blue-green water of the inlet as the waves made their way toward shore. Cory stood entranced, watching the unfamiliar sight.

Kieran nudged his partner, and they resumed making their way to the place where they would spend the next week. The pathway wandered along the coastal cliffs at the edge of the forest and followed a gradual slope down to a secluded and sheltered sandy beach. When they arrived on the beach, Kieran set down his pack and helped Cory out of his. They took the tent from Kieran's pack and got the shelter set up. Kieran set up a fire ring of stones. Together, the lovers gathered wood from the forest at the edge of the beach and built a fire. While Kieran started getting things ready for dinner, Cory settled the rest of their equipment in the tent. He set up the sleeping bags as one big bag and settled the pillows on top of their packs. With their camp set up and dinner cooking, Cory settled in beside Kieran on a blanket, watching as his boyfriend cooked over the open fire.

"You're a regular boy scout," Cory teased.

"Something of the sort at least, Wolf. I've been trained to survive in the wilderness by all my uncles. Uncle Brom taught me how to craft and use about anything as a weapon; my mother's brothers and my great-uncles taught me how to track, fight shifters, and how to recognize edible plants as well as how to trap, kill, and prepare wild game."

"The best I can do is push a cart around the grocery store if you want me to hunt down meat. I'm pretty handy in the garden though."

"I wouldn't expect anything less, farm boy. I think I would enjoy being a farmer's partner."

"I'm thinking I would be happy living a life on the coast."

"You would hate the winters up here. We measure the snow in feet, and the winter storms on the coast are fierce."

"I want to experience what winter is like up here. Do you think your grandparents would let us come for Christmas?"

"I'll ask them when I'm on speaking terms with Gramps again, but I warn you, this family celebrates the older traditions as well as the ones you're used to, Wolf."

"I don't care as long as we're making traditions of our own, Kieran."

"Cory, if I survive all the things I need to do this summer, you and I will build a lifetime of traditions. I promise you, we will live our own lives on our terms."

"Kieran, we survive the summer together or we die together. I want whatever time we have together to be lived to the fullest."

"We will live life to the max, Cory. Now let's eat. We're going to need our strength for all the lovemaking I have planned for tonight."

The young lovers ate to the sounds of the waves splashing against the shore and the hooting calls of owls in the woods. After they'd finished, Kieran sent Cory to the tent to grab a couple of towels from his pack while he cleaned up the dishes and banked the fire. When Cory returned, towels in hand, Kieran led him down toward the edge of the surf, drew him into a deep kiss, and slowly began to undress him. Cory started to move his hands to do the same to Kieran but was stopped when Kieran trapped his hands behind his back with his tangled t-shirt. Kieran kissed his way down Cory's throat and across his shoulder and back along the collarbone to the hollow of Cory's throat before working his way down Cory's chest to kiss and lave first the right nipple and across to the left one. Kieran sank to his knees as he worked his way down Cory's torso to his belly button where Kieran's tongue played in the hollow. Cory finally managed to free his hands from the tangle of his t-shirt as Kieran reached down and lifted Cory's left foot to remove both the sneaker and the sock. Cory used his newly freed hands to balance himself on Kieran's shoulders as his lover repeated his actions with the right foot. Now, Cory stood barefoot on the rough sand, clad only in his cargo shorts, and gazing down at his lover. Kieran surprised Cory by turning him around so he faced the sea as Kieran rose up behind him and held him tight, his arms wrapped around Cory's waist above his belt. Kieran rested his head on Cory's shoulder and took in the scents of his lover and the sea air for a few moments before his fingers unfastened Cory's belt and opened the fly on the cargo shorts. Kieran's hands quickly skimmed the shorts and the briefs beneath them off his lover, leaving Cory's body naked and gleaming in the moonlight. Cory turned around after stepping out of the shorts pooled around his ankles and slowly undressed Kieran with the same care and tenderness Kieran had showed him. When Kieran stood naked before him, Cory discerned how evident the scars across Kieran's chest became under the moonlight.

Cory made to speak, but Kieran silenced him with a kiss before leading him into the swirl of the sea. Cory shivered for a moment, unused to the cold waters of the Atlantic, but soon found warmth in Kieran's embrace. The lovers lost themselves in a kiss, which traveled to the depths of their souls.

Kieran's hands slid down Cory's body to cup his lover's ass and pull him in tight before pulling them both off balance and under the surface of the water. Cory broke free and surfaced, sputtering and spitting out salt water. He glanced around, looking for Kieran to surface, only to have his legs pulled out from under him by the still submerged Kieran. Cory crashed back into the water with a shout as Kieran surfaced between his legs. Kieran laughed as Cory rose up coughing up salt water and dove out of reach as his lover lunged for him. The two lovers dodged and splashed around in the surf until Cory finally snagged Kieran's braid and caught a finger in the chains, which held the braid together. He cursed as his finger bent backward before he pulled his finger free. Kieran caught his hand and kissed the injured finger before running his tongue across the palm of Cory's hand. He led Cory out of the water, where they scooped up their clothes before going back to the fire and settling on a log to dry off before crawling into their tent. Cory reached for Kieran's hair again but stopped at the top of the braid and gave Kieran a glance. Kieran grinned at Cory.

"I'll take the chains out of my hair and leave this mess loose for now. I have to do something with this mop or the length gets in the way. I should get my hair cut short and donate the braid to one of those charities, which makes wigs for cancer patients."

"As much as I believe in supporting charities, Kieran, don't you dare cut your hair."

Kieran reached up and popped the catch of the chains holding his braid together, and carefully slid the silver chains out of his midnight black hair. He ran his fingers through his hair and let his mane fan out over his back. The lovers settled into their sleeping bag and cuddled up for the night with Cory resting his head on Kieran's chest. Before long, they were asleep.

INTERLUDE: A WARNING, WHICH GOES UNHEARD

Richard St. Martin sat in the office of his antique store, listening to the message on Kieran Belle's voicemail.

"Hey, I'm busy and can't take your call now. Leave a message at the beep."

"Kieran, this is Richard St. Martin again. Word in the community is Alex Kincaid has been hired to hunt you down. He's already killed your witch contact in North Carolina, so don't rely on the cloaking spell she cast for you. Be careful. No one is sure where Kincaid is at the moment, and no one is sure how much magical help he has for backup." Richard disconnected the call and turned to figure sitting on the other side of his desk.

"Ambrose, I want Kincaid found before he finds Kieran Belle."

"And if finding Kincaid first isn't possible, Lord Hunter?"

"Rescue the boy and kill Kincaid, but do not turn him. I want the bastard dead."

"The task will be done as you command, Lord Hunter."

Richard St. Martin sank into his office chair once his right-hand vampire left the office. His own fangs elongated as his hunger at last overrode his control. Bright Goddess, how he hated his new existence. He called one of the many vampire sycophants from the former leader's court into his office. When the vampire entered, he was surprised to find an empty office, or so the room seemed. Richard pounced from behind the vampire and sank his fangs into the poor fool's neck and drank until the vampire began to crumble into dust. Hunger sated for the moment, Richard went back to worrying about Kieran Belle's safety.

13

———————

Kieran stood on the beach holding his camera, watching Cory and Billy playing fetch along the edge of the surf. Cory was only wearing surfer style board shorts as he tossed a stick for Billy to chase. Kieran regarded the two playing and rough housing as Billy tired of chasing the stick, pounced on Cory, and knocked him on his butt in the sand. He raised his camera and began snapping pictures. Cory was his favorite model to photograph. Cory possessed a quality the camera loved, or perhaps the quality was the fact the photographer was in love with the subject the camera caught. When the camera stopped advancing the film, Kieran put the camera away and went to join Cory and Billy.

Cory noted Kieran's approach down the beach and marveled at the play of Kieran's muscles beneath his skin. Kieran's swim trunks were a square cut boxer style and outlined his bulge and ass to perfection. Since their first night on the beach, Kieran had left his hair loose or tied back with a single leather thong at the base of his neck. As Kieran jogged down the beach toward where Billy and he were playing, Cory noted his lover had left his hair unbound and the waist-length mane fluttered out behind him. Billy spotted Kieran and raced down the beach toward him. The wolf leapt and collided with Kieran, driving the wind from the young man's lungs, and knocked him to the ground. The two rolled down the beach, getting covered in sand. Watching the pair, Cory thought about the small box buried in a side pocket of his pack. He'd carefully kept it hidden from Kieran since they left the Cooper family farm. All he needed was the courage to ask a simple question. Cory laughed at the pair and jogged over to help his lover back to his feet. Both Billy and Kieran shook themselves off, sending sand everywhere and making Cory cover his face as the sand flew his way.

"Hey, you two, stop."

Kieran laughed at the expression on Cory's face before grabbing his hand and dragging him into the surf. The lovers swam for a while before heading back up the beach to their campsite to dry off and prepare lunch. When they'd finished eating, Cory reached out and ran his fingers through Kieran's hair as he pulled him close for a kiss. His fingers caught in the salt-matted hair, and Kieran winced in pain at the tug.

"Sorry, babe. I didn't mean to pull your hair."

"Everything's okay, Wolf. The hazard of hair this long around the ocean, I'm not even sure why I ever grew my hair this long other than to spite Grandmother's sense of what's proper for men."

"Well, I love the length and the silky texture of your hair under normal conditions, but we're going to need to get the salt out before your hair is a total wreck."

"Let's grab our kits, towels, and some clothes. I've got a place I want to show you and we can soak in something besides salt water."

"What is this place?"

"A surprise I think you'll enjoy."

The young men grabbed their shower kits, towels, and changes of clothes and threw on their socks and boots. They tossed the gear into daypacks before heading out. The path Kieran set them on climbed the cliffs further down the beach from where they'd come down to the shore from their cabin. After about an hour of hiking, they arrived at the opening to a cave high above the ocean surf. Kieran lead the way inside, and when the way twisted around a corner and the sun was blocked, he stopped for a moment to let Cory's and his eyes adjust to the darkness and the faint traces of bioluminescence. Cory's indrawn breath of surprise after his eyes adjusted confirmed to Kieran choosing to show him this place was the right thing to do. Kieran took Cory's hand and led the way deeper into the cave system. Cory made out the sound of running water in the distance. Soon, a different source of light brightened the cave and reflected off a pool of water. The light came from veins of quartz in the walls stretched to the surface. Cory's gaze penetrated the dark to recognize where places for torches were set around the walls of the cave.

"This is beautiful, Kieran."

"If you will tolerate my magic for a moment, Cory, I can truly bring the beauty here to life for you."

"For you, I'll endure anything."

Kieran kissed his lover, turned, and made a strange gesture with his hands before slapping his left hand against the wall. Silver magic spread from his fingers to form a spider web of illumination as the magic flowed around the cavern. In the places where his magic touched the crystals set into the walls, they burst into silver light, brightening the cavern to early afternoon illumination. Before Cory, stretched a series of natural pools and a small waterfall, the source of the running water sound he'd made out as they made their way here. A couple of the pools appeared to be steaming hot springs.

"This can't all be natural."

"No, everything is shaped by magic, mostly Emerald, Sapphire, and Ruby. The lighting system is shaped with Silver magic, which also acts as a ward against intruders when activated."

"This place is amazing, but I thought your family only possessed Silver magic."

"The men of the family only possess Silver magic. Like your father, Grams practices Sapphire magic. My late great-aunt had Ruby magic and her husband had Emerald; they're the ones who shaped this place along with Gramps."

"Well, this place is beautiful."

"We can put our things over here."

Kieran lead the way over to a stone bench in a nook designed with hooks for towels and clothes around the walls. The young men stripped off their boots, socks, and shorts. Naked, they followed a smooth path down to the level of the pools. They made their way over to the pool at the base of the waterfall and eased themselves in. The water came to their waists as the walked across to the waterfall. To Cory's amazement, the water temperature hovered around body temperature instead of being ice cold. He followed Kieran under the waterfall and helped him rinse as much of the salt out of his hair. They realized they left their kits back on the bench. Kieran lead Cory back toward where they left their things and settled him into a warm pool with carved benches around the rim about a foot below the surface. Kieran walked back to their things and grabbed their kit bags. Cory admired the beauty of his naked lover's muscles flexing beneath his skin as he walked away to get their kits. The play of Kieran's waist-length hair across the top of his firm bubble butt made Cory's cock firm up fast. Watching Kieran's soft, thick cock swaying over his plump ball sack gave Cory a hard-on. As Kieran stepped down into the pool near where Cory sat, Cory moved enough to take Kieran's soft cock into his mouth and began to tease the head with his tongue. Kieran moaned as Cory's tongue bathed his cock and brought the shaft to its full length and hardness. Cory buried his nose in Kieran's well-trimmed pubic hair and inhaled the scent of his lover as he worked over the hard shaft with his tongue, lips, throat, and using his teeth to tease.

Kieran buried his hands in Cory's thick blond hair as he giggled as his lover's beard tickled his balls on each downward motion of Cory's head. He remembered complimenting the bearded appearance when Cory first started to grow one. He complained about the beard the first time they made out when Cory started letting the beard grow, when the beard scratched in those early stages of growth. Now Cory's thick, soft beard added an extra layer of pleasure to their lovemaking when Cory applied his oral skills to either Kieran's cock or ass. With a deep moan of pleasure, Kieran filled his lover's mouth with his seed. He stepped back enough to free his sensitive cock from Cory's ministrations. Cory loved to work Kieran's cock beyond his orgasm to keep him hard and to try to coax a quick, second load from Kieran's still tingling balls. If Kieran didn't leave room or leverage to withdraw, Cory would win the mini battle and enjoy the cries of pleasure-filled anguish coming from deep in Kieran's chest.

This time Kieran had room to escape, though he didn't go far. Once his cock was clear of Cory's mouth, Kieran dropped to his knees in the pool between Cory's legs, and leaning forward, captured his lover's throbbing cock in his mouth to return the favor. Kieran enjoyed the sensation of Cory wrapping his fingers into his hair, one of his favorite things to do to softly guide Kieran's pace. Cory's moans of pleasure increased when Kieran relaxed his gag reflex and let his lover's thick cock slip deep into his throat. Before long, Cory was on the edge, and his tightening grip dragged Kieran down to the root of his cock, driving the head into the younger man's throat as he blew his thick load. After the first blast rocketed down his throat, Kieran was able to slide back up Cory's shaft and take the rest of his lover's load into his mouth. Despite the number of times he'd swallowed, Cory's load was still a strange burning sensation and bitter flavor in his mouth. He didn't care this was a part of Cory, and for a while, it would be a part of him. When Cory's orgasm ended, Kieran licked his lover clean before pulling off and dragging Cory into the pool.

The lovers went under the surface and emerged locked in each other's arms in a deep kiss. Kieran's hair formed a soggy curtain around both of their faces and kept them from noticing a shadow move across the cavern and into a hidden alcove. With reluctance, they separated from each other before they waded back to the edge of the pool, and Cory grabbed the shampoo from the ledge before Kieran reached the bottle. He turned Kieran so his back was to him and squirted a decent amount of shampoo into his hand before proceeding to lather up Kieran's hair. Having his scalp massaged always put Kieran into a trance-like state of pleasure. Cory loved listening to Kieran's faint moans as he worked his fingers over his head and down his neck. He was never sure how Kieran managed to keep his hair clean on his own but suspected magic played a role in the process somehow. Once Kieran discovered how much Cory loved to play with his hair, he'd become shameless in allowing Cory to wash his hair for him at least twice a week. Cory used his handhold on Kieran's hair to bend his lover's head back and steal a kiss before dunking him to rinse the shampoo out of the midnight locks. Once they washed away all traces of salt and sand, Kieran led them over to another pool of warm clean water. It was big enough for two people to share while lying down. The lovers entwined on the low shelf, which put most of their bodies underwater as they began to tease and caress each other. They brought each other to climax and viewed their seed flowing and mixing in the water before drifting off to the pool's drainage system. Kieran and Cory pulled themselves from the pool and padded over to where they'd left their towels and clothes to dry off before Kieran picked up his kit and led Cory naked into a smaller side chamber designed for sleeping or making love, he never quite decided what his grandparents, great-aunt, and great-uncle had crafted this chamber for. Here, he dug out lube and condoms, and set them on the small shelf beside the large padded outcropping, which served as a bed. Now in this smaller chamber, Kieran's dominate personality slipped away as he let Cory take the lead in their lovemaking. Cory bent Kieran over the edge of the outcropping forming the base of the bed. He spread Kieran's ass cheeks, and kneeling behind his lover, began to lick and rim the exposed hole. Kieran gave himself over to Cory's ministrations. Pleasure soon overwhelmed any thought process in Kieran's mind as Cory relaxed the muscles of his hole and began to slide a finger in to begin loosening him for entry. Kieran wanted to reach down and take himself in hand but remembered from previous experience if he did, Cory would stop and replace tongue and fingers with the flat of his hand in a spanking. During one of their nights of passion back in Little Rock, Cory had stopped rimming him, flipped him face down, made Kieran count the spanks, and thank him for them afterward. Their agreement stated, unless otherwise arranged, Cory was the boss in the bedroom.

Cory reached up with his other hand and pulled Kieran's cock and balls back between his legs to tease them with his tongue as he worked on his lover's ass. The tongue traced upward from the tip of Kieran's cock, along the shaft, over the tightening ball sack, and along the taint into the crack before circling the edge of the hole. Tongue plunged deep into the hole elicited deep moans of pleasure from its owner and a copious amount of pre-cum to leak from the tip of the cock. Kieran shivered as his lover teased him again and again to the brink of coming, only to back off and deny release. Before long, he found himself begging Cory to fuck him. Taking mercy on his prostrate lover, Cory rose and grabbed a condom from nearby. He suited up, added enough lube to make entry painless, and slid his cock into Kieran's ass to the hilt on the first push.

"Oh, Bright Goddess, yes! Oh, how I've needed you to do this to me, Wolf. Take my ass and make me yours," Kieran wailed in pleasure.

"You crave these times I take full control like this, don't you, lover? You need to let go of everything and be. To be owned by someone who will never let you go."

"Yes, yes. Take me, own me, and never let me go. I need you more than you will ever realize, Wolf."

Cory slid in and out of Kieran's ass until his lover shuddered beneath him, and with a silent sob of joy, exploded in a full body orgasm. Kieran's cock still pinned back between his legs exploded as his whole body achieved orgasm and splattered the back of his legs and Cory's feet to the ankles. Cory pulled out and removed the full condom, making sure not to let the contents spill, as Kieran collapsed on the bed and slid to his knees. Once the condom was disposed of, Cory returned to his lover and helped him stand. They made their way back down to the bathing pools where Cory cleaned them both up. Kieran revived as Cory ran the washcloth over his still sensitive cock head. He grabbed his lover's hand and stopped the torment. He wrestled the cloth away from Cory, and with lots of love, washed his body from head to toe, taking extra care around Cory's cock and balls. When they were cleaned up, they went back to the bedchamber and cleaned the room up before turning in for the night. Cory settled in first, and Kieran climbed in beside him, settling in with his head resting on Cory's furry chest. Cory's steady breathing soon had Kieran drifting away on the edges of sleep. Strong fingers stroked through Kieran's hair; finding the places on his scalp relaxed him and sent him to sleep.

Cory lay watching his lover drift off into peaceful sleep.

14

———

Kieran and Cory spent the last day of their escape swimming and playing along the ocean shore. They packed away all their gear and stowed the equipment away in the cavern before cooking dinner together.

"I think you're extra special. You have a second magic about you when you're in the kitchen."

"I spent a lot of time in the kitchen both here and at home with Mom's family. Cooking at the Belle estate kept me out of the way of Grandmother and the rest of the Matriarchs. Here, Grams loves to cook and she loves to teach. When we get back to Little Rock, I'm going to spoil you with a proper home-cooked meal."

"I need to increase my exercise regiment if I let you do the cooking."

"We're both going to have to up our exercise routines, Wolf. I want you to start training with me so you can pick up some decent self-defense skills."

"Kieran, I've never been a fighter. I'll train with you, but I'm never going to be anywhere near your level."

"I'm not worried about you matching my skill level, Wolf. What I want is for you to be able to hold off an attacker long enough either for me to get to you or for you to find a way to escape."

"As long as we agree you aren't training me to enter any *Fight Club* events."

"I promise this will be a strict bully deterring 101."

Wrapping his arms around Kieran's lean waist, Cory pulled his lover back against him and nuzzled his nose into Kieran's neck in the wolfish way, which drove his lover nuts. Cory turned his lover's head and kissed him before letting him go to finish cooking. Kieran sighed and refocused on their dinner. After dinner, they retired to the sleeping chamber, and they made love.

* * *

IN THE MORNING, they packed up their clothes and personal gear, and headed back to the main residences of the compound. At the top of the path leading back to their cabin, Cory stopped to gaze out over the ocean one more time. Kieran came up beside him and wrapped an arm around Cory's waist.

"When we finish the rituals, which will grant me proper access to the powers of the Silver Witch, we'll come back here, Wolf. In the family grimoire is a ritual, which will let us complete our mating bond without worrying about what the magic in our blood might do to each of us. This is a full moon ritual, so we'll have to wait until next month before we try the ritual."

"So we can be mated, I can wait another month for whatever we need to do."

"Well, I found this one ritual we might do with a quick trip into town, Wolf."

"What ritual do you mean, Kieran?"

Kieran dropped his pack, sank down on one knee, and presented Cory with a small box. Cory glanced at Kieran, stared at the box, and back at Kieran again. His heart fluttered. Was Kieran thinking the same thing he'd been thinking all week? Kieran smiled and opened the box to reveal a gold ring set with a moonstone and a matching set of gold rings etched with the Gaelic phrase, *Deo mo chroí,* forever my heart.

"Corwin Samuel Cooper, will you do me the honor of becoming my husband?" Kieran said as he took the moonstone ring from the box and placed the ring at the tip of Cory's left ring finger, since the soul mate band, which had once occupied the finger, was gone.

Cory eyes, actually brimming with tears, gazed down into Kieran's silver eyes. He smiled and answered with one word. "Yes."

Kieran slipped the ring on Cory's finger and kissed his lover's hand. Before he rose to take Cory in his arms, his lover's pack was on the ground beside his own, and Cory was now gazing into his eyes from the same level. Amber eyes burned with love and devotion as Cory raised a similar small box up into Kieran's line of sight.

"I guess I'm silly to ask you the same question in return," Cory said as he opened his box to reveal a gold ring set with an uncut canary-yellow diamond and placing the ring at the tip of Kieran's left ring finger. "But, Kieran Samuel Belle Oisín, will you do me the honor of becoming my husband?"

Silver eyes locked with amber eyes across the tiny distance, and Cory realized he needed no vocal response as he witnessed the love burn for him in Kieran's eyes. Kieran struggled to speak around the lump, which was wedged deep in his throat, so he nodded his head in the affirmative. Cory slipped the ring on Kieran's finger, and he too kissed his lover's hand. Reaching out, Kieran drew Cory into a deep kiss, which only broke when the lovers ran out of air in their lungs.

They stared at each other and laughed.

"I can't believe we both came up with the same idea," Kieran said between giggles.

"This is a crazy situation, although I didn't pick out matching wedding bands. I thought we would pick them out together."

"Actually, I didn't pick them out. I inherited them from my mother. She left me hers in her will, much to Grandmother's annoyance. Dad put his in the box on the day they read mother's will, and he understood her wish. She also left me the engagement ring, which is an heirloom as well."

"Well, the ring I gave you isn't an heirloom, but I did find the diamond myself down at the Crater of Diamonds State Park, back home in Arkansas. I mounted the stone uncut so the person I gave the ring to would understand my love is as raw as the diamond on his finger."

"Such a beautiful ring, Wolf, and the diamond will always remind me of your eyes."

"So what does the writing say on the wedding bands?"

"*Deo mo chroí*, which means 'forever my heart.' The man Beauty chose to be her eldest daughter's husband gave her these bands when they married in his native Ireland. Rumor says the prince gave this engagement ring to Beauty. I don't how much is true and how much is legend. All I care about is my parents used these wedding bands last, and Mother broke tradition by giving them to me. They should have gone to my eldest sister."

"It's an honor to be married using your parents' rings. I don't care who else legend says wore them. So, I'm guessing the ritual in town is to go before the clerk of the court and do the paperwork and say our vows."

"Yes, we'll go to the town offices, do the paperwork, and appear before a notary to get our marriage recognized. You realize, of course, we'll need to have witnesses, because Grams, for one, will never forgive me if I elope."

"Oh no, we are not getting your grams upset with us. I don't care what the rest of your family thinks of me. I'm not upsetting Grams. Come on, let's get back so we can surprise your family at dinner tonight."

* * *

AFTER RETURNING TO THEIR CABIN, the young lovers got cleaned up and put on dressy clothes before heading over to the main house for dinner with the rest of Kieran's family. While Kieran's grandmother finished getting the food ready, the boys joined Kieran's grandfather, father, and uncle in the family room. None of the older men paid attention to the near idiotic grins of joy on either of the young men's faces. Grams entered the family room to announce dinner and stopped short when she spotted the excited expressions on Kieran's and Cory's faces being ignored by her husband and sons.

"Honestly, I'm amazed at how dense the men of this family can be. I've told you that all your attempts to hurt or separate the boys are over. They've both passed all of your tests, so get over your plotting. I'll not have Cory thinking this family is anything like the House of Beauty. Shame on you, Kellen Kieran Oisín, for failing to recognize your own son and his boyfriend have news."

Kellen and Brom turned to face the boys and espied Cory standing in a possessive position behind Kieran, their left hands clasped over their right hands. Brom spotted the Belle engagement ring on Cory's left ring finger first. He also spotted the unusual ring on Kieran's hand on the same finger.

"So which of you asked the other one first?" Brom asked.

"What are you talking about, Brom?" Kellen asked.

"For the super witch of the family, you are so dense, little brother."

"What am I missing?"

Kieran raised his and Cory's left hands and held them out to his father so the rings appeared under his nose, and the boys said in unison, "He asked me to marry him, and I said yes."

Kellen dragged both boys into a fierce hug, which quickly turned into a family hug as Brom, Grams, and Gramps joined in to congratulate the boys. All the tension of the past few weeks seemed to melt away over the joyous news. When the hug finally broke, Grams urged everyone into the dining room so they might eat while they discussed the plans for Kieran and Cory's handfasting. Cory appeared confused by the terms Grams and Gramps tossed around. Kieran took pity on his fiancé and leaned close to explain after stealing a quick kiss.

"A handfasting is the old religion's version of marriage, only more than the church or the state's version of marriage, Wolf. Both parties declare their intention and they're marrying of their own free will, not reciting forced vows."

"Oh, I like the sound of this. So I guess this means no one in your family was ever forced into a shotgun handfasting."

"No, Wolf. You can't force anyone into a handfasting; the goddess and the god would never bless a forced union. The choice is up to you if you want to go through the ceremony. If you don't want to because of a conflict with your own beliefs, I'll understand, and we won't be any less married because we didn't get handfasted."

"I've never been much of a church goer. I've only ever gone because Mom and Dad were big on us doing everything as a family. I'm about to become a member of your family, or we're starting our own family, so we should have our own traditions, and if they're a blend of both, I don't think the divine will be too upset with us."

"You'll find our traditions are pretty blended in this family. I don't think we're going to get much say in how the ceremony is done, only whether we want to participate. As I said, they can't force us to be handfasted. They didn't even insist on offering ceremony to Mom and Dad when they announced their engagement."

"What about your mother's family? Will they attend?"

Kieran snorted in indignation. "No, Grandmother Belle would never lower herself to attend a ritual of the old religion. She's High Church."

Cory was sad; part of Kieran's family wouldn't be in attendance, but the expression on Kieran's face said he was glad they wouldn't be around to disrupt the ceremony. A cough from Grams' end of the table dragged both boys' attention to the Matriarch of the Oisín clan.

"I'm asking, dear boy, if you and Cory both agree to be handfasted. Do try to pay attention."

"Sorry, Grams, I was trying to explain to Cory what everyone else was talking about before you got him to agree to something he doesn't want."

"Of course, so now he understands what we're talking about, what's your decision?"

"We agree to be handfasted, Grams. Will you and Gramps consent to be High Priestess and High Priest for our handfasting?"

"Of course, we would be honored to serve in those roles, Kieran.

We will need to invite a few other mages to properly call the quarters. Do you have anyone you want to attend the ceremony?"

"If the ceremony doesn't offend them, I think we need to invite Cory's parents, and if we blend traditions enough, Cory's dad might agree to serve as the Western Guardian, since he's a Sapphire mage. What do you think, Wolf?"

"I think they'll come because they'll be mad if we don't at least invite them."

"I want to invite Professor Mason, which will give us an Emerald mage for the Northern Guardian. I don't recall any Ruby mages I can call or...wait, I can ask one if he'll come. Mr. St. Martin would be perfect for the Southern Guardian since he's a hunter as well as having Ruby magic."

"Good, Kieran, after dinner, let's call Cory's parents and invite them, and if you'll let me speak to Cory's father, Sapphire mage to Sapphire mage, I think I can convince him to serve."

"Oops, I almost forgot to ask, Wolf. We need to take precautions to protect the barrier spell. Can your mother control the shift? This is a full moon ritual, and if she shifts, the ceremony won't be ruined, but the shift will cause other problems."

"Yes, she's only ever shifted when she's wanted or needed to do so."

"Okay, filling the Eastern Guardian's position is the only thing left. Dad, I gather from reading the ceremony in the family's grimoire, by tradition, the heir to the Silver Witch stands as the Eastern Guardian, but I need you at full strength for the other ritual Cory and I want to undergo during the full moon, so would you mind if Uncle Brom stood in the East for our handfasting?"

"Since I think I can guess the other ritual you're talking about, Kieran, I don't mind letting Brom take my place in the East. I think perhaps your grandfather and I should switch roles and let me be the High Priest for your handfasting while he serves as guardian for your second ritual."

"What is this second ritual, Kieran?" Gramps asked.

"The mate-binding ritual. Cory and I need and want to mate at least once without barriers so his mating drive is locked into me and I'm locked into him. We can't make love to mate if I retain my magic, because we wouldn't be able to tell what would happen if our opposing magic touched when our body fluids meet inside either of us. Only you or Dad are powerful enough to draw out my magic during the night of the full moon."

"You're choosing a perilous ritual, Grandson. Not only for the two of you, but for the guardian of the ritual. If anything happened to me during the ritual, you might never get your magic back."

"I understand, Gramps. This is why I asked Dad to stand as guardian. Health wise, he's younger and stronger than you are. Magic wise, he's between us in power, and as your direct heir, he is able to call on your power to help him if something goes wrong. I'll leave the decision up to you two to discuss and decide."

The discussion ended as everyone began to dig into dinner. After dinner, Cory and Grams retired to the kitchen to call his parents while Kieran went with his father and Gramps to the library to discuss the mate-binding ritual in further details. Brom left to return to his own cabin near his forge.

INTERLUDE: THE BARRIER DISCOVERED

Alex Kincaid and the small group of shifters they gave him searched for weeks along the back roads of coastal Maine for a trace of Kieran Belle and Cory Cooper. The special compass he possessed didn't work to specifications. The needle kept spinning madly around, never settling in to point out where his quarry lay. At the directions of the mysterious Master, several additional shifters arrived from the dark Alpha's pack to help him locate his prey. He didn't trust any of the shifters to guard his back beyond this mission, and one of them he didn't trust at all. The girl, Marissa Holden, didn't seem ruthless enough to be a member of the dark Alpha's pack and survive.

The little female shifter came wrapped in Ebony magic. Control spells wrapped around Marissa so tight she only followed certain outside orders. Kincaid didn't understand why the mysterious Master sent this particular shifter since she, unlike the others he'd been sent, needed so many controls.

At the next turning on yet another dusty dirt road, Kincaid learned why the girl was sent.

"Stop here. Kieran passed by here."

"How can you tell?"

"By his scent and his power. Let me out so I can find his path."

Kincaid stopped the van and let the Marissa and two other shifters out to locate the path. Sniffing the air, the girl moved around and came to a stop about two hundred feet to the right of the van. She pointed. "His trail goes this way."

Kincaid stared at where she pointed and surveyed only trees. He gestured to one of the shifters, and the man raced ahead. About a hundred feet past the girl, he slammed into a barrier of some sort, screamed, and burst into flames.

"What the hell?" Kincaid screamed at the girl.

"Defense spell. Only the invited may cross."

"Why didn't you say something?"

"You didn't ask or order me to give you a warning."

After a brief moment of confusion, Kincaid's fiery temper burst. He lost control and smashed his fist into her solar plexus, driving the wind from her lungs and sending her to the ground where he beat her until she lost consciousness. He ordered his remaining shifters to check how far the barrier ran. *This is going to take longer than planned.* Time to come up with a plan B, in case he needed one.

15

———

A couple of days after getting engaged and setting the date for his handfasting to Cory, Kieran checked his cell phone for the first time in a couple of weeks and discovered the message from Richard St. Martin. He listened to the warning the hunter left him, and his blood grew cold, causing a shiver to run up his back. He quickly found Richard's number and returned his call.

"St. Martin's Antiques and Collectibles. How can we help you today?" came Richard's voice over the phone.

"Mr. St. Martin, this is Kieran Belle."

"Kieran, I've been worried sick. When I didn't get a call back from you right away, I feared the worst, but when I couldn't find you by magical means, I realized Kincaid wouldn't be able to do so either."

"Yes, a locator spell to find me would take a powerful Ebony mage to cast to pierce the spells I'm under. Thank you for the warning, Mr. St. Martin. I'll keep an eye peeled for any signs of him."

"Good, I realize you'll be careful. You possess the instincts to make a spectacular hunter, even if you are a male of the House of Beauty."

"I'm glad you think so, because I'm the current hunter-candidate of the House of Beauty. All my sisters failed the test."

"I'm sorry to learn your sisters failed Kieran, and I'm sorry for your loss. I trust you will lead the House of Beauty into a new era."

"Thank you, Richard. I need to ask a favor of you if you can travel and don't mind participating in a Pagan ritual. I would like you to stand as Southern Guardian at my handfasting to Cory on the 31st of July."

"I'm honored to be asked, Kieran, but I'm sorry, I made a promise to my fiancée before her death to give up my Pagan ways, and even though she's gone, I intend to keep my promise in honor of her memory."

"I'm sorry, I didn't even consider the idea you might be engaged. Of course I wouldn't want you to break a promise, and I understand."

"Well, you be sure to bring your husband by so I can meet him when you're out this way."

"I will, Richard. Thank you."

"You're welcome, Kieran, and congratulations."

The phone clicked off from Richard's end, and Kieran turned his phone off again. They would need to be careful when they went into Bar Harbor to get the marriage license and appeared before the notary to make their marriage legal under Maine law.

16

———

Later in the afternoon, following his call to Richard St. Martin; Kieran and Cory sat on the couch with Kieran between Cory's legs and leaning back against his lover's chest as they filled out Maine's Intention of Marriage form on a laptop perched on Kieran's knees. As they filled out the forms, Cory made mental note of Kieran's fast approaching birthday, knowing he'd need to arrange something with Grams and the rest of the family. They wanted to have everything ready for a trip into Bar Harbor to file for their marriage license and certificate. They were double-checking their information on the form before printing the form out when Uncle Brom knocked on the door to their cabin.

"Come on in, Uncle Brom. The door is open," Kieran called.

"Hey, guys, I realize you have rings and everything for your handfasting, but I wanted to do something for you," Brom said.

"You're doing enough by being the Eastern Guardian, Uncle Brom. You don't have to do anything else," Kieran told his uncle.

"Well, I thought you guys should have an honeymoon after we get all the paperwork done and filed. I figured you'd have to go before a judge or notary in town for an official marriage since neither Mom nor Dad is a licensed member of a clergy. Therefore, I booked you three nights at the Black Friar Inn. The inn is only a block away from the town offices and walking distance to all the attractions of Bar Harbor."

"Uncle Brom, this is a wonderful gift. What do you think, Wolf? Want to play honeymooning tourists with me?" Kieran teased Cory.

"I can think of several things I'd like to play with you, future Mr. Cooper."

"Oh you think so, future Mr. Oisín, or would you rather be the future Mr. Belle?"

"Okay, boys, I'm going to escape before I get drawn into this one," Brom said, raising his hands as he backed away from the boys. "Oh yeah, one last question. Which one of you gets the bachelor party and which one gets the bridal shower?"

Brom ducked and dodged the pillows, which were hurled his way as he stepped out of the cabin.

"So, in all seriousness, do we pick one family name or the other, or do we choose to hyphenate our names in some fashion?"

"I guess we're going to have to hyphenate names. I'm not sure I want to be Kieran Samuel Belle-Cooper-Oisín though, too much of a mouthful."

"Yeah, all those names are a bit much. I guess the question is which family will be the most disappointed in not being in our family name."

"Well, I don't have a problem with dropping the Belle part of my name, even though I'm likely to be the hunter for the House of Beauty by the end of the summer. I'd be happy being Kieran Samuel Oisín-Cooper or even plain Kieran Cooper," Kieran said with a grin.

"Well, as much as I'd like to have you take my name, I don't think we should drop your father's family name from our new family, so I can be happy with Oisín-Cooper as well," Cory said before kissing the top of Kieran's head.

Kieran set the laptop down on the coffee table and turned so his cheek was pressed against Cory's chest, and his lover wrapped him tighter in his arms.

"I like the sound of Mr. and Mr. Oisín-Cooper, Wolf, although the name change is going to create a nightmare of paperwork back at school."

"I like the sound of the new name too. We'll deal with the paperwork when we get back to school, if we're going back to school. Won't you have to stay here if you're the next hunter?"

"No, I can move the family seat wherever I choose to claim as my territory. We can even put the scare into your brother Jeff and his pack by claiming your parents' farm as the new seat of the House of Beauty."

"Oh my, you would rock his Alpha ass back a few steps. I think we should find someplace we can call our own, especially if we're going to raise a family to keep the House of Beauty going."

"Let's not worry about the future of the House of Beauty for now, Wolf. Let's enjoy some normal time together before we start worrying too much about the future."

Kieran snuggled in tighter to his lover, and Cory stroked Kieran's hair and enjoyed the warmth of his lover's body against his own. The two of them drifted off to sleep on the couch, content and safe in the other's arms.

When they woke later in the afternoon, they kissed and stretched to get the kinks out from their somewhat awkward sleeping arrangement. Kieran scooped up his phone from the coffee table.

"I should call Professor Mason and ask him if he will participate in our handfasting."

"Go ahead, Kieran. I'll go fix us a light snack while you talk to the professor." Cory kissed Kieran on the forehead as he got off the couch and headed to the kitchen.

Dialing his professor's number, Kieran waited as the phone rang several times before Professor Mason answered. "John Mason Photography. How can I help you?" The professor's deep baritone voice rumbled through the phone.

"Professor Mason, hi, this is Kieran Belle."

"Kieran, I thought you and Cory were in Maine for the summer. Are you guys okay?"

"We're fine, professor. Actually, we're getting married in a couple of days. We wondered if you might be available to come to Maine for a few days to participate in our handfasting ceremony on July 31?"

"Congratulations, Kieran, and please give my congratulations to Cory as well. I think I can get away around your date for a few days. What do you need from me by way of participation? I'm pretty rusty on the handfasting front."

"We would like you to stand as the Northern Guardian. We would also love for you to do our wedding photographs after the ceremony."

"Let me check into flights and make sure I'm not committed to anything else, and I'll call you back in a day or so to give you an update, Kieran."

"Thank you, Professor." Kieran hung up as Cory returned with a plate of cheese and summer sausage and two bottled waters.

"From the grin on your face, I gather Professor Mason said yes," Cory said as he set down the plate and handed Kieran a bottle of water.

"Well, he didn't say no. He has to check to make sure he doesn't have other plans and can get away around the date. He's going to check flights and call back. He sends his congratulations," Kieran replied as he cracked open the water bottle.

"I'm glad you asked him. Mom and Dad are coming, and Dad was excited about having a part in the ceremony. Mom said Dad is enchanting a special necklace for her, which will keep her shift at bay until she takes the pendant off."

"Glad we checked in on their plans. I don't want to cause your mother pain, but shifting once she's inside the barrier spell would be a bad thing. A shift would bring the barrier down and leave the whole compound vulnerable to attack."

"Babe, what a terrifying thought. No wonder your grandfather was so anxious when he learned Billy was a shifter. If anything happens to the collar while we're here—"

"Everything is okay, Wolf. The collar isn't coming off unless Billy agrees to have the collar removed or an Ebony mage equal to me in power breaks the spell."

The young men dug into their snack and relaxed on the couch until the food was gone. When they were finished, Kieran took the plate and the empty bottles back to the kitchen to clean up before they headed out to visit Uncle Brom at his forge.

INTERLUDE: THE RENEGADE HUNTER'S PLAN B

Alex Kincaid left a pair of his shifters behind to keep an eye on the barrier spell and the supposed path into the area where his target was hiding. He took the rest of his forces and headed into Bar Harbor to set up a base of operations since the town was the closest one. Kincaid figured the target or someone supporting him would have to leave and get supplies at some point. The watchers would alert Kincaid, and he would set a trap for the boy or whoever came to town. If he captured the boy, he might finally get paid; if they captured someone else, he'd have leverage to get the boy where he wanted him. He set his shifters up in various parts of the town, or village as the place called itself, and got himself a room at the Harborside Hotel. Once he settled in, he contacted Professor Simms to update him on the changes to the plan. To say the man wasn't happy was an understatement, but Kincaid informed him of everything. Unless a powerful Ebony mage was handy, they wouldn't get past the barrier spell. Now a waiting game began.

17

On Friday, the Oisín family along with Kieran and Cory piled into the family's large passenger van for the trip to Bar Harbor. The excited young men put their weekend bag in the back of the van before taking the bench seat at the rear of the van. Uncle Brom got behind the wheel to drive with Kellen in the front passenger seat. Kieran's grandparents took the middle row of seats. When everyone was buckled in, Brom started the van and headed for the gates of the estate. As the van passed through the gates of the estate and out on the road, which would take them out to Highway 3, none of the passengers spotted the watchers who noted several people leaving the hideaway. The family chatted away during the drive to Bar Harbor and recommended activities for the young couple in the back to think about doing during their short honeymoon.

"Make sure you take Cory out on the whale sighting and lighthouse tour, Kieran. You always loved going when you were a boy," Grams said.

"I promise I will make sure Cory gets the full Bar Harbor experience. I hope everything goes right in town today. Grams, did you manage to contact your friend about standing as the Southern Guardian?"

"Yes, dear. Emma. You remember Mrs. Handler, don't you, dear? You had her in school the year you and your father stayed with us."

"She was my fifth grade teacher, Grams. Does Mrs. Handler still remember me?" Kieran appeared a little worried.

"Okay, what did you do to this woman when she was your teacher?" Cory asked, knowing if Kieran didn't give him the answer, Grams would.

"Oh lord, this is embarrassing. Grams and Gramps sent me to the private school where Mrs. Handler taught gifted students how to control their magic. I was a horrible showoff because I'd been learning to use my magic for a couple of years. I also had the horrible problem of wanting to be the center of attention. So, Mrs. Handler decided one day I needed a special lesson." Kieran turned bright red in embarrassment and couldn't continue.

"So what happened?" Cory grinned, enjoying watching his fiancé blush and squirm.

"Dear Emma decided—since Kieran liked to showoff and acted like a bully—to let all the other kids get in a magical whack at him. She slipped a special training potion into Kieran's drink at lunchtime, which blocked his magic for the afternoon. When he started to bully one of the other boys and went to back his threat up with magic, he found himself defenseless. That's when the boy got mad and lashed out at him with a fireball. When the other kids he bullied realized he couldn't defend himself with magic, Kieran learned firsthand what he put them all through. Mrs. Handler made Kieran apologize to each student he bullied. The experience humbled our poor Kieran the way he needed."

"She was right to do what she did. I was so in the wrong, and I moped for hours afterward. When she figured I'd learned my lesson, she had all the other kids apologize to me for doing back to me what I'd done to them. I'm still not sure some of them forgave me. Afterward, I went out of my way to stop other powerful kids from bullying those with less power."

"Well, the lesson stuck with you. I've seen you face bullies on campus, plus the time you rescued Billy when Johnson got mad at him."

"Yeah, bullying isn't right. One of my classmates in high school was ready to commit suicide because the head cheerleader and her crew were bullying her. I caught her before she took the pills. To prove to her how easily bullying can be overcome, I recruited the help of a few friends at school, and we got her elected Junior Prom Queen and the president of the chess club elected as her Prom King. The expressions on the faces of the so-called in-crowd were priceless. Last, information I received, they were planning their wedding."

"Yes, they got married before you boys left Arkansas to come up here," Grams said.

"Hey, we'll be in town in a few minutes, so make sure you have everything," Brom called out.

Kieran and Cory reached for each other's hand and laughed as they both realized how nervous the other one was. They turned to gaze at each other, and their eyes spoke volumes about how much they loved each other. The van made the turn from the highway to Cottage Street and pulled into the parking lot for the city office building. Once the van was parked, they all climbed out and made their way into the office building to find the correct office for filing the Intention of Marriage form and pay the fees to get their marriage license and certificate. Only one other couple was in line ahead of them, so the wait to file and get the forms was only about the forty minutes the website mentioned the process would take to get the license, the certificate would be sent to them after the license was signed and turned in by the official who performed the service. Kieran asked if a notary was on duty to perform the brief civil service and deal with the paperwork, and they were directed to an office downstairs. After exchanging brief vows and signing the license before witnesses and the notary, Kieran and Cory were pronounced married by the laws of the State of Maine. For once, Cory moved faster than Kieran. He grabbed him and kissed him when the notary said they were now legal spouses.

"I love you, Mr. Oisín-Cooper," Cory said when he broke the kiss.

"And, I love you too, Mr. Oisín-Cooper," came Kieran's breathless response.

"Congratulations, gentlemen," the notary said as he handed them their copy of the license. "I'll get this filed, and you should receive your marriage certificate in about thirty days."

"Thank you," Kieran replied as he took the form, and with care, put the license away in the file folder, which held all the original paperwork before handing the folder over to his father.

The newlyweds and family exited the town office building and piled back into the van to head around the block to Summer Street where the Black Friar Inn was located. Uncle Brom informed them he'd reserved the room under Cory's name, guessing they might take at least Cory's family name. The young men laughed as they slid from the van and gathered their bags from the back of the van. They headed inside to the check-in desk, and the clerk found their reservation.

"Mr. and Mr. Cooper, welcome to the Black Friar Inn. We have you booked in room four. Here are your keys; take the stairs to the third floor. Breakfast in the restaurant is included in your room rate and the full menu is available. If you need anything, please make us aware and enjoy your stay."

"Thank you," they said as they picked up their bags and made their way to the stairs and up to their room.

When they arrived at their room, Kieran took the bag off Cory's shoulder and set both bags down in the hall before opening the door, sweeping Cory off his feet, and carrying him into the room to deposit him on the queen-sized bed. He grabbed their bags from the hall and toed the door shut. A stunned Cory lay on the bed, watching as a dominant Kieran moved toward him. Kieran's movement made Cory shiver as if he was watching a wolf stalking its prey or its mate. Kieran climbed up over Cory so his new husband was pinned to the bed by his weight. He proceeded to claim Cory's mouth in a deep kiss, which melted his lover into the mattress. Cory gave over everything to Kieran, letting him claim Alpha status.

Kieran broke the kiss and sat back, his ass resting on Cory's hips with his knees keeping Cory's arms pinned to his side. His silver-eyed gaze locked with Cory's amber eyes and bore into his soul, letting the older man understand who was in charge. Cory raised his head, exposing his neck in the traditional wolf sign of submission, and Kieran leaned down and sucked a hickey on his husband's neck, marking his territory. Moving enough to begin undressing his husband, Kieran peeled away Cory's shirt, exposing the beautiful sculpted chest, furred with its firm pectorals and erect nipples, which he leaned down and licked before taking the left one between his teeth and chewing lightly, eliciting moans of pleasure from his lover. He kissed his way across Cory's chest to the other nipple, which received the same treatment and drew forth more moans of pleasure. Knowing Cory wouldn't move, Kieran rose up and slid off the bed to divest Cory of his shoes, socks, pants, and underwear, leaving his glorious body naked. Kieran undressed himself before licking his way up Cory's left leg to nuzzle into his crotch and lick and suck on his lover's furry balls and tease the tip of his cock before the object of his attention filled with blood and lifted the object of his attention away to lie on Cory's firm stomach. Kieran returned his oral attention to Cory's balls, watching and listening as his lover tried to hold himself still as he moaned his passion at the attention his husband was lavishing on him. After spit soaking Cory's balls, Kieran licked his way up his lover's hard and thick shaft to capture the throbbing cock in his mouth as he slicked his fingers by stroking Cory's saliva soaked balls. Those slick fingers stroked down across Cory's furry taint into his ass crack to tease his hole until the muscle opened to admit first one finger, followed by two fingers, and after much teasing and edging Cory's hole, swallowed three of Kieran's fingers. Cory was begging between moans for Kieran to claim him.

"Please, babe, I can't take any more teasing. Please, I want you inside me. I need your cock buried in me."

"I'll decide when I'm ready to claim you, Mr. Corwin Cooper. I'm not done making this incredible body moan and ride the edge. You're not ready to be claimed yet, not while you can still string together full sentences. Only when your mind shuts down and you can't speak will I consummate this marriage."

True to his word, Kieran drove Cory to the edge of spending again and again until Cory couldn't speak at all, let alone string a sentence together. Drenched in sweat and pre-cum, Cory couldn't even plead with his eyes for Kieran to take him. Kieran stood and retrieved a condom and lube from his bag. He slicked his cock, rolled on the condom coated with lube, before pulling a rubbery Cory across the bed so his ass rested on the edge of the bed. With his legs lifted to resting on Kieran's shoulders, Kieran slid his hard cock into the exposed ass. As soon as the head of his cock stroked over Cory's abused prostrate, Kieran regarded his husband as he blew a massive load across his abs and furry chest. So hyped up was Kieran, the spams of Cory's ass on his cock had him filling the condom in only a few strokes. When his own orgasm subsided, Kieran slid gently out of his lover's ass. He picked Cory up and resettled his lover on the bed before going to the bathroom, cleaning himself up before returning with a warm damp cloth and cleaning up Cory. Once he'd rinsed off the washcloth, Kieran returned to the bed and curled up beside Cory, and drew his limp lover into his body, resting Cory's head on his chest and wrapping his arm around Cory. He stroked the sweat-damp hair back from Cory's forehead and kissed him on the forehead before they both drifted off to sleep.

Around six o'clock, the alarm on Kieran's phone went off, waking both young men from their long nap. Cory tried to snuggle back in against Kieran's chest, but his husband wouldn't let him.

"Wolf, time to get up, shower, and get something for dinner."

"Not hungry. I'm too worn out to move."

Cory's stomach chose to gurgle its own opinion on the matter of food. He groaned and with reluctance, sat up.

"I'm still as limp as a wet noodle. I did not realize what I was getting myself into when I decided to marry you. Where did my virgin lover learn such a skill?"

"Internet porn. I figured I needed to learn something to keep you interested in me once we were married."

"I will never lose interest in you, love. I never imagined being kept on the verge of orgasm for so long. I don't think I'll be able to come again anytime soon."

"Oh, I think you'll be surprised how many orgasms I can pull out of you over the next couple of days."

"You might want to wait until I write a will before you try and fuck me to death." Cory chuckled as he rose.

Kieran smiled at his husband and wrapped him in a hug before ushering them both into the bathroom to get cleaned up. Kieran reached up and undid the clasp holding the chain, which bound his hair at the nape of his neck. Flexing his shoulders, Cory caught a glimpse of the large bruise on his neck from Kieran claiming his territory. Kieran moved behind him and wrapped his arms around Cory's waist as he rested his chin on Cory's shoulder, tracing the mark he'd left with his tongue, and let a trickle of Silver magic flow over the spot. Kieran smiled. While Silver magic couldn't heal, the magic aided the body's natural processes; the bruise now appeared to be days old instead of only a few hours. Their eyes locked in the mirror, and Cory grinned as he wove the fingers of his left hand into those of Kieran's left hand. He leaned his head back on Kieran's shoulder as his husband licked across his neck and shoulder. Amazing how good letting go and trusting someone else to make the decisions for a while was. He shivered as Kieran's teeth took hold of his earlobe and nibbled the flesh to get his attention.

"You're thinking instead of enjoying, Wolf."

"Only about how wonderful letting my husband make all the decisions for a while is."

"We'll make all the important decisions together. Time to get in the shower, clean up, get dressed, and go down to the restaurant for dinner."

"Okay you'll have to let go for a moment so you can start the shower while I get our kits."

"Oh, who's becoming a feisty pup now?" Kieran chuckled into Cory's ear as he let him go and ducked as Cory laughed and swung at him.

"I'll show you feisty, Mr. Oisín-Cooper." Cory mock lunged at

Kieran and slipped out to get their shower kits while Kieran turned and got the shower going.

Cory laughed at how playful Kieran had become. Before he got their kits, Cory picked outfits out of their luggage and laid them out on the bed. While in the bedroom, Cory experienced a tingle of energy all over his body and shivered when he glimpsed the condom Kieran had used glowing silver where the used item hung on the lip of the trashcan. What Cory failed to spot was the small puddle at the bottom of the trashcan also glowed silver where small drips from the tip of the condom pooled. He padded back into the bathroom to gaze at a wet Kieran attempting to wash his hair without, Cory suspected, resorting to magic. Cory stepped into the shower and took over washing Kieran's more than waist-length hair. Kieran sighed and moaned as Cory's fingers worked magic along his scalp and neck. If not for the fact Cory refused to let him cut his hair, Kieran would be tempted to have his hair cut down to a short style.

"However did you manage to wash all this hair before I came along, love?"

"I admit I cheated and used magic. Not how I should be using Silver magic, but I bind the dirt to the shampoo and bind the shampoo to the water and let soap and dirt flow away down the drain." Kieran peered over his shoulder at Cory. "I enjoy having you wash my hair though. You find all these magic spots on my scalp and neck, and the tension flows away."

"I love washing your hair and your body. I can't get enough of being able to touch you. You are made to fit against me."

"I think the same way about how we fit together, Wolf. You came into my life when you did so you would catch me and put me back together when I fell apart."

"I haven't seen you fall apart yet, babe. You're strong, but I will be here to catch you should you fall, and I will hug all the pieces back together. Let's get finished in here and go downstairs so we can eat. I want to walk on the beach in the moonlight with you after dinner."

Kieran turned and embraced Cory. Cory experienced a strong tingle along his skin, which signaled that Kieran had used Silver magic on both of them. He did seem cleaner than he'd ever been before and shot his lover a puzzled glance as Kieran reached behind him and turned off the water.

"All clean. Magic is useful when you're in a hurry; the spell even exfoliates for a deep clean." Kieran grinned and grabbed a towel, proceeding to dry Cory and himself.

They padded out into the bedroom area and dressed in the outfits Cory picked out. For Kieran, a dark blue polo shirt—this brought out the almost blue highlights in his hair—khaki shorts, and leather sandals. Cory drew on a green polo shirt, khaki shorts, and tan boat shoes. Neither young man wore underwear. Cory grabbed his wallet, room key, and phone, and slipped them into his pockets before doing the same for Kieran. Hand in hand, they left the room and descended to the Friar's Pub on the first floor of the inn. They found a table toward the back of the pub and settled in. Cory's confidence waivered a little when confronted with a menu of mostly seafood dishes he'd never experienced before.

"Relax, the food isn't going to eat you. Will you let me order for us both?" Kieran asked.

"Yeah, I'll let you order for us. This is beyond me. Seafood back home is fried catfish or crawdads."

"Yeah, neither of those is seafood. You're on the coast, so let me introduce you to real seafood."

The waiter arrived in a moment. Kieran glanced up at him, his eyes shining silver in his amusement at Cory's idea of what seafood was.

"Welcome to the Friar's Pub. I'm your server, Friar Tim. What can I get for you guys?" he asked.

"Two bowls of cioppino and a bottle of Pinot Noir. We're celebrating." Kieran's voice took on the same thick Maine accent as their waiter.

"So, what are you celebrating, guys?" Tim asked as he jotted down their order.

"We got married today." Kieran beamed as he captured Cory's left hand across the table so their matching gold rings caught the waiter's attention.

"Well, congratulations, guys. I'll be back with your order in a few minutes." He turned and headed off to the kitchen.

"You're showing off, babe. Your accent got so thick, following along got difficult in places. What is cioppino?"

"Cioppino is a hearty seafood stew, full of mussels, clams, scallops, crab, and fish. Trust me, the Friar's Pub is famous for their cioppino." Kieran's Maine accent vanished while he talked with Cory.

Tim returned with their order a few minutes later and set the steaming bowls of stew in front of each of them with care before breaking the seal on the wine and pouring a splash in Kieran's glass for him to sample. Taking a sip, Kieran let the red wine swirl around his tongue for a moment before swallowing and nodding his head in approval for Tim to pour two glasses. Once the wine was poured, Tim went off to check on his other customers, leaving the guys to dine in peace. Kieran eyes were on Cory as he dug in and tried the cioppino, waiting to find out what his reaction would be. The hearty combination of flavors washed over Cory's taste buds, and after swallowing, he smiled at Kieran. They sat and ate; looking at each other with all the love they had for each other. When they were finished, Tim came and cleared their dishes, and checked to discover if they wanted dessert.

"Thank you, but we'll pass on dessert, Tim. If you'll bring the check, we'll be good," Kieran told the young waiter.

Tim left with the dirty dishes and returned a short while later with the folder containing the check, which he placed in front of Kieran before going to check on another customer. When Kieran opened the folder, he was surprised to find a note inside instead of a bill. He held the note up for Cory to read as well.

"Congratulations on your wedding. Another couple has paid for your meal. They wish you the best as you start your new life together. The Management."

"Wow, how sweet of this other couple. I didn't think we did anything to attract a lot of attention," Kieran said as he slipped a twenty-dollar bill into the folder as a tip for their waiter and slipped the note into his pocket.

Cory and he left their table and headed outside to walk down to the harbor and the beach.

Kieran and Cory stood out on the public pier overlooking the ocean, enjoying each other's company and the cool ocean breeze. Cory's gaze swept across the pier and spotted a tourist type sign mounted on a railing. Taking Kieran's hand, he tugged his husband over to the wayside sign. Cory was amazed to discover they were actually inside a huge national park.

"I didn't realize all this was a national park, Kieran."

"Well, the town isn't part of the park but most of the land around here is, including where the compound is part of Arcadia National Park. The park is close to forty-eight thousand acres in size."

"Wow, this park has a lot of land," Cory said as he pulled Kieran against his chest and hugged him tight.

"Yeah, the park is big. We can get the tour of the islands out in the bay, which are part of the park, tomorrow along with the whale watching tour, or if the weather is good and the tides are at reasonable times of the day, we might cross the land bridge over to Bar Island and spend the time between low tides out on the island's beach."

"We have time to do both before either your dad or your uncle comes to pick us up to take us back out the compound."

"I'm sure if we talk to the front desk clerk we can extend our stay in town a few days, so we don't have to cram everything into a couple of days."

"Don't you need to do more training? And what about the plans for our handfasting?"

"Training can wait, Wolf, and as for planning our handfasting, Grams is in control, so everything is well in hand. All we need to do is come up with any personal vows we might want to make. No, the only thing I still need to do is travel over toward Bangor to the Belle family estate and deal with Grandmother and the rest of the Matriarchs."

"I'm happy to stay in town longer then, Kieran."

"Lets go down to the beach and walk along the water's edge."

18

A few hours after their return to the compound, Kieran and Cory got cleaned up before heading up to the main house to have dinner with the rest of the family. Kieran and Cory went along the pathways, which led to the back of the house and in through the kitchen gardens to the kitchen proper. Líadáin was delighted to find both boys in her kitchen after their absence and put them to work shelling peas for dinner. She did a scan of Cory while the boys worked and stopped them both.

"I realize you're married and monogamous boys, but did you give into temptation during your honeymoon and have unprotected sex?"

"Grams?" Kieran was shocked by his grandmother's blunt question. "No, we used condoms every time, especially when I was entering Cory. Why? What's happened?"

"Our *mac tíre óg* here has no trace of Ebony magic left in his bloodstream. He's flooded with Silver magic. Do you have any of the condoms you took with you left?"

"Yes, ma'am, we put what was left back in Kieran's kit when we packed to come home from the Black Friar," Cory replied.

"*Mo stór*, go back to your place and bring me the condoms that are left. I have a theory about what might have happened."

Kieran sped from the house and raced back to their cabin, taking every shortcut to speed his journey. Cory sat dumbfounded at the worktable in Líadáin's kitchen until she prodded him to action.

"Keep shelling those peas, *mac tíre óg*. When Kieran gets back, we will have our answers to how your transformation was accelerated, and I suspect we'll also learn who the culprit was. Meanwhile, those peas aren't going to shuck themselves, so get busy."

"Yes, ma'am."

Kieran raced in through the front door of the cabin and headed up the stairs into the master bedroom where he collided with his father as the man emerged from the master bath, condom packets in hand. Guilt spread across Kellen's face at being caught red-handed. Kieran regained his physical balance while his emotional balance was still off kilter.

"Dad! What the hell are you doing here and why are you stealing condoms from our place?"

"Ugh, you caught me. I've got a hot date tonight, and I'm all out."

"You do realize, Dad, you're a horrible liar. Grams wants those so she can find out how and by whom Cory's blood transformation was accelerated, but I don't think I'll have to wait for Grams to work her magic on them to find the answer."

"No, you won't, Son. I pricked holes in them and put a tiny Silver magic spell on them, which allowed your loads to pass thorough but not Cory's. I wanted you to have the happiness your uncle didn't get. Now you and Cory can have all the raw sex you want without ever having to worry about accidents damaging your magic the way Brom's was damaged."

Kieran's anger flashed silver in his eyes, and Silver magic ignited around his hands and formed a binding spell around his father. Kellen attempted to break the spell, but to his surprise, he found he couldn't.

"While I love you dearly, Father, I cannot believe the lengths you and Gramps are going to, trying to force me to fit your stupid prophecy. I can't believe after you and Gramps promised to leave us be that you would deliberately put us at risk." Kellen was struggling to breath as Kieran's anger tightened the binding spell around him.

"Luckily for us, Cory's Ebony magic was already bound and weakened by his father's Sapphire magic or this would have been disastrous. Come on, let's get back up to the main house, so you can confess to Grams and Cory."

Kellen groaned when Kieran loosened the spell enough that he could follow Kieran back to the kitchen of the main house. Kellen was forced to stand, sheepishly looking at his mother like he was a naughty schoolboy as he confessed his role in Cory's transformation. With a look from Grams, Kieran dropped the binding spell on his father once the man's confession was out in the open.

"Kellen Kieran Oisín, I am so cross with you. Do you realize how much danger you put the boys in?"

"No, Mother. I wanted them to have the freedom to love each other fully without worrying about whether or not they were going to ruin Kieran's magic. I wanted Kieran to have his shifter and love him completely, in all the ways Brom couldn't love his."

"If Cory had not been as far along in his transformation, you might have killed him or Kieran. Lucky for everyone, I reinforced the failing binding spell on Cory's shifter genes. I can't predict what will happen since his blood carries only Sapphire and Silver magic. I can't foresee whether he'll shift or not. So you will keep an eye on these boys for me, Kellen."

"Yes, Mother."

"One more thing. None of us will mention this to anyone else, especially my husband or my other son."

The three men in the kitchen nodded their agreement, and Kellen beat a hasty retreat while Kieran and Cory returned to helping get dinner ready. Once they prepared everything to be cooked, Líadáin sent Kieran off to the living room to hang out with the rest of the men. Kieran entered the living room and was swept into fierce hugs by his uncle and grandfather, while Kellen held back.

"Okay what's the occasion for all the hugging?" Kieran asked as Uncle Brom released him from the hug.

As if Kieran's question triggered a response, Cory and Grams came in each carrying an armload of gifts.

"Happy Birthday, Kieran," everyone shouted.

"Oh, wow, I can't remember the last time anyone celebrated my birthday. Last year, I tested to become a full tracker. Thank you." Kieran turned and was wrapped in Cory's arms. Kieran kissed his husband. "I'm betting you're behind all this, Wolf."

"Well, partly, but I had Grams help me. I needed her help to get everything ready while we were off on our honeymoon. She told me you hadn't had a real birthday party in years, and I wanted to do something special."

Cory pulled Kieran over to the couch and settled in with Kieran resting against him as their family piled gifts around Kieran's feet. Cory reached to the top of the pile and handed Kieran a small gift-wrapped in bright paper.

"This one is from me, babe. Uncle Brom helped me make the pendant, but this is from my heart."

Kieran unwrapped the gift with care to find a black velvet jewelry box. Opening the box, he found a pendant shaped in the form of two wolves running side by side, one amber-eyed, the other diamond-eyed. The beautiful but imperfect forms of the figures told Kieran his uncle did the metal pour for the process while Cory created the actual wax pieces and the mold used to make the pendant.

"This is beautiful, Wolf. Would you put this on me?"

Cory took up the silver pendant, and everyone discovered he didn't flinch from the metal anymore. He pushed Kieran's hair out of the way, put the chain around Kieran's neck, and fastened the clasp. When the pendant was in place, Kieran turned far enough to be able to kiss his husband once again.

"Thank you, Wolf."

"You're welcome. Now you have lots of presents to open."

Kieran dove into the pile of presents like he was ten years old. The expression of joy on his face lit the room. In the midst of his excitement, Kieran plunked one of the bows from his presents on Cory's chest and mock whispered, "I'll save this present for later."

The family erupted in laughter, and Cory blushed a deep crimson. Once all the presents were opened, the family adjourned to the dining room for dinner and birthday cake. When everyone was groaning from how full they were, the family retired to the living room and were sitting down to relax when Kieran's phone rang with a tone he'd set but never expected to ring.

"Who in the world is calling you at this time of night, and what is with the horrible ring tone, Kieran?" Grams asked.

"The tone is howler monkeys and the bigger surprise the caller is Grandmother Belle."

"I didn't even realize she had your cellphone number," Kellen said.

"Actually, I think I left the number with Great-Aunt Desdemona on the off chance the rest of the Matriarchs might decide to overrule Grandmother. Well, I'd better play the game and answer her call," Kieran said, putting the phone on speaker as he answered.

"Huntress-emeritus, how may I be of service?" Kieran's voice almost broke.

Cory and the rest of the family beheld the strong, handsome young man, who was husband, son, nephew, and grandson transform for a moment into the frightened hesitant boy he'd been in one spoken line. Cory wrapped Kieran in his arms to lend him his strength. Bolstered by Cory's presence and the love of the rest of his family, Kieran drew his resolve back together and waited for his grandmother's reply.

"Your year is almost up, Tracker Kieran. The time has come for you to return home and resume your duties to this house."

"To which of my sisters do I report, Huntress-emeritus?"

"You will report to myself and to the Council of Matriarchs, Tracker Kieran. All your sisters failed the test."

"I shall return home and present myself as Hunter-candidate Kieran in a weeks time, Honored Grandmother."

"The Council does not choose to give you such status boy. You will respect your elders in the proper fashion."

Everyone in the room caught the ice and derision in the tone of the woman's voice when she called Kieran boy. Kieran's tone as he replied should have frozen the entire compound and the old woman on the other end of the line.

"The time has come, Honored Grandmother, for the Council to

respect me. The fact remains whether this Council chooses to recognize me or not, I am the last child of the last Huntress of the House of Beauty, which makes me the candidate for the test, regardless of my gender. I will be addressed as such until after the test."

"I'm impressed you developed a spine, boy. Come before the Council by the end of the week, and we will decide your standing in the House of Beauty."

"My father and I will arrive at the end of the week, Honored Grandmother, please make sure our quarters in Mother's suite are ready and waiting for our arrival."

"Do not presume to dictate to me, boy. You and your father will stay where I choose to put you. Until such time, Tracker Kieran, you will respect the Council's and my orders."

"As always, Huntress-emeritus, I am the Council's servant. A pleasant day to you, Honored Grandmother."

Kieran disconnected the call before his grandmother said anything more. He leaned back into Cory's embrace and let out a deep sign of relief as he tossed his phone on the coffee table. Cory hugged him tight and nuzzled into his neck.

"Well, as usual, a pleasant conversation. Interesting to note the old battle axe didn't thaw out any over the last thirty years," Grams said as she rose to go get beverages.

"I should come with you, babe. We can face her together."

"I love you, Wolf, and I want to take you with me, but you wouldn't last five minutes in the harpy's lair. I need to do this on my own, even Dad isn't going to be able to enter the Council chambers with me."

"You will need everything we can give you, Kieran, including the full powers of the Silver Witch. In two nights, your father and I will conduct the ritual to transfer the power and title of Silver Witch to you," Gramps said.

"But I didn't cast my personal energy into the barrier spells here to earn my place as an heir to your power, Grandfather."

"You, Cory and Brom will perform the ritual tomorrow at noon."

"Cory? Gramps, you're often coming up with bad ideas, and this is one of them. You realize exposing him to so much Silver magic at once will cause him harm."

"Kieran, your grams is a wise lady, but I can read your husband's aura from here, and he no longer possesses even a trace of Ebony magic in his system. He is the other half of your soul, so he should be part of these rituals as well. You will need him by your side when the time comes."

"If Cory's participation is what you require, he'll be part of the ritual. We'll meet Uncle Brom in the clearing at the center of the compound tomorrow before noon."

"Take the family grimoire with you tonight, Kieran. You will need to read up on the barrier spell and how to merge your power in with all the power of your ancestors," Kellen said.

"Okay, this is a lot to take in, so I think Cory and I will call an end to the evening. I will grab the grimoire on the way out. Thank you all for making this the best birthday ever."

Kieran and Cory hugged everyone and gathered up all the presents into a couple of bags Grams provided them. On the way out of the main house, Kieran detoured into his grandfather's library and crossed to the lectern, which held the Oisín family grimoire. The massive tome held every spell, potion, and history notes ever learned by the family from the time before the ancient war. Some of the languages in the book had been dead for millennia, while others were in such ancient dialects they were hard to comprehend. Kieran touched the book's cover and jumped back as the grimoire glowed before bursting open and flipping to a beautiful illuminated page of a man in silver armor battling a dark, undefined figure. Written in a language Kieran couldn't read was a passage that glowed with importance. Cory moved to stand behind Kieran and peer over his shoulder.

"Is this the prophecy, babe?"

"I'm not sure, Wolf. I can't read the language this passage is written in. Taking a wild guess, I think this is the ancient prophecy about the Silver Hunter. I will need to cast a translation spell on this page to be able to read what's written here."

Kieran closed the book, and the grimoire shrank in size to fit into one of the bags they carried.

"Well, at least the book doesn't make you carry around the deluxe family size," Cory joked.

"Yeah, if the grimoire stayed full-size, I would strap the thing to my handy pack wolf's back for him to carry home for me," Kieran said from behind one of his brilliant smiles.

"You do realize, Mr. Birthday Boy, you're still going to receive the traditional birthday spankings. How much they sting is up to your attitude." Cory's grin carried a huge trace of hungry wolf.

Kieran wisely decided to pick up the bag containing the grimoire to carry back to their cabin. The young men returned to their cabin and put away Kieran's gifts. Kieran set up the grimoire on a desk in the small office off the kitchen. Once in place, the book returned to its normal size and flipped open to the page containing the prophecy.

"Somehow, I get the idea the grimoire isn't going to let me ignore the old prophecy. I don't get what the book wants me to understand about the subject. The language is so old I'm not sure I can find a translation spell in the book that would work."

Kieran glared at the ancient book, almost as if willing the book to speak to him.

"Leave the prophecy for the night, babe. You didn't collect your last present yet."

Kieran turned to find Cory standing in the doorway of the kitchen with his shirt off, his jeans unbuttoned, and the zipper pulled down enough to reveal the top of his blond pubic hair and barely containing his swelling cock. Between the front door and the kitchen, Cory ditched his shoes, leaving him standing in the doorway barefoot. Kieran's eyes went to his lover's fur-covered chest and down the washboard abs to the invitation of the open jeans. With the grace of a hunting cat, Kieran pounced and locked lips with Cory. Tongues dueled for dominance until Kieran gave into his desire and let Cory assume control. The next moments made Kieran glad his current shirt didn't number among his favorites. The sound of ripping fabric was all the warning he received as Cory tore the shirt off him. His jeans soon pooled around his ankles, and he managed to toe off his shoes before finding himself hoisted over Cory's broad shoulders, being carried to their bedroom.

On the way up the stairs, Cory administered Kieran's twenty-two birthday spanks as they reached the massive bed. Cory shrugged Kieran off his shoulders to the bed, where he landed face first, leaving his crimson glowing ass exposed to Cory's viewing pleasure. As Kieran reached back to rub his ass, Cory caught his hands and held them away from his husband's body.

"You keep your hands on the bed, mister. I'll tend to your ass in a moment. You passed up your chance to be in control of how you received your gift downstairs. I'm the boss tonight." Cory's voice was deep and carried the edge of a growl, which never failed to drive Kieran mad with lust.

"I promise I'll behave, Mr. Oisín-Cooper," Kieran purred back.

"You can bet your sweet ass you'll behave, Mr. Oisín-Cooper," Cory growled back.

Kieran listened as Cory's jeans hit the floor before wet warmth and the bristle of facial hair began working over the red globes of Kieran's ass, working their way toward the split between the firm mounds. Soon, firm hands gently spread the flesh as the probing tongue established its presence by swiping along the exposed flesh and returning to pay particular attention to the rosy hole at the center. Teasing the pucker flesh, the firm tongue worked its way inside to the obvious pleasure of its owner as evidenced by the deep moans. Soon, Kieran was a molten puddle of flesh as Cory slid his finger in to massage the prostate as his tongue teased the flesh of Kieran's perineum. Kieran did his best to stay still beneath Cory's provocative activities. Much too soon, he found himself moaning he was going to come.

Cory stopped all his actions and let Kieran cool down from the edge before flipping him over, exposing his husband's raging erection. Cory slid up Kieran's body, making sure his chest hair touched all Kieran's most sensitive spots, until their cocks were rubbing next to each other and their chests rose and fell in a rhythm. Leaning down, he brushed his beard along the side of Kieran's neck before licking his way up long the exposed flesh to his lover's ear, which he drew into his mouth and nibbled on the lobe, driving Kieran mad with lust. Taking some pity on his whimpering husband, Cory moved his head so their lips lined up, and he clamped down in a fierce kiss, which threatened to suck the air out of Kieran's lungs. When breathing became a desperate necessity, Kieran found the one spot Cory was most ticklish and used the spot to break the kiss.

"Understanding we promised to love each other until death do us part, Wolf, don't you think we should save this kind of killer kiss for when we're old and gray?"

"Sorry, babe, you have me so turned on I couldn't help myself."

"Well I've got a better idea. Why don't you put your raging hard cock to good use and make love to your husband?"

"I like your thinking. Do you think we're safe making love to you flesh to flesh?"

"Gramps confirmed you're free of all Ebony magic. I think we're safe to go without the condom, if you're comfortable about doing so."

"Better play safe a while longer. I'd rather claim you as my mate under the power of your ritual when we're sure everything is safe."

Cory reached across the bed to grab the lube and a condom from the nightstand, and Kieran took advantage of his stretch to latch his mouth and teeth gently on Cory's right nipple to tease his lover. Cory lightly swatted Kieran away before hooking his arms under his lover's legs and hoisting them up over his shoulders. Slicking his cock, he slipped the rubber on before slicking the condom as well. Cory rose up and slid his cock into Kieran's ass slow and deep; he set up a gentle rhythm, intending to make the evening last. He leaned forward, bending Kieran's legs back until he locked lips and kissed his husband as they made love.

"Happy Birthday, babe."

"Thank you, Wolf. This is the best birthday I've ever had."

"I plan to make them all special from now on."

Cory rose up and adjusted Kieran's legs so they were wrapped around his waist and resumed his thrusting, speeding up as he drew closer to the edge of orgasm. Soon, Kieran's breathing matched Cory's as they reached climax together. Kieran's load splattered both young men's chests as Cory's filled the condom. Careful to make sure he had a grip on the condom Cory withdrew his spent cock from Kieran's ass and collapsed beside his husband. They kissed before Kieran found a spot on Cory's chest, which wasn't sticky with spent cum, and rested his head on the spot. Cory's fingers found their home in Kieran's hair, stroking the spot at the base of his neck, which always relaxed his lover. Despite all their relaxing activities, Kieran's neck muscles were already beginning to tense up.

"You're thinking deep thoughts already."

"I'm sorry. Thinking about dealing with my Grandmother Belle later this week, she's never been an easy person to be in the same room as. I'm pretty sure I always cower or give deference to her. I'm not sure how to oppose her and earn her respect without blowing a hole through the council chamber or one of my great-aunts."

"Are you sure you don't want me to come with you? What if we redirected their focus on to your shifter-stock husband?"

"Bright Mother, the thought of the cascade of heart attacks lightens my heart. I want to show you where I grew up, but now is not the time. I need to make them accept me as the Hunter-candidate, and as much as I love you, Wolf, I won't be able to convince them if I walk into the council chamber with you and Billy in tow."

"What's Billy got to do with all this?"

"If I take you as my husband, I will need to take Billy as my dark shifter and claim a title as yet unearned. I would be forced to walk into the House of Beauty as the Silver Hunter. No, for now, I need to be Tracker Kieran, petitioning for my place as Hunter-candidate."

"Okay, we'll do this your way. You must approach the Alpha of your family, showing enough respect to keep her from guessing you're challenging to take the pack away from her."

"Something along those lines. Let's go take a shower. I want to cuddle properly and not get all sticky. Besides we need to get some sleep. We're going on a long hike and working a long day tomorrow."

"The barrier spell?"

"Yes, I need to read up on the spell if the grimoire will let me turn the pages."

"Is the book alive, babe?"

"To tell you the truth, Wolf, I wouldn't be surprised if the book was alive. I think the grimoire has been the focus of so much high-level magic over the centuries, perhaps the thing has developed an awareness."

"Let's shower; then, we'll go check out your living book."

* * *

HOURS LATER, Kieran rose in frustration as the grimoire refused to allow him to turn the page from the prophecy. He wanted to hurl the book into a fire, but suspected the tome was protected from such actions. Pacing across to the kitchen, Kieran snarled when he reached the fridge and started reaching for yet another soda. He was wired on caffeine enough. He rounded on the book, snarling in rage, Silver magic flaring in his eyes.

"What is in this fucking prophecy you want me to understand, you stupid book? I don't want to be the blasted Silver Hunter. I want to be Kieran Oisín-Cooper and go live on a godforsaken farm far away from the never-properly-cursed House of Beauty. To be honest with you, book, I don't even want to be the heir to the Silver Witch. I want to be a normal gay guy. Where is the spell in your pages for granting such a wish?"

To Kieran's surprise, the book slammed shut, and a ghost-like figure emerged from the grimoire. Silver magic swirled around Kieran's hands as he raised them to ward of the ghost.

"For someone who doesn't want his Silver magic, you're pretty quick to raise magic for defense."

"Who are you?"

"I don't suppose you would buy the genie of the lamp here to grant you three wishes," the figure teased.

"You're in the wrong book of wonder tales. I think Aladdin lives about five thousand miles east of here."

"Well, at least you still possess a sense of humor. I figured humor died out of my sister's line a long time ago."

"You're Beauty's brother, the one who became the first male Silver Witch."

"Yes, Kieran Samuel Belle Oisín-Cooper, my what a mouthful. I think I'll call you Kieran. I am or I used to be Johan Kaufmann, and like you, I was destined to be the Silver Hunter. I'm the one who should have slain the Beast; instead, I acted the coward and let my little sister go and face the monster."

"So I'm not the first person cursed to fulfill this prophecy. Is this some sort of reoccurring curse or did everyone before me chicken out?"

"I guess you would say I chickened out. Most of those called to do the job never answered the call for one reason or another, mostly because they grew up repressed by the women of my sister's line. Ten generations ago, a glimmer of hope appeared when the first man became the Hunter of the House of Beauty."

"He didn't fit the requirements, did he? Wouldn't take a shifter for a mate for starters, even though several were offered to him."

"Well, I gather the Historians of the House of Beauty still keep two sets of books."

"Yes, and Great-Uncle Jonas showed me the 'this is the true account' set regarding the male hunter. If I'm going to deal with this prophecy, I need to understand what is in the blasted thing. I can't even begin to read this language."

"Let me translate the prophecy for you. You might want to write this down."

From behind him, Cory handed him a pad and pen. Kieran turned and stared at his husband.

"Thanks, Wolf. I'm sorry I woke you."

"I told you we would do this together. I should've realized you couldn't let this go, so I got up when you started shouting at a book. Somehow, I didn't expect a ghost to be answering you back."

"I didn't expect an audio answer either, but here's Johan, Beauty's youngest brother and the first male Silver Witch. Johan, this is my husband, Corwin Samuel Cooper."

"I like how Kieran calls you Wolf. Now do you boys want the translation?"

"Okay, go ahead and translate," Kieran replied.

"When the lines of white do twist and twine, the firstborn of the second son shall of two Houses be. Child of the White Witch thy path doth wind, like the goddess a threefold way, Tracker, Witch, and Hunter thee. A lone journey to the city named for a small stone, leads the Child of Beauty to his soul's mate. From the ever-shifting line of the Ebony beast, shall a never-changing pup's soul bind to your fate? When bound are two souls, which cannot part, 'ware to those who work the dark art. The hour draws nigh to confront the heir of the dark beast. One whose shape shifts shall claw the light to bring on the dark feast. Boundaries of magic and of flesh shall shatter, and white will shift its shape. Hunter in white thy time has appeared, call forth thy mate and thy guard, this fate thou cannot escape. Slender chains of white bind you, yours the mage's burden to bear. Bound or free, only the rising gold shall reveal your fate by its rising glare."

"Okay, this is the usual nonsense of a prophecy." Kieran tossed the pad down in frustration.

"No, babe. This whole thing does seem to point to us. These lines here describe you to a T. You're the firstborn of a second son of one line with Silver magic, and I guess the House of Beauty would be considered a second line with Silver magic."

"Those lines contain the first problem. The prophecy says white, not silver," Kieran said.

"If I might interject. Some of the translations use silver instead of white. We used to debate this back in my day when Silver magic families were more numerous," Johan offered

"So what was our family's position on the matter? Gramps seems to side with the silver translation," Kieran asked.

"Silver has always been our position, given no one's working white magic," Johan replied.

"Okay, so for argument's sake, let's go with silver instead of white.

Now I can relate to the prophecy talking about me. I guess this part about a never-changing pup might refer to Cory since our souls are bound together," Kieran mused aloud.

"The heir to the dark beast must be the Alpha who's taken over the pack in the forest on the Belle estate and ordered the murder of your sisters," Cory offered.

"Yes, now I must take the test, which means facing him in combat. These lines about the Hunter in silver calling forth his mate and his guard sound similar to another verse I learned elsewhere about a dark shifter on his left and a light shifter on his right—or was the line an ebony shifter and a silver shifter? Those don't work either, because silver shifters don't exist," Kieran explained.

"What's this one about boundaries of magic and flesh shattering and silver shifting its shape? Would the passage mean I'm eventually going to shift since I still have the genes for shifting, even though all the Ebony magic is gone from my blood?" Cory asked.

"I never considered your genes. I suppose we might interpret the passage in such a way. All right, I can't wriggle out of the prophecy. Johan, I need every drop of power I can get. First, I need the barrier spell. Time to tinker with the spell, we need to separate the spell from the bloodline and tie the barrier to an object each Silver Witch candidate can add power to." Kieran's voice now held determination.

Cory withdrew to the kitchen to make a light breakfast and coffee for himself and Kieran, while Kieran and the ghost of Johan read over the barrier spell. Kieran began making notes on the spell and adapting changes to refocus the power from the living bloodline to an artifact to be charged by each new generation. Afterward, he focused on the ritual for becoming the Silver Witch's formal heir.

"Well, this one I'm going to have to do by all the traditional methods, because Gramps will be in charge, and if I mess up, things will go wrong."

"Yes, this is perhaps the one ritual you cannot change to suit your own style, Kieran," Johan said.

"Thank you for your help, Johan. How do I return you to your rest within the grimoire?"

Johan didn't reply to Kieran's question, and his ghostly presence was gone. Kieran closed the grimoire and made his way into the kitchen where Cory was getting ready to pour two mugs of coffee. He stopped Cory before he poured the first cup and waited while his love set down the pot before he wrapped himself in Cory's arms. They stayed wrapped up in a hug for several moments before Kieran broke the silence.

"I'm sorry, Wolf, but we have to fast for the next couple of days. These spells all call for fasting before they're cast, and I don't understand them well enough to attempt changing them up more than I'm going to. Everyone wants you included in these spells and rituals, so I'm afraid you have to starve along with me. Pure water is all were allowed until after I'm invested as Gramps' heir."

"Okay so forty-eight hours or so of fasting. I think I can survive, babe. What clsc do I need to be aware of or do?"

"Well, we're going to be spending a lot of time out in the woods naked with Uncle Brom."

"Are you worried I'm going to start drooling over your uncle, babe?"

"Ugh, you're learning to read our bond to well, Wolf."

"Nope, I remember how your sexy uncle is the only thing we've ever fought over. You don't need to worry. We may not have done any fancy rituals—aside from my pledging my faithfulness to you until death does us part when we got married in town—but because your seed has been in me and changed me, our bond is even deeper than you think. I'm your mated partner."

Kieran turned in Cory's arms so they were face to face and drew his husband in for a deep kiss.

"Pack up as much bottled water as you can carry comfortably, Wolf. I'm going to go get the items I need to work with and talk with Uncle Brom about bringing a few items as well. Oh, and grab a couple of towels as well. We have to take a ritual bath at the spring before we begin working magic."

The lovers separated, going to get themselves ready for their day. Kieran filled a backpack with a serious array of magical tools, including the family grimoire. He strapped on his silver sabers and loosely bound his hair with a simple silver clasp. Going back downstairs, he found Cory waiting for him with a daypack filled with bottled water and a pair of towels. Beside Cory was a staff of oak capped at each end with silver, which Kieran recognized as his uncle's work. Cory stood, shouldered the pack, and took up his staff. The lovers kissed one more time before Kieran led them outside where they we're met by not only Uncle Brom, but Kellen and Gramps as well. Kieran was surprised to find his male relatives dressed and ready to go.

"I thought only Uncle Brom was going to go with us to do the barrier spell," Kieran said.

"Brom told us about your innovation to the spell, and we thought our help would make the spell even stronger if we added our power to your new version."

"You're testing me, evaluating if my spell is up to the task of proving me worthy to be the Silver Witch if the need arises. I suppose this happens with every generation, even though Johan didn't say anything about these kinds of tests last night while we worked on the changes."

"Johan? Who is Johan, Son?" Kellen asked, looking puzzled at his son.

Kieran glanced back at his father and grandfather, as puzzled as the two older men.

"The spirit of the grimoire, the first male Silver Witch, the youngest of Beauty's brothers, the guy who didn't take the job as the Silver Hunter. Are you telling me you never interacted with him?"

"I don't think we were ever suppose to interact with him if he was destined to be the Silver Hunter. Neither your father nor I were ever fated to be the Silver Hunter," Gramps replied.

"Freaking awesome. So how about you, Uncle Brom? You're being too quiet on the subject."

Brom swallowed a lump in his throat and tears formed in his silver eyes, which he tried to blink away.

"Only once. He appeared right after I recovered from having my magic ruined by my foolish bout of unsafe sex with a shifter. He said I tried to take on a destiny that belonged to another, and told me I'll recognize the chosen one when he comes crying to me for love and attention. I've been aware of your destiny since you came to me at age ten, *mo stór*."

"Oh, *mo mhúinteoir*, my teacher and beloved uncle, he's right you tried to take on too much." Kieran wrapped his uncle in a fierce hug. "You sacrificed your place as Gramps' heir for a nephew you'd never even met. Why did you think I'm worthy of such a sacrifice?"

"Because you are my little brother's son. I would give anything to keep you from such a destiny, and my own foolish notions of love blinded me."

"Well, I love you dearly, Uncle, ever my wise counsel since I was bawling child of ten. Because of you, I found the strength to face my destiny. Now, we need to get hiking if we're going get to the center of the property with time to set up. This is the last chance to back out or ask questions. Once we leave here, silence must hold until we begin the ritual to cast the new barrier spell."

Kieran paused and glanced at everyone in turn from his grandfather around to his husband. They merely nodded their agreement, and silence settled over the group. Kieran gestured for Brom to lead the way and let his father and grandfather precede Cory and himself. Cory smiled at his husband and fell into place behind him as the group set off single file. Billy popped up and fell in beside Kieran, butting his head against Kieran's hand for attention. Kieran let his hand caress Billy between the ears. Receiving a magical nudge, he paused and bent down to meet Billy's eyes. The boy/wolf nodded his head, licked Kieran in the face, and resumed trotting along beside the group. Kieran rose, resuming his trek with Billy at his side. The spell he was planning on casting played in his mind and shifted form before his mind's eye as Billy's part became clear in the new pattern of the spell. The woods of the Oisín compound were filled with the sounds of wildlife as the men and the wolf made their way to the sacred center of the property. When they reached the edge of the clearing, they stopped to gather as a group. At a gesture from Kieran, they all stripped off their clothes and waited while Kieran entered the clearing with one of his silver sabers bared. Moving to the north, Kieran saluted the giant quartz pillar with his sword before bowing to honor the Guardian of Earth. Proceeding clockwise, Kieran repeated his ritual before each of the other pillars until he once more faced the northern pillar. Here, he raised his arms and the saber above his head, and with a silent cry, released Silver magic to form a dome around the clearing. He moved to the place inside his dome where the outside path met the edge of the dome between North and East. Saluting the dome, he placed his saber at ground level and traced upwards, across, down, and back across to his point of origin. Where the sword cut, the dome faded away, creating a doorway. Kieran bid each member of his party to come forward and challenged each with the tip of his sabre until each nodded his agreement to enter in silence and reverence. In silence, his directed Cory and Billy to the center of the circle as his grandfather, father, and uncle each moved to their favored quarter. Gramps moved to the North as Guide, Kellen to the East as Rover, Brom to the South as Guardian, leaving the West open for Kieran as Hunter, each man representing a facet of the god.

Kieran swept his saber back across the entrance he'd cut and sealed the dome once more before laying his saber across the path to cut a door in case of an emergency. Moving clockwise around the circle, Kieran took up his position in the West. The four men of the Oisín clan raised their hands over their heads and joined their magic in a silent evocation to the goddess and the god to bless their working. Surprising everyone, especially Cory, Billy remained silent despite the outpouring of Silver magic all around him. Kieran merely smiled at his husband and nodded to his family. Each of the Oisín men stepped forward to the center from their quarter of the circle until they were linking hands in a circle around Cory and Billy. The ground shivered a moment, causing Cory and Billy to shift toward Kieran, as a flat stone rose from the ground braced on two pillars of quartz to form an altar. When the altar settled into place, the Silver mages released their circle and waited for Kieran's next instruction.

Wordless, Kieran gestured for them to stay put while he crossed to his saber and reopened the doorway to the outside. He crossed the threshold and gathered up his backpack before returning inside the dome and resealing the doorway. Moving to stand before the altar, Kieran pulled out several items from his backpack and placed them on the altar, the grimoire, a bell, a plate, a chalice, a pair of candles, a silver dagger, a silver flask, and a small silver box. Gramps took the candles and set them into small indentations in the surface of the altar, while Kellen took the plate and the chalice and set them on the center of the altar. Brom picked up the flask and the box, setting them to the side. Kieran set the bell on the opposite side of the altar from the flask and the box. He set the grimoire into a rest at the front of the altar and opened the book to the page containing the ritual for barrier spell, resting the silver dagger in the seam of the book as a bookmark. Still silence reigned over the group as Kieran knelt before the altar and bowed his head in prayer. When Kieran arose, he picked up the flask, twisted of the cap, and poured the contents into the chalice before returning the flask to the altar and taking up the box. Opening the box, he removed a strike anywhere match, which he struck and used to light the candles. Kieran removed a piece of flat bread from the box and placed the bread on the plate. He tore the bread into five pieces and spoke for the first time.

"We are gathered before the goddess and the god to ask their aid in our work. When our working is completed, we shall partake in this offering to the ancient ones."

The Oisín men replied, "So mote it be."

Kieran reached over his shoulder as if reaching for a sword, and when he pulled his arm back, a silver sword gleamed in his hand. He held the sword upright for a moment before setting the blade on the altar.

"This is the sword of my sister Rosalind Belle, who died a huntress of the House of Beauty. This sword will anchor the barrier we craft this day. Cory and Billy, please come here," Kieran, said the last part as he took up the silver dagger. "All magic comes at a price, and every spell must contain a way for the magic to be broken. The barrier, which protects these lands, is meant to keep out shifters, but can be shattered if a shifter transforms from one shape to another within the barrier.

Today, we will craft a new barrier, which can only be shattered by the use of an item enchanted by an Ebony mage, whose power is equal to or greater than the power of the Silver Witch, to shatter this sword. To invoke this power, I need a drop of blood from each of you."

Cory held out his hand, and Billy raised a paw, both of which Kieran swiftly pricked with the point of the dagger. He touched the tip of the dagger to the blade of the sword and began a chant, which his family took up and repeated three times. Power surged and swirled around the domed circle until Kieran drew the power in and took hold of the sword's pommel, directing the power into the sword. Lifting the sword, Kieran slammed the blade point first into the ground in front of the altar, burying the sword to the hilt in the earth.

The spell's power flowed out to the pillars of the circle and sucked away the dome the Oisín men had raised before releasing a sphere of power outwards with the sword at the center. All four Silver mages collapsed to the ground as their power was drawn into the spell in the initial phase before rushing back into them like a surging tide. Brom recovered first, because he was the least powerful of the four men. He prevented Cory from rushing to Kieran's side and touching him.

"Cory, stop. Don't touch him until he starts to come around on his own or you'll kill him. He has to recover his balance with his power, and an outside touch will upset the balance within him."

Kellen and Gramps eventually recovered and sat up. They stood watching as Kieran's body lay twitching from the power surging around and through him. Long minutes passed, and worried expressions grew on the older mages' faces, as Kieran still didn't revive. Before anyone tried to stop him, Billy surged forward and licked Kieran's face, shocking the young mage back to reality. Slowly, he sat up, blinking his eyes back into focus. Kieran glanced around and smiled at his family.

"Well, how did I do with my first major working?"

Cory grabbed him from behind in a tight hug and said, "You scared us all half to death, babe. We feared for you until Billy licked your face and woke you up."

Billy nudged his head into Kieran's chest, and Kieran ruffled his fur from ears to neck.

"So I get woken up by true love's doggie slobber instead of a kiss." Kieran chuckled as he scratched Billy behind his ears.

"Impressive, Grandson. You proved you can cast a spell in the traditional manner, even if you did bend the spell all out of shape while doing the casting. Come, let us partake of the offering to the gods, and give thanks."

Gramps took up the plate and handed each of them a piece of the bread. They all ate, and Kellen took up the chalice and passed the cup around until they all drink from the cup. With some help, Kieran rose on wobbling legs and hobbled over to where his saber lay across the path. The blade was a twisted, darkened wreck. Kieran picked sword up and reverently laid the saber on the altar along with the undamaged twin blade. After extinguishing the candles, Kieran cleaned and packed everything up. With a gesture, Kellen sent the altar back into the ground, taking the sabers as well. The group got dressed, and Cory handed out bottled water to everyone.

"I do not believe this. I lost another set of sabers to magic." Kieran sighed as they left the clearing to return to their cabins.

"We'll forge you a new set after your initiation as heir to the Silver Witch, *mo stór*."

"Thank you, Uncle Brom."

They reached a point on the trail where three separate trails branched off. Brom took the trail to the left, Gramps and Kellen took the path to the right, and Kieran led Cory and Billy along the center path back to their cabin. Cory didn't understand how three paths now existed when on the way in only one existed. Kieran gave him a brief explanation of the magic of the path as they returned to their cabin. The young couple and their wolf arrived back at their cabin and went in to clean up and rest. Cory put the remaining bottled waters back in the fridge to chill before heading upstairs to join Kieran in the shower.

INTERLUDE: THE MASTER WATCHES AND PLOTS

Many miles away, the Ebony mage, who styled himself the Master, awoke from his meditative trance as he experienced the power of Kieran's massive working. He trembled in sudden fear as proof of the existence of at least four Silver mages of vast power hit home. Reaching out with his own dark power, he explored around the edges of the monumental working. Yes, four Silver mages, one old and vastly powerful, two middle aged, one his equal and tied to the old man like an apprentice. The other was damaged in some way; he couldn't tell why, but definitely weaker. The forth proved to be the boy Simms kept promising to deliver to him. The tracker from the House of Beauty, who shouldn't possess magic or at the best a weak one-shot talent, turned out to be related to the other three mages by blood and possessed their talent in full measure. The boy ranked as his equal in power, and the Master trembled as he read the potential for greater power than even the old mage of the group. The boy must be captured and broken before his potential became unlocked. Time to put his apprentice into the field again. His apprentice would make sure Kincaid and his group of ragtag shifters didn't make a mess of the capture of the boy. From his lair, the Master redirected Marissa Holden, the little owl shifter, from her task aiding Kincaid to finding a way to get inside the enemy stronghold and break the barrier spells on the hidden compound. He needed to go down to his vault and check the inventory of enchanted items left over from his predecessor's reign.

The boy's untapped potential troubled the Master. This foe's creative use of magic terrified the Ebony mage in a way not experienced since his time as a slave-apprentice. So much power pulsed in the sword, which held the inner barrier spell in place; the mage didn't think he possessed a single dark object with enough power to break the spell. He would need to merge two or more objects to get the power. Rising, from his bed the Master found his eager new slave-apprentice waiting to serve him. The mage cuffed the boy aside and wrapped his body in the shadow robes he preferred before striding from his bedchamber headed for his library and the vault, which lay beyond. This new slave-apprentice didn't possess a large potential for Ebony magic, but he made a pleasant diversion in bed, and William Harkrider proved his usefulness when he brought his family's enchanted compass in trade for his apprenticeship.

19

After an exhausted night's sleep, Kieran woke still snuggled up to Cory and giggled when he caught his husband's stomach growling. Cory groaned as his stomach complained about its empty status. Kieran's fingers began stroking through the hair on his husband's chest, roaming down the abs to skirt along his waist before traveling back up to play with first one nipple and then the other before resuming their teasing travels. A low possessive growl rumbled from the back of Cory's throat as Kieran's fingers slipped below the sheet to wrap around his cock. The gentle tugs took him from soft to stiff in mere moments. His husband's fingers released their grip on his now solid manhood and trailed down to play with his full balls before slipping lower to tease their way back to his hole. Kieran, lying next to him, let his fingers do all the work. Cory realized Kieran was doing everything as if on autopilot, his mind elsewhere.

"Kieran, you're distracted. I can tell your mind is off someplace else."

"I'm sorry, Wolf. I love touching you, and normally, doing so takes my mind off my problems; this time the reverse seems to be happening."

"Talk to me, babe. What's got you distracted from loving your husband?"

"I sense a darkness encroaching on our time together. Those lines of the stupid prophecy we couldn't figure out are nagging at me, Wolf."

"Babe, I don't think trying to figure them out on an empty stomach is a good idea. I understand we can't eat for several hours yet, so why don't we go out back and swim in the lake."

"I guess some sort of physical activity would be a good idea. We've got a couple of hours before we need to join Gramps up at the house for the ritual to tie me into the powers of the Silver Witch."

"Well, if physical activity is what you need, lover," Cory said with a sexy grin.

"After the ritual, Wolf, I promise we can fuck like bunnies in heat."

"No food and no sex. This ritual better be impressive."

"I have no idea, Wolf. The grimoire says the ritual is performed however the current Silver Witch chooses. Considering how much of a traditionalist Gramps is, I would imagine all sorts of crazy prayers and magic gestures."

"Like all the things you did yesterday?"

"Yeah, only about ten times more showy, Wolf. Let's grab our trunks and hit the lake."

The guys got out of bed and crossed the room to the dresser where they rummaged for their swim trunks. Once they were dressed, they grabbed towels and headed downstairs and out the back door of their cabin. The back porch opened on to a long pier, which extended out into the lake. A small fishing boat was tied up at the end of the pier next to a ladder for getting back out of the water. When they got to the end of the pier and had set down their towels, Kieran grab Cory in a fierce hug and kiss as he launched them off the end of the pier and into the icy waters of the lake. He held them both under the water for a moment before breaking the kiss, and with a powerful kick, he sent them to the surface. When they broke the surface, Cory glared at him, which caused Kieran to break out in laughter.

"What's with you and water? Every time we go swimming, you try to drown me."

"Oh no, Wolf. I love watching your reactions when we break the surface. Your inner wolf doesn't like being near this much water, and he sort of surfaces when I dunk you."

"Deep inside you is a part that enjoys toying with a dangerous beast. You're an adrenaline junkie."

"Trust me, Cory, I'm not chasing an artificial high. Being with you charges my batteries in ways I can't begin to express. If I didn't grasp the complexity of my family bloodlines as well as I do, I'd swear shifter blood crept in somewhere way back. I want to howl at the moon, run, and chase you—or be chased by you—through the woods."

"Um, Kieran, I can't keep this from you, even though your Gramps and Dad made me promise never to tell you."

"What are those two up to this time?" Kieran's voice was tinted with annoyance.

"Beauty's prince and the Beast shared a mother who was part shifter. They said her daughter used her one shot of Silver magic to bind the shifter blood in her children so they'd never be able to shift but they'd have all the strength and tracking skills of a shifter."

Silver magic flowed around the young lovers as Kieran raised them on a platform out of the water. He didn't appear angry, but Cory experienced the tension through the bond. He drew Kieran into a hug and turned him so they both stood on the silver platform looking out over the lake. Cory rested his chin on Kieran's shoulder so his beard tickled the side of Kieran's neck.

"I upset you. I shouldn't have said anything, but I think this is the reason for our ability to bond at all, love. The tiny amount of shifter blood in you calls to the massive amounts of shifter blood in me."

"Actually, what you told me explains a lot of things I wondered about over the years, Wolf. I always wondered how the members of the House of Beauty managed to keep up with the shifters we hunted. My tutors said our ability comes from the Silver magic in our veins, but their answer didn't explain why even my non-gifted relatives are able to track shifters so easily."

"I guess even the House of Beauty hid the truth from itself."

"Only one person would have been privy to the truth, Great-Uncle

Jonas the family historian. His line kept the history of the House of Beauty from the day Beauty charged her firstborn son with the job until Jonas' death. I always suspected the existence of more secret chronicles hidden away in the archives besides those on the only male hunter."

"Do you think your great-uncle left a clue to where they were hidden?"

"I can only hope he did. He died about a year after Mom did of extreme old age and without a successor. I think he wanted me to be his choice, but I'd already taken the tests and proven I possessed the talent for tracking. All my other male relatives were two young for the task. I can't help but think that under different circumstances, Rosie would have been the Jonas' successor if either Selene or Celeste passed the test and became the Huntress. She was the only one besides me to give the old man more than a passing nod. We used to sit for hours listening to stories from the chronicles when we escaped our lessons." Kieran's voice grew hushed and raspy as he tried to fight his emotions back under control.

"I wish I could have met your sister Rosie. I can tell by the tone in your voice and experience through our bond how special she is to you."

"Rosie was special, Wolf. She would have been the first one to welcome you with open arms, and she would have beat me with whatever she laid her hands on for letting out relationship fade out between Thanksgiving and Christmas."

Cory laughed as a vivid picture of the petit but beautiful and powerful Rosie surged up out of Kieran's mind and across their bond. Kieran's image of a miniature Amazon warrior chasing him with a lamp was too cute. A tear escaped from both of them as Kieran fondly remembered his sister. Sensing his lover was trying hard not to loose control of his emotions, Cory hugged Kieran tighter for a moment before taking advantage of Kieran's distracted thoughts to push him off the platform. The shock of the cold water broke Kieran's concentration, and Cory yelped as he plunged into the water a moment after Kieran went in. Sputtering to the surface, Cory couldn't help but laugh at Kieran's expression this time around, as his lover trod water, trying to get his hair out of his face. The lovers abandoned all serious thoughts and began chasing each other through the water, dunking, groping, and kissing as the mood took them. Eventually, they grew tired and cold, so they climbed out on the pier to dry off and grab some sun. After awhile, Kieran shifted so his head rested on Cory's chest with his arm draped over Cory's waist. Feeling tears drip on his chest along with flashes of grief through their bond, Cory wrapped his arm around Kieran's shoulders and pulled him in tight. They settled into a true Alpha/Alpha partnership, with each of them taking the lead as needed. Knowing his lover needed peace and a quiet release of some of his grief, Cory held him, letting love and contentment flow through their bond while lightly stroking Kieran's hair. They lay in silence until the heat of the day began to get to them.

"Do you want to go for another quick swim or head in and shower, Wolf?" Kieran said as he wiped the last of his tears from his eyes.

"Let's head in, love. I think we've both gotten enough sun for the day. I'll grab us a couple of bottles of water while you go start the shower."

They padded their way back down the pier to the cabin and headed inside, separating in the kitchen as Cory stopped at the refrigerator to grab a couple bottled waters. Kieran continued upstairs into the bathroom to start the shower. The young couple downed their waters before shucking their trunks and stepping into the shower enclosure. Cory took up the shampoo once Kieran had soaked his hair. He soon had his husband moaning in pleasure as he worked up a thick lather and worked his fingers into the scalp and down into the neck muscles. When Kieran backed up against his husband so Cory's cock slipped into the crease of his lover's ass, Cory reached around and killed the hot water. The shock of the sudden cold water snapped Kieran out of his trance and reminded him they couldn't have sex until after the ritual tonight. Kieran restored the hot water for Cory to finish rinsing the shampoo out of his hair before they shut down the shower and dried off. In the bedroom, they pulled loose-fitting clothes from the closet and dressed, put on sandals, and headed downstairs. Cory stopped Kieran and slipped the silver wolf pendant Uncle Brom helped him make around Kieran's neck. They kissed and walked hand in hand up to the main house for the ritual and dinner.

20

G ramps sat in the library of the main house looking over various formats of the ritual for passing the power of the Silver Witch from one generation to the next. His own father put him through a ritual of such complexity; he still didn't believe either of them came out of the ceremony with their sanity intact. Aodhfin's original investiture plans got tossed when Brom ruined his personal magic. He redesigned the ritual with Kellen in mind, ending up with a convoluted mess, which somehow fit Kellen's makeup and casting style. He read the requirements in the family grimoire again. He was a warrior, and his magic reflected the ways of the House of Beauty more than they did the style of the Oisín Clan. *Fine*, Aodhfin decided, *we will make a warrior's ritual; I will initiate Kieran using the old blood brother oath.* Aodhfin sat back in his chair with a grin on his weathered face.

Forty-eight hours of fasting for both himself and his boyfriend for a five-minute ritual. Yes, Kieran's scream of outrage and disbelief might well reach Little Rock.

The boys arrived about half an hour after Aodhfin had made his decision, and he made out the sounds of their stomachs growling as they caught the scent of dinner. Kellen showed them into the library where Brom and Aodhfin were waiting. Kieran hugged both his uncle and his grandfather before taking place in the center of the library.

"Give me your right hand, Kieran," Aodhfin said.

Kieran held out his right hand and shuddered in shock as his grandfather slashed his palm with a silver dagger before cutting his own. Gramps grasped Kieran's bleeding palm with his own bleeding palm.

"Brothers of blood and magic are we now. By this exchange of blood and magic, I, Aodhfin Oisín the Silver Witch, name you, Kieran Samuel Belle Oisín-Cooper, heir to my power and to the lineage of the Silver Witch."

"By the bonds of blood and magic, I, Kieran Samuel Belle Oisín-Cooper, accept the power, the lineage, and the responsibilities of the Silver Witch."

Silver magic swirled around the men's joined hands and was gone. Aodhfin released his grip, and Kellen wrapped Kieran's hand with a cloth to slow the bleeding while Brom did the same thing for his father. Cory still stood by the door to the library with a stunned expression on his face. He was actually the first to react to the brief ritual.

"You're done? The entire thing was over in five minutes max. I had to starve for two days for a ritual that was over in five minutes."

"Well, I couldn't keep dinner waiting. Kieran's grandmother would never forgive me," Aodhfin replied.

"Yeah, right, and she's going to be happy you slashed our hands open, got blood on the carpet, and made her favorite grandchild and his husband starve for two days. I'd say you're going to be sleeping in one of the spare bedrooms, Gramps," Kieran retorted.

The men left the library and headed for the dining room where Grams was busy setting out the last few side dishes. She stopped and stared as the Oisín men and Cory entered the dining room. Her eyes were immediately drawn to her husband's and grandson's bandaged hands. She crossed the room and took each man's hand between hers and let her Sapphire magic swirl around the wounded hand, bringing its icy, healing touch. With the magic, Kieran unwrapped his hand and flexed his fingers and palm before hugging Grams.

"Thanks, Grams. I figured you wouldn't let me suffer for long."

"I hope you boys didn't get blood on the carpet in the library."

"I didn't. Gramps was the one wielding the dagger," Kieran said, dodging a swat from Gramps.

"Ungrateful whelp," he said with a laugh as Kieran stuck out his tongue from the safe location behind his grandmother.

Cory laughed at Kieran's antics. His husband was playing around like he was twelve, not twenty-two. The whole family burst into laughter before settling down to dinner and serious planning for Kieran and Kellen's trip to the Belle estate. Neither man was looking forward to dealing with Grandmother Belle, but Kieran's attempt at the test needed to be scheduled in order for him to take control of the House of Beauty. Cory tried once again to get himself included in the trip, and Kieran once again explained the reasons Cory's coming along would be a bad idea. Eventually, everything was settled, and the family did their best to enjoy the rest of the evening before returning to their respective cabins.

Back at their cabin, Cory tried one more time to convince Kieran to take him along on the trip to the Belle estate.

"Babe, I understand we all agreed, but I can't shake the sensation something is going to happen to you, and I should be with you."

"Wolf, taking you with me would put you in danger. Grandmother and a couple of the Matriarchs still have their Silver magic, and the one-shot spell granted to women of the House of Beauty is in league with the barrier spell I cast yesterday. I might block one of them from hurting or killing you, but I couldn't stop them all."

"I want to make sure you're safe, babe."

"I realize you do, Wolf. Trust me, I'll be safer with the knowledge you're here safely behind all these barrier spells and under the direct protection of Gramps, Grams, and Uncle Brom, not to mention Billy the guard shifter." Kieran acknowledged the wolf, and Billy bumped his head into Kieran's side for attention.

"Okay, I'll be good and keep an eye on the home front."

"Thanks, Wolf. You have no idea how much your being here sets my mind at ease. Now if I can convince Grandmother as easily, all will be well."

"Well, we have a couple of days before you have to head out. You can practice your speech on me."

"I think no matter how much I practice a speech, everything will go out the window when I have to deal with the Council and Grandmother. So, I'll save you the agony of me pacing pathetically up and down the living room."

"Let's go soak in the hot tub and have some naughty fun, Mr. Cooper."

"I like your thinking, Mr. Cooper." Kieran grinned and raced off toward the back porch and the hot tub, shedding his clothes as he went.

Cory was hot on his heels with Billy at his side. The lovers were both naked as they climbed into the hot tub. Billy put his paws up on the edge, panting for attention until a wave of water washed over the edge and splashed him. The wolf rumbled deep in his throat before stalking off in a wolfish huff. The lovers laughed at the wolf and lost themselves in each other.

* * *

THE FEW DAYS after the ritual naming Kieran heir to the power of the Silver Witch passed quickly, and he found himself packing madly a few hours before he was due to depart with his father. As he was attempting to jam his tracker leathers into the duffle bag he was using to take his clothes, Cory reached around and took the heavy leathers from his husband's hands. He took them and hung them in a garment bag Grams had loaned him so Kieran's clothes wouldn't be all wrinkled when he arrived at the Belle estate. Cory quietly repacked Kieran's clothes in the garment bag before closing and folding the bag neatly in half. He placed Kieran's hand on the handle of the bag, drew him in, and kissed him one more time before sending him downstairs to meet with Kellen. Father and son hugged briefly before Kellen wrapped Cory in a hug before he and Kieran walked out to Kellen's SUV. Kieran turned and waved to Cory before getting into the passenger seat of the SUV. Father and son drove off as if they were headed to face down a dragon in its lair.

* * *

THE TRIP STARTED with strained silence between Kellen and Kieran, as both men tried to find a way back from the hurt and betrayal that had come between them. Finally, Kieran broke the silence.

"We really need to settle a few things before we get to Grandmother's estate, Dad. This whole visit has been very close to being a nightmare of epic proportions—between you and Gramps making attempts on Cory's life, the crazy tests and rituals, not to mention your stunt with the condoms during our honeymoon."

"I know I can't apologize sufficiently for my actions, especially the ones I took on my own initiative. I'm afraid I got caught up in your grandfather's enthusiasm for the prophecy when I saw how far along the path you'd already traveled. I'm not trying to excuse or justify my behavior, just explain where my thinking has been coming from."

"I don't get this fascination with the damn prophecy. There are parts of it, which can't possibly happen. I don't know what the person who first envisioned the thing was on, but silver shifters will never exist. Grams doesn't think Cory will ever shift now that his Ebony magic is gone. Still, I want you to promise me no more plotting behind my back or threatening Cory. If I wanted to live my life dealing with family intrigue and plots, I would have stayed on the Belle estate."

"I promise, Son, no more plots or intrigue against you and your family. I'm glad you kept the Oisín part of your name. Despite your grandfather's and my own actions, it really is a noble heritage."

"I know, and I'm proud of that heritage. You know I'm expecting you to start dating again and to find someone who can make you happy. Plus, I'm going to need lots of half brothers and sisters to carry on the family line."

"Once we've had a proper time to mourn your sisters—something we both need to do—then I'll think about dating. You and Cory could think about using a surrogate to make me a grandfather."

"I'll promise to think about it when we get past all the current mess we need to deal with. Bring me up to speed on where things were when you left the Belle estate. I need a rough idea of who's siding with whom."

Kellen began to review for Kieran the state of family politics within the House of Beauty, as he knew them to be when he'd left after the deaths of Kieran's youngest sisters. In particular, he warned Kieran to keep an eye on his cousin Justine Belle-O'Niall, an avid supporter of the Council of Matriarchs. Kieran listened but eventually fell asleep to the sounds of his father's voice. Hours later, Kellen nudged Kieran awake as the SUV slowed at the turn off before the gates to the Belle estate.

"You'll need to be the one to announce who we are and why we're here, Son."

"I guess we should switch places," Kieran said as his father pulled the SUV to a stop.

After switching places, Kieran drove the SUV up to the guard post where one of his cousins by marriage stood on guard.

"What business do you have here?" the guard challenged.

"Tracker Kieran Belle, returning to report to the Council of Matriarchs."

"I don't have you on the list of authorized visitors, Tracker Kieran."

"Since when is a returning Tracker required to be on the list? I'm here on a direct request from the Huntress-emeritus. Do you want to get on her bad side, Cousin?"

"No, Tracker Kieran. Let me get the gate open for you."

When the gates opened wide enough, Kieran drove the SUV through and headed for the mansion. After another half hour of driving, the massive log mansion loomed up before them. The massive house sat perched on the edge of the river, which ran through the property. Kieran sighed as he parked the SUV in front of the mansion's main doors. Two of his younger cousins came out the front doors to attend to his and his father's baggage. Both boys stopped when they recognized Kieran and bowed to him.

"Tracker Kieran, what an honor to have you back. Will you be staying long?"

"Rise, Cousins. I've told you before, I don't expect you to bow to me. How long we're staying is a decision for Honored Grandmother and the Council. Take our bags to our quarters in the Huntress' suite."

The boys scrambled to get Kieran's and Kellen's bags and carry them off to their quarters.

"You're assuming your grandmother assigned us to your mother's suite."

"No, I'm staking my claim to Mother's suite as part of pushing my position as Hunter-candidate. The time for being timid around Grandmother is over. I'm a full tracker and now the only candidate left with a rightful claim to take the test. Time for the Council to show me the respect I'm due as my mother's son and heir, and I hope they choke on the fact."

"Be careful how far you push them, Son. They still have teeth, and your grandmother's tongue didn't soften while you were off at college."

"They're about to discover the meek little boy they despised, grew up and became a man with teeth and a spine. Let's go make sure no one redirected the boys to some other set of rooms."

Inside, Kieran and Kellen came face to face with one of his great-aunts who had stopped the boys on their way to take their burdens to the Huntress' suite.

"Where do you two think you're going with those bags? The Tracker and his father are assigned to the green guest suite."

"No, Great-Aunt Hilda, the Tracker and his father will be staying in the Huntress' suite as is their right as the family of the Huntress. As my mother's only heir, I claim my right to the suite as the Hunter-candidate. Do as I asked you, boys. Matriarch Hilda, you will inform the Council I am here and will await their summons to appear, but stress this, I will only wait one day for their summons before I invite myself to Council. You are dismissed."

"Don't put on airs with me, boy. You're a tracker and nothing more."

Kieran locked eyes with his great-aunt and let his anger blaze forth in his silver eyes.

"I am so much more than you know, but I am a full tracker of the House of Beauty, Matriarch Hilda. I will, however, have the respect I am due as a full tracker of this house. If you won't give me the respect as a person, I am due respect for the position I hold. None of your sons or grandsons possesses the skills or the calling to ever be a tracker. Once again, you are dismissed, Matriarch Hilda."

Kieran crossed his arms over his chest and stared at the old woman until she finally turned on her heel and headed off to meet with the rest of the Council. When she was gone, Kieran and Kellen grinned at each other before heading to their claimed suite. Both men understood the council would keep them waiting as long as possible before summoning Kieran to appear before them.

Kieran strode the halls of his former home with a confidence beyond Kellen's experience with the young man. Beside him no longer walked the frightened boy or the teen granting everyone respect whether they deserved respect or not. This young man held himself with the confidence of a trained warrior-mage. This man will be the Silver Hunter. Kellen smiled with pride as they reached the suite of the Huntress of the House of Beauty.

The two boys opened the doors to the suite and ushered Kieran and Kellen inside. Each disappeared to a different bedroom to set down the bag they carried. When the boys returned, they started to bow to Kieran until they caught his expression and stopped mid-bow. Kieran smiled at both of them and motioned them to join him as he walked out on the balcony overlooking the river. He'd always loved this view and had spent hours often with Rosie standing out on this balcony.

"I want you to fetch your group of trainees. My father and I will have need of your services while we're here. Bring food and drinks with you when you come back, enough for everyone. If the cook gives you a hard time, tell her I'll share a secret and special recipe with her— one she's seen me make but will never figure out for herself."

"We'll be back as quick as we can, Tracker Kieran. Will you be resuming our lessons?"

"Not this visit. Things are going to be changing soon. I also need one of you to go to the archives and bring me the chronicle of the—no, never mind. I'll go fetch the tome myself. Jonas would have hidden the book I want."

The boys scampered off to go and fetch their group mates and raid the kitchen. Kellen chuckled at the unbridled hero worship the boys had for Kieran. Even the boys who realized they had no talent worshiped the ground Kieran walked on as a full tracker. Kellen grinned as he realized Kieran didn't recognize how the boys copied his mannerisms. The boys took him as their role model, the first strong male in their life full of powerful women and cowering men.

* * *

KIERAN WAS PACING THE SUITE, waiting for the Council to summon him. The swish of his heavy leather coattails was beginning to get on Kellen's nerves. He glanced at his son and wondered if Cory shared Kieran's anxiety back at the Oisín compound through the bond they shared. As if sensing his father's question, Kieran came to a complete stop and stared into the huge mirror in the sitting room. The glass shimmered as Silver magic flowed over the surface and settled to reveal a view of Cory standing before a mirror in the boys' bedroom in their cabin. The lovers stared at each other for a moment with so much love in their eyes the emotion made Kellen tear up as he remembered what the experience was like. A lot of time had past since he'd stared at someone with equal love. The boys blew each other a kiss before the spell faded, returning the mirror to its normal function. Right on time, a knock on the door to the suite sounded before Jeremy, the oldest of the group of trainees, entered the suite.

"Tracker Kieran, the Council of Matriarchs sends their compliments but refuse to receive you. They ask you and your father move to the green guest suite."

"Thank you, Jeremy. We won't be moving. The Council's time is up anyways. Time for me to go present myself to the Matriarchs, whether they wish to receive me or not."

"Be careful, Son. I'll keep the boys here so they aren't in the line of fire."

"Thanks, Dad. I'll be back when I'm done with the Council."

Kieran strode from the room, every inch a tracker of the House of Beauty. *No*, Kellen corrected his thoughts, *every inch a hunter of the House of Beauty.*

21

—————

Kieran strode into the council chamber with such force the doors slammed into the walls. The Matriarchs rose at the interruption of their meeting. All except Kieran's grandmother who remained seated in her throne-like chair. When he reached the end of the conference table, Kieran smacked his hand down on top of it, and the room echoed with the sound.

"We did not summon you, boy. A tracker does not bring business before this council."

"Shut up, Aunt Fiona. I'm not here as a tracker of the House of Beauty. I'm here as the hunter-candidate. Time is up, Grandmother. You are all out of granddaughters to send to their deaths. The pact is broken, and the mongrels of the forest murdered my sisters."

"Sit down, now! My grandson makes a valid point. We lived to witness a cursed generation when we must allow a male to test as a hunter. We must also resign ourselves to this fate. Kieran is the last of the House of Beauty. With his death, our line ends."

"I'm not dying anytime soon, old woman. I've got too much to live for. Oh, I'm so much more than my sisters."

"A disappointment is what you are, boy."

"Only to a closed-minded old woman, who couldn't do what was needed to be done before she let an entire generation of huntresses be slaughtered. Serena and Rosie both died as full huntresses. My other sisters were never given the chance to properly test. The Alpha who rules this pack now is a direct descendant of the Beast himself. I'm the only one who stands a chance to defeat him."

"Male arrogance. Your chances of defeating a monster of such an ancient a lineage are less than even your sisters."

Kieran stepped back from the table, taking a defensive stance before the assembled Matriarchs. Silver magic wrapped him for a moment to encase him in silver armor. Scythe-like blades ran from his elbows to his wrists and spanned a similar length past his hands. Many of the Matriarchs drew back in their seats. Before them stood Kieran, a figure out of legend, the Silver Hunter.

"You waste whatever Silver magic you have, boy. You should save your magic for the curs of the forest."

"I'm aware Father told you who he is, or I should say what he was. I now hold his position and all the position entails. Silver magic is mine to use at will. I am the heir to the Silver Witch. On the first full moon of August, I will test to become the Hunter of the House of Beauty. When I return, I will be the fulfillment of prophecy. I will be the Silver Hunter."

"We do not agree to let you take the test, boy."

"Will you stop me, Grandmother? Better yet, can you stop me? None of you have the power to oppose me. When I return, I will head the family council. We will be relocating, so I suggest you all start packing. Contact the family lawyers and start selling this estate."

"This is my home, and I will not leave here, boy."

"My name is Kieran Samuel Belle Oisín-Cooper, the heir to the Belle of Belle. I will no longer tolerate your tone or your attitude, Grandmother. Your days of ruling over this family are over." Grandmother Belle opened her mouth to interject, only to be silenced by Kieran. "Be quiet, I'm talking. Aunt Celeste, until I return to take the test, I leave you in charge of the family council."

Kieran started to turn when he caught a flash from the corner of his eye and spun out of the path of a throwing knife aimed at his back. His movement took him out of the path of two more knives and face to face with one of his cousin's husband. The man stood stunned by Kieran's swift movement, another knife in his hand poised to throw. Kieran lashed out with a right uppercut to the man's jaw, rocking him back. Instead of closing on the man for a physical attack, Kieran picked the man up with Silver magic and hurled him across the room to smash into one of the massive log columns, which supported the roof of the chamber. His cousin-in-law didn't rise. Silver magic blazing around him like a fiery aura, Kieran turned to face the Council of Matriarchs.

"Get him a healer!" he ordered. "Which of you put him up to such a foolish attack?"

Silence reigned around the council table as most of the women cowered in fear at the massive display of Silver magic from a man. Finally, from behind the council, a younger woman emerged from the shadows, the cousin whose husband lay unconscious at the base of the massive column. Defiance and hatred filled her expression as she faced him from across the expanse of the oaken table.

"I bid my husband defend the honor of the council and the House of Beauty."

"You send a man to defend the honor of the House of Beauty, Cousin? You trained to take the test of the huntress, Cousin. Why not face me yourself? Why didn't you go to take the test? By looking at you, you're more than old enough to have gone before most of my sisters."

"I don't possess the magic. I am considered unworthy to take the test, Cousin."

"Respect your betters, child, and address the Hunter-candidate by his title, Justine," Kieran's grandmother chided the young woman. "I will not allow family to kill family. We've lost enough family this year."

"Thank you, Huntress-emeritus. Come forward, Cousin Justine, I will check if you are lacking the magic or if the magic is dormant in your branch of the family."

A healer entered the room and crossed to the unconscious man to examine him, while Justine screwed up her courage and came around the table to face Kieran who still stood with his Silver magic flaring around him. As she drew closer, Kieran doused his magic and smiled at her.

"I promise, Justine, I don't bite, despite whatever tales they're telling about me around here. You are close to Celeste's age and training, are you not?"

"I am closer to her in training; age wise, I'm a year older than Selene. I married early, which slowed down my training, Hunter-candidate," Justine said with a proper bow.

"Rise, Cousin. Hold still, this may tingle a bit," Kieran said as he raised one hand wrapped in Silver magic to touch her head.

Justine shivered as the magic washed over her from head to toe. When the magic faded, Kieran smiled at her before giving her a big hug. He whispered in her ear so only she comprehended his message.

"Congratulations, Cousin, you're pregnant with a daughter. Your magic is too latent to activate, but I will open the gift in your daughter if you wish me to."

"You would do this for me after I challenged your place?"

"I'm a scary legend come to life, Justine, but I'm the only hope for the House of Beauty. I still possess one problem though I'm still gay and not likely to produce children of my own. I will give your child the gift of the main line in exchange she will be raised as my designated heir. What do you say, Cousin?"

"Stop, Husband! I was wrong about Hunter-candidate Kieran," Justine said, putting herself between her revived husband and Kieran. She turned her back on her husband, dropped to her knees before Kieran, and took his right hand between both of hers.

"I, Justine Belle-O'Niall, do hereby swear my fealty to Kieran Samuel Belle Oisín Cooper as my liege, and pledge my family to the service of the Belle of Belle and the House of Beauty."

Collective gasps echoed from around the council chamber as Justine gave her fealty to Kieran as if he were already the Hunter of the House of Beauty. Her husband recovered from his shock at his wife's sudden change of heart and moved to kneel beside her and do the same.

"I, James O'Niall-Belle, do hereby swear my fealty to Kieran Samuel Belle Oisín Cooper as my liege, and pledge my family to the service of the Belle of Belle and the House of Beauty."

"I, Kieran Samuel Belle Oisín Cooper, the Belle of Belle, Hunter-candidate of the House of Beauty, do here by pledge my protection to the Belle-O'Niall of Belle. I acknowledge and accept your oaths."

For a moment, Silver magic shimmered over both Justine and James before forming into a bracelet on each of their right wrists and solidified into metallic silver.

"By this bracelet, let all recognize this couple is sworn to my service and under my protection. From this day forth, they and their line will be the Belle-O'Niall of Belle. Cousins, consult with each other how you would like your boon granted."

Justine took her husband aside and gave him the news of her pregnancy along with Kieran's offer to not only grant their daughter the gift of the House of Beauty, but to also name their child his heir. James thought for a moment and added a caveat to the deal; if Kieran ever had a child of his own, their daughter was to be trained as a tracker to serve her cousin. Justine agreed, and they approached Kieran with their request.

"Hunter-candidate Kieran, we ask for the gift for our child, a daughter, and we offer her to serve as your heir should you never produce a child of your own, or to serve as tracker should an heir of the main line be produced."

"I accept your request and grant your boon," Kieran said as a small twist of Silver magic entered Justine's womb and the child within, activating the gene that gave the women of the House of Beauty their gift of one-shot magic. "My business here is done, Huntress-emeritus, Matriarchs. I leave you to prepare for my test on the first full moon of August. Until the appointed time, I will be reachable by phone."

Kieran turned and walked out of the Council chamber. He returned to his suite where he found his father conducting a lesson on the history of the last male hunter. Kieran stopped and listened as his father recounted how the hunter defeated a terrible dark shifter who came to the Belle estate and directly challenged him. Kieran learned this version of the tale out of the hidden chronicles from Gramps when he turned fifteen and again from Great-Uncle Jonas when he turned sixteen. When Kellen finished the tale, he glanced up and caught Kieran's eye. He dismissed the boys to their regular duties and studies. One of the boys started to ask Kellen a question until he caught sight of Kieran coming to speak with his father. The boy started to bow and withdraw until Kieran stopped him with a hand on his shoulder.

"Ask your question, Cousin. Father is wise in the history of our family, for all he is an outsider," Kieran said with a wicked grin.

"I wondered why he didn't take up the mantle of the Silver Hunter. By his actions, he seems to deny his destiny."

"An excellent question, young Ian. The only answer I can give you is he was afraid. Being the Silver Hunter calls for a special person, one who can be afraid but use his fear to make himself stronger," Kellen replied.

Ian appeared as if he was going to ask another question when Kieran broke his concentration.

"In my room, you will find the ancient chronicle on the last Hunter from the special archive. Why don't you go and read while I talk to my father?" Kieran said, easing the boy in the direction of his bedroom.

"Thank you, Tracker Kieran." Ian dashed off to Kieran's room.

"Do you think letting the boy read from this version of the chronicles is a wise choice, Son?" Kellen asked.

"I don't think the knowledge should be hidden, Dad. The boys of this family need to understand they're as good as the girls. They need a role model to emulate."

"They practically worship the ground you walk on, Kieran. You're a living example of how badly the Matriarchs have treated men in this family and how a man can still achieve his dreams."

"Well, if I'm going to achieve any dreams, we need to get back to Gramps' compound so I can study the grimoire and find out if I can get Johan to tell me more about the original Beast. Not even the hidden chronicles of the House of Beauty ever mention how Beauty used her one shot of Silver magic against the Beast."

"I'm hoping he might have a clue. It's bad enough I'm going to have to put down the entire pack in the forest, including all the pregnant females. We can't have another generation of the Beast's lineage born."

"You're right, Son. I'll go pack my things, and we can leave when you're packed and ready."

"I'll be packed and ready in about ten minutes, Dad."

Both men went to their rooms and were surprised to find their luggage already packed and waiting for them. The young boy in Kieran's room glanced up from the dusty tome of the chronicles.

"We suspected you would be leaving again once you met with the Council, Tracker Kieran, so Joey and I took the task upon ourselves to get your father's and your bags packed and ready for your departure."

"Thank you. When you're finished reading, leave the book on the table. I placed a spell on the book so you can't take the thing from this room."

"Thank you, Sir."

Kieran grabbed his bag, met his father in the outer siting room, and together, they headed downstairs and to the estate's garage. After tossing their bags in the SUV, Kellen got behind the wheel and started the car. Kieran hopped in the passenger side and buckled up. They drove off without a backward glance at the massive mansion.

On the drive back to the Oisín compound from the Belle estate, Kieran's phone rang. He glanced at the number before answering and clicked accept when he recognized the call came from Richard St. Martin.

"Hello, Mr. St. Martin, how can I help you?"

"Hello, Kieran. One of my associates called to inform me he found a young woman in Bangor asking for directions to the Belle estate. She said she needed to get to the estate as if was a matter of life and death."

"Did your associate get a name from this woman?"

"She said her name is Marissa Holden."

"She's an acquaintance from school. Last, I checked she was still in Little Rock. Why did she come all the way to Maine? She has my number. Why didn't she call me?"

"My associate says she seemed compelled to find you, almost as if she is under a spell. He also said she's a shifter, and he didn't trust her reasons for asking directions to the estate of a hunting family."

"My father and I are almost to Bangor. We can meet with your associate and Marissa to find out what's going on."

"I'll text you the address where you can meet my associate. His name is Jordan Sinclair."

"Thank you, Mr. St. Martin."

"Be careful, Kieran. Something about all this seems off, even from several states away."

"We'll take every precaution, sir. Thank you for your assistance. I owe you a favor."

"I'll save the favor for a rainy day, Kieran. Call me if you need anything."

"I will, Mr. St. Martin," Kieran said as he disconnected.

His phone chimed a moment later with a text message containing the promised address.

"So where do we need to go to find this friend of yours, Son?"

"I'm programming the address into the GPS. Considering the neighborhood, we're not in a good section of Bangor, Dad."

"Seems St. Martin took the advice your mother gave him years ago to heart, and developed an information network."

"Somehow, his network seems an extensive one, almost as if he's taken over someone else's network."

"I think if he's willing to share his information with you, Son, you don't worry how he created or acquired his network."

"Your destination is on the right," interrupted the voice of the GPS unit.

Kellen pulled the SUV over into the parking lot of an old warehouse. Kieran stopped him before he got out of the car.

"I think things would be better if you stayed out here and kept an eye on things."

"I don't like the idea of you going into a meeting alone. We don't possess any information on this associate of St. Martin's," Kellen said.

"You do realize in two months time I'm going into the heart of the Belle woods alone to face down an entire pack of shifters. I think I can handle a lone human. Besides, if he works for Mr. St. Martin, he'll be one of the good guys."

"When did you get so grown-up? Be careful. If I don't bring you back home in one piece, your husband will get your nephew to bite me."

"I'll be all right, I promise."

Kieran strode away from the SUV and approached the front of the warehouse. Pulling open the door to the warehouse office let the man waiting inside get a chance to recognize him.

"I'll assume you're the tracker Richard said would be coming."

"Tracker Kieran of the House of Beauty. Mr. St. Martin tells me you're in possession of a shifter here who asked for directions to my home."

"Yeah, she's in the back office. The chick's got a mouth on her that would make a sailor blush."

"Most likely because you called her a chick or some other term she finds offensive."

"She's a shifter and a pretty dark one from her aura."

"She's a friend, and while she carries a large trace of Ebony in her, the Ebony is balanced by Emerald."

"I didn't sense any Emerald in her."

"Well, why don't you let me sort her out and get her out of your hair?"

"Sounds like a plan to me. Oh yeah, here's the key to the cuffs. She's all yours. Don't bother to lock up; the place hasn't been used in years, and the locks are all busted anyways," the man said before heading out the door.

Kieran made his way into the back office where he found Marissa sitting cuffed to a chair with a gag in her mouth. Kieran untied the gag before unlocking the cuffs. Marissa rubbed her wrists where the cuffs chafed against her skin. She rose and hugged Kieran. The close contact was enough for Kieran to sense all the dark spells wrapped around Marissa. He broke the hug and stepped back, Silver magic barely held in check.

"What the hell happened to you, Marissa?"

"The campus pack was betrayed to an Ebony mage by someone we thought trustworthy. The mage is holding Bruce and the rest of the pack hostage until I find you and bring you back to him wrapped in chains."

"And you figured the best way to do this was to head for an estate filled with people who kill shifters on sight, and ask for me by name?"

"I've been compelled. I'm still being compelled, Kieran. Believe me, if he left me enough freewill, I'd have called and begged you to come back to Little Rock to help us."

"Hold still. Let me check if I can break the spells binding you. This will hurt since your nature tends toward Ebony."

"Hurry and do this. I suffer enough each month when the change comes."

Kieran joined his hands together as if about to pray. When he pulled them apart, Silver magic flowed between them like a pulsing electric current. He lifted his hands above Marissa's head and spread his hands as he passed them along her body from head to toe. As he passed her heart, she screamed in agony while the spells anchored to her heart burned away. When Kieran finished, she sagged back into the chair for a moment to recover.

"What a relief, getting those spells broken. Thank you, Kieran."

"So what do you recall about this Ebony mage?"

"You want to do this here and now, Kieran? Surely, we can find someplace more civilized."

"Fine, we'll go to a diner in town, and you will tell me everything you recall about this mage."

"Thank you, Kieran."

Kieran led the way back to the SUV and introduced Marissa to this father, although some little nagging sensation made him introduce Kellen as his uncle instead of as his father. Was he imagining things or did a tiny flicker of Ebony go dull in her eyes? Kellen for his part played along, urging his nephew and his friend to hop in, and they were on their way out of the bad section of town. They drove for a while before Kellen pulled the SUV into an all-night diner. The three of them got out of the car and headed for the diner. Once inside, they grabbed a booth at the back of the place, ordered sodas and burgers, and waited before beginning their conversation.

"So, Marissa, what can you tell me about this Ebony mage?" Kieran asked.

"He's incredibly powerful, and several lesser mages of various colors work for him. Everyone only refers to him as the Master, and he never shows his face. He always keeps his face cloaked in shadow."

"Why does he want me?"

"One of his associates promised you would be delivered to him as a sex slave by one of the mages working for him. In part, he wants you for your beauty, but I gather from rumors that he also wants you for some ritual to break the ancient spell binding all shifters, Kieran."

"So what are his plans involving you?"

"He wanted me to plead with you to come back to Little Rock and rescue the pack. He said I needed to get you to kill the Alpha of the pack in the woods on your family estate, and then bring you and the head back to Little Rock. Once he gets both you and the head, he holds all the components to break the spell."

"Sounds more like he's trying to eliminate a troublesome ally or a dangerous opponent," Kellen added to the conversation.

"Might be, Uncle Kellen. He may have discovered he's not a strong enough Ebony mage to face me directly. I'll do what I can to help the pack out when I get back to Little Rock, Marissa. You should head back, but keep a low profile."

"I can't go back without you, Kieran. He'll kill them all if he finds I'm back and you're still here in Maine. I realize you must be planning to deal with the dark Alpha. Let me help. I can scout things out in advance for you on the next new moon. Nobody will take heed of an owl flying around the woods."

"I'm not challenging the Alpha yet, Marissa. I have to go consult some other mages about how the spell that binds shifters was cast, and even for a Silver mage, consulting the dead is a full moon spell."

"At least let me come with you. I can help with research or keep an eye out for shifters trying to sneak up on you."

"Well, I suppose we could let her stay in one of the guest cottages, Kieran," Kellen put in.

"Can you control your shift, Marissa?"

"Yes, I learned how to when I was a little girl."

"Good. I'm not keen on taking you where I'm going, but I don't have an alternative. Uncle Kellen is right. We can lodge you in a guest cabin until we're ready to make our move against the dark Alpha. Let's get back on the road. I miss Cory, and I'd like time with my husband before diving into all the research I'm going to have to do."

Kellen picked up the check and headed to the register, while Kieran and Marissa headed for the SUV. Kellen called the compound and alerted them to the unexpected guest and Kieran's rouse with identities before heading out to the car to drive back to the compound. The ride back to the compound was quiet, with only the music on the radio playing softly to break the silence. Marissa dozed in the back seat until the SUV passed through the gates of the Oisín compound and thus the barrier spells. She woke screaming as the Silver magic washed over her, challenging her presence. The SUV stopped, held by the spells, until Kieran reached back and grabbed Marissa's hand, granting her temporary passage through the barrier spells.

"Oh, God, my head fucking hurts. I've never experienced a spell of such intensity before."

"I doubt you will again, Marissa. Those spells have been woven by generations of mages. They're the reason I asked if you can control your shifting. You're not allowed to shift here. If you do, you'll break the outermost barrier, and I'll be forced to treat you like any other dark shifter and kill you."

"I promise not to shift, Kieran."

Kieran released his hold on Marissa, and she sank back in the seat. Wariness lit her eyes for a moment before she composed herself again. Neither Kieran nor Marissa were aware of what happened from miles away. The Master participated in everything via a spell buried deep in Marissa's shifter DNA. His control links were also buried in her genes. The barrier spell had burned him more so than Marissa, and he'd lost his concentration for a moment from the pain. When he refocused, his puppet was well inside the barrier, and a large log home was coming into view before her eyes. Marissa blinked and refocused on what Kieran was saying about dropping his uncle off at the main house before he took her to the guest cabin he shared with Cory.

They'd put her up with them until they cleaned and aired out another guest cabin. When the SUV stopped before the stairs to the main house, an older version of Kieran came bounding down the steps to meet them. Kieran glanced at the expression on his uncle's face and realized Brom was having too much fun over the idea of teasing his brother over the sudden change of relationship between them and Kieran. When Kieran got out of the SUV, Brom grabbed him in a fierce hug and actually lifted Kieran off his feet.

"Glad to have you home, Son. I hope the trip wasn't too much time with your uncle," Brom said as he set Kieran down.

"I survived. At least Grandmother didn't have all your faults to harp on along with my own. Dad, I'd like you to meet Marissa Holden, a friend from college."

Brom extended his hand to shake Marissa's. "A pleasure to meet a friend of Kieran's. Welcome, Marissa."

"Thank you, Mr. Belle. What a pleasure to meet you as well."

"Marissa, we don't stand on formality around here. You can call me Brom. Kieran, why don't you take Marissa to your cabin and get her settled in while your uncle and I catch up on some of what's going on?"

"Sure, Dad. Come on, Marissa. I'm sure Cory will be happy you're here."

The two young people climbed back into the SUV and headed off to the cabin where Kieran was living with Cory. The crunch of the SUV's tires on the road alerted Billy, who started howling from the front porch of the cabin until Cory appeared beside him in a pair of shorts. Marissa regarded Kieran, watching his face light up as he caught sight of Cory, and her heart grew heavy thinking of Bruce and the other members of her pack chained up in the Master's cells. Kieran hopped out of the vehicle and rushed up the stairs to engulf Cory in a hug and a deep kiss. Kieran broke the embrace and gestured over his shoulder, so Cory spotted Marissa climbing from the SUV. Billy's hackles raised, and his pants of joy changed to growls of warning as he bared his fangs. Kieran reached down and put his hand on Billy's head.

"Everything's okay, Billy. She's not going to hurt anyone."

The boy/wolf didn't appear convinced as he settled down on his back haunches. Marissa grabbed her bag and approached with care. Even Cory appeared leery of her presence. She passed Billy and gave

Cory a brief hug before going inside to wait in the living room of the cabin.

"Why is Marissa here, babe?" Cory asked.

"Safest place to keep someone you don't trust is where you can keep an eye on them, Wolf. She's been under the control of the dark mage we've been hearing about, and I'm not sure I broke all the spells on her."

"Wouldn't we be better of tossing her on a bus back to Little Rock?"

"I'm not sure. This mage is holding the rest of the campus pack hostage against Marissa's success. Until we possess more information, I'm afraid we're stuck with her."

"I'll leave the decision up to you, Kieran. Let's get her settled into the downstairs guest room, and we can all get ready for dinner at the main house."

"Yes, I've got a lot to discuss with Dad and Uncle Kellen, not to mention Gramps," Kieran said, cluing Cory in on his deception.

"Of course, your dad's been showing me some tricks with the forge, but Grams is a miracle worker in the kitchen, and she's kept me occupied helping her in the gardens and cleaning vegetables."

"She's taken a real shine to you. Come on, I want to grab a quick shower before dinner," Kieran said before giving Cory a quick kiss and heading inside.

While Kieran went upstairs, Cory showed Marissa to the downstairs guest room, got her fresh towels, and made sure she settled in.

"Dinner is in about half an hour up at the main house with Kieran's family."

"Okay, I'll freshen up and be ready to go in a few minutes. I'm sorry to intrude on you guys like this. I guess having an unwanted guest show up wasn't how you planned to welcome your husband home."

"Not in the slightest. You understand Kieran will do whatever is needed to rescue the rest of the campus pack. He has a soft spot in his heart for your little zoo."

"Says the big bad wolf! Who would ever imagine a shifter shacking up with a tracker from the House of Beauty? You're as much of a lapdog as your nephew out in the hall."

"Unlike Kieran, Marissa, I've never cared for you or your pack of misfit shifters. You have no idea how many generations my family has spent trying to purge the taint of being a shifter from our bloodline. You, Bruce, and the rest of the merry menagerie enjoy reveling in your shifter heritage. Get ready for dinner; we'll leave in ten minutes."

Cory turned and stalked out of the room. He headed upstairs to join Kieran in a fast shower and to get ready for dinner. Kieran sensed the deep mood Cory was in and opened his arms to his husband. They hugged under the water for a few moments before Kieran turned the shower off and dried them both off. They dressed in silence and headed downstairs where they met up with Marissa and a still growling Billy. The group left the cabin and piled into the SUV for the drive back up to the main house. Silence hung thick in the passenger compartment of the SUV on the short drive to the main house. Kieran parked and everyone got out to climb the stairs up to the front doors where Brom and Kellen waited for them. They escorted the group in to the dining room and showed them to their seats at the expanded table. Kieran introduced Marissa to his grandparents before the family and guest sat down to dinner.

Tension mounted around the table as the members of the Oisín clan tried to keep from lashing out at the dark shifter sitting at their table. Marissa's presence was an affront to everyone but Kieran, even though he was worried about what her true motives were and how free from the dark mage's influence she was in reality. He rose to help Grams clear the table and bring out dessert. As he walked back into the dining room, hands full of the chocolate cake Grams baked to welcome him home, he sensed the tension snap as Marissa grabbed up a stray steak knife and slashed across his grandfather's throat. Blood spurted everywhere as Grams screamed behind Kieran, and time slowed to a crawl as Marissa threw the knife at Brom before diving for the open window, shifting as she went through. Kieran came out of his shock as he experienced the outer barrier shatter under the ancient condition, which allowed the barrier to exist. He regarded his father and uncle trying to stop the bleeding from his grandfather's wound before diving out the window in pursuit of Marissa. As he rolled to his feet from his dive, he spotted a huge gray owl stooping to try to rake him with her claws. Silver fire leapt from his hand, forcing Marissa to veer off from her attack. While he never amounted to much of an archer, Kieran's training included all weapons. Magic answered his will and formed into a silver bow and a silver arrow. As Marissa wheeled for a second pass, Kieran drew back the magic bowstring and fired. The Silver magic arrow sliced through Marissa's right wing, and she whirled, trying to stay airborne. Ebony fire wrapped around her as Kieran drew back a second arrow. Marissa vanished from sight, and the Ebony magic faded away. Kieran cursed, trying to get a sense of where Marissa went. He reeled as a huge surge of power flooded into him. His scream ripped the air as the mantle of the Silver Witch settled around him. The power burned as it flowed into the channels created in him during the rituals.

Part of Kieran urged him to race back into the house and to the dining room, where somehow he knew he'd find his family kneeling beside the body of his grandfather. The magic of the Silver Witch showed him the scene inside: blood soaked the ancient carpet beneath the old man, who'd taught Kieran so much wisdom. Grams knelt beside her fallen husband; despite her efforts, Sapphire magic had failed to heal her beloved husband. Kieran saw the deep wound in his grandfather's throat and realized only a powerful Emerald mage would stand a chance of healing such as the one that claimed Gramps' life.

Kieran locked down his emotions for his grandfather, shoving them into the same place as his unshed tears for his sisters, before he redirected his new powers. The magic showed him his family drawing together to support Grams. Mere moments had passed as he refocused and cast his senses far and wide, trying to find Marissa. He sensed her darkness along with a deeper darkness in the one place he couldn't afford a dark shifter armed with dark objects. She appeared in the central clearing where Rosie's sword held the power of the inner barrier in place. Even as he moved to stop her, he projected a fragment of his new powers into his family.

"I'm sorry, this is all my fault. I'm going to set this as right as I can, but I need you all safe, and here isn't a safe place."

"Kieran, this is not your fault. How would anyone predict she would attack your grandfather?" Kellen said, reaching for his son.

"Her actions don't matter. They sent her to capture or kill me. I'm sending you to the cave now. She's about to shatter the second barrier, and my guess is a horde of shifters are waiting to overrun this place. When you arrive, weave the strongest wards you can manage over the entrance."

"Kieran, don't send us a—" Cory didn't get to finish his sentence as Silver magic wrapped around Kieran's family, and they vanished from the house.

The surviving Oisín found themselves on the ledge at the entrance to the seaside caves where Cory and Kieran spent a week not long ago. Brom ushered the family inside and raised the first barrier by triggering the wards already built into the place. He swapped with Kellen the task of escorting their mother out of harm's way. Kellen raised powerful wards along the passageway. Nothing left for them to do but wait.

INTERLUDE: THE MASTER INTERVENES

In his lair, far away from the Oisín compound, the Master gloated over the death of the old man as he sensed the man's life and power vanishing. His renegade hunter and the various dark shifters he recruited paced around the edges of the barrier spells. They advanced when the ancient outer barrier went down, only to lose one of their numbers as the cougar shifter slammed into the second barrier and burned to ash. The Master risked revealing his location, wrapped the wounded Marissa—still in her owl form—in an Ebony transport spell, and deposited her in the clearing holding the sword, which powered the second barrier. Beside her appeared the bag of items enchanted with Ebony magic. Under his total control, she shifted back to human form and began to wrap the sword in dark magic.

23

———

Unused to the new channels of magic, Kieran crashed into the clearing as he released the transport spell and realized he'd arrived too late to stop Marissa from destroying the barrier. He shuddered when the spell shattered as he cast silver fire at Marissa, driving her back from the rapidly melting sword. He stalked into the clearing as Marissa rose to face him.

"This time you can't escape, Marissa. Your death is going to be slow and painful."

"My death doesn't matter. You'll all be as dead as the old man soon. I served my purpose in the Master's plan."

"Burn in hell, shifter scum," Kieran screamed as the ancient knowledge of the Silver Witch showed him a powerful spell. The raw power burned through him; making Kieran scream in pain before he locked down the new channels, sealing off the powers he'd inherited with his grandfather's passing.

Silver magic wrapped around Marissa, binding her in chains, which burned her everywhere they touched bare flesh. Slowly, the chains tightened, burning deeper and deeper into her flesh and toward her bones. Kieran turned and walked away, knowing Marissa was finished. Time to face the dozens of other shifters headed his way. Kieran raced

for the main house where he figured the shifters would head first.
When he arrived in front of the house, Kieran summoned his magical
armor but not the scythe blades. From the house, he took his father's
silver long sword.

* * *

IN THE CAVERN by the beach, Kellen, Brom, and Cory took turns
keeping an eye on the entrance while Grams rested in the sleeping
chamber. The men would check on her from time to time to make sure
she rested. On one of his visits to check on Grams, Cory found her
sitting up and alert.

"Can I get you anything, Grams?" Cory asked.

"Bring me up-to-date on Kieran please, Cory."

"All I can tell through our bond is he's still alive, but I think he's
getting tired. Otherwise, all I sense is determination."

"As long as he's still alive, there is hope for us. Keep supporting
him with your love, Cory."

"I will, Grams." Cory crossed the room and hugged Grams, trying
to project not only his love, but also Grams' as well, to send to Kieran
via the bond.

* * *

KIERAN SPUN and dodged as he ran through the forest, trying to find
a good place to make a stand. He played the ambush game as much
as possible and had taken out seven or eight shifters already. When
the fifth shifter went down, he sensed another change come over
him, and realized he'd passed the test of the Huntress. Now, all he
needed to do was survive. Knowing he'd become the Hunter for his
generation freed Kieran to use his magic. Silver fire arced out,
catching two shifters dead-on and leaving their smoldering corpses
lying on the ground. Onward he raced, trying to find a good place to
make a stand. Magic leapt from one hand while he slashed with the
long sword in the other hand. Behind him, several shifters crashed

through the underbrush, close on his heels. Leaping over a fallen tree, Kieran crashed to the ground as a sudden wave of exhaustion hit him and his armor flared and vanished. Kieran rose and came to a halt when he found himself surrounded by shifters. He found himself facing five shifters with only a sword, dressed in street clothes. His father's silver long sword flashed, driving back the pair before him, but leaving him open to the trio behind him. They jumped him, claws raking fire across his back and legs. Kieran cursed not having his leathers or enough energy to re-summon his armor, and barely managed to throw off the shifter pinning him to the ground. He rolled and slashed at an exposed foreleg with the long sword. Goddess, if only he had his sabers. He bit back a scream as his wounded back rolled across an exposed root. Kieran's attempt to rise put him off-balance, and a cougar shifter pounced, sinking its teeth into his thigh.

Never had Kieran experienced such pain. Ebony fire burned through his flesh and blood, and Kieran experienced his lock on his grandfather's magic falter. Another shifter darted in, clamping its jaws on his right wrist with enough force to break the bones, and causing him to loose his grip on the sword. Sensing their prey was weakening, the next shifter lunged for Kieran's throat, while its partner sank its teeth into Kieran's right calf. Slowed by pain and the disruption of his magic, Kieran barely managed to get his left arm up and between his throat and the shifter's jaws. A dark shadow leapt in from the left and locked its jaws on the shifter trying to get to Kieran's throat. Kieran was crippled, and the shifters recognized the condition as they circled, trying to get past the dark wolf, which blocked their path. Kieran spotted the collar around the wolf's throat and recognized Billy.

"Billy, run. Go find Cory on the beach. Go now. My magic is about to explode."

Billy glanced at Kieran and bolted straight for the lead shifter, throwing the beast off its chosen path. The shifters circled in for the kill, and Kieran prayed Billy was far enough away.

His failing mind flashed to the memories pulled from Rosie's sword about her death and her bravery. Kieran thought Rosie spoke to him in his poison ravaged mind. *Go out fighting, big brother. Take the bastards with you.*

Kieran's also thought to himself, *I'm sorry, Gramps. I failed to get them all. I can't die with no one to take my place. Cory, I love you.*

Kieran's final coherent thought ripped through the Ebony poison of the shifters' bites and unlocked all the powers of the Silver Witch and unleashed the ancient Silver magic in one titanic blast of energy. The area around Kieran for a hundred yard radius was blasted into ruins. Trees shattered and burned; the shifters vanished in blood-red explosions as devastation radiated from Kieran's shattered body. Mercifully for Kieran, he passed out before the giant pine tree fell on him, breaking both legs and pinning him to the ground.

* * *

As Kieran brought down the forest, his agony and desperation smashed into Cory, who let out a blood-curdling scream, which transformed in the middle into an anguished howl. For the first time ever in his twenty-six years, he shifted shape into a beautiful silver wolf. Kellen and Brom tried to calm the agitated beast down, but Cory growled and snapped at them, trying to get past them to the exit. Grams stepped out of the sleeping chamber at this moment and went to her knees, opening her arms to Cory. The silver wolf gently thrust his head into her arms and whimpered as she stroked his fur.

"Reach for him, *mac tíre óg*. Find Kieran and find your humanity. I won't let anything happen to you. Come back to us for Kieran's sake." Grams rocked the wolf until he transformed into a sobbing and naked Cory.

Brom found a pair of shorts the boys must have left on their last visit. He helped Cory dress. Kellen gathered them all and urged them to the entrance of the cavern where they found a howling Billy. Cory did for Billy what Grams had done for him, and the wolf eventually took Cory's wrist in his jaw, tugging him in the direction that led back to the forest and the main house. The party of survivors followed the wolf back to the forest where they witnessed firsthand the destruction wrought by Kieran's magic. They picked their way carefully through the fallen trees and around the smoldering stumps until Billy lead them to a giant fallen pine. With a cry, Cory leapt toward the pine and landed beside Kieran's mangled body. Somehow, despite all the burning trees, Kieran's beautiful hair remained untouched. Cory called out to the others.

"He's over here under this tree. He's barely breathing."

Grams took charge, using her magic to stabilize Kieran, while Kellen and Brom worked to get the tree off him.

"Kellen, do you have enough power to transport us to the hospital?" Grams asked.

"No, Mother. Father severed my connection to the powers of the Silver Witch, so Kieran would have everything if anything happened to him. I can get you, Kieran, and myself back to the house, and we can load him in the van. Can you keep him stable long enough to get to the emergency facilities at Mount Desert Island Hospital in Bar Harbor?"

"I'll have to do my best, even if I need to lower his temperature until he's in a coma."

"Brom, you and Cory will have to go by foot back to the main house. Take the SUV and meet us in Bar Harbor."

"We'll be as close behind you as we can manage," Brom replied as Kellen began the transport spell, wrapping the magic around his mother and son as well as himself.

"Come on, Cory, we need to be around when they get to the hospital."

"Kieran will need clothes, and I'd better grab something besides these shorts."

"Your cabin is on the way. We'll pack a bag with clothes for both of you."

Cory, Brom, and Billy raced back toward the cabin. The real race, the one against death, had just begun. *Would they be able to get Kieran to medical treatment in time? Could the doctors save Kieran?* Cory wondered as he put on more speed, trying to get back to Kieran's side.

PLACE OF INTEREST MENTIONED
IN WITCH

Cory mentions in the story that he found the diamond for the ring he gives Kieran at Crater of Diamonds State Park back in Arkansas. This Arkansas State Park is unique among diamond sites anywhere in the world. It is open to the public and is the only site where you can hunt for diamonds and keep what you find. The diamonds from this park come in three colors: white, brown, and yellow. As I was writing *Witch,* a park visitor found an 8.52-carat white diamond, which became the new record holder for the fifth largest diamond found at the park since the property became a state park in 1972. For more information about Crater of Diamonds State Park and other Arkansas State Parks, visit www.ArkansasStateParks.com.

VOLUME THREE

Kethric Wilcox

Hunter

Legend of the Silver Hunter

Book Three

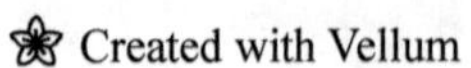 Created with Vellum

PUBLISHER'S NOTE

ACKNOWLEDGMENTS

Thank you once again, Tiger, for giving me a chance to express my creativity. Your love and support makes every day brighter.

A big shout out to my Beta Reader Lisa Cullinan and to all the fans of Kieran and Cory, this one is for you.

PART I

BEAUTY'S TALE

He was within thirty miles of his own house, thinking on the pleasure he should have in seeing his children again, when going through a large forest he lost himself. It rained and snowed terribly; besides, the wind was so high, that it threw him twice off his horse, and night coming on, he began to apprehend being either starved to death with cold and hunger, or else devoured by the wolves, whom he heard howling all round him, when, on a sudden, looking through a long walk of trees, he saw a light at some distance, and going on a little farther perceived it came from a palace illuminated from top to bottom. The merchant returned God thanks for this happy discovery, and hastened to the place, but was greatly surprised at not meeting with any one in the outer courts. His horse followed him, and seeing a large stable open, went in, and finding both hay and oats, the poor beast, who was almost famished, fell to eating very heartily; the merchant tied him up to the manger, and walking towards the house, where he saw no one, but entering into a large hall, he found a good fire, and a table plentifully set out with but one cover laid. As he was wet quite through with the rain and snow, he drew near the fire to dry himself. "I hope," said he, "the master of the house, or his servants will excuse the liberty I take; I suppose it will not be long before some of them appear."

He waited a considerable time, until it struck eleven, and still nobody came. At last he was so hungry that he could stay no longer, but took a chicken, and ate it in two mouthfuls, trembling all the while. After this he drank a few glasses of wine, and growing more courageous he went out of the hall, and crossed through several grand apartments with magnificent furniture, until he came into a chamber, which had an exceeding good bed in it, and as he was very much fatigued, and it was past midnight, he concluded it was best to shut the door, and go to bed.

It was ten the next morning before the merchant waked, and as he was going to rise he was astonished to see a good suit of clothes in the room of his own, which were quite spoiled; certainly, said he, this palace belongs to some kind fairy, who has seen and pitied my distress. He looked through a window, but instead of snow saw the most delightful arbors, interwoven with the beautifullest flowers that were ever beheld. He then returned to the great hall, where he had supped the night before, and found some chocolate ready made on a little table. "Thank you, good Madam Fairy," said he aloud, "for being so careful, as to provide me a breakfast; I am extremely obliged to you for all your favors."

The good man drank his chocolate, and then went to look for his horse, but passing through an arbor of roses he remembered Beauty's request to him, and gathered a branch on which were several; immediately he heard a great noise, and saw such a frightful Beast coming towards him, that he was ready to faint away.

"You are very ungrateful," said the Beast to him, in a terrible voice; "I have saved your life by receiving you into my castle, and, in return, you steal my roses, which I value beyond any thing in the universe, but you shall die for it; I give you but a quarter of an hour to prepare yourself, and say your prayers."

The merchant fell on his knees, and lifted up both his hands, "My lord," said he, "I beseech you to forgive me, indeed I had no intention to offend in gathering a rose for one of my daughters, who desired me to bring her one."

"My name is not My Lord," replied the monster, "but Beast; I don't

love compliments, not I. I like people to speak as they think; and so do not imagine, I am to be moved by any of your flattering speeches. But you say you have got daughters. I will forgive you, on condition that one of them come willingly, and suffer for you. Let me have no words, but go about your business, and swear that if your daughter refuse to die in your stead, you will return within three months."

The merchant had no mind to sacrifice his daughters to the ugly monster, but he thought, in obtaining this respite, he should have the satisfaction of seeing them once more, so he promised, upon oath, he would return, and the Beast told him he might set out when he pleased, "but," added he, "you shall not depart empty handed; go back to the room where you lay, and you will see a great empty chest; fill it with whatever you like best, and I will send it to your home," and at the same time Beast withdrew.

Beauty and the Beast, Jeanne-Marie LePrince de Beaumont, English translation, 1757

Mother never refuted this section of the tale. She loved her father, the last man she ever really loved, and I think she wanted to remember him as someone who loved her after the rest of her family abandoned her to her fate. Family rumors abound. The youngest of my uncles, Johan, supposedly had a destiny he chose not to face or was forbidden to face by Grandfather. Whatever the case may be, Johan gifted Mother with the ability to channel Silver magic once in her lifetime in her greatest hour of need. We all suspect she used her spell during the fight with the Beast, but even on her deathbed, she wouldn't revel what she'd done with the spell. Father past many years after Mother. I believe his fear of her kept him from revealing the truth.

From the First Chronicle of the House of Beauty, translated from the original French, 1998

PROLOGUE: THREE WEEKS AGO

John Mason was surprisingly excited when he got off the phone with Kieran Belle. The boy's excitement about his upcoming wedding and handfasting was contagious. The photography professor dialed his travel agent to arrange for a trip to Maine. As he gave the travel agent his details, John wandered through the living room and stopped before the photographic portrait of Kieran's fiancé hanging over the fireplace. A shirtless Cory Cooper, leaning on a piece of construction equipment, looked back at the professor with a deeply felt love for the man on the other side of the camera. The boys hadn't even begun to admit their feelings for each other when the picture had been taken, but you didn't have to know them to sense what they felt in that moment in time. John's daydreaming was broken by the voice of the agent.

"Sir, are you still there?"

"Yes, I'm sorry. My mind wandered off. What were those flight times again?"

The agent rattled off the flight information between Little Rock and Maine, along with the cost. John agreed and added in a rental car booking, and then gave the agent his credit card information. The agent let him know his reservations were complete and could download his tickets when he was ready. John thanked the man and hung up. He decided he'd call Kieran back when he had his tickets in hand.

1

PRESENT TIME

The transport spell faded, depositing Grams, Kellen, and an unconscious Kieran in the garage attached to the main house. Kellen and Grams made Kieran as secure and comfortable as possible in the back of the family van. Grams stayed in the back with Kieran using her Sapphire magic to heal what damage she could. She was fighting a desperate battle to save her grandson. Between the damage the falling tree had done and the wounds inflicted by the shifters during his defense of the compound, Kieran was an unrecognizable mess. Ebony magic surged in his system from the numerous bites he'd received fighting off the shifters, and now it was fighting her efforts, keeping Kieran on the edge of death.

She dug in. Recalling how some Sapphire mage had locked away the Ebony magic within Cory's blood, she crafted a binding spell. It began to chase down the Ebony magic and corral it, driving it away from Kieran's vital organs. Kellen drove like a mad man, using the reserves of his own magic to keep the tires attached to the road as he raced to the hospital in Bar Harbor.

Back at the Oisín compound, Cory, Brom, and Billy raced back to the cabin Kieran and Cory had been living in, so Cory could get dressed and pack clothes for Kieran to wear. When Cory burst through the open door just ahead of Brom and Billy, he found a man sitting on the couch in the front room. The stranger, who'd brought the attacking shifters to the compound, bristled with weapons and reeked of Ebony magic. Without thinking, Cory leapt at the man, shifting shape in mid-leap to become a silver wolf. He crashed into the stranger, sending him over the back of the couch. Brom snatched up a fire poker as he raced past the fireplace to pin the man down.

"Who are you?" Brom snarled.

"Alex Kincaid, I've come to collect the Master's prize. Where is young Belle?"

"No place you need to worry about, murdering scum," Brom said as he slammed the poker down on the man's head until he was sure Kincaid was unconscious.

Brom turned to find Cory caught in a midway form, between his wolf shape and his human form. Brom couldn't help himself. A vision of the character from the animated version of Beauty's story superimposed itself over Cory's figure. Hysteria got the better of him, and he started laughing at Cory. From his perspective, Cory couldn't figure out what was so funny about the situation until he turned and caught a glimpse of himself in the mirror over the fireplace. His own laughter burst forth, and his shift completed back to human.

When Brom finally got himself under control, he urged Cory to get dressed. Blushing, Cory dashed upstairs to get dressed and toss some clothes in a bag. As he opened the closet, he was confronted by Kieran's tracker armor. Tears sprang to his eyes as he thought about how Kieran might not be hovering on the edge of death if he'd been wearing those enchanted leathers. He tried to sense Kieran through their bond, but only sensed pain. He poured his love down the bond, hoping it would strengthen Kieran's spirit to fight through the pain. Cory dressed in his own clothes, even though he would have loved to toss on one of Kieran's shirts, but while they were the same height, Kieran was narrower in build than he was. He tossed a couple of changes of their clothes into an overnight bag before heading back downstairs. After setting down the bag, Cory wrapped Uncle Brom in a hug, which caught the older man off guard for a moment.

"Are you okay, Cory? This has been a rough day for all of us, but . . ." Brom didn't finish elaborating. They both knew Cory's husband was fighting for his life; toss in Cory's sudden ability to shape-shift at will, who wouldn't be having a rough day.

"I just needed to hold something of Kieran's for a moment to ground myself again. He mentioned a couple of times how much he liked it when you'd hold him when he was here and sad. I guess I needed to feel what he felt for a moment."

Brom hugged Cory tight as he'd done for Kieran so often as a boy.

"I get it, Cory. Kieran is the son I never had. Now, before we go to him, we need to take care of this piece of trash. The sad part is he's human. I want you to go on ahead to the hospital. I'll catch up after I've taken care of Mr. Kincaid and the coroner has come and collected Dad's remains."

"Do you think Kieran caught up to Marissa?"

"Yes, I'm sure he did. My magic is limited at this distance from my forge or another Silver mage, but I can sense a very ancient and nasty Silver magic spell active in the center of the property. I think he cast a spell, which borders on being forbidden. If he did cast that particular spell, neither you nor I want to see it in action. Pray he doesn't remember what he did when he wakes up."

"Okay, I'm going to go to the hospital now."

"Make sure you take a copy of your marriage license with you. In the rush to get Kieran medical treatment, Kellen and Mom may not remember, but you have as much right to make Kieran's medical decisions for him as they do."

"I packed it, figuring I'd need to prove I'm his husband so I could even visit him. I didn't stop to think about medical decisions."

"Kellen and Mom won't let anything bad happen to him, but they aren't going to be thinking about what might happen to you if Kieran isn't going to recover. In that event, their first priority is going to be to transfer the power of the Silver Witch back to Kellen."

"I won't let them hurt Kieran. He has to recover. I can't live without him, but I won't trap him on life support forever."

"Cory, listen to me. Kieran is very tough; he's a descendant of two of the most powerful families in history. I'm sure no one's ever told you how his mother died."

"No, but I assumed she was killed by a shifter while on a hunt."

"No single shifter was ever a match for my sister-in-law. To bring her down took an entire pack of the darkest shifters anyone had ever encountered. In the end, fifty shifters died to take her out. Kieran's maternal grandmother wanted him to be with his mother on that mission, but his two uncles—Eric and Stephen—said he wasn't old enough or ready to go. They went in his place. While they were skilled trackers and experienced fighters in their own right, neither of them was gifted. Miranda used her one shot of Silver magic trying to save them instead of herself."

"But you think if Kieran had been there she would have survived?"

"No, I honestly think Miranda was destined to die that night," Brom said, opening his mouth to continue, but Kincaid groaned. He hit him with the poker again, and then sighed. "Kellen brought Kieran here to get him away from his grandmother because she blamed him for her daughter's and sons' deaths." He paused as if considering his next words, but never took his eyes off Kincaid. "She blamed a ten-year-old boy—for failing to be old enough or skilled enough to go out and die. I spent months convincing Kieran their deaths weren't his fault. Months." He kicked Kincaid for good measure. "I don't want him falling into that pattern over his grandfather's death. There was no way to know Marissa was going to attack any of us like she did." He looked up from Kincaid to meet Cory's amber eyes. "We have to keep him from blaming himself, or we will lose him."

* * *

KELLEN WHIPPED the family van into the patient drop-off for the Emergency Room at Mount Desert Island Hospital. After he parked, he hopped out of the van and raced inside to get medical personnel. Once the desk nurse heard about Kieran's injuries, she summoned immediate assistance, and a gurney was rolled out to the van. Grams withdrew her magic the moment the doors to the back of the van were pulled open.

With her magic gone, Kieran began to seize as the pain came crashing back into his body. The emergency team slid a full body board into the van and got Kieran transferred to the board and then onto the gurney. They rushed him into the hospital and into an exam room. Grams moved as quickly as she could to stay with Kieran while Kellen dealt with paperwork, registering Kieran as Kieran Oisín without even thinking about it. Once the paperwork was filled out, Kellen moved the van to the parking lot before going back to find his mother standing in the hall as a team of doctors worked to stabilize Kieran. Monitors beeped and pinged as doctors called out orders for blood typing, meds, and X-rays. The surgical team and operating room were prepped.

Kellen could tell his mother wanted to use her magic to hold Kieran stable so the doctors didn't have to deal with it while they treated his injuries. One glance at his mother and he could see her exhaustion. She'd already pushed herself beyond her limits.

"Mother, come, let's find a place to sit—out of the way of the trauma team. Brom and Cory should be here soon."

"I could still be keeping him stable, Kellen. I can hold him while they fix all the broken parts."

"You're exhausted, Mother. You won't do Kieran any good if you kill yourself trying to do what the doctors can do. He's going to need us all when he wakes up."

"I can't lose him too, Kellen. Not after loosing Aodhfin like that."

"We're not going to lose Kieran; we can't even think those thoughts. He's well-anchored to this world, Mother, by his bond with Cory." His own words gave him pause. "Oh, hell. I wasn't thinking when I registered Kieran into the hospital. I put his last name down as Oisín."

"We need to go fix that right now, Kellen. Cory will be frantic when he gets here. He won't think to ask under only Oisín, not at first anyway."

They quickly made their way back to the Emergency Room admission desk to correct Kellen's error only to find an agitated Cory. He demanded to know where his husband was. Kellen caught him around the shoulders.

"Cory, calm down. They have him in a trauma unit, trying to

stabilize him so they can get X-rays and prep him for surgery. I'm sorry I wasn't thinking when I filled out the paperwork and signed him in under Oisín. Mother and I were just coming to fix that mistake and get him registered under Oisín-Cooper."

"Cory, come with me. We'll get something to drink while we wait for the doctors to let us know when we can be with Kieran," Grams said, taking Cory's arm to lead him away from the desk.

"But I need to talk to registration."

"Kellen is taking care of that."

"I have the right to make Kieran's medical decisions. I'm his husband, and see, here's the paperwork, plus his insurance cards, and a copy of his medical records from Little Rock. Please don't take him away from me."

"We're not trying to take him away from you, *mac tíre óg*. I promise you, we'd never do that to you. Kellen will fix the paperwork and get you put down as the primary contact."

Kellen came over with a clipboard full of paperwork and handed it to Cory.

"As his lawful spouse, you need to fill these out and sign them. I'm sorry, Cory. I was worried about my son, and I didn't stop to think about my son-in-law. Let's get these filled out, and let the nurse make a copy of all your paperwork for their records." His eyes shifted away. "Where's Brom? I thought you two would be together."

Cory filled them in quietly, "We ran into a human hunter waiting in our cabin to collect Kieran for someone called the Master. Brom stayed behind to take care of him and to arrange for the coroner to come and take care of Gramps' body. He sent me on ahead, figuring that something like this would happen," he said. "I'm sorry I'm being rude. I don't mean to be."

"We're all on edge, Cory. Once you finish the paperwork, you have full control over what happens to Kieran. We will support your decisions."

"Even if I decide to let him go without letting you take back the power of the Silver Witch?"

Both Grams and Kellen gasped at the thought; it hadn't even

crossed their minds yet. They looked at Cory in horror for a moment before Kellen spoke in hushed tones.

"If that's the price I must pay to keep peace in this family, so mote it be."

* * *

CORY BENT his head to focus on the paperwork and in acknowledgement of Kellen's sacrifice. He wondered if Brom had misjudged his brother or if Kellen had a secret plan to draw the power out of Kieran. No time for such thoughts; he needed to focus on Kieran and his treatment. He finished the paperwork and took it to the front desk along with his marriage certificate, Kieran's insurance cards, and the medical records from Little Rock. He signed a few more papers in front of the desk nurse and then watched as she entered the corrections in the computer to generate proper paperwork for Kieran.

When it was complete, Cory went back to sit with Grams and Kellen to wait for the doctors to tell them something about Kieran. Brom arrived a short while later and joined the family in the waiting room. Control of the situation was out of their hands now.

Three hours later, the lead doctor on the trauma team headed out to the waiting room to find the boy's family. The admitting nurse handed him new information on the young man. He flinched when he read the young man was married to another man.

"I should have known someone that pretty and with that much hair was a faggot," the doctor muttered loud enough the nurse heard him.

The nurse remained silent.

"Go get Dr. Mihaylova, and have her come deal with the family."

"Yes, Dr. Miller," the nurse said before leaving to find the young Russian doctor.

The nurse found her in conversation with Dr. Thomas Waffe, the chief surgeon for their tiny hospital. From what the nurse overheard, the patient's chances did not sound good.

"I'm sorry to interrupt, but Dr. Miller sent me to get Dr. Mihaylova to do the consult with the family and bring them up to speed on the patient's condition."

"What brought this about?" Dr. Waffe asked instead. "Dr. Miller was already on the way to meet with the family and brief them on the boy's condition."

The nurse handed over information to explain. "Here's the updated patient information, Dr. Waffe."

"Oh, this is beyond belief. Miller and his prejudices." Dr. Waffe sighed. "So what if the young man is married to another man? Uphold your damn oath." Dr. Waffe turned to Dr. Mihaylova. "Anna, would you prefer to let me handle the family?"

"We can go meet with the family together, Thomas. I think they will appreciate access to two doctors."

The doctors followed the admissions nurse back to the waiting area for the emergency room. They were met with four faces in various states of worry and concern. Relationships were easy to discern for the doctors, the two dark-haired men and the older woman were blood relatives, which left the handsome young blond man as the husband.

"Mr. Oisín-Cooper, I'm Dr. Anna Mihaylova, and this is Dr. Thomas Waffe, our chief of surgery. Let's sit and talk about your husband's condition and how he got injured so badly."

"We were out hiking in the forest and this huge tree began falling," Cory explained. "Kieran shoved me out of the way, but the tree caught him and pinned him to the ground."

"What actually happened, Mr. Oisín-Cooper?" Dr. Mihaylova was short. "He has what appear to be bite wounds on his arms and legs, and his back is torn up with what appear to be claw marks."

"Dr. Mihaylova," Kellen interjected, "if you don't mind, my son-in-law—like the rest of us—is very worried about Kieran. There will be time later to talk about how he received his injuries. Please, Kieran's condition."

The doctor looked up at the tall man and felt a sudden shock of recognition as her amethyst eyes met Kellen's violet eyes. Where did she know him from, and why was she suddenly drawn to him? She sat in stunned silence for a moment until she realized Dr. Waffe was talking to the family. She ripped her gaze away from Kellen's and refocused on the rest of the family and Dr. Waffe.

"Kieran's condition is critical," Dr. Waffe said. "He's taken a lot of damage. Most of his injuries are internal. We need to get him into surgery as quickly as possible. We're only holding off for his CT scan to come back, so we can know if he's suffering from any intracranial bleeding. Honestly, I think it's possible he may have a subdural hematoma since he hasn't regained even the slightest trace of consciousness while we've been running our tests."

"What do you need from us, Dr. Waffe?" Cory asked.

"You'll need to sign the paperwork to give us permission to operate on your husband."

"Of course, Kieran gets whatever medical treatments he needs." Cory practically shouted from the relief of being able to do something for Kieran.

"Good, I'll have the nurse start prepping his head in case we have to relieve pressure in the skull."

"I take it you mean you're going to shave off his hair."

"Yes, please understand, Mr. Oisín-Cooper, we're hoping we won't have to do anything, but we should be ready in case we have to open his skull to stop any major bleeding."

"I understand. Can you save his hair? He always said if I let him cut it, he wanted to donate the length to one of those charities that make wigs for cancer patients."

"Of course we can. I'll have the nurse bag it for you."

"Dr. Waffe, besides the possible head injury, what other injuries does Kieran have?"

"Well, he has several broken ribs, none of which appear to be endangering his internal organs, but both of his legs have suffered severe fractures, which we'll have to set and very likely hold together with pins and rods until the bones knit. Both wrists are fractured too, plus all the damage done by those possible bite and claw wounds. He has a lot of bruising, and until we can get him on the table, I can't be sure how much damage has been done to him internally."

"Thank you, doctor. Please keep us informed," Cory said. "I'll go sign the required forms."

The doctors left to get Kieran prepped for surgery. Cory sat stunned by the extent of the damage. He tried to hold himself together, but the first tear escaped, and after it fell, he couldn't hold them back any longer. Líadáin was quick to wrap Cory in a hug.

"Why didn't he escape before they cornered him? I would have expected him to summon his armor. Why didn't he use his magic to join us in the cavern? We could have helped him hold them off. I can't live without him. He has to live."

"*Mac tíre óg*, he's strong, and while Silver magic can't heal like Sapphire or Emerald can, his magic will hold things together once the doctors get everything back in place."

"Grams, why couldn't you heal him?"

"My Sapphire magic did what it could, dear one. His injuries are beyond my healing abilities. To heal him magically we'd need a powerful Emerald mage who'd be willing to take the risk of burning out his magic in Kieran's healing."

"We'd better get the paperwork signed, so the doctors can do their work, Cory," Kellen coaxed.

"Of course, do you think they'll let me see him before they shave off his hair?"

"We can only ask, Cory," Kellen said, offering his hand to help Cory stand.

The entire Oisín clan rose and went with Cory to the admissions desk. The nurse looked up at Cory's tear-stained face and the grim looks of the three people with him.

"What can I do for you, sweetheart?" the nurse asked.

"I was hoping we could see my husband before they prep him for surgery."

"Oh, honey, of course. Come with me, and we'll try to see if we can do that right now. Sally, will you cover the desk for me, while I take the family back to see the boy in 501?"

"Sure, no problem, Trudy. You go on back. I'll buzz June and let her know you're bringing them back so they can hold off prep for a few minutes."

INTERLUDE: DURING THE ATTACK

Professor John Mason sat in his living room, staring at the photograph mounted above the fireplace. There was a tension in the air, as if something terrible had happened, and Kieran was involved. The professor had some connection to his student since their magic had touched during the Thanksgiving dinner Kieran had helped him with. Without thinking, John found himself dialing Kieran's number, hoping everything was all right. Kieran's phone rolled directly to voicemail. John's worry only grew. He called his travel agent and set about changing his travel plans. After he had new travel arrangements, John called the dean of his college to change his request from vacation time to a sabbatical for the coming academic year. The dean wasn't happy about the short notice, but John's performance was above all the standards, so he granted the sabbatical.

John began packing the things he felt he would need, including a battered old book he'd been writing in since he was a young boy and learning magic from his grandmother. He also made a phone call to his sister Vivian. Her phone rolled to voicemail too, so he left a message for her to call him. He hoped she'd come meet him in Maine.

2

HOURS AFTER THE ATTACK

Cory entered into the patient room where the hospital staff was prepping Kieran for surgery. He stared at his husband's battered and broken body. Bruising covered Kieran's beautiful face like a Halloween mask. Monitors beeped and pinged, tracking his vital signs. Tubes and wires were everywhere, and Cory could hardly hold back tears as he moved closer to his husband's bedside. Gently he stroked a strand of Kieran's hair away from his face. Tears rolled down his face as he softly placed a kiss on Kieran's forehead.

"Please come back to me, babe. I need you," Cory whispered in his husband's ear.

Grams, Kellen, and Brom each took a brief moment with Kieran before they gathered up the shattered Cory and led him back out to the waiting room. Elsewhere in the hospital, Dr. Waffe was prepping for surgery and examining the latest round of X-rays and the CAT scan. He sighed in relief as he noted there was no sign of subdural hematoma in Kieran's skull. He had his surgical nurse call down to the room where they were getting Kieran ready to cancel the head shaving. The nurse who took the call was glad not to have to remove the boy's hair, and she carefully coiled it into an extra large surgical cap to keep it from getting into any incisions the doctor made. She then called out to the front desk to let them know the good news. The surgical team came shortly after that and wheeled Kieran off to the surgical bay.

* * *

CORY PACED the waiting room of the small hospital waiting for news on Kieran's surgery. He'd been relieved when the doctor had cancelled the need to shave Kieran's head. News that there was no apparent injury to his brain had brought the whole family relief. Now Dr. Waffe and Dr. Mihaylova were trying to put all the broken pieces back together and stop the internal bleeding around his kidneys. Their goal was to get Kieran stabilized in order to transport him to Eastern Maine Medical Center in Bangor for better care in a larger facility. Dr. Mihaylova had admitting privileges there, so she would be able to transfer with Kieran to monitor his condition, especially if he grew worse.

INTERLUDE: KELLEN PLOTS TO RECLAIM THE MAGIC

As the days passed after Kieran's initial rounds of surgery with no signs of him regaining consciousness, Kellen began to worry that the ancient legacy of the Silver Witch would be truly lost. He regretted giving Cory his word that he'd let the magic be lost if Kieran didn't recover. Pacing the hallways of the hospital, Kellen began to plan a way to recover the powers and knowledge locked away inside his own son.

Father used a blood bond ritual to give Kieran access to all of his power in case something happened to him. Maybe I can work a similar ritual to let the power pass back to me should the unthinkable happen and Kieran dies. I have to do something. I can't let the heritage of the Silver Witch die with my son.

After swapping places with his brother Brom at Kieran's bedside for a while, Kellen gladly turned over the sad task of watching over his son to Cory. As he was leaving the hospital, Brom stopped him.

"You have that look you get when you're plotting something you shouldn't be, Brother."

"I'm just going home to collect the Grimoire to see if there's anything in it that might help us fix Kieran."

"Be sure that's all you're planning to do, Brother. Remember, you gave Cory your word you wouldn't attempt to reclaim the power of the Silver Witch from Kieran."

"And I intend to keep that promise, Brom. I want my son alive and well, more than I want the legacy of the powers that left him in this state."

Kellen turned and strode out of the hospital under the watchful eyes of his older brother—an older brother who did not trust him in the least.

3

____

After hours of surgery to repair Kieran's internal injuries and to begin setting his fractures, he was finally wheeled into a private room. Cory made sure that Grams got the one visitor chair in the room so that she could sit and rest while being close to Kieran. He stood on the opposite side of the bed running his hand over his husband's head, stroking his long black hair. Kellen and Brom sat on the couch beneath the window. The floor nurse came in to check on Kieran's vitals and meds, taking notice of the worn-out family scattered around the room.

"It's going to be some time before we see if he comes around after everything wears off. Why don't you go home, grab a shower, eat something, and get some rest? We'll call you if anything about his condition changes."

"I brought clothes, this room has a shower, and I can sleep on the couch," Cory protested. "I'm not leaving my husband's side."

Kellen and Brom rose from the couch and moved to help their mother up.

"I picked up a change of clothes for myself and my mother when I went back to the house," Kellen said. "We'll go get a couple of hotel rooms and be back in the morning so you can rest, Cory."

"I'll go back to the compound and pick up some of my things after we book the hotel," Brom stated as he helped his mother from the room.

Cory moved around the bed to settle into the visitor chair. He pushed it up against the side of Kieran's bed so he could rest his head on the mattress and be close to Kieran. The stress of the day didn't take long to catch up to Cory, and he soon drifted to sleep. The nursing staff came and went as quietly as they could, trying not to wake the sleeping young man.

"They're such an adorable young couple," the day nurse said to the evening nurse. "It's so sad to see the shape the poor boy is in."

"What on earth happened to the poor boy?" the night nurse asked.

"The report says a tree fell on him, but he has other injuries consistent with being attacked by animals. Nobody pushed for more details because the boy was in such bad shape, and neither his husband nor his father would answer any more questions until after the doctors had done their job."

"Well, maybe when the boy wakes up after the anesthesia wears off, we can get the full story. If his injuries are that bad, then a police report should be filed." The night nurse's face grew pale as she began to read the patient's chart her. "Oh, this is horrible. I thought the name on this chart sounded sort of familiar. There was a story on the local news about an attack on the Oisín compound and that Mr. Oisín was killed. The police say the attacker used a pack of dogs to try and hunt down the rest of the family."

"The boy was originally registered under the name Oisín before his husband arrived to correct it to Oisín-Cooper. Do you think that the dogs got to him after the tree fell and pinned him?"

"I don't know. It doesn't explain why he's still alive."

"Shouldn't one of you ladies be on rounds?" Dr. Mihaylova asked as she entered the nursing station.

"Yes, doctor, I was just getting up to speed on the new patients."

"Is that what they're calling it these days in Maine? Where I went to medical school, it was called gossiping. I'll take Mr. Oisín-Cooper's chart; there are some items to update while I check on his recovery status."

Dr. Mihaylova walked out of the nurse's station and into Kieran's room. Both of the occupants were asleep, so she tried to remain quiet as she moved across the room. But it only took one step for all that to change. Cory woke suddenly and snarled at her like a wolf protecting its injured mate. At first, she even thought she saw claws at the end of Cory's fingers before a soft silver light seemed to wash over him, and he sank back in his chair.

"I'm sorry, Dr. Mihaylova." Cory mangled the pronunciation of her name. "You startled me."

"Why don't you call me Dr. Anna? It will be easier to pronounce, Mr. Oisín-Cooper," she replied with a small smile.

"If you will call me Cory and my husband Kieran. We're not used to the new last name yet; it's still only a few weeks old." Cory's smile was weak but stunning.

"Then we have a deal, Cory. I'm going to check Kieran's vital signs and make sure everything is going well after the surgery. Have you noticed any sign of his regaining consciousness?" she asked as she proceeded to check vital signs, bandages, and the latticework of rods and pins holding Kieran's shattered legs together.

"No, if he'd stirred, I would have known and buzzed for a nurse," Cory replied around a yawn.

"I'll have the nurse come and make the couch for you to sleep on, Cory."

"Thank you, Dr. Anna. I'm tired, but I don't want to leave him all alone."

"Nobody's throwing you out, Cory. We just want you to be comfortable, so you can be well rested. If Kieran is still in stable condition by late tomorrow, I'll check and see if there's a room available for him at the hospital in Bangor as we discussed before he went into surgery."

"Thank you, Dr. Anna. Please know that the Oisíns have said that cost is not a concern." Cory's response was hesitant when talking about Kieran's family money.

"Just relax, Cory. We're doing everything we can for Kieran. Get some sleep if you can. His vitals are looking good. I am a little concerned about the fever he's running, but it's likely due to his body trying to fight to heal itself. If it doesn't break in a day or two, I'll put him on additional medications."

Dr. Anna finished checking Kieran over, making notes in his patient chart before she left to finish her rounds. She stopped by the nurses station and directed the duty nurse to get the couch in Kieran's room set up as a bed for Cory. Afterward, she continued her rounds, trying hard not to think about what she might have seen.

* * *

LATER IN THE EVENING, after the Oisíns had left Cory sitting beside Kieran's bed, Father Ivory de Beauchamps, the hospital chaplain, was wandering the halls checking on patients and family members. He made his way up to the floor where Kieran's room was located and noticed a different feel to this floor; the peaceful calm was disturbed by the ebb and flow of magic. He followed his senses until he stood outside of Kieran's room where he saw the faint glow of Silver magic wrapped around the joined hands of two young men. One was a patient swathed in casts and bandages, the other an attractive blond with red-rimmed eyes from abundant tears. As if sensing Father Ivory's presence, the blond looked up and focused bleary amber eyes on the young priest.

"I'm sorry to intrude. I'm Father Ivory, the hospital chaplain. Would you like someone to talk with?"

"I wasn't expecting anyone other than the nurses to be wandering around this late at night, Father. Neither of us is Catholic, and I doubt you'd approve of us."

"This young man is obviously important to you, and while my church's doctrine frowns on such things, I can tell you're very much in love with him . . . and I think from the way Silver magic shines around your hands the feelings are returned."

"You can see our bond? Kieran told me that only the two of us could see it," Cory replied. Fear of discovery tinged his voice.

"I have a gift related to magic called second sight. While I can't work magic myself, I can see it in those who have it or when it has been used. I think in your case, your love for Kieran is visible to anyone who looks at the two of you."

"What else does your sight show you about us?" Cory asked.

Father Ivory's face went blank for a moment as he looked at the young man in the hospital bed. A vision washed over his sight, showing a glimpse of a glowing man in medieval hunting attire bending over the young man as if to whisper in his ear. Father Ivory blinked, trying to focus on what appeared to be the patron saint of his order, but as he did, the vision vanished. He came to himself as he felt Cory's hand on his shoulder.

"Are you okay, Father Ivory?" Cory asked. "You seemed to have blanked out for a moment."

"Just a momentary dizzy spell. I've never been near anyone so gifted in magic before. I had a vision of my order's patron saint, Saint Hubert."

"Sorry, not a Catholic, I have know idea who Saint Hubert is or what he's a patron saint of."

"Hubert is the patron saint of hunters and protection from rabies, among other things. Kieran was bitten by something; that's how the darkness got into him."

Cory took Father Ivory by the arm, turned him around, and escorted him from the room. "Thank you for your visit, Father, but I think it's time for you to go check on other patients. It's been a long day, and Kieran is scheduled for more tests in the morning. I'd like to get some rest before they come to take him down."

Before he could speak, Father Ivory found himself staring at the closed door to the hospital room. Something told him he'd be back again. He could still feel the magic inside the room.

4

———

ellen, Brom, and Grams found Cory curled up on the couch asleep when they returned the next morning. Grams quietly settled into the chair at Kieran's bedside while her sons went to see if they could find some additional chairs. Líadáin stroked her grandson's right hand, trying to work the healing aspect of her Sapphire magic into the shattered wrist, but she found her power blocked by a swirl of Ebony magic. She focused and let her power scan Kieran's body. She shivered as she discovered the pools of Ebony magic near all of Kieran's major injuries, especially one waiting at the base of his skull, blocked by a powerful shield of Silver magic. So deep was she in trance that when Cory's cellphone rang, she nearly screamed.

Cory groped blindly for his phone as he struggled to wake up. He thumbed it into accepting the call and answered. "Cory Cooper, can I help you?"

"What's wrong, baby?" Cory could make out the sudden concern in his mother's voice.

"Kieran's in the hospital, Mom." Cory's voice cracked as tears began to flow. "He's been through a massive round of surgery, and he still hasn't woken up."

"Oh, Corwin, are you all right? What happened?" Tamara asked.

Cory knew his mother would be pacing the kitchen at home, trying to figure out how she could fix things from Arkansas.

"I can't give you all the details over the phone, Mom. We were attacked, and Kieran ended up pinned under a massive tree. The doctor hopes to move him to a larger hospital over in Bangor this afternoon if he's still stable."

"Oh my god, Cory, I'm so sorry. Why didn't you call us sooner? Your father and I will change the flight plans we made to come for your wedding and be there as soon as possible."

"I haven't had time to focus on calling anyone, Mother. I've been busy filling out paperwork and dealing with doctors and trying to understand all the things they've been telling me regarding Kieran's condition, and today will be filled with making the arrangements to move him to a different hospital."

"Corwin, take a deep breath and slowly let it out." His mother soothed him over the phone. "That's better. Now, sweetheart, why don't you let his family do what they need to do—"

"I'm the one who has to make the decisions," Cory exasperated.

"What?" she asked. "You two aren't getting married until the end of the month."

"No, Mom, we're getting handfasted at the end of the month." The reminder shook Cory. "Oh lord, that will have to be postponed and all the guests notified." Cory started pacing the room until Grams stopped him and sat him in the chair by Kieran's bed. She took the phone from him and placed Kieran's battered and broken hand in Cory's hands before speaking into the phone.

"Mrs. Cooper, I'm Líadáin Oisín, Kieran's grandmother."

"Mrs. Oisín, where's Corwin?" Tamara asked.

"Cory is sitting beside Kieran's bed here in the hospital," she said, ready to break the rest of the news. "The boys married three weeks ago in a civil service at the courthouse here in Bar Harbor. As Kieran's husband, Cory has the right to make the medical decisions, and he has us here to support him. I think, however, he could use some support from his own family."

"My husband Jonathan is changing our travel arrangements as we speak, Mrs. Oisín. We'll call Corwin as soon as everything is set. Would you please have him call us with an update when you get Kieran settled into the new hospital?"

"Of course, Mrs. Cooper. Someone will call you as soon as all the arrangements are made. Please let us know what your flights are, and we'll arrange to have someone meet you at the Bangor Airport."

"Thank you for looking out for Corwin. I know you have a lot to worry about while taking care of Kieran."

"Cory is my grandson's husband, and even before they married, I considered him family, so don't worry. He's in good hands," Líadáin said, seeing the nurse entering the room. "I'm sorry though. I need to let you go so I can hear what the nurse has to say about moving Kieran."

As Grams hung up, the nurse handed a clipboard full of documents to Cory. The paperwork needed to be reviewed before Kieran could be transferred. Cory looked overwhelmed by all the forms and records. He looked up from the clipboard as Líadáin reached over to take it from his grasp. She looked at the forms and the invoice for the cost of moving Kieran to Bangor.

"These fees and charges are ridiculous. I know we've said cost wasn't an issue, but we won't be robbed by a bean counter padding the bill," Líadáin said, thrusting the clipboard back into the nurse's hands. "Take these back to your hospital accountant and tell them to try again without all the phony extras."

When the nurse left, Cory leaned forward. "Grams, do you think we really need to move Kieran?" Cory asked. "It seems like Dr. Anna has everything she really needs here."

"I don't know, Cory. We'll discuss it with Kellen and Brom when they get back, and then talk it over as a family with Dr. Mihaylova. Staying here would certainly be easier on us to drive back and forth from the estate and to put up guests there."

And when Kellen and Brom returned, the family did just that.

"What did we miss, Mother?" Kellen asked while setting his chair down next to the one Cory sat in.

"The hospital just brought the paperwork and the invoice to move Kieran to the hospital in Bangor. I sent it back when I saw how many unnecessary items they'd tossed in on just the first page. Cory and I were just discussing the possibility of keeping Kieran here and using the compound to house Cory's family and any other guests."

"Well, the compound isn't in bad shape physically, just the broken window in the dinning room of the main house. The only area to take major damage is where Kieran made his last stand," Kellen replied, quick to lower his voice on the next part. "Our major problem is all the magical defenses are gone, and without Kieran or the power of the Silver Witch, the best I can do is ward each building separately."

"We could ward a bigger area if we work together using my forge as the focus of the spell," Brom said. "I'm nearly at my original power level when I'm working at the forge. We could use Kieran's new warding spell and tie it to the physical structure of the forge; that way it would be harder to destroy."

"I'm not sure we could work Kieran's spell without him," Kellen argued. "It took four of us to cast it the last time, and one of those people was the Silver Witch. Dad's gone and Kieran's powers—along with those of the Silver Witch—are locked in his head. We're safer moving to Bangor and warding hotel rooms."

Brom held back a glare. "I've worked spells Kieran's created before without him being present, Kellen. The warding spell is just a spell. Ours won't be as big and powerful as the one Kieran cast when he had all of us helping him."

"What about the shifter blood?" Kellen asked.

"Cory, would you be willing to come back to the compound with us for a day and give us some of your blood so we can make the place safe again?" Brom asked.

Cory's eyebrows shot up. "Don't you need to ward against dark shifters, Brom? My blood is only laced with Silver magic, and you want to stop shifting based in Ebony magic . . ."

"It has to be fresh blood in order to work." Brom sighed, defeated.

Cory remembered his nephew. "Billy is still at the compound, because I didn't think the hospital would have appreciated a wolf camped out in Kieran's room. He might be locked in wolf form, but if you ask him and tell him it's for Kieran, I'd bet he'd let you draw some of his blood."

"Oh, dear goddess, I forgot all about Billy!" Grams had a sudden look of panic on her face. "The poor dear must be frightened and hungry. Brom, please take me back to the house. I'll ask Billy if he'll help us."

Behind them, a sudden silver glow around Kieran's right hand caught their attention but quickly faded away. Beneath his hand on the bed, a small silver hatpin appeared. Cory turned in his chair and leaned close to Kieran.

"Babe, are you awake? Can you hear me?" Cory pleaded with his husband.

Kieran laid still; the only sign of life was the slow rise and fall of his chest as he drew breath. Cory took up the hatpin and handed it to Kellen. Kieran's father looked at the pin closely, and his face grew blank as he was drawn into a trance. The rest of the family watched as his eyebrows shot up in surprise.

"Somehow, Kieran has channeled the essence of the spell into this hatpin. If Billy will let us draw his blood with this, then Brom and I can cast Kieran's warding spell over Brom's forge and cabin, my cabin, and the main house since they're the closest structures," Kellen said as he came out of the trance.

"How can he do magic but not talk to us?" Cory asked, his voice cracking.

"I don't know, Cory. I'm just worried it might cost him dearly," Líadáin said. "Kellen, I had to push Ebony magic away from all his wounds when we were bringing him here. I thought I'd driven it out of him along with the blood that was pooling. Now, I can sense that there's a pool of it at the base of his skull, as well as around his wounds. Kieran has his brain shielded to keep the Ebony out."

"That may explain why he's still unconscious," Kellen said. "He's holding off the Ebony poisoning his system and trying to keep it from damaging his magic. I'll check the grimoire; perhaps there's a spell for removing it."

Kieran's body suddenly tensed and started to convulse, setting off all the monitors keeping watch on his vitals. Nurses came running, and Dr. Mihaylova wasn't far behind them. The Oisíns drew Cory back out of the way of the hospital staff so that they could help Kieran. Líadáin sent a trace of Sapphire magic into Kieran to try and sense what was happening. Inside her grandson, a battle raged between Silver magic and Ebony magic as Kieran fought to seal the tiny breach created when he'd shaped the magic hatpin. Still in great pain from his injuries and weak from battling the poisonous effects of the Ebony magic in his system, Kieran was having a hard time focusing on closing the breach. Líadáin thrust a block of Sapphire magic into the breach to buy Kieran time, and realized as she did so that the Ebony magic in his system was a dark spell that was learning as it acted. Kieran sealed the breach, but the Ebony magic had learned to block and destroy Líadáin's Sapphire magic. The monitors returned to their normal sounds as Kieran's body settled down and his heart slowed to a normal pace. His temperature was still high, as if his body fought off an infection.

When she was sure Kieran was out of danger from cardiac arrest, Dr. Mihaylova turned to face the family. The expressions of worry and fear on their faces tugged at the doctor's heart. She wanted to promise them that Kieran would be just fine, but she didn't know what was keeping the young man in his catatonic state. By every test she'd run, the young man should've been awake and talking by now. Behind her, the nurses cleaned Kieran up and made him comfortable again before leaving the room.

"Dr. Anna, please," Cory begged. "Tell me what's wrong with Kieran."

Tears were streaming down Cory's face as he looked desperately at the doctor, hoping for some miracle of science to save his husband. Cory could barely sense Kieran's pain through their bond now. Something deep inside him told him that Kieran must have been shielding the bond to protect Cory from the pain.

"Honestly, Cory, I don't know what just caused that. I'd like to run a new MRI and CAT scan on him. I'm worried we missed some kind of internal trauma."

"Whatever tests you need to run, Dr. Anna, just please save Kieran," Cory said as he collapsed on the couch in tears. "I can't lose him."

"My son-in-law is correct, Dr. Mihaylova. Run whatever tests you need to run." Kellen added.

"I'll go order the tests right now. An orderly should be up to get Kieran in about an hour. Why don't you take Cory and get him something to eat?"

"No!" Cory screamed. "I'm not leaving Kieran."

"Sshh, Cory," Líadáin urged, wrapping Cory in her arms. "You and I will stay right here, *mac tíre óg*, while Kellen and Brom go find us something to eat and drink. I'm sure that Dr. Anna will make sure you can go with Kieran for all his tests."

"Of course, I was only suggesting you keep your strength up, Cory. It won't make Kieran better if you collapse from hunger or dehydration. You have to take care of yourself while I take care of Kieran. Okay?"

Cory sniffed. "I promise I'll eat something."

"That's all I ask. Now, let me go get these tests scheduled."

Dr. Mihaylova left the room, and the members of Kieran's family looked at each other with deep concern, both for Cory and for Kieran.

"I know you scanned Kieran while he was having that attack, Mother. What did you sense?"

"The Ebony magic in his system isn't just residual poison from shifter bites. It's a spell, a powerful one that can learn how to fend off lesser magic. I won't be able to use my magic to help Kieran until the Ebony magic is gone from his body. I had to buy him time to rebuild his defenses, so the spell now knows the feel of my magic."

"We'll need to keep Kieran from using his magic outside of his body until we can break this spell," Cory said.

"Let's hope he doesn't need to do so again, Cory," Kellen said. "I'm going to go down to the cafeteria and bring back food and water for all of us. Brom, I think we're going to have to try Kieran's warding spell. I don't want to risk moving him to Bangor."

"I'll go back to the compound and start making preparations after you get back with the food and we've all eaten," Brom replied.

"I'll go with you and take care of Billy," Grams said. "Cory, is there anything we can bring back for you so that you will be comfortable here with Kieran?"

"Would you bring back his hairbrush and comb? I'd like to keep his hair clean and free of tangles. My brushing his hair always seems to help him relax."

Her face softened. "Of course, dear. I'll make sure to get those for you and maybe a couple of leather strips so you can braid and tie his hair back, so it's out of the way for the nurses."

Cory gave the older woman a big hug. "Thank you, Grams."

* * *

DEEP beneath the drugs coursing through his system to keep the pain dulled and to fight off any infections, Kieran's mind drifted. He was torn between active defense against the Ebony magic pulsing through his system with every beat of his heart and thoughts. Emotions ranging from sadness about his grandfather and his sisters to pleasant ones of being curled up with Cory followed. He needed strength to maintain the shield he'd built up around his mind, so he focused on the pleasant thoughts. His happiest memory was of Cory accepting his marriage proposal. His heart swelled with joy when the love of his life had said yes to becoming his husband. His mind began to flow along the memory path leading to their brief honeymoon in Bar Harbor.

The memory replayed, *Kieran dropped his pack, sank down on one knee, and presented Cory with a small box. Cory glanced at Kieran, stared at the box, and back at Kieran again. His heart fluttered. Was Kieran thinking the same thing he'd been thinking all week? Kieran smiled and opened the box to reveal a gold ring set with a moonstone and a matching set of gold rings etched with the Gaelic phrase, Deo mo chroí, forever my heart.*

"Corwin Samuel Cooper, will you do me the honor of becoming my husband?" Kieran said as he took the moonstone ring from the box and

placed the ring at the tip of Cory's left ring finger, since the soul mate band, which had once occupied the finger, was gone.

Cory eyes, actually brimming with tears, gazed down into Kieran's silver eyes. He smiled and answered with one word. "Yes."

With these happy memories playing in his mind, Kieran drifted off to sleep.

5

The ride back to the family compound was quiet. Each of the Oisíns was lost in thought. Kellen was focused on trying to figure out a way to convince Cory to let him try to tap the powers of the Silver Witch locked away in Kieran without hurting his son in the process. Brom was trying to figure out if there was a way to extend the area they could cover with Kieran's warding spell using only the personal power of two Silver mages. Líadáin was trying to keep her thoughts focused on getting Billy the wolf's assistance in their plans and reassuring the boy trapped inside the wolf that his Uncle Kieran would be all right. She fought desperately to keep her thoughts away from images of her husband lying dead on the floor of their dining room.

"Brom, what did you do with your father's body?" Líadáin asked her eldest son.

"The county coroner came and collected it, Mother. It wasn't easy, since the coroner notified the sheriff, who sent out a deputy to take a statement. I lucked out that the coroner sent Joey McIntire to collect dad's body and the deputy who came out was Sammy Petersen. Together we came up with the report about wild animals attacking Dad."

"How did you explain away the human hunter's body, Brom?" Kellen asked.

"Joey and Sammy were too busy with taking care of Dad and making sure his remains were given proper respect that they didn't bother to search the rest of the buildings. When we get back home, you'll have to use a transport spell and dump the body someplace out to sea, Kellen."

"We were very lucky that Aodhfin commanded so much respect in the community, otherwise we might be stuck in a very messy investigation," Líadáin said.

"Yes, and with Joey and Sammy having been part of my circle back when I could work magic helped as well. I just needed to remind them that exposure of Dad's magic could expose them as well. No one wants a modern-day witch hunt," Brom said.

"How long is the coroner going to hold Dad's body?"

"Until one of us calls in to claim it. Despite the obvious cause of death, he still has to perform an autopsy. Goddess, I hate the idea of anyone doing anything further to Dad's body."

"It's just an empty shell now," Líadáin replied with a hitch in her breath. "Your father's spirit is with the goddess and the god. We will celebrate his life once Kieran is recovered. I'll call the coroner and have him turn the body over to the Bragdon-Kelly Funeral Home. Your father and I prearranged our basic funeral services with them."

"Okay," Kellen said, voice cracking as tears began to seep from his eyes. "Let's change the subject before I wreck the car. Besides some shifter blood from Billy, what do we need to work Kieran's warding spell?"

Wiping back tears, Brom replied, "From what I recall of the casting, the blood and the focus item were all the material components to the spell. I already have a hiding place in the forge where we can stash the focus and ground the spell the way Kieran did with his saber."

"Do you have whatever you need to bring your magic to full power, Brom?" Kellen asked.

"I already have all the materials to begin working on new sabers for Kieran. If you can help out Mother, I'd like to add Sapphire magic to the blades this time to keep them from being melted."

"You know I'll do whatever is needed. Perhaps, I can get Emma Handler to come out and help you as well. Can you add Ruby magic to your plans for Kieran's blades?"

"Yes, I think I can adapt the enchantment on the blades to add Ruby to the Sapphire and Silver magic mix. I'm not quite as good at adapting magic as Kieran is, but I've picked up a few tricks from my nephew."

"I'll see what I can do to help you adapt the spells, Brom. The grimoire has a few enchantments for binding multiple forms of magic together for stronger results. I don't know if I can work them without being the Silver Witch, because they're very old spells and very powerful."

"Kellen," Líadáin warned, "don't even think about trying to link to Kieran to get the power back. From what I saw while I was helping him after he created the focus, any breach in his defenses puts him in danger of losing to the Ebony magic."

"I have no intention of going back on my word to Cory. I won't put Kieran's life in danger." Kellen choked. "He's all I have left."

"He's going to be fine, Kellen," Brom tried to reassure his brother. "Think about it. Once we get the Ebony magic out of his system, he's going to heal rapidly, in part because of the latent shifter genes in the House of Beauty's bloodline."

"Kieran also invited an Emerald mage for the Handfasting," their mother added. "Perhaps he'll be able to help us heal Kieran."

"That's asking a lot from a stranger, Mother. Let's find out what information is in the grimoire and go from there. Right now, we need to focus on getting some of the defenses back up if we're going to use the compound as a base of operations," Kellen said as he turned the SUV onto the long driveway leading up to the Oisín home.

"It will take me a while to get the furnace in the forge up to a working temperature, Kellen," Brom said. "That should give you and Mother time to find Billy, get his cooperation, and check over the grimoire. When you come to the forge, bring water and food besides whatever supplies you need for working the ritual. I'll set the forge's wards and then leave the doorway open for you."

Once the SUV was parked and they'd gotten out, the members of Kieran's family spread out, each going to their chosen task. Líadáin went to her kitchen without passing through the dining room. Kellen headed for his father's library where he'd put the family grimoire after reclaiming it from Kieran's cabin on an earlier visit. Brom headed for his cabin and the forge nearby to begin lighting and heating the furnace. What time they had to prepare was short

INTERLUDE: THE MASTER GETS A REPORT

The Master lounged in his giant four-poster bed. Between his outstretched legs, his current apprentice-slave—blindfolded and bound in tight leather—sucked on his thick, uncut cock. Once known as William Harkrider, the slave had traded away his freedom and his family's greatest treasure to obtain lessons in the dark arts. It had been with great delight that the Master had plundered Harkrider's virginity in all forms. The mewling mass of flesh could barely recall its name these days. While he was being serviced, the Master received a message spell from his primary apprentice, whom he'd sent to watch over the operation to collect the Belle boy from Maine.

Master, it is with great displeasure that I must inform you of the failure of the hunter and the shifters to secure your prize. While the owl-bitch managed to destroy the defenses and kill one of the Silver mages, she paid for it with her life. Kincaid and his shifters tore the place apart looking for the targets, but only found the boy you wanted as a prize. The boy is the most powerful Silver mage I've ever felt. He's also something else besides a mage, because he fought off the majority of the shifters with weapons. The boy cut them down like he'd trained with hunters. In the end, the pack took him down and infected him with Ebony magic from their bites, but he unleashed a spell of destruction that nothing could have survived. His family found Kincaid and dispatched him. I'm sorry, Master, but your prize is dead.

Ebony magic swirled around the Master's hands and hurled the helpless slave across the room, smashing him into a wall. The mage stormed from his bedroom, dark magic swirling around him to cloak his appearance as he moved to his ritual chamber. Slaves and servants alike fled in terror from their dark master. He seethed, and those not fast enough to escape his path died. When he reached his ritual space, he uttered a few syllables of an ancient language, and a pool of Ebony magic glimmered before him like a mockery of a magic mirror.

"Show me where the boy I seek is. My dark magic dwells in his blood now thanks to the bites of those shifters. Show me!"

The magic pool swirled and rippled before parting to show Kieran lying in a hospital bed hooked up to monitors, arms heavily bandaged and legs under the blanket. His beautiful face was a mass of bruises, and his long silky hair was a mess. Beside him, the Master glimpsed a blond youth, but before he could focus on either boy further, his spell shattered. His vision was lost, but not in memory.

6

John Mason paced in the terminal of Little Rock's William and Hillary Clinton National Airport, hoping that Kieran would pick up his phone. Professor Mason's nerves were nearly shot when a female voice answered the phone.

"Hello?"

"Hello, I'm trying to reach Kieran Belle." John fought to keep his voice calm. "Do I have the right number?"

"Yes, this is my grandson's phone. How do you know Kieran?" the woman asked.

"I'm his photography professor at the University of Arkansas at Little Rock, and he invited me to participate in his handfasting, Mrs. Belle?" John's voice rose in question, not sure of the woman's identity aside from her mention that Kieran was her grandson.

"Oh heavens no, I'm not his maternal grandmother. I'm sorry, Professor. I'm Líadáin Oisín, Kieran's paternal grandmother. I didn't catch your name."

"It's John Mason. Am I correct in guessing Kieran isn't available to come to the phone?"

"Yes, I—I—I'm going to give the phone over to Cory. He'll explain."

John listened as the phone went static for a moment before a young man's voice came across the line. As the young man started to speak, the airline began to announce the boarding of John's flight.

"Hello, Professor Mason? Are you there? This is Cory Cooper."

"Cory, I'm at the airport in Little Rock, and they've just announced that they're ready to board my flight. What's happened to Kieran?"

"There was an accident, and Kieran was severely injured. The doctors are doing what they can, but there are conditions I can't talk about over the phone. Are you coming here to Maine?"

"Yes, I have to change planes in Charlotte, North Carolina and Washington D.C., but I'm suppose to arrive around five o'clock tonight in Bangor."

"Keep us posted on your progress, Professor, and I'll have Kieran's uncle pick you up at the airport when you arrive in Bangor."

"I'll call again from D.C., Cory." John ended the call and shut off his phone as he moved to get in line to board the flight from Little Rock.

Flying from Little Rock to Charlotte was uneventful, and there was plenty of time for his layover. On the flight to D.C., John fidgeted in his seat, seeking a comfortable position as chills crept up and down his spine. The feeling of Ebony magic made his skin crawl as he tried to locate the source without giving himself away. His nerves had been on edge from before he'd talked to Cory and learned of Kieran's accident. Somehow, he felt it was something more than a simple accident, especially since Cory wouldn't give him details over the phone. The chills grew stronger. *Where the hell was the blasted Ebony mage?* With caution, he let a trickle of Emerald magic loose to seek out the dark magic. *It's in first class, third row, not a mage, but a dark object.* John was thinking he needed to get closer when two men boarded the plane. They wore dark suits, sunglasses, and had an ear bud in their right ears. The lead flight attendant escorted him and his carry-on baggage to the two dark suited men. They escorted him off of the plane. With them went the dark object, and John found he could relax and breathe easy again. The flight departed shortly afterward, and John stretched in his seat as much as possible. He tried to focus on his book, but his mind kept drifting to the question of what had happened to Kieran. *Nothing you can do until you get more information, John. Stop trying to figure it out*, he thought to himself.

When he arrived in D.C. and found his gate, John placed a call to Kieran's phone and waited for Cory to answer. He was surprised when a deeper, older, and seriously sexy voice answered the phone instead.

"Kieran Belle's phone, can I help you?"

"Um, this is Professor John Mason. I was calling for Cory Cooper."

"Cory is finally getting a little rest now that Kieran is back in his room from the latest round of testing. I'm Kieran's uncle, Brom Oisín. Cory said you'd call when you reached D.C."

"Yes, my flight arrived just a few minutes ago. I won't depart for a while if everything stays on schedule. I was hoping to get an update on Kieran's condition and what happened, Mr. Oisín."

"Call me Brom, Professor."

"Only if you'll call me John. Kieran won't call me anything but professor or sir."

"No problem, John. I can't tell you too much over the phone; it just isn't safe right now."

"I get it. Did Kieran tell you why he chose me for his handfasting?"

"Yes, he mentioned your photography uses a *green* process." Brom emphasized the word green.

"That's correct, Brom. He requested my services to capture their ceremony so they would have something to admire on their *silver* anniversary," John replied.

"Well, we're glad you're coming, although it looks as if the ceremony will have to be postponed. Kieran's accident was severe, and unfortunately, my father was killed in the same accident. I will meet you at the airport when you arrive in Bangor. Give me your flight information, and I'll keep an eye on the arrival status so you don't have to hang around the airport long."

"My condolences," John said before giving Brom his flight information. "I appreciate your help."

"I appreciate yours," Brom replied, and the two hung up.

After the conversation, John went to a food court near the gate. He picked up a sandwich and drink to hold him over until the airline announced boarding of the plane for the final leg of his trip to Maine. John was amazed as his last flight arrived in Bangor, Maine on time. He hadn't flown in several years, and it surprised him that—despite all the additional security measures—the airlines could still manage to get a plane where it was supposed to go on time. Once he was off the plane, he made his way down to baggage claim to retrieve his luggage and look for Kieran's uncle. John wondered what he looked like, and he'd been daydreaming up an image since hearing his voice. *Brom Oisín, the man has a voice for audio romance novels. I didn't talk to him long, but that voice could induce orgasm just reading the phonebook,* John thought as he scanned the crowd for someone who might match the voice.

Behind him, the warning buzzer sounded as the carousel began to move. John turned his attention to finding his luggage. His bag came around the carousel, and John snatched it up and then turned to see if he could find Brom. Having seen all the crime shows where the person on the other end of the phone sex line had the voice of an angel and then turned out to be someone's grandmother instead of the hot twenty-something-year-old, John scanned the crowd looking for a short, dumpy guy, who looked like he'd be cast as a homeless guy. He spotted a man fitting that description not too far away and was headed toward him when he stopped short as a man in jeans, a light blue dress shirt, and hiking boots entered the terminal and turned toward baggage claim. He lifted a sign with John's name on it. The man was stunning in his looks. Before John stood Kieran, grown and mature, or at least he was a possible future version. Short dark hair merged into a neat and trimmed beard, framing the face of a model. John drew near enough to see the man's silver eyes as they locked with his own emerald green eyes. The man's eyes lit up as he smiled at John. *Oh bright goddess, he's even more attractive than Kieran,* John thought as he pushed himself forward to meet the man.

"I'm John Mason, you must be Brom."

"I am, a pleasure to meet you in person, John. I'm sorry it couldn't be under the happier circumstances you were expecting," Brom replied while extending his hand to shake.

"It's still nice to meet some of Kieran's family," John replied as he shook Brom's hand and felt a tingle of very faint magic. It left John puzzled, because he figured a relative of Kieran's would be a powerful mage, but it seemed as though Brom had the barest trace of Silver magic.

"What hotel do you have reservations at, John?" Brom asked as he led the professor out of the airport and toward one of the family SUVs.

"Oh my, I didn't think about a hotel. To be honest, Kieran offered me the guest room in his cabin at your family's place, but if that's out of the question, I'll see what's available."

"Sorry, I should have realized Kieran would do something like that. You can take the guest room in my cabin at the compound. Kieran and Cory's cabin is currently beyond the limits of the wards."

"I don't want to impose on you. I'm sure I can find something in town."

"You won't be imposing, John. If the room isn't to your liking, I'm sure Mother can put you up in the main house."

"If you're sure I won't be in the way."

"I'm sure. We've hardly been home the last couple of days. Between the rounds of testing and surgeries Kieran's been through, the whole family has been living at the hospital."

"Well, I'll try to stay out from underfoot," John replied.

They reached Brom's SUV, and he opened it, allowing John to stow his bags in the back of the vehicle. While John was lifting his luggage into the car, Brom was studying the man. He estimated John was about six foot two, maybe two hundred and ten pounds; his emerald green eyes had captivated Brom from the moment they'd met. John looked to be in good physical shape, not a gym rat, but someone who took care of himself. His dark hair was a little messed up from his traveling, but he was a very striking man. Then there was the feel of the man's Emerald magic; he was incredibly powerful. Brom could see why Kieran had been taken with the man. Moreover, there was the man's tenor voice, which glided across Brom's brain like silk. Once John's luggage was stowed, they climbed into the vehicle, and Brom started the engine. They drove out of the parking area and headed for Bar Harbor and the Oisín compound. When they were well on the way, John turned enough to look at Brom as he asked about what had really happened to Kieran.

"If I'm going to be of any help, Brom, I'll need to know what really happened to Kieran."

"First, tell me how much you know about Kieran, John."

"I know he comes from a hunting family, although I don't know which one. Kieran has a very powerful gift for Silver magic. I know this, because his gift has touched my own gift for Emerald magic. He's the most talented student I've ever had the pleasure to teach, and if he wasn't my student and didn't have Cory, I'd very likely have found a way to have him in my bed. Is that what you'd like to know?"

"I appreciate your honesty, John. Kieran is my only nephew, but he's more like a son to me. I want to make sure you're the man he said you were. I think you're everything he said you are and more. Ask your questions, John. I'll do my best to answer you with all the truth."

"What happened to him?" John asked.

"Long story short, we were betrayed by someone Kieran thought he could trust within a few given limits. Do you know Marissa Holden?"

"Yes, she's a ceramics student and teaching assistant. A very talented young woman."

"Did you know she was a shifter?"

"No, I never sensed it in her. What did she do?"

"She murdered my father, destroyed the magic barriers protecting our family home, and let a hoard of shifters attack us."

"By the Creator, that's horrible, and again, I'm sorry to hear about your loss, Brom."

"Thank you, John. Kieran chased her down and killed her with an ancient spell that borders on the forbidden. Then, he whisked all of us off to a hidden sanctuary on our estate before taking on every shifter that came with Marissa and a human hunter by the name of Alex Kincaid. We're not sure, but we think that Kieran wasn't able to properly channel all of the new powers he inherited when Dad died, and eventually, it interfered with his personal powers and abilities as a tracker. The shifters ran him to ground, and in the fight for his life, he was mauled by the pack and lost control of his vast reserves of Silver magic. He devastated a huge swath of forest, killed all the shifters, and then couldn't get out of the way of a very large tree, which landed on him, adding to his already considerable injuries."

"What kind of powers could Kieran have inherited that would cause him such problems?"

"Our side of Kieran's family is the last descendants of the most powerful ancient Silver mages. Father was the Silver Witch, and Kieran had only just become his direct heir about a week before the attack. My father bypassed my younger brother Kellen—Kieran's father—as his heir, because he was afraid something might happen and Kieran would need the full powers of the Silver Witch."

"I've only ever heard vague myths and rumors of such a being. The Silver Witch is a character out of fairy tales."

"You don't know the half of it, John," Brom said with a dry chuckle.

"What do you mean?"

"Originally, the Silver Witch was always a woman until some twenty generations back, when the last woman to hold the title decided the best way to preserve her line was to transfer the gift from females to males. She tied the full potential of her gift to the Y chromosome of her youngest son. All of her children carried the potential for Silver magic, but only that one son would ever wield the power and the ancient lore. Shortly after his birth, she vanished. The tales say she died in childbirth, but those tales have been edited by both our family and Kieran's mother's family over the ages."

"I'm lost, Brom."

"Have you ever read the original version of *Beauty and the Beast*, John?"

"I can't say that I have. Why?"

"The original tale by Madame De Beaumont, begins, 'There was once a very rich merchant who had six children, three sons, and three daughters...His daughters were extremely handsome, especially the youngest. When she was little everybody admired her, and called her The little Beauty; so that, as she grew up, she still went by the name of Beauty, which made her sisters very jealous.'"

"Okay, so what does that have to do with all of this?"

"The youngest of the brothers was the child the Silver Witch gave her powers to. Beauty, the focus of the tale, went on to found a line of women, who hunt shifters known as the House of Beauty, or to use the French, *la Maison de Belle*."

"Belle, as in Kieran's last name. Are you telling me that Kieran is a descendant of the Beast and Beauty?"

"Of Beauty, yes. She didn't transform the Beast back into a man; she killed him. Don't ask, nobody really knows how she took down such a powerful dark shifter. She found the real prince locked away in the castle dungeon and eventually married him to found her line."

"Wow that's a lot to take in. If this House of Beauty is all female hunters, how does Kieran fit in?"

"That's the tricky part of all of this. Normally, Kieran would have served as a tracker for whichever one of his sisters succeeded his mother as huntress. Unfortunately, all of Kieran's sisters either failed the test and died or were overwhelmed and killed."

"Are all these deaths recent?" John sighed. "I don't see how poor Kieran could stand up under all the grief."

"Yes, all his sisters died within the past year. I don't think Kieran would have been able to withstand the grief if he didn't have Cory by his side. With my father's death added on top of everything, I'm not sure what shape my nephew will be in mentally when he wakes up."

"I'll do whatever I can to help Kieran. I promised him I'd be his ally."

"Thank you, John. Get some rest if you can. It's about an hour and a half drive back to our compound."

INTERLUDE: THE MASTER BEGINS WEAVING A TRAP

The Master stood in the center of his workroom gathering his magic around him. A giant sphere of black onyx stood on a pillar before him. With a gesture, Ebony magic wrapped around the sphere and created a link to Elihu Hayes, his chief apprentice in Maine.

"I have a task for you, apprentice."

"I hear and obey, Master."

"You must go to the hospital in town and pose as an orderly. Gain access to the boy's room and work on increasing the Ebony magic in his system. We must overwhelm his defenses, so corruption may take root.

"Yes, Master. I will do as you command."

The Master broke the connection to his apprentice and then recast the spell to connect to the dark shifter.

"Child of the ancient Beast, hear me, I am the Master."

"So the spider comes calling from its web. What would you have of me, mage?"

"The son of the House of Beauty lies defenseless in a hospital in Bar Harbor; you could destroy him there and end your curse."

"Once that would have been true, but a condition here has changed. I no longer have the ability to leave this cursed forest. Some of this pack speak of a magical pact between the shifters of this forest and the House of Beauty."

"You aren't of the bloodline of that pack. How is it that you are bound?"

"I am not of their bloodline, but they are of mine, mage. I am the Beast of legend, sent forward in time twice. First by the whining little bitch Beauty and then by a male hunter of her line who was too much of a coward to face me in battle."

"You've somehow been caught up in the magic woven in your bloodline. Something of each side must be bound to the spell. Most likely, it's blood bound and done so with Silver magic. You will have to find out what the other half is in order to break the spell. Send some of your pack to kill the son of Beauty."

"No, I will have the joy of destroying the last of the bitch's bloodline. Have your minions bring him here to me, or better yet, prove your worth to me and bring him here yourself. Now be gone, mage."

7

———

Kellen Oisín stood just outside his son's hospital room, trying to convince his son-in-law Cory to go to the Bangor Airport to pick up his parents. Mr. and Mrs. Cooper were due to arrive in a couple of hours, and driving took an hour and fifteen minutes if traffic wasn't crazy.

"Cory, you're the best person to go and pick up your parents. They won't know who to look for if Brom or I go to pick them up."

"I've been away from Kieran for an entire night, Kellen. I don't want to be away from him any longer."

"You still don't trust that I won't try and take back the powers of the Silver Witch while you're gone. I get that, and both my mother and I have told you it can't be done without killing Kieran. I'm not going to lose my son, Cory."

"You're right that I don't trust you not to make the attempt," he confessed. "If I'm not here, there's nothing to prevent you from trying."

Kellen and Cory paused their conversation as a nurse went by on her rounds. The sounds of monitors both in Kieran's room and from other rooms along the hall filled the silence. Once the nurse was gone, Kellen resumed the conversation.

"Cory, there are several things preventing me from trying, one of which is the fact that both Kieran's and your own life would be lost should I try and fail. There's also the massive amount of Ebony magic in his system, which is actually a spell that won't hesitate to attack both Kieran and myself. If we both die, the only person left holding the ancient spell binding shifters to their one form is Brom."

"You can still go get my parents from the airport. Just do what Brom did when he picked up Professor Mason; use a sign with my parents' names on it."

"They're going to be looking for you, Cory, not someone they don't know with a sign. Besides they'll want to ask all kinds of questions, some of which only you will be able to answer. I give you my word on Kieran's life that I will not attempt to make any kind of magic connection to Kieran while you're away."

"I don't trust you after everything you've conspired to do over the past couple of months, but I'll go. You're right about the questions my parents will ask, and I should be the one to tell them all their plans to keep me from shifting have gone to hell in a handbasket." Cory started to turn away but stopped. "If anything happens to him while I'm away, Kellen, I'll tear you apart with my bare claws."

"I promise you, nothing magical will happen to him on my watch."

Cory walked off toward the elevators for the trip down to the parking levels. Kellen went into Kieran's room and sat in the visitor's chair beside his son's hospital bed. Hospital sounds intruded into his thoughts as he watched his son battered and broken body fight for existence. He'd read and re-read everything the family grimoire had on transferring the power from one Silver Witch to another and had concluded that it wasn't possible to do it, not with the conditions that existed. The presence of the Ebony magic in Kieran's system made it impossible to establish a link between them. He was glad he was alone with Kieran for the moment so that no one else could see his frustration over being powerless to help his son. Tears stung his face as Kellen finally let himself feel the loss of his daughters as he faced the possible loss of the last of his children.

Kellen leaned forward and took Kieran's right hand between his own. He brought the heavily bandaged hand to his face and held it against his cheek. His tears continued to flow. "I'm so sorry that we forced you down this path, Kieran. I wish I could undo everything that was done to bring about this outcome. I should have done more to help your sisters pass the test. I could have—No, I should have given at least Rosie a protection spell to help her become the Huntress of the House of Beauty."

Kellen put Kieran's hand back down on the bed before he buried his face in his own hands. The dam on his emotions finally broken, Kellen let his tears flow.

* * *

A FEW HOURS EARLIER, Cory had let Kellen convince him to go and pick up his parents from the Bangor Airport. Against his better judgment, Cory had taken the minivan and made the drive to Bangor, relying on the GPS to get him to the airport. He checked the arrival board and found he was early; his parents' flight wouldn't arrive for at least another half hour. He found a coffee stand and ordered a coffee and a muffin. After his order was ready, he found a bench where he could keep an eye on the arrival board while he ate. He reached for the bond between himself and Kieran and poured his love down it. There was the faintest of responses back down the link. Cory could tell his husband was focused on fending off the Ebony magic in his system, but Cory wished there was something he could do to help Kieran.

Cory tossed his trash and began wandering the airport, trying to kill time and not worry about Kieran under Kellen's watchful eye. If Brom or Grams had said they'd watch over Kieran while he was here waiting for his parents, Cory wouldn't be so worried, but Kellen and Gramps had been plotting events in Kieran's life all summer. Kellen hadn't expected his father to cut him out of the succession for the power of the Silver Witch when he'd made sure Kieran would inherit directly from him. While it was true Kellen was the most likely person to preserve the ancient bloodline by having children, Cory worried he'd sacrifice the last of his previous family in order to make sure any new family he eventually sired wouldn't have any rivals. No matter how many times Kellen swore Kieran's life was more important than the power, Cory didn't believe him; after all, he'd let all five of his daughters die so that Kieran would be forced to take up the mysterious destiny of the Silver Hunter in the prophecy. *No, I'm not going to let him toss Kieran to the wolves just to fulfill some ancient prophecy. Kieran doesn't want that life for himself, and I'm going to see that he gets the normal life he wants.* Cory looked up and found that the board was showing his parents' flight had just arrived and that their baggage was slotted for baggage claim on carousel six. Shaking himself from his gloomy thoughts, he made his way to the baggage claim area to wait for his parents.

Jonathan and Tamara Cooper made their way down the concourse from their plane to baggage claim. Tamara spotted Cory hanging about the baggage carousel watching the bags come down the shoot and onto the conveyer belt. She ushered Jonathan forward to greet their son.

"Corwin, here we are," Tamara called out.

Cory turned at the sound of his full name. *Only mother calls me Corwin,* he thought. He waved to them and then wrapped his mother in a hug when she was close enough. "Mom, Dad, it's good to see you. Was your trip okay?"

"We managed two layovers, but the long layover in Washington D.C. was a bit much. We're here for you now. How are you holding up?"

"Honestly, I'm dead tired, and I'm worried that Kieran isn't going to ever wake up."

"What about his family? Aren't they taking turns watching him so you can get some sleep and eat something?"

"Yes, Mom. Kellen, Kieran's father, is with him right now. Can we please wait until we get to the car? This isn't something we should be discussing in public."

"Of course, Corwin." Tamara then turned to find Jonathan trying to catch their bag. "Go and help your father with the bag, please, Corwin."

Cory moved with a grace his mother had never seen in him, and she watched as he swiped up his parents' suitcase with ease. Jonathan looked as his son with a stunned expression before thanking him for getting the bag. Cory led the way out of the airport and over to where he'd parked the minivan.

"Well, I see you boys made it up here with that thing still in one piece," Jonathan remarked as Cory opened the back hatch to put away his parents' suitcase.

"We had to stop a couple of times to have some repairs made, but Kieran managed to get a tracking job wherever we happened to be," Cory replied as he closed the hatch.

The Coopers got in the van, and Cory started it up and headed back to Bar Harbor.

"So why didn't you call to tell us you and Kieran were getting married in a civil ceremony before the handfasting?" Tamara asked. "You know we would have come up sooner."

"We got married on the spur of the moment. Kieran didn't want to wait until the handfasting to have the civil ceremony, and I agreed with him. We wanted something that was just ours. The handfasting is more for Kieran's family," Cory replied.

"It's okay, Son. Your mother and I understand," Jonathan said. "I'm sure the Belles are happy you're already married."

"I don't know about the Belle family, Dad. We've been staying with Kieran's father's side of the family, the Oisín side. Kieran used his mother's last name to keep his father's family hidden. When we got married, he decided to combine his father's family name with our family name. We're Mr. and Mr. Oisín-Cooper."

"We're both happy for you, Corwin," Tamara said. "We just wish we could have been there when you took your vows."

"Mom, you will be there when we exchange our real vows. What we've already done was mostly legal paperwork. There wasn't any major ceremony. This handfasting is the big deal, so you will be there for the main event in my life."

"I'm thinking we're skipping over the shifter in the car, Son," Jonathan said.

"I wasn't the one the gene for shifting was bred out of, but you knew that already, Dad. Your binding spell on my shifter gene broke."

"I can't sense any Ebony magic in you. You're all Silver magic, but your ability to shift still exists. There's never been a silver shifter before."

"Nope, I'm the first. It seems I'm part of an ancient prophecy that has Kieran trapped in a life he doesn't want. I'm Kieran's soul mate and the silver shifter at his right hand. Billy is the ebony shifter at his left hand."

"The prophecy regarding the end of the binding on shifters . . ." Tamara faded away as she thought for a moment. "None of this should be possible if all the stories about Beauty slaying the Beast are true. The Beast is required for the breaking of that ancient spell."

"Well, the Alpha whose taken over the pack that tests the candidates of the House of Beauty is rumored to be a shifter of the Beast's direct line—"

"Cory, Son, you don't understand," Jonathan interrupted. "The shifter version of the prophecy you just referred to clearly calls for the Beast himself to be present. Not a descendant. Something is off with the histories of our family and those of the House of Beauty."

"Are you trying to say that the Alpha might be the Beast from the story?" Cory asked. "How? He'd be hundreds of years old. No shifter lives that long."

"He'd be over a thousand years old if he arrived here following a normal flow of time. And you're right; he'd have died ages ago of old age. Magic must have been involved," Jonathan said.

"I don't know, Dad. That sounds like it would be a very powerful spell. I don't think even Kieran, with all the powers of the Silver Witch at his command, could cast an immortality spell."

"He couldn't. A spell like that would require a caster who could work all the colors of magic, and no mage can do that anymore."

"So, if no mage currently living couldn't extend the Beast's life, who or what could?"

INTERLUDE: A TOUCH OF DARKNESS

Elihu Hayes, the dark apprentice, sat on a stool in a bar near the hospital where he'd learned a couple of the orderlies liked to hang out after work. He was in a dark and frisky mood as he sat nursing a long neck beer. The Master had given him an important task to increase the dark magic within the prize. Elihu relished the idea of breaking the young Silver mage into a sex toy for the Master. He spotted the young orderly, who—according to his sources—had just started working on the floor where the target was kept. The boy had prey practically written on his innocent face. The orderly was new enough that the duty nurses on the floor wouldn't be familiar with his face. He gave the young man a while to relax before having the bartender deliver a fresh beer to the young man. When the young man looked over to where Elihu sat at the bar, the apprentice flashed him an inviting smile. Elihu's prey smiled back and waved the man over to his table. Elihu gave the bartender an order for a pitcher of beer. He asked that the beer and two mugs be delivered over to the booth where the orderly was sitting. The dark apprentice rose from his stool and sauntered over to meet his prey.

"Hi, I'm Elihu, and you'll be taking me back to your place tonight, so I can fuck your brains out," Elihu said as he slid in beside the stunned orderly instead of across the table from him.

"Wha-a-at?" The orderly shook his head like he hadn't heard correctly. "I think you got the wrong impression, Elihu. I'm not looking for anything like that."

"Oh, sorry to hear that." Elihu pouted. "But tell me, how often do you have a hot guy not only buy you drinks, but also tell you he plans to fuck you into a coma? If I'm not the first one, then I'll just go back to my place at the bar and the pitcher that's headed this way is all yours."

"No, no, you're the first guy to do that; it's just that I have a blind date coming, and well, I guess when you sent the drink over, I thought you were him."

"But up close I don't match the image of this mystery stud? Am I sexier looking than mystery guy?"

"Oh god, by a huge factor. You have to be the hottest guy I've ever seen."

"Then take me home and let me fuck your brains out. I promise I'll be the best you've ever had."

"Wow, so much confidence. What happens when I say no?"

"Oh, but we both know you're not going to say no to me." Elihu's dark eyes focused on his hapless victim, and the boy sank into the depths of the dark pools. "You're going to tell me you're ready to go home with me."

"Let's go back to my place," the young orderly said.

Elihu slid out of the booth, drawing the entranced young man with him. The waitress was just arriving with the pitcher and two mugs as they got out of the booth. Elihu drew the orderly closer to his body. He reached into the young man's back pocket and found his wallet, which he drew out and opened. He pulled out some cash and handed it to the waitress.

"There should be a guy coming in and looking for his blind date; settle him in here and pick him out a cute boy toy," Elihu whispered into her ear with a trace of Ebony magic.

The waitress looked blank for a moment before grinning at the young couple before her. She nodded and turned back to her work.

Elihu lead the entranced young man outside and then whispered the command to lead the way home. The orderly started walking toward his apartment while holding Elihu's hand. The walk was only a few blocks from the bar and close to the hospital. He led the dark mage up the outside stairs to his apartment. Elihu gave the place a sneering once over as he entered behind his little toy. He gave the boy a sharp twist and brought them face to face as he released the enchantment while he locked lips with the startled kid. The boy gasped when Elihu broke the kiss for a moment. The man's hand on the back of his neck squeezed as it drew the poor little toy in for another kiss. Elihu's other hand reached up and grabbed the neckline of the kid's T-shirt, and he pulled down with enough force to rip the shirt open from neck to naval. The boy squirmed in Elihu's grip as he struggled for the air the man was drawing out of his lungs. A fist slammed into his solar plexus, driving the last of his air from his lungs. As the boy struggled to breathe, Elihu dropped him to the floor. He kicked the kid in the ribs a couple of times. When he was sure the boy wasn't getting up in a hurry, he moved on to the kid's bedroom and found a couple of pairs of hospital scrubs and a backpack. He stuffed the scrubs into the backpack before going back out to the living room where his victim was finally starting to draw a deep breath. Fear drove the kid's eyes wide open like a deer in the headlights. He tried to scramble back away from Elihu, but the man made a gesture, and Ebony magic wrapped around the boy's body and pulled him into the bedroom.

8

———————

Cory had taken his parents by the hospital for a brief introduction to Kellen and so that Tamara and Jonathan could see Kieran for a moment. They'd arrived at the Oisín compound and driven to Cory's cabin, where he'd shown them to their room and given them a brief tour of the cabin. He also showed them the path to the main house and let them know that dinner was served at six o'clock at the main house. Cory then left his parents to settle in while he went to visit with Grams.

Brom stood at his forge pumping the bellows to get the burning charcoal within the desired temperature for forging. He'd gotten up earlier than usual and had waited until he was outside to put on his heavy socks and steel-toed boots. His jeans came down over his boot tops to keep any stray coals or hot metal from dropping directly into his boots. He wore a lightweight cotton T-shirt that stretched tight across his chest and biceps. Over all of this, he wore a heavy leather apron. As the temperature of the forge rose toward the desired levels, Brom felt his magic rising with it. He gathered the materials he needed to continue his work on Kieran's new swords. The blades were already taking shape, and both Líadáin and Emma had added magic to the swords to help protect them from the kinds of damage Kieran often did to swords. With the help of some of Kieran's notes on adapting magic and Kellen's research in the grimoire, Brom had been able to wrap both the Ruby and Sapphire magic into the weave of Silver magic to create a protection spell. It would keep Kieran's blades from being melted once they took on their final form.

Brom checked the heat of the forge and found it where he wanted it. He drew on heavy leather gloves before picking up his tongs and using them to grip the steel of the first blade. He slid the blade into the forge to heat it up so that it could be worked. Brom wanted to be working when Kellen came to cast the barrier spell. They would need their powers at full strength, and only when he was actually working metal did Brom's power come to its full potential. He let his mind begin to drift into the trance state he often entered when working.

* * *

THE RINGING of metal on metal woke John Mason from his restless sleep in the spare bedroom of Brom's cabin. It took him a moment to focus on what had awoken him before he recalled that Brom and Kellen were supposed to be working a new barrier spell over the compound today. He wanted to watch the working, because he'd never seen Silver magic being cast before. John also wanted to watch Brom's muscles flexing as he crafted Kieran's new weapons. The man was haunting his dreams in a way no one had done since before his long-time partner had passed. John dressed in the clothes Brom had suggested he wear if he ever came out to the forge. Jeans, heavy socks, a cotton T-shirt, and leather work boots borrowed from Brom. John grabbed a cup of coffee from the pot in the kitchen on his way outside to the forge. As he neared the forge, the sound of ringing metal grew louder and was mixed with the sound of chanting. Just as he reached for the handle of the door John felt powerful magic wash over him as it rippled outward from the forge. The hammering stopped for a moment, and John overheard Kellen and Brom in conversation.

"I wish we could do something to restore your magic to what it should be, Brom. You so seldom use it, I forget how powerful you are."

"I sacrificed my magic a long time ago to try and keep Kieran from the path destiny and Dad seemed to feel he should walk. I don't regret it. Besides, I'm more focused here doing useful things."

"Well, thank you for helping me cast the new barrier spell again. I didn't sleep well knowing I'd let Cory's parents stay in the boys' cabin when it was outside the barrier. I'm going to walk and see if it extended as far as we thought it would. We need to know how far the perimeter goes past the boys' cabin now."

John knocked as he pulled open the door to the forge. "I'm not interrupting anything, am I?" he asked as he nodded to Kellen and Brom.

"No, Professor Mason, I was just leaving. If you'll excuse me, I have some things to do around the property," Kellen said, heading for the door without waiting to hear a reply.

"You will have to forgive my brother, John. Kellen is trying to keep himself occupied. I think he regrets giving Cory his word that he wouldn't try to regain the powers of the Silver Witch from Kieran. He wants access to the ancient lore that's not in any of the books we have. That way, he can find a way to bring Kieran out of that spell."

"I've been giving it some thought, that spell, and I'd like to carefully scan Kieran with my magic. I think if several of us work together we might be able to pull the Ebony magic out of Kieran and dispose of it."

"Let me get things cooled down enough to leave them unattended and then grab a fast shower. I don't think the hospital staff would be happy if I came in all covered in sweat and soot."

"Well, it's a sexy look, but I don't think they'd let you in the front door of the hospital," John said as a suggestive smile stretched his lips.

"So you find sweaty and dirty guys . . . attractive, Professor?" Brom said with a smirk made brighter by the soot covering his face. "Must be that ivory tower existence you lead."

Brom leaned in close to John and slipped his hand behind the man's neck; drawing him in for the kiss they'd both been shying away from for days. One of John's hands came up and wrapped around Brom's neck, holding them together in their kiss as it deepened into a war of tongues. His other hand slipped down the broad back, tracing the spine until he reached the top of the tight-fitting pants. At the same time, John felt Brom's free hand cupping his ass and felt his body collide with Brom's. It was hard to tell through the thickness of the leather apron and the jeans beneath if Brom was physically as excited as John himself was, but he'd guess from the way the other man was refusing to let go that the attraction was mutual.

Brom finally broke the kiss he'd wanted to steal since he'd picked this gorgeous stud up at the airport. He had to have this man in his bed or at least his shower. John had started to back away to regain his breath and balance when Brom reached out and grabbed him just as he was about to lean against the anvil and the blades resting on it.

"Careful, John, that anvil is hotter than it looks, and so are those blades."

"They aren't glowing like they're hot," John said, stretching his hand toward the anvil and blades.

Brom captured him by wrapping him in a hug from behind, which pinned John's arms to his sides.

"Both the anvil and the blades are still very hot, about 700 degrees or more. They're in a state known as black heat, where they look cool but would leave you with a very nasty burn. Trust me, I've got a couple of scars to prove how stupid it is to assume metal around a blacksmith's forge is cool enough to touch."

"I'll have to trust the master knows his craft and its dangers," John said, leaning back against Brom's chest.

Brom let his hands begin to wander across John's body while his tongue traveled across the man's neck, tracing a trail up to his left earlobe where he gently began to nibble the soft flesh, eliciting a moan. He stroked his left hand up to grip the firm right pectoral while his right hand slid down across firm abs to rest just above the man's belt buckle. John moaned and ground his ass back against Brom's body, only to be frustrated by the leather apron still between them. Brom's fingers tweaked the firm flesh of John's right nipple through his T-shirt while his tongue snaked into John's ear, making the man squirm and bring his crotch right into the grip of Brom's questing fingers.

The deep moan that escaped from John's throat as Brom's fingers gripped his cock through his jeans only served to enflame Brom's lust further. John felt the hand fondling his nipple slide down his body to join its partner at his waistline. He felt himself being pulled tighter against Brom's body as the man wrenched open John's belt and then went to work on the fastener of his pants. Soon, the jeans, a wallet, and a cellphone went sliding down John's legs, and he was moaning even more as he felt Brom's calloused hands grip his raging hard cock through the thin cotton fabric of his boxers. Before he could focus, there was skin on skin contact, and a rough calloused hand was wrapped around his hard cock and stroking, pulling back the already partly withdrawn foreskin. John gave up any hope of taking control of the situation and melted back against the firm body, which was the only thing keeping him upright. The hand stroking him dragged his foreskin back up and over the head of his cock, lubricating it with some of the copious pre-cum that was leaking from his aching shaft. This man knew his way around a cock, and it wasn't long before John found himself panting on the edge of orgasm only to find that the talented hands bringing him there also knew how to stave off that same orgasm and prolong the pleasure. Twice, Brom brought John to the edge of orgasm only to ease him back from the brink before leading him back to the edge. When Brom felt that he'd ramped the sexy professor past the point of all control, he teased the man to the point that even though Brom removed his hand from the man's hefty cock and locked it around his waist, John still blew his pent up load totally hands free. Brom watched the thick heavy load blast from the man's throbbing cock in five jets, reaching to the base of his anvil before subsiding into minor pulses. Those landed in the jeans pooled around the man's ankles. John signed deeply as the last traces of his orgasm finally faded and let his mind return. He turned his head toward Brom and found his mouth captured by a deep kiss.

Brom broke the kiss and whispered into John's ear, "Pull up your pants and follow me to the shower."

It took John a moment longer than he would have liked to focus enough to follow the directions Brom had just given him. He'd never been so out of it during a sex act. This man was addictive and commanding. John had always been the more active partner with his late lover, always the one in control, but Brom had ripped away any thought of control John might have thought he had. He bent down and grabbed his jeans, hiking them back up to his waist before he followed Brom's muscular ass. Thankfully, Brom's cabin wasn't very far from the forge. John wasn't sure he'd survive the embarrassment of being caught like a naughty teenager.

He slipped in the backdoor and made his way to Brom's room where he heard the sound of water running from a shower. As he walked into the bedroom, he found himself wrapped in Brom's strong arms, but at least this time he was facing the man. Silver eyes locked on the beautiful face of the sexy professor. Brom drank in the features of this man who was perfection personified. The slightly curly hair was matted to the man's forehead by sweat generated by both the heat of the forge and the heat generated while getting a load jacked out of his cock. Brom brought their faces closer together, and then teased the already sex-swollen lips with a gentle sweep of his tongue. They parted of their own accord. John lost his grip on his jeans, and they slid back down his legs as he reached around Brom to hang on for dear life. This man was going to be his undoing. At least the heavy apron was gone and he could feel the heat and the thickness of the other man's package. John slid his hands down first to cup the muscular ass and then to move them to where he could fumble with Brom's belt and pants.

Brom let his own hands wander down John's back to slip beneath the man's boxers and let his calloused hands roam over the soft and lightly furred ass. Slowly, he stroked in toward the cleft and gently gripped each cheek, pulling them apart slightly, just as his own pants slipped loose to pool around his ankles. John was moaning into his mouth as their tongues danced. Both men let their hands roam upward, catching the T-shirt the other man wore and working it up until they were both trying to remove the offending garment from the other and getting twisted up in them because they didn't want to break the kiss. Brom used his strength to break the kiss and strip John's shirt away before removing his own. Now both men were naked to the waist and panting with deepening lust.

John let his hands roam over Brom's work-defined chest and through the heavy coating of hair that covered his pectorals before narrowing into a trail over his abs to the waistband of his boxer briefs. The bulge in that underwear promised a cock at least as thick and long as John's own. Brom, for his part, was taking in the lighter covering of hair on John's defined chest. There was just enough hair dusting the upper chest to make him sexy. John's treasure trail began at his naval and vanished into his boxers. Brom used his bigger frame to move John back toward the king-sized bed that dominated his bedroom. John found himself falling backward as his knees connected with the bedframe. He lay sprawled on Brom's bed, reminded that he was wearing heavy boots as his feet dangled off the edge of the bed. Just as he was about to try and sit up to remove them, he watched Brom drop to his knees and begin unlacing them. They were soon undone, and Brom gripped them and John's jeans. He pulled them off, leaving the man in his socks and boxers. Brom then fumbled with the laces on his own boots as he gazed up the long muscular legs of the smoking hot professor sprawled on his bed. Once his laces were loose enough, Brom rose and toed the boots and his jeans off, leaving himself in his socks and boxer briefs. Soot from the furnace left him with a pseudo farmer's tan. He reached his hand out and drew it up the inside of John's left leg until it slipped into the underwear and came to rest cradling John's balls. The professor's thick, heavy cock started to regain its hardness as Brom teased his calloused fingers over the shaft. John tried to reach over to give attention to Brom's cock, but found his hand captured and pinned. Brom leaned down over John and whispered in his ear, "I want to watch you melt in pleasure again, John. I'll let you have a chance to service me later." The bigger man then locked his lips over John's, keeping him from replying as Brom took a firmer grip on the professor's throbbing cock and began to stroke.

John melted under the sensations coming from his cock, as the rough calluses were so different from his own smooth hands. The feel of Brom's bearded face against his own clean-shaven one was very different from the last time he'd kissed anyone. His partner had always kept his face smooth. With all the differences from the last person he'd ever had sex with, John was rapidly on the edge of a second orgasm. This time, Brom didn't tease him by stopping when he sensed the moment was near. Instead, the man increased the friction and brought John over the edge in a smashing orgasm. If Brom hadn't had his lips locked to John's, both men were sure John's scream of pleasure, as his load fired from his cock, would have reached the main house. As Brom slowly released John's now sore cock with a few last strokes to milk out the last bits of his load, John shuddered at how sensitive his cock was. Brom stroked his hand up John's abs to his chest, smearing cum as he did so. John shivered under the touch as Brom kissed him once more before standing up and offering his hand to John.

"Come on, sexy professor, time we hit the shower so we can get to the hospital before Cory thinks we've abandoned him."

"I'm not sure I can stand up after all that. Are you sure you don't want me to return the favor now?"

"We need to talk about a few things before I let you have your way with me, John," he replied, kindly. "Right now isn't the time for that discussion. Let's get cleaned up, go check on Kieran and Cory, and then I'll take you out to dinner and we'll talk about safe sex between mages."

INTERLUDE: A TOUCH OF GOLD?

Elihu Hayes double-checked that the sedative had been added to the food he was bringing to the mongrel shifter that watched over the Master's prize as he pushed the trolley of hospital meals toward Kieran's room. The dark apprentice needed to be sure he could work undisturbed while enhancing the Master's dark spell inside the prize. He'd been quietly studying the routines of the floor staff as well as the prize's family. The one he most needed to watch out for was the prize's so-called husband. The shifter very rarely left the prize's bedside and spent each night sleeping on the couch in the room. The dark apprentice knew he had to strike tonight because the local news had reported the discovery of the orderly's body earlier in the day. It wouldn't be long before the cops started asking questions at the hospital. Elihu arrived at the prize's room and knocked to announce his arrival with the dinner tray.

"Come in," Cory called from his usual spot next to Kieran's bed. "Hello, Joshua." He'd read the man's nametag earlier in the week. "So what are they serving tonight?"

"Hello, sir. Dinner is soup, a roll, pudding, and a coke," Elihu replied.

"Not very filling, but it's nice that Dr. Anna lets me order in."

"Yes, sir. Has there been any change in your husband's condition?"

"No, no change. Thanks for asking. You can leave the tray over there," Cory said, pointing at the moving tray table.

The dark apprentice set down the tampered tray and then left the room to continue his routine.

* * *

Late that evening, Elihu made his way quietly back to his target's room, where he checked to make sure the shifter was fast asleep from the drugs. Slipping into the room, the dark apprentice made his way to the bedside where he examined the prize. He could sense the stalemate between Silver and Ebony magic inside the young man. The Master's spell was powerful, but the prize seemed to have vast reserves of power to draw on to prevent the spell from taking hold. Elihu pulled back the sheet covering Kieran's waist and then flipped up the hospital gown to reveal Kieran's flaccid cock. The catheter tube running from the end spoiled the view, but it was still an impressive cock.

"I hope you enjoyed your little shifter's ass, because once the Master has you in his possession, that pretty cock is going to vanish into a permanent chastity device. Now let's start breaking down those shields of yours so the Master's spell can do its work."

Elihu began to chant the enhancement spell, and Ebony magic started swirling around his hands. As he reached out to touch Kieran's forehead and groin, he sensed another presence in the room. He looked up to find Father Ivory standing in the doorway.

"What are you doing?" Father Ivory called out as he spotted Elihu hunched over a nearly naked Kieran.

Snarling in frustration, Elihu raised his magic-shrouded left hand, and threw a bolt of Ebony magic at the priest. Father Ivory instinctively raised his hands in a warding gesture as he muttered a prayer to St. Hubert. The room was engulfed in brilliant flash of gold. Elihu screamed as the gold washed over him, snuffing out his Ebony magic. Cory awoke as the light cleansed the drug from his system, and Father Ivory passed out, slumping to the floor. Both Cory's and Elihu's eyes were drawn to Kieran's body as the golden light lifted him from the bed. They watched as the Ebony magic within Kieran was burned away and the broken bones knit together. The light set Kieran down on his feet right in front of Elihu, whose eyes grew large with terror when he realized Kieran was wide awake and his eyes were glowing with Silver magic. Before Elihu could scream, Silver magic wrapped around him and he heard Kieran's voice. They were the last words he ever heard. "Be my message to your master."

* * *

Over a thousand miles away, Elihu's smoking corpse crashed to the floor at the foot of the Master's throne-like chair where the Ebony mage sat holding court over his minion. They all drew back at the feel of Silver magic wrapped around the body. Before their eyes, a silver shade arose in Elihu's form and faced the Master.

"I bring a message for the mage who calls himself the Master. The Silver Witch is done dealing with your pathetic minions. You have a choice: leave him and his alone, or suffer the fate of your lowly apprentice."

The shade vanished, and the body exploded, spreading gore across the room.

9

Magic raged just outside the barrier he'd created to protect his mind and powers from the poisonous Ebony magic in his system. Kieran felt and heard everything the dark mage was doing to him but couldn't respond. He knew that something must have happened to Cory since this mage didn't seem worried about him. Then had come the shocking surprise in the form of Father Ivory's arrival. The dark mage had tried to attack the priest only to be stopped by a blast of a magic that shouldn't exist anymore. Gold magic had flooded the room, canceling out all the Ebony magic and freeing Kieran from his self-imposed mental prison. It healed his shattered bones and other injuries, including the burned control channels over the powers of the Silver Witch. He found himself standing and facing his would-be assassin. Power blazed through him and fueled an ancient spell that used the enemy as a message. It surged up, giving him just enough time to tell the enemy mage to fuck off before it sent the burning remains back. Not quiet as nasty as the spell he'd used on Marissa but not pleasant either.

Now he stood wobbling on legs weakened from disuse. Kieran tried to turn to face Cory, but that proved too much for him. He started to fall. Cory caught him in a fierce embrace, keeping him from hitting the floor. His husband held him tight, drowning his hospital gown in tears.

"Wolf, can you set me back on the bed?" Kieran's voice sounded drier than he remembered it being. "I'm not really ready for all the standing."

He felt Cory lift him up and gently place him back in the bed. As his head sank into the pillow, the shrieking alarms from his vital sign monitors finally made its presence known. Cory had just settled Kieran when the first responding nurse arrived, nearly tripping over the fallen Father Ivory.

"We need a gurney; something's happened to Father Ivory," the nurse called out as she jumped over the priest to get to Kieran. She was surprised to see the young man staring at her with bright silver eyes.

"I seem to have dislodged a couple of my monitor leads when I came to," Kieran said with a weak version of his normally devastating smile. "Is Father Ivory okay?"

Before the nurse could answer, Dr. Anna arrived along with a trauma team. Part of the team stopped to check on the fallen priest, while Dr. Anna crossed the room to begin examining Kieran. Cory stood out of the way, but Kieran could feel his anxiety through their restored bond. He pulsed his love down the bond and watched Cory relax a little bit.

"So give it to me straight, Dr. Anna, will I be able to dance the Viennese Waltz?"

"That will have to wait until your legs heal, young man."

"Well, I guess I have something to look forward to, since I couldn't do it before my legs were broken." Kieran's grin was a mile wide as he heard Cory groan at his lame attempt at a joke. He focused on the doctor again. "Do you think we can get the casts off and the rods and pins out soon? They itch something fierce."

"It will be weeks before the bones in your legs have healed enough for us to think about removing the pins and rods. Then you'll be doing months of physical therapy to recondition the muscles."

"I think you'll find that my legs and other injuries are healed, Dr.

Mihaylova." Kieran's tone was harsh. "Perhaps we can at least schedule some X-rays."

"Which one of us is the doctor and which is the patient?" Dr. Mihaylova snapped back, her Russian accent starting to thicken.

"Better question, doctor, which of us is the mage who knows the condition of his body down to the cellular level?" Kieran said as his eyes began to blaze solid silver and a glow began to form around his right hand.

Dr. Mihaylova drew back as the silver glow dissolved the cast around Kieran's right hand, and it flexed like it had never been broken. The glow spread to his left hand and repeated what had happened with his right hand. Kieran then flexed both hands through the motions of a person used to wielding a bladed weapon. The staff was drawing back in fear. Cory darted forward and took Kieran's left hand in his own so that their wedding rings touched.

"Babe, calm down. You're scaring everyone." He leaned in and whispered, "They don't know what you are." In a louder voice, he continued, "All they know is that you came in here with devastating injuries. They didn't witness the miracle Father Ivory's prayers to St. Hubert brought about."

Kieran blinked at Cory in confusion, which was enough to break his focus on his magic so that it faded away. Suddenly, comprehension dawned on Kieran.

"I'm sorry, Dr. Mihaylova, I'm still in shock over my sudden recovery. I do believe I felt the touch of St. Hubert bringing me a miracle. Please, is Father Ivory all right?" Kieran turned a pitiful look on the doctor.

"He seems to have fainted. I'll check on him in a little bit. I want to check all your vitals personally; then I'll order some tests, including X-rays and a full CAT scan. I don't believe in miracles any more than I do in magic."

Dr. Mihaylova pulled herself up, her logical and scientific mind already erasing the strange events as the shock of finding her unconscious patient fully awake and able to engage in conversation. The realist in her already shoved all thoughts of miracles out of her conscious thought. She walked out of the room and began issuing orders regarding tests for Mr. Oisín-Cooper. Once the duty nurse had finished reattaching all of Kieran's monitor leads and had left, Cory turned to his husband.

"Okay, we both know that you're totally healed, but Kieran, you don't have to go ballistic on these people."

"I'm sorry, Cory. I'm still a bit stressed about coming out of that nasty spell face-to-face with a dark mage out to kill or enslave me. Then, there's the shock of being saved by a priest with Gold magic. Nobody has Gold magic anymore, Cory."

"Well, I guess it really was a miracle then. Maybe that's what the prophecy was referring to when it talked about the rising of the gold revealing your fate?" Cory said.

"I don't even want to think about it. What are the odds of a priest dedicated to the patron saint of hunters being assigned to this hospital just when someone like me is admitted? Especially when said saint's area of miracle working is curing people infected with rabies. Trying to figure out this prophecy gives me a headache."

"Just rest, babe. I'm sure Dr. Anna will be back to start running her battery of tests on you sooner than we'd like."

"One thing before I try and get some real sleep."

"You know all you have to do is ask, Kieran."

"Kiss me, Wolf."

Cory leaned over the bed and bent down to kiss Kieran deeply. When they broke their kiss, Cory scooped Kieran up and shifted him over in the narrow bed. He then slipped in beside him and pulled him tight against him.

"I'm not letting you sleep alone, babe," Cory said as he wrapped Kieran in his arms.

"Thanks, my love. I don't think I could sleep without you by my side."

"Sleep, Kier. I'm here to keep watch."

The lovers managed to get a few hours of sleep before Dr. Mihaylova returned with an orderly to help get Kieran ready for the first few tests. Cory was just stepping out of the restroom when she came in.

"Mr. Oisín-Cooper, we're going to start with X-rays and the CAT scan before we start drawing blood and doing more invasive tests."

Kieran looked up at Dr. Mihaylova with a faint smile. "Mr. Oisín-Cooper is my husband; you can call me Kieran."

"Well, at least your sense of humor seems to have survived the injuries," she replied.

"Can you do something to fix that, Dr. Anna? He tells the worst jokes, and he's not half as funny as he thinks he is," Cory said.

"Maybe you should ask that question to Father Ivory, since you claim he can work miracles."

"How is Father Ivory?" Kieran and Cory asked in unison.

"A little dehydrated and confused. He doesn't remember a thing about last night past visiting with Mrs. Hyde-Green on the third floor."

"That's a shame. He won't be able to report the appearance of St. Hubert to his order."

"Probably for the best. I don't think the administration would be happy about the hospital suddenly becoming a pilgrimage site. Have you called your family to let them know that Kieran's awake, Cory?"

"Oh, no, I'd better do that right now," Cory said, reaching for his phone and punching Kellen's contact line.

While the phone rang, the orderly set about moving Kieran's IV from the stand next to the bed to a pole attached to the bed. The monitor cords were unhooked and laid beside Kieran on the bed. He then unlocked the wheels of the bed and raised the rails on both sides. Kieran just relaxed as he listened to his husband talk to his father on the phone. When Cory hung up, the orderly began pushing the bed out of the room and off to X-ray. Shortly after their departure, the elevator chimed, and a burly sheriff's deputy exited. He made his way over to the nurses' station, flashed his badge, and identified himself as Deputy Petersen.

"Have you seen this man?" He showed a picture of the real Joshua. "I'm told he works as an orderly on this floor."

* * *

KIERAN WAS EXHAUSTED when the orderly wheeled his bed back into his room. Dr. Mihaylova was talking with Cory, Kellen, and Líadáin as the orderly got him hooked back into the monitors and moved the IV bag back to its separate stand. Líadáin moved to the bedside and took Kieran's hand.

"We were all so worried about you, *mo stór*. It's good to see you awake again."

"It's nice to be able to interact again, Grams. How are you holding up?"

"Like the trooper your grandmother is," Kellen interjected. "Once we got her to rest and eat, she was back to her usually busy self. She's thrilled to have people to look after and feed. Between Cory's parents and your Professor Mason, she's having a blast entertaining."

"Professor Mason is here?" Kieran asked. "I figured he'd stay in Little Rock when someone told him I was injured and the ceremony would have to be postponed."

"When he heard you'd been hurt, he changed to earlier flights and put in for sabbatical instead of vacation time," Kellen said. "He's staying in the guest room in your uncle Brom's cabin. They seem to enjoy each other's company. Brom says they'll be along later; he was trying to finish up something at the forge when Cory called with the news. The Coopers should be here soon."

"Could you ask them to come back later? I'm worn out from all of Dr. Anna's poking and prodding," Kieran said.

"I'll let Mom know that maybe tomorrow would be better," Cory said.

"Thanks, Cory," Kieran said around a yawn.

"Okay, time to let the patient get some rest. Cory will let you know when Kieran is up to visitors again," Dr. Anna said, ushering Kellen and Líadáin out of the room and closing the door behind them.

Kieran was starting to drift off when he felt a surge of love and worry through the bond as Cory settled down in the chair at his bedside. He forced his eyes open and gave his husband a smile as Cory took his hand. Cory reached out and stroked Kieran's hair. Kieran drifted off to sleep at his lover's touch.

* * *

CORY BOLTED upright at Kieran's screams of pain. He groped around and found the call button, pressing it to summon the duty nurse. He gently stroked his husband's hair trying to calm him down enough to learn where the pain was most intense.

"Sshh, love, the nurse will be here in a moment with something for the pain. I'm right here with you; share the pain through our bond if you can."

Kieran whimpered in pain and tried to reach for the bond with his husband. Cory fell back into the chair as pain from the pins and rods in Kieran's legs took his own out from under him. Cory ground his teeth and hung on to his sense of self as the nurse arrived.

"What's the matter?" the nurse asked.

"The pins and rods are causing him a lot of pain. Can you get him something to ease it, please?"

"Let me check his chart. Dr. Mihaylova was supposed to leave instructions. Yes, here they are. Okay, you hold on, dear. I'll be just a moment."

Cory continued to hold Kieran's hand and bear his part of the shared pain as they waited for the nurse to return. It wasn't a long wait, and she added pain medication to the IV drip. After a few minutes, Cory felt the pain fade from his own legs and knew that Kieran was relaxing back toward sleep. The nurse checked Kieran's vitals and made a note on the chart about giving the pain medication.

"He should sleep now. Dr. Mihaylova should be by on her rounds soon."

"Thank you," Cory said as he settled back in the chair still holding Kieran's hand.

10

———

D r. Mihaylova waited to check on Kieran as the last patient on her rounds. She still couldn't believe the X-rays and the results of the CAT scan. Kieran was totally healed. She'd have to schedule an operating room to get the pins and rods out of him so that the bones in his legs could finish healing. He'd still need to do physical therapy to restore his muscles. The doctor had figured that by the time she reached Kieran's room his family would be visiting, and she was right. The room was packed with visitors. She entered, and most of the people moved back out her way as she started checking Kieran's vitals. Pleased with what she found, Dr. Mihaylova faced the family.

"I'm not a believer in miracles, but we seem to have experienced one, because Kieran's X-rays and CAT scan came back showing that all of his injuries have been healed. All that remains to do is to remove the rods and pins we put in to hold his legs together when they were shattered."

"How soon can you schedule the surgery, Dr. Anna?" Cory asked.

"We can do it as soon as I can get a surgical team together. I know you must be starving, Kieran, but can you go a while longer without food?"

"I can manage, Dr. Mihaylova. Grams and Mrs. Cooper have promised to stuff me to the gills with food when I get home from here."

"Well, you wont be leaving right away, Kieran. Your leg muscles will need exercise to get strong enough to support you again after being immobilized for the last couple of weeks."

"I promise to do my exercises, Dr. Mihaylova. I have an important event I plan on walking to," Kieran said as he took Cory's hand in his own.

"Okay, I'm going to go secure an operating room and a team. I think your visitors should say their good-byes for now so you can rest before my team comes to prepare you for the surgery."

Dr. Mihaylova left, heading off to schedule the OR for Kieran's surgery. The Coopers, Kellen, and Líadáin followed her out in short order. Brom and Professor Mason stayed just a while longer before heading out for their dinner and discussion. Cory scooted Kieran over in the bed and curled up beside his husband.

"I can't wait to get home to a real bed," Cory said as he laid his head on Kieran's shoulder.

"Yeah, this bed is way too small for both of us. Besides, if we're home, it will mean I don't have all this metal in my legs, and we can make love," Kieran replied.

"I think that Dad, Grams, and Professor Mason will help speed up your healing, Kier."

"You know I like the new pet name you have for me, Wolf," Kieran said, turning his head enough to kiss his husband.

"Good, because I plan to use it a lot," Cory replied when the kiss broke.

"When we get back to the compound, I want to see you as your wolf," Kieran said, taking Cory by surprise.

"How did you know?"

"I can feel him through our bond. He's as curious to meet me as I am to meet him."

"Kier, you realize the wolf is still me and not a separate entity, right?"

"It is and it isn't you, Cory. The ability to shift is still new to you, and you haven't really accepted your wolf as part of who you are. When we get out of here and I'm strong enough, we need to go spend time in the woods. You can let the wolf out and get used to him."

"But we'll have to wait for a full moon to do that."

"I don't think we will, Cory. You're something new, a shifter whose power comes from Silver magic. You aren't bound by the spell my ancestors cast. Focus on your right hand and will the change."

Cory turned his gaze from his husband to his right hand, and he willed it to become a wolf's paw. Pain flowed through his hand as the bones shifted and flesh reshaped itself. In just a few moments, his right hand was a wolf's paw, complete with fearsome claws. He stared in awe at his transformed hand, and then willed it back to human shape.

"That's going to take some getting used to."

"Well, we now know that you're the shifter on my right, which makes Billy the shifter on my left. We're going to have to relocate to the Belle estate once the doctor clears me. I'm going to have to find the hidden archives the family historians have kept. I need to know the secrets they've kept from each huntress."

"We'll do the handfasting, and then send Mom, Dad, and Professor Mason home to Arkansas. Then we can take your dad, grams, and uncle Brom to the Belle estate with us," Cory said.

"Actually, Professor Mason and your dad might be useful, but we can discuss any plans later, Wolf. I need to rest," Kieran said, snuggling into Cory as best as he could.

Some hours later, the surgical prep team knocked on the door before entering. A couple of them grinned at how cute the two young men looked curled up together in the tiny hospital bed. The lead nurse of the team gently woke Cory.

"Mr. Oisín-Cooper, we've come to prep your husband for surgery. I'm afraid you'll have to slip out of bed. Dr. Mihaylova feels the surgery will last about four hours, so if you'd like to go get yourself something to eat . . ."

"Will you be bringing him back here after the surgery?" Cory asked.

"As soon as he comes out of the anesthesia in the recovery room, we'll bring him right back here," the nurse replied.

Cory slipped out of the bed, trying not to wake Kieran, but he found his husband's silver eyes locked on him. He leaned over and kissed Kieran.

"Go get something to eat, grab a shower, and change your clothes, love. I'm in good hands here," Kieran teased Cory.

"Awake only one day and you're already getting bossy," Cory teased back.

"Your stomach is growling, you stink, and you've been wearing those clothes for at least two days. Go home; spend some time with Grams and your parents. Tell Uncle Brom and Professor Mason to come and stand watch. They can wear the pacing path deeper in the tile of the waiting room." Kieran flashed one of his irresistible smiles.

"Okay, but I'll be back before the doctor is done," Cory said as he left the room and called Brom's phone. "Uncle Brom, they're getting him ready for surgery, and he's sending me home. He wants you and Professor Mason to come and pace in the waiting room. Yes, I'm just heading downstairs. Let Grams know I'm headed back. No, he didn't ask for Kellen for some reason. I don't know, I think his mind is on other things. Thanks, Uncle Brom." Cory hung up and stuffed his phone in his pocket as he headed down and out to the minivan.

As Cory crossed the waiting room headed for the exit, he caught a fragment of the local news.

"Police are still looking into the brutal slaying of local hospital orderly, Joshua Prescott, who was found dead in his apartment two days ago by his landlord. If you have any information on Joshua Prescott, please call . . ."

11

____

While Elihu Hayes—the dark apprentice—had been attacking Kieran the previous evening, Brom and John had been out to dinner at the Black Friar Inn. Brom treated John to fresh seafood. After dinner, they'd gone for a long walk along the shore so they could have the private talk Brom had promised regarding safe sex between mages. John stopped Brom when they reached the end of one of the piers. Reaching out, he took one of Brom's calloused hands between his own smooth hands.

"So we were going to have a conversation about safe sex between mages," John said, raising one hand to place a finger on Brom's lips to forestall his speaking. "I want you to know that what you did earlier was absolutely amazing. I also want you to know that whatever the reason you're afraid of someone returning the pleasure, you don't have to be afraid I'll walk out. We haven't had a lot of time to get to know each other, and you have things that are more important on your mind than a casual hook-up with a random professor. So just tell me what's on your mind, and we can build something from there."

"You're an amazing man, John Mason," Brom said, looking into John's emerald green eyes. "The last guy I was with got up and walked out before we even really got started when I mentioned safe sex. It seems like nobody practices it anymore. He wasn't much of a mage, more of a hedge witch at best. His talent made what's left of mine look vast, but he seemed to think mages were immune to things being transmitted via sex."

John locked his gaze with Brom's silver eyes. "Go ahead, Brom. I promise to hear everything you have to say, and then I ask that you return the favor."

"I will listen to anything you have to say, John." Brom gave the man a quick kiss before resuming his story. "You know how much I love Kieran; he's the son I never had. When he was born, Kellen was so excited, and it was infectious. In those days, I was father's heir to the powers of the Silver Witch, and my magic ranged free. Father discovered a prophecy in our ancient grimoire that he was afraid referred to Kieran. We investigated, we found that Kieran seemed destined to fulfill this prophecy or at least have to attempt to fulfill it. I was dating a young man at the time that I didn't realize was a dark shifter until I brought him home for dinner to meet the family. He couldn't pass the defense spell that used to cover the grounds. Father met us at the gate when the alarm spell went off. We argued, and I left with my so-called boyfriend and went back to town. We rented a hotel room, and I deluded myself into thinking we were making love—" Brom's choked.

"It's okay, Brom." John ran a hand up his arm to soothe him. "It's in the past. Let it go."

"I thought by taking up with a shifter I could take Kieran's place in the prophecy. I didn't realize that the shifter had known I was a Silver mage and had dark plans for me. We fucked for hours, always with condoms because he insisted on them, afraid of what Silver magic might do to him if it got into his bloodstream. Sometime in the early morning hours, we were going at it one last time before having to split up for some reason. He was fucking me, and I wasn't paying attention. He slipped the condom off and fucked me bare. When I realized what was happening, it was too late; he was blowing his load deep in my ass. The Ebony magic in his blood infected me, battling with my Silver magic, warping and twisting it. I managed to get off one last spell at full power before my magic was crippled forever. I killed him and took most of the hotel with him. I staggered to my car and managed to drive home somehow. Father found me slumped over the steering wheel with a raging fever just inside the gates. He got me back to my cabin and worked some spell that stripped me of my connection to the powers of the Silver Witch. He stopped the spread of the Ebony magic in my system. When we tested my magic after I recovered from my fever, he found that my channels had been ruined. I went out to my forge to console myself by working with hot metal. Something in the process of working metal opened my magic channels, but only while I was working at the forge."

"Brom, I'm so sorry."

"Don't be, I really didn't want to be the Silver Witch, because I wouldn't have been allowed to remain true to myself. I would have been expected to take one for the team and wed a woman to produce a blood heir. Father shifted the heir status to Kellen who already had an heir of the bloodline. I honed my craft, traveling to learn from the best blacksmiths around the world, and fulfilled family tradition by making a fortune in order to inherit my share of the family fortune. I'd tried to take Kieran's place, but magic prevented me. The problem is that I'm still infected with a taint of Ebony magic, and anyone I have sex with can be infected and lose their powers if we don't use condoms for everything. Over the years, I've learned to enjoy giving my partner pleasure without having them reciprocate."

"I thank you for being honest with me, Brom. I did wonder why you didn't want me to help you get off," John said. "May I ask if you'll let me scan you magically? Silver magic isn't noted for it's healing spells, but Emerald magic is."

"If you wanted to scan me with magic, you could have done so at any time."

"I could have, but my family has always striven to have permission before we do a scan as invasive as this one will be. I think it would be best to go back to your place, as the magic will take a lot of both of us. I want to test out the spell I plan to use tomorrow on Kieran."

"So I get to play guinea pig to your magic?" Brom shrugged at the thought. "Well, for Kieran, I'd do anything, so let's go find the SUV and head home."

John reached out and pulled Brom in for a kiss. When he broke the kiss, he whispered in Brom's ear, "You're the sexiest guinea pig I've ever met."

12

———

Kieran was resting peacefully in his hospital bed when Uncle Brom arrived. His uncle slipped into the room as quietly as possible, and he settled into the visitor's chair beside the bed, casually opening a book.

"You seem happier than I've seen you in a long time, Uncle." Kieran's raspy voice startled his uncle.

"I didn't realize you were awake, *mo stór*."

"You and Cory are a lot louder than you think you are. Even when you don't say anything for fear of waking me."

"I'm sorry for disturbing your rest, Nephew."

"So what—or should I guess whom—has you walking on clouds, Uncle Brom?"

"I'm overjoyed by your miraculous recovery, *mo stór*."

"Okay, like everyone else in this family, Uncle Brom, you're a terrible liar, even when what you're saying is true but not the real answer. I think you're seeing someone you've met since we've been here at the hospital. Did you find a sexy nurse to ease your pain, or is there a smoking hot doctor giving you a special physical exam?"

"Kieran! It's none of your business."

"Well, that confirms you've found someone who rocks your world. Am I sensing more magic around you?"

Kieran's abrupt change of topic caught Brom off guard. However, before he could respond or Kieran could press further, John Mason knocked on the door to the room before he entered.

"Am I interrupting something important?" John asked.

Kieran caught the gleam of joy in his uncle's silver eyes and turned to find a matching sparkle in the emerald green eyes of his photography professor. His own silver eyes lit up as he started to laugh with happiness. His laughter cut off when a jolt of pain reminded him of his recent surgery. He smiled at both of the older men who were blushing like schoolboys.

"So cute." Kieran chuckled. "You two as a couple is just too much to handle."

"We're not a couple, *mo stór*."

"What a thing to imply, Mr. Belle." John's voice was in professor mode.

Kieran looked at both men as they tried hard to look sternly back at him. His smile got bigger as their blushing got redder and ruined the effect they were going for.

"Right! So not a couple!" Sarcasm dripped from Kieran's tongue. "But I bet you two have been spending a considerable amount of time together, and Uncle Brom has made you lose your mind at least twice with his reputedly skilled hands. However, I sense the dynamic is changing. You've been working Emerald magic on my uncle, Professor. Uncle Brom has never felt this powerful in all my life. I'd have to get Dad to tell me if you're anywhere near your old potential."

The look that passed between the two men told Kieran he'd hit the nail on the head. Both of them started to say something, but Kieran stopped them both.

"I approve. I think you're exactly what the other needs, even if you're only friends with benefits while Professor Mason visits. I want you both to be happy."

"Well, thank you for your approval, Nephew. Not that we need it since we're both grown men and choose who we see for ourselves."

"You might be my elder, Uncle Brom, but as the Silver Witch, I'm the head of the family." Kieran suddenly choked on a huge lump in his throat as his statement reminded him that he was the Silver Witch because Gramps was dead. Marissa murdering the old man flashed through his thoughts. Tears began to flow. Both Brom and John reached out and gently wrapped him in a hug between them.

"Let it out, *mo stór*. You haven't had time to process your grief. We all miss his strength and presence. He was always so proud of you, Kieran. You were his favorite grandchild."

"I failed him. In the end, I failed him. I brought his killer past the barrier and destroyed him and the only place I've ever felt safe—all at the same time." Kieran sobbed.

"You couldn't know Marissa would turn on you like that. She was your friend, and you gave her the measure of trust you give all your friends. I've watched how you made friends with Mr. Harkrider in class even though you didn't like him taking pictures of you," Professor Mason added in a gentle voice.

"All I've ever wanted to do was create, not destroy, but it seems I leave a trail of destruction in my wake. I should have just stayed home and trained young boys to fight monsters until I died."

Cory's voice cut through the grief and self-loathing. "Kieran Samuel Belle Oisín-Cooper, if you'd done that, then the most beautiful thing in the world would never have been created."

Kieran looked up as the two men holding him let go. His husband was standing at the foot of his bed.

"You created the most beautiful love anyone could have ever known. I'd just be a lonely college student drifting through life if you hadn't come along. Billy would be a tormented kid shifting into a raging monster every full moon if you hadn't met him. Your uncle would not have met the man who's made him not only happy, but also magically whole. Yes, some stuff has gotten broken along the way, but that's life, Kieran. Gramps wouldn't have wanted you to be any different than you are now. He loved you as we all do. So cry for his loss, but do not question your decisions to live the life you chose for yourself."

Tears flowed down Kieran face as he opened his arms for his husband. Cory moved into his embrace and gently hugged his husband, stroking his hair as Kieran cried himself to sleep in his arms. John pulled Brom out of the room so the boys could be alone.

"I was going to speed up the rest of Kieran's healing, but I think he needed this release of his grief even more."

"We can come back later, John. Right now, he needs Cory and rest. I think that since the dam has broken on his emotions, he'll finally mourn his sisters as well as Father."

"What about you, Brom? When will you mourn for your father?"

"It's not time for me to mourn yet, John, but I promise that I'll let you comfort me when the time comes."

13

It took another week before Dr. Mihaylova was convinced that Kieran was healed enough to be discharged. He'd been getting antsy once he'd started physical therapy. He'd been upset when his legs wouldn't hold him up on the first day. However, each day he got stronger, and each night Professor Mason, Jonathan Cooper, or Grams worked to speed up his healing. By the end of the week, Kieran was wandering the halls under his own power. Now, he was sitting on his hospital bed, dressed in his own clothes and waiting for the nurse to arrive with his discharge papers. Cory sat watching his husband try not to fidget. A huge grin spread over Cory's face as Kieran gave up trying to sit still and began pacing around the room.

"Grin and laugh if you want. You haven't been trapped motionless in a bed for over a month, Wolf."

"Kier, relax, the nurse will be here any minute, and then you can enjoy the nice wheelchair ride downstairs and out to the car. Then, you can enjoy the ride home to the compound and our cabin." Cory's grin was evil.

"You're being mean, Cory. I've got so much energy pumping through me I need to move. I want to be free in the woods to move and dance with a sword in my hand."

"You're catching some of that from me through our bond, Kier. The full moon is only a few days away, and my wolf is clamoring to get out and run."

"I want to run with your wolf, Cory. I want to know him, learn how he moves."

"Likely I'm going to trip over my own tail and fall on my muzzle. I have no clue how to be a werewolf."

"Billy can come and run with us. He can show you how to be the wolf. We need to learn how to move as a group, how to hunt and fight together."

"Babe, settle down. We aren't going shifter hunting any time soon. You have to build all of your strength back up. We still have to honor Gramps, so that Grams, Kellen, and Brom can all mourn. Then there's our delayed handfasting and the claiming . . ."

When Cory mentioned the claiming, the burst of sexual desire that flowed from him stopped Kieran in his tracks, and a moan of pleasure escaped his throat. He turned to look at Cory, his silver eyes blazing with animalistic lust. Cory felt the lustful sensation rebound on him down the bond, and it was all he could do not to grab Kieran and rip his clothes off right then. Only the fear of being discovered by the nurse kept him from pouncing on Kieran. If he felt this wild a few days before the full moon, what would he be like when the moon was full?

The lovers were saved from being caught in a compromising position by the return of the nurse. She had Kieran's discharge papers, prescriptions, and an orderly with a wheelchair. Kieran groaned at the need for the wheelchair but knew it was hospital policy. He took his seat in the chair and let the orderly set the foot rests. Kieran nearly gagged at the scent of the orderly's cologne. His sense of smell seemed heightened; it must have been part of sharing the bond with Cory and his wolf senses. *I wonder if all that Ebony magic triggered something in my own dormant shifter genes,* Kieran thought as he fought down the urge to vomit at the cloying aroma. Mercifully, the elevator ride was short as was the section of hallway to the exit. Out front in a parking space near the door, the minivan he'd bought with Cory sat waiting for them. Once they were close to the van, Kieran practically launched himself from the wheelchair to escape the overpowering smell. Cory looked amused as he clicked the button to unlock the van so that Kieran could escape. He thanked the orderly for his assistance and then made his way around the van to the driver's side. He opened the door and then slid in behind the steering wheel. He glanced at Kieran and had to bite back a laugh. Kieran was pinching his nose, trying to erase the foul smell from the cologne. Cory reached across the seat and pulled Kieran over and into a kiss, making sure to leave his own scent all over Kieran's face to block out any other smells. When the kiss broke, Kieran visibly relaxed back into his seat. Cory started the van and then backed out of the parking space before putting the van in drive and heading back home.

* * *

IN THE KITCHEN of the main house on the Oisín's compound, Líadáin was hard at work putting the finishing touches on a special welcome home dinner for Kieran. She'd made all of his favorite foods and now was frosting the carrot cake she'd made with cream cheese frosting. Tamara Cooper had been helping earlier with some of the cooking and now was out in the garden setting the large table. The construction crew had done a remarkable job of repairing the window in the dining room, and Brom and John had done a remarkable job of getting the stain of Aodhfin's blood out of the oriental carpet and the floor beneath it. Líadáin just couldn't make herself enter the room yet, but maybe once they'd held his memorial service tonight, she'd feel better about entering the room where he'd died. This place had been her home for over fifty years, but perhaps it was time to move on and settle closer to Kieran and Cory in Arkansas. Tamara had already offered her the use of rooms in the Cooper's home on their farm. The gesture was nice, but she was still a very independent woman, even after sixty years of marriage. She set down the frosting knife and pulled a handkerchief from her pocket to wipe away the tears that threatened to get out of hand. *Tonight, I can let them spill during the ceremony. Aodhfin, my dearest, I miss you, but right now, I have to celebrate the living.*

Forgive me, my love, but your grandson and heir needs me more than your spirit does. Líadáin dried her eyes and then picked up the frosting knife and resumed her work on the cake.

* * *

THE CRUNCH of gravel beneath the tires and the smell of clean pine woke Kieran from the nap he'd taken on the way home from the hospital. It was good to breathe in the clean smells of home. He rubbed the sleep from his eyes and watched as the familiar forest engulfed them. It wasn't long before Cory was pulling up in front of the main house and parking. Kellen came down the front steps and opened Kieran's door before he could do it himself. Kieran emerged from the van and into a huge hug from his father. When Kellen let go of his son, Kieran took a small step back and looked at his father from head to toe.

"Okay who are you and what did you do with my real father? You don't get emotional and hug, Dad. What's up?" Kieran said with a puzzled look on his face.

"I'm finding all the emotions I buried along with your mother," Kellen said. "I realized when we almost lost you that I'd repressed the side of me you and your sisters needed most. I buried the caring and loving father along with the loving husband."

"Then I'm glad to have my loving and caring father back," Kieran said as he wrapped his father in a hug. "We need to talk about a few things in the next couple of days."

"I know, Son. Let's honor your grandfather first; then we can deal with the rest of things life has to throw at us. Now come inside before your grams decides to give all the food away to the homeless."

"I think she'd enjoy feeding all of them, Dad. Come on, Wolf, let's go eat. I'm starving," Kieran said, taking his husband's hand and dragging him into the house.

Kellen laughed and followed the boys inside. He caught up to them, and then led them out to the garden where a huge table groaned under the weight of all the food his mother had prepared for her grandson's homecoming. Kellen smiled as their combined family

engulfed his son and son-in-law. The entire family laughed when Billy
—with all the enthusiasm of a giant puppy—pounced on Kieran,
knocking him backward into Cory as he slobbered all over the
young man.

"I'm happy to see you too, Puppy. Thank you for leading everyone
to me," Kieran said, ruffling the wolf's fur between his ears.

Cory handed Kieran a napkin so he could wipe off some of the
wolf drool. Kieran then found himself being hugged by Jonathan and
Tamara, before being passed to Uncle Brom and Professor Mason. At
last, he stood before his beloved Grams. He swept her up in a hug that
lifted her off the ground as they both dissolved in tears of mixed joy
and sadness. After a moment of shared emotions, Líadáin thumped
Kieran on the shoulders so he would set her down. She then turned to
her guests and picked up a glass from the table.

"Today is a day of celebration, both of life and of death. It has
always been the tradition of the Oisín clan to mourn a birth and to
celebrate a death. We mourn birth, because it separates us from our full
participation with the divine, and we celebrate death, for it reunites us
with the divine until we are needed again. We also celebrate the living
and the miraculous healing given to Kieran. *Mo sheacht mbeannacht
ort, mo stór*!"

Kieran, Brom, and Kellen all leaned over and whispered a
translation to Cory, John, Tamara, and Jonathan.

"It means, 'My seven blessings on you, my treasure,'" Kieran
whispered in Cory's ear before taking up his glass and returning the
toast with a blessing in return. "*Go riabh míle maith agat, Maimeó!*
May you have a hundred thousand good things, Grandmother."

The combined families settled in to eat dinner and enjoy being
together. Kieran made a huge dent in the piles of food before him. He
couldn't believe how hungry he was; he even managed two huge slices
of cake. When dinner had been demolished, the gathering broke up as
each pairing went to get ready for the ceremony to honor Aodhfin
Oisín's life and passing.

Cory drove Kieran and his own parents back to their cabin. When
they entered the cabin, Tamara and Jonathan withdrew to the guest

room so that Kieran and Cory could have some privacy. Cory led Kieran upstairs to their bedroom, where he slowly undressed his husband and then stripped off his own clothes. Kieran drew Cory into a full body hug, and their hands were soon caressing and exploring each other's body, getting reacquainted with each other. When Cory reached for Kieran's raging hard on, Kieran stopped his hand with one of his own; his other hand touched one finger to Cory's lips to prevent a protest.

"After the ceremony for Gramps, my heart. Then, we can give ourselves over to our passion for each other. Come shower with me, and then we need to get dressed."

"What should I wear, Kier?"

"Wear the nicest clothes you brought with you, Cory."

"What are you going to wear?"

"My tracker armor," Kieran replied as he pulled the heavy leather outfit and boots from the closet.

After they'd laid their clothing out on the bed, they went and showered, each lathering the other and Cory washing Kieran's hair before braiding it as Kieran directed, weaving in the silver chains. They dried off and then dressed in silence before returning downstairs where they met up with Tamara and Jonathan dressed in their nicest clothes. Silence reigned over the group as they returned to the car and drove back to the main house. Kieran led them inside to the library where they were met by Kellen and Líadáin and joined shortly afterward by Brom and John. Kieran picked up the urn containing his grandfather's ashes and handed them to Uncle Brom as the eldest son. To his father, he handed the family grimoire, and to his grandmother, a bell and a candle. He gathered everyone into a tight circle around him and then cast the transport spell, whisking the group to the beach.

14

Kieran stood at the center of the family group on the beach staring out at the sea. Above them in the cliff was the cavern system his grandparents and great aunt and great uncle had created with their magic. *Here is where I will give your ashes to the sea, Gramps,* Kieran thought as the rest of the family withdrew to give him the space he needed. He turned and scanned the faces around him as a large furry body pressed up against his leg. Kieran glanced down to find Billy sitting on the beach leaning against him for support. He reached down and scratched the wolf between the ears for a moment. *Will Cory's fur feel this soft when he's in wolf form?* Kieran wondered. With a sigh, he shrugged back his shoulders, casting his tension to the winds. His eyes fell on Professor Mason, standing very close to Uncle Brom.

"Professor Mason, may I call on your Emerald magic for some assistance in erecting an altar?" Kieran asked.

"Of course, Kieran. Where would you like it and what dimensions?" John asked.

Kieran made a gesture with his hands using Silver magic to sketch the form he wanted John to create. "Just like this if you would, Professor," Kieran said.

Professor Mason took a relaxing breath and focused his magic. Emerald magic swirled the sands of the beach into the shape of the altar defined by Kieran's Silver magic. When he was done, he sagged a bit, but was caught by Brom and led to a log so that he could sit.

Concern made the creases in Brom's forehead deepen. "Are you okay, John?"

"I haven't stretched my powers like this in a long time, Brom," John managed as Brom massaged his shoulders. "The healings I've worked on you have taken a little more out of me than I thought. Shaping earth shouldn't have been so taxing. I just need a little rest and I be fine."

Kieran had turned to Jonathan Cooper and Grams for the next items he wanted. In a few moments, candelabras of ice stood at the four cardinal points of the compass. Kieran then took the grimoire from his father, collected the bell and candle from his grandmother, and lastly claimed the urn containing Gramps' ashes from Uncle Brom. All of these items he set on the altar before making the motion of drawing a sword from a scabbard over his shoulder. As his hand came away from his shoulder, a gleaming blade of Silver magic formed. Kieran then walked to stand just outside the area marked by the four candelabras. Finding east by some internal compass, he began to walk clockwise around them with the point of the sword in the sand scribing a circle. When he arrived back at his starting point, he took a step back to stand before the candelabra. Raising his sword of Silver magic, Kieran saluted the candelabra and spoke.

"All hail the Watchtower of the East. The Element of Air, I do summon and call you forth to guard and protect this Circle." On the top of the candelabra, a small swirling cyclone began to form, and Kieran continued, "Be Here Now." The cyclone became a physical presence, confined to the little platform designed to hold a candle.

Kieran moved to the south and repeated his formula, calling fire. In the west, he called the element of water, and finally, he moved to the north.

"All hail the Watchtower of the North. The Element of Earth, I do summon and call forth to guard and protect this Circle. Be Here

Now," Kieran said before returning to the east and completing the circle. He then moved and placed his sword of magic on the altar before taking a pack of matches from his coat pocket. Kieran set the candle upright in the center of the altar and lit it. He took up the bell and rang it three times before setting it back down. Lastly, he placed his hand on the grimoire and chanted a call to the goddess and the god.

"By Bell, Book, and Candle, I call to thee, oh ancient guides of life and death. I call thee to attend this circle and stretch forth thy protection that none save those who serve the light shall enter or leave this sacred space, which stands outside time and space. Into thy care I place this circle and all who enter."

Kieran raised his hand from the grimoire and raised both hands above his head. From his fingertips, Silver magic flared upward until it reached the apex and flared out to form a dome of magic with its edge defined by the circle Kieran had scribed in the sand.

"As defined above, so be it below, by my will, so mote it be."

Everyone present felt the dome of magic become a sphere, and they watched Kieran vanish inside as the dome became opaque. After a few moments, an opening appeared just north of where the eastern marker stood, and Kieran appeared holding his sword.

"Let those who would honor the passing of he who was the Silver Witch come forward and prove their commitment to the light," Kieran said to them.

Kieran's family was approaching the opening when they watched him shudder as if fighting off a possession. When the shuddering stopped, the tip of his blade came up, pointing at Líadáin's throat. They met the fire in his eyes and knew another entity currently held sway. Ancient and powerful, this entity would brook no lies. It spoke now, and the voice was groaned from Kieran, as if air was escaping from a tomb. Cory turned and looked at his mother and Billy, fear in his eyes.

"I am the guardian of the mortal remains of the Witch of Silver. I was called to serve the first Witch, and I will come when the last Witch breathes their last breath. All who would pass must prove their service to the light. The dark may not pass."

"Tamara, I think it would be best if you took Billy and went back to the cabin," Jonathan said.

"We honor the light as much as you do, Jonathan," Tamara replied.

"Honey," Jonathan said, "that being inside Kieran isn't going to understand. It will sense that you're both shifters, and it will kill you."

"Billy and I will just wait here," Tamara replied. "I don't know how to get back to the cabin from this beach."

"Dad, it's okay," Cory said. "Billy will keep an eye on her. This beach is pretty secluded from the rest of the estate."

Jonathan hugged his wife then moved to join the rest of the family before the ancient guardian.

"Speak only the truth of your person and relationship to the Witch of Silver," the guardian rasped.

"I am Líadáin MacGregor Oisín, Sapphire Mage and wife of he who was the Witch of Silver."

"Hail helpmate of Sapphire, enter and be welcomed."

"I am Kellen Kieran Oisín, second son and former heir of he who was the Witch of Silver."

"Hail child of Silver, enter and be welcomed."

Brom hesitated a moment before stepping up to the guardian.

"I am Brom Padraig Oisín, first-born son and former heir of he who was the Witch of Silver."

The guardian's blade flamed bright silver, and it started to draw back to attack Brom; it sensed the Ebony magic within him. Kieran stopped the blade short. His body froze as an internal combat seemed to ensue until Kieran stepped to the side, leaving a ghastly being standing frozen in place.

"Enough, I am the Witch of Silver now," Kieran said. "You will do my bidding and depart from this place. Your service is over. I thank you for it and dismiss you."

"Thank you, master. You are the first to defeat me, as did the first Witch of Silver. You have shown a kindness no witch has ever shown me since she who bound me guard her dead. My name is hidden in your memory. Should you have need of me, you may call on me once without the need to conquer me anew."

"Again," Kieran emphasized, "I thank you for your service, and now I bid you return directly to your realm."

The horror vanished in a swirl of multicolored magic. Kieran looked over everyone still standing outside the barrier. Then he turned to see his father and grandmother standing within. He raised his hand, and with a word of thanks, banished the entire summoning. Everyone looked at him and blinked as all traces of Silver magic vanished from the beach.

"This is what you get when you do things the way Gramps would have wanted it done. Rituals and strange guardian creatures, family and friends in danger when all they want to do is honor a man who has died. Well, screw it, Gramps. I'm done with mumbo jumbo rituals; it's not my way of doing magic." Kieran bent and scooped up the urn holding his grandfather's ashes. "You were Irish to the core, old man. We should be going bar hopping, getting rip-roaring drunk, and telling stupid stories about you, not fighting off demons from the dawn of time."

Kieran bent his arm back, and with a twist of his body, snapped his arm forward, hurling the urn on a burst of Silver magic into the ocean.

"Rest in peace, Gramps." Kieran called after the urn.

Kieran turned to face his stunned family. Grams walked up to him and slapped him across the face. Kieran rocked back in shock; his gentle Grams never hit him. Grams was always his shelter from the vicious world.

"Kieran Samuel Belle Oisín-Cooper, that was the most disrespectful send off I've ever witnessed. Aodhfin loved you more than you will ever realize. You were his pride and joy. Not your father or your uncle. You. I cannot believe you just tossed him away like that." Grams sobbed as she fell into Kieran's open arms.

Kieran wrapped his beloved grams in his arms. All of his love for her and Gramps surrounded her.

"Grams, I'm sorry. The person I disrespected was you. I casually tossed away the love of your life as if he didn't matter to you. I can fetch his remains back for you."

"Don't be daft, boy. Aodhfin's spirit is long gone to the

Summerlands. What could I possibly want with his ashes? I have my memories of all our years together and the promise that when it's my turn, he'll be waiting for me in the Summerlands. No, I'm mad at you because you beat me to tossing the old coot into the drink," Grams said with a laugh and a twinkle in her Sapphire eyes.

Everyone around them laughed, breaking the tension as they looked at the stunned expression on Kieran's face. Cory took pity on his husband and moved to stand behind him. He wrapped him in a hug, making sure that his beard rubbed across Kieran's neck in just the spot that sent shivers down his lover's spine. Kieran kissed his grandmother on the cheek and then let her go as he relaxed back into his lover's strong arms. The group gathered around in a circle surrounding the two young men.

"Take us back to main house, *mo stór,*" Grams said. "We'll gather in the living room and tell stories about your grandfather."

In a swirl of Silver magic, the group was transported back to the living room of the main house, where they spent the evening swapping stories about Aodhfin Oisín.

15

A few days had passed since the memorial service for Brom's father, and John Mason was watching Brom working at his forge through the lens of his camera. There were some small details, which seemed to nag at the back of John's mind. He watched the man who wasn't quite his lover but was more than a friend-with-benefits. It was awkward not knowing what their relationship was. Early on, Brom had opened up to him about why their physical relationship could only be one-sided, Brom giving pleasure with hands or mouth but never full-on intimacy. Ever the healer as his family traditions with Emerald magic required, John had asked Brom for permission to magically scan him to see if his problem could be fixed.

John thought back to that night Brom had brought him home from their dinner date and conversation. He was nervous at the thought of being scanned by another mage. Brom is such a proud man, and it took a lot for him to open up and share his story with me. I had to show him a demonstration of how skilled a healer I am. I remember watching him jump when I slashed that razor-sharp letter opener across my forearm. Who the hell keeps their letter openers razor sharp? The shocked look on his face as the wound glowed green and sealed up before his eyes without leaving a trace was priceless. I melted when he pulled me into that fierce kiss and then held me at arm's length, admonishing me to never do that again. I wonder if that fierce protective streak is a family trait. I think I convinced him I was a healer. He let me do the scan, and he was right about the Ebony magic infection in his blood. I'm not sure how he's lived all these years with the kind of pain it must generate, especially since Ebony magic clashes constantly with his natural Silver magic. Whoever struck that balance between them saved his life, but he became a dull and badly mended blade. He burns so bright when he's working metal, but away from his place of power. He's barely got the power to light a candle. He needs to be melted down and reforged.

They'd spent that night just cuddled up together in Brom's giant bed, eventually falling asleep in each other's arms. In the morning, John had figured out what to do to begin healing Brom properly. He'd dragged the bigger man out to the forge naked, grabbing a small bag from his own room on the way, despite Brom's protests about safety. The furnace hadn't been lit in days, and all the metal in the place was cold. John dragged Brom over to the anvil and looked him straight in the eye.

"Do you trust me to know my craft as well as you know yours?"

"I trust you, but it's not safe to be naked out here, lots of sharp objects."

"Sshh, I trust that you know how to safely secure everything in this place so that no random item can hurt someone, even by accident. For the healing you need, it has to be here in your place of power. Your magic has become tied to this place. I have to melt you down and reforge you, burn away the impurities until your bright shining Silver magic again."

"John, I'm concerned about what that entails."

"It means letting me have control of your pleasure and passion for awhile. It means I'm going to take your body to the heights and depths you've taken others to. Now bend over that anvil."

"John, it's not safe to bring me to orgasm or to fuck me, even with a condom on."

"Did I say I was going to let you orgasm or that I was going to fuck you? No, I said I was going to bring you to the heights and depths of pleasure and passion. Now bend over that anvil."

Brom sighed and bent over the anvil as directed. He felt a whisper of Emerald magic run over his body. It wrapped around his wrists and ankles, binding him to his anvil. Tough vines wrapped themselves around his arms to the elbow and up his legs to the knees before they reached out and twined around each other, holding him firmly in place.

"I never pictured you as the kinky type, John," Brom said.

"Silence, Brom. The only thing I want to hear out of you is moans of pleasure. Your safe word is actually an action. Use your magic and everything ends; the vines will release you the moment they feel Silver magic," John said as he slid his hand between Brom's legs to grab hold of the man's rapidly hardening cock.

John pulled Brom's cock back between his legs, and more vines wrapped around it, holding it in place. A thinner vine wrapped around the man's balls, pulling them away and then wrapping them so that they couldn't draw up and ejaculate. Brom started to speak, but another vine wrapped around his head and forced his jaw apart, thickening into a makeshift ball gag. Brom moaned into the gag as John stroked his cock from his tied off balls to the tip of the blunt head. John let his hands roam all over Brom's naked and helpless body, drawing moans of lust from the man. He toyed with the idea of letting one of the vines penetrate the man's ass and stroke his prostrate, but felt that would be too much of a violation. He could feel the Ebony magic pulsing along with Brom's heartbeat and Silver magic. He so wanted to run his tongue over many of the places his fingers trailed, tingling pleasure, but knew the danger of contact beyond what he was doing now. It was time to focus on torturing Brom's throbbing cock and overloaded balls until the man exploded. John focused his earth sense and formed a special container that the vines picked up and held just below the tip of Brom's cock. John began to milk the hefty cock. So thick, and those veins will bring so much pleasure rubbing against a prostrate. This beautiful cock will reach so nice and deep. I hope some day I can feel it inside me.

Brom was getting close, and John could feel the fires of passion ramping up to a fevered pitch. Brom was bucking and straining against his bonds, trying to get just the right friction to allow him to fire off his pent-up load. Silver magic was driving Ebony magic before it as it raced to fill the semen churning in Brom's aching balls. This was the moment John had been driving Brom to by bringing him to the edge several times and then denying him release. This treatment would have broken a lesser man, but Brom Oisín was not a lesser man. When he sensed that Brom's churning balls were filled with an Ebony-tainted load, John commanded the vine around Brom's balls to release, and then he made sure all of Brom's tainted cum was captured in the special vessel he'd conjured. Once the vines milked the last of Brom's load from his now-aching nuts, the vessel sealed itself, trapping the Ebony magic within. Brom flexed his hands, and Silver magic flowed effortlessly around him. The vines withdrew as promised. Brom stood and flexed tired muscles before he turned, grabbed John, and drew him into a deep kiss. When the kiss broke, John looked at the silver fire gleaming in Brom's eyes; his magic was free and untainted for the first time in years.

"You, sir, are a knight in shining armor," Brom teased as he sketched a mock bow in John's direction.

"Nay, milord, I am but a humble country healer, peddling the latest in potions and poultices."

The men collapsed against each other laughing. Brom wrapped John in his arms and drew the man close so that they could enjoy the feel of each other's body. Brom nuzzled his bearded chin against John's neck as he caught the healer's ear between his teeth. John's moan of pleasure reminded Brom that this amazing man still hadn't had his own release. He let his left hand stroke down John's body to wrap around the man's throbbing cock and gently drew the foreskin the rest of the way off of the dripping cock head. His right arm wrapped around the man's chest and pulled them tightly together as his fingers found John's stiff left nipple and toyed with it. John was so close that it only took Brom a few firm strokes to bring him over the edge into orgasm. Once his orgasm subsided, John slumped in Brom's arms, lying as if boneless against the other man's strong chest.

"You, my friend, are a menace. When I'm in your grip, I'm of two minds, wanting to never to be free and wishing to escape at the same time," John whispered.

"Well, you will just have to stop being so sexy and easy to capture, mo fíníunacha," Brom whispered into John's ear, making him shudder.

"What does that last bit mean?" John gasped between shudders as Brom's warm breath continued to tease his ear.

"Mo fíníunacha, means my vines, you're a very kinky little witch, John."

"I'm a very kinky mage when I choose to be, Brom. I haven't indulged that side of me in ages. It was the best way to get you to the place you needed to be in order to get the Ebony magic out of your system. Speaking of which, we need to dispose of that quickly," John said, pointing at the sphere held aloft by the last remaining vine in the forge.

Brom glanced at the furnace of his forge, and it came to life under his freed magic. Soon, both men were sweating profusely from the heat of the furnace. When the temperature rose to over 2500 degrees, Brom grabbed his tongs from the rack, grabbed the sphere, and dropped it into the furnace. The sphere melted away in the heat, and the Ebony magic vaporized along with it.

"Now that that's done, let's go inside and get cleaned up before we go soak in my hot tub," Brom said, drawing John out of the forge building.

16

The day of Kieran and Cory's handfasting dawned clear and bright. The young men had spent the previous night in separate locations with their families. While it wasn't traditional or even required, they'd agreed to spend one night apart to increase the impact of the ceremony, not just for themselves but for Cory's family who'd missed their actual wedding. Kieran stood in the center of the main house's kitchen as Grams made final adjustments to his wedding outfit.

"Stop fidgeting, Kieran," Líadáin scolded her grandson. "Your hem will be uneven if you don't stand still."

"I'm sorry, Grams. I just never expected to be nervous about going to my handfasting. I guess it's because I figured Gramps would be waiting in the circle to join me with my other half."

"I'm sorry, *mo stór*. You know he's with us in spirit, even if it's a bit soggy," Grams said with a laugh.

Kieran joined her laughter as they both recalled the night of Gramps memorial service when Kieran had flung the urn containing his grandfather's ashes into the depths of the bay.

"I'm sorry, Grams. I really should have let you have the honors of pitching Gramps into the ocean. Have I told you how grateful I am to you for helping speed up my healing so I could get out of that hospital sooner?"

"You have, *mo stór*. Just remember to do the same with Mr. Cooper and Professor Mason. Bringing you back to full health and healing your Uncle Brom took more out of your professor than any of us thought."

"I know, Grams. I'm grateful for what all of you did. I just have to wonder what good it is to have shifter genes if they aren't going to speed up my healing."

"Your father and I think that if Gold magic really did heal you, it pulled all the Ebony magic out of you and turned off your shifter genes."

"I haven't had a chance to question Father Ivory. I only vaguely remember him coming into the room while that dark mage was attempting to pour more Ebony magic into my system and finish the job. Then, there was this sudden flash of golden light, and I was free of the horrible spell and Cory was awake. I'm not sure what the spell I used to get rid of the dark mage was. It's like I know all this information is up here in my head, but I just can't access it at will."

"Your grandfather mentioned a time or two after he first came into the powers of the Silver Witch that the most ancient of spells only seemed to come to mind when they were needed. He never could access any of the ancient lore he knew was hidden in his mind."

"So all the ancient stuff is locked away like a fire hose in a tall building; you just break the glass in case of emergency." Kieran chuckled as he pictured a giant spell book in a glass case.

"Yes, something like that," Grams said as she smiled at the sound of Kieran's chuckle. "Now let's finish getting you ready. Your Uncle Brom should be along soon to take you to the circle."

Kieran reached out and pulled his grandmother into a tight hug. "I never say this enough, Grams, but I love you."

"And I love you, *mo stór*."

A knock at the backdoor to the kitchen let Kieran and Líadáin know that Brom had arrived. Brom crossed over to his mother and Kieran taking in the scene.

"So, nephew, are you ready for me to give you away?" Brom asked.

"I guess I'm as ready as I can be since tradition requires a male relative of the Silver Witch or his heir to give him away in marriage," Kieran replied.

"Well, then we should get this show on the road. Mother, the rest of the celebrants are waiting for you out in the garden."

"Thank you, Brom. I will see you in just a little while Kieran," Grams said before making her way out the backdoor to the garden.

"So any last-minute doubts about committing to this handfasting, Kieran?" Brom asked as he moved beside his nephew to escort him out to the clearing they'd chosen for the handfasting ceremony.

"No, Uncle. This handfasting is one of the few things in life I've never doubted. I love Cory with all my being, and I can't picture not getting handfasted to seal that love. I know we're legally married by the state, but being handfasted has that spiritual connection I don't want to miss out on."

"Then let's get you out to the clearing so you can be complete, *mo stór*," Brom said as he led Kieran out into the garden.

* * *

"KIERAN AND CORY, know now before you go further, that since your lives have crossed in this life, you have formed eternal and sacred bonds," Kellen spoke in his role as High Priest. "As you seek to enter this state of matrimony, you should strive to make real the ideals that, to you, give meaning to this ceremony and to the institution of marriage. With full awareness, know that within this circle, you are not only declaring your intent to be handfasted before your friends and family, but you speak that intent also to your creative higher powers. The promises made today and the ties that are bound here greatly strengthen your union and will cross the years and lives of each soul's growth. Do you still seek to enter this ceremony?"

"Yes."

"We invite you all to please stand as we ask for the blessing of the Guardians of the four quarters." Grams voice carried a welcoming lilt.

"Blessed be this union with the gifts of the East and the element of air, for openness and breath, communication of the heart, and purity of the mind and body. From the east, you receive the gift of a new beginning with the rising of each Sun and the understanding that each day is a new opportunity for growth," Uncle Brom voice rang out.

"Blessed be this union with the gifts of the South and the element of fire, for energy, passion, creativity, and the warmth of a loving home. From the fire within you, generate light, which you will share with one another in even the darkest of times," Grams' friend, Gertrude said in a raspy voice.

"Blessed be this union with the gifts of the West, the element of water, for your capacity to feel emotion. In marriage, you offer absolute trust to one another, and vow to keep your hearts open in sorrow as well as joy." Jonathan Cooper's voice almost seemed to sparkle.

"Blessed be this union with the gifts of the North, the element of earth, which provides sustenance, fertility, and security. The earth will feed and enrich you, and it will help you to build a stable home to which you may always return," Professor Mason's deep voice trembled as he spoke.

"We thank the Guardians for their blessings, and now we invite you to sit and witness Kieran and Cory bind themselves in joyous union," Grams spoke with delight. "Kieran and Cory, I bid you look into each other's eyes. Will you honor and respect one another, and seek to never break that honor?"

"We will," the boys said in unison as Kellen draped the silver-colored first cord over the couples' hands.

"And so the first binding is made," Uncle Brom said from the East.

"Will you share each other's pain and seek to ease it?" Kellen asked them.

"We will," came the boys' reply as Grams draped the ruby-colored second cord over their hands.

"And so the binding is made," came the response from the South.

"Will you share the burdens of each so that your spirits may grow in this union?" Grams asked them.

"We will," the boys again responded as Kellen draped the sapphire-colored third cord over the couple's hands.

"And so the binding is made," Jonathan's voice rang from the West.

"Will you share each other's laughter, and look for the brightness in life and the positive in each other?" Kellen asked.

"We will," the boys replied for the final time as Grams draped the emerald-colored forth cord over their hands.

"And so the binding is made," Professor Mason's voice rumbled from the North.

Kieran's grandmother tied the four cords together, binding the boys' hands as they bound their lives together.

"Cory and Kieran, as your hands are bound together now, so are your lives and spirits joined in a union of love and trust. Above you are the stars and below you is the earth. Like the stars, your love should be a constant source of light, and like the earth, a firm foundation from which to grow." Grams and Kellen said in unison as they blessed the couple.

17

F ollowing the ceremony, the newly blessed couple led the way back to the main house and celebrated with their family and friends over a lavish dinner created by Líadáin and Tamara. Kieran couldn't resist drawing Cory into a kiss in front of everyone. The level of excitement, joy, and happiness between the young men was at its all-time high. Their families and friends toasted them and wished them luck and blessings. As the evening was winding down, Kellen came forward carrying a tray with two small glasses on it. He stopped before his son and son-in-law and offered the glasses.

"What is this, Dad?" Kieran asked while looking at the glasses.

"You asked me before you got married to cast the spell of the claiming for you and Cory so that you could cement your bond and establish the hierarchy of your relationship. This is how I chose to cast it. Once you drink this potion, you will be transported to the caverns by the sea where you will battle for dominance until one of you claims the other through sexual conquest."

"Kieran, you could easily mop the floor with me with a single spell," Cory said.

"Cory, you could tear me limb from limb if you shifted into a halfway form," Kieran replied.

"This potion will block Kieran's magic and prevent Cory from shifting until the sun rises. You will both be normal humans, filled with all the unbridled lusts and drives man to seek dominance over others," Kellen said.

"We don't need this anymore, Dad. We have everything we ever wanted, and we're happy," Kieran said.

"You don't have a choice, Son." Kellen stiffened. "This potion comes in two parts, and you drank the first part during the first toast. If you don't drink the second part and complete the spell, you'll die."

"Why did you do this, Dad?" Kieran's voice shook. "If I die, the powers of the Silver Witch are gone forever."

"It was never about the powers of the Silver Witch, Kieran. I never wanted them, and I was never meant to wield them. Look at my eyes, both of you. They've always been violet or amethyst as some have called the color. I was meant to fall in love with a witch or a mage of that kind of magic. I did meet her, and my soul knew we were supposed to be together, but I put duty to family first. This is your test, Kieran. Prove which you love more, Cory or power." Under the light of the full moon, the gray in Kellen's hair seemed more pronounced, and his amethyst eyes seemed duller under the strain as he explained.

Kieran and Cory felt the first twinge of pain from the potion in their system, and with a look, each grabbed a glass from the tray and downed the contents. Silver magic swirled around them, and they were whisked away.

18

Cory found himself on the ground deep in the cavern of pools. A rage burned within him that he was yet again the victim of Kieran's crazy family and their magic. He got up and pulled off the robe he'd had to wear for the ceremony, leaving him dressed only in a pair of shorts. The lights in the cavern dimmed and then flared bright as Kieran appeared with a crash in the entrance to the caverns. A barrier sprang up between the two, separating them from each other. His rage grew as he watched Kieran rise, still looking like he could step out of a fashion catalogue. *Perfect as always,* Cory thought. *Why the hell are we here anyways? What do we really have together?*

"What do you really want with me, Kier? Do you really think we have a chance together, shifter and hunter? Are we really trying to make the story of *Beauty and the Beast* over into one that ends happily ever after?" Something felt off to Cory. *Was this part of the effects of Kellen's potion? Did the man add some of his own anger to the potion?* "Do you think you can dominate me, little virgin boy? What are you offering me?"

"I'm offering you a true mating, including the fight for dominance, Wolf. We both have shifter blood in our veins, so a mating either way will bond us both to the other. I'm offering what I've always offered you, Cory. My heart and all the love in my soul."

"Love? No, you're more your father's son than you'd like to believe. This potion was your suggestion, and he tailored it to be a test. He wants to see if you measure up. I don't think either of you have it in you to truly love anything but power, Kieran. So, come fight me if you can do it without your fancy silver weapons or your stinking magic."

I think Cory's partly right, I read over the formula for this spell, and it shouldn't be causing this kind of reaction. Dad did something to twist the intent. I'm going to have to do something to prove to Cory that he's wrong about my loving power, Kieran thought.

During their conversation, Cory had crossed the cavern to stand facing Kieran across the barrier. Kieran stripped to his shorts and lunged through the barrier, wrapping his arms around Cory's waist and dropping them both to the ground. They rolled and split apart, and Kieran bounced to his feet as Cory tried to grapple him. The lovers dodged and swung at each other, getting more and more worked up. On one lunging pass by Cory, Kieran sidestepped and sent a sidekick into the back of Cory's legs, sending him sprawling into the nearest pool. Kieran leapt and landed on Cory's back, pushing him under. Wrapping one arm around Cory's neck, Kieran used the other to reach into Cory's shorts and grab a handful of ass cheek. Cory bucked and rolled, sending Kieran to the bottom of the pool. Cory's right foot came down on Kieran's chest and pinned him to the bottom. Kieran struggled to breathe then thrust his right arm up, grabbing for Cory's cock and balls. Forced to dodge, Cory jumped back, freeing Kieran to rise to the surface and grab a lung full of air. Rage and lust burned in Kieran's eyes. His gaze flashed bright silver as they locked with the equally lust-filled amber-eyed Cory. Kieran grappled Cory and drew him into a soul-shattering kiss before biting Cory's lip and drawing blood. They both felt the jolt as the loose bond between them rose up and fused into a solid chain anchoring them soul-to-soul, but lust, anger, and frustration still roiled within them.

Cory reared back, and his fist slammed into Kieran's jaw, driving him back. Cory then grabbed Kieran's hair and yanked his head back before slamming his mouth down over Kieran's and returning the kiss and bite. Kieran jammed his elbow into Cory's solar plexus and then drove a knee into his groin. The farm boy collapsed to his knees, trying to get his breath back and cradle his injured manhood at the same time. Kieran pushed Cory forward and shredded Cory's shorts, leaving him naked. He dropped his own shorts, and grabbing Cory's hips, slammed his rigid cock into his lover's ass.

"This was never how I imagined we'd do this, Wolf, but you were meant to be mine, and so mine is what you will be."

Cory bucked and threw Kieran off. Kieran crashed backward, striking his head against the edge of the pool. Cory took advantage of Kieran's dazed state, scooped him up, and dropped him on the edge of the pool before lifting Kieran's legs up, exposing his hole. Cory slammed his cock into Kieran's ass and was rewarded with a moan.

"This is the more natural state of things, little hunter. Just lay back and surrender that sweet ass; it's what you were really born to do."

Recovering, Kieran twisted his legs into a headlock and threw off the balanced Cory, driving him back into the pool. Kieran followed, and his fist met Cory's jaw as his lover rose to fight back. Grabbing the remains of Cory's shorts, Kieran tied Cory's hands behind his back before bending him over the edge of the pool and slamming his cock back into the blond ass.

"Enough of the foreplay, Wolf. It's time for you to give in and be a good husband. Just relax, and this will be over in an hour or so."

"Like you could last that long, babe."

"So now you're calling me babe again? Well, at least the spell seems to be fading. Now let's finish it off and make it so no one can ever break our bond. Time for you to become my unquestioned mate, Wolf."

Kieran's raging hard cock began sawing in and out of Cory's ass, driving both men into a heated passion they hadn't had since the early days of their relationship. The fight hadn't completely gone out of Cory yet, and he reared backward, slamming the back of his head into Kieran's face and knocking his lover off balance, causing his cock to slip out of Cory's ass. The binding shorts ripped apart, freeing Cory's hands, and he darted forth, lifting Kieran out of the water. He carried him up to the sleeping nook. There he laid Kieran out on his back, straddled his lover's hips, and impaled himself on Kieran's cock. The young lovers both moaned as Cory roughly fucked himself on Kieran's thick prick. Even though he was bottoming, Cory was in complete control of the situation—the Alpha of the relationship, as he'd been from the beginning of their lovemaking.

"Fill me with your seed, babe; bind us together so that we can never be pulled apart again. Please, love me forever and forgive me."

"I claim you as my Alpha lover, Corwin Samuel Cooper. By blood, sweat, and semen, I bind you to me."

"Oh god, yes, Kieran. God you feel so good. Please fill me with your seed, bind us heart, body, and soul. By blood, sweat, and semen, I bind you to me. Transform us."

Kieran finally gave into his pending orgasm and blew his load deep into Cory's ass. He kept his cock buried deep until finally it softened and slid out on its own. He felt the huge pool of cum on his stomach from Cory's still-leaking cock. He grinned and then pulled Cory down and kissed his lover. Cory wrapped his arms around Kieran and held him tight. Kieran drew back and placed his left hand over Cory's heart, and Cory did the same thing. Silver magic streamed out of their chests and formed a sphere between them. They each reached out, and their hands sank into the sphere until they touched inside. They grasped each other's hand, and then the sphere split in half and flowed down to their wrists where the magic transformed itself into bracelets of woven silver with a pair of wolf heads pointing down toward their hands. Kieran and Cory drew each other in for a deep kiss, and the eyes of the wolves opened, reveling that each wolf had one amber and one diamond eye. Cory slid off of Kieran and scooted up the bed to lean his back against the wall. Kieran followed and settled in against his chest as they rested in the sleeping alcove and drew the covers over both of them. Kieran shifted and snuggled his head down on Cory's chest, wrapping his arm over his husband's waist.

"I love you, Kieran. Thank you for fighting for me. I was a jerk."

"I love you too, Wolf. I will always fight for you."

Cory linked the fingers of his left hand with those of Kieran's and stared at the new bracelets on their wrists.

"Are these replacements for the rings we use to have? Is this the same magic that Brom forged into the old rings?"

"That magic broke when we let jealousy destroy our original connection, Wolf. All magic has a condition under which it will fail. The rings only lasted while our hearts were true."

"These feel different somehow," Cory said.

"I think these are a manifestation of our soul bond, Cory. This isn't magic forged by one person looking for his true love; this is magic forged by two souls bound for all time to each other. Nothing save death can break these bracelets. Whatever happens, we're one soul, now and forever."

"I love you, Kieran Oisín-Cooper. I'm honored to be yours."

"I love you, Corwin Oisín-Cooper. Will you make love to me now? I want to be equally yours. We aren't meant to be anything but equals. Claim me as yours as I've claimed you as mine," Kieran said.

"I think we'll do this without all the combat. I want to make sweet love to you as you deserve," Cory said as he bent down and kissed Kieran as a prelude to their lovemaking.

PART II

THE HOUSE OF BEAUTY

INTERLUDE: A SECRET HISTORY

I have discovered a terrible secret regarding Great-Grandmother's pact with the shifters of the forest. She gave her youngest sister to the leader of the pack as a mate. From what I have been able to discover, Great-Great Aunt Ophelia was totally without the gift of Silver magic, a very rare thing only three generations removed from the first of our family. The most terrifying part of this pact is that it must continue each time a new huntress takes over the family. She must give a non-magical sister or cousin of the same generation to the leader of the forest pack as a mate, or the compact between these dark shifters and the House of Beauty will be broken. I am afraid for my twin sister as neither of us were born with the gift of Silver magic. Our eldest sister goes for the test tomorrow night, and if she becomes the huntress, then I fear my sweet sister is doomed to this horrid fate.

From the Second Chronicle of the House of Beauty, translated into English in the 21st century

Fifty Years Ago

Theresa Belle stood with her oldest sister Camille, the new huntress of the House of Beauty, at the edge of a clearing deep in the dark forest on the family estate. In the center of the clearing stood a cottage, which looked like it had been built using plans from a fairy tale. *Why is this here in the forest, and why did Camille bring me here?* Theresa wondered as her sister led her deeper into the clearing. For a brief moment, she thought she felt a tingle on her skin, but it was gone before she could be certain. The door to the cottage opened and a tall, broad-shouldered man stepped out and stood waiting. Theresa felt Camille move to stand behind her and gently urged her forward.

"Camille, what's going on? I don't understand why you brought me out here. Please tell me what's going on. I'm scared."

Camille refused to answer her sister's questions until they were within reach of the strange man.

"Theresa, this is Eugene, leader of the forest shifters. I brought you here today to honor our family's obligation to the compact. You will be Eugene's mate, although you will never bare his children. This arrangement will last so long as I am the huntress or Eugene is leader of this pack."

"What? Why? Camille, I don't understand what you're talking about."

"I'm sorry, Theresa. This is the way it has to be. We must all serve our function to the House of Beauty. You were born without even the potential to pass on our gift of Silver magic. When you were five, your appendix became inflamed and had to be removed, but that wasn't all that was done. Mother ordered your ovaries removed as well. You are barren. She knew you would be the one to take Aunt Mildred's place."

"Why, Camille?" Theresa screamed. Her thin body shook with fear. "Why would you give me to this filthy shifter? Who is Aunt Mildred, and why can't she stay to do whatever it is she's been doing out here?"

"Aunt Mildred was Mother's eldest sister. Like you, she was born without the gift for magic. She can't continue serving, because when mother died and I came to test, Eugene snapped her neck after I killed the previous leader of the pack."

"And this is the fate you condemn me to? So long as you live as huntress, I live as a whore for this abomination?" Theresa's fear was fast becoming anger. "Why don't you kill all the shifters in this forest? Why do they exist at all when our family is dedicated to killing their kind? Why don't you do what you're supposed to do as huntress?"

"Because we must train against their kind if we are to kill them, so that the rest of humanity doesn't have to face their threat. Because you were born useless for any other duty a woman of our house would do. This is your fate, Sister. All your needs will be met, and as long as you live here in this cottage, the Belle side of the compact is honored. The shifters of the forest must honor their side of the bargain and leave the rest of the family in peace."

"I may be a dark shifter, but I still honor my word," Eugene said. "I promise I will never force you, and you may live out your days a virgin."

"What's to keep me from just running away from here?" Theresa asked her sister.

"Magic, for starters. I know you felt it when you crossed the boundary of this clearing. The spell that guards this place prevents all shifters save the pack leader from entering, but in exchange, it prevents those without magic from leaving. Get to know Eugene, Sister; he will be your only contact with the outside world from this day forth."

Camille turned and strode out of the clearing, hardening her heart to the pleas, cries, and screams of her baby sister. She knew the sounds of Theresa's screams and curses would haunt her for the rest of her life.

19

The Oisín family, Professor Mason, and the Coopers arrived at the Belle estate a week after Kieran and Cory returned from finalizing their bond. Kieran strode up the stairs leading to the main doors of the great house that had been his boyhood home. Just behind him, Cory walked at his right shoulder, and Billy the wolf was pressed against his left leg. Behind them, Kieran knew his family and allies watched and followed his lead. He pushed the doors opened with a shove of magic. A mob scene waited for Kieran inside the huge entrance hall. Massive timber support columns reached up to the roof three stories overhead. The Council of the Matriarchs jostled each other, with the exception of Kieran's grandmother and his great-aunt Desdemona, who stood waiting as the forefront of chaos. Around the perimeter of the great hall, Kieran caught sight of his young cousins, both male and female, peeking out around columns for a look at the first male to become a hunter-candidate. Four young boys ranging in age from twelve to fourteen stepped forward from the sidelines and stopped when they were directly in front of Kieran's party. In unison, the boys bowed to Kieran.

"Welcome home, Hunter-candidate Kieran. We await your approval to resume our training so we might aide you as your trackers."

"Greetings, former tracker-candidates. I look forward to continuing the training of those of you who wish to continue when you reach the appropriate age to begin the full training. Until such time, you will resume your regular duties and return to school. When you enter your junior year in high school, I will retest those of you who wish to continue as a potential tracker-candidate. Go and be boys for a while longer."

Beside Kieran, Billy sniffed and whined as the oldest of the candidates approached and knelt at Kieran's feet. The black wolf edged closer to the kneeling boy and sniffed his scent. A huge pink tongue lashed out and licked the boy's face. The boy, taken completely by surprise, fell backward onto his ass and looked up into the glowing amber eyes of the wolf. Billy nudged the young boy, trying to get him to pet him, but the boy cowered in fear until Kieran spoke up.

"It appears that Billy likes you, Cousin. You have nothing to fear from my nephew. Now, if I recall correctly, you are Ian, the boy full of questions. I feel bad for not remembering your full name, Cousin, but you boys have all sprouted in the year I've been gone from this house. I didn't get the time to relearn which branch of the family you come from. Tell me your full name and rank."

"I am probationary tracker-candidate Ian Belle-O'Connell, Hunter-candidate Kieran."

"And how old are you, Cousin Ian?"

"I just turned fourteen last week, sir."

"Well, Ian, you and Billy are close in age. Perhaps you might even convince my nephew to become a boy again instead of remaining a wolf."

"He's a shifter?" came the startled cry from one of the Matriarchs. "You brought a shifter into the House of Beauty?"

"Do not question my actions. I may not look the part right now, but I am the salvation of this house. I don't enjoy it, but I am the Silver Hunter. I have already passed the test of the huntress on my father's family estate and survived. I lead the House of Beauty as Hunter and Belle of Belle, my word is law in this house."

Cory's hand on Kieran's shoulder stopped his tirade at his great-aunts and kept him from crossing the room. His grandmother, still proud in her heritage, came forward from the gaggle of women to meet Kieran.

"Forgive me for not greeting you properly, Huntress-emeritus, but these boys needed attending to first," Kieran said, extending his hand to his grandmother.

The old woman took his hand and stiffened for a moment before bowing as best as she could, given her bad leg. Rising from her bow, she spoke, "Forgive the Matriarchs and I for not giving you the proper courtesy due your rank, Hunter Kieran." There were gasps from the crowd in the hall. "The Matriarchs and I are at your service, my honored grandson."

Kieran was wishing he had been sitting down. Never had he heard such respect in his grandmother's voice. The woman was sincere in her newfound respect. Before he could reply, she turned, stood at his side, and addressed the gathered family.

"Know this, all members of the House of Beauty, this day I acknowledge a new Hunter and leader of the House of Beauty. I present to you my grandson, a hunter who in his test has slain a dozen shifters and retains his magic. Kieran Samuel Belle, I acknowledge you this day as Hunter, Belle of Belle, and head of the House of Beauty. We are yours to command."

"Thank you, Grandmother. The time has come to clean out the forest of the shifter pack and to put an end to the lineage of the Beast. Go about your regular duties and rest tonight. Tomorrow, the House of Beauty prepares for war," Kieran said before turning to face Cory, Billy, and Ian. The young boy had his arms wrapped around the wolf's neck and his face buried in Billy's fur. Cory stood over them looking proudly at Kieran.

Sensing eyes on him, Ian lifted his head from Billy's fur, but kept a tight hold on the wolf, as if he was afraid the wolf would vanish.

"You two seem to have become fast friends, Cousin," Kieran said to the boy.

"We've never had animals in the house before. Is he really a shifter?"

Billy gently pulled loose from the young boy, padded over to Kieran, and rubbed his collar against Kieran's hand. Kieran looked down at the wolf, and silver eyes met amber ones.

"Not here, Billy," Kieran said to the wolf. "I'll consider it once we're settled in." The wolf whined before padding back over to sit pressed against Ian's leg. "Grandmother, will you please have our baggage sent to the hunter's suite. We also need to make arrangements for our guests as well."

"Of course, Desdemona and Fiona will take charge of the arrangements. Where do you want the beast housed?" Grandmother Belle asked.

"If you're referring to Billy, he'll stay with Cory and I in my suite unless we agree to allow him to shift back to human form." Kieran paused to consider his options. "If that is the case, he'll be assigned a bed in the cousins' wing with the other boys his age."

"Very well," Grandmother Belle replied. "Desdemona, see that Hunter Kieran and his husband's things are taken to the huntress' suite, and put Kellen and Líadáin in the blue suite. Fiona, please find suites for the rest of our guests and make sure there is a spare bed in the boys' dorm if it should be needed. Will you take dinner in your suite, Grandson, or would you prefer something more formal?"

"We will all dine in the hall tonight, Grandmother," Kieran said.

"I'll have the cooks prepare for a family gathering then. Will there be anything else?"

"No, Grandmother, that takes care of everything for now," Kieran said as he turned and led Cory, Billy, and Ian off toward the hunter's suite.

20

Kieran and Cory had taken the suite of rooms reserved for the Huntress of the House of Beauty after their initial meeting with the Matriarchs and the rest of the Belle family. The four boys Kieran had released from their training as tracker-candidates still waited on them as personal servants. It made Cory uncomfortable having servants waiting on him, and he was starting to get surly. On the second full day of their stay, Kieran had finally agreed to remove Billy's collar with Ian as the only outsider present. Kieran knelt and unfastened the clasp on the collar. With a howl, Billy the wolf returned to being Billy the boy. Billy, the naked boy, shivered as the cool air of the house hit his skin. Cory quickly wrapped him in one of his sweatshirts and tousled the boy's hair. Billy rose on shaky legs and walked over to Ian, and then wrapped the startled boy in a hug. Kieran and Cory glanced at each other with huge grins on their faces as the two boys hugged.

"I think you're about the same size as Cousin Henry. Come on, Billy, let's go see if any of his clothes fit you," Ian said to Billy.

Billy glanced over his shoulder at his uncles, who nodded their approval before allowing Ian to drag him off to find clothes. Despite being a year older, Ian was smaller than Billy both in height and body mass.

Ian helped Billy settle into the male cousins' dormitory by rearranging. A couple of the older cousins were reassigned to the servant quarters attached to Kellen's suite, so it was easy. They would see to Kellen's and Líadáin's needs. Once they'd been moved, Billy was moved into the open bunk in Ian's quad. Over the next couple of days, Billy learned the routines and got to know Ian and the other two boys in the quad better. On Billy's third night in the dormitory— around the time dinner for the main family was being called—Cory wandered the halls of the cousins' living quarters looking for Billy so that the boy could eat with them. He found Billy and Ian sitting in the strangest position. Billy was on the floor wedged in the narrow hallway with his bare feet pressed to one wall and his shoulders and upper back pressed against the opposite wall. On his legs, seated in a lotus position, was Ian who was bent over and whispering to Billy. *Wow,* thought Cory, *these two move fast. Wonder if Billy sensed a potential mate. They look so cute like this. I have to get a picture for Kieran to see.* Cory took out his cell phone and snapped a picture of the two boys before he disturbed them.

"It's time for dinner, guys. Kieran wants you both at our table tonight."

Ian looked up with grass green eyes as wide as saucers. Billy merely grinned at his uncle. He'd known Cory was there the entire time and had kept Ian unaware of his approaching uncle. He liked Ian a lot. There was something special between them, and Billy knew that after Uncle Kieran dealt with the evil shifters in the woods, he was going to ask about the possibility of using his collar's magic to lock him in human form instead of wolf form.

After dinner, both boys were invited back to Kieran and Cory's suite, so Kieran could assess how Billy was fitting in. Ian had automatically settled into servant mode when they'd arrived until Kieran had practically ordered his cousin to sit down. There'd been tension in the air, especially around Uncle Cory until that point. Once Kieran was satisfied that Billy was fitting in with the cousins, he'd sent them back to their room. Whenever he was visiting his uncles, Billy paid attention to the mood in the room when Ian or the other trainees were present.

A couple of days later, Billy stopped them just outside their room and checked that no one else was close by. He kicked off his shoes before settling down on the floor with his upper back braced against one wall and his legs braced on the opposite wall. Ian kicked of his shoes and settled himself on top of Billy's powerful legs in the lotus position. He leaned forward to be close to Billy so their conversation wouldn't be overheard, only this time, Billy pulled him even closer until their lips touched and met in a kiss. Ian was startled and almost fell off of his perch. Billy's strong arms caught him and kept him in place.

"Why did you kiss me?" Ian asked, his grass green eyes wide with surprise. "I don't think we're that close."

"I've wanted to kiss you since I switched back to human form," Billy said, locking his deep amber eyes on Ian's. "I really like you, Ian, and I wanted to show you how much I like you. I hope you like me, too."

"Yes, I like you a lot!" Ian gushed.

Billy put a finger to Ian's lips to curb his enthusiasm. "Ssh, we don't want to disturb anyone. We need to have a talk about how you and the rest of your group act around Uncle Kieran and Uncle Cory."

"What? Are we doing something wrong? We've been serving the hunter since we were deemed old enough to begin training to be trackers." Ian was blushing in embarrassment.

"You're so cute when you blush," Billy said as he tapped Ian's nose lightly. "I know this will sound strange to you, but maybe you should let them fend for themselves."

The shocked look on Ian's face at the suggestion stunned Billy who wasn't used to human reactions after several months locked in wolf form. He'd gotten so used to scents telling him what was going on around him that Ian's reactions were confusing.

"I don't understand why you're so shocked at the idea of letting two grown men look after their own needs, especially when your waiting on them hand and foot is driving Uncle Cory nuts," Billy said.

"It's the duty of tracker-candidates to attend to the needs of the Huntress of the House, so she can attend to the larger, more important tasks. Hunter Kieran and his friend are due that same consideration," Ian replied.

"Uncle Cory isn't Uncle Kieran's friend, Ian," Billy growled. "They're married and mated. You aren't a tracker-candidate anymore. Uncle Kieran released all of you from that position. So, it follows that he's not expecting you or the others to wait on him or Uncle Cory. He wanted you to have a childhood, to come hang out with me and play games or read books."

"Billy, I can't ignore what I'm supposed to do just to hang out and do frivolous things. I'm supposed to take care of the hunter, so he can protect the family and the world from shifters." As soon as the last word left Ian's mouth, his hand slammed over it, trying to bite back what he'd just said.

"Right, because we're all evil nasty monsters who are going to attack you and rip your throats out while you're sleeping," Billy snarled. "I thought you'd be different from all the others. My wolf smelled something that drew me to you, but I guess it was wrong. You're as much a bigot as the rest of your family. Only Uncle Kieran seems to be able to get passed his hatred of shifters and see us as people." Billy rose so abruptly Ian was dumped on the floor. Billy stormed down the hallway.

Ian sat horrified that the boy he'd developed a crush on was mad at him. His stomach felt as if he'd taken a punch. He couldn't leave things as they were, so he raced down the hall to follow Billy to try and apologize. The room they shared was at the very end of the hall, so it was easy to follow Billy until he came to the cross hall. *I didn't think he could move so fast. I can't tell which direction he . . . Wait, what's this sensation? It's like I know he went left.* Turning, Ian followed the strange sensation within him right up to the door of the hunter's suite. Loud voices were coming from within. Billy's was one of them, and he thought that Hunter Kieran's voice might be the other voice. He raised his hand to knock on the door to the suite when it was flung open, and he found himself staring at a furious Billy.

"Why are you following me?" Billy snarled. "Come to throw some more insults in my face?"

"How did you know I was out here?" Ian asked.

"I felt your presence. I just . . ." Billy reached out and grabbed Ian, dragging him into the suite as he turned to face his uncles. Ian was swept around in front of him and held protectively tight against Billy's chest. "I don't understand what's going on, Uncle Cory. Part of me wants to beat him to a pulp for thinking shifters are all monsters and part of me wants to protect him from the real monsters."

"I'd say there was a bond forming between you on some level. I also think part of this is an age thing," Cory comforted. "You're still a puppy, and you're seeing Ian as a playmate and rival for attention. We're also in the middle of a strange pack, and we don't know our place in the hierarchy yet."

"It's going to take some time to adjust the thought patterns around here, Billy," Kieran added. "Hatred and fear of shifters has been drummed into the every fiber of poor Ian since he was born. Give him time and patience. He'll come around and be the partner you need in time." Kieran turned to his cousin. "Ian, how did you know where to find Billy? Did you just assume he'd come here, or was there something else?"

"I realized I needed to apologize for my words as soon as I said what I did," Ian replied. "I ran to follow Billy, but didn't know how fast he could move. There was no trace of him in the hallways when I got to the junction, but then I just felt this pull toward the left hallway, and I followed it here."

A look passed between Kieran and Cory before they looked back at the two boys still in an embrace much like they shared. Kieran gestured for the boys to take a seat on one of the couches in the sitting room of the suite. Cory and he watched in amusement as Billy sat first and then drew Ian into his lap, back against his chest. Cory and Kieran then took the couch across from the boys. They watched as the understanding suddenly dawned on the youths as Kieran sank into the protection offered by Cory's embrace. Kieran couldn't help laughing at the expressions on the boys' faces.

"They're just too cute for words." Kieran laughed as Cory hugged him tight. "Now we know what everyone else sees when they look at us."

"You're right, babe. They are adorable. I think they'll make a wonderful pair," Kieran said before turning his attention back to Billy and Ian. "I have been thinking about your futures. I want you to listen carefully to what I'm proposing. This is a long-term plan, so take a few days to discuss my offers between you. Then, when you've reached an agreement between the two of you, come back to me and tell me which path you wish to pursue."

"You really are kicking me out of the tracker-candidate class, aren't you, Hunter Kieran?" Ian asked.

"Yes, Ian, I am removing you from that path to offer you one I think you're better suited to walk. I am, however, offering you a choice of paths. One leads to lifelong service to the House of Beauty in a very different capacity; the other leads you both away from service to the family and sets you free to make your own way in the world."

"Service or exile is the choice we have to make?" Ian asked.

"No exile, Ian. I have plans to change up how the House of Beauty does business, and some members of the family fit what's coming and others don't. My vision for you and Billy is for you to fill a very important role if you choose to accept it. If you choose to go your own way instead, you will always be family and welcome wherever you come across family. There will always be a set of rooms ready for you both in Cory's and my house."

"Okay, then I think we can listen to your offer, Hunter Kieran," Ian replied.

"When I visited here several weeks ago, you showed an interest in the old chronicles, Ian. Therefore, option one is this: the position of House Archivist is currently vacant and needs to be filled. If you choose this path, the House will pay you to go to school and complete at least your Master's degree in Archival Studies. Once you present your degree to the Council of Matriarchs, you will be confirmed as Archivist." Kieran held up his hand to forestall Ian's question. "The Archivist is very important to this family. Great-Uncle Jonas helped keep me on the path I needed to be on by sharing certain stories with me. If you choose this option, there are traditions that will have to be kept up, but we'll discuss those if you take the job. Now, option two is this: you are free to choose whatever you'd like to be in life, free of any and all obligations to the House of Beauty."

"These both sound like choices for Ian, Uncle Kieran. What are my options?"

"You're both sensing a connection to each other that may well lead to a permanent partnership like I share with Cory. I want to try letting you live your life without the collar. Your ability to shift will be for you to master control of, as part of your schooling."

"You think I can master my wolf?" Billy asked.

"If you apply yourself, we think you can do anything, Billy. If this connection between you develops, I'd like you to study alongside Ian so that you can assist him—if you take option one, that is. If you decide on option two, what you study is totally up to you."

"I don't think you want us both to become professional bookworms, Hunter Kieran," Ian said.

"No, I would like to see you both physically active as well as academically challenged. My recommendation is while you, Ian, get your Masters, Billy goes to the police academy or bodyguard school. That way, he can protect you."

Both boys looked thoughtful for a moment; then, Ian turned to face Billy. He looked up at the dark amber eyes with his own grass green eyes. Kieran and Cory watched as the boys seemed to silently communicate with each other. Ian tilted his head back, and Billy leaned down for a quick kiss before they both focused on the older couple across from them.

"We've decided to take option one. You're right. I'm not cut out to be a tracker, but I do love the archives. I'll need someone to look out for me, but I think we're agreed that whatever self-defense training Billy takes, I'll take it as well. He can't protect me all the time, and if

I've had the same training, I'll be able to move as he needs me to move."

"Thank you, Cousin. I do want you both to understand that you can change your minds at any point up to the day you're handed the keys to the archives. Knowing that the archives will be in the hands of someone as interested in them as I am makes me feel a lot better about their future," Kieran said. "Now, both of you run along and be boys; the future will be here before you know it."

21

E very seat around the council table was occupied, except the chair reserved for the Huntress of the House of Beauty. Camille Belle sat one seat down from what had once been her chair, waiting for her grandson Kieran to arrive. There was plenty of murmuring going on, mostly complaints about the presence of the Oisín family at the table. Camille was practically glaring daggers at Líadáin, knowing the other woman had the one thing she'd cheated herself out of years ago: Kieran's loving respect instead of the fear she'd instilled when he was a boy. Now, the women who'd run the House of Beauty for generations sat waiting for the man who would tell them how to they were going to help him save the family.

A small bell, which announced visitors to the chamber, rang, and one of the male cousins opened the great double doors to reveal Kieran with his husband Cory at his side. Kieran was dressed in his impressive set of armored leathers. Cory was wearing heavy denim jeans and a thick denim shirt; sturdy hiking boots completed the outfit. It was hard to decide if the second young man should be considered a threat or a decoration. He was handsome, even next to the beauty that was Kieran. Rugged looks where Kieran was smooth. Then, he moved in Kieran's wake; his stride screamed predator on the hunt. Kieran strode across the room with a glide that reminded Camille of her daughter Miranda and her son-in-law Kellen. Here was a man who could kill you just as easily as let you look at him. The impression of a deadly killer came to an abrupt end when Kieran flung himself into the great chair at the end of the table and sprawled one elegant leg over an arm of the chair. He slouched against the back of the chair. *He's amused that he's annoying me, and those silver eyes of his have always given away his mood,* Camille noted to herself.

"Welcome to the Council of Matriarchs, Hunter Kieran. We are honored to have you grace us with your presence," Camille said, managing not to choke on the words.

Kieran's smile grew larger and his eyes brighter as he watched his grandmother speak the ritual words of welcome. He knew he was already riding her last nerve by his carefree posture and mischievous grin. He caught a small frown of disapproval from Grams and decided he could behave himself. He straightened in the chair before returning his own ritual formula.

"Honored Grandmother, Matriarchs, and guests, I thank you for taking the time out of your busy schedules to attend this meeting. The House of Beauty is in great danger; the pact between our family and the shifters of the dark forest is broken. My sisters have been slaughtered during their attempts to take the test of the huntress. Shifters have ventured to attack me beyond the testing grounds. I have been put to the test of the huntress and come out the other side as the Hunter of the House of Beauty. The time has come to dispose of the shifters who have lived in our woods under our protection in exchange for their taking part in the test. They have broken faith with us and must be put down."

"How do you propose to do that, Hunter Kieran? If you're truly the Hunter of the House of Beauty," one of the Matriarchs said.

"Come and take my hand; you can sense the change in me. I'm more than just the Hunter of the House of Beauty. I'm the Silver Hunter, a child of the line of Belle and of the line of her younger brother, the one who inherited their mother's magic."

"That ancient prophecy called for a three-fold path—tracker, witch, and hunter. Men in our family don't have magic."

Kieran raised his hand, and Silver magic swirled around his hand in sparks like fireflies chasing each other. The magic swirled around him and his chair, and suddenly, he was across the room seated at the other end of the table.

"Does that satisfy you that I have magic? My father, uncle, and other grandmother are here to testify to my having become the Silver Witch. So, shall we get down to business and discuss a plan to clean out our forest?"

There were gasps of surprise from Matriarchs who hadn't been present during Kieran's last visit home. From those Matriarchs who'd been on hand for that last visit, there were both murmurs of approval and disapproval, depending on where they stood in the hierarchy of the council.

"We figured you'd do what huntresses do and just go in and kill them," a Matriarch said.

"Do we have an accurate count of how many shifters live in the woods? From what the magic revealed to me when Rosie went to the test, there were hundreds of them. It took twenty of them to take her down. It took fifty to take down Mother. I don't know if I can take on the entire pack alone, and then there is the mysterious Alpha and the question of a dark mage helping him. I'm going to need backup."

"But if you're entering the forest to face the pack, it will be during the full moon, and they will think you've come to test. You will have to go alone."

"What is with all of you? You let my sisters go into those woods alone to be slaughtered; now you'd send me to the same fate? This is supposed to be a family that hunts shifters. How did it come down to being one person in each generation doing all the fighting while people like you spend your time making the decisions? You old ladies need to go take up knitting or something, save for Grandmother; you aren't worth taking advice from. It's time for a new Council to lead the House of Beauty; this one is dissolved."

The Matriarchs looked at each other and then at Kieran. Voices of protest started to rise against him until Camille slammed her cane down on the table.

"Enough! Kieran is the Hunter; the Council of Matriarchs serves at the will of the Hunter. He has dismissed us from our service. You will accept this and go."

Chairs scraped over the wooden floor as the Matriarchs pushed back from the table and rose. They departed in a parade of long skirts and outraged looks. Kieran only stopped three women from leaving, Grandmother Belle, Great-Aunt Fiona, and Great-Aunt Desdemona. All women who still had their one-shot gift of Silver magic.

"I know you can no longer fight, and I know you don't approve of what I've done, and you certainly won't like my plans for the future, but I need your wisdom, Aunt Fiona, and your knowledge, Aunt Desdemona, and your experience, Grandmother. You three have led this family through some dark times, and we're about to experience something beyond dark. Will you stay and help me?" Kieran asked.

"You ran away a boy, but you have returned a man, Kieran. We were hard on you, because we feared that this is what would come our way. We will do what we can to help you, but we fear that it will come down to you standing alone to face the pack in the end," Great-Aunt Fiona said.

"What do you need from us, Kieran?" Great-Aunt Desdemona asked.

"Of everyone living, Aunt Desdemona, you know the archives the best. I need you to work with Ian and Billy in tracking down everything about Beauty's fight with the Beast and the last hunter's fight with the dark Alpha of his time. I want to know what they did to defeat their opponents. Aunt Fiona, I want you to go play peacemaker with the other Matriarchs and let them know that there are better things ahead for the family. Grandmother, I want you to choose candidates from the younger cousins for a new council. Pick both males and females with a potential to be trackers or hunters. Change is coming to the House of Beauty, and they will help usher it in."

INTERLUDE: THE MASTER COMES TO MAINE

The Master was pissed. The capture or destruction of Kieran Belle could no longer be left in the hands of underlings or beasts. It was time to deal with this personally.

The Master packed a few things he felt he would need before casting a sleep spell over his minions in his lair. Once he was sure none of his servants or slaves would attempt to escape, he cast a transport spell and whisked himself across the miles from Little Rock to Bangor. The spell deposited him in an alley near a major hotel. With a gesture, he altered his appearance from his concealing robes to a finely tailored business suit. His bag became a small suitcase, and he walked around the corner from the alley and made it appear to the valets as if he'd just emerged from one of the cabs. The young valet who was the next on deck took his bag and escorted him inside to the front desk. Here the Ebony mage became the suave businessman he was normally.

"Hello, sir, checking in?" the front desk clerk asked.

"If you have a vacancy, yes. I'm afraid I was called to attend to business at the last moment and didn't have a chance to book in advance."

"We have a couple of suites available, sir. How long will you be staying?"

"That will depend on how long it takes to deal with the business that called me here. At least a week if you have a suite available that long," the mage replied.

"Yes, sir, the Arcadia suite is available for the next two weeks," the clerk replied.

"Then please book me for the two weeks," the Master said, handing over a credit card.

"Yes, sir, if you'll please fill out this registration card please." The clerk handed him a card and a pen, and then waited so that she could enter his information into the computer to book the room.

Behind the mage, the young valet stood holding the man's bag. The mage noted the boy's eagerness and build. He was slender but muscular, somewhere between a gymnast and a swimmer. The tight slacks showed what promised to be a hefty cock and heavy balls. He'd noted the beautiful bubble butt on the way into the lobby. Perhaps he'd indulge himself later. He handed the completed card back to the desk clerk. She smiled at him, hoping maybe she could make an impression. He merely nodded back at her. After a few moments, she ran a pair of blank keycards through the machine and coded them for his suite. She slipped them into an envelope and handed them to the man. She then slid a copy of his receipt to him for his signature.

"Here are the keys for your suite. It's on fifteenth floor. Kevin will show you the way, Mr. Locke," she said. "If you'll sign here, everything will be charged to your card when you check out."

"Thank you, my dear," Mr. Locke, better known as the Master, said as he signed the receipt and slid it back to her.

"Kevin, please show Mr. Locke to the Arcadia suite," the woman said.

"This way please, Mr. Locke." Kevin turned, showing off his tight bubble butt as he headed toward the elevator.

Mr. Locke followed closely behind the young valet. The elevator arrived almost as soon as Kevin pushed the button. Holding the door, he let Mr. Locke enter first and then followed and pressed the button for the fifteenth floor. Once the doors slid closed, Mr. Locke made eye contact with Kevin in the reflection of the highly polished doors. With little effort, he had Kevin turning around to face him directly and locked his gaze on the young man. Kevin was soon in a light hypnotic trance and leaning against the older man. The mage whispered in Kevin's ear, and the boy stood up straight and turned back to face the doors. He remained that way until the elevator chimed to announce their floor, which seemed to break the trance the boy was in. He stepped out and led the way to the Arcadia suite, where he took the key from Mr. Locke and opened the door for the man. He followed the man inside and placed the suitcase on the luggage rack by the door.

"Is there anything else I can do for you, Mr. Locke?" Kevin asked.

"Yes, Kevin, tell me when you get off your shift. I may have some errands for you to run for me."

"I'm off my shift at eight o'clock tonight, Mr. Locke. If you need something before then, I'm happy to be of service," Kevin replied.

"No, that will be fine. Once you're off the clock, come up here and let yourself in," Mr. Locke said, slipping the extra keycard into Kevin's back pants pocket, getting a feel of the tight muscular butt cheek at the same time.

Kevin smiled at the man. "Yes, sir. I'll be here as soon as I've changed and clocked out."

Mr. Locke peeled a twenty-dollar bill out of his money clip and handed it to Kevin for his services so far. Kevin started to thank the man and then froze in place when the man's hand touched his. Mr. Locke maintained his touch on Kevin's hand as he moved around behind the boy and pressed his body up against the frozen youth. He slipped his hand into Kevin's back pocket and pulled out his wallet. Flipping the wallet open, he checked Kevin's age on his driver's license. Finding the boy was actually twenty-one, he put the wallet back and then released the boy. He was the perfect age to meet all of his dark desires. Kevin shook his head when he found Mr. Locke behind him, but he just figured he was tired from working long shifts.

"I'll see you tonight as soon as you can get here, Kevin," Mr. Locke said, ushering the boy out of the suite.

Once his reward for the evening was out of the way, Mr. Locke stepped over to his suitcase and then opened it to retrieve his crystal ball and its stand. He set these up on the table in the suite's siting room, loosened his tie, and undid the top couple of buttons on his dress shirt. Ebony magic began to swirl around the crystal ball, and then the connection snapped into place. Staring back at him was one of the most brutish men he'd ever seen. Here was the human form of the legendary Beast.

"So you finally decided to show yourself, mage," the Beast growled, even in human form.

"Yes, I've come to Maine to deal with this in person. I will join you in a few days once I have the lay of the land and an assessment of the defenses around the boy."

"The bitches don't have defenses, mage. The pact between them and this pathetic group of mongrels keeps these sheep bound to the forest. They don't need defenses against shifters."

"As I recall, you're just as trapped by this magical binding as the mangy cur you're trapped with. I want to know what protections the boy has put in place to deal with outside magical threats. He will expect at least my agents to make another attempt. Actually, I'm sure he's expecting me to take a direct hand after his little message drop."

"So do something about him. Once he's gone, the binding spell will begin to unravel, and my kind will be free to shift at will to any shape. I will have my revenge on the bitch's family at long last."

"Soon, one of us will have what we want," the mage said as he broke the spell.

22

After many days of being cooped up in the Belle mansion, Kieran had finally had enough of meetings with various members of the extended Belle family. Kieran was tired from more than fruitless meetings; he hadn't been sleeping well the last few nights. Dreams and nightmares were plaguing his sleep. The nightmares of a dark-furred monster—half-man, half-beast—were ones he hadn't dreamed since he was ten. To escape the mad house, he grabbed Cory out of their suite, scooped up the new swords Uncle Brom had forged for him, and led Cory outside. He took Cory into a set of woods near the house that wasn't part of the greater forest around them. When they reached the clearing in the center of the grove, Kieran stopped and raised a barrier of Silver magic around the clearing.

"I don't want us to be disturbed. Only you and I can cross that barrier," Kieran said.

"We need one of those on our suite, or at least the bed room," Cory joked.

"Cory, I need to watch you shift. I need to get used to you doing that, so I don't reflexively strike out at you."

"It's not the full moon, Kieran. I can't shift during the day."

"You're different from every other shifter in existence, and I think that if you put your mind to it, you'll find that you can shift at will."

"Is this really necessary, Kieran? You know I'm not much of a fighter," Cory said.

"You're going to have to become something of a fighter or at least learn to let your wolf-instincts take over for you before we go to face the dark pack. You have to be at my side when I face down the Alpha," Kieran replied.

"I'll give it a try, babe," Cory said.

Cory closed his eyes and tried to still his mind to find his wolf within, as his mother had taught him just in case he ever felt the urge to shift. It started as a tingle in his fingers and toes, and it became an itch he couldn't scratch, and then it was a burning pain. His body rearranged itself. He twisted and howled until a beautiful silver wolf stood before Kieran. Until the pain of a cramp in his hands hit his brain, Kieran didn't realize he'd drawn both swords and gripped them so tight his knuckles were white. Slowly, he forced himself to relax his stance and his grip. At the moment, Kieran sheathed his swords, and Cory leapt. His huge front paws crashed into Kieran's shoulders, knocking him backward. Cory's wolf body pinned him to the ground. Silver magic swirled and struck at Cory the wolf, but the power just flowed back into Kieran through their bond. Amber wolf eyes locked on silver mage eyes, and Kieran realized that his magic couldn't hurt Cory in anyway when he was in this shape. Wolf jaws opened, revealing sharp canine teeth before a long wet tongue lashed out and licked Kieran's face. Cory bounded away from Kieran with a wolfish grin on his muzzle as his husband wiped his face on his sleeve.

"I'm going to die by drowning in wolf slobber," Kieran said, rising to his knees. He held out his arms to Cory. "Come here, Wolf."

Cory trotted over and then sat facing Kieran, who moved closer and wrapped his arms around Cory's neck as he buried his face in the thick, soft silver fur. After a few moments, Cory lightly nipped Kieran's shoulder, and Kieran released his hold. He sat back staring at Cory in his wolf form; then, he rose and drew his swords.

"I know this is alien to you, Cory, but we need to learn to move together and to fight side by side. I need to adjust to having a shifter fighting at my side. Will you work with me before we bring Billy out here to work with both of us?"

Cory looked at his lover for a moment before standing and shaking himself before yipping in the affirmative. He padded over to Kieran's right side and waited for Kieran to begin. Kieran began with warming up through several sword katas, partly for himself since he hadn't worked out heavily since his accident and extended hospital stay, and partly so Cory could get a feel for how he moved. Several times, they collided and crashed to the ground before they started to rely more on their bond to sense how the other was going to move. Eventually, they were moving in sync and at greater speeds until Kieran finally reached his full attack speed. They became a whirling blur of swords, boots, claws, and teeth as they lashed out at invisible enemies. Cory urged them to a greater speed as he shifted shape into the halfway form and became a beautiful beast. Cory's movements changed as he became Kieran's opponent in their dance of death.

Claws slashed past soft targets, never striking but showing openings an enemy wouldn't hesitate to rip open. For his part, Kieran's swords blurred past Cory, turning so that the flat of a blade would strike an open target in warning that a shifter could be vulnerable as well. Their sparing went on and on with Kieran moving faster than he'd ever moved before by drawing on his bond with Cory. The bond worked both ways, and Cory seemed to have figured out a way to use it to flow with Kieran's grace and to predict Kieran's moves. Cory noticed that Kieran was tiring, and the scent of a possible victory was driving Cory's hormones into over drive. He wanted to defeat his mate and claim him.

Kieran took a couple of steps back trying to gain some space to reset to go on the offensive, but he stepped into a hole and fell, twisting his ankle in the process. Before he could raise any kind of defense, Cory was on him and not only had him pinned but was actively shredding his clothes. Kieran could feel Cory's intense desires, but his lover was still in partial beast form, and Kieran didn't want to admit it, but this form frightened him.

Silver magic flashed between the two lovers and shoved Cory away from his mate. He landed and then pounced toward his mate again. He crashed into a barrier of Silver magic, but it only slowed him down a little bit. Cory saw Kieran rising to his feet, clothing hanging in rags from his beautiful body, and it inflamed him even more. *Naked, his mate should always be naked,* he thought.

Cory crashed into Kieran, knocking him face first into the ground, and then Cory finished ripping away his mate's clothes. He heard sobbing beneath him as his cock slid along the crease of his mate's ass. He rose up enough to flip Kieran face up. Then, he looked at his mate's eyes and saw fear, not a matching desire. *My mate is afraid of me. Why is my mate afraid of me?* Confused, Cory stopped trying to enter Kieran and forced himself back to fully human. He wrapped Kieran in his arms and felt his husband's body tremble with the fear of his half-beast form; that's when he began to make out the words Kieran kept repeating.

"Please not in this form. Please not in this form," Kieran whispered between sobs.

"Sshh, babe, it's safe. You know I would never hurt you. Please don't be afraid of me."

Kieran wrapped his arms around the human form of his husband and buried his face against the hairy chest. Cory rolled to his back, bringing Kieran to rest on top of him, and caressed his husband until the sobbing and trembling passed.

"Talk to me, Kier. Why are you so scared of me making love to you in my midway form?"

"The nightmares. Always in my childhood nightmares, I saw that form come out of the darkness to rape and abuse me. It was so real that I'd wake up covered in sweat and cowering in a corner."

"Oh, Kier, I'm sorry. The wolf in me saw a victory over my mate and wanted to claim his prize. I didn't know that my midway form was a thing of terror for you. I promise I'll never use that shape when we make love." Cory lifted Kieran's face so that his husband could see the sincerity in his eyes.

Kieran shifted slightly so that he could kiss his husband before snuggling back against him. They stayed like that for a few moments before Kieran looked up at Cory again.

"I didn't know the shift was painful. I felt your pain during the shift from human to wolf form. Once you were moving, the pain was gone when you shifted to your halfway form or when you shifted back to human. Is it because you had to force the change to wolf form?" Kieran asked.

"I think the pain was because I went directly from human to wolf instead of using the midway form first. There are so many anatomical differences between wolves and humans that it's painful when you're consciously making the shift. On the night of full moon, it may not be so bad. The last time I did it, the change happened so fast. I didn't even know I'd changed until Grams talked me down enough to change back."

"You changed the night Gramps died?" Kieran asked.

"Yes, I think it must have happened at the moment you cut loose with all of your power to kill those attacking shifters, or it may have been when the tree fell on you. All I know is that you were in great pain when it happened, and all I could think about was getting to you," Cory replied.

"I love you, Cory."

"I love you too, Kieran."

"Will you do something for me?" Kieran asked.

"You know I'd do anything for you, Kier."

"Shift back to your midway form and just hold me."

"Is that a good idea, Kieran? I've never seen you so afraid before."

"I need to face my fears, to grow stronger. It helps that your fur is bright, not dark like the fur in my nightmares. Please help me to grow stronger, Cory."

Cory gave off a sexy growl; he loved it when Kieran needed him. In a moment, he began the shift toward his midway form. He let his hair thicken into fur, and slowly, he let his muscles and body shift afterward. Kieran snuggled in tighter as Cory's fur thickened, and tried to will himself to remain calm as Cory's body shifted beneath him into the monstrous midway form. Fingernails shifted and became claws, tracing careful lines against his skin as Cory stroked him, trying to help keep him calm. It seemed as if everything was going along fine until Kieran looked up at Cory's face to find the face so like the monster in his childhood dreams. He recoiled in horror. Cory stopped the shift and returned to his human form. He tried to reach for Kieran, but his husband wouldn't let him touch him. Kieran rose unsteadily to his feet and wrapped himself in Silver magic. The magic shifted and molded to Kieran's body starting at his feet. It began hardening, forming boots, and then as it moved up his body. It formed itself into form-fitting armor. As the magic flowed down his arms, part of the magic separated and formed wicked scythe blades starting at Kieran's elbows and extending beyond his hands a matching distance. Cory watched as the magic slowly swallowed Kieran's beautiful face, leaving a mirrored mask facing him. From the shoulder guards, the magic took the form of a cloak and flowed outward to billow in the breeze. Cory had seen Kieran in armor like this before, but there was something different about it this time. As much as he wanted to approach Kieran, Cory knew that any move in Kieran's direction would likely prove fatal.

"Kieran, we can face your fears together. The face scares you the most. You see the monster of your nightmares. Even though you know that the person behind the face you're seeing here is your loving husband, who will never hurt you, that face has promised to do horrible things to you in your dreams for years. Don't hide in that shell of magic. Come share my strength and love. I'll never let the monster get you."

"You can't stop it. The monster comes and he's so strong. I have to be stronger. So many people want me to be so much stronger than any one person can possibly be. This monster is powerful; everyone who was supposed to fight him has run or passed the problem on to someone else. I don't get that choice, Cory. Everything has conspired to leave with only two options: fight and win, or fight and die." Kieran's voice was muffled by the magical armor, but the sob that wracked him was loud, and he crashed to the ground, armor fading away. "I don't want to die, but I can't face that monster."

"We're in this together, Kieran," Cory said as he wrapped himself around his love. "I'm not going to let you face the monster alone. Besides you have an advantage your sisters didn't have when they went to take this test."

"What advantage do I have besides nearly unlimited Silver magic?"

"You're forgetting you've already passed the test. The shifters in the forest are going to be expecting a moment of weakness or something when you've cut down the magical fifth shifter."

"They may expect me to stop fighting since the pact calls for the test to end after five shifters have died. Since we already know they aren't going to stop, we're ahead of the game. You know you're very smart for a big scary monster," Kieran teased, bringing a big smile to Cory's face.

"Well, you're not too bad for a tasty monster snack," Cory teased back before running his tongue across Kieran's neck.

"Oh my, are you going to eat me, Mr. Monster?" Kieran squirmed in such a way that his ass rubbed against Cory's cock.

"Mmm, yes, I'm going to gobble you up, little boy," Cory said as his grip tightened with one hand while the other glided down to stroke Kieran's own rampantly hard cock. "Can you take us back to the cavern at Gram's place?"

Kieran twisted in Cory's grip so that they were face-to-face. He could see the lust and love in his husband's eyes. He nodded and then kissed Cory deeply as Silver magic wrapped around them and whisked them away to the cavern where they'd claimed each other. Kieran even managed to land them gently on the sleeping shelf in the bedchamber. With a groping hand, Cory found the bottle of lube they kept on the little side shelf and flipped the top open. He kept the kiss going as he squeezed lube out to slick up his lover's hole and his own cock. Slowly, he settled so that his cock slipped into Kieran's welcoming ass. Moans of passion began to echo in the chamber as Kieran broke the kiss and let his head roll back against the bedding. Being held in Cory's strong arms or being pinned beneath the strong body always made him feel safe and loved in ways he didn't understand and didn't care to explore further. He just let himself go and let Cory have control of their lovemaking. His skin began to tingle as Cory leaned over him and let his chest hairs brush over his smooth skin. The sensation was different this time, softer somehow. Kieran reached up and ran his hand across Cory's chest and through much thicker hair, the feeling of a dense but soft fur pelt. Kieran opened his eyes and found that Cory had shifted at least part way toward his midway form. The face that looked down at him was still that of his human form, beautiful as always in Kieran's eyes. He watched as Cory slowly let his shift take him from human to half-wolf. The blond hair shifted color to bright silver and spread down his throat and back beneath Kieran's clutching fingers as his lover increased the pace of his thrusts. Soon, Kieran was staring into the face of the monster from his childhood nightmares, but this wasn't the face that caused blind panic; this was his husband who'd never let anything happen to him. He pulled down the face above him, awkwardly kissing the strange mouth that was more wolf than human. When he felt Kieran relax in the arms of his midway form, Cory let the shift fade back to full human, and then set to bringing both of them to the edge of climax several times before finally taking them over the edge. When they came down from their mutual orgasm and had control of their legs again, they made their way down to the pools in the main cavern and set about getting clean. Once they were clean, they rummaged to find something to wear, coming up with a couple of pairs of shorts.

"These are enough to not be embarrassed if there's someone in our suite when we arrive back there," Kieran said.

"That's good. I don't want to scare off the kids. I'm not used to them waiting on us hand and foot, but I do like that they feel so free to come and ask us things. I don't know . . ." Cory paused. "Maybe we should look at having kids of our own someday."

"If it's something you want, Wolf, I'll certainly think about it. I'm not sure I want to inflict my bloodline on an innocent child though."

"We can discuss it another time. We should get back before someone starts sending out search parties, babe."

"Thank you, Cory."

"You're welcome, Kieran."

Kieran stepped into Cory's embrace, and Silver magic swirled around them, whisking them back to their suite in the Belle mansion.

They stepped apart at the sound of a throat being cleared to find Kellen and Grams sitting in a couple of chairs in the main sitting room. Both young men blushed at being caught.

"You're both adorable when you blush like that. Now, go put some real clothes on. We have some important things to talk about," Grams said, while Kellen tried not to laugh aloud at his son and son-in-law.

"Be right back," Kieran said as he turned and fled to the safety of their bedroom, Cory right on his heels.

The lovers found clothes and dressed quickly before returning to the sitting room of the suite. They took their customary place on one of the sofas and waited for either Grams or Kellen to begin the conversation. Silence stretched, making Kieran uncomfortable, but he held back from breaking it, practicing the skills he needed for facing down the Council of Matriarchs. Finally, Kellen cleared his throat.

"Mother and I are worried about the whispers we're hearing from some of the staff about opposition to you from the Council."

"What have you heard, Dad?" Kieran asked.

"Several of the Matriarchs are conspiring to put Camille back in charge of the family, because they don't believe that you've passed the test of the huntress," Grams said. "They refuse to believe that any man could pass the test."

"They're willing to challenge Grandmother's own acknowledgement of my status?" Kieran leaned back. "Wow, I knew they were stubborn old women, but I never thought they'd challenge Grandmother in order to keep things the same."

"Fear of change, *mo stór*," Grams said. "They'd challenge Camille for her seat if any of them had passed the test themselves. You didn't go into their sacred woods and pass the test there, so they don't believe you've faced down a hoard of shifters and emerged the victor."

Kellen settled against the back of the sofa he sat on and crossed one long elegant leg over the other. "You're going to need to convince them that you're in charge and beyond their challenges."

Kieran snorted. "Short of going into the dark forest tomorrow and returning with five shifter heads, I don't think I can convince them I've passed the test. Actually, I'm not even sure they'd believe that evidence,

Dad. They'll think I used magic, because only a woman is strong enough to take on five shifters without using magic. Especially since they know I can use magic at will. I don't have to hoard my magic for a really big need."

"You need to do something before you have a challenge on your hands," Kellen said.

"The Council's days are numbered already, Dad. I have a plan to protect and spread the House of Beauty. Like the Oisíns, the Belles have become dangerously concentrated in one place. I'm going to set up each of the cadet branches in their own regions, with training for both men and women as hunters. There will be a new Council made up of the chief regional hunters. This will give us better coverage. I'd like to set up a training school for hunters and huntresses, that will even train non-family members," Kieran said.

"That's a marvelous idea, *mo stór*. Now, all you have to do is convince your current Council to step down and let you get on with the job of transforming everything they've ever known," Grams said.

"I've already started a redesign of the Council. Everyone save Grandmother and Great-Aunts Desdemona and Fiona has been removed. I've asked Grandmother to replace them with younger women and men."

"Well, that will keep Camille busy for a while," Kellen said. "Now we need to find out how to defeat this dark Alpha and the entire pack."

"Plus there's still the Ebony mage out there to be dealt with," Grams added.

Kieran looked around the room, realizing that one of his normal voices of advice was missing. "Has anyone seen either Uncle Brom or Professor Mason since we got here? I'm not even sure what suite Great-Aunt Fiona put them in."

23

John Mason stood in the sitting room of the suite he was sharing with Brom at the Belle estate. The huge house made him feel uncomfortable. The place was cold, emotionally. Then, there was Brom. The man was just about everything John wanted in a partner, but Brom was beginning to become the one thing John didn't want above all things, possessive and controlling.

The last few times they'd had sex, it had become a battle for dominance, and if John didn't submit, Brom suddenly wasn't in the mood. Just last night John decided enough was enough, and he moved his things into the second bedroom of the suite and slammed the door in Brom's face. It couldn't go on, but John didn't want to desert Kieran when his student might need him most. With one last glare at the door to Brom's bedroom, John stormed toward the door leading to the hallway only to smack straight into Brom as he entered the suite. Angry emerald eyes meet storm-gray silver eyes, and both men's tempers flared.

"Get out of my way, Brom," John growled.

"Where do you think you're going, John?" Brom snarled back.

"To talk with Kieran. I think it's time I went back to Little Rock."

"So after all your talk about being his ally, you're going to cut and run when he's going to need all the help he can get to face an entire pack of shifters that want to rip him to pieces?" Brom pressed up against John with every word.

John shoved Brom away and moved toward the door. Brom grabbed him by the elbow and slammed him into a wall. Emerald eyes flashing with intense anger locked on Brom as every plant in the room tripled in size. Several vines lashed out and wrapped themselves around the man. Silver magic slammed John against the wall and held him there as the vines were slashed. Brom closed in on John and attempted to kiss the man, but John slammed his head into Brom's nose, breaking the man's concentration along with several blood vessels in his nose. When he came free of the wall, John followed up his head butt with a right hook to Brom's jaw.

"Stay away from me, Brom. I won't be manhandled, and I'm not your personal property. I decide when and if I will be the submissive during sex. I am not and will never be a slave or a plaything. If you want to be more than friends with benefits, you will respect my position and limits on the matter."

"Go back to your darkroom then. Kieran needs fighters at his side, not whining little boys." Brom turned his back on John and stormed into his bedroom. He slammed the door behind him.

John looked at the mess he'd made and sighed, sorry for the extra work the maid who took care of the suite would have to do. Turning, he left the suite and went in search of Kieran.

* * *

KIERAN WAS SITTING in the library, reviewing several of the most ancient of chronicles in his search for information on how Beauty defeated the Beast. He even looked for how the last male hunter had defeated the powerful dark shifter of his time. But he wasn't having much luck with the task. When Professor Mason found him, Kieran gave a huge sigh of relief.

"Kieran, I'm sorry to interrupt your research, but we need to talk," John said.

"I always have time for you, Professor. What did you need to see me about?" Kieran asked as he gestured to the empty chair beside him.

John sat down and then looked at his favorite student, trying not to see a younger version of Brom. It was actually easier to focus on Kieran's appearance and block out Brom's, because he'd known Kieran longer.

"I think it's time for me to go back to Little Rock, Kieran."

"I'm going to guess that Uncle Brom is part of the reason," Kieran said bluntly. "I heard part of the argument you had with him last night when I was on my way back to my suite. If you need me to knock some sense into him, I will, Professor."

"That's kind of you, Kieran, but I can fight my own battles on the relationship front, and I think your uncle will realize he's messed up a good thing eventually. However, that's only part of why I think it's time for me to leave. Something about this house doesn't sit right with me. The place is emotionally empty, and for an Emerald mage, it's uncomfortable."

"Let me guess, it feels like all the joy and happiness has been sucked out of the place?"

"Yes, at least in the majority of the house. Around your suite and here in the library, I get a sense of your happiness at least. In here, you were very happy listening to stories told by a very kind old man."

"Yes, Great-Uncle Jonas, the family archivist, whom I deeply miss. Ian kind of reminds me of him. Jonas was the last of his branch of the family, and I think he wanted me to inherit his position. I used to hide in here for hours when I wanted to escape my training to be a tracker," Kieran said, a sad note ringing in his voice despite the smile on his face.

"I don't really want to abandon you when I know you're about to face a great darkness, but I'm not sure how much help I can still offer," John said.

"I think you've done more than enough, Professor. You helped speed up my recovery, and you've given me back the uncle I lost even before I was born. He'll wise up eventually, because I think you two were meant to be together. If he doesn't do it soon, I'll kick his ass until he does."

"Thank you, Kieran. Do you think you'll be back in time for the fall semester?"

"If I survive what I have to do here, Professor, I'll be back for fall semester, so save me a spot in class." Kieran smiled at his professor with one of his dazzling smiles.

"There's always a spot in my class for you, Kieran, just as there will always be a place at my table for you and Cory during the holidays."

"When you get back to Little Rock, Professor, will you do something for me?" Kieran asked.

"I'd be happy to do just about anything for you, Kieran," John replied.

"Find Mrs. Jones for me and ask her how much she wants for the house where Cory and I have been renting," Kieran said.

"I'll see what I can do, Kieran. Do you really think that she'll sell you the place?"

"I'm hoping that she will. It has a good set up for the few members of the family I want living near Cory and I."

"Then I'll see you at the beginning of the semester, Kieran," John said.

"I'll see you in class, Professor Mason," Kieran said.

They both stood up, and Professor Mason grabbed Kieran into a hug before letting him go and escaping the library. Kieran stood there stunned for a moment before returning to his research.

INTERLUDE: THE MASTER MEETS THE BEAST

The Master was irritated Kevin the valet hadn't returned to visit his suite last night as promised. He'd wanted that ripe body to work out his tension on; now he must go and meet with the shifter claiming to be the legendary Beast. He rented a car through the front desk of the hotel, and after getting directions to Belle Lumber, he made his way toward the vast Belle estate. When he felt he was close enough, he pulled the car off the road and into the woods. Stepping out of the car, he shifted his clothes from his business suit back to his all encompassing robes. Ebony magic swirled around him, and he vanished and reappeared in the clearing at the center of the dark woods. Before him stood the throne of bones. His apprentice had created it months ago when he'd come here to meet with this shifter, and it still stood. He gathered his robes about him, seated himself in the throne, and waited for the Beast to arrive.

"So the Master mage finally comes to get his hands dirty," a voice rumbled from the edge of the clearing.

"Don't act all high and mighty with me, mongrel. You and your pack of puppies had ample opportunities to kill the entire family and didn't act," the Master replied. "For what you want, you need me, and for what I want, I do not need you."

A huge and brutish man stepped in front of the seated mage and looked down at the smaller man. He reached to grab the front of the mage's robes and haul him out of the throne, but his hand collided with a barrier. He pulled it back as a burning sensation spread from his fingers up his arm. Several lesser shifters, all in human form, moved to attack the mage, but a mere flick of his fingers froze them all in place.

"You cannot hurt me, Beast, but I can kill you and all of these pathetic strays."

"You can't kill me, mage. Hurt me, I will acknowledge, but your Ebony magic can't kill me. I don't even think Silver magic can do the job. So far, all it's ever done is fling me across time from the bitch to her coward of a descendant and now to a mere boy. I'm not afraid of the House of Beauty."

"This boy is more than just a mere hunter. I've been in contact with his magic, and it is old and powerful. He isn't limited to one spell like those you've faced up until now. I've never sensed a mage like him before."

"I do not fear him. He doesn't fulfill either prophecy. No child of the House of Beauty will ever take a shifter for a mate nor are they going to knowingly associate with a shifter."

"You need a better spy network, dog. This boy is very different. He has a shifter for a guard dog, and his husband comes from the same shifter family as his pet."

"It won't matter in the end. He must fight his way through this pack to face me before sunrise on the day he comes to the test. He'll become more of a challenge if he kills five of them before they take him down. Something in the bitch's lineage seems to unlock when they've killed five shifters."

"I gather from all the bones here that this is the place where the test takes place. I shall weave trap spells here; that will slow or stop the boy's progress. I shall also weave a general protection spell from Silver magic over all those who will fight this hunter. On the night of this test, I will also offer the boy a challenge, and he may choose which of our challenges he wishes to accept."

"Do not fail in your tasks, mage, because if he doesn't kill you, I will."

"That's a threat that goes both ways, dog. I bet in your beast shape you'd make an excellent throw rug. In this form, you might make a passible slave once you were properly broken in. I'll be back in two days to begin casting my spells," the Master said as Ebony magic swirled around him, and he vanished. The bargain was struck.

24

The stack of ancient manuscripts teetered on the table in front of Kieran. The pile had grown over the last few days. He'd read them all and still hadn't found the information he was looking for. The equally high pile of translations and historical notes didn't make any more sense than the dusty old tomes. The tension in the library grew. Kieran's sigh was louder than ever before.

"Does everything have to be couched in riddles and metaphors? Why couldn't the family historians just admit they didn't know what the hell happened?"

"You're only looking at what is available to the whole family, Cousin Kieran." Ian's reply was muffled because he was buried deep in the stacks.

"I don't have much choice in the matter, Ian, unless you or Billy have discovered where Great-Uncle hid the second set of books," Kieran shouted back.

"Where did you get that one on the first male hunter? The one that talked about his choices of armor and why he wouldn't marry the woman his aunts picked for him?" Ian called back.

"Fourth floor, fifth set of shelves, third shelf up from the bottom of the case," Kieran's answered in a mechanical tone. "Why?"

Ian came out of the stacks, dragging Billy with him, which made Kieran laugh considering the size and weight difference between the boys. Billy just grinned at his uncle over the top of Ian's head. The smaller boy was bursting with questions, and both Kieran and Billy knew they wouldn't stop until he had satisfactory answers. When Ian was practically in Kieran's face, Billy drew him back a couple of steps and wrapped his arms around him.

"Easy does it, bookworm. Uncle Kieran will answer your questions. No need to get in his face. I thought your family taught you respect for the hunter," Billy said into Ian's ear.

"Listen, fleabag," Ian hissed back. "This is important, and it must have escaped your notice, so look up and count how many floors there are to this library."

"Boys, no need to fight about this." Kieran pointed up. "Just look. You can see the three floors above this one."

Billy glanced up toward the ceiling and then looked at his uncle before looking up once again. Ian followed Billy's line of sight and then fixed his gaze on Kieran.

"Uncle Kieran, I only see two floors above this one," Billy said, looking back at his uncle.

"I can only see two additional floors as well, Hunter Kieran," Ian said.

Kieran looked at the two boys as if they were playing a joke on him. He turned and whistled toward the stacks on the far side of the room. A moment later Cory, followed by Kellen and Líadáin, emerged from the stacks.

"What's up, babe?" Cory asked as he approached his husband.

"Would you all look up and tell me how many floors you see above this one?" Kieran said to his family.

Cory, Kellen, and Líadáin all looked up toward the ceiling, not really understanding what Kieran was getting on about the number of floors in the library. It wasn't until they looked back down and gave their answers that the confusion began. Cory reported only seeing two floors while both Kellen and Líadáin said they saw three floors above them. Everyone in the group looked at Kieran in confusion.

"All right, Son, what's going on here?" Kellen asked.

"Active magic, or to be correct, the sight of those who have actively used magic. Neither Cory nor Billy have magic, Ian's magic is dormant, and for his and Billy's future, it's better that it stay that way. The rest of us are all active mages in a house where the use of active magic is discouraged save in an emergency," Kieran replied.

"Okay, so if there really is a fourth floor to this library, and you got a book from it that isn't normally available to the rest of the family, why aren't you looking for more such books up there instead of down here?" Ian asked, exasperated with his older cousin.

"Because, until you asked me where I got the book from, I'd forgotten that's where it came from. Great-Uncle always made sure I passed by a particular spot in the library any time he let me borrow a book like the one on the last male hunter. Oh bright mother, I bet that spot has a spell of forgetting on it," Kellen answered.

Kieran paced around the reading area of the library for a moment as if searching for something before he stopped in front of a statue of Beauty. He blinked a couple of times as if something was trying to make him look someplace else. He stepped back a few steps before stepping forward again. When he felt satisfied that he had the right place, he turned and faced his family.

"I take it you found the hidden entrance to the fourth floor, Kier," Cory said.

"Yes, and there is definitely a spell of forgetting on it. The spell isn't very powerful, but it's subtle, and it's Amethyst magic. I'm not going to break it, but I can give Ian and Billy the key to bypassing it. They can keep their memories of the entrance and the fourth floor," Kieran said.

"What about the rest of us?" Kellen asked.

"Neither you or Grams need to remember the place exists once we're done here, Dad. Besides, once Ian and Billy are old enough, I imagine that the library will move to wherever I establish the hunter school," Kieran replied.

"If you'll key us into the spell, then Billy and I can go up and explore the fourth floor and see what we can find," Ian said.

"Come here and I'll give you the key," Kieran said.

The boys crossed the room toward Kieran, and each took a hand he extended when they started to stop and turn away from the statue. Kieran drew them in close and then whispered a phrase to them. They suddenly straightened up and looked at the statue for a moment before moving forward and through the statue. Behind the illusion of a statue, they found an old elevator cage. They got in and started the elevator on its journey toward the fourth floor. The rest of Kieran's family looked at where the boys had vanished and then crossed the room to where Kieran stood. A sharp indrawn breath from both Kellen and Líadáin let Kieran know that the magic had whispered across their minds and coaxed them into forgetting what they'd seen. It raised an illusion of a lower ceiling in the room to hide the fourth floor from their sight. Cory just took Kieran in his arms and nuzzled his beard into Kieran's neck, making his husband giggle with the knowledge that the magic hadn't worked on Cory as well as from the tickle of the beard.

Kieran led his family back over to the reading table he had buried under books and got them to sit. Cory was the first to come around.

"Where did Billy and Ian get off to?" Cory asked as he snuggled Kieran into his lap.

"You don't have to pretend with me, Wolf. I know because of our bond that the spell of forgetting didn't work on you." Kieran grinned as he leaned in and stole a kiss from his husband while waiting for his father and grandmother to come out of the minor trance they were in due to the spell.

"You're being sneaky and giving the boys someplace nobody will disturb them when they want to sneak away," Cory said after their kiss broke.

"Well, they do have to share their room with a couple of other boys, and the whole hall is packed with boys in groups of four. There's no privacy for the occasional kiss or hug. As I recall, there's a private room up there that Great-Uncle used when he wanted to hide out from the rest of the family."

"You really think that they're like us, a bonded pair."

"Yes, they clicked that day we arrived. Just watch them closely the next time they come to our rooms. It's almost like looking into a mirror of us together," Kieran said.

Kellen and Líadáin came out of their trances about that time, and after remembering where they were, they looked around for the two boys.

"Where did Ian and Billy go?" they asked together.

"I sent them off to go be boys for awhile. Plenty of time for them to be locked in dusty old libraries when they're older. For now, they need to have some fun away from the grown ups. I think it's time we all packed it in for the day. What we're looking for is carefully hidden, and my eyes are tired from all the horrible penmanship I've had to read," Kieran said, stretching and grinding into Cory.

* * *

WHILE the older folk were gathering up their notes and leaving the library's ground floor, high overhead on the mysterious fourth floor, Ian and Billy were just emerging from the elevator. They exited onto a balcony overlooking the rest of the library.

"Okay, so where do we start looking, bookworm?" Billy asked.

"Hunter Kieran said he got the book on the last male hunter from the fifth set of shelves, so I guess we should start there, fleabag," Ian replied with a grin.

The boys made their way to the entrance to the fourth floor's stacks and counted in five sets of shelves. The books here seemed to match the one Kieran had in his suite so they began checking entries in books. The first books they checked were all written in foreign languages they didn't have a clue about, so they kept looking.

"Do you think there's an index or card catalogue around here someplace, bookworm?" Billy asked after a half an hour of looking for books in English.

Ian stood up and brushed dust off his pant legs. "Let's see if there's an office or something up here. I imagine the Archivist must have spent lots of time up here to escape the family squabbles."

The boys started walking up and down the rows of books until they came into an area with several tables and chairs scattered around like some ancient gentleman's sports club. Off to one side was what looked like an office door. Together they made their way toward the door, which they carefully opened. The door opened into a suite of rooms, the first of which was set up as an office of sorts. With a quiet reverence, they entered the room and shut the door behind them. One side of the room was dominated by a huge fireplace of beautiful marble, above which hung a painting of a beautiful woman with hair as dark as midnight and skin as pale as moonlight. Along the entrance's wall stood a heavy bookcase filled with books and scrolls. The far wall had a door leading into the rest of the suite, and the final wall was made of glass and looked out over the library.

"Maybe what we're looking for is here on these shelves, Ian," Billy said.

"Let's be careful. We don't know what other kinds of magic the last Archivist might have used to protect this place," Ian replied.

Together the boys started to carefully check the books on the shelves. The first shelf of books proved to be diaries of the last three Archivists. They found notes in the last diary about Kieran and his sister Rosie.

I have had the joy of finding two potential Archivists in the family of the late Huntress—her son, Kieran, and her middle daughter, Rosalind. They both have a love of history and family lore. The only drawback to either of them is that they have active magic, being of the main line of descent. Young Kieran would be my primary choice, but he's already been in training several years to become a tracker. Only rarely does this post go to a daughter, but if Rosalind could be persuaded to use her magic and then be free of it, she would be a perfect candidate.

Kieran came to me battered and bloody after his test to earn his tracker certification. He told me that the pack had broken the rules of the test and sent two shifters. I worry, the last time a pack broke the rules was during the time of the male hunter. There is an air of destiny about young Kieran. While I don't have magic, I am sensitive to it, and the boy is bursting at the seams with Silver magic. I don't know where it comes from. It can't be the boy's father, not with those amethyst eyes of his, but Kellen MacDonnell has never let me get to close to him. Kieran is a mystery for the next Archivist, since I do not believe that I will live to see the New Year.

Ian noticed that the last entry was in a very different hand.

I came up to say good-bye to Great-Uncle Jonas to discover he's gone quietly in his sleep. I know that he wanted me to take up his position as Archivist, and I would have enjoyed hiding here among all these marvelous books, but my magic calls me to other things. I have a destiny I do not want calling me out into the world. Someplace out there is the other half of my soul. To whoever takes Jonas' place as Archivist, I wish you much joy, but I hope you're not as alone as Jonas was. This will be the only entry I ever write in these journals. I hope they will remember me fondly if I'm ever written about in them.

Kieran Belle, son of Huntress Miranda Belle and a full Tracker of the House of Beauty

"Oh wow, Uncle Kieran was the last person to write in these diaries. He sounded sad that he wasn't going to get to do it full time," Billy said.

"That's because the Archivist is one of the few men in the family that gets to leave to go further their education beyond high school. They have to learn a lot of languages and how to maintain the archives and stuff like that," Ian replied.

"He's offering you his dream job, bookworm. I think you have some big shoes to fill," Billy said as he hugged Ian.

"Well, he's actually offered it to both of us. He didn't want me to be lonely like the last office holder. So we both have a lot to live up to, fleabag." Ian chuckled as he hugged back. "Let's see what's in these other books."

The boys dug into the books on the next shelf and hit a jackpot in the fifth book. Before them, was the story of *Beauty and the Beast* as recorded by the first known author of the tale, broken into sections and interwoven with notes from various chronicles of the family history.

Many of the entries were translations from the very first Archivist's chronicles. As they flipped through the book, they found the ending of the tale and the notes from the chronicles, and they were stunned by what they read.

BEAUTY'S TALE

She put on one of her richest suits to please him, and waited for evening with the utmost impatience, at last the wished-for hour came, the clock struck nine, yet no Beast appeared. Beauty then feared she had been the cause of his death; she ran crying and wringing her hands all about the palace, like one in despair; after having sought for him everywhere, she recollected her dream, and flew to the canal in the garden, where she dreamed she saw him. There she found poor Beast stretched out, quite senseless, and, as she imagined, dead. She threw herself upon him without any dread, and finding his heart beat still, she fetched some water from the canal, and poured it on his head. Beast opened his eyes, and said to Beauty, "You forgot your promise, and I was so afflicted for having lost you, that I resolved to starve myself, but since I have the happiness of seeing you once more, I die satisfied."

"No, dear Beast," said Beauty, "you must not die. Live to be my husband; from this moment I give you my hand, and swear to be none but yours. Alas! I thought I had only a friendship for you, but the grief I now feel convinces me, that I cannot live without you." Beauty scarce had pronounced these words, when she saw the palace sparkle with light; and fireworks, instruments of music, everything seemed to give notice of some great event. But nothing could fix her attention; she

turned to her dear Beast, for whom she trembled with fear; but how great was her surprise! Beast was disappeared, and she saw, at her feet, one of the loveliest princes that eye ever beheld; who returned her thanks for having put an end to the charm, under which he had so long resembled a Beast. Though this prince was worthy of all her attention, she could not forbear asking where Beast was.

"You see him at your feet, said the prince. A wicked fairy had condemned me to remain under that shape until a beautiful virgin should consent to marry me. The fairy likewise enjoined me to conceal my understanding. There was only you in the world generous enough to be won by the goodness of my temper, and in offering you my crown I can't discharge the obligations I have to you."

Beauty, agreeably surprised, gave the charming prince her hand to rise; they went together into the castle, and Beauty was overjoyed to find, in the great hall, her father and his whole family, whom the beautiful lady, that appeared to her in her dream, had conveyed thither.

"Beauty," said this lady, "come and receive the reward of your judicious choice; you have preferred virtue before either wit or beauty, and deserve to find a person in whom all these qualifications are united. You are going to be a great queen. I hope the throne will not lessen your virtue, or make you forget yourself. As to you, ladies," said the fairy to Beauty's two sisters, "I know your hearts, and all the malice they contain. Become two statues, but, under this transformation, still retain your reason. You shall stand before your sister's palace gate, and be it your punishment to behold her happiness; and it will not be in your power to return to your former state, until you own your faults, but I am very much afraid that you will always remain statues. Pride, anger, gluttony, and idleness are sometimes conquered, but the conversion of a malicious and envious mind is a kind of miracle."

Immediately the fairy gave a stroke with her wand, and in a moment all that were in the hall were transported into the prince's dominions. His subjects received him with joy. He married Beauty, and lived with her many years, and their happiness -- as it was founded on virtue -- was complete.

Beauty and the Beast, Jeanne-Marie LePrince de Beaumont, English translation, 1757

* * *

Dear Lord, the fabrications that went into crafting the happily ever after of Mother and her beastly prince. All of it was created out of whole cloth. The entire time Mother spent in that palace was spent trying to hide from the monster that impersonated the prince under a spell. Even in his human form, he was the Beast. Brutish, crude, and violent, nothing could redeem this monster of a shifter. One night, Mother stumbled into the dungeons searching for a hiding place for the night, seeking to escape his attempts to capture and rape her. In a cell far to the back of the dungeon, she found the real prince chained to the wall. She searched the dungeon until she found the keys to his chains, and then she returned and freed him from his bondage. She tended to him until he was strong enough to move on his own. Together they found a way to ambush and destroy the monster. To her dying day, Mother never spoke of how they managed to kill an Alpha shifter of such power. Father never spoke of that day either. I've gone back to the abandoned castle of the Beast, searching the ruins for some evidence of how they freed us from the terror of the Beast. I've concluded that they didn't actually kill the Beast. I'm no mage, I'm not even a hedge witch, but there are traces of a magic so powerful even someone ungifted like me could sense it. I touched the spot where the magic was still strong and saw a vision of a place and time I didn't know or understand. I saw people bowing to a man in strange metal clothes who had the look of my mother in his facial structure. If I had to guess, Mother used her spell to hurl the monster forward to another time where someone stronger could face the creature.

Entry from the first chronicles of the House of Beauty, translated from the original German in the 21st century.

* * *

The creature came out of nowhere and tore into my trackers as if they'd never fought a shifter before. I've never seen a shifter so dark in color before. This beast was huge and black, as the night itself. I closed with it as quickly as I could, swinging my great sword for its head. The creature swatted my blade aside as if it were a child's toy. It flung me through the air and came at me looking to tear me apart. I reached deep inside and drew on the magic my family is said to posses. Silver swirled from my hand and surrounded the creature. With a twist, the magic ripped the creature away as if he'd never been there to start with. I touched the spot where it had been and where magic still swirled. A vision filled my sight of the beast in a clearing facing off against a young man in silver armor, flanked by wolves, one the brightest silver and the other darkest black. I think this is what I was supposed to have done as the Hunter of the House of Beauty. I'm sorry some future descendant must undertake the task.

A first person account from the hidden chronicles of the first male Hunter of the House of Beauty, translated from the original Spanish in the 21st century.

* * *

"We need to get this book to Uncle Kieran." Billy found the words. "He needs to know that he's not facing some random dark Alpha shifter; he's facing the legendary Beast himself."

"I don't know how we get the book out of here. I can feel magic on them. It's like they aren't supposed to leave this room, never mind this floor. It might be better to bring Hunter Kieran up here instead," Ian said.

"We're—or at least you—are the new Archivist, so I bet you can take things out of this room if you want to, Ian."

Ian picked up the book and walked toward the door. He reached out to turn the knob, but it began to glow bright red and put off intense heat. He quickly retreated.

"There must be something I haven't done to prove to the spells that I'm the new guy on the job," Ian said.

"Hey, there's blank pages in the last diary after Kieran's entry. Maybe if you write something in the book the magic here will know you've got the job," Billy said.

They looked back to the beginning of one of the earlier diaries and found an entry much like what they'd been thinking about doing. They realized that Kieran's entry had sort of been an introduction to the book as the next writer.

Billy found a pen and a bottle of ink on the desk. He scooped up the last diary and brought it over. He set it on the desk, open to the page with Kieran's entry.

"Time to decide for real, bookworm. Do we want the job and the future Kieran sees for us like we told him we do, or do we want to forget all about it and be on our own with no magic and no shifting?" Billy said as he pulled the desk chair back to let Ian sit.

Ian sat in the chair and stared at the book, pen, and ink for a moment before glancing up at the boy he knew would eventually be his lover when they were older. His decision would affect both of their lives for the long run.

"If we do this, Billy, it's you and me together forever. There's no turning back, no splitting up, and no regretting we committed to this path," Ian said.

"In case you haven't already noticed, bookworm, it's already you and me forever. There's a mate bond like Uncle Kieran and Uncle Cory have growing between us. We're too young for the full effects of it, but in time, the only place I'm going to be found is at your side. The choice is dusty library or the open road, Ian. What do you want?"

"I want this, Billy. I want this dusty library and all the wonders it contains."

"Then make our entry in the book, Ian Belle-Cooper," Billy said.

"That isn't my name," Ian replied.

"It is now. We're not old enough for me to claim you as my bonded mate, Ian, but I'm staking my claim to you, and I hope you'll stake your claim to me and let me be William Cooper-Belle in these journals and eventually out in the real world as well."

Ian swallowed hard to keep back the tears of joy he felt. He grabbed the pen, dipped it into the ink, and began to write.

August 15, 2015

On this day, William Cooper-Belle, my life partner, and I, Ian Belle-Cooper, take up the duties of the Archivist of the House of Beauty. We have been asked to take up this task by Kieran Samuel Belle Oisín-Cooper, Hunter of the House of Beauty, and we hereby accept. We release all other candidates from this role to pursue their own dreams as we now pursue ours.

Both boys felt a tingle of magic as Ian made the last period in his entry and knew the library had accepted them as its new custodians. They left the journal open on the desk so that the ink could dry. Ian picked up the journal they needed to show Kieran and once more headed for the door. This time the door swung open before he'd even reached for the handle. When they were both back out in the reading area, the door swung shut behind them. Billy drew Ian in and gave him a quick kiss on the cheek.

"What was that for?" Ian asked. "Not that I mind you kissing me."

"A promise for our future together," Billy said with a smile. "Now let's go show Uncle Kieran what we've found."

25

While Ian and Billy were exploring the fourth floor, Kieran and Cory had returned to their suite of rooms. As Kieran crossed the sitting room to the table and chairs set up out on the balcony, Cory flipped the lock to the outer doors so that no one would disturb them. He had plans for Kieran and would tolerate no interruptions. He toed off his sneakers and then padded silently across the room to come up behind Kieran and wrap him in a tight hug. Kieran sighed and relaxed into Cory's embrace with a giggle.

"What's so funny, babe?" Cory asked.

"You trying to be all sneaky and silent. Even in socks, you walk like an elephant, and all your emotions flow down our bond like water down a drain," Kieran replied.

"Ah well, as long as you always know how much I love you, I'm happy to be a leaky sink."

"You have mischief in mind, Wolf. I can tell."

"Mmm, I might have a little bit of fun in mind," Cory whispered in Kieran's ear as he leaned in to run his tongue around the shell of that pretty ear.

Kieran shivered as first Cory's breath and then his tongue caressed his ear. He couldn't hold back the moan when Cory caught the lobe of his ear between his teeth and lightly tugged. Cory released the tender flesh for a moment and blew warm breath over the damp skin, making his lover tremble. Slowly, he nuzzled along Kieran's neck, eliciting shivers, sighs, and moans from his lover as he undid the buttons of the shirt the man was wearing, exposing the scarred but beautiful flesh beneath. He slipped the shirt down Kieran's arms, kissing and licking along the exposed flesh of the left shoulder before retracing his path, lifting the long ponytail out of the way so that he could trace across the exposed nape to repeat his treatment on the right shoulder. Cory slipped the mass of Kieran's ponytail over his shoulder, leaving his beautiful back bare. Slowly, he licked his way down Kieran's spine, taking occasional side trips to follow one of the many faint scars the crossed his lover's back. In order to continue his journey down Kieran's back, Cory had to kneel behind his lover. He slowly reached around, finished pulling the shirt from the waist of his lover's pants, and then unbuttoned the cuffs to pull the shirt free of the wrists. He teased his way down to the top of Kieran's jeans and then slowly turned his lover around while keeping his tongue pressed to the exposed flesh. Kieran shivered and moaned as Cory turned him around so that they were facing each other, but Cory didn't stop until Kieran was once again facing away from him. The next thing he felt was Cory undoing his belt and the fastenings to his jeans before they were eased down his body to pool at his ankles to reveal that he was wearing a jockstrap. Cory growled in appreciation of his lover's tight ass framed in the straps of the jock. The beautiful curves of Kieran's ass called out to be licked, and Cory began running his tongue over them from where they met the top of Kieran's muscular legs up to his waist. He closed in on the crease between the firm cheeks from the right-hand side before switching and starting over on the left side. Once he'd paid attention to both sides equally, Cory began to tease the crease of his lover's ass with tongue and beard. Kieran was whimpering with pleasure and beyond words as Cory began to spread his ass cheeks apart so that his tongue could have access to the hidden treasure in the center. If there was a coherent thought left in Kieran's head, it shorted out when Cory's tongue laved over his hole. He was holding onto the table for dear life as his husband ravished him with his tongue. His cock was rock hard, and his balls were drawing up as the need to release his load flooded his body without Cory ever coming near to touching his cock. Cory teased the muscles of Kieran's hole until they fluttered open, and let his tongue slide in to tease the inside of his lover. It was more than Kieran could take, and his body arched and tightened in orgasm. Cory caught Kieran as his lover went boneless with his orgasm. While Kieran recovered, Cory finished stripping his clothes off and carried him to the bedroom. He gently laid Kieran on the bed before beginning the tongue bath over again, starting at Kieran's feet and working his way upward until he'd brought his husband to a second hands-free orgasm.

Cory was just starting to remove his own shirt when a frantic pounding on the outer door interrupted. *Oh well, at least I gave Kieran plenty of pleasure before the hoards descended again,* Cory thought as he pulled his shirt back down and headed for the door to the suite. He glanced back, taking in the beauty of his sated husband lying naked on the bed. With a sigh, he went to open the door to the hallway and tell whoever was out there to go away. It seemed like a nice plan, which failed to take into account the two excited young boys on the other side of the door. They blew past him into the sitting room. Billy caught the look of annoyance on his uncle's face and then spotted the pile of clothes on the balcony. Ian was clueless and beginning to babble when a barely coherent Kieran wandered into the sitting room totally naked. Ian stopped in mid-word, blushed, and turned to face in the opposite direction. Billy turned his attention to Ian, while Cory swiftly crossed the room and ushered Kieran back into the bedroom. The two younger boys heard Cory admonish Kieran, "Clothes, babe, we have underage company." Ian looked at Billy with eyes as big as saucers. Billy was as amazed by Kieran's naked beauty, but tried to play it off to help Ian calm down.

"He was naked. I've seen the hunter naked," Ian was muttering.

"Hey, bookworm, it's not like you've never seen a guy naked before considering the showers in our wing are communal. Okay, so Uncle Kieran is a lot hotter than any of the boys in our wing, but he's just another guy," Billy said.

"But he's the hunter," Ian moaned. "It just seems so wrong to see him naked."

"He's human, Ian. He puts his pants on one leg at a time just like you do. I bet he's just as embarrassed at being caught naked as you are at seeing him naked."

"Actually, I'd be surprised if Kieran is embarrassed at all. He has a beautiful body that he likes to show off," Cory teased from the doorway to the bedroom.

"Shut up, Wolf. The boy doesn't need to be teased," Kieran said as he pushed Cory out of the way so that he could reenter the room properly dressed. "Sorry about that Ian, Billy. Cory left me a little out of my senses. I just hope that whatever brought you down here in such a state is worth all the fuss."

Ian gathered himself and picked up the book he'd dropped. "We found a really old record in a one of the journals that shares how the story of *Beauty and the Beast* was created, and it talks about what the first Archivist pieced together about Beauty's battle with the Beast." Ian spit out in one breath.

"Okay, that's important enough to forgive the interruption," Kieran said. "Sit down and show me what you've found, Archivist Ian Belle-Cooper."

"How did you know how I signed my entry?" Ian said, stunned by Kieran's knowledge.

"Because I was the last person to make an entry in those books, and your entry freed me from the obligation to have to go back and fill in all the details of my own life as hunter. Your magic is dormant and buried deep, Ian, but it leaves you with a sensitivity to magic being used around you and to ancient spells that have been laid over items to protect them. All of the spells in that library are delicate; active magic would destroy them all and the library along with them," Kieran said.

"That's why Great-Uncle Jonas wanted Rosalind to use up her magic and why—as much as he wanted you to be his heir—it wasn't possible. Your magic is different from the rest of the House," Ian said.

"Yes, Ian that's correct. Now tell me what you and Billy found."

"Beauty didn't kill the Beast," the boys said in unison.

"What?" Kieran asked, sinking onto the couch in shock. "That can't be right. Everything I've read says that she killed the Beast but would never talk about how she managed to do it. What did she do if she didn't use her magic to kill the Beast?"

"She used her magic to hurl the Beast forward in time," Ian said.

"How far forward did she hurl him?" Cory asked as he sat down on the couch and drew a stunned Kieran up against his body.

"To the age of the first male hunter. Didn't anyone record the man's name? You'd think someone would have written down his name. After all, he was the first guy on the job," Billy huffed.

"The Archivist to his successor did record his name. I found it in later book. He was called Simeon. Why do I have a feeling that history repeated itself and that Simeon did the same thing Beauty did?" Kieran asked.

"Because that's what happened. Simeon fought the Beast, but couldn't defeat him. He panicked and used the same spell Beauty had used," Ian said.

"So the dark Alpha out there in the forest isn't just some powerful shifter that wandered in and took over. The creature out there is the most powerful shifter in recorded history," Kieran said. "No wonder I've had nightmares about facing him since I was a kid."

"You're not facing him alone, babe," Cory said as he hugged Kieran tighter to him. "Billy and I will both be there at your side, just like prophecy says."

"I don't understand why he's out there lurking in the woods then. Why not come and attack us here at the house directly? I'm missing something. I've never understood why this house isn't warded to the max, yet the pack never emerges from the woods," Kieran said.

"They can't leave the woods; it's a part of the pact between the huntress and the Alpha. See, right here in the chronicles," Ian said as he flipped to a page he'd marked in the book.

I have discovered a terrible secret regarding Great-Grandmother's pact with the shifters of the forest. She gave her youngest sister to the leader of the pack as mate. From what I have been able to discover, Great-Great-Aunt Ophelia was totally without the gift of Silver magic, a very rare thing only three generations removed from the first of our family. The most terrifying part of this pact is that it must continue each time a new huntress takes over the family. She must give a non-magical sister or cousin of the same generation to the leader of the forest pack as mate, or the compact between these dark shifters and the House of Beauty will be broken. I am afraid for my twin sister; neither of us was born with the gift of Silver magic. Our eldest sister goes for the test tomorrow night, and if she becomes the huntress, then I fear my sweet sister is doomed to this horrid fate.

From the Second Chronicle of the House of Beauty, translated into English from the original French in the 21st century

"If this is how the pact is maintained, how is it holding right now? Mother didn't have any sisters, and all of her children had magic. Could Grandmother have made the pact with one of her siblings?" Kieran wondered out loud.

"It doesn't sound like it should have held up when your mother replaced your grandmother as huntress," Cory said.

"Ian, has there ever been a case like Mother's and Grandmother's where a huntress was injured and unable to continue in the field?" Kieran asked.

"How would I know? I haven't . . ." Ian's voice trailed off for a moment, and he got a far away look in his eyes, as did Billy. "No, Hunter Kieran, your mother and grandmother are unique in the annals of the House of Beauty," Ian and Billy said in eerie unison.

"How did they do that?" Cory asked.

"We are the Archivist, and we are connected to the knowledge of the library. Ask your questions, Hunter Kieran," the boys spoke together.

"Who did Huntress Camille take to bind the pact?"

"Her youngest sister, Theresa, was offered as the House of Beauty's side of the bargain," the boys answered.

"That would have been over fifty years ago. If the Alpha is killed and replaced by another Alpha, does the pact remain intact, or must the House of Beauty send a new person?" Kieran asked.

"Only if the Alpha is of a bloodline not bound to the pact. Only the death of the huntress or of the sacrifice can free the Alpha from the pact."

"Well, then if Great-Aunt Theresa is still alive, the pact would hold. Grandmother is still living, so her sacrifice would still be valid; the spell that created the pact still views her as the huntress. It doesn't explain how the Beast is bound in those woods though. He can't be of the bloodline of that pack."

"Is the pack of the bloodline of the Beast?" Cory asked.

Ian and Billy hesitated for a moment as if consulting some internal rulebook before answering. "Because you are the mate of the hunter, we shall answer. Yes, this pack like all the packs before them is of the bloodline of the Beast."

"That's how he's bound to the woods. The spell was worked on his bloodline," Cory said.

"That's not a good thing, Cory. Because either he was once able to move in and out of the woods, or he traveled here within the last couple of years," Kieran said.

"What make you say that, Kieran?" Cory asked.

"Billy. Think about how dark his wolf form is. A shifter strong enough to have and hold a midway form raped your sister. My mother died at the hands of a huge pack led by a very dark shifter. I think the Beast was loose and then made his way here. When he took over the pack in the woods, he became trapped by the spell of the pact. Even if Great-Aunt Theresa died, the pact wouldn't be broken, because Grandmother lives and still has her magic," Kieran said before he asked, "Would the pact spell still recognize Camille Belle as the huntress if she uses her one shot of Silver magic?"

"If Camille Belle uses her Silver magic, the pact will be broken until Kieran Belle brings a suitable sacrifice to the Grove of the Secret," came the eerie unison reply.

"I thank you for your advice, Archivist. I have no further need of your counsel at this time," Kieran said.

The distant look in Ian's and Billy's eyes faded, and the boys returned to the present. They looked confused for a few moments as they sat there staring at Kieran and Cory.

"It will take some getting used to, guys. I'm actually surprised that I could trigger the effect. Since Grandmother still has her magic, she's still the huntress. The enchantments around here shouldn't respond to me while she has magic. I'm not fully the Hunter of the House of Beauty. I'm going to have to put an end to that before I go into the forest," Kieran said.

"What do you want us to do, Uncle Kieran?" Billy asked for both boys.

"Stay here with Cory for now. I'm going to go goad Grandmother into using up her one shot of Silver magic, or actually, I'm going to go ask Grams to do it," Kieran said.

"Is that a wise thing to do, Kieran? Grams could get hurt," Cory asked.

"Silver magic isn't going to hurt Grams; she's the widow of the Silver Witch and the mother of his children. There's some Silver magic still in her bloodstream. Should be enough to protect her from Grandmother's one-shot spell. No, if anyone needs protecting from magic, it will be Grandmother," Kieran said with a malicious grin on his face.

Kieran went to search out Grams, Kellen, and Uncle Brom. It was time for the Oisín clan to have a little council.

26

Líadáin Oisín made her way across the expansive dinning hall the Belle family used for dinner. She went toward where Camille Belle held her minor court with several of the Matriarchs. Kieran had explained the secrets the boys had uncovered last night over a small family dinner in her suite. He was concerned that Camille knew that all the enchantments around the estate still only acknowledged her as head of the family and was using that knowledge to plot against her grandson. Líadáin was boiling with anger by the time Kieran had laid out all the evidence supporting his theory, including summoning Cory, Billy, and Ian to join them. He'd even put the two younger boys into Archivist mode to convince his father and uncle. By the time they'd finished their dessert, the younger boys were curled up together asleep on one of the couches, and even Kieran was beginning to fade. Wrapped up in Cory's arms, the couple was an older copy of the younger boys. Líadáin smiled at the memory before her frown returned as she thought of all the people, including her late husband and her youngest son, who'd plotted against Kieran all his life. Líadáin was tired of people plotting against her favorite grandchild; it was time some justice was delivered. She paused just outside of the group around Camille and drew herself up to her full height.

"Camille, it's time you and I had a conversation, grandmother to grandmother, about Kieran," Líadáin said.

"Líadáin, of course, please have a seat." Camille waited while Líadáin settled into a chair. "What did you want to discuss about Hunter Kieran?"

"Give some actual respect when you talk about him in that role, Camille. You're holding out on the young man you've proclaimed is the head of your family, and he knows it."

"I have know idea what you're talking about, Líadáin. I've given Kieran all of my support."

"But you haven't truly given him control of the House of Beauty; all the big family enchantments still only acknowledge you as the huntress. I wonder if that little fact is what got your daughter killed, never mind the slaughter of our granddaughters. Why didn't you use your Silver magic to prevent the accident that put you out of commission as an active hunter, Camille?" Líadáin asked.

"Because there was no one else to be offered in place of my sister Theresa to maintain the pact. Miranda was my only child, and she had the gift of magic. All the girls of her generation were gifted. Then, she married your son, and every one of her children came up gifted. I'd hoped that Kieran could be goaded into using up his magic so that he could be sent to take Theresa's place, but his magic proved different, and I figured one of the girls would have to sacrifice her magic and take Theresa's place."

"Then, Miranda died and the girls became more important as potential huntresses, but you still had the question of what to do with Kieran, because you knew he was more than just a gifted tracker-candidate."

"The boy was too talented for his own good, and then he came back from his tracker test with the first real proof that something was wrong with the pact. Two shifters attacked him that night, but the pact of the test allows for only one," Camille said.

"So you started sending the girls in to become the next huntress, knowing something was wrong. Why didn't you go yourself?" Líadáin asked.

Camille gestured for her hangers-on to leave them before she continued. "Because I was afraid that Theresa might be dead, and if I used up my magic, the pact would be broken until a new huntress made the sacrifice. I didn't think about the fact that the test of the huntress doesn't usually take place while the previous one is still living and still has her magic. If I give up my magic, the test must take place immediately; the full moon is only days away. If Kieran doesn't complete the test and make the sacrifice, the pact will be shattered forever."

"Camille, you need to let go of the magic and let Kieran take his rightful place as head of this family. His magic can't be exhausted, and if need be, there are cousins of his generation who can be sacrificed to the pact. I don't think he'll allow it to happen; his plan is to wipe out the entire pack, down to the last pup."

"Líadáin, that's been done before, but the next huntress must be tested, and the use of a pack of shifters makes the magic of the pact necessary."

"Camille, Kieran is the child of two very powerful magical families, and he's very gifted at adapting magic to suit his needs. He's fooled you all for years with the various ways he's used magic to enhance his skills. Now, he has all the power my husband once wielded; give him the last piece he needs to save the House of Beauty from itself."

"I can't take the risk of what happens if he fails," Camille said.

"Then, you leave me no choice, Camille. Your magic has to go so that Kieran can come into his full inheritance as the Hunter of the House of Beauty," Líadáin said.

"You'll have to kill me, Líadáin. I'm not going to waste my magic fighting you. I know your magic isn't over in one spell like mine is," Camille replied.

"Actually, Grandmother, Grams doesn't have to do anything," Kieran said from behind Líadáin. "The brother of Beauty gave your line the gift of one active Silver magic spell, and his line has always held the power to take it back. Give me your hand, and I'll make this as painless as possible."

"Your kindness will get you or those around you killed someday, boy," Camille said.

"It already has, Grandmother, but I choose to remain kind to honor those that have fallen. Now it's time for you to lay down your burdens and let younger shoulders carry the load," Kieran said as he took his grandmother's hand and withdrew her Silver magic.

With the removal of Camille's magic, Kieran found himself overflowing with a new power and perspective on the House of Beauty. The household enchantments locked on to him, and he could sense the bond of the pact. At the moment, he sensed it, the old bond attached to his grandmother shattered, but a new bond attached to him. It somehow took its place, as if the perfect sacrifice had already been on hand in the Grove of the Secret. It was a mystery for another time.

INTERLUDE: THE PACT REBOUND

In the heart of the dark forest lies the Grove of the Secret, where the newly proclaimed Huntress of the House of Beauty brings the chosen child of the Belle line. In this grove, the Alpha of the forest pack comes to accept his chosen mate. For over fifty years, Theresa Belle had served in this role, sacrificed to secure the peace between her family and the dark shifters of the forest. Unknown but long suspected by Camille, Theresa had died around the time of the accident that sidelined Camille as huntress. The magic didn't recognize a change of huntresses, because Camille still had magic, so it held until the day Kieran Belle Oisín-Cooper stripped away Camille's magic and claimed the full heritage of the House of Beauty. The magic shattered, alerting the Alpha of the pack that the old huntress was no longer in place. The time of the test was at hand.

The Beast felt the magic that had bound him to the forest since the day he'd challenged and killed the old Alpha shatter. However, much to his surprise, the binding spell reformed. He remained a prisoner in the forest.

"I do not understand this strange magic that binds me to this forest," he bellowed.

"Ancient One, it is the magic of the pact between the House of

Beauty and the pack. It binds the Alpha and the pack to this forest. We are bound by a blood spell tied to the lineage of the Alpha," replied the shaman of the pack.

"I am not of the lineage of your last Alpha. How does this spell bind me?" the Beast demanded.

"You are not descended from the line of our Alphas; they are descended from your line. Blood calls to blood and binds all of the bloodline," the shaman said.

"Then there is some ritual involved to seal this pact with each Alpha?" the Beast asked.

"There has been in the past. If the binding has broken, then the huntress who made the sacrifice is no longer among the living or has used her Silver magic. A new candidate will come to the test, and if successful, will bring a new sacrifice to the Grove of the Secret to meet with the Alpha and renew the pact," the shaman answered.

"The binding broke, but then it was renewed in an instant," the Beast retorted.

"Then the House of Beauty had a hidden huntress and a new sacrifice already in place in the grove. It is not required that the Alpha receive the sacrifice, only that one is made."

"Where is this grove?" the beast demanded.

"It is known only to the Alpha and his designated successor," the shaman replied.

The Beast's rage was terrible to behold as he ripped the shaman to shreds. He'd killed both the old Alpha and the one who came forward to challenge as the Alpha's chosen successor. The location of the Grove of the Secret was lost. There was no way for him to go and break the binding spell. He would have to wait for the last child of the bitch to come to him. He took little solstice in knowing that his opponent's hidden secret was exposed. The boy was already the hunter, and with his death, all the enchantments both of Beauty's line and of the cursed ancient Silver mages would break.

FIVE MONTHS BEFORE

Five shifters lay dead at her feet. She'd felt a shift inside her, but none of the expected additional powers came to her, and more of the pack was closing in on her. She swept around her with the silver sword Kieran had given her, slicing through any shifter that got within reach. They were circling her now; it wouldn't be long before they attacked her from all sides. A huge dark gray wolf pounced on her from the left, knocking her to the ground and jarring the sword from her hand. She whipped out a dagger and tried to protect herself, but they were all over her, and claws were tearing through her leathers. God, was this the pain Kieran had felt when the shifters had mauled him during his tracker test? There had to be something she could do; she couldn't die here, not like this.

The magic tingled within her, and a spell of ancient might came into her head. She knew her time as a huntress was over whether she cast it or the pack tore her apart. Therefore, Rosie reached out and grasped the spell, letting the magic flow. She vanished from beneath the pile of the pack and spiraled across the forest to crash into a grove that contained a cottage, a dormant garden, and the remains of a corpse that might once have been a woman. Biting back a scream of terror at practically landing on the corpse, Rosie rose up and made her shivering way into the cabin.

27

The ancient forest seemed gloomier than ever. Only two days after Camille's magic had been taken away, the full moon flickered through the waving branches of the trees. Dark shadows stretched from tree to tree, blocking all but the faintest hint of light. A young man stepped on the path leading to the heart of the woodland. The scene felt familiar to Kieran. Was it only four years ago that he'd stood here waiting for a shifter to come and begin the test for his status as a tracker? The dark forest didn't look any less daunting now than it had back then. This time he would follow the track to the clearing in the center of the forest to face the pack and its Alpha for the test of the huntress. There was a big difference for this test; he would not enter the forest alone.

At his left was the dark wolf that only a few hours ago had been Billy; at his right the bright and shining form of Cory in wolf shape. Kieran stood in his dark leathers, armed with not only his knives and new matching sabers, but also his father's silver long sword. He would have to start with the long sword since the sabers were heavily enchanted and the rules of the test only allowed minimal enchantments.

Behind him, he knew that his father, uncle, and grams were standing in silent support. They couldn't enter the forest, and unless he was victorious and broke the enchantment on the forest, Cory and Billy wouldn't be able to leave it because they shared part of the bloodline of the pack with their common descent from the Beast. Kieran drew a deep breath and then took the first steps along the path to his destiny.

The path ran straight through the forest to the clearing at its heart, and it took Kieran, Cory, and Billy only an hour to make the journey. Before they broke the cover of the forest, Kieran stopped Cory and Billy from going any further. He knelt between the two wolves and pulled them both close.

"I have to do this first part on my own. Once the first five shifters have gone down, then you can join in the fight. They're going to keep coming. Don't spare any of them, because they won't spare any of us," Kieran said to both wolves.

Both wolves whined but didn't move when Kieran rose, turned, and walked out into the clearing. When he stood near the throne of bone crafted by the Master, Kieran stopped. His anger rose when he saw the three human skulls, two of which were child sized. Here were the remains of Selene, Savannah, and Amanda. Callie's had been recovered from the edge of the forest nearest the house, but where were Rosie's remains? He would have all of his sisters back for proper burial.

"I am Kieran Samuel Belle, Hunter-candidate of the House of Beauty, and I've come for the test. Send forth your five chosen warriors, Alpha of the pack."

"Don't seek to fool me Child of Beauty, you passed the test of the huntress over a month ago when the minions I sent with the little owl attacked you. The magic of this forest tells the tale. The sacrifice made by the last huntress no longer holds us bound to this forest, but a new sacrifice by a new hunter does," came a growled response from the far edge of the woods.

"I have made no sacrifice; none of my generation meet the requirements for the ritual, and you've killed all of my sisters," Kieran replied through gritted teeth.

"Yet the sacrifice was made to and accepted by the forest. There shall be no test. Prepare to die Hunter of the House of Beauty," the voice called out.

The forest shifters poured out of the forest and raced to attack Kieran. He dropped into a defensive position and drew forth his sabers. The first shifter leapt to drive Kieran to the ground only to go flying in two directions as Kieran sliced it in half. His blades became a whirling wall of death, and shifter parts went flying in all directions. When it seemed as if the shifters would surround him—long after five shifters had died on his blades—Cory and Billy came racing out of the woods to tear into the shifters trying to get behind Kieran. Shifters howled and burst into flame from Cory's Silver bite or claws. Billy tore his victims apart with his greater strength. Soon, the pair of wolves was fighting off shifters right beside Kieran.

The number of shifters attacking doubled, and the weight of them drove the trio back for a moment. At one point, the shifters managed to separate Kieran from Cory and Billy, and he went down under their weight. Claws tore into his leathers, and despite the heavy enchantments, the claws reached the skin on his legs. Rolling to avoid a set of jaws trying for his hamstring, a bleeding Kieran reached a spot from which he chose not to be driven beyond. Silver magic swirled around him, driving back the shifters for a moment before it formed into his familiar silver armor, minus the wicked scythe blades. The shifters regrouped and came again. He began the dance of death. Ebony magic ripped across the clearing to blast Kieran from his feet, and the shifters leapt to try and pin him down, but Billy and Cory blocked their way. Kieran rose, and with a gesture, sent Silver magic racing across the clearing to burn anything with Ebony magic. Shifters burst apart as the magic cut through them, and at the edge of the forest, the magic hit a barrier of Ebony magic. It exploded, taking out a chunk of the forest.

Whirling back around, Kieran cut away several shifters trying to get close enough to take down Cory. Billy flashed past Kieran's shoulder and tore out the throat of a shifter going for Kieran's back. Kieran signaled to Cory and Billy, and the pair hit the ground at his feet as he set off a second Silver magic burst, illuminating the entire clearing and finishing off all of the shifters in the attacking force. A second bolt of Ebony magic came searing Kieran's way, but he was able to deflect it away.

"Come out and fight me, mage," Kieran called out. "I know you're the one behind most of the attacks against me on and off campus. I don't really know what you want from me, but I'm not going to let you keep attacking me or those I care for."

Silence greeted him.

28

The Master and the Beast stood watching the battle in the clearing. When he thought he had an opening, the Master threw blasts of raw Ebony magic in Kieran's direction, hoping to put the boy out of commission. Nothing he'd observed of the boy in class, on campus, or his escapes from lesser foes had prepared the Master for Kieran's power. The blast of Silver magic the boy had flung in his direction took just about everything he had. The best he could manage was to deflect it and dodge the trees that came crashing down around him. Then came the boy's challenge.

"Come out and fight me, mage. I know you're the one behind most of the attacks against me on and off campus. I don't really know what you want from me, but I'm not going to let you keep attacking me or those I care for."

"This is what you wanted, mage, a chance to take on the boy. If you defeat him, then your plans move forward while mine will be impeded," the Beast said.

"Yes, and if I lose to him, then you have your shot at freedom," the Master replied.

The Master drew his darkest shadows around himself and stepped out into the clearing to face the boy. It was easy to find the boy; he was a gleaming beacon of silver in the center of the clearing, standing next to the throne of bones. The Master stopped when he was about twenty feet away from Kieran.

"Well, I'd say the evil mastermind finally steps out of the shadows, but since you're wrapped up in them, that would be a tall tale," Kieran said.

"I'll give you the chance to kneel before me now, boy. Surrender to me and you will know only pleasure as my slave," the Master said.

"I know pleasure, and it comes freely from my husband. No slave can know pleasure, only a lack of pain. The only option here is which one of us will walk away from this place alive."

"When I walk out of here, boy, it will be with you on a leash," the Master replied.

"You aren't walking out of here alive," Kieran retorted.

"Then, as challenged, I call weapons for our duel, and I choose magic only. You will have to get rid of your weapons."

"Fine." Kieran began removing his weapons.

"Lose the armor as well, Mr. Belle," the Master added.

Silver magic swirled around Kieran, and his armor reverted to his now battered leathers. A nagging voice in the back of Kieran's mind said he knew the voice of the mage and the way he'd called him Mr. Belle. Only his professors at school called him that. He knew it couldn't be Professor Simms; the man was a Ruby mage. Professor Mason was an Emerald mage, so who could it be? At last, Kieran stood in just his leathers; all his weapons leaned against the throne of bones near his sisters' skulls. *Keep an eye on those for me, my sisters. I'll need them later.* Kieran silently pleaded to his sisters' spirits. He stepped forward to face the Master once again, and spread his arms to show that he was unarmed.

"Well, at least you can still follow directions, Mr. Belle, even if you do still have a smart mouth."

"It's been mentioned that my mouth gets me in trouble. It's a family trait on both sides. You might as well drop the shadows. I know who you are under them, Professor Jaynes," Kieran said.

The shadows unwrapped from around the Master, and he pushed

back his cloak to reveal that Kieran had guessed correctly. Before him stood his English professor, who gave him a mocking bow for having figured out the puzzle.

"What gave me away, Mr. Belle?" Professor Jaynes asked.

"Little things, Professor, like calling me Mr. Belle. What clenched it was referring to my smart mouth. Only two professors have ever commented on my snide comments. You and Professor Mason. No mage can fake the powers of another kind of mage, so I knew it couldn't be Professor Mason," Kieran replied.

"You are a star student, Mr. Belle; that along with your beauty sparked my desire to own you, and when Professor Simms offered to procure you, I couldn't resist. I grew leery of you when you gave your explanation of *Beauty and the Beast* and how reluctant you were to take it as your paper topic. I loved how you hid all kinds of tidbits in the paper you turned in, such a fascinating read. I had no idea how much truth was hidden in it until I discovered the Beast by accident."

"I don't really care, Professor. You've attacked me and mine. Your agents caused the death of my grandfather, and for that, I'm going to rip your heart out with my bare hands. Let's get on with the duel. I have a real monster to face," Kieran snarled.

Professor Jaynes made a gesture, and a wall of Ebony magic rose up behind him. Kieran mirrored him, and a wall of Silver magic rose up to match up and lock with the Ebony wall. The magic of the two walls swirled and formed into a dome of magic.

"Only the winner leaves this dome with his freedom," Professor Jaynes said.

"Only the winner leaves this dome alive," Kieran replied.

The two mages squared off, and the Master fired off a testing bolt of Ebony magic, trying to find out the power of Kieran's personal shields. He was caught by surprise when Kieran merely danced aside and let the bolt be absorbed by the shielding dome of magic. Kieran moved with fluid grace, and the spell he fired back wasn't a testing spell. Silver chains wrapped around his opponent and latched on with fiery hooks of Silver magic. Professor Jaynes screamed in pain and tried to muster a counter spell, but it was as if his own magic made the chains draw tighter. He watched in terror as Kieran approached.

"You should have heeded the warning I sent back to you with your dead apprentice, Professor. I am the Silver Witch, and your agents killed my predecessor and beloved grandfather. I'm going to do for you what I didn't do for Marissa when I trapped her in this same spell. I'm going to do as I promised and rip your heart out with my bare hand. I grant you a swift death," Kieran spit out.

Professor Jaynes screamed as Kieran's Silver-magic-wrapped hand slammed into his chest, piercing flesh and bone to grasp his heart. He felt Kieran grip his heart and squeeze before he tore it from the man's chest. Kieran looked up from the beating heart in his hand and watched as the spell, sensing the death of the victim, caught with tightened and incinerated the remains. Silver fire wrapped around Kieran's hand, burning away the heart and blood of his enemy. The magic in the dome swirled on last time before flashing pure silver and vanishing. Kieran staggered and fell to his knees as the vast use of magic caught up to him.

Across the clearing, Cory and Billy began to race toward him from one direction as more shifters poured out of the forest from the opposite direction. On hands and knees, Kieran didn't see either group heading his way. The howl of the approaching pack roused him to the danger headed his way. He pushed himself back up to his knees and raised his hands just as the first wave of shifters crashed into him, biting and clawing him. Cory and Billy crashed into the pile of shifters burying Kieran. Teeth and claws tore into the enemy shifters. From the bottom of the pile, a blaze of Silver magic came, driving off the pile and revealing Kieran in his full Silver magic armor, including the wicked scythe blades on each arm. Getting his legs under him, Kieran executed a powerful flip and landed on his feet, braced and ready to fight once again. A new dance with death began and continued until the corpses of shifters were piled high around Kieran, Cory, and Billy.

Out of the dark forest, a huge shape emerged. The Beast had finally come to fight. Kieran was reeling from blood loss, magic drain, and pure exhaustion. He braced himself to meet the Beast in combat.

29

———

Kieran, Cory, and Billy stood facing the massive figure of the dark Alpha in his midway form. Fur as dark as midnight covered muscle double Cory's size in his own midway form. Kieran looked at the face out of his childhood nightmares and froze. This could only be the legendary Beast, whom both Beauty and the last male hunter had faced and banished across time. Now the darkness stood before him.

"So the latest of the bitch's descendants comes to face me. Are you braver than the rest of your family, little boy?" the Beast growled at Kieran.

"I've slaughtered my way through your pack and you doubt my bravery?" Kieran tried hard not to let his fear show through.

"I can smell your fear, little boy. All that strength, power, and training, you went through, and it's all for nothing. You're quaking in your boots, just like the last man to face me. Will you banish me to face another as the bitch and the coward did?"

"The time for running is over," Kieran growled back.

"You're drawing strength from this mongrel who smells of my lineage but is polluted with your Silver magic. Then, there is the more interesting pup at your side. My direct progeny, even if he smells like your mongrel lapdog here. You must be the child of that little bitch I caught trying to get it on with the human boy. They were both so much fun to play with. To bad the boy was so fragile, but that's the trouble with pure humans, they break easily."

"This is between us, monster," Kieran shouted to try and drag the Beast's attention back.

"No . . . these two are much more interesting than you are, Child of Beauty. They are the key to prophecy. They're a set of keys that will either lock or unlock the great spell. Silver to relock the spell, Ebony to unlock it forever. You, little hunter, are merely the lock. The choice of key is mine." The Beast's tongue lashed across his maw like he was licking his lips after savoring a tasty morsel.

Kieran screwed down his fear of the image from his nightmares of just that happening and lashed out, aiming to take the Beast's head from his shoulders with the swing of the scythe blade attached to his left arm. The monster dodged and slammed a huge fist into Kieran's back, sending the tired hunter sprawling face first into the pine needles covering the forest floor.

"Stay down, little hunter. I'll deal with you once I've locked away your little pets."

Kieran pushed himself to his knees. "If you're hoping that your Ebony mage is going to help you, monster, you're out of luck, because he's already dead."

"It doesn't matter. Once I make the little Ebony pup bred your ass, the binding spell will be broken," the Beast snarled. "Then, your Silver mongrel will rip you apart to finish off the House of Beauty once and for all."

"Well, that's not going to happen," Cory growled, shifting to his own midway form.

"You have no concept of the power of my bloodline, you pathetic pup. I'm an Alpha of an original shifter line; it gives me control over all descendants of the bloodline regardless of how diluted the bloodline has become. Bow to me, both of you," the Beast commanded.

Kieran had made it back to his feet only to watch in horror as Billy shifted to a midway form and bowed down before the Beast. He turned to see Cory struggling to fight the reflex to bow to a superior Alpha. Deep down in Kieran, he felt the tug as well through his bond with Cory. Kieran drew himself to his full height and banished his armor and clothes. He stood naked before the Beast, Cory, and Billy.

"You're mistaken about the requirements that break the binding spell. I am the last of the prime line that cast the spell. An Alpha of a founding line is the required key to unlock the spell. Billy just proved he isn't an Alpha by bowing to the Alpha of his line. Take me if you can, monster," Kieran said.

The Beast whirled with incredible speed to lunge at Kieran, thinking that he was vulnerable in his naked state. As he grabbed the naked hunter, Kieran drove his right hand into the Beast's gut just below the ribcage. Wrapped in Silver magic, his hand cut through the monster's flesh. The Beast reflexively drew Kieran closer, trying to rip out his throat, but only succeeded in making it easier for Kieran to change his angle and drive his hand up toward the heart of the Beast. He transformed the Silver magic from blade to fire and burned away the Beast's internal organs. Claws began to dig into exposed flesh, but Kieran ignored the pain as he wrapped his left arm around the Beast to hold them together as the monster struggled to break free.

"Kill him, my children." The Beast's words were a command neither Billy nor Cory could refuse.

"You've lost, monster. Killing me without having bred me leaves the spell in place." Kieran bared his teeth in a fierce grin as Silver magic burst forth from his body.

The pair leapt for Kieran with Billy howling as he tasted Silver magic; he tried to sink his jaws into Kieran's thigh. The Beast was surprised when Cory stepped through the Silver magic. Cory shifted to his own midway form and pressed up tight against Kieran, sinking his raging hard-on into Kieran's ass. There was an increase in Silver magic as the two lovers joined, becoming one, physically and magically. The Beast felt the mating bond between the two become a physical thing as Cory's strength flowed into Kieran.

"I am the Silver Shifter who is the key that closes the lock that is the Silver Witch. Together we make the binding. This night we choose to reseal the binding of old. To one animal form are those who were born to shift their shape bound. By the sacrifice of this Alpha of a first line, we bind and seal." Cory's voice was an odd cadence.

"I am the Silver Witch who is the lock that closes at the will of the Silver Shifter. Together we make the binding. This night we choose to reseal the binding of old. To one animal form are those who were born to shift their shape bound. By the sacrifice of this Alpha of a first line, we bind and seal," Kieran's voice answered.

The three became a blazing column of Silver magic that shot skyward and touched the moon before spreading to wrap around the world. Shifters everywhere felt the power of the binding spell clamp down on them and howled, hooted, growled, or made whatever cry of longing and pain as they felt the loss of potential freedom.

When the spell was completed, the Silver magic vanished, leaving Kieran standing only because Cory was holding him upright. Of the Beast, there was no trace.

* * *

BILLY SHIVERED and forced himself to finish shifting back to human form. He stood facing away from his uncles who were still locked in an adult position he shouldn't be watching. Eventually, he coughed to draw their attention.

"Umm, Uncle Kieran, Uncle Cory, are you guys done being a mystical lock and key?" Billy asked.

"Just a moment, Billy," Kieran said as Cory released him.

Billy felt the tingle of Silver magic he'd grown used to around Uncle Kieran, and then he felt a daypack being handed to him. His uncles had insisted he pack a change of clothes for moments like this. It suddenly dawned on Billy that he was as naked as his uncles. He practically ripped open the pack to drag out his clothes, and he dressed faster than he ever had in his life. He could feel the blush heating his face as he turned to face his uncles who were both at least dressed from the waist down.

"I think our nephew is shy, Wolf, although I bet if Ian were here, he wouldn't have been quite so quick to get dressed," Kieran teased.

"Nope, I'd have been even faster, Uncle Kieran," Billy replied. "Honestly, we're saving that stuff until we're of age. We change separately in the bathroom, and we each sleep in our own beds."

"Relax, Puppy. I'm teasing, and I'm glad you two are saving things until you're older. Now, on a serious note, what has to be done next is something you shouldn't see or be involved in. Your part is done. Go back to the clearing and carefully take the three human skulls out of that horrible throne and put them in our packs. Then, follow the trail we came in on back out of the forest. You will have to wait at the edge of the forest until I can bring down the magic binding the pack."

"Those skulls belong to your sisters, don't they, babe?" Cory said.

"Yes, Selene, Savannah, and Amanda. I don't know where Rosie's is, but it's not in that clearing," Kieran replied.

Billy gave both of his uncles a quick hug before heading back out into the clearing. Over his shoulder, he said. "Don't worry, Uncle Kieran. I'll be very careful with my aunts' remains." Then, Billy was gone. Kieran and Cory finished dressing, Kieran in a second set of his tracker leathers and Cory in heavy denim clothing and hiking boots.

"Kieran, do we really have to slaughter all of the rest of the pack? All the males and the Beast are dead; there's only females and pups left. Haven't we done a enough killing for a lifetime?" Cory asked.

"I wish I could spare them, Cory. They're as tied into the spell as the males and the Beast were. One side or the other has to be eliminated for the pact to be dissolved. I don't know about you, but after everything we've done, I'd like to live a lot longer," Kieran said.

"Yeah, I want you around for a long time," Cory said, hugging Kieran close. "Let's get this over with."

Kieran found the track to the lair of the pack, which was actually a small village deep in the woods. Tidy little cottages ranged around a clearing, where all of the remaining shifters were gathered. Young pups, gravid females, older females, and males too old to be of use in a fight. Kieran and Cory stepped into the village clearing and waited for the remains of the pack to focus on them.

"The Beast and your males are dead. Who ranks highest in the pack?" Kieran called out when he had their attention.

An aged female and limping male made their way to the front of the remaining pack and forced themselves to shift back to human. When their shift finished, they rose to face the Hunter of the House of Beauty and his shifter mate.

"I am the *Cainteoir don phacáiste*, speaker for the pack. This is *Eolas ar an phacáiste,* knowledge of the pack. We will lead now that the Ancient One is no more. What would you have of the pack, Child of Beauty?" the aged female said.

"How many of those now gravid with pups were bred by the Beast, *Cainteoir*?" Kieran asked.

"All of those you see, Child of Beauty. The Ancient One made sure that no other male came near a female in her season," the speaker admitted.

"And how many of these pups are the get of the Beast?" Kieran asked, feeling sick to his stomach.

"Again, Child of Beauty, since the coming of the Ancient One, no male save he has mounted a female when she entered her season. All of these pups are of the direct blood of the Ancient One."

"I'm truly sorry to hear that, *Cainteoir*. I had hoped there might be those I could spare. I promise to make this as swift and painless as possible for the pack."

"Child of Beauty, the pact between your house and the pack is still in force. A sacrifice was made and accepted on behalf of the current huntress. We cannot leave this forest," the lame man said.

"*Eolas ar an phacáiste,* I am the Hunter of the House of Beauty, and I did not make the sacrifice, although I know one was made. Unfortunately, my mate and nephew share the lineage of the pack and are trapped here as well unless the pact is dissolved."

"The House of Beauty would purge this pack in order to remove the pure taint of the Ancient One? There is another way."

"What is this other way, *Eolas ar an phacáiste*?" Kieran almost begged.

"You could sterilized the entire pack, from the pups in the womb to those males still fertile enough to bred. Then we will die out naturally," the lame male said.

"That leaves my mate and nephew trapped in here until they die as well. This is not an acceptable solution," Kieran replied.

"Then go to the Grove of the Secret and give magic to the one who has none," the speaker said.

Kieran started to say he didn't know where the grove was when the knowledge flooded his mind. Along with the location also came the awareness that giving the sacrifice magic wouldn't be enough to break the pact. The pack still had to die. Kieran closed his eyes for a moment, and when he opened them, they were pure silver. He raised his hands, and Silver magic glowed around them.

"I'm truly sorry, but the protection of the House of Beauty is withdrawn. I am Kieran Samuel Belle Oisín-Cooper, Silver Hunter of the House of Beauty and the Silver Witch. By my hand and magic, I pronounce your death sentence and carry it out."

Silver magic leapt from Kieran's hands and struck every shifter of the pack between the eyes, killing them instantly. Kieran wept tears of silver fire as he struck down the pack. When it was done, he turned on his heels and walked to the path that lead to the Grove of the Secret. Cory stayed behind, knowing that his husband and mate needed time and had to face the Grove of the Secret alone.

30

Kieran entered the secret grove hidden away from the community of the shifters. He felt the tingle of magic as he crossed the boundary. In the center of the grove stood a cottage with a small garden plot in which a figure moved, tending the flowers and herbs growing there. The shape of the figure seemed familiar to Kieran as he moved closer. Hair as dark as his own hung in a braid over the figure's left shoulder, and the floppy hat this person wore obscured their face with shadow. Kieran called out so that he wouldn't scare the person by suddenly appearing by their side.

"Hello, I'm Kieran."

"I know who you are, silly," a familiar voice called out to him. "I've been waiting for you to come and find me, Brother."

Kieran stopped in his tracks. It wasn't possible. He'd seen her die, buried under a pile of shifters. Her throat had been torn out, and her sword had come to him when summoned, which it shouldn't have done if she was still alive. This couldn't be his beloved sister Rosie.

"Who are you?" Kieran called back.

"Did the shifters hit you so hard you don't know your own sister, Kieran?"

"You can't be who you sound like. Her sword came to me and showed me her death. It wouldn't have done that if she was still alive."

"It would if part of the spell that saved me also severed my connections to magic. It was the price I had to pay to survive."

The mystery woman turned to face Kieran as she removed her hat to reveal the familiar features of his beloved sister Rosie. Shock froze him for a moment before he was racing across the distance between them. He swept her up into a hug that lifted her off her feet. He spun her around until they were both dizzy.

"Kieran, stop spinning. You know I hate when you do that."

"Bright goddess, it really is you. How is it possible, Rosie? How are you here?"

"My one shot of Silver magic. I used the spell to shift me to the nearest safe place in the dark forest. I woke up to find myself in this grove and unable to leave," Rosie said.

"No, you wouldn't be able to leave once you no longer had magic. It's the nature of the Grove of the Secret. This place was used to maintain the pact between our family and the shifters. Every generation, the huntress would bring a relative with no magic here as a symbolic mate to the pack Alpha. The relative was always infertile, so there couldn't be any children."

"I'm not infertile, Kieran. I've had my—"

"I don't need to know, Rosie. It's because you lack of magic that you're trapped here in this grove. Are you alone, or is there another trapped here? I know Grandmother left her sister out here when she became huntress, but that was ages ago. I couldn't find any reference to Mother having done the same thing."

"I'm the only one here. I think our great-aunt was the last one to occupy the cottage; everything in there is about as old as the stuff Grandmother prizes."

"Well, it's time to get you out of here and back home. I have someone I want you to meet."

"I don't have magic anymore, Kieran. If what you've said is true, I'm here for the rest of my life."

"Oh, little sister, how I've missed your lack of faith in my men's magic. I'm the head of the family now. The pact shattered when I put down the last pup of the dark pack. The magic of this place is already fading and is easily swept away."

"You're the Huntress of the House of Beauty?"

"The Hunter of the House of Beauty, and more. I'm also the Silver Witch, and after all that's gone down over the past couple of weeks, I've become that old legend Gramps always talked about, the Silver Hunter."

"My, you've been busy since you escaped. You'll have to catch me up," Rosie said.

"I will, because there's a lot you've missed out on, being dead and all." Kieran laughed as he scooped his sister up and swung her around again.

With the wave of his hand, the warding spell shuddered and collapsed. Kieran led Rosie to the path leading back to the main house, and they stepped over the boundary together. Rosie laughed and slipped her hand from Kieran's and started racing down the path toward home.

"Last one home has to do all the explaining to Grandmother," she called out over her shoulder with a laugh.

"You'll have to do all your own explaining, Sister," Kieran called back as he passed her.

"No way, you've never been that fast," Rosie remarked as she pushed to catch up with her brother.

As they came around a bend in the path into a small opening in the trees, a handsome blond man stepped out of the woods and caught Kieran in an embrace that quickly became a very intimate kiss. Rosie stopped dead in her tracks as she realized the man kissing her brother was a shifter. She reached for the knife at Kieran's belt, but he moved with a grace much like their father. He turned in the blond man's embrace so that he was facing her and his weapons were out of reach.

"Oh no you don't, little sister. No sticking pointy silver weapons in my husband," Kieran admonished. "This is one of those things we have to catch up on."

"Did you say husband?" Rosie asked at the same time Cory was questioning him about calling this young woman sister.

Kieran grinned impishly at his sister and snuggled against his husband's chest.

"Corwin Oisín-Cooper, I'd like to introduce you to my not-deceased sister, Rosalind Oisín Belle. Rosie, this is my shifter husband, Cory." Kieran chuckled as Cory growled in his ear.

"It's a pleasure to meet you. Kieran has talked a lot about how special you were to him," Cory said while keeping Kieran close.

"I'd like to say the same thing, but Kieran and I have a lot of catching up to do. Like how you ended up married to a shifter?"

"We met at school and one thing led to another. We fell in love, discovered we were each other's mortal enemy, and said screw it because we loved each other more than opposing heritages between us," Kieran replied. "Oh yeah, there was Gramps' ancient prophecy that said we needed to be together in order to defeat the Beast."

"This is more than I can take. A shifter with free range of the family estate? What's next? Kieran moving the family some place else?" Rosie was close to screaming.

"Let's go back to the house, Rosie. Dad, Grams, Uncle Brom, and Grandmother will want to see you. We can talk when you've had a chance to catch up on everything that's happened since you took the test."

"I have as much right to lead this family as you do. More so since I'm a Huntress of the House of Beauty and took the test before you."

"Actually you don't, Rosie, but I'm not going to argue with you out here. I've been out in these woods all night. I've fought or just plain slaughtered the pack. Men, women, and children. I'm not the big brother you knew before, Rosie. That person died the day you went to take the test without my support. I'm the head of the House of Beauty, and I won't tolerate a challenge."

"I passed the test, and I'm the oldest living daughter of the last huntress; leadership of the family is mine by birthright."

"You're wrong on so many counts, Sister. Mother was never actually the huntress; the powers that make a true huntress never passed to her, because Grandmother never used her magic while mother was alive. I stripped Grandmother of her magic; you've used yours. Neither of you is qualified to lead this family by all the ancient traditions of this house," Kieran replied.

"As much as I love you, big brother, you can't lead this family. No man has ever truly led this family," Rosie retorted.

"It's time to go home so you can let the family know you're alive, and then we will find a role for you in my plans for the future of our family." Kieran's tone brooked no argument, and he and Cory turned, starting back toward the mansion.

* * *

TWO NIGHTS after Kieran's victory over the Beast, the House of Beauty laid to rest the mortal remains of his sisters—Selene, Savannah, and Amanda—beside the remains of his sister Callie and their mother Miranda. A cousin, who was a minister, carried out the funeral service. Kieran did his best to hold back his emotions as he always had before the women of his family. It wasn't until the last ringing passages of scripture that Kieran felt the tears begin to escape his control. When the final prayer had been said, Kieran walked out of the family chapel and back to his suite, where he collapsed in tears and sobs against Cory. Now that his sisters were laid to rest, he could finally let go of his grief and mourn them.

31

A week had passed since Kieran's defeat of the Beast, his discovery of Rosie in the Grove of the Secret, the burial of his sisters, and the departure of the Oisíns. The House of Beauty was in disarray as they attempted to adjust to the new reality. Kieran had been closeted in meetings with Grandmother Belle, Rosie, and several of the senior Matriarchs discussing the future. Factions were forming, and he knew the Council of Matriarchs had also been meeting without him present, debating his suggested course of action for the future of the House of Belle. His grandmother, Camille Belle, was still a formidable woman, with opinions of her own regarding the future of the family and their duties as the foremost hunting family. His plan set her on edge, and she was digging in to oppose it, because it meant leaving her home of nearly eighty years. He was sitting curled up in Cory's embrace on a sofa, in the suite reserved for the Huntress of the House, thinking. He was pulled from his thoughts by a knock on the door to the suite.

"Enter," Cory called out as he stroked Kieran's hair to keep his husband relaxed.

The door opened, and Rosie, Kieran's beloved younger sister, poked her head in.

"Kieran, can I speak with you in private?" Rosie asked.

"Come in, Rosie. This is as private as it gets. I don't have secrets from Cory," Kieran replied.

"Okay. I wanted to offer a suggestion for a compromise with Grandmother," Rosie said.

Kieran snuggled in tighter against Cory, hiding behind his own hair, as his sister pulled a chair closer to the sofa. He'd developed a weird tick over the last couple of days due to the stress of dealing with his grandmother and the Matriarchs. He tried to make himself relax, but Cory merely pulled him in tighter.

"Sorry, even though I'm head of this family now, she still has a way of making me feel like a little boy again."

"I never understood her hostility toward you, Brother. It was never rational, and it only got worse after Mom died," Rosie said.

"The list is so long, Sis. Trust me, Mom's death wasn't what she was angry with me about. She went over the edge when her brothers died with Mom. If she'd had her way, I'd have been on Mom's last hunt with her. Never mind I had barely started my training as a tracker. I'm the one who should have come home in the body bag, not her brothers and certainly not Mom." Kieran turned and tried to burrow beneath Cory.

"I'm sorry, Kieran. I know you were miserable here. We all missed you when you ran away, but most of us understood why you did it. I think Amanda was the only one who never really understood, but considering how young she was, it was forgivable that she was mad at you for leaving without saying good-bye."

"I wanted to say good-bye, but there wasn't time, and I didn't dare risk getting caught by the Matriarchs. I wanted to be here when Selene tested. I begged Dad to let me surrender to Grandmother when he told me you were going to the test before your time. He wouldn't let me. Told me you wouldn't want me to do that."

"He was right about that, Kieran. You escaped, found the man of your dreams, and had a chance at being happy. I still want you to be happy and free," Rosie said.

Kieran had surfaced, pushed back his hair, and turned to face her, but he was still snuggled in tight to his husband's chest, and Cory wasn't letting him go. She tried to hide a smile over how adorable her brother looked snuggled up with his husband. It didn't help when Kieran caught a glimpse of her hidden smile and stuck his tongue out at her. Laughter erupted from both of them, and Cory merely sighed. These two could reduce each other to giggles with a look.

"You said something about a compromise between Kieran and your grandmother?" Cory prodded when the giggles had gone on for several minutes.

Rosie drew in a deep breath to control her giggles. "Yes, let her keep this place; it's her home. Better yet, let me stay here to run the finishing school you want for your regional hunters and huntresses. It's my home as well, and as Huntress of the House of Beauty, I have the right to determine my own future."

At the fire in Rosie's voice, Kieran sat up straight, silver fire flashing in his eyes at her challenge. Cory was as alert as Kieran, and his amber eyes flashed a warning at Rosie. She drew herself up, refusing to back down from her position.

"You may be a huntress of the House of Beauty, Rosalind, but I am the Silver Hunter and head of this family. I know about the senior Matriarchs' plan to form a breakaway group centered here and on you. You all have no secrets in this house. Have you stopped and wondered why I haven't given you back your one shot of Silver magic? I could, you know, I'm the Silver Witch, heir of the woman who gave birth to both lines. I didn't do it, because I knew the traditionalists would rally around a daughter of the main line."

Rosie cringed back in fear as Kieran began to glow. His anger grew. The look of fear was what snapped Kieran out of his anger, because it was the one thing he'd never wanted to inspire in his sisters.

"Part of your advice is sound, Rosie. I don't need the money this estate would bring at sale. Grandmother will never support me if I don't let her keep something she values. I'm not sure about using this place as the finishing school for future hunters and huntresses, because our enemies already know where it is and I have to no desire to find another pack of shifters willing to make a deal for its protection."

"Actually, if you can ward this place, we can just let shifters roam into the forest and then use them for hunting practice without having to reestablish the pact."

"Wild shifters might be a better plan. We don't owe them anything, and we can test more than one hunter at a time. All right, Rosie, you have a deal with just two conditions in exchange for my giving you and Grandmother this place."

"Why do I hear wedding bells in my future?" Rosie looked at Cory for support.

"Don't look at me, Rosie. I support Kieran in this. I want lots of Belle nieces and nephews to spoil."

"Ugh, sappy love. I should have known you'd gang up on me," Rosie said.

"You and I are the last of the main line, Rosie. Your first-born child will become my official heir, superseding all my other arrangements with the cadet branches. I'm not going to arrange your marriage. I'm not even going to force you to get married. Just pick someone worthy to be the father of your children," Kieran said.

Rosie sighed and nodded her head. "Fine, I'll keep the line going, and I'll even bring my choice to Arkansas so you can approve or disapprove of him. What's the other condition?"

"All of the Matriarchs who support splintering the family by supporting you as a rival must step down. They will retire to the various estates in Europe, never to return to America."

"It's a deal," Rosie agreed without hesitation.

Kieran stood up and opened his arms to his sister. Rosie bounced out of her chair and wrapped herself around her brother. She felt herself wrapped in a double embrace as Cory hugged them both. Kieran looked down at her with a goofy grin on his face.

"You'll get used to it, Sis. Cory and I are a package deal, but I have a request to make of you as the new headmistress of the Belle Academy of Hunting," Kieran said. "I want you to seal off the library until Ian and Billy return here to take over the archives. They are Great-Uncle Jonas' true successors, and I've confirmed them as such."

"I'll do it on the condition that you agree to send me potential hunters and huntresses who aren't related to the House of Beauty. I don't think we should hoard our training anymore."

"I agree with you on that one, Rosie. Now I think it's time to go face Grandmother and see if she'll take the bait."

* * *

KIERAN, Cory, and Rosie walked down the hallway to Camille's quarters. Kieran knocked on the door to his grandmother's suite. It creaked open, and the face of one of the younger cousins peered out. Seeing Kieran, she opened the door wider and bowed to him.

"I've come to speak with the Huntress-emeritus," Kieran said.

"I'll see if she will receive you, Hunter Kieran," the girl replied.

"Of course I'll see Hunter Kieran, girl. Send him in," Camille's voice called out.

Kieran and his party entered Camille Belle's elegant sitting room, tastefully decorated with heirlooms handed down over the generations from huntress to huntress. Camille herself was seated in a high-backed chair of Victorian provenance; legend said it had been a gift from the queen for services rendered.

Kieran glanced around the room quickly before focusing on his grandmother. This formidable woman had controlled his life since before he was born. Even though he was now the true head of the family, she still scared a part of him as if he was the little boy or even the teenager she'd dominated and hated. He drew strength from his bond with Cory and the presence of his sister.

"Honored Grandmother, thank you for taking the time to see us," Kieran said with a small bow to the seated woman.

"It gains me nothing to make you cool your heels, Kieran. I've acknowledged you as head of this family and tried to make up for some of my past actions by supporting your plans for the future. I'm willing to listen to what you have to say as you've been willing to listen to what I've had to say, even if all you really wanted to do was flee the room."

"You know me well, Grandmother. I listen because you have

something I can only hope to have someday. You have the wisdom that comes from age and experience. Right now, I have knowledge that spans the ages on Father's side but not the wisdom needed to use it correctly. I've come to offer you a compromise that I hope will keep the peace in our family."

"You have wisdom, Grandson, to know that you lack experience. Your mother would be proud of the man you have become. Please sit. I will listen to your proposal."

"Is it safe to sit on the furniture, Grandmother? I'd hate to break something given to the family by King Solomon."

"Now you're being cheeky, boy. There's nothing older than Victoria's reign in this room. Sit. The couch is sturdy enough for you and your husband. Rosie, come sit beside me here."

Kieran and Cory settled on to the couch, an Edwardian settee from the look of it, and waited for Rosie to settle in beside their grandmother. Camille sent the cousin attending her to fetch tea and cookies.

"After a few discussions with Rosie and many with Cory, I've decided it isn't worth the fight to make you sell this place and move. Rosie also pointed out that this place with proper warding spells around the main buildings would actually make a good location for my proposed finishing school for hunters and huntresses. Rosie asks to be in charge of the school, but I'd like to add a twist to our agreement. I'd like Grandmother to administrate the school and train a select group in the administration of the vast wealth of the family."

"You want me involved in the future you envision for the family?" Camille said in surprise. "I thought you'd rather I retired to some small country home to be forgotten in all, save a name in the chronicles."

"You've been running the family business empire since you were a young woman, Grandmother. It would be foolish of me to retire you out of the financial end of things. Besides, someone needs to inspire a little fear in future generations of hunters and huntresses. Rosie and I are too soft to do that right now," Kieran replied.

"What about the stubborn faction that opposes all the changes you propose?" Camille asked.

"Exile back to Europe, where each branch of opposition will be given a different estate. We need to spread the family presence out as much as possible. I'm going to do a ritual to restore the Silver magic to each branch of the family. It should last several generations before it will need to be renewed," Kieran said.

"A masterful plan, Kieran. You are showing wisdom. I agree and accept your plans. In truth, Kieran, I would have given into your plans in the end. This place has many happy memories for me, and I hated the idea of parting with them. I hope you will come to forgive a stubborn old woman someday," Camille said.

"Perhaps in time I'll come to forgive you for the terror you inflicted on my childhood, but for now, you'll have to make do with my respect for your wisdom and experiences. Thank you for your support, Grandmother. I will see you tonight at the council's meeting."

* * *

KIERAN HAD SENT a couple of family members into the clearing at the center of the forest to clean up all the bones and corpses. They gathered them into a pile around the throne of bones. When all the remains had been gathered, they'd poured gasoline on the pile and set it on fire to cleanse the forest of its dark taint. Other family teams had gone to the shifter village and done the same thing. On the night of the dark of the moon, Kieran led a procession made up of a man and a woman from each branch of the family. He'd studied the family records, and with Great-Aunt Desdemona's assistance, had paired up couples that were far enough apart to marry without breaking laws. These couples would form the new Council of the House of Beauty. They would establish the regional houses and oversee all hunting activities in their regions. Once a year, they would come to Little Rock for a general council meeting with Kieran or his successor. Tonight, these couples would be touched with Silver magic, which would pass on down the generations. Tonight was just part of the new beginning for the House of Beauty.

32

Once everything had been settled and set in motion on the Belle estate, Kieran, Cory, Ian, and Billy had returned to the Oisín compound on the Maine coast to spend the rest of the summer. One night on the beach, Kieran stood in a circle of power and cast the spell that would set the potential for Silver magic in the exiled lines of the Belle family. The family spent time making arrangements to move to Arkansas and plan for the future of the lineage of the Silver Witch. During their final week in paradise, Kieran, Cory, Ian, and Billy were packing up their belongings for their return trip to Arkansas. To Cory, it seemed as if Kieran didn't want to leave Maine . . . or was it just the Oisín estate he didn't wish to leave?

"We could keep this place, Kier. You don't have to sell off all of your memories."

"I wish that was true, Wolf. Our enemies know about this place, so it's never going to be as safe as it was before Marissa destroyed the original wards. Better to turn it over to the National Park Service than try to maintain it."

"What about Grams? Where will she go?" Cory asked.

"She and Uncle Brom are coming with us to Arkansas. Uncle Brom found a place for sale up in Eureka Springs that he and Grams are going to turn into a bed and breakfast as well as setting up a store to sell his creations. They're both going to take Grams' maiden name as their last name," Kieran replied with a sigh.

"Well, they won't be that far away from us then. We can visit on weekends," Cory said, trying to cheer Kieran up.

"We won't be able to visit all that often, Cory. I'm sure we'll be busy taking the boys to various activities," Kieran said with a look at Ian and Billy. "There's also the fact that I'm now the Hunter of the House of Beauty; the last thing I want is to put Grams and Uncle Brom in danger.

"Babe, don't cut yourself off from Grams and Uncle Brom; they can protect themselves, especially since Brom's magic is coming back to him."

"I don't want to, Wolf, especially not after I do what I have to do to Dad to ensure the survival of the line of the Silver Witch. They need to forget me, at least for a while. When it's safe, I can send the counter to the memory spell."

"What about the relationship between your uncle and Professor Mason? If you alter memories, won't you mess with that?" Cory asked.

"Considering the explosive argument they had just before the professor got on the same plane as your parents to go back to Arkansas, it might be for the best if Uncle Brom forgets him too."

"You don't mean that, Kieran Oisín-Cooper." Cory stopped for a moment and made eye contact with the boys, who left the room to find someplace else to be. "You care too much for both of those men. They need a chance to work things out for themselves. I know that what you're going to have to do to Kellen is tearing you up, but don't make it harder by doing this to Grams and Uncle Brom. There are members of my family's pack that would jump at the choice you gave Billy. Offer some of them the collar in exchange for becoming guards on your uncle's new place."

"All right, Wolf, I'll leave it be on most of the recent memories for Grams and Uncle Brom. I'm still going to kick Uncle Brom's ass for messing up with Professor Mason. Those two are meant to be with each other."

"I know, and I'll help. There's a question the professor asked that nobody's ever answered," Cory said.

"What question is that, Cory?"

"He wanted to know why your father's eyes were the violet of an Amethyst mage when his magic was Silver."

"Silver eyes mark the heir to the power of the Silver Witch in our family. Dad wasn't supposed to be Gramps' heir. Uncle Brom was always meant for that role, at least until I was born. Dad was meant to marry an Amethyst witch or mage; that's why his eyes are violet."

"But he met and married your mother, who wasn't an Amethyst mage."

"Yes, but that was on the orders of Gramps. When Uncle Brom came out as gay and then ended up with his powers all messed up, Dad had to take Brom's place in everything. Gramps wasn't paying attention to the prophecy he set so much store in."

"When the lines of white do twist and twine, the firstborn of the second son shall of two Houses be."

"Yep, that would be the part Gramps missed. You want to know the real kicker, Wolf?"

"Somehow, I bet this is a major plot twist in our little personal fairy tale," Cory replied.

"Dad met the Amethyst witch at the same school where he and Mom were going to school. He told me she was the most beautiful woman he'd ever met. He knew they were supposed to be together, but he did his duty to the family instead of making himself happy. Don't get me wrong, he loved Mother, but they weren't soul mates. The real kicker is the witch went on to become a fashion model, a career Dad wanted to pursue."

"He'd have made a fortune with his looks and those eyes. So who is this witch?"

"Vivian Mason."

"The one they compare to Elizabeth Taylor because of the color of her eyes?"

"She's the one."

"Vivian Mason is beautiful."

"You're not catching the plot twist, Wolf."

"Okay color me dense, Kier."

"Vivian Mason is Professor Mason's older sister, and if things hadn't gone the way they did, I might be calling the professor Uncle John."

"Wow, that is a twist. You may end up calling him that anyways if he and Uncle Brom patch things up," Cory said with a grin.

"I'm going to end up calling him that for two reasons it seems."

"What's the second reason?"

"I'm going to give Dad the life the prophecy took from him. I'm going to give him his dream of being a fashion model and let destiny take its course on the runway."

"But won't that undo the magic you're going to work on your father tonight?"

"No, only Professor Mason will know the truth, and I'm pretty sure he'll never tell his sister that her boyfriend—or whatever status they're at when she brings him home to meet the family—has a son and a daughter from his previous marriage still living."

"That's putting a lot of trust in the man and giving him a terrible burden to carry."

"I know, and I hate to do it, but I want my dad to have the life he should have had twenty-two years ago."

"Well, I'm glad he's getting it now, but I'm glad he didn't get it back then, because I wouldn't have you." Cory sniffed back tears.

Kieran stepped around the bed and wrapped Cory in a tight hug. "I'm glad too, Wolf, because without you, my life wouldn't be worth living."

Kieran turned Cory around so they were face-to-face and drew him in for a kiss. Their embrace shifted as they each reached to undress the other. They didn't take long in getting each other naked and then fell on the bed together. Kissing and stroking each other, they rolled around the bed until Cory pinned Kieran to the bed, his cock hard and ready in the crack of Kieran's ass. His husband's equally hard cock was trapped between their bodies. It had been awhile since Cory had been in the dominant role, but they'd promised each other equality in their relationship. They were family, not pack; there was no hierarchy between them, just as there were no barriers between them. Cory leaned down and took his weight on his forearms as he pressed his body along and on top of Kieran's until they could kiss again. Cory's hips rocked, dragging the head of his cock over Kieran's hole and drawing a moan from the man pinned to the bed. Kieran adjusted his hips and wrapped his legs around Cory's waist, lining up his hole with the head of Cory's cock. The next thrust of his husband's hips pushed cock into ass, and Kieran bit down on Cory's shoulder as his muscles gave way to the hard cock. The burn helped to center him on his husband. Cory lifted up enough to lock his amber eyes on Kieran's silver ones, making sure he wasn't hurting his husband. A warm smile greeted him as hands moved down his back to cup his ass and encourage his rhythm. It was amazing to be inside the heat of Kieran's ass with no condom in between them. They lost themselves in each other's pleasure until finally Kieran's spine arched and a wet heat pulsed between them as he moaned loudly in pleasure; his orgasm soaked both of their bodies. Kieran's spasms tightened the muscles in his ass and pushed Cory over the edge, pumping his massive load deep into Kieran. The lovers collapsed together on the bed.

* * *

AFTER DINNER that evening at the main house, the family sat around the dinner table talking. Kieran excused himself and asked his father to meet him in the study.

"We need to have a very serious talk, Dad."

"Of course, Son. I know you're worried about protecting your grandmother, but Brom and I can protect her."

"Grams' safety is important, Dad, but so is the future of the lineage of the Silver Witch. I know you were forced to marry Mom when your heart had found a different match. I want you to have the life you should have had," Kieran said.

"That life is long gone. I'm sure Vivian found someone else and married. I'm beyond the fashion model age range. I can manage the family fortune for you and Cory and help Brom and Mother run their bed and breakfast."

"No, Dad. Vivian didn't find anyone and get married. She's a major fashion model, and her agency is looking for a semi-mature gentleman to work with her on several shoots and as her escort to events. I checked up on her, and when I found out she was Professor Mason's sister, I asked him about her."

"She never married?"

"There wasn't any reason for her to do so, Dad. She and the professor are the youngest of five children, and their siblings have already given their parents lots of grandchildren. You two were meant to be together. The only drawback is that I need you to continue the family line. You'll still have to father the next Silver Witch."

"All right, Son. What's the catch to this perfect life with the woman I should have married?"

"You can't be allowed to remember your old family until after I'm dead. You'll be heir to the power of the Silver Witch in a caretaker role for your children—and you'll have to have several. The line has become too narrow with just you for breeding stock. All of your children will inherit the full powers of the Silver Witch, with the eldest inheriting the title regardless of gender."

"Time to do what our ancestress did when she gave the power to a male line: mix it up and hide it. It's a very practical plan, Son." Kellen drew a deep breath to steady himself before asking, "What happens if I die before you do?"

"Then I'll find your eldest child and unlock the channel myself." Kieran's breathing became ragged for a moment, before he continued, "I'm sorry it has to be this way, Dad."

Kellen sat in one of the leather chairs his father had decorated the study with. He picked up his wine glass and took a large swallow. "Do Brom and Mother know what you have planned for me?"

Kieran moved one of the other chairs closer to his father. He settled into it and rested a hand on his father's knee. "No, and they'll believe you died in the same accident that claimed Mom and my sisters. If we ever meet again, you won't recognize any of us as family, nor will

Grams or Uncle Brom remember your relationship to us. That will only change if Professor Mason and Brom reconcile and the professor chooses to unlock their memories and yours."

Kellen leaned forward to lay a hand on his son's knee. "When will you do this?"

Kieran pointed to the wine glass his father held. "It's already done. I enchanted the wine. Only you, Uncle Brom, and Grams had it with dinner tonight. When you leave this room, your new memories of the last twenty-two years will come into being. You'll find a suitcase and briefcase by the front door along with the keys to your SUV," Kieran said as the tears started to flow.

Kellen wrapped his son in his arms and hugged him as both of them wept over their mutual loss.

"I'm sorry it has to be this way, Dad. I have to protect the future of two houses, and I can't spare anyone's feeling, even my own. I love you, and I will always remember you."

"I love you too, Son. Tell your sister that I love her too. Good-bye, Kieran."

"Good-bye, Dad."

Kellen walked out of the study, and his memories shifted until he only knew himself as Kellen MacDonnell, up-and-coming male model. Unseeing, he picked up his suitcase and briefcase and walked out of his old life and into his new one. Behind him in the study, Kieran sank to his knees weeping for the loss of his father. In many ways, Kieran had just given Kellen the kind of life he wanted for himself. One free to be his own person.

About a half an hour after Kellen left for his new life, Cory entered the study to find his husband a soggy mess, eyes red-rimmed from his tears. He pulled Kieran into a tight embrace and let him compose himself. Kieran finally lifted himself off of Cory's shoulder and looked at his husband with red-rimmed silver eyes.

"It's done, babe. Grams and Uncle Brom only remember your dad, mom, and the rest of the family as dim memories."

"I only wanted to create, not to destroy. Where did I go wrong, Wolf? How did I end up destroying so much?"

"You haven't destroyed things, Kier. Altered them beyond recognition maybe, but not destroyed. We still have a future to build, and we're going to start by going back home to Arkansas and finishing our college degrees. You'll never get a good job and be able to support me in my old age if you don't have a college degree." Cory tried to lighten the mood.

"Wolf, between the fortunes I'm inheriting, neither of us will ever have to work a day in our lives if we don't want to. Do you think my dad will be happy in his new life?"

"I do. You've given him his dream, even if he never learns it was you who did it. Be happy for him. Come on, let's get you cleaned up before Grams and Uncle Brom wonder what you've be doing in here and why you were crying."

They stepped into the half bath off of the study, and Kieran took one look at his reflection in the mirror and knew there was no cleaning up the blotchy mess he'd made of his face with his crying. He ran the cold water and soaked a washcloth to try and cool down his eyes. It didn't really do much to help. There was no hiding his red-rimmed eyes without the use of magic. A minor disguise spell would allow him to safely make an exit from the family evening. Cory watched as Kieran swiped a glowing hand over his face and the damage from his tears vanished. Cory hugged him again before they returned to the dining room where Grams was just setting out dessert at the four places. Kieran looked at the dessert and almost lost his magical covering. Grams had set out a dessert that had been the favorite of both Gramps and his father, Apple Brown Betty with vanilla ice cream. Kieran choked back the new tears that threatened to flow, drawing his family's attention.

"What's the matter, *mo stór*? I thought we'd honor those who have passed. This was your grandfather's favorite, because it reminded him of your father. I wish you'd had more time with Kellen; he'd have been so proud of you."

"I'm sorry, Grams. I just miss Gramps so much. There's so much to do, and now I don't have him to turn to for advice. He was always such a good balance to Grandmother Belle. I just feel like the weight of the world has been dropped on my shoulders."

"Well, you don't have to worry about your uncle and I, *mo stór*. We'll be close to you in Arkansas."

"I know, Grams, and I promise Cory and I will come up to visit every chance we get. There will just be times when we won't be able to get away."

"Kieran, we know you still have your own life to live, and we want you two to find your happily ever after. We love you, and there will always be a place for you come and hide when the world gets to be too much for you," Brom said.

"Thank you, Uncle Brom. Grams, dinner was wonderful as always. I think Cory and I are going to head back over to our cabin for the night. We still need to make plans and figure out what things we want to ship back to Little Rock," Kieran said as he pushed back from the table.

Both of the young men stood and then hugged Grams and Uncle Brom before leaving. Cory took Kieran's hand in his own as they walked back to their cabin. He could feel the tension in his husband. He pulled Kieran to a stop when they'd gone far enough from the main house to be out of earshot.

"Babe, take us to the cave. I can tell you still need to scream and yell about how unfair life is, and you can't do that here where Brom or Grams can hear."

They walked forward into a swirl of Silver magic, and their next step carried them out into the entrance of the caves above the beach. When they'd made their way into the main cavern of the system, Cory stopped them and turned Kieran to face him. Cory looked into his husband's beautiful silver eyes, which were dimmed to a dull gray and red-rimmed from all his earlier crying. He cupped Kieran's face in his hands and brushed away a pair of tears that fell from his eyes with his thumbs before drawing him closer and kissing the love of his life. Kieran shivered in Cory's grip, not from cold but with the repressed sadness inside. Stroking back strands of Kieran's amazing midnight locks, Cory drew his husband down toward the hot pools. At the edge, he stopped and began to undress an unresisting Kieran. He then eased his lover into the hot pool before quickly stripping off and slipping in behind. He pulled Kieran in close and settled them both on the bench submerged beneath the water. Instinctively, Kieran settled between Cory's legs and curled into his lover's chest, hiding his face behind a curtain of hair as sobs wracked his body. Cory held onto him, stroking his hair and back, just letting him cry himself out. When his sobs dissolved into hiccups, Cory rocked him gently, encouraging him to breathe with him until they settled into the same breathing pattern and the hiccups passed. When he'd settled, Kieran brushed his hair out of his face and looked up at Cory who read the loss in his lover's eyes. A quick kiss and then Cory resumed stroking Kieran's hair.

"I understand, babe. I know how much doing what you did tonight hurt you, and I share your pain. I'm so proud of you for doing this incredibly brave thing. Right now, you feel like you ripped out your own heart and stomped it into a paste, but we both know that your heart is protected and sheltered in me. In time, you'll see that this is a good thing. Your father is going to be happy in his new life. Grams and Uncle Brom are excited about their future, and I think with a gentle nudge, you can get Professor Mason back into Brom's life where we both know he belongs. We have time for just us. You can give the various branches all but the most important or highest paying hunts. Plus, you have your favorite sister back among the living."

Kieran stretched up and kissed Cory. "Thank you, Wolf, for being my anchor. You have no idea how much I wanted to drink that potion right along with Dad, Grams, and Uncle Brom tonight. To make myself forget all the pain we've been through. Your unconditional love is the only thing that kept me from reaching for that glass."

"Would it have worked on you? You made the potion and cast the spells. I thought you couldn't work magic on yourself."

"That potion and those spells would have worked on me just like they worked on the rest of my family. I might even have forgotten I was the Silver Hunter and all that entails."

"I can sense a 'but' in there, even if you haven't said it out loud, Kier."

"The 'but' is I'd have forgotten you as well. You'd have been a stranger to me. You're the best thing that's ever happened to me, Cory, but you're also wrapped up in the thing I'd most like to forget, and because of that, the potion and spells would have stolen the memories of you from me along with all the crap that went down because of the prophecy."

"Let me be your potion and spells then. I'll help you forget all the darkness and only remember the good times. We're going to build a bright new future for ourselves, Kieran Oisín-Cooper. You promised me a happily ever after."

"The happily ever after starts by us dropping the Oisín from our name, Wolf. The Oisín clan died tonight. Would you object to being Mr. and Mr. Belle-Cooper?"

"Shifters and hunters, please welcome to the world Corwin and Kieran Belle-Cooper." Kieran was laughing at Cory's silly introduction as Cory continued, "I like the sound of the new name, and I love hearing you laugh again, *mo chroí*."

"My heart, I see you had Grams teach you a bit of the old tongue. With you at my side, *mac tíre óg*, I plan to laugh a whole lot more," Kieran said as he snuggled in closer.

"I think we should dry off and go to bed, Kier. We have a lot to do tomorrow."

"Five more minutes like this, Cory," Kieran murmured against Cory's chest.

"Now, babe. In five minutes, you'll be asleep," Cory replied.

"Spoilsport," Kieran said as he disengaged from his perch and made a gesture.

Silver magic wrapped around both of them and whisked them and their clothes from the cavern back to their bedroom in the cabin. Both men were dry when they arrived back in the bedroom. Kieran pulled Cory over and into the huge bed, and they snuggled into the covers and were fast asleep before either of them could tell the other good night.

EPILOGUE

Kieran and Cory looked at the huge Christmas tree, which filled the corner of the front parlor of their stately Victorian home. It was their turn to host the friends and family party this year, and they'd been busy getting all the decorations out, food cooked, and the table set. It was hard to believe that four years had passed since they'd defeated the Beast and the evil mage known as the Master. They'd both finished college, earning their bachelor's degrees. Cory was weighing plans to go for his Master's degree in economics, so he could help Kieran better understand the vast family fortunes he controlled. Of all those coming to their home for the holidays, they were most excited for the arrival of Billy and Ian, who'd started their first year of college. Under Ian's influence and the stern eyes of his uncles, Billy had become an excellent student, and both boys had been accepted to Oxford. Kieran and Cory were looking forward to hearing all about their studies and lives in England.

The doorbell announcing the arrival of their first guests interrupted their study of the tree. Cory went and answered the door to find his parents loaded down with presents and food.

"Mom, Dad, we said no bringing food this year. Kieran and I have done all the cooking."

"That's why your mother insisted on bringing food; she didn't want your other guests to starve to death," Jonathan Cooper said with a laugh.

"I wanted you to have your favorite pecan pie, Corwin," Tamara said.

"Well, since it's pie, I'm sure Kieran will forgive you," Cory said as he took a stack of gifts from his father's arms. "You know where the kitchen is, Mom; just set it on the counter with the other desserts."

Once presents were settled under the tree and the pie found a home in the kitchen, Jonathan and Tamara wrapped both young men in a hugs before settling in with a glass of eggnog. They were just beginning to relate all the news from the farm when the doorbell rang again. Kieran went to answer the door and was engulfed in a double bear hug from Billy and Ian.

"Well, look who's here, our Oxford scholars," Kieran proclaimed loudly.

Billy and Ian were swept up in hugs and kisses from Jonathan, Tamara, and Cory.

"You boys know where your room is; go drop off your things and come back down. You can unpack later," Cory said.

Up the stairs, the boys vanished to put their suitcases and coats in their room. They noted that the twin beds had been replaced with a queen-sized bed, and they grinned at each other. They set down their suitcases and pulled out the presents they'd packed away before heading back downstairs to join the family. They arrived downstairs to find that Grams and Uncle Brom had arrived and were piling presents under the tree as well. More hugs and kisses were exchanged as the boys put their gifts under the tree as best they could.

"Boys, will you take Grams' and Uncle Brom's bags up to their rooms please?" Kieran asked as he came back into the parlor from the kitchen.

"We've got it, Uncle Kieran," Billy called out.

Ian and Billy grabbed Grams' and Brom's luggage and carried it upstairs to the rooms assigned to Kieran's family. Kieran had left the suites on the second floor like they'd been when he first met Cory. He'd given Grams the suite on the left-hand side at the front of the house overlooking the street. Uncle Brom had the suite on the same side at the rear of the house and across the hall from the boys' suite. Jonathan and Tamara usually occupied the front suite on the right-hand side. This year they'd opted to get a hotel room, leaving the suite available in case of unexpected guests. The boys came back downstairs just in time to catch the door as the bell rang.

"Professor Mason, wow, Uncle Kieran didn't tell us he'd invited you this year," Billy said as he stepped aside so that John and two others could enter the house.

"My goodness, Billy and Ian, I didn't know you were back from England already. Kieran mentioned you were coming home for the break," John replied.

"Can we take your coats?" Billy asked.

"Of course. Viv, Kel, these are Kieran's wards, Billy and Ian. Boys, this is my sister Vivian Mason and her friend Kellen MacDonald," John introduced his guests.

Both boys stopped in their tracks as the pair removed the coats and dark glasses. Both had to take a moment before blurting out a wrong word at the sight of Kellen. Because of their role as the Archivist of the House of Beauty, Kieran couldn't wipe or even fade their memories when he'd done so to Kellen, Grams, and Brom. Ian regrouped first.

"Ms. Mason, Mr. MacDonald, a pleasure to meet you both. We've seen several of your promotions, and your last appearance during Milan Fashion Week was all over the television at school," Ian said as he took their coats.

"Oh, they're just as adorable as you said they'd be, John," Vivian said as she hugged a still stunned Billy.

"Uh, everyone's in the parlor, Professor," Billy said when Vivian released him.

"Professor, you should know that Brom is here," Ian said.

"I expected he would be. Kieran was kind enough to warn me in advance," John said before leading his guests into the parlor.

"Professor, you made it. I was hoping you'd come," Kieran cheered.

"I told you I'd come, Kieran. You know you're not my student anymore; you can call me John now."

"Nope, not the way I work, Professor. Besides. I'm thinking of coming back to school for my Master's in photography," Kieran replied.

"Well, if you do, I'm going to work you even harder as my lab assistant teaching freshmen," John replied.

"Ugh, freshmen. Now who are your guests?" Kieran asked as he turned to greet the professor's friends. He stopped when he saw his father behind the woman. "Oh bright goddess, Vivian Mason and Kellen MacDonald in my house. Be still my heart, and where the heck is my camera?"

Cory came out of the kitchen with a tray loaded with glasses of eggnog to catch the end of Kieran's conversation. Hearing the extra names was the only thing that saved him from dropping the tray at the sight of Kellen.

"Never mind the camera. Just get them to sign any available piece of paper, babe," Cory called.

"John, you didn't tell me this was a house of fans," Vivian said, blushing slightly at all the attention from such beautiful men.

"We should have been more better prepared, Viv. If we'd known we had so many fans stateside, we could have brought press kits for them," Kellen said. His familiar voice ripped away the scabs that had grown over the wound in Kieran's heart.

Swallowing hard, Kieran remembered his hosting duties and introduced the newcomers to the rest of those gathered. He marveled at how well the spell he'd crafted four years ago was holding up under the surprise arrival of his father under the same roof as his uncle and grandmother. It was as if all of them were meeting for the first time. The reunion between Uncle Brom and Professor Mason even seemed to be going smoothly. He was glad he had given both men a heads-up about the other being invited. Cory finished handing out the eggnog and stepped up beside Kieran, slipping one arm around his husband's waist as he raised his glass of eggnog.

"Everyone, Kieran and I want to say thank you all for coming to spend the holiday with us. It's a joy to have friends and family with us at this time of the year," Cory said.

"We have a very special announcement and someone we'd like you all to meet. Angelina, would you come join us?" Kieran called out.

A young woman waddled out into the parlor from the kitchen. Her advanced pregnancy was obvious to everyone gathered around the beaming couple as they parted to wrap her between them.

"This is Angelina Belle, one of my distant cousins on my late mother's side of the family. She very kindly volunteered to be the surrogate mother for the child Cory and I decided we wanted to have. Much to all our surprise, Angelina is pregnant with twins, boy and a girl, who will join our family in February."

Kieran, Cory, and Angelina were swamped with hugs and kisses from a very excited pair of grandparents, a great-grandmother, a great-uncle, and a pair of cousins to be. The questions and suggestions competed with each other until Kieran finally managed to get Angelina to a chair so she could get off her feet.

"Please, we'll answer questions in due time. Let Angelina get some air, please," Kieran said. "This is our big Christmas gift to everyone."

"How did you two manage to keep this a secret from everyone?" Grams asked.

"By going up to Maine for our last vacation. Grandmother Belle and Rosie were a big help in helping us find a cousin willing and able to become a surrogate mother. Angelina came down here just last weekend, which is why we couldn't come up to Eureka Springs or down to the farm," Kieran replied.

"We were busy getting the old servants quarters cleaned up and ready for Angelina's arrival. Not to mention all the work we've been doing converting my studio into a nursery," Cory said.

While all the women gathered around the happy couple and their unborn children, Professor Mason drew Brom aside. Jonathan had taken Kellen aside to pump him for details on his modeling career.

"I think you and I should talk, Brom. We had some pretty harsh words for each other when we last saw each other," John said.

"I know, and I've really taken a long hard look at myself over the last couple of years. Kieran kicked my ass around the new forge a few times too," Brom said.

"Yes, he's talked to me in the darkroom a couple of times as well," John replied.

"I'm sorry for treating you like you were less than a person, John. I was an idiot, and if you never want to have anything to do with me again, I'd completely understand," Brom said.

"Thank you for that, Brom. I was just as big of an idiot for not standing my ground on some things before they got out of hand. So if you'd rather not deal with me after this, I'll also understand," John replied.

"I think what I'd really like is for us to start over on equal footing. We kind of rushed into things. I enjoyed talking with you when we just talked, not that I didn't enjoy all the other things we did together, but I really miss having another guy to talk with," Brom said.

"I miss our conversations as well, Brom. How long are you staying in town?" John asked.

"Through the New Year. Mom and I closed the B&B for the holidays this year," Brom replied.

"Good. How about we start slow, and meet for coffee, say the day after tomorrow?" John suggested.

"That sounds like a plan to me, John," Brom said, extending his hand to the other man.

John and Brom shook hands, and only John noticed the smile on Kieran's face that had nothing to do with the fact that he was going to be a father soon. The family and guests all gathered around the dinning room table, which Kieran quietly expanded with a little magic so that Vivian Mason and his father could be seated with them. Kieran and Cory—with help from Billy and Ian—brought out all the food, and the gathering fell silent as they blessed the meal and then began to dig in. When everyone pronounced themselves stuffed, they adjourned back to the parlor to do a round of gift exchanges. Vivian and Kellen found a quiet corner out of the way of the chaos of family gifts—or so they thought. They were surprised when Kieran came over and presented them with a gift each.

"Kieran, you didn't have to give us gifts. You didn't even know we were coming with John today," Kellen said.

"We have a funny family tradition in this house. Well, it's something Cory and I came up with, and we've done it every year since we got married. We get a couple of gifts and set them aside in case we have unexpected guests or we hear of a family in need. This year we have unexpected guests. Please come and join in the family chaos," Kieran said.

"Thank you, but we don't have anything to give you in return," Vivian said.

"Actually, you've given me a gift just by being here, but if you feel you need to do something, would you consent to pose for me sometime while you're in town?" Kieran asked.

"We'd be honored. If you and Cory join us in a couple of the photos, I'm sure I can get John to shoot them for us," Vivian said.

"Would you include Angelina in the group shot?" Kieran asked. "She'll be the envy of all the family back in Maine."

"On one condition," Kellen said.

"Name it," Kieran replied.

"You let us come back to visit and take a picture with you, Cory, and your children," Kellen said.

Kieran choked, trying to hold back the tears he so wanted to shed. Cory came to his rescue. "Of course, we would. My goodness, the children will be famous before they're able to crawl," he joked, taking the attention off of Kieran.

"I have one other favor to ask of you as our hosts?" Kellen asked.

"Sure, you've made our day special already," Cory said.

"Everyone, I don't want to upstage the happy parents to be, but I'd like you all to witness something for me," Kellen said, drawing the focus of the room to their little group as he sank to one knee before Vivian.

"Kellen MacDonald, what are you doing?" Vivian asked.

Kellen pulled a small velvet box from his pocket and held it out to Vivian. He then opened the box to reveal a gleaming diamond and amethyst engagement ring.

"Vivian Mason, before all of these witnesses, I ask you the question I've wanted to ask you for twenty-six years. Will you marry me?" Kellen said as he took the ring from the box and held it toward Vivian.

Vivian was struck speechless until Kieran leaned in and whispered in her ear. "The correct answer is yes." She was galvanized, and her amethyst eyes locked onto a matching pair staring back at her. "Yes," she replied.

Kellen slipped the ring on her finger and then drew her into a kiss. Cheers broke out as the newly engaged couple broke their kiss and looked at the assembled room.

"So how big of a deal do you want to make of this marriage?" Kieran asked. "You are both famous after all."

"Oh my, I really hate the idea of being swarmed by the press on our wedding day," Vivian said.

"Well, this is your lucky Christmas. Grams is a licensed minister. We can slip down to the county courthouse on Monday when they reopen and get all the documents squared away. Then, we can do everything here at the house. Kellen can spend the night before the wedding here, so he doesn't see the bride before the big day," Kieran said.

"You are a keeper, Kieran," Vivian said. "Thank you so much."

"See? You got us a gift after all." Kieran gave her one of his famous smiles. "Now, speaking of presents, there are way too many under that tree. Billy, would you and Ian please play Santa's helpers and start passing out the loot?"

Finally, the holiday Kieran had dreamed of all his life, and he let all the joy fill his heart. When all those who weren't staying at the house had departed—and Kieran and Cory had seen Angelina to bed—they retired to their own suite on the third floor. In their private sanctuary, Kieran finally let all of his emotions slip free. Tears streamed down his face, and he cuddled into Cory. Some of the tears were from the sadness of not being able to fully share the truth with Kellen about how much the photos would mean to him. Yet, many of the tears were tears of joy at having been witness to his father's happiness and the prospect of having a family photo of three generations. His children would have at least one picture with their grandfather.

"It seems so odd, being around Dad and yet not being able to share all of our joys with him," Kieran said.

"I'm glad for the surprise guests. Too bad Grams won't know that she's performing the wedding ceremony for her youngest son," Cory said.

"I know, but this is still all for the best. You know I never realized just how famous Vivian and Kellen were in the modeling world. If any of those photos we're planning go beyond the family, we'll be swamped with press and modeling contracts," Kieran said.

"Send them to Grandmother Belle. She'll drive such a hard bargain they'll run for the hills and leave us alone," Cory replied.

"I like that idea," Kieran said. "This has been a perfect Christmas."

Cory reached over, grabbed their water bottles off the nightstand, and handed one to Kieran before tapping them together. "Here's to many more prefect Christmases."

They took a drink and put up their waters before snuggling in for a long winter's nap.

DEAR READER,

Thank you for reading my first series. I hope you enjoyed it. Please take a moment to leave a review. I hope you'll join keep following my stories. Coming up next, I'll be exploring the vampires of my world from their origins into the far future looking through the eyes of shifter and vampire hunter, Richard St. Martin, and Cain, father of all vampires.

Thanks,

Kethric Wilcox

ABOUT THE AUTHOR

Kethric Wilcox (1966-) was born in Melrose, MA to average middle-class parents. Growing up, he did normal kid things, cub scouts, and boy scouts earning the rank of Eagle Scout. He graduated high school, went to college as a computer graphic design major, in the days when the field was more programing than design, for a while before dropping out to go work in the travel and tourism industry for four years. Kethric relocated to Little Rock, Arkansas in the early 1990s and went back to college earning a B. A. in both graphic design and history. He currently lives with his partner, whom he officially started dating in 2008, in a 1923 house they renovated in 2012, and works as a graphic designer doing museum and trail exhibits. In his spare time, Kethric writes church dramas and paranormal gay romances. When he's not at a computer, writing, designing, or doing research, Kethric enjoys playing in the kitchen, creating healthy versions of some of his favorite desserts and dinners. He is an avid camper and loves to get away from technology from time to time to recharge his spiritual and creative energies.

For Upcoming Releases
www.kethricwilcox.com
kethricwilcoxauthor@gmail.com

www.ingramcontent.com/pod-product-compliance
Lightning Source LLC
Chambersburg PA
CBHW071956110726
47910CB00005B/1551